RUPERT THOMSON

DREAMS OF LEAVING

BLOOMSBURY

First published 1987
Copyright © 1987 by Rupert Thomson

Bloomsbury Publishing Ltd, 4 Bloomsbury Place, London wc1a 2qa

British Library Cataloguing in Publication Data

Thomson, Rupert
Dreams of leaving.
I. Title
823'.914 [F]   PR6070.H68/
ISBN 0-7475-0023-1

The author and publishers are grateful to the following for permission to reproduce
song lyrics in the text: p.260, two lines from 'Strangers in the Night' by Bert
Kaempfert, Charles Singleton and Eddie Snyder. Copyright © 1966 Champion
Music Corporation/Screen Gems Columbia Music. Reproduced by permission of
MCA Music Ltd. International copyright secured. All rights reserved; p. 284, four
lines from 'Falling in Love Again' by Friedrich Hollaender and Reg Connelly.
Copyright © 1930 by Ufaton-Verlag GmbH, West Germany; Campbell Connelly
& Co. Ltd, 78 Newman Street, London w1. Used by permission. All rights
reserved; pp. 314 and 315–16, extracts from 'So What!' by The Anti-Nowhere
League, reproduced by courtesy of Head Music Publishers Ltd.

Designed by Newell and Sorrell Design Ltd
Printed and bound in Great Britain by
Butler & Tanner Ltd, Frome and London

There was a village somewhere in the south of England, a village cut off from the rest of the country, a village nobody had ever left. Mr and Mrs Highness decided to change all that. They wanted to give their son, Moses, something they had always been denied – freedom. But, where they came from, freedom was a dangerous ambition, a dream that had been outlawed by the police.

Moses Highness? Not a very typical English name, you might think. Nor did Moses, growing up alone in the outside world, as he began to scour the phonebooks for some clue to his origins. He moved to London and found a flatmate, Eddie, who was so beautiful he could make people faint. He also found Gloria, a jazz-singer, and fell in love with her because her eyebrows told the time like the hands on a clock.

But he had still to unearth the bizarre and chilling secrets of his past. He had yet to learn of his mother who ate raw yeast because she wanted to rise out of her misery, his father who spent eight years in bed, the greengrocer who disguised himself as a section of ploughed field, the postman who thought he was Tarzan.

And, most threatening of all, the brutal obsessive figure of Chief Inspector Peach, head of the village police, who had an old score to settle.

Rupert Thomson explores the fine line between normality and madness as the two worlds of Peach and Moses slowly converge. Farce, terror, magic, they all have a part to play as this mesmeric first novel builds towards its climax. Because nobody can escape the past. Least of all Moses.

TO MY FATHER
SORRY AND THANK YOU

TO MENISHA
JUST THANK YOU

CONTENTS

STRANGE TIME
FOR A DROWNING (1956)

It was a hot day to be wearing black. The coffin-bearers counted themselves fortunate. The coffin resting on their shoulders measured less than four feet in length. It was also empty. The child's body had never been found.

Very few people had turned out for the funeral. A gaunt bearded man, an ungainly blonde woman and five police officers. Two men in shabby black suits took up the rear of the procession. One of them, Dinwoodie by name, wore a sling on his right arm. He had pale swivelling eyes and long hair that was prematurely grey. The other ran the village greengrocer's shop. Their heads tilted sideways and inwards like two halves of a reflection so they could hear each other without raising their voices. They had allowed a small gap to open up between themselves and the five policemen. That they were linked, as if by an invisible cartilage, to the main body of the procession was obvious from their conversation.

'So what do you think?' Dinwoodie spoke in a hoarse whisper.

'Think?'

'About the baby. Do you think he really drowned in the river?'

The greengrocer squinted into the sun. 'Well,' he said, 'that's the story that's going round.'

'That's not what I'm asking.'

'Is he really dead, do you mean?'

Dinwoodie nodded. His eyes lit like hot ashes.

'Well, if he's not,' the greengrocer said, 'where is he?' A logical man, the greengrocer.

'That's what I'm getting at,' Dinwoodie said. Sweat oiled the working parts of his face. It was sweltering outside, but it was not the heat that he felt.

The greengrocer waited for his friend to elaborate. They passed a marble cross that had been carved to look like wood. A heap of stone fruit and vegetables adorned the base. The greengrocer's grandfather.

'What I'm getting at is, could he have escaped?' Dinwoodie said.

The greengrocer raised an eyebrow. 'A thirteen-month-old baby?'

'All right. Could his escape have been – ' and here Dinwoodie paused, searching for the appropriate word – 'have been,' he continued, '*engineered*?'

'Ah,' the greengrocer said. A logical man, but not an excitable one.

'Well?'

'Well what?'

'Well what do you think?'

'It's never been done before,' the greengrocer said.

'So far as we know,' came Dinwoodie's fierce whisper.

'So far as we know,' the greengrocer agreed.

One of the police officers walking in front of the two men twisted his head and glared in their direction. Dinwoodie lowered his eyes. He examined the flagstone path as it passed beneath his feet. The stones were uneven. Weeds pushed through the cracks like mysteries demanding solutions.

'There seems to be some tension,' the greengrocer observed, 'among certain members of our local police force.'

Dinwoodie's pale eyes glowed. His hand, trembling, clutched at the air. 'Is it any wonder?' he said. 'They never found the baby's body, did they? The mystery hasn't been solved. It's just being buried, that's all.' He drew a large yellow handkerchief out of his pocket and began to mop his forehead and his upper lip. 'We're burying an empty coffin here. *An empty coffin.* Don't you see, Joel? They're admitting they've failed. The police have failed – maybe for the first time. Do you know what that means? It means there's hope for us, Joel. There really is.'

Joel sighed. As if the sun had slid behind a cloud, gloom moved over his face. 'You'll never know.'

'How can you be so sure?'

'I'm telling you,' the greengrocer said. 'You'll never know. Who are you going to ask? The police?' He snorted. 'There's no way you'll ever find out.'

'Ah, this fucking village,' Dinwoodie snapped. 'You too.'

Chief Inspector Peach (known behind his back as 'The Fuzz') swung round, his lower lip jutting, his face pink with indignation. 'Gentlemen, please. This is a funeral.'

The two men covered the remaining distance to the open grave in silence.

*

George Highness stood, gaunt and bearded, beside his son's grave. How he loathed New Egypt, he was thinking. How he loathed and detested the place. Hate massed in his fists, drew the blood out of his knuckles, tightened the stringy muscles in the back of his neck. He looked older than his twenty-nine years.

He was facing north. The cemetery fell away in front of him, sank to its knees, offering a view. Tombstones rough as dead skin. Yew trees almost black against a flawless sky of blue. Then, at the bottom of the hill, a wall which contained, if you looked closely enough (and as a child he had), every colour in existence. Beyond the wall, a row of brick cottages. Above their rooftops, the elm that told him where he lived; it stood in his front garden. Away to the left and anchored in a dip in the land, the church. Unusual stonework: green on grey days, grey on bright days like today. Timeless, ancient, solid. He didn't believe in it. Further left, a lane dodged the pub and ran downhill past the village green. Behind him all the time, the police station. As it should be, he thought. A brief smile twisted one side of his mouth.

He turned back to the grave. He watched the empty coffin being lowered into the ground. What a farce this was. He glanced across at Alice, his wife. Tension bunched in her shoulderblades so that, in profile, she looked almost hunchbacked. Strands of green–blonde hair lay lank against the nape of her neck. Behind her veil her eyes were blank as stones. Her face like bread, spongy and pale. An echo of the girl he had married.

*

The first time he noticed her she was eight, a white floating girl, a twist of smoke against the grey trees on the western edge of the village. He began to run across the field. Twice he turned his ankle on a furrow. It didn't matter. He ran on. He had to close the distance between them. Catch her before she vanishes, he had told himself. A curious thing to say. But so right, so instinctively right, he would realise later.

He must have been eleven. Even then he had felt the pull of her strangeness and how magnetic somehow her frailty was. Close up, among tree-trunks veined with ivy and bindweed, her feet lost in leaves the colour of rust, she had the awkward grace of a bird. A stork, perhaps, or a heron. She had the same elongated neck, the same brittle stumbling legs.

He stood in front of her getting his breath back. She wasn't looking at him. He asked her name.

'Alice,' she said. Without moving her feet, she turned away so he could no longer see her face. Rooted to the ground she seemed. A bird that would never fly. He could have seen it then. In that first meeting.

'What are you doing out here?' he asked her.

'I was alone.'

Her hands moved among the folds of her white dress. Three years younger than he was, she seemed wiser, more adult. Like blotting-paper she soaked up the messy ink of his questions.

Still something possessed him to say, 'Not any more,' and she turned towards him and looked at him as if he had just spoken for the first time.

They had met by chance and their friendship continued as a kind of planned coincidence. This understanding arose: he looked for her, she waited for him. He always knew where to find her – by the river, in the woods beyond the allotments, up on the hill behind the police station (from there, you could see the village as it really was, a group of houses huddled in a hollow in the land, bound on one side by the river's thin grey cord and on the other two by trees which, from that distance, all too closely resembled fences) – and soon they were spending so much time together on the village boundaries that people began to think they were up to no good. The truth was simpler, though still ominous, perhaps. They wanted privacy, secrecy. They needed territory they could call their own. So they went to the edge of the village. Had to go to the edge. There were no halfway houses. They both understood this early on and recognised it in each other. Peach recognised it too. He wrote a short memo regarding the two children. The police were alerted. Gently.

An endless source of fascination for George, those boundaries. Marked on the map, but invisible in real life. Invisible but concrete because people had believed in them for so long. He was overawed by the power beliefs could generate. He could even hear it. Like electric fences, the boundaries seemed to hum when he approached. He knew them off by heart, as he knew the names of the twenty-nine policemen who took turns to patrol them. The twenty-nine real policemen, that is. How many dummy policemen there were he had never been able to work out. They were always moving them around.

One of Peach's inspirations, the dummy policemen. They were built out of straw, as scarecrows were, but instead of being dressed in rags they wore proper uniforms – helmets, truncheons, the lot. They stood in realistic positions throughout the village and the surrounding countryside. Their eyes always seemed to be staring at you. In poor light they looked as real as real policemen. It was an immensely cunning, uncanny and economical device.

They terrified Alice. She said they looked like dead bodies propped up. Whenever she saw one she had to poke or tickle it just to make sure it wasn't alive. She was convinced that, sooner or later, one of them would begin to wriggle and giggle on the end of her finger. She dreaded the moment. She had another theory. She thought their faces resembled the faces of policemen in the village. 'Look,' she would cry, 'here's Peach.' And George would tilt his head on one side, try to see the likeness. He wanted to believe her. She invented nicknames for them too. Peach she called 'Melon' because he was 'much bigger than a peach' or 'Gooseberry' on account of his short prickly hair. Marlpit was 'The Waterfall' because he dribbled so. Hazard she described as 'the one with a face like a shovel' so he became 'Shovelhead'. But when she heard their heavy boots come crashing through the undergrowth she would flatten herself against the ground until it seemed the earth would open up and swallow her. Her eyes staring, her blonde head pressed sideways into the leaves, she would always whisper the same words:

The world is a dream
It will always be so –

It was the beginning of a nursery rhyme that every child in the village knew off by heart. It was what the boots meant.

*

By the time she was fifteen Alice was already moving out of reach, her mind a wild garden where only weeds grew. Their age-difference was beginning to count now. George tried with his own sharpening intelligence to cut through to her, to clear some ground, but no matter how hard he tried the jungle always grew back. Rain would fall overnight and in the morning he could no longer tell where he had been.

He remembered finding her once that year sitting in the tall grass on the hill behind the police station. He sat down beside her. She acknowledged his presence with a slow hydraulic turning of her head, so smooth and slow that, horrified, he thought of a machine.

'Who are you?' she asked him.

It wasn't a joke, and he didn't try to laugh it off.

The jungle always grew back.

It was during the same year that Tommy Dane made his famous escape attempt. Everybody knew about Tommy Dane. He was a phenomenon. So much so that a new word had been invented to describe him. *Juvenile delinquent*. George remembered thinking how complex, how grand, that sounded. Like a title or something. Tommy obviously thought so too. He certainly did his best to live up to it.

When he was seven years old he cut a rat's throat during needlework class. A live rat. He used a pair of nail-scissors. The rat died theatrically on the scarred lid of his desk. When he was twelve he got a 22-year-old girl pregnant. The girl claimed that he had tied her to a tree with coat-hanger wire and then raped her. Tommy denied it, but people believed the girl. At sixteen he set fire to his parents' house while they were asleep inside. They survived. The house burnt to the ground. Tommy decided it was time to leave home.

Rumour had it that he had staged a fake accident on the main road outside the village, using a stolen hayrick, his father's bicycle and a gallon of fresh pigs' blood. He arranged the hayrick and the bicycle so it looked as if the two had collided, then lay down on the tarmac with his head in a puddle of blood. He hijacked the first car that stopped for him. He climbed into the back seat and, brandishing a fiendish homemade bomb, shouted, 'Get going, you bastards, or I'll blow us all sky-high.' Accounts of exactly what followed vary, but, somehow or other, the bomb exploded in Tommy's face. The driver of the car (a spirited chap from the south coast, retired brigadier apparently) pulled into the side of the road, sprinted to a public phone-box, and called the nearest police station. Which just happened to be New Egypt.

George would never forget that afternoon. He was standing outside the post office with Alice when they brought Tommy in. It didn't look like Tommy. Glossy yellow blisters, smooth as mushrooms, swelled on the left side of his face and the palms of his hands. One eye was a bloated purple slit. His hair must have caught fire at some point because it had shrivelled, coiled into a few black springs. He had no eyebrows any more. Invisible slings held both his arms stiff and crossed in front of his chest.

'Where am I?' he whimpered. Poor Tommy really didn't seem to know.

Peach glanced round as if he too wasn't quite sure, the sarcastic bastard. He took a deep breath and let the air out again in several tense instalments. By the time his answer came, it had acquired immense dramatic power. 'New Egypt,' he said.

Tommy Dane began to cry.

Peach put an arm round the boy's shoulders, then looked up as if he expected cameras to be rolling. It was a historic moment, certainly. The rebel tamed, the system triumphant. The record intact. Nobody had ever succeeded in escaping from the village. And nobody ever would, Peach's smile seemed to say. Later that day he threw a small drinks party at his house in Magnolia Close.

And Tommy? He went back to live with his parents in temporary accommodation, a pre-fab hut behind the vicarage. He died at the age of twenty-four. Some said he had committed suicide. According to the doctor (a more reliable source, perhaps), he simply lost the will to live. The events of that day closed a whole avenue of fantasy for George. If Tommy couldn't leave the village, he reasoned, then nobody could. He was stuck there for life and he had better get used to the idea. He had just celebrated his eighteenth birthday.

Two years later he asked Alice to marry him.

They were sitting by the river. Side by side, as usual. Nine years of rehearsal for this moment. The month was September, the sunset that evening almost Victorian in its coyness, layer on layer of respectable black and grey. Then, unexpectedly, just as he spoke, the sky lifted its huge gathering skirts to reveal an inch of pink flesh, the hint of a calf. His scandalous proposal. Embarrassed, he glanced across at her. But she was staring at the river, her eyes flicking left to right, left to right, trying, it seemed, to follow separate pieces of water as they floated downstream. He knew she had heard him. He gave her time, as he had always done. He waited. The sky's lights dimmed, the darkness of a cinema then. Side by side, their elbows almost touching, their dim profiles silver-lined. And then, when he could no longer see her face, she whispered, simply, 'Yes.'

Afterwards he never asked her why she had accepted him. He could only suppose that he had got closer to her than anybody else, so close that she had been able to show him how far away she was from most people. A curious basis for a marriage, perhaps, but not untypical of the village where they lived. In those days, of course, he had still believed that her darkness would lift, that some kind of wind would spring up inside her and blow it all away like so many clouds. He had never imagined that it would thicken until the air of their marriage became impossible to breathe, until it was suffocation for her to live in the same house with him.

In bed she froze before he even touched her. Her body locked, keys turned in all her muscles. He could find no way to open her. He talked to her, but there were no magic words.

One night, months after the wedding, she called out. 'Help me.'

He thought she was talking in her sleep and lay still.

'Help me,' came her voice again. 'Please.'

He climbed out of his bed and into hers. He put his arms around her, but he could no more bend her than he could have bent a plank of wood. She would snap first. He held her, tried to still the trembling beneath her rigid surfaces. He held her until dawn came, watched the grey light wash into the shallow trough of her forehead, felt her nearest leg twitch under her nightgown, twitch again, then slowly begin to thaw, to stretch and flex until, curled into a foetal ball, she slept.

Aching and exhausted, he dropped away into a deep well of sleep, daylight a silver hole the size of a coin somewhere far above. He woke three hours later. Rose up through many layers of sleep in one breathless second. This sudden consciousness felt like vertigo. The bed was empty on Alice's side, moulded but cold. Brushing the covers aside, he stood up, stumbled on to the landing.

'Alice?' His voice came to him as if through undergrowth.

He tried again. 'Alice? *Alice?*'

Her face floated, bland and round, into the darkness at the bottom of the stairs. 'What is it, George? What's wrong?'

7

'Nothing. I just thought – '

'I was in the kitchen. Making breakfast. I wanted to surprise you.' She smiled up at him.

Sometimes he wondered which one of them would go mad first.

*

After eight years of marriage Alice became pregnant. They couldn't believe it. They had long since resigned themselves to a life barren of children. And given the village they lived in, perhaps it wasn't such a bad idea. It was no place for children, they told themselves. In fact, it could be seen as selfish, cruel even, if not actually criminal, to want to bring a child into their bleak doomed world.

But when Alice's tests proved positive those layers of justification fell away like scaffolding no longer needed. Their marriage rose into the air, sheets of glass and gleaming steel, founded in rock, challenging the sky. They were giddy for days.

And Alice changed. It was like the simple tilt of a Venetian blind: she suddenly afforded views into herself that he had never known (or even guessed) existed. She sang in the mornings, she came down to breakfast naked, she altered her hairstyle. A new woman. Was it because there was now somebody inside her beside herself to think about? He didn't know – and, superstitious where Alice was concerned, didn't ask either. He remained astonished and grateful. They both felt rewarded. They made all kinds of plans.

'We'll plant roses in the garden,' George said. He hated gardening.

'We'll paint the house,' Alice said. She hated decorating.

'We'll shoot Peach,' George said. They both hated Peach.

They began to laugh.

'We'll shoot the whole bloody lot of them,' George said.

'We'll go away,' Alice said.

Neither of them noticed the transition.

'We'll buy a caravan,' George said.

'A gypsy caravan.'

'We'll travel all over the country. Like gypsies.'

'We'll go everywhere. We'll see things.'

'We'll get married again.'

'A gypsy wedding.'

'Jump over a fire hand in hand.'

'You playing a Spanish guitar.'

George laughed. 'You in one of those big whirly skirts.'

'We'll live happily ever after,' Alice said. 'Like in fairy stories.'

Roses were planted and the house was painted, but they skilfully ignored the point at which their fantasies failed to face reality. Happiness had turned them into children. The mood of innocence lasted, swept them into 1955.

On May 22nd, almost two weeks late, Alice went into labour. After thirteen hours she gave birth to a healthy baby boy. He weighed 11 lbs 3 ozs (a local record) and he had a widow's peak which, according to George, signified a life of great good fortune. Otherwise there was nothing particularly unusual about him. Because both George and Alice had always liked the story about the Israelites crossing the Red Sea – in their eyes, of course, the pharaoh was a policeman – they decided to call their son Moses. There was hope in a name like that.

Alice returned home.

Two weeks later George found her in the scullery cupboard. She was vomiting. On the floor beside her stood an empty tin of baking yeast.

'I wanted to rise,' she whispered, when she could speak again. 'I wanted to rise out of this place.'

He could almost have laughed, but a weight descended, crushing all humour, however bitter, crushing all thought. In the squalid darkness, squatting among hoes and rakes, smells of compost and turpentine, jamjars of nails, his wife's face gave off the palest light. He knelt beside her, took her awkwardly in his arms. It wasn't resistance that he encountered then, it was fear, stealing like a numbness through her flesh, stiffening her limbs. He heard the distant jangle of keys.

After that he would often hear her sobbing behind locked doors or see her crouching by the hedge at the end of the garden, the sun pouring its harsh light on her like scorn. She was sliding backwards and he couldn't get a grip on her. She had lost interest in everything, Moses included. His size frightened her. His demands made her feel powerless: he was so *strong*. She wished, she told George once (her face caged in her hands, tears trickling through the bars of her fingers), that she had never had him. George could only gaze at her. It was such a brutal transformation.

When Moses was six weeks old, Alice drew the curtains and went to bed. In desperation George consulted the village doctor, a fussy bald man with a moustache like Stalin's. The doctor used reassuring phrases – nothing to worry about, it's only post-natal depression, perfectly normal – and prescribed a course of iron pills. 'Time,' he said to George. 'Give her time.' But time had always been difficult for Alice, and George wasn't reassured. Meanwhile Moses was growing, changing, almost oblivious, as if his life had an uninterruptable momentum of its own. He slept the whole night through without waking and, for the first two months, slept in the mornings too. Once he had mastered the art of sitting up, he seemed content to spend the day on the floor, one hand on his stomach, thumb in his mouth, smiling. He had one solemn expression which he put on rather deliberately, like a cap. He seldom cried and seldom moved. In retrospect, then, a most unusual baby.

George had to learn motherhood. He sterilised bottles, changed nappies, wheeled Moses around in his new maroon pram. He even knitted Moses a simple romper-suit. He told Moses stories about New Egypt, and Moses often looked as if he was listening. Piece by piece, an extraordinary idea occurred to George. The picture, when he had assembled it, shocked him, shook him with its implications, but as the months went by it tightened its hold. First it became possible, then logical, and finally the only alternative. He realised that regardless of, *because* of Alice's condition, he would have to share it with her.

'Alice,' he said one evening after a dinner that he had cooked and she hadn't touched, 'there's something I've got to say.'

'What.'

'We have to let Moses go.'

Her eyes flickered, widened, but she said, 'Yes.'

George's patience had been fraying for days. Now it tore. 'Jesus Christ, Alice,' he shouted. 'Don't just say yes. Say what you mean.'

She sat motionless. Then she began to shiver. The wave of his anger subsided. Shame flowed into the spaces it had left.

'Listen to me,' gently now. 'We have to get Moses out of this village. I've been thinking about it. I've got a plan.'

Alice said nothing.

'I know there's only an outside chance, but it's the only chance he's got. It's worth it, for him. For us too, in a way.'

'In what way?' Her voice was so soft that the silence bullied it.

'We'd be thinking about something other than ourselves. Maybe that would bring us together again. Maybe it would – ' but he broke off, aware that he was walking into fantastic territory. 'We *have* to do it. We have to try and give him what we never had. We owe it to him.'

'I don't know – '

'We *owe* it to him. What have we got to lose? Fuck all.'

His language had coarsened recently. The frustration, he told himself. The sheer bloody frustration of it all. He looked across at Alice. Her unwashed hair hung in limp greenish strands. Her centre-parting had the pinkness of a scar. She avoided his eyes.

'You hate me,' she said.

He sighed. 'Alice, you know that's not true.'

'You're bored with me. You hate me.' Her voice had grown hard, serrated, but when she lifted her eyes to his the water in them warped and trembled like the air above a fire.

'No.' He reached across the table and took one of her hands. 'I love you, Alice. I always have. You know that.'

She looked down again. Tears began to splash on to her skirt. Because he couldn't see them falling from her eyes, they seemed to have nothing to do with her. This tyrant sadness had invaded her, was running her. She lacked the strength to fight it.

'I love you,' he repeated. 'We only have each other. What else do we have?'

Her mouth tightened, shrank. 'You want to take my child.'

George climbed to his feet. He paced round the kitchen. He let his eyes travel over things: the chipped spout on the teapot; the cobwebs slung between the cooker and the fridge; the lino floor curling at the corners as if stale; cracks, like black hairs, on the cups and plates; the window a tiny dribbling pane of glass. He felt as if he was walking on the ocean bed. If he opened his mouth to scream, he would drown.

'Look at us,' and he was still circling the room, 'just look at us. We're pitiful. Absolutely bloody pitiful. What can we do? Nothing. Not a damn bloody thing, Alice.' He rested one hand on the back of a chair, pinched his eyes with the other. 'But Moses – ' and, using the boy's name, his voice lifted as if in prayer. He sensed a change in the quality of his wife's silence. He took it as approval. Or, if not approval, acquiescence at least.

The next day he dressed warmly in his old sheepskin coat and walked down to the river. It was a raw sunless afternoon in January. His breath streamed out behind him, a white scarf in the wind. It had been raining for days and the mud track sucked at his boots. He passed the tree-house that he and Alice had built fifteen years before. A few lengths of wood, blond and curiously straight, among the sinuous green branches. Dismantled by the wind, by other children. Almost unrecognisable now. When he reached the river, he squatted down and began to pick the bulrushes, snapping them off at the waterline so he would have a good length to work with. He kept going until he could no longer feel his hands. He held his hands out in front of him, red up to the wrists, and smiled. Something was happening. Something was actually happening. He gathered up his bundle of rushes and walked home across the fields.

He visited the river almost every day for five or six weeks. Sometimes lithe, sometimes sluggish, it was always there, alive, developing, like the drift of his thoughts. It gave him lessons in momentum, it taught him persistence. Some days he would sit on the bank and watch it go by, watch an endless array of objects twist and roll and jink their way downstream – sticks, cans, leaves and once, improbably, a wardrobe, its slim mirror bright as a knife in a drawer. Downstream. That was where Moses was going. In a basket made of rushes and sealed with pitch. That was the plan.

Alone on the bank, he would run through the mechanics of the plan, weigh up the coincidences it depended on, wonder, above all, at the cheek of it, and slowly it would begin to flow in his head, washing obstacles away, and he would know then that it was right, that it could work, that if he didn't at least give it a try then the rest of his life would be a cowering, a ritual of flagellation, a bottomless pit of remorse. He knew the dangers too. They showed themselves often enough. Policemen appeared from nowhere, propelled by curiosity. They scrutinised his armfuls of rushes. They asked innocent loaded questions.

'Rushes, Mr Highness?'

'Yes, officer.' And then, 'My wife, you know. She loves having greenery around the place.' Absolute crap, of course. In her present state, she couldn't have cared less. And how he longed to sound defiant. To say, for example, 'That's right, officer. They're rushes.' Or even, 'Yes. So what?' He resisted. These would have been cheap victories. He forced himself to think in campaign terms.

But it wasn't only the police he had to contend with. Once he came back from the river to find Alice waiting, hands on hips, in the kitchen. It was Valentine's Day.

'Hello, Alice,' he said, kicking off his Wellington boots. 'God, it's beautiful out there.' He felt good after his walk, his mind honed by the wind and cutting cleanly.

'Don't tell me,' she snapped. 'More bloody rushes.'

He looked up at her in surprise. She so rarely swore. And the air in the kitchen suddenly seemed compressed, squeezed into a space too small for it.

'I need them,' he explained. 'I need them to practise with. I'm still learning, you see.'

'You can say that again.'

'What do you mean?'

'Learning,' she mocked, and waved a hand in the air, palm up, as if scattering seed. 'Learning, he says. You've got a lot to learn if you ask me.'

'I'm sorry, Alice. I just don't follow you.' His mind not cutting quite as cleanly as he had thought.

Her sudden fury released a blast of heat in the cold room. 'Spending all your time with these,' she screamed and grabbing a handful of rushes from a vase on the dresser hurled them, stiff and dripping, at his face. They landed on the floor with a slap. 'And none of it with me,' she went on. 'Now do you *follow*?'

George wiped his face with the back of his hand.

'If you want to *learn* something,' Alice sneered, 'why don't you try learning something about marriage?'

Still George said nothing. He was staring at the rushes. They lay on the floor like a prophecy or an omen.

Then her voice sank back into listlessness as she told him, 'They're beginning to drive me mad.'

He decided that, from then on, he would only pick what he needed. He would hide the rushes out of sight at the top of the house. If the police came round and asked where all the 'greenery' was, he would have to dream up a new story.

As he watched Alice fly from the room, her arms angled back like wings, it struck him that this plan of his could be seen as nothing more than an attempt to set some vivid daring achievement against a marriage that had become lack-lustre, irredeemable. But he loved Alice. He still loved her. And her unhappiness hurt him all the more because he lacked the power to alter it. He had tried. God knows he had tried. He now knew that her only happiness lay in sleep, in unconsciousness, and finally, he supposed, in death. Moses, though. He could do something there. However risky, however far-fetched, however painful it might prove to be.

He locked himself in the attic at night and worked for hours at a stretch. He had never been practical so he took a certain pride in the acquisition of this new and utterly manual skill. He suffered untold setbacks and began to understand why he had heard so little about basket-weaving. Awkward, monotonous, maddening work.

Then, one night, he found himself watching in fascination as the rushes began to flow from between his clumsy hands, braiding, interlacing, repro- ducing in their twisting plaits, in their infinite and subtle shades of green, the currents of the river they had grown in. His confidence rose, bobbed on the surface of his darker thoughts. He knew he could build a basket that would float, he knew the river would carry his son. He became impish and for the first time in years looked as young as he really was, if not slightly younger. He danced a jig in the spotlight of his desk-lamp. He unleashed silent cries of jubilation. He saw a policeman turn into the street below, a truncheon swinging from his wrist. From his attic window, the chink in the curtains narrowed to an inch, George mocked the policeman as he passed.

'You fool,' he hissed. 'Fool bobby. Look at you. Bobby fool.'

It was four in the morning before his excitement died down and he could sleep.

During the hours of daylight he hid the basket under a torn sheet in the corner of the room. It looked like a miniature ghost – the ghost Moses would become. It looked capable of uncanny things. It radiated power. The various materials he had used lay scattered on the floor – dried rush-stems cut to length, coils of thin blond rush-stems stringy as hair, pots of rush-glue that he had made by boiling the base of the stalks – and the reek of pitch hung in the air, so acrid that it was almost visible. How long before it crept downstairs, spread through the house, filtered out into the village? How long before the police started poking their noses in?

In ten days he had finished. He took Alice by the hand and led her up to the attic. A drab spring day. Wind nagging the wet trees. When he drew the cover off, she held her face in both hands as if it contained something that she was afraid she might spill. She examined the basket with nervous fingertips, her left eye twitching. He had been standing close to her, his arm touching hers, but now he stepped back, allowed her room to speak.

'It's beautiful. It's – ' and she hunted for more words with her hands as if they might be found on her person somewhere, in a pocket, perhaps, or up a sleeve. 'It's, it's,' and they came tumbling out, 'it's like an ark, isn't it, George?'

George clapped his hands, then brought them to his lips. 'That's exactly what it is,' he cried. 'It's an ark. Of course. Oh, Alice. You're – '

He couldn't speak. In that moment he had seen his wife transformed again. She had forgotten herself so rarely during their nine years of marriage. He opened his arms, offered her an avenue. She closed her eyes and turned into it, blind. They clung to one another. Just there and then, the room darkening, rain closing in and shutting out the world, she was with him.

'Alice,' he murmured. 'I love you.'

*

A misty dawn in the June of that year. Trees' branches blurred, hands gloved in white lace. The fields beyond the trees invisible.

The sun, the world, invisible.

Ideal conditions.

Since his birth, Moses had been growing at a startling rate and now, at thirteen months, he already measured over two and a half feet. George knew he had to act fast. If he left it any longer the whole thing would be impossible.

He turned away from the bedroom window. Alice was still asleep, her many anxieties holding her down, weights on her body, weights on her eyelids. She slept late these days. After that morning in the attic she had curled in on herself like a snail, all her life inside, withheld. When he tried to speak to her, she flinched, backed away, hands muffling her ears. She didn't want to listen any more.

He crossed the landing to his son's room. Moses lay on his back. He was gazing at his fish mobile. The window stood open a notch and cool air flowed in. Finned shapes swam in the gloom. When he noticed his father standing above him, one of his hands began to strike the air. Sounds that had the feeling of words and the complexity of sentences bubbled from his mouth. He would be talking in no time.

George reached down and lifted him out of his cot. The baby's feet pumped the air like someone treading water. A trickle of silvery drool spilled from the corner of his mouth and ran down George's sleeve. Moses grinned.

'Thank you, Moses,' George said. 'Thank you very much.'

He carried Moses downstairs. He opened the kitchen door and groped one-handed for the light. The window jumped back, turned blue. The mist a bandage on the sky. The sun would soon bleed through.

He changed Moses on the kitchen table then set him in the high-chair while he made breakfast. Baked beans, toast and tea for him. Porridge with brown sugar, blended banana and a bottle of milk for Moses.

'All your favourites, Moses,' he said. 'A real feast.'

Where would his next meal come from? What would it be? Who would be holding him? George squeezed his eyes closed for a moment, tilted his head back. His mind bustled with questions, a thousand voices babbling at once. He looked down at Moses, ran his hand through the widow's peak. The hair stood up in a dark crest then fell forwards in wisps on to the baby's forehead.

Remember these final moments.

The night ebbing. Trees rising out of the sky – dark islands, jagged coastlines.

Daylight beginning to heat the crimson roses in the kitchen window.

The taut click of the electric clock. The knocking of a waterpipe. The shudder of the fridge.

His nerves tightened and Moses, sensing tension, pushed the teat away from his mouth.

'It's all right, Moses. Everything's all right. Here.' His soothing voice as he touched the bottle to Moses's lower lip. Moses began to suck again, his eyes drifting out of focus.

Later there would be no way to bring this close again or make it seem real. Memory is a museum. Events mounted on pedestals, faces in Perspex boxes, emotions behind looped red ropes. Everything temperature-controlled, sealed off, out of reach. Looking only. No touching. That alone is distancing enough but sometimes, after a difficult journey, you arrive at the bottom of the steps, those grand stone steps with lions sprawled on either side, and you look up and the museum is closed. New hours, renovation work, an obscure public holiday. There is nothing for it. You turn away. Later in George's life there would be times when he doubted whether he had actually ever had a son.

The church clock struck six. George eased the back door shut, winced as the loose glass rattled. He moved across the damp grass, a suitcase in one hand, the basket in the other and Moses, snug in a one-piece suit, lying peacefully in the crook of his right arm. Nervousness turned his belly on a spit but he no longer feared anything. Now he was outside and under way, now he felt his plan begin to stir, to breathe, to come alive, he passed through fear into excitement. His eyes flicked from side to side, missing nothing. The row of marigolds, mist frosting their warm orange glow. The top of the fence a giant saw-blade. The hinges on the garden gate coiled like springs and burgundy with rust. The way he was looking around he might have been leaving the village himself. Seeing it for the last time. The one thought that had sustained him for the past six months now lifted him again. Moses was leaving New Egypt. Leaving the place where apathy lay like a fine dust over everything. Where people gave up, broke down, turned their faces to the wall. Where lips had forgotten how to smile and danger wore a blue uniform with silver buttons. Absurd. Pathetic. Criminal.

He glanced down. Moses lay still, but his eyes seemed lit from the inside. That's because he knows something good is happening, George thought. Babies always know.

Mist clung to the world like a new dense air, like sweat on skin. The gate didn't creak for once. No lights in any of their neighbours' houses. The inanimate was on their side. They had accomplices everywhere. It was going to work.

George slipped across the lane that wound behind their house. He cleared the stile. Ahead of him now stretched the bridleway where girls sometimes rode horses. Blackberry bushes banked high on either side. A ditch offered a hiding-place, should they need one. One hundred yards on, the hedgerow subsided, merged with the undergrowth. The track narrowed, ran into a copse, lost its identity. Trees meshed overhead, weeds sprang up. Now he was walking through a dim green tunnel. Birds sang in harsh sporadic bursts. Otherwise only the creak of the basket and the soft thudding of his shoes on the packed mud.

Five minutes later, as they were leaving the cover of the wood, some instinct made George look over his shoulder. And there, wrapped in shadow, casual and terrifying, stood a policeman. The policeman stared at George and George, transfixed, stared back. Neither of them moved or spoke.

It was several long seconds before George realised that it was only a dummy. It hadn't been there two days ago. They must have moved it. They were always doing that, the bastards. Even when he had turned his back on the dummy, he could feel its supernatural presence, the pressure of those blank white eyes.

He stood at the edge of an open field. Cows often grazed there in the daytime. Now it seemed empty, an arena of dull grass, occasional highlights of dew. Beyond this field, another field. Beyond that, the river. This was the most dangerous part. He could imagine the colour blue appearing, on the very border of visibility, but spreading like ink until it surrounded him.

He began to walk.

He had to stop every so often to alter his grip on the basket, to switch Moses from one arm to the other, to wipe the lenses of his glasses, but he never stopped for long and when he started again he always walked faster than before. His eyes probed the mist and it broke up into marbles, weightless, grey and white, jostling, colliding. After that he kept his eyes on the path. At last the ground began to slope down and he heard the trickling of the river.

When he reached the place where the rushes grew he squatted down. He opened the lid of the basket and laid Moses inside. He left the lid open while he fitted the suitcase into the brackets he had built on to one side of the basket. He used the leather strap that bound the suitcase to lash it into position. There were two makeshift pockets on the other side of the basket. These he filled with stones to act as ballast. He sat back on his heels and pushed at the suitcase with spread fingers. It seemed secure enough. His only lapse into sentimentality, this suitcase. He had packed it the previous night. It contained a few mementoes of their all too brief family life together. Also inside the suitcase was a carefully worded (and unsigned) letter instructing that the contents were to be 'held in trust for Moses George Highness until he attains the age of twenty-five'. No reasons were given for the abandonment of the baby. The fewer clues, the better.

The sky had expanded above their heads. The mist was beginning to lift. A tractor snarled two or three fields away. He had to get back.

He bent down and kissed Moses. Moses tugged at his hair.

'Moses,' he whispered. 'That hurts.'

Moses gurgled.

George tried to imagine his son's future face, the face this face was a blueprint for, but nothing came. He fastened the lid and waited. He couldn't form the word goodbye – not even silently. It stuck like a fishbone in his throat and would choke him. He lifted the basket in both hands and set it down in the shallows. The rushes, stiff, abundant, held it fast. He rolled it from side to side to test for buoyancy and removed two or three stones from the right-hand side. It was as stable as it would ever be. He gave it a firm push. The rushes parted. The basket floated out into the current, stern swinging anti-clockwise, and began to slide downstream. He watched it dissolve into the mist.

He stood up. Wiped his forehead with the back of his hand. Brushed some mud off his coat. A greyness invading him, gloom in his blood. He turned away and, walking fast, reached home in ten minutes. So far as he could tell nobody saw him return.

Alice was sitting at the kitchen table. She had been staring at the door. When he opened the door and appeared in the gap, she stared at him with equal blankness. Sleep had swollen her eyelids, creased one side of her face.

'Is it done?' she asked. Her voice flat and neutral. An automatic pilot through the storms in her head.

He nodded. 'It's done.'

*

At midday George called the police and reported his son missing. The Chief Inspector would be there in fifteen minutes, he was told. He replaced the receiver and looked across at Alice. He had talked to her earlier that morning.

'Alice,' he had said, sitting down at the kitchen table, 'I've got to talk to you.'

Her face, sullen, lifted an inch. 'Talk then.'

'Now we've got this far, I don't want to risk ruining the whole thing.'

Her resentment crystallised. 'We've?'

'We did this together, Alice. We thought it would be the best thing for Moses, remember?'

Alice frowned.

'What I wanted to say was, let me do the talking. When Peach comes, I mean.'

The skin of her face seemed to stretch thin with fear. 'Peach? Is he coming?'

'Probably. But don't worry. I'll talk to him.' He took her hand. It felt soggy. Her entire body was soaked in grief. 'You're upset,' he said. 'If he asks you anything, you're upset. Do you see?'

'I am,' she said.

Too intent on his own line of thought, he didn't grasp hers.

'Upset,' she added.

'I know.' And then, not liking himself, but seeing a necessity, 'That should make it easier, shouldn't it?'

The rims of her eyes, red as they were, registered a faint irony.

'We wanted this for Moses,' he reminded her, aware that this wasn't the whole truth.

Her face collapsed again.

'I don't know,' she wept. 'I don't know.'

From an upstairs window he watched Peach arriving. Peach was a burly pear-shaped man. He wore his grey hair in a crewcut. His lower lip jutted. He could look brutal or avuncular at will with scarcely an alteration in expression. His legs moved smoothly (and independently, it seemed, of his body) as he negotiated the garden path. He was flanked, as always, by two officers. Dolphin and Hazard. Both hard men.

When the bell rang George answered the door. He ushered the three policemen into the lounge. Alice shrank against one end of the sofa, her hand closing round the sodden ball of her handkerchief. Ignoring George's offer of a seat, Peach stood in silhouette against the window. Dolphin and Hazard took the armchairs on either side of the fireplace. Peach wasted no time in coming to the point.

'When,' he said, 'did you last see your son?'

'At around eleven-thirty,' George told him. 'It was a sunny day and we'd left him at the bottom of the garden in his pram. Alice was upstairs cleaning. I was in the kitchen preparing some lunch. When I went out to check him the pram was still there but he was gone.'

Peach massed at the far end of the room. Absorbing information. Blotting out the light.

'I couldn't have been more than twenty yards away from him the whole time,' George added, 'but I never heard a thing.'

Don't talk so much, he told himself.

Peach could be heard jingling a selection of keys and small change in his pocket. 'And you, Mrs Highness, were upstairs,' he said, 'cleaning.'

Alice whispered, 'Yes.'

'I beg your pardon?' Peach said.

'Chief Inspector, please,' George said. 'This has been a terrible shock for my wife. She's very upset.'

'And not for you?' Peach enquired.

'And not what?' George asked, though he had understood.

'Never mind.' Peach moved from the window. Light invaded one half of his face. He seemed, unaccountably, to be smiling. 'You have no idea who could be responsible for this?'

'No idea.'

A long silence followed. George could hear the rustle of Dolphin's notepad and the scratching of his fountain pen. Hazard was fidgeting in his armchair. He seemed to be trying to contain violence of the most unpleasant kind. Peach stared out of the window.

'Unusual, don't you think,' Peach said eventually, 'the disappearance of a baby?' His voice light, almost conversational.

'Not especially,' George replied. 'Babies disappear all the time.' Only to realise that he had fallen for one of Peach's tricks. A truly grief-stricken parent would never have answered with such apparent objectivity. 'But,' he rushed on, wanting now to convey courage in the face of adversity, giving himself, as it were, a stiff upper lip, 'we haven't given up hope, Chief Inspector.'

Peach moved across the room on extraordinarily light feet. 'And what about you, Mrs Highness? Have you given up hope?'

Alice flinched. Eyes staring. Hands clenched. Still that girl in the woods, her head pressed into the leaves. The boots, the boots.

'I told you,' George stepped in, 'she's very upset.'

Peach said nothing. He looked at Alice, then at George, then at Alice again. His lower lip moved out and back. Once. Smoothly. 'Well,' he said, 'that'll be all for the time being,' and, gesturing to Dolphin and Hazard, spun like a huge lubricated top in the direction of the hallway.

George followed them out and suddenly couldn't breathe. The three policemen packed the narrow space to suffocation point. They had arrested all the light, all the air. The coarse rasping blue of their uniforms everywhere. Even their breathing seemed blue. God, how he loathed that colour now. He couldn't even look at the sky without thinking of policemen. Peach opened the front door and passed through. A draught flowed into the house. George gulped it down.

'Not feeling too good,' he muttered.

Dolphin made a note of the fact on his pad.

As George closed the door, he heard Alice run up the stairs.

*

The next day, at nine in the morning, the phone rang. The Chief Inspector would like to see them. Separately. Mr Highness at two p.m. Mrs Highness at three p.m. Was that convenient?

'What is this?' George cried. 'A trial? We've lost our son, for Christ's sake.'

'I'm sorry, Mr Highness,' came the official police voice. 'It's the Chief Inspector's request.'

'Well, it's out of the question. Absolutely out of the question. Please inform the *Chief Inspector* that we'll be coming together.'

The official police voice sighed. 'At two p.m., Mr Highness?'

'At two p.m.'

George replaced the receiver.

Peach didn't refer to this telephone conversation when they were shown into his office that afternoon. In his mind he had probably already turned their refusal to appear separately into an admission of weakness. Which it was, of course. Instead of taking them apart one by one, in isolation, he would now attempt to play them off, one against the other. Peach sat behind his desk, his lower lip drooping with scepticism. His eyelids looked heavy, ornately wrinkled, curtains that rose and fell on mysteries that ran for years. His fingers, plaited together on the surface of his desk, reminded George improbably of the rush basket. Peach asked them both to be seated. There was a pause while he adjusted the position of a document. Then he began.

'You know, of course, that I'm suspicious.'

George assumed a puzzled air. Aware beforehand of just how exacting this interview was likely to be, he had been practising all morning in the bathroom mirror. He felt his eyebrows slide into position, he felt ridges forming in the skin above the bridge of his nose. Perfect.

But Peach turned away from him, making an irrelevance of his expression. 'Mrs Highness,' he said, 'I think *you* know what I mean.'

Alice's eyes rolled sideways in their sockets.

'You mean,' George rushed in, 'that someone might have kidnapped Moses? Abduction. Is that what you suspect?'

'Abduction?' Peach pretended to be dealing with a possibility that hadn't occurred to him. 'No, not abduction.'

'What then?'

Alice sniffed. (George had told her to sniff as often as possible. At awkward moments she should cry. But only at awkward moments. Strategy, you see. Anything to distract Peach.)

'Deception,' said Peach, yet to be successfully distracted, 'might be one way of putting it – '

21

George altered the angle of his head. He wanted to appear just that little bit slower than he really was.

'Subterfuge would be another,' Peach went on. 'Intrigue. Finagling. Machination.' A pause. 'Conspiracy.'

George couldn't resist. 'Nice words,' he said. '*Roget's Thesaurus*?'

Peach's steady gaze dropped in temperature. 'Where's Moses?' he snapped.

'I don't know.'

'I don't believe you.'

The two men's eyes locked.

Alice began to cry. George silently applauded her timing then, looking at her, realised that her tears were genuine. He put an arm round her and drew her towards him.

'If we knew where Moses was,' he said, 'we would hardly be sitting here, would we?'

Peach considered this. 'I don't know,' he said.

'I thought you knew everything.'

Peach eased his chair backwards. His mouth widened in anticipation of a smile. The smile never arrived. He folded his hands across his belly. Somehow he managed to make this otherwise homely gesture look threatening. Another silence began. George stared out of the office window. To kill time he counted the thorns on a rose-bush. He had reached thirty-six when Peach spoke.

'We found a toy dog,' he offered casually.

George shifted in his chair. 'Oh?'

'By the river.'

'By the river,' George repeated. He wondered how Peach knew that Moses had a toy dog.

'A white toy dog,' Peach said. Leaning forwards, he reached into an open drawer, produced the white toy dog and stood it upright on the desk.

George gasped. It was Moses's toy dog. Alice began to cry again. This time George didn't notice. He couldn't understand how the toy dog had fallen into Peach's hands. He thought he had put it into the basket with Moses. He had certainly intended to. Did this mean that Peach had found Moses too? Was this interview just another of Peach's sadistic charades? He reached out and picked up the toy dog. He turned it over, playing for time. He was trying to remember. He knew that he had slipped it into his coat pocket that morning. He had wanted Moses to have something to hold, something to comfort him on his lonely journey downstream. But, now he thought about it, he couldn't actually remember *handing* the toy dog to Moses. It must have fallen out of his pocket then. So. Peach knew nothing.

'Yes,' George admitted, 'this is my son's toy dog.' He put it back on the desk. His hand was shaking. The dog toppled over. He smiled. He had never been able to make the dog stand up.

'You don't seem particularly overwrought,' Peach observed.

'What do you want me to do? Break down? Would that satisfy you?' George's voice had lifted an octave in sudden anger.

'Just an observation,' Peach said. Two shelves of Pelican psychology ranged behind his head. Nasty little blue spines. Titles like *The Hothouse Society* and *Alienation and Charisma*. Something of an expert on the subject, Peach.

'Just in case you haven't noticed, Chief Inspector, my wife's in a terrible state,' George said, calmer now, 'and the way you're conducting this interview isn't exactly helping matters.'

'I know your wife's in a terrible state.' Peach's tone of voice implied that, in his opinion, this 'terrible state' had nothing whatsoever to do with the disappearance of the baby. Implied, therefore, that he was privy to the secrets of their marriage. Implied, in fact, omniscience. Such a very cheap yet complex remark. Vintage Peach.

George said nothing.

The Chief Inspector shrugged. He stood up. Walked to the window and back, twisting one palm against the other. 'Believe me when I say this,' he said. 'If there is anything irregular going on here, I shall discover it. Believe me.'

'I believe you.'

'Good.'

'We've been here over an hour,' George said, 'and my wife's exhausted. May we go now?'

Peach spread his hands. They were empty of questions.

As George guided Alice towards the door (grief had made an invalid of her), Peach appeared to relent. 'We'll do everything in our power,' he assured the couple, 'to find your son.'

'I'm sure you will,' George muttered.

Whichever way you looked at it, it was true.

*

Nobody could have predicted the effect that the news of the baby's disappearance would have on New Egypt. During the last two weeks of June the apathy lifted. Rumours flew the length and breadth of the community on giant wings. At first people talked of a kidnapping, a ransom – even a child molester. But then talk of an escape crept in. Stealthily, very stealthily. The few who still harboured dreams of escape themselves gathered in obscure corners of the village – under the disused railway bridge, behind the cricket pavilion, at the back of the greengrocer's shop – to discuss whether it was possible and, if so, how it could have been done. Dinwoodie held the floor, his bony hands marshalling facts, attacking the air, his extravagant grey hair tumbling on to his high shoulders, into his eyes. The greengrocer also advanced several interesting theories. The two men could often be seen returning through the summer dusk to the privacy of Dinwoodie's garage. In the light of a single naked bulb, surrounded by tools and grease and the dismembered limbs of motorbikes, they would squat on fruit crates, they would whisper and gesticulate, they would rail and connive. 'It is time,' Dinwoodie had been heard to say, 'to make a stand.'

Towards the end of the month things began to escalate. Dinwoodie founded a secret revolutionary organisation. He called it the New Egypt Liberation Front. It was dedicated, he said, to one simple political goal: freedom from oppression. He was just hours away from distributing the first copies of his manifesto when Peach led a dawn raid on his house. Hazard broke Dinwoodie's arm in a scuffle by the garage door. The greengrocer, who had stayed overnight to assist with the printing, escaped unseen over the garden wall. The police confiscated (and subsequently burned) all the political material they could find and Dinwoodie, clutching his useless arm below the elbow, was arrested and hauled off to the station for questioning. The NELF was officially disbanded. It had lasted slightly less than twenty-four hours.

But the unrest spread. Several crimes were committed. A police officer was attacked by an unknown assailant in the dark alley that ran behind the post office. Dinwoodie's repeated cries of *Fascists* carried from his cell in the police station to the road outside where his mother and his sister waited with blank faces and nervous hands for his release. Even more disturbing, perhaps, PC Fox reported the existence of 'a number of wreaths and assorted bunches of flowers' on Tommy Dane's grave in the churchyard. The story of that desperate bid for freedom in the forties had been revived and was being retold in graphic and inflammatory detail through the village. They were witnessing, Fox suggested, the first stirrings of a Tommy Dane cult.

Once again Peach reacted with speed and efficiency. He imposed a curfew. Anybody found on the streets of New Egypt after nine p.m. would be arrested immediately. The offender would be liable to the severest penalties. Peach called an emergency meeting in the church hall to explain his decision. He had introduced the curfew, he maintained, in order to safeguard 'our future', the children of the village.

'We cannot risk another tragedy,' he declared in his most sombre voice. George wasn't fooled.

Two days later the discovery of the white toy dog beside the river became common knowledge and people began to talk of a drowning. George smiled to himself at this shift in public opinion. Rumours of escape were dangerous, subversive. Rumours of death, on the other hand, were quite harmless and acceptable. Peach must have leaked the information with that specific end in mind. George shook his head. How gullible, how fickle people were. How shrewd Peach was.

At the beginning of July a heatwave hit the area. The sky burned white and the clouds hissed like steam. The sun beat down on the drum of the land. People retreated indoors complaining of headaches. Volunteers for the search-parties dwindled. The gossip withered and died away. Now everybody had forgotten about him – even his mother and his sister had given up their vigil – Dinwoodie was quietly released. As apathy descended with a vengeance on the population, so the pressure on the police department began to lift – a perfect example of what Peach liked to call *the scissor effect*. The grass on the village green turned brown. The leaves on the trees were so dry that they clicked as if they too were made of wood. Rain became a memory. Peach declared a drought. He issued a comprehensive list of instructions pertaining to the use of water: no washing of cars, no lawn sprinklers, no baths. Now people really had something to moan about, something nice and trivial. The search-parties continued, consisting entirely of police officers. Lines of sweat-drenched uniforms could be seen combing the long grasses and the bramble-patches in the vicinity of the river. Peach ordered Dolphin, a powerful swimmer, to drag several hundred feet of the river-bed. No new clues turned up. No fresh evidence. One white toy dog. That was all that remained of Moses Highness. It was a strange time to talk of a drowning but no other conclusion could be drawn.

Towards the middle of the month, almost five weeks after Moses's disappearance, George was summoned to Peach's office, alone this time. A far less combative, far wearier meeting. One look at Peach's face and George guessed.

'Nothing new, then.'

'Nothing new,' Peach admitted. 'We've tried everything, exhausted every possibility.' He sighed. 'I can only conclude that Moses, your boy, drowned in the river. We shall never know exactly how.'

George hung his head for an appropriate length of time. When he looked up, the necessary tears filled his eyes. 'There's really no hope?'

'I'm afraid not.'

'Of course I knew there was a possibility that Moses might have, might have drowned. I just never – ' His voice faltered and he looked away. His acting had definitely improved.

'Well,' Peach said, 'I'm making it official, as from today,' and he consulted his calendar, 'July the fourteenth. We can't have any loose ends, you understand. Not in a matter like this.' He paused. 'There will be the funeral to take care of.'

'I know.'

'If there's anything I can do – '

George scanned the Chief Inspector's face for its usual irony. Not a trace. Genuine compassion then. Peach could be almost likeable at times. That was what made him so dangerous.

'Thank you,' George said.

Any elation he might have felt as he walked to the door of Peach's office had been dismantled by the preceding weeks of pressure and suspense. And, for all he knew, Moses might really have drowned in the river.

That would have been the cruellest irony of all.

*

The priest sprinkled a handful of token soil on to the coffin lid. The grave gaped. A mouth in the ground not saying anything. Soon the sexton would arrive. Stop it up with spadeloads of earth. Stop it up for ever. Eternal silence.

George wondered.

His grandfather and his father were buried here. Now his son. In a way. He had a sudden urge to laugh, to screech with laughter, to guffaw. He coughed instead.

He glanced round. So few mourners. A dozen, if that. And half of them policemen. Things were definitely back to normal. Even now he was being watched. Perhaps he would always be. He caught Dinwoodie's eye and felt the tug of the man's curiosity. He would like to have let Dinwoodie into the secret (imagine his face!) but Dinwoodie had a mouth on him, everyone knew that. If it wasn't his escape plans, it was his revolutionary party. No, he would never be able to tell Dinwoodie. Or anyone else, for that matter. He turned back in time to see the priest close his prayer-book. The priest's sacred words were already evaporating in the heat.

The service over, there was a general adjusting of collars and veils, a general shuffling and clearing of throats. As George steered Alice away from the grave, Peach loomed, a mass of blue curves, vacuum-packed into his dress uniform.

'Please accept my condolences,' he said, 'my sincere condolences,' and rested a heavy hand on George's shoulder.

The resonance of this gesture was not lost on George. So devious this Peach. Even now his mind would be on the move, bristling with suspicions as an army bristles with spears.

'Thank you,' George said. The briefness grief allows you.

But Peach was unwilling to let go just yet. 'We did everything we could,' he said. 'As I'm sure you know.'

'Oh, we know that, Chief Inspector. We know that.' George considered the sky, its empty unblemished blue, Peach's face a pale blur in the foreground. And he smiled. 'If you could've found him, you would've done. I can only thank you for all you did on our behalf.' Overdoing it a bit, perhaps, but in a kind of trance. He had climbed, it seemed, into thin exhilarating air.

Peach shielded his eyes and fell back on convention. 'Not at all, Mr Highness,' he said, and pleasantly enough, 'not at all.' Tugging at the front of his tunic he turned away to rejoin his colleagues.

Relief drifted upwards through George's body, the faintest of breezes, cooling him, refreshing him, but not visibly disturbing his outer surfaces. He couldn't allow relief to register. He would always be careful.

He turned to Alice, took her arm.

'Let's go,' he said, 'shall we?' Secretly rejoicing that his plan, against all odds, had worked.

THE BUILDING
OF MANY COLOURS

The sun falling across the tables of the Delphi Café that afternoon was pure and white, as dazzling as a vision. The proprietor leaned against the back wall, his legs crossed at the ankles. He was leafing through a paper. A fly described an unearned halo in the air above his head. It was a Sunday.

His only customer was an old woman dressed in a crumpled mackintosh. Her mane of grey hair, so long that it tickled the small of her back when she unpinned it, wound in a chaotic bun beneath her transparent plastic headscarf. A bag, also plastic, nestled against her left foot. Her wrinkled fingers held a cup of tea as settings hold precious stones. Her name was Madame Zola and she had printed cards to prove it. MADAME ZOLA, the cards said. FAMOUS CLAIRVOYANT AND PSYCHIC CONSULTANT. APPOINTMENTS ONLY. Never mind that the cards were twenty years old. She could still touch somebody and feel sadness or ambition or fear, the tremors of a life as it ran along its own unique track towards an unknown destination. Sometimes, too, she got flashes. She would never forget the night when she felt the death of Christos, the man she worshipped, her religion.

Rain on the windows and she had trickled fingers down his face, his neck, his arm, and she had felt death like a fine powder on his skin, she had felt his life speeding towards some collision, and she had drawn back, biting her wrist, it seemed so strange, this strong Greek, he looked more like a wrestler than a pianist, and he had stared at her across the black curls on his chest, his eyes had reeled her in, fish-hook eyes, and he had said *What is it?* and she had pretended to be thinking of her sister, the one who had just lost her baby, and he had believed her because she was a woman and women are sentimental, and he had pulled her towards him, one of his piano hands playing in her hair.

How she wished she hadn't touched him that night – but how could she not touch him?

In any case, he had believed her lie and one year later, in the same room, he had died. His head resting in her hands, his hands still for ever. Fifteen years ago now, but she still returned once a year, sometimes twice, sometimes with flowers and nowhere to leave them, because she thought of Kennington as his cemetery and the building where he had died as his mausoleum, and when she stood in front of the building she could still hear the music pouring from his fingers, running up her spine and into her hair, every note a shiver, and when darkness fell she would turn away and travel home, this frost around her heart, an old woman on the bus with flowers.

Yes, she could predict the future. Her husband's death was proof of that. She could also make a cup of tea last a very long time. The proprietor had already sent one or two unpleasant glances in her direction. She had ignored him, of course. And even as she sat at her table in the shadows, her various powers combined to produce a vision of the café in ruins. There was no malice in this. Visions came unsolicited; they appeared out of thin air, as poems do. It was unmistakably the Delphi Café, though. She recognised the strawberry formica and the concrete stump where the pillar had been. And there, perched high on the rubble and miraculously intact, stood her cup of tea, filled to the brim with twigs, cobwebs, the bones of small animals, wood-splinters, fragments of plaster and brick, the remnants of a nest, and an unidentifiable grey dust (had bombs fallen?). With fingers that were nimble for their age, she unearthed about 0.02 cl. of petrified tea, scarcely more than a stain really, but proof none the less that she could make a cup of tea last almost indefinitely (whether the proprietor liked it or not), prolonging it into a future which, it had to be admitted, she had herself predicted, but which all the same seemed real enough. For one nasty moment she took this vision as a warning – the destruction of the café might occur this afternoon, her life was in danger – but when she searched the wreckage she could find no trace of her body. She could only assume that she had already left the café and would die (had died?) peacefully somewhere else.

Some minutes later she passed a hand across her forehead. Another vision intruded. Time had wound back into the present. She saw a man standing beside a phone-box somewhere in the immediate vicinity. A tall dark man. She recognised the phone-box, but she didn't recognise the man.

A tall dark stranger?

Madame Zola frowned. All her basic instincts told her this was nonsense. Worse than that – a cliché. She adjusted her plastic headscarf, a nervous fluttering of her left hand, then peered down into her cup as if to extract some guidance or advice from the few tea-leaves floating on the surface. They told her nothing. She glanced up at the proprietor. His paper closed then opened again with a loud rustle of its intricately marked wings. She shuddered at the vision of a giant butterfly alighting on his face.

Tall dark stranger indeed.

When you worked on such a vast scale, when your materials were the past, the present and the future, you often fell victim to vivid but random images, maverick phenomena. Pieces of fantasy, dream, or memory would break loose, float free, generate their own electricity, their own atmosphere, as stars do. Madame Zola had a word for this kind of thing when it happened. She called it *interference*. This tall dark stranger, she decided, lips twisting as if she had just bitten into a lemon, almost certainly fell into that category. Lifting her cup, she sipped at her cold tea. She was getting old. Her gift was breaking up. She felt herself crossing the fine line between clairvoyance and hallucination.

All the same, as the minutes passed, she was unable to dismiss an obscure feeling of excitement, not unlike moths brushing against her stomach walls. Interference or not, she was becoming increasingly convinced of two things: one, that the tall dark stranger was going to walk into the café, and two, that she would be able to make her cup of tea last until he did.

*

Madame Zola needn't have doubted herself. A tall dark stranger was indeed standing beside a phone-box in the immediate vicinity. His name was Moses Highness.

Moses seemed to be in some kind of dilemma. He opened the phone-box door, closed it, then opened it again. It looked as if he was fighting the pull of a magnetic field. In the end he capitulated. Opened the door, edged in sideways and did what he always did: thumbed through the directory until he reached the letter H.

'Now then,' he muttered, his right eye twitching. He began to run his finger down the thin columns of names –

Heart
Heaven
Hemlock
Henna
Henry V
Hercules
Herod
Hey
Hey Gary
Hey Raymond
Hi-Tension Tattooing
Hidalgo
Hien Chul Oh A
Higgins Prof
Highgate Literary Scientific Institution

Highjack Video
Highmore – only to sigh as he witnessed that nimble, almost imper-
ceptible, but oh so familiar leap to –
Higho Belinda
Hikmet
Himmel
Ho
Hogbin –
Hopeless. It was always the same. The same disappointment. The crucial
name missing, that gap invisible to eyes other than his own. For that was
what he was looking for when he succumbed to the lure of the phone-box:
another Highness. Not necessarily his parents, not even a relative. Just
another person with the same name. Just *one person*, that was all he asked.
He had checked the London directories a thousand times, and whenever
he travelled to other towns he checked theirs too, but so far he had drawn
a blank. Literally, a blank.

He must have been about eight the first time. Still living at the orphanage,
anyway. They used to go for walks with Mrs Hood every afternoon –
outings, she called them – always the same walk, long too, real drudgery,
until one day he noticed something different. A phone-box standing near
the entrance to a wood. So red against the dusty summer green of the
hedgerow. And those directories, fat and pink, lolling like dogs' tongues
in the heat. He had dropped out of the crocodile and slipped inside.

He was always losing things, Moses. That afternoon, it was his sense of
time. Those phone-books, the names. They revealed new worlds, they cast
spells, they mesmerised. They were open sesame and abracadabra and look
into my eyes. And that gap where his own name ought to have been but
wasn't. Not so much a gap, really, as an absence, an invisibility, a having-
gone. As if he didn't belong at all, not in this world. As if he only existed
in another dimension, *between the names*. Everything swam away from him
with great gaping strokes. A black wake in his vision. The oily swell of
waves. He supposed he must almost have fainted. He surfaced with the
smell of hot dust and stale breath and dried urine in his nostrils, and black
fingers from the print of those magic pages. When he arrived back at the
orphanage, Mrs Hood summoned him to her clinical white office. She
examined his hands and asked him what on earth he had been up to.
'Reading the phone-books,' he said. Her plump glossy face (which ought
to have looked kind, but didn't) darkened. She told him he was insolent,
and sent him to bed without any tea. He had associated looking for his
name with hunger ever since.

Sixteen years later he still found phone-boxes irresistible. They stood like sirens on street-corners, their doors inched open for him, their glass panes winked and beckoned. And, after all, phone-books were constantly updated so there was always an outside chance. He had heard that people in America had strange names and one day, when he was rich, he planned to tour the country state by state, directory by directory, until he found another Highness, a Highness he would probably be related to in some fantastic circuitous manner, and he, Moses, sole English bearer of the name, would visit this Highness and they would drink to their common burden and talk late into the night, exchanging tall stories, stories that arose from having a name as unusual as theirs. (God knows, he had enough of those. When he was fifteen he had tried to change his name. The town hall clerk, a man with hands like tarantulas, had actually laughed at him; one of the tarantulas had crawled across the man's lips, but too late to frighten the laughter away. Moses had called him several names – they weren't in the phone-book either – and stalked out.) It was a dream, of course, an American dream, but one that Moses cherished and meant to translate into reality. In the meantime the search continued on this side of the Atlantic. He no longer had the slightest desire to change his name. Some things you inherited, even as an orphan.

Besides, he thought as he stood in the phone-box, what would he have called himself instead? He could have called himself Moses Pole, after his foster-parents, but that would only have opened another bag of jokes. It could have been Moses anything. Or anything anything. It was that arbitrary. He closed his eyes, thumbed blind through the directory and jabbed with his finger. He opened his eyes and glanced down at the page. Fluck, Brian. Jesus. He let the directory swing back into place and left the phone-box smiling. He suddenly felt very hungry.

*

Madame Zola's eyes had blurred from too much staring. The frosted-glass door and the smeared windows of the café swam beyond their contours, mingling lazily like Martini in gin, until a sudden injection of movement and colour, a flurry of blues and blacks, made her jump. She blinked her eyes back into focus just in time to recognise the tall dark stranger she had never seen before. He was bigger than she had been led by her vision to expect – an enormous assembly of legs and arms held together by a torn leather jacket and a pair of oily worn jeans. He positively dwarfed the café interior. She wondered how he had fitted into that picture in her head. He was the one, though. No doubt about that. She took a sip of tea that was, for her, almost profligate.

Moses paid for a cup of coffee and a ham roll and carried them to the back of the café. He placed his camera on the table (exploring London and taking photographs was something he often did on Sundays) and, after a series of improvised contortions, managed to sit down. It was one of those places where they screw everything to the floor. The tables, the chairs, the waste-bins, even, in this case, the hat-stand. Nothing moves. Sometimes you wonder whether the people who work there have been screwed to the floor as well. And they always screw everything just that little bit too close together. Places like the Delphi Café reinforced his feeling that the world had been designed for other people: phone-boxes were too narrow, baths were too short, chandeliers were too low, and tables and chairs were too close together. It was a world of barriers and partitions. It seemed to divide into areas of confinement that caused him discomfort and, on occasion, pain. It pinched like a shoe that didn't quite fit. How he longed sometimes to sweep the whole cautious miserly clutter aside. To run barefoot, as it were. Being so tall, of course, he felt it more acutely than most. Moving the tip of your finger across his forehead was like reading a braille history of his life. Bumps and swellings everywhere. It wasn't that he was accident-prone; it was just that he stuck out like a sore thumb which, because it stuck out, became still sorer. It had taken him until now – twenty-four years old and 6′ 6″ – to learn the words *duck* and *stoop*, to become accustomed to his size in relation to his surroundings, to begin to make the necessary compensations. Hopefully that was it, at least as far as vertical growth was concerned, and from now on, year by year, millionth of an inch by millionth of an inch, he would shrink, as his foster-father (once 6′ 1″, now 5′ 11½″) had done.

His thoughts were interrupted at this point by the pressure of a hand on his arm. Looking round, he saw an old woman sitting at the next table. Worn face. Sombre eyes. On the breadline, he thought. There were a million like her.

'I've seen you before,' she said.

He studied her. 'I don't remember you.'

'No, of course not.' She looked away from him with a smile that was almost coy. 'How could you?' Then, though her head remained in profile, her eyes slid sideways until they rested on him again. 'My name is Madame Zola.'

'And mine's Moses.'

'An unusual name,' Madame Zola observed. 'A name with a destiny. You see this cup of tea?'

Moses nodded, smiling.

'I made this cup of tea last until you came.'

33

Moses leaned over and peered into the cup. Three-quarters full. 'You can't have been waiting very long.'

'Ha.' Madame Zola's face broke into a complex smile made up of an infinite number of lines. 'You're right. I've only been here for four hours.'

'*Four hours?*'

Madame Zola dismissed his surprise with a casual wave of the hand, and turned down the corners of her mouth to register, presumably, great scorn. 'Four hours is nothing,' she said. 'Nothing. One time I made a cup of tea last for three days.'

'*No*,' Moses gasped.

'Yes, really.' She told him how she had walked into a café on Portobello Road one Monday morning and had suddenly been struck by a vision of herself leaving the same café three days later. She had settled at a table, ordered a cup of tea and waited to see if the vision came true.

'It's like you say. People, they don't remember me. They don't *see* me. An old woman in old clothes,' she pushed out her bottom lip, lifted an arm away from her side, 'that's like being invisible, no?'

'I suppose so.'

Madame Zola chuckled to herself. 'I exaggerate a little, but the story is true. I stayed in the café from Monday morning until Wednesday in the evening. I slept two nights on a plastic chair. Because I had to know, you see? I heard the Italian man, the owner, I heard him say to his son, "Why you lock her in? Why you no see her?" ' She twirled her hands in the air, a parody of the Italian, and Moses grinned. 'And you know what the son said? He said, "I don' know. How can I know that? How can I know why I din' see her? If I knew why I din' see her, I would of seen her. Wouldn' I?" And he tapped his head with his finger. Like this.' Madame Zola demonstrated. 'They tried to throw me out and I smiled at them. They couldn't throw me out. None of them. I leave when I want to leave. Wednesday evening. My vision, it came true.' She smiled a smile of private triumph at the memory.

'I could never do that,' Moses said. 'I could never be invisible. I'm too –' and he squared his shoulders to illustrate his point.

'Listen,' Madame Zola said, laying a hand on his forearm, 'you don't understand. What I'm talking about is, what you have, you have to use. You see what I mean?'

Moses nodded, almost following.

And watched, fascinated, as she sipped at her tea, barely disturbing the surface with her top lip. It was an act of infinite delicacy and skill, like origami or levitation. Years of practice and belief had gone into it.

'And now,' she put her cup down, and leaned towards him with the air of a conspirator, 'there is something I must show you.'

'Show me? What?'

Madame Zola waved his questions away like flies. They were tiresome questions. He hadn't understood.

'I have to show you,' she said, 'not speak about it. I cannot speak about it. Come. It's not far.'

Abandoning her cup of tea with a wistful smile – it was still more than two-thirds full; she could have waited another two days for him – she rose to her feet.

'Yes,' Moses was saying, 'but why me?'

'Because you,' and her smile became indulgent, 'you came through the door.'

He followed her across the café.

'Who knows,' she joked, as they stepped out into the September sunlight, 'maybe it's your future I'll show you.'

She was taking him to the building, the building where she had lived with Christos, the building where Christos had died. In those days it had been as white as the keys on a piano and she had told Christos that and he had said *That would be strange music*, meaning music played on a piano with no black keys. Since then the building had changed colour many times. It had been grey, cream, green and brown. Now it was pink. So many disguises. To forget the past and be young always. Like a soul passing through its different reincarnations. Some buildings had souls, she decided, and she had told Christos that too. He had laughed and she had seen the secret part of his beard that grew, black and soft, on the underside of his chin. *Soul*, he had scoffed. *You have a head full of wool and no knitting needles*. But she *knew*, you see. She knew the building would go on changing colour until it had been through every colour of the rainbow. Only then would it be allowed to die, to rest. She had seen visions of its destruction, but she had never been able to place them in time. It hadn't surprised her to receive a vision of the building again that afternoon – she often saw it; it contained the ashes of her happiest years – but it was curious how it had merged with the vision of the tall dark stranger, Moses, who now walked beside her. She didn't understand precisely in what way the two were connected, only that some connection must exist. She felt impelled to bring them together.

'You see,' and she stopped Moses with a light touch just below the elbow, 'I knew you were coming.' And then, a minute later, with a quizzical tilt of her head, 'but I never believed you would be tall and dark. *That* is extraordinary.'

Moses grinned at her without understanding the reference. He had the feeling he was learning something, though he couldn't have said what exactly. He couldn't take his eyes off her hands. She clasped them together in front of her as if they contained something precious or fragile which she was in the process of delivering.

'There.' She had lifted one finger, and the blood rustled in her veins. 'That's what I wanted to show you.'

*

She was pointing at a pink building on the other side of the main road. It was so pink, this building. Almost fluorescent. He couldn't understand why he hadn't noticed it before. Perhaps it had only recently been painted. Not only pink, but triangular too, dominating the junction. It reminded him of a ship, the way it ploughed through the drab sea of surrounding shops and houses. Yellow flowering weeds fluttered on the roof like tiny pennants.

He crossed the road and tested the double-doors. Locked. He tried to peer through the ground-floor windows. The smoked glass, opaque and black, gave nothing away. Like somebody who answers a question with a question, they offered him only a few different reflections of himself. He turned. The old woman was standing beside him. One hand on her throat, she stared up at the pink façade.

'I'm leaving now,' she said. 'You'll never see me again probably, but maybe I'll see you.'

'I'll keep a look out for you,' he said.

'That won't make any difference.'

Reading between the lines around her eyes, he realised she was smiling, but with difficulty, through tears. He looked at the ground, then at the building again. This time he noticed a flysheet taped to the side-door. He moved closer. *The Revelation Sisters*, it said. A gay cabaret. The small-print told him more. The building was a nightclub, and its name was The Bunker.

When he looked round again, Madame Zola had vanished. He crossed the street and began to take pictures. He wanted to remember the building and, by remembering the building, remember her too.

He had almost finished the film when the double-doors slammed open. A black guy appeared. He was leaning forwards, hands bunched at thigh-level. Well-dressed. Furious. Without thinking, Moses snapped off another couple of pictures. He watched the black guy through the camera as he locked the double-doors, threw wary glances left and right, noticed Moses, and walked towards him, growing larger, more detailed.

'What the fuck're you doing?' The voice was smooth and venomous, anger planed down.

Moses lowered his camera. 'Taking a few pictures. Of the building.'

The black guy's eyes were pools of yellow acid. Moses felt them eat into his face. 'I don't like people taking pictures, all right?'

'All right.'

The black guy spun on his heel, and walked over to a white Mercedes parked in the shadow of the side-street. He drove past Moses in low gear, tyres trickling on the tarmac like something about to explode. Moses wound his film back thoughtfully, his eyes following the car as it turned the corner.

*

He returned to The Bunker twice that week. It was closed both times, lifeless. He wondered whether it had closed for good.

Two weeks later he was driving up to Soho to meet his flatmate, Eddie, for a drink when he happened to pass the club again. This time he noticed a few people clustered round the doorway. It was raining. A slab of violet light glistened on the slick black pavement. The place looked open. He stamped on his brakes and pulled into the side of the road. A horn blared behind him, headlights flashed full beam. Fuck you too, he thought.

Leaving the engine idling, he crossed the pavement. It *was* open. £2.50 to get in. The blonde girl selling tickets smiled at him. Change of plan, he decided.

He parked his old Rover in the side-street and ran back to the club in case it closed while he wasn't looking.

'Is there a phone in here?' he asked the girl.

'Down the corridor on the right,' she said.

But he postponed the call to Eddie (Eddie was always late anyway) and, moving down the corridor, turned left into a room with a small bar and a dance-floor. Black walls. The usual barrage of lights. Iggy Pop's 'No Fun' slammed out of head-high stacks of speakers. A Mohican danced alone, fists clubbing the air. Already damaged sofa-seating seemed to shrink back against the walls. A short flight of stairs led to a second room, also painted black. Lengths of ripped black netting gathered like stormclouds on the ceiling. White neon tubes fizzed above the bar. The facing wall, a solid mass of mirror-tiles, glimmered a dim silver. There were black tables, sticky with spilt drinks. His kind of place.

He walked back through the club to the main entrance. The blonde girl was talking to a man whose name, if Moses had heard it right, was Belsen.

Moses waited for her to notice him. His size made that inevitable.

When she turned her head, he said, 'I'm sorry, where did you say the phone was?'

She laughed. 'Have you been looking for it all this time?'

'Sort of.'

'Come on, I'll show you.' And then, to Belsen, 'Won't be a second.'

Belsen's watery eyes followed them down the corridor. His face looked as if it had been made of wax which had melted, run, then hardened again. He was wearing a Crombie and drinking Coke out of a can.

'Who's that man?' Moses asked the girl.

'That's Belsen. He's the bouncer.'

'I don't think he likes me.'

The girl smiled. 'He doesn't like anyone. That's his job. There's the phone.'

Moses thanked her. He dialled the pub where he was supposed to be meeting Eddie and when Eddie came on he said, 'New venue, place called The Bunker.' He gave Eddie the address and hung up.

On his way to the bar, he bumped into somebody he recognised from a club in the West End. Moses knew him as The Butcher. The Butcher wore a naval cap and a belted leather apron. A meathook earring swung from his left ear. His sleeves were rolled up past his elbows, exposing a pair of scarred white forearms. The Butcher sold speed. Moses bought a £5 deal and headed for the Ladies. 'The Ladies is cool,' The Butcher had told him.

The Butcher was right. Chinese-red walls. Hairspray and smoke instead of air. Men slumped in wash-basins. Girls with their eyes on the mirror. Moses stood in line for one of the two cubicles.

When his turn came, he squeezed inside and bolted the door.

A couple of minutes later somebody wondered what he was doing.

'Wanking, probably,' another voice suggested.

Derisive laughter.

'I'm not,' Moses called out.

'What's taking you so long then?'

He didn't answer this time. He had to chop the speed on the sloping top of the cistern and that wasn't easy. One clumsy movement could send the whole lot cascading into the toilet bowl. He cut the powder into four crude lines with his Cashpoint card, rolled a £5 note and, bending his right nostril to the paper, vacuumed them up one after the other. No sense in running the gauntlet of all those beautiful jeering girls again. He dropped the paper into the toilet and flushed. Cynical applause from the other side of the door.

'About fucking time.'

Moses emerged, hands raised, warding off abuse. 'Really sorry about that.'

'You would've been,' a girl muttered as she pushed past him, 'if I'd done it on the floor.'

He had forgotten all about Eddie. He had two or three drinks, talked to the blonde girl (whose name was Louise), and once, much to his astonishment, for it was something he rarely attempted, danced. The speed, he thought. OK stuff. He'd have to use that butcher again.

At least an hour had passed when a smile appeared.

'Oh dear,' the smile said, 'you look a bit fucked up, Moses.'

'Hello, Eddie.'

The smile handed Moses a whisky. 'Swallow that and we'll go smoke a joint.'

Moses tipped the whisky into his mouth and handed the glass back. The smile became a grin. They occupied a dark corner, lit the joint. A crush of bodies soaked up the music now. It was hot.

'Vince and Jackson've come along too,' the grin said, 'but I lost them.'

Moses didn't answer. He was beginning to feel strange. A smell had risen in his nostrils, a smell he couldn't identify or explain. Something like rotten meat, something like shit. But it wasn't so much the actual smell that affected him as the idea that he had *noticed* the smell and would now be unable to *not* notice it. The smell was like the symbol of a stage he had reached in an extremely unpleasant and irreversible process. It told him there was no going back. Not now. Oh dear indeed.

His skull began to revolve of its own accord inside his scalp. His forehead became the target for a volley of tiny ice-cold missiles. He touched his hairline and sweat glistened on his fingertips. He stumbled towards the exit.

Half an hour later Jackson ran into Eddie. 'Have you seen Moses?' he asked.

'Last I saw of him,' Eddie said, 'he was going that way.' He pointed to the corridor. 'Seemed to be in a hurry.'

They exchanged a knowing look.

Jackson eventually found Moses in a skip on the main road. Moses was lying on a heap of rubble, his head halfway inside a TV set. He had lost a shoe. His arms and legs were flung out, crooked, the shape of a swastika. He looked as if he had fallen out of an aeroplane. Jackson sighed. He went to fetch Eddie, but Eddie had disappeared. With some girl, knowing Eddie. He found Vince instead. Led him outside. They stood on the pavement and stared at Moses.

'What are we going to do with him?' Jackson asked.

Vince climbed into the skip. 'Hey, Moses,' he said.

Moses didn't move.

Vince poked him with the toe of his boot. Absolutely no reaction. Vince kicked Moses several times in various parts of his body. Including once in the groin, for good measure. A faint groan came from inside the TV.

Vince climbed down shaking his head. 'Better call him a cab.'

Jackson nodded wisely. 'Usual procedure. Leave it to me.'

He ran back to The Bunker and asked the blonde girl where the phone was. She showed him. 'Is your friend all right?' she asked him. 'I saw him leave. He didn't look very well.'

'He'll be all right,' Jackson said. 'You know. Tomorrow.'

He called the cab company they always used and explained the situation. 'Yes, that's right,' he said. 'The skip on Kennington Road.'

Ten seconds.

'Don't worry about that,' he said. 'I'll pay you this end.'

Another five seconds.

He grinned. 'No,' he said, 'he doesn't usually do that.'

When Eddie arrived home at three that morning, he found Moses asleep on the sofa in the lounge with both shoes on his feet and a smile on his face.

Cab-drivers are amazing.

*

Moses had been living with Eddie for almost two years. When he first moved in, somebody had told him that Eddie would be the perfect flatmate. Sociable, loaded, out a lot. Perfect.

Not so.

Eddie was too good-looking to be the perfect flatmate. He had blue eyes and a symmetrical white smile. His skin was so smooth that an American girl had once asked him whether he oiled his body. He walked on the balls of his feet, so he communicated purpose, energy, sexual hunger. He worked in the City, some job whose mystery he preserved by using phrases like *interest differential* and *liquidity ratio*. Most people thought him just too good to be true. The phone rang constantly. So did the doorbell. Lying in bed at night, Moses soon learned to recognise the sequence of sounds that meant Eddie had come home: the giggles on the stairs, the gulp of the toilet, the three-syllable squeal of Eddie's bedroom door. It seemed that, sooner or later, half the world's population would pass through that ground-floor flat in Battersea. It could have been worse, of course. As Moses said to Eddie after their first exhausting week together: 'Thank Christ you're not bisexual.'

The months went by and Moses developed a theory about Eddie. He became secretly convinced that Eddie had once been a statue, that Eddie had been released from his immobility, activated, as it were, but only for a limited period of time, and that, sooner or later, Eddie would have to return to his pedestal (somewhere in the Mediterranean, no doubt) and readopt his classical pose (involving, Moses imagined, a discus or a javelin). This explained Eddie's smooth skin, his sculptured features and his athletic physique. It explained the hectic dyslexic way he lived. It explained his attitude to women (for which Moses could find no other possible explanation). Above all, it explained why he never got home until three or four in the morning. Life was short for Eddie.

Whenever one of Moses's friends travelled abroad, he asked them to keep an eye out for empty pedestals. Nothing of any significance had turned up so far. There had been a brief surge of hope, the glimmer of a breakthrough, when he received a postcard from Vince's girlfriend, Alison, reporting the existence of an unoccupied plinth on one of the remoter islands in the Cyclades. However, the missing statue had been removed to a museum in Athens, and Alison assured Moses, in a second postcard bought at that very museum, that she had seen the statue in question and that it definitely wasn't Eddie.

During the summer and autumn of 1979 Moses kept Eddie under constant surveillance. When they passed a statue in the street, he watched Eddie's face, but it never registered even the slightest flicker of recognition or unease. Either Eddie was a natural actor, or he was like Moses and part of his memory had been erased.

Once, Moses – a casual Moses, studying his fingernails – had asked Eddie a trick question.

'Where were you born, Eddie?'

'Basingstoke,' Eddie said.

Basingstoke indeed. What kind of fool did he take Moses for?

Then, a few days before their first visit to The Bunker, Moses forced a confrontation. Uncertainty and frustration had been eating into the fabric of his life like an army of moths. He opened colour supplements and Michelangelo's David would be standing there, eyes averted, as if he knew. He went for long walks through parks only to see stone Neptunes frozen in the act of climbing out of artificial lakes. He dreamed about football matches attended by capacity crowds of 100,000 statues, scarves wrapped round their cold necks, rattles in their dramatic outstretched hands. He couldn't take it any longer. He had to know the truth.

It was a weekend. Moses had been sitting at the kitchen table when Eddie ambled in wearing his blue towel dressing-gown. Eddie had a loose-muscled way of moving about, even first thing in the morning. His eyes were heavy, though. He had slept alone and that always took a lot out of him. What you aren't used to can hit you pretty hard.

Eddie poured some cornflakes into a bowl, added milk and sugar, and sat down opposite Moses. These movements tortured Moses. Their slowness, their relaxed simplicity, crackled through him like electricity. He felt as if he was about to short-circuit. The first spoonful was halfway to Eddie's mouth when Moses spoke:

'Eddie, were you ever a statue?'

There. He had said it. After all these months.

'I mean, you know,' he went on, 'have you got to go back sometime and be one again? And, if so, how long have you got exactly? Because if you are going back, I think I should know, really. After all, I *am* living with you.'

A puzzled expression, remote, barely defined, moved across Eddie's face, but left it undisturbed. Wind over stone.

'All right then,' Moses said, 'just tell me where it is. The pedestal, I mean. I'm curious, you see.'

'Moses,' Eddie said slowly, 'it's very early in the morning and I'm trying to eat my breakfast, OK?' He shook his head. The first spoonful of cornflakes completed its journey to his mouth.

Moses rubbed his eyes with the heels of his hands. Eddie's cereal made a rhythmic crunching sound in the silence of the kitchen. Moses saw a battalion of statues with stiff arms and stony faces marching through the darkness towards him.

The next few days had proved awkward for them both. Moses hated the tube – it was too small for him – but when he wanted to go to the Trafalgar Square post office to check the directories he had to use it. What else could he do? His Rover had broken down again and there were seventeen statues on the bus-route.

Eddie seemed distracted too. Why did Moses keep going on about his past? What was all this crap about statues? And where had last week's colour supplement gone? He could often be seen sitting around the flat deep in thought, his forehead resting on his fist, his elbow resting on his knee. That was the last straw for Moses. The idea that Eddie could have been a famous sculpture all along explained the failure of his various Mediterranean investigations. It had never occurred to him to explore the art galleries. He had been too limited. This, coupled with Eddie's talent for evasion, made the task of arriving at any kind of truth almost totally inconceivable. Moses realised there and then that he would have to resign himself to never knowing the answer.

*

Midnight in the flat at Battersea. Recuperation time. Moses had arranged himself in front of the TV. Three cans of Special Brew beside his left foot. Cigarettes on the arm of his chair. Then the front door slammed. Eddie and Jackson breathed a mixture of whisky fumes and cold air into the room. Jackson leaned his bicycle – a black pre-war Hercules – against the wall. Eddie collapsed in a chair and spread himself as if he had acquired great power.

'So who's this old lady?' he said.

Moses glanced up from an Open University programme about logarithms. 'I'm watching TV,' he said.

'Jackson's been telling me,' Eddie said. 'You met some old lady.'

'She was a clairvoyant,' Jackson said, 'apparently.'

'Of course she was,' Eddie scoffed, 'and she could make a cup of tea last for a week.'

'Three days,' Moses said.

'I thought you were watching TV,' Eddie said.

Moses turned back to the screen. He swallowed some beer from his can. Jackson placed himself carefully at one end of the sofa and crossed his legs.

'So who is she?' Eddie asked.

Moses was watching a professor scrawl a series of hieroglyphics on a blackboard. The professor wore gold-rimmed spectacles and a violent green shirt. His hair was about to take off. Moses didn't understand a word he was saying. Great television.

'What?' he said.

'This old lady who took you to The Bunker,' Eddie persisted. 'Who was she?'

'I don't know. Just an old lady. Look at this professor.'

Jackson threw a quizzical glance at Eddie. 'He's changing the subject.'

'Avoiding the issue,' Eddie said. 'Pretending not to know.'

'Something to hide, I expect.'

'He's embarrassed. Look at him.'

'Old ladies, you see.'

'Well, we all know what Highness is like.' Eddie always called Moses 'Highness' when he was drunk.

'No taste.' Jackson adjusted the cushions on the sofa with a dispassionate hand. 'No taste at all.'

'Anything in a skirt,' Eddie leered. 'Absolutely anything.'

'Incredible, really.'

'Too drunk to notice, you see. Too fucking wasted.'

'Yes,' and Jackson became solemn, 'a drunk.'

'An animal. A real animal.'

'I'm afraid so.'

'Taking too much speed.'

'Lying in skips.'

'Picking up old ladies.'

Moses sighed.

'Picking up old ladies,' Eddie repeated. He leaned forwards, his pupils floating in a pink surround. 'And watching programmes about logarithms.'

Jackson chuckled.

'If you must know,' Moses said, '*she* picked *me* up.'

More mockery, more laughter. In the end, of course, he had to tell the story, a story that concluded with the words, 'And then she vanished into thin air.'

Eddie and Jackson exchanged looks.

'Strange,' Moses said, 'don't you think?'

Eddie stubbed out his cigarette. 'I don't believe it. Clairvoyants and black gangsters and cups of tea that last for ever. It's too much. You made it up, didn't you, Highness?'

'I didn't.'

Eddie grinned. 'Come on, Highness.'

'Every word I told you is true. I promise you,' but Moses couldn't help smiling at the expression on Eddie's face.

'Do you believe him?' Eddie asked Jackson.

Jackson made an n-shape with his mouth.

'Neither do I,' Eddie said. 'Look. He's smiling. You can't trust him, you know. He's always making things up.'

Almost two weeks, Moses thought, since their little conversation about statues. Had he touched a nerve in Eddie?

'He probably just drove past the place,' Eddie was saying, 'you know, completely by chance, and stopped because he thought it looked interesting.'

Jackson was staring at the ceiling. 'It wasn't *that* interesting.'

'Exactly. So he had to make up a few stories, didn't he. Make it *sound* interesting.'

'Pretty sad, really.'

'Very sad.'

Moses switched the T V off and stood up. 'Jesus, you two talk a lot of shit. I'm going out.'

Eddie looked up, all drunken innocence. 'Where are you going, Highness?'

'Anywhere. To the pub.'

Eddie turned to Jackson. 'What do you think, Jackson? Do you think he's telling the truth?'

Jackson glanced at his watch. 'The pubs are closed,' he said, 'aren't they?'

Eddie gloated up at Moses. Moses shrugged and went out.

To The Bunker.

*

During the next two months, the November and December of 1979, Moses saw very little of his friends. Jackson had started working at an occult bookshop, and spent his evenings and weekends pursuing his interest in meteorology. Vince was taking a lot of heroin in his squat at the bottom of the King's Road. Eddie flew to New York on business. Moses received a postcard. *Met any more old ladies?* He needed air. New air. He began to go to The Bunker once, often twice, a week. As he drove east through the city, past the power-station and the huge refrigerated warehouses, along those stark grey four-lane roads, he thought of Madame Zola sometimes, the way you might think of a key that has unlocked a door.

He quickly became a regular, a face, a name. He leaned against walls. He talked to anyone. He heard things. The nightclub hadn't always been a nightclub. It had been a wine-bar called Florian's, a fishing-tackle shop and a printer's studio in its time. Nothing lasted. Very high turnover of owners. Some said it was an unlucky building. 'Sliker fuckin' ker*me*lion, init,' a drunk told him one night, brandishing an empty bottle in his face, and Moses chose not to point out that a 'ker*me*lion' blended rather than clashed with its surroundings; he didn't want any trouble.

Between frequent drinks and awkward dances he began to find out about the present set-up. Belsen had done time for armed robbery. One of the barmen, Django, beat his wife. Elliot, the guy who ran the club, was a pimp. Louise had slept with him. How much truth these rumours contained Moses couldn't have said, but he listened all the same. When he asked why the club had closed in September, people told him there had been some kind of break-in. Nobody could give him the details. Elliot would know, they said, but Elliot, they added in the same breath, didn't like to talk about it, know what I mean? He suddenly realised that Elliot was the guy who had told him not to take the pictures.

He began to narrow his focus, and found there was more gossip about Elliot than about everybody else put together. Take the gap between his front teeth. 'Yer know what that means, dontcher,' Gladys said (Gladys owned the petshop three doors down). 'What does it mean, Gladys?' Moses asked. Gladys showed him her own diminishing collection. 'Wimmin,' she leered. 'That's what.' (One woman it didn't mean, Moses soon discovered, was Louise. He had mentioned the rumour to her one evening, and she had laughed and said, 'Nobody gets that close to Elliot.')

No one seemed to know where Elliot had come from originally – though there were a few predictable theories about the jungle. He had a South London accent – Bermondsey, somebody said. People often mistook him for a famous West Indian cricketer, and once, so rumour had it, Elliot had signed the great man's autograph for a group of young fans outside the Oval (Moses made a mental note: sense of humour?). Many accused Elliot of arrogance. The evidence? Flash suits, flash car, flash attitude. Elliot didn't seem to care whether he made enemies or not. 'The way I see it, right,' he had been heard to say, 'you make deals, you make enemies. That's the way it goes.' His pleasures? He drank brandy, preferably Remy Martin. He smoked Dunhill King Size. He listened to Manhattan Transfer in his office late at night ('He likes that soft music,' said Dino, a spry and ageless Greek who ran the delicatessen opposite the club, 'but he plays it so *loud*'). He had his own private pool-table too, and he saw himself as a bit of a hustler. If he thought you were all right he invited you up to the office for a game. When asked what they thought of him, most people used colourful language. *Wanker* cropped up more than once. So did *bastard*. Moses realised that if he wanted to know Elliot better he would have to meet him again. In the flesh. People were beginning to repeat themselves and contradict themselves. People were beginning to ask, 'Why all these questions?'

He had been voyeur for long enough.

*

Elliot shaking Belsen's hand. Elliot at the wheel of his white Mercedes. Elliot dyed red by a dance-floor spotlight. Elliot in an upstairs window, a cigarette bouncing on his lower lip.

But no contact. No real opening.

Once, as Moses paid to get in, Elliot seemed to be staring straight at him, but when Moses tried a smile, Elliot gave no sign that he had recognised him. It wasn't that Elliot stared at you as if you weren't there.

No, he stared at you as if you were there – *but not for much longer*. He stared at you as if you were about to be removed. Permanently. It made you feel nervous and disposable. Moses had the feeling it was meant to. In that moment the roles reversed, and Moses began to feel watched.

Then, one Friday just after New Year, Elliot wanted a light and Moses happened to be nearest. As Elliot dipped his head towards the match, he glanced up sideways through the flame.

'So how did they come out?' he said.

Moses was thrown for a moment. In the ultraviolet light of the corridor Elliot looked supernatural. Only the whites of his eyes and the gold of his medallion showed.

'The pictures. How did they come out?'

'Oh, the *pictures*.' Moses relaxed. 'Fine. Yeah. They came out fine.'

'I'd like to see them sometime.'

'Sure. There are a couple of good ones.'

Elliot fired smoke out of the side of his mouth.

'This is your place, isn't it?' Moses risked.

Elliot nodded.

'It's good. I come here a lot.'

'I know.' Like the hand that conceals a razor-blade, Elliot's face gave nothing away. His wide unflinching eyes seemed to be sizing Moses up. Moses began to understand why people talked about him the way they did.

They saw each other again five days later. Moses was standing in the foyer when Elliot appeared at his elbow, Belsen in attendance.

'Well, fuck me,' Elliot said, 'if it isn't the photographer.' He was wearing a maroon suit and a silver tie. He eyed Moses with a kind of teasing hostility.

'I've got something for you,' Moses said. He handed Elliot an A4 envelope.

Belsen's cold face glimmered in the corner like the light from an open fridge. He lit a Craven A and sucked on it so hard that his cheeks hollowed out and all the bones rose to the surface.

Elliot frowned. 'What's this then?'

'Open it,' Moses said.

Elliot glanced at Belsen, then tore the envelope open. The first two pictures were views of The Bunker shot from the front and the side. The third showed Elliot in close-up, chin lifted, snarling. Elliot nodded, and his top lip peeled back to reveal the gap between his teeth that meant wimmin to Gladys and nothing to Moses.

'Nice,' he said. And made as if to hand the pictures back.

'No,' Moses said, 'they're yours.'

47

Elliot blinked. 'Yeah?'

'Yeah. They're for you. Hang them in your office or something.'

'How much?'

Moses smiled. 'Nothing. I developed them myself.'

'How about a drink then?'

'Now you're talking.'

'What do you want?'

Moses knew the answer to that one. 'Brandy,' he said. 'Remy, if you've got it.'

Of course he'd got it.

Moses bumped into Louise again on his way out. 'I didn't know Elliot was a friend of yours,' she said.

'He isn't.' Moses paused, smiling, by the door. 'But I've got the feeling he will be.'

*

One night in January Moses was standing outside The Bunker. He couldn't find his money. The air prickled with a fine drizzle. A chill wind rumpled the surfaces of puddles. There was nobody in the fish and chip shop across the road. London in winter.

Jackson waited while Moses ran through his pockets once again. Jackson was wearing a short-sleeved shirt. The wind seemed to be trying to untie the knots in his hair.

'Moses? Hey! Moses!'

It was Elliot. He was dressed in a double-breasted suit of soft grey cloth. He looked warm and expensive, and his forehead shone like bronze. He had a problem, he said. His regular DJ for Wednesday night had called off sick. He needed a replacement. Strictly a one-off. There was twenty quid in it. Did Moses know anyone?

Moses poked a crushed Coke can with the toe of his shoe. 'Funny you should say that. I worked as a DJ one summer. Up in Leicester. I'd be glad to help you out. And I could use the money.' He kicked the can into the gutter.

'You sure about that?'

Moses nodded. They shook on it.

Elliot turned to go into the club. 'You coming in or what?'

'In a minute. Got to find my money.'

'It's on me,' Elliot said.

Jackson tugged on Moses's shirt as they walked in. Teeth chattering, he whispered, 'You never worked in a disco.'

'What do you know standing there in a short-sleeved shirt on a night like this?'

'It's going to warm up later on,' Jackson said. 'A ridge of high pressure moving in from the west.' But his lips had already turned blue, and his conviction was beginning to fade.

'Later on?' Moses said. 'July or August, maybe.'

'Anyway, what's that got to do with whether you've worked in a disco before or not?'

'You're always wrong,' Moses said. 'That's what.'

*

When Moses arrived at The Bunker on Wednesday night, Django pulled him to one side. Django had bushy orange sideburns and a boxer's nose that turned left halfway down. He looked Scottish but claimed to be Italian, hundred per cent. But then he also claimed he didn't beat his wife.

'Listen, Mose,' Django said, 'how about doing us a favour?'

'What favour?'

Django shifted from one foot to the other. 'Just a couple of requests, that's all.'

'Yeah?'

'Yeah, and if you play them for me, maybe I'll send a few double whiskies your way, you follow me?'

Moses studied the barman with new interest. 'What requests?'

Django mentioned two Beatles songs.

'What d'you want to hear *them* for?'

Django grinned. He looked very sly when he grinned. 'Like I said, Mose. Double whiskies.'

'How many?'

'One for each request.'

Moses nodded. 'See what I can do, Django.'

He walked over to the DJ's booth and installed himself in front of the two turntables. He put on the headphones. Jackson had been wrong the other night, but not that wrong. Moses had only been a DJ once in his life, five years ago now, and he had already drunk a bottle of red wine that evening because he had only been a DJ once in his life. Nerves.

The buckles on Elliot's shoes glinted gold as he moved across the dance-floor and into the corner of Moses's eye.

'How's it going?'

Moses was casual, even though Elliot had surprised him. 'It's coming back to me,' he said.

Elliot lifted and dropped his shoulders as if to adjust the fit of his jacket. 'If you need me, I'll be upstairs. All right, Isaac?' He grinned and walked away.

'Isaac,' Moses muttered, 'I'll give him Isaac.'

Once he had mastered all the knobs and dials he began to enjoy himself. He played all his favourite music – The Sex Pistols, T. Rex, The Temptations, Iggy Pop, Françoise Hardy, Killing Joke, The Anti-Nowhere League, Aretha Franklin. He didn't talk between tracks except for once when he said, 'And here's something you might remember from when you were very young,' and put on 'Practising for Childbirth', an educational EP on the CBF label. One girl, who reminded Moses of a famous German actress – she wore a simple black dress and no shoes – actually danced to the syncopated gasps and sighs, her eyes closed, her hair a dark blonde waterfall, and yes, Moses had to agree, the record did have a certain obscure rhythm of its own. After that hypnotic solitary dance, Moses couldn't stop looking at her. He tried to steer a smile towards her, but her eyes slid away and his smile sailed on into a sea of faces that weren't hers. There was a man with her, of course. There always is.

At first, and out of longing, he had played Dusty Springfield's 'I Only Want To Be With You'. Then, with savage irony, he thought, he put on 'Stand By Your Man' by Tammy Wynette. He swayed miserably behind his Perspex shield.

Eddie came over. 'What's this shit you're playing?'

'Go away, Eddie.'

'Jesus, you look strange, Moses.'

'Leave me alone.'

'You look like a dinosaur in a museum.'

'Fuck off, Eddie. I'm working.'

'Been a while, hasn't it?'

'Eddie,' Moses said patiently, 'fuck off before I kill you, all right?'

Eddie sauntered away, grinning. Django appeared.

'You haven't played any of my records yet,' he complained.

Moses sighed. 'Hey, Django,' he said, 'you see that girl over there in the black dress?'

Django had already noticed her.

'She's a German actress,' Moses said. 'Famous German actress.'

'Yeah?' Django looked impressed. Then suspicious. And, finally, sceptical. 'You're rat-arsed, you are.'

'She's beautiful, Django. I'm in love.'

'I can understand that, Mose. So what's the problem?'

'She's ignoring me.'

50

'Want me to have a word with her?'

Moses examined Django for a moment, then shook his head. 'No, it's all right,' he said. 'Is there something wrong with me, do you think?'

Django looked Moses up and down. 'Not that I can see. Apart from you being out of it, that is.'

'I mean, I'm the *DJ*, Django.'

'So?'

'Well, I thought girls always fell for the DJ.'

'Apparently not, Mose.'

Moses sighed again. He tried to forget about the German actress. The lights coloured his face an appropriate blue. 'All right, Django. I'll play your records now.

'Cheers, Mose.'

During the next hour Moses played both the records twice and the drinks kept coming. He saw Django dancing with a girl, and the girl Django was dancing with wasn't Django's wife. Moses began to understand. The requests. The whisky-bribes. Crafty bugger. A Scotsman definitely. A Scotsman and a wife-beater. He wished the German actress would go. Her beauty was ruining his evening. His smiles reached out to where she stood. She didn't notice. His smiles were like love-letters that get lost in the post.

Eddie came over again. 'You're making a fool of yourself.'

'What do you mean?' Moses said.

'Staring at that girl in the black dress.'

Suddenly Eddie's grinning face irritated Moses intensely. 'If you don't like it, Eddie, why don't you fuck off home?'

Eddie fucked off home ten minutes later – with the German actress. Moses felt that something had gone badly wrong somewhere. He needed a drink.

'Anything else you want to hear?' he asked a passing Django.

' "Knock on Wood". Ami Stewart.'

Moses played that twice too and drank himself into a vast indifference to everything.

The Bunker closed at two that night. While Moses was clearing away, Elliot strolled up and laid three £10 notes in a fan on the mixing-desk.

'I thought you said twenty,' Moses said.

'You did a good job.' A smile tugged lightly at the corner of Elliot's mouth. 'I thought maybe you could take over on Wednesdays. Permanent, like.'

'Not a chance.'

'How come?'

'Too painful.'

Elliot looked puzzled. He scratched his head at the point where his hair was receding. Maybe that was why it was receding, Moses thought. Maybe Elliot got puzzled a lot.

'I can't go into it,' Moses said, 'not now. I'd just rather be a normal person. You know, one of the crowd. Inconspicuous.'

Inconspicuous made Elliot laugh. 'You seem a bit down. Fancy a game of pool?'

Moses, slow tonight, said, 'Where?'

'In the office. Got my own table.'

Now Moses remembered. 'Sure,' he said.

He followed Elliot up the carpeted stairs to the second floor. Outside the last few people were stumbling home. Standing by the office window, Moses saw Belsen fold the gaunt scaffolding of his body into a battered white Cortina and drive away.

Elliot selected two glasses with heavy bases and poured them both a large Remy. The green baize, lit from above, lived up to its reputation. So did Elliot. There was something carnal about the way he chalked his cue, the way his eyes feasted on the position of balls on the table. He won two games on stripes. Then he was on spots, and the spots disappeared as if he had some kind of miracle cream on the end of his cue. He crept towards the black on soft predatory feet and killed it in the top right-hand pocket. Moses had lost again. Three games in a row.

Elliot slapped him on the back. 'You need to sharpen up, Moses.'

Moses stood his cue against the wall. 'It's been a long night.'

Elliot went and sprawled in his executive leather chair. Moses took the dralon sofa under the window. He surrendered to the deep soothing reds and charcoal greys of the office. Wall-lamps built nests of warm light in the corners. Two glasses of brandy glowed in the shadows.

The traffic had slackened on the street below. The occasional truck. The still more occasional bus. Moses was sober now – the soberness that comes from hours of drinking. Elliot must think I'm all right, he thought. He only invites people up here if he thinks they're all right. He reached for his brandy, and smiled as he swallowed.

Elliot propped his feet on the desk and talked about the club. He offered Moses cigarettes. They smoked until the corners of the office disappeared. Then the conversation touched on the break-in last September, and Elliot, without any prompting from Moses, began to tell the story.

There had been two men, apparently. They had climbed in the back way – over the wall and into the yard where the dustbins were kept – and forced a ground-floor window.

'Professional job,' Elliot said. 'Very professional.'

One of the men had been carrying a plastic bag of shit. He had scooped it up in handfuls, and plastered it over the walls, the tables, the bar. Afterwards he had wiped his hands on the curtains in the foyer. The second man had brought along one of those plastic tubs you buy paint in. Instead of being full of paint, it had been full of blood. Ten litres of the stuff. That too had been smeared over everything in sight.

'Right fucking mess,' Elliot said. 'You can imagine, right?'

Moses shuddered.

Elliot went on with the story. The next day, a Sunday, he had pulled up outside The Bunker in his motor. Two flicks of his wrist and the double-doors were open. The stench had flung him back into the street, an arm over his nose, gagging. It was as if everything that was bad in his life had caught up with him at once.

He had rushed up the stairs to his office. It had been left untouched. He had grabbed the phone and almost called the police. Almost. Instead he had picked up the Yellow Pages and dialled a firm of industrial cleaners. After hanging up, he had noticed some shit on his shoes. He must have trodden in it on his way upstairs. At that moment, he said, he had wanted to kill.

Later in the day he called a couple of friends of his, forensic experts. The only clues that had been left behind were the plastic bag and the paint-tub. The plastic bag had come from Safeway's. The tub had once held Crown White Matt. No fingerprints on either of them. According to Elliot's forensic friends, the shit in the plastic bag had been human, possibly belonging to the man who had done the job, and collected over a period of several days during which time he had eaten, among other things, a McDonald's, two Indian take-aways and a Chinese. More than that, they couldn't say. The chances of tracing the man, they told Elliot, were slim. Very slim indeed.

'You know, it's funny,' Moses said, 'but the first time I came here I smelt shit. I thought I was imagining it.'

'You weren't imagining it.' Elliot smiled grimly. 'This place was so full of shit I could've opened a sewage farm. I had to close for three weeks.' He sighed, leaned back, massaged his neck. 'Three weeks is a fuck of a lot of money.'

Moses wanted to ask why it had happened; he chose not to.

'Yeah,' Elliot went on, 'that's why I laid into you that afternoon. You know, when you were out there taking pictures.'

'What? You mean that was the same afternoon?'

Elliot nodded.

'No wonder you were in such a foul mood,' Moses grinned. 'I suppose you could say it was shit that brought us together.'

Elliot winced. 'Hey Moses, I don't want to think about it, OK?'

Moses apologised, but his grin lingered.

He stayed at The Bunker until four in the morning. Partly because he liked Elliot's company, and partly because he didn't want to risk running into the German actress who hadn't noticed him smiling at her. Especially as she was with Eddie, who had.

*

Then it happened again.

One evening at the end of February Moses turned up outside The Bunker to find Elliot prowling up and down the pavement as if held by an invisible cage. His face twitched with rage. His lips were forced back over his gums.

'What's wrong, Elliot?'

'*Fuck*,' Elliot snarled. 'Fuck Jesus fucking *fuck*.' He pointed at the pavement just to the left of where Moses was standing. Somebody had painted a big white arrow on the ground. It was aimed at the entrance of the club.

Elliot jerked his head, and disappeared through the double-doors. Moses followed him inside. A trail of similar arrows led across the foyer, up the stairs, along the corridor, leading, inevitably, to Elliot's office. Elliot pushed the door open, then stepped aside to let Moses in first.

It was a scene of such violence that Moses found the stillness unnerving. As he gazed into the room, he kept expecting something to spring out at him from a hiding-place in the debris. It was the kind of stillness that had recently been havoc and had only just returned to being stillness again. Moses took a deep breath, and let the air out slowly through his mouth. The entire office had been systematically and viciously destroyed. Torn paper, broken glass and long splinters of wood buried the carpet ankle-deep. The red drapes lay on top, cut into sinister neat pieces. The red lamps had been ripped loose and smashed. Wires trailed from the empty sockets like torn ligaments. The two black holes in the wall made the room look blinded somehow. The desk, the sofa and the executive chair, dismembered, hacked almost beyond recognition, reared up from the chaos as if trying to break free. Blood inched down the window-panes. The bitter smell of urine trickled into Moses's nostrils. But worst of all – and Moses groaned when he noticed it – was what they had done to the pool-table, Elliot's pride and joy. They had sawn the legs off, all four of them, and slashed the green baize into strips, with a razor-blade by the look of it, and then peeled it back to reveal the slab of grey slate, showing like bone through flesh, beneath.

'The same people?' Moses asked.

Elliot shrugged.

It couldn't be kids, that much was clear. And remembering what Elliot had told him about the previous break-in, Moses thought he recognised the style. The blood, the shit, the piss. The same sadistic premeditated violence. It had the feel of a vendetta, a psychotic vendetta, and, once again, Moses wondered exactly what truth lay beneath the rumours he had heard about Elliot. This kind of thing didn't happen to just anyone.

'I suppose it's no good getting the police in,' he said.

Elliot didn't even hear. His face had clenched like a fist. He was, Moses saw, one of those people who feel fury rather than fear.

He took Elliot by the arm. 'Come on. Let's go and get a drink somewhere.'

He drove Elliot to a pub in Bermondsey. The jukebox was playing early Sinatra to an interior of dark wood. They drank in near silence. An idea occurred to Moses – or, rather, recurred, because it had first begun to hatch when Elliot told him what had happened in October. The idea now grew, spread wings, though, even as it did so, Moses realised that he would have to save it for a more propitious moment.

*

Winter eased. Spring became a possibility.

When the vital conversation took place, Moses had been waiting almost a month. Insurance had restored the office to its former sleek condition. The windows were wide open. The roar of rush-hour traffic competed with the squeak of the blue chalk cube on the end of Elliot's cue. The pool-table was playing as beautifully as ever, though Elliot still winced sometimes when he looked down at the green baize and remembered. Moses sat on the arm of the sofa, cue in one hand, a brandy in the other. A typical evening on the second floor of The Bunker.

Elliot was telling Moses about a trip he had made to West Germany. 'I was in this town, right?' he was saying.

Elliot in West Germany? 'What were you doing there?' Moses asked.

'Business.'

'Ah,' Moses said.

'Anyway,' Elliot went on, 'there was this bloke going on about a dome – '

'The cathedral?' Moses suggested.

'Yeah, probably, but he called it a dome. Anyway, this bloke, he's sort of a guide, right? He points at this dome and he says, "You see that?", and I go, "Yeah". "You see that?" he says, second time, OK?, and I'm thinking *What is this?* but I go, "Yeah," anyway. Then he says, "Ugly," he says. "Ugly ugly ugly". And I'm cracking up but he hasn't finished yet. "In the war," he says, "boo boo boo, everything falls down, but that," and he points at the fucking dome again, "that no bombs touch." I'm thinking *Yeah, OK, so?* And then he says, "You know why no bombs touch?", and I go, "No," and he says, "Why God inside".'

Elliot shook his head. 'God inside. *Jesus.*'

'You shouldn't mock,' Moses said, with the air of somebody who has just thought of something. 'There's a moral in that story.'

'Moral?' Elliot said. 'What moral?' But he wasn't really listening. He was loping round the table, running his cue back and forwards through his left hand, intent on victory.

Moses smiled. His moment had come. 'I mean, maybe you need God in here, Elliot.'

'What the *fuck* are you talking about?'

'Well, if you had God in here, maybe you wouldn't get broken into any more.'

Elliot paused in mid-shot and straightened up. There was a shrewdness in his gaze that Moses recognised as confusion in disguise. He stepped forwards out of the shadows. He couldn't risk obscurity. Not when he was this close.

'I was thinking,' Moses said, 'that maybe I could be God, you see.'

Elliot rushed his shot, and missed for once.

'You going to talk English or what?' he snapped.

He hated missing.

The setting sun reached through the window, showed Moses standing in the centre of the room, his cue upright in his hand like a shepherd's crook. I could be God, he was thinking. Just a couple more sentences, that should clinch it.

He took a deep breath, became precise, factual. 'Listen, the top floor's empty, right? You're not using it for anything, so what I thought is, suppose I live up there. Sort of keep an eye on the place when you're not here. I mean, you can't be here all the time, can you? Not a man with your interests. And if somebody was actually *living* here all the time, then maybe you wouldn't get broken into any more – '

Moses bent over the table. He lined up a spot and knocked it into the left-hand side pocket. Like a sort of full stop.

Elliot stared at the place where the spot had disappeared. 'Maybe you have something there,' he said.

They carried on playing in silence. A siren cut through the quiet of the street below like a reminder of violence. It was more than five minutes before Elliot spoke.

'I've been thinking,' he said. 'If you were normal size, like me, for instance, I'd say no way.' He paused. 'But since you're so fucking big – '

He didn't have to finish the sentence. They shook hands, and slapped each other on the back. Moses leapt into the air, his legs revolving as if he was riding a bicycle. When he landed, the floor trembled. He was big all right. Out came the brandy. Elliot poured two. Trebles.

''Course,' Elliot said, 'you could be one of them, couldn't you?'

'That's right,' Moses said.

They held each other's glances for a few long seconds, their heads very still as if the slightest movement could cause something terrible to happen, then they began to laugh, both at the same time.

'You really think you can handle it?' Elliot asked.

'Let's put it this way,' Moses said. 'You're not going to be any worse off, are you?'

Ten minutes later Elliot had to go downstairs to attend to something. He left Moses sprawling in his executive chair. The look on Moses's face was one of pure fruition. He forgave everyone for their cruel jokes about his size. He even forgave his unknown parents for having created the problem in the first place.

It was all worth it.

*

Who to tell, though?

First would have to be Eddie. His life in Eddie's flat in Battersea would now be coming to an end. Well, that had been part of the plan, really. No more voices at night. No more statues in the kitchen. No more Jackson Browne (like most beautiful people, Eddie had absolutely no taste in music).

Not that they hadn't had some good times, of course. How could he forget the night Eddie had come in and thrown up all over the TV?

'Eddie,' Moses had said the next morning, 'what's *that*?'

'What?' Eddie said. 'Oh, *that*. That's breakfast television.'

Moses smiled as he dialled the number that had been his for the last two years. They had been avoiding each other recently. Putting a bit of physical distance between them might bring them closer together. Something like that, anyway.

He glanced at his watch. Nine twenty-five. Hang on. If it was nine twenty-five, Eddie probably wouldn't be in. Unless he was having sex. At nine twenty-five, though? Yes, what about the time Moses had come home, it must have been around seven in the evening, to find a pair of pearl earrings placed, all neatness and innocence, on the arm of the sofa – the first in a trail of female clues that led with unerring logic, with unfaltering resolve, across the carpet, along the hall and up the stairs, only to disappear with a wriggle of black elastic under Eddie's bedroom door. Yes, he might well be in.

Moses let the number ring just in case Eddie was struggling, irritable, half-dressed, but still unbelievably good-looking, towards the phone. After two minutes he gave up. Either Eddie was out, or the sex was uninterruptable. He replaced the receiver.

*

He thought of Jackson next.

Jackson would almost certainly be home. Jackson was *always* home. Jackson wasn't interested in women. Once, when drunk, Jackson had suddenly announced that he was asexual. The laughter he had been expecting never arrived. Everybody simply agreed with him.

Women held no fascination for Jackson. He was far more interested in the weather – its beauty, its caprices. He watched the way the clouds walked across the sky. He listened to what the north wind said. These were his women.

Yes, he would be at home now, in his dark basement flat, his tense wiry frame bent over an antique weather-vane, or staring tenderly, myopically, at the latest reading on a barometer. He would be crouching at his desk, one hand plunged into his coarse, curly hair, calculating the exact position of an isothermal layer, or puzzling over the sudden prevalence of millibars in the air above the city. He would be totally absorbed in making yet another totally erroneous weather forecast.

Moses dialled the number and waited. Sure enough, three rings and there was the quavery tenacious voice he knew so well.

'Hello?'

'Jackson?'

'Yes.'

'It's Moses.'

'Who?'

'Moses. You know. Six foot six. Size twelve feet. Likes old ladies – '

'I'm sorry, it's not that Jackson.'

'What?'

'You've got the wrong Jackson. This is Jackson's brother. The Jackson you want isn't here.'

There was a pause while Moses assimilated this sudden glut of information: one, Jackson had a brother, two, Jackson and Jackson's brother sounded identical, three, Jackson's brother also called himself Jackson, and four, Jackson, the Jackson he knew, was out.

Jackson? Out?

'Where is he?' Moses asked.

'The Amateur Meteorological Society.'

Moses smiled. Few things could persuade Jackson to leave his cluttered basement flat. The AMS was one of them. 'Could you tell him that Moses called?' he said.

'Moses. OK. Any message?'

'Just tell him that I've got some good news.'

'Good news. Right. Goodbye.'

Very dry brother, Moses thought. Probably a very good meteorologist. Either that or very successful with women. As he pondered the differences between Jackson and Jackson's brother Jackson, he realised that he still hadn't actually *told* anyone.

*

Who else was there?

Vince! What about Vince? Vince would probably tell him to fuck off. Vince was like that. Still.

He dialled Vince's number.

A sullen voice said, 'Who's that?'

'Moses.'

'Fuck off, Moses.'

You see?

Moses sighed. 'What's wrong with you, Vince?'

'Why should anything be wrong?'

'What's wrong, Vince?'

'Lots of things. Everything.'

'Like what?'

'Alison's left.'

Oh Christ, not again. People were always leaving Vince. Especially Alison was always leaving Vince. Moses didn't blame her either. If he was going out with Vince, he would leave him too. There was some great disparity between Vince in your memory and Vince in the flesh. Moses was very fond of Vince when he was somewhere else. The imagined Vince was impish, controversial, photogenic; the real Vince was boorish, truculent, morose.

But, real or imagined, you couldn't forget him somehow. His blond hair, dark at the roots, stuck up at all angles, unbrushed, unkempt, stiff with gel, lacquer and soap. His mouth turned up at the corners even when he wasn't smiling, so he gave the impression of being good-humoured when, actually, nothing could have been further from the truth. And he always wore this black waistcoat, glossy with age and stains, and prolific with insulting badges; it was almost as if these badges had sprouted, like toadstools, from the black soil of his clothes, they were so much a part of him. His trademark, this waistcoat. Vince wouldn't have been Vince without it.

He was forever being turned away from places – wine-bars, clubs, restaurants, pubs (he had been banned from his King's Road local twice), cafés, shops, parties, you name it. If asked, he would recite, and not without a certain pride, a list of all the famous places he had never been allowed into. 'I'm sorry, you're drunk,' doormen would tell Vince as he swayed, leering and malevolent, on the pavement – but they would always be looking at his waistcoat. In the end Moses decided there had to be a connection.

One night he tried an experiment. They had taken some angel dust at Vince's squat, and were on their way to a private party at The Embassy Club. In the back of the cab, he turned to Vince. 'You don't need to wear that waistcoat tonight,' he said in a gently persuasive voice. 'Why not leave it behind for once?' He should have known better. Gently persuasive voices didn't work with Vince. Gently persuasive voices made him puke. He glared at Moses. The lights of Chelsea coloured his face green then red. 'Who the fuck're you?' he snarled. 'My mother?' This was not a role that Moses was suited to. He dropped the subject and they went back to being friends. Naturally Vince didn't get into The Embassy.

That they were friends at all sometimes seemed extraordinary to Moses, not least when he had to scrape the remains of Vince off the floor after a fight or stop Vince jumping out of a tower-block window. Driving Vince to St Stephen's at four in the morning with a six-inch gash in the back of his head and his blood pumped full of drugs may have made a good story the first time round, but when you had to deal with it on a monthly basis it got pretty fucking tedious. Go and kill yourself somewhere else, you felt like saying. The things he did for Vince. He sometimes hated himself for being so good-natured, and wondered whether in fact he wasn't Vince's mother after all.

'Why?' he asked. 'Why's Alison left you this time?'

'I don't know.' Vince was talking through a mouthful of clenched teeth. 'She said something about she couldn't stand it any more.'

'Where is she now?'

'She went home. To her fucking parents.'

'Is she OK?'

'She was crying.'

'You want me to ring her?'

Vince didn't reply. Anger made him autistic.

'I'll find out how she is and call you back,' Moses said.

Vince said something about not caring, then slammed the phone down.

Moses dialled Alison's number.

'Hello?'

Only one word but, like the single toll of a bell, the woman's voice had resonance, hung on in Moses's head, bright, droll. Not Alison then. Alison's mother, maybe. But he had delayed too long, making her suspicious. She probably imagined Vince on the other end.

'Could I speak to Alison, please?'

'Who is this?'

'Moses. I'm a friend of Alison's.'

'Will you wait a moment? I think she's upstairs.'

Moses heard footsteps on a tiled floor, the opening and closing of a door, a faint *Alison?* and, in the distance, the quiet fretting of a string quartet. He had no idea what he was going to say to Alison. He didn't even know her that well. She had a dry sense of humour and a head of striking, natural red hair. Some total stranger had once come up to her in the self-service restaurant above Habitat and asked her how she got her hair that amazing colour and Alison had said that her parents were responsible for that and the total stranger, gushing now, had said, *Wow! Your parents are hairdressers?* and Alison had said, *No, my parents are my parents,* and the total stranger had dried up, backed away, evaporated. The soft Indian-print skirts, the cluster of thin silver bangles on her wrists, the bohemian vagueness acted as elements of Alison's cover. Underneath, she was pretty tough and sorted-out – almost, at times, Moses felt, predatory. He alternated between liking her a lot and mistrusting her. He couldn't really understand why she had chosen Vince, but he knew that if one of the two got hurt it wouldn't be Alison.

A fumbling sound at the other end and Alison picked up the phone.

'Hello?' She sounded wary, bruised.

'Alison, it's me. Moses. I just thought I'd ring you, see how you were.'

'You've spoken to Vince, then?'

Moses said he had.

'How did he sound?'

'Pretty pissed off. What happened?'

'Oh, you know, another argument. He wants me to live with him and I don't think I'm ready for that. Not at the moment, anyway. I told him that and he went mad and hit me.'

'Oh shit,' Moses muttered.

'Not hard or anything. He was too drunk for that.' She laughed – a half-laugh; the other half was bitterness. 'Well, I'm pretty fed up with all that shit. So I left.'

Moses sighed. 'Are you all right now?'

'Yes, I'm all right. Bit shaky.' She paused, sniffed. 'I don't know what's wrong with him. Just because I tell him I don't want to live with him, he starts thinking there's some kind of conspiracy going on – '

'That's typical Vince,' Moses said. 'He likes it better when he's fighting the whole world.'

'I'm not the world, I'm me,' Alison said tearfully. 'Why's he have to make everything so complicated?'

Moses didn't know the answer to that.

After Alison rang off, thanking him, he tried Vince again. No reply. It was as he had feared. Vince had gone out to wreak terrible vengeance on an innocent city. He would probably end up in hospital again. Moses didn't want to think about it.

He sat in Elliot's chair for a while longer. Too many phone-calls had taken his elation apart piece by piece until nothing recognisable was left. He felt tired as he unlocked the door of his old Rover, slid into the seat and drove home.

So much for telling everyone the news, he thought.

*

'Do you like pigeons?'

Elliot asked the question casually as he walked Moses round to The Bunker's side entrance.

Moses scratched his head. What was all this about pigeons? Elliot had called Moses at nine that morning and offered to show him the rooms on the top floor of The Bunker. 'I'll be here until twelve,' Elliot had told him.

Moses had driven over at eleven, his lungs still misty with smoke from the previous night. Too much whisky with Vince had laced the suspense he might otherwise have felt with irritation.

They had reached the black door. Wind blew dust and grit into the back of his neck. He folded his arms and drew his shoulders together.

'What do you mean, do I like pigeons?' he said.

Elliot didn't appear to have heard. It was an annoying habit of his.

Seconds later he said, 'You'll see.' His grin was half grimace as he grappled with a muscular rusty padlock.

The padlock had resisted his first efforts, but now the key slid in and gripped. It snapped open, almost jumped out of his hands. He pushed at the door. It swung inwards to reveal a pile of crumpled newspapers, a few circulars, and a steep flight of wooden stairs.

'Nobody's been in here for bloody years,' he said.

There was a light-switch on the wall. One of those round protruding light-switches with an inbuilt timing-device. He jabbed it with his thumb. It began to tick quietly like a shy bomb. He set off up the stairs, two at a time. Moses followed.

Halfway to the top, the light clicked off. Moses heard Elliot mutter *Fuck* somewhere up ahead. They reached a door.

'You really don't like pigeons?' Elliot asked Moses again.

'I hate pigeons,' Moses said. And said it with feeling, because it was true.

Elliot's laugh was soft, so soft that it was hardly louder than a smile. Moses didn't like the sound of it.

Elliot put his shoulder to the door. A groaning splintering sound. The wood gave. Light poured into the stairwell.

At first, Moses thought he was seeing some kind of optical illusion – the result of being in the darkness for too long. But then he realised that what he was seeing was real. He blinked his eyes several times. Yes, it was definitely real. They had walked into a room full of about five hundred pigeons. The pigeons were moving about with extraordinary speed and abandon. It seemed to Moses as if fifty per cent of the air had been siphoned off and replaced with moulting grey feathers. He took a deep breath. It was like breathing pigeon.

'Oh,' he said.

He backed away towards the stairs.

'Do you like it?' Elliot shouted. He thought the whole thing was a big joke.

Moses didn't answer. He was gazing at the floor – or the place where the floor would have been if it hadn't been inches deep in pigeon shit.

'Oh,' he said.

He had had a dream and his dream, after all these months, had finally come true. But there hadn't been any pigeons in his dream. No pigeons at all. They had come as something of a shock to him.

'Oh,' he said, for the third time.

When he returned three days later, the party was still in full swing. He winced in the darkness of the stairwell as he heard the whirring and clattering of five hundred pairs of grey wings, as he thought of the task that lay ahead of him, but at least he had the grim satisfaction of knowing that he was prepared.

*

This was how Moses had spent his dole cheque that week:

  1 broom
  1 dustpan and brush
  1 mop
  1 plastic bucket
  1 pair of Torpedo swimming-goggles
  3 scrubbing-brushes
  1 wicker carpet-beater
20 giant black plastic bin-liners
  1 bottle of non-scratch cream cleanser with ammonia
  1 bottle of scratch cream cleanser with ammonia
  1 bottle of new thicker Domestos
  1 bottle of new stronger Vim
  1 aerosol of new improved instant double-action double-strength easy-to-use 30% more free Blast insect-killer with new perfume in new giant family-size can as seen on TV
  1 aerosol of Supafresh air-freshener with new alpine fragrance
  2 grams of speed
  5 packets of Increda Bubble – the popping bubble-gum (Feel the pop! Chew the soft juicy bubble-gum! Blow the fantastic bubble!)
  1 case of Merrydown Vintage Cider (dry)
  1 cassette of Liszt's *The Dance of Death*
  1 Second World War hand-held air-raid siren
  1 shovel

That, he thought, should just about cover it.

*

The pigeons seemed to have some collective premonition of their impending fate. They began to whirl round the room twice as fast, colliding with each other, slamming blindly into walls and windows. Even the more casual of the pigeons left their mantelpieces and sills and mingled in mid-air, exchanging theories about the new situation and discussing possible courses of action.

Crouching low, with his arms wrapped round his head, Moses crossed the room and opened all three windows. Then, returning to the door, he switched his cassette-recorder on. The first bars of *The Dance of Death* thundered out at top volume. Moses began to shake the can of insect-killer. He glanced ominously at the pigeons. Some of them seemed to have taken the hint and headed for the open air. The others didn't seem to understand the significance of the music they were listening to. Moses leaned back against the door and sprayed clouds of new improved Blast into the room. No effect whatsoever. We are not *insects*, the grey wings seemed to say. We are *birds*.

Eyes streaming, Moses tossed the can to one side. He reached for the carpet-beater. It was a sturdy article, a relic from Victorian times when carpets took some beating. It didn't look as if it was going to stand for any nonsense, especially from a handful of twentieth-century pigeons. Things turned out differently. For ten minutes Moses thrashed and flailed. But the pigeons had never seen a carpet-beater before. They didn't know what it was. They circled the room, wondering why this large man was attacking the air with an old wooden implement. It was strange behaviour, certainly, but not necessarily threatening. Some of the pigeons who had left even flew back into the room again to find out what was happening.

Moses was beginning to feel tired and foolish, he was beginning to feel as if he was playing a game of surrealist tennis that would last for ever, he was just reaching for the Second World War air-raid siren when help came from an unexpected quarter in the shape of a cat, a street-cat by the look of it, jet-black, with a blunt nose and fierce yellow eyes. It slid into the room from one of the window-ledges and crouched by the wall, eyes scouring the busy air, its rangy haunches tense and trembling. Moses stopped beating pigeons and stared at the cat. Where had it come from? And what did it have in mind?

Everything seemed to go quiet as Moses watched the cat begin to move slowly round the edge of the room, its eyes never leaving the pigeons, not for a moment; it seemed to know exactly where the walls were without looking. Halfway round, it paused, spread itself flat on the floor, hindlegs shuffling, and unleashed a haunting guttural cry that cut through the silence its entrance had created. It made Moses think of a seagull. Yes, now he thought about it, the cat sounded *exactly* like a seagull. How extraordinary.

The pigeons, meanwhile, had reacted with consternation and frenzy.

They were clambering over one another in a desperate effort to reach the windows. In a matter of seconds they were gone. The cat sat up, lifted its left leg, scratched its ear, then licked its flank. In the light of its recent eerie display of control, this was reassuringly catlike. The washing over, it shrugged its shoulders, turned tail, and left the way it had come, without so much as a backward glance. Moses was impressed.

During the days that followed, the black cat patrolled the edges of his mind with a casual power, uttering its uncanny seagull cry from time to time as if it could still see the ghost of a pigeon there. The thought of this cat sustained him as he shovelled shit, chiselled and scraped at it, tipped it into buckets and bags, and hauled it down eight flights of stairs and out to the dustbins in the cobbled yard at the back of the club. Sometimes Elliot would be there, lounging against a wall, the spring light picking out the bracelet on his wrist, the mockery in his grin.

'How's it going up there, Abraham?' Elliot asked once as Moses passed. He lit a Dunhill. His gold lighter flashed like a piece snapped off the sun.

Moses looked at him. 'Was that suit expensive, Elliot?'

'Two hundred.' Elliot glanced down, brushed at a lapel.

'Well, in that case, it'd be a shame to get shit all over it, wouldn't it?' Moses said, gesturing with his bucket.

After that Elliot often backed away in genuine alarm whenever Moses trudged past.

*

That April Moses worked harder than he had ever worked for money. Every day for three weeks he undid the padlock on the black door and climbed the eight flights of stairs and, gradually, the shit cleared. Areas of clean floorboards opened up before him like a whole new life. The sight of all this unfurnished space ignited him all over again, and his face would glow through a spattering of dust and filth. Hands blistered, dirt embedded in every crevice of his skin, he returned to Eddie's flat each night with a larger vision of his future.

There were four rooms altogether. He decided to call them bedroom, lounge, kitchen, bathroom, though there were very few clues as to which was which. No cooker in the kitchen, for instance. No bed in the bedroom. The rooms led one into the next through doors that opened unwillingly, dragging on their hinges, as if children had been swinging on the handles. The walls and ceilings had been painted different shades of grey. The plaster had come loose in some places, leaving patches that looked like scabs. In the bedroom, there was a long brown stain where the rain had leaked through.

Of all the rooms Moses's favourite was the one he had walked into with Elliot on the morning of the five hundred pigeons. It had a black fireplace surrounded with dark-blue tiles, and a trio of arched windows that reminded Moses of railway stations. They looked out over a clutter of rooftops, treetops, chimney-pots and TV aerials out of which, toffee-coloured in this landscape of red and grey, and surprisingly close, rose the intricate spires and crenellations of the Houses of Parliament. Away to the west a pair of pale-green gasholders stood among the rows of terraced houses like giant cans of paint. Modern offices blocked the view eastwards with their coppery glass façades. Even though it faced north, the room felt bright owing to the size and elevation of these three windows. It had possibilities, this room. Definite possibilities.

The real find, though, was the bath. (Moses loved baths, even though he had to fold himself double to get into one.) Deep-chested, eight feet long, it stood on four flexed metal claws. A lion of a bath, it was. Its pristine antique enamel seemed unmarked but for the faintest of yellow stains running from the overflow down to the plug-hole. Sometime during his second week of work Moses walked into the bathroom and turned on the hot tap. A moment's silence, as if the machinery was gathering itself. Then a clanking, a subterranean clanking deep in the foundations of the building, like a metal bucket hitting the bottom of a dry well, followed by a gurgling that seemed to be ascending, growing louder, that built to a crescendo as the tap coughed a few brown splashes into the bath. Seconds later a powerful flow of water was crashing on to the enamel. Steam lofted into the chill air. Moses began to take off his clothes.

Through the small window above the taps he could see the planes easing down into Heathrow. They slid silently from left to right, dropped two hundred feet as they hit a swirl in the glass. He lay in the water until it had turned cold for the third time, pleasure written all over his face in invisible ink. In future, when crisis threatened or exhaustion softened his bones, he would retreat to the bathroom. It would be his sanctuary from the world. It had the power to heal, soothe, replenish him. Sometimes he would climb into the empty bath and lie on the cool enamel, fully dressed, with his eyes closed. Other times he would open those fierce taps and run a bath so deep it swamped the floor. But he would always feel better afterwards – calmer, more objective. A sense of proportion would descend, as silently as planes. If he ever left The Bunker, he would have to take the bath with him – somehow.

On the day of his first bath, the black cat appeared again. He paused on the window-ledge, one paw raised in the air, disappointed, perhaps, by the absence of pigeons. His glowing yellow eyes raked the room and fixed, eventually, on Moses. Such was the hypnotic power of the cat's gaze that Moses thought, for one terrifying moment, that he might throw himself from the window as the pigeons had done. He concentrated on one simple thought: *I am not a pigeon.* The black cat eyed him without blinking. He seemed to be listening, taking the information in. When Moses thought the cat had understood, he relaxed.

'Bird,' he said affectionately.

He had decided to give the cat two names, one formal, one familiar. His formal name would be Anton, after Anton Mesmer, who believed that any one person can exercise influence over the will of another by virtue of the emanations proceeding from him. Any one person or cat, Moses had decided, after that exhibition of control over the will of five hundred pigeons a week or two back. His nickname, however, would be Bird. Moses had toyed with the name Seagull, but you couldn't call a cat Seagull, could you? Bird, he felt, was a nice compromise. Bird the cat.

Bird responded with a cry worthy of his new name. Bird was hungry, perhaps.

Moses fetched the old green and gold cake-tin he had found under the kitchen sink and covered the bottom with milk. He placed the tin in the middle of the living-room floor. Bird stared at Moses with suspicion as Moses moved back to the kitchen doorway. Then, dropping down to floor-level without a sound as if he weighed nothing, he began to creep towards the tin. Stalking it, as if it might be dangerous. Once there, he squatted over the tin, neck extended, and lapped at the milk, his tongue moving out and back like a tiny pink clockwork toy.

Halfway through he suddenly stopped. Black chin sprinkled with white drops, he looked at Moses, seemed to be appraising him.

'It's good milk, Bird,' Moses whispered. 'It's Dino's milk.'

Bird dipped his blunt head into the tin again. When he had finished he paused, as if thinking, then turned, sprang back on to the window-ledge and vanished, as before.

Moses still hadn't moved. He gazed round the room with its clean floorboards and its grey decaying walls and its open window through which the black cat came and went.

It was beginning to feel like home.

*

As if somebody had splashed petrol around and tossed a lit match, the end of April caught fire. Car tyres crackled on the sticky tarmac of main roads. Clouds rolled along the horizon like smoke. The temperature, unbelievably, touched eighty. HEATWAVE, the papers roared, HEATWAVE.

Moses hired a transit van and moved out of Eddie's flat in a single day, sweat tickling his forehead, trickling down his spine. He saw roadworkers with red backs. Girls in bikinis. In *April*. The world seemed out of kilter – surreal, delirious.

Elliot watched him unload from the shadow of a wall.

'I would've given you a hand,' he said, 'but you know how it is.' He adjusted the lapels of his excuse.

'I know how it is,' Moses panted, a mattress balanced on his back.

'So what's it like up there?'

'It's luxury. It's what I've always wanted.'

Elliot threw his head back and swallowed hot sky.

But Moses meant it. Those empty rooms on the fourth floor dwarfed what few belongings he had. He had never had so much space to himself before. The place might have been designed specifically with him in mind, might have been waiting for him to arrive and take possession.

He drove back to Eddie's that night to return the keys.

'Finished already?' Eddie said. 'I was going to help you.' He opened the fridge and handed Moses a cold beer.

'Eddie,' Moses said, 'the thought never crossed your mind.'

As he tore the ring-pull off the can, he watched Eddie smiling. The damage Eddie had caused with that smile of his. Moses had long since pushed the statue theory aside, stored it away in the museum section of his mind for re-evaluation at a later date. He had begun to see Eddie's beauty in wider terms. As a magnetic force. As disruption unleashed on men and women alike. Once, he remembered, Eddie had brought the entire cosmetics department of a famous London store to a standstill simply by smiling as he stepped out of the lift. The air vibrated softly as fifty murmurs of desire coincided. Then fifty tongues emerged to moisten fifty upper lips. One salesgirl let a bottle of perfume slip from her hand. It shattered on the tiles with a crystal sigh and the ground floor of the department store smelt of Opium for several days. In memory of Eddie. Another time Moses and Eddie were walking along a quiet street in Kensington. A red sports saloon, some foreign make, slowed and drew alongside. The woman at the wheel wound the window down. Moses thought she was about to ask for directions. Instead, with her eyes on Eddie, she cried, 'You're beautiful.' The car sped away again, its pert rear-end pointing in the air. 'What is it about you?' Moses had asked. Eddie shrugged, smiled. A young man on an old-fashioned bicycle glimpsed the smile on Eddie's face and rode straight over a traffic island without even noticing. There ought to be a sign, Moses thought. CAUTION: MAN SMILING.

*

That was the really curious thing, Moses thought, as he walked out of The Bunker two days later. Eddie could never be accused of being conceited or narcissistic. He didn't keep a record of his lovers, as some men did, because he wasn't trying to prove anything. Girls passed in and out of his life without changing him in the slightest. Their presence was necessary, continuous, and taken for granted – like time itself; Lauren followed Connie as Tuesday followed Monday. Nostalgia had no place in his scheme of things. Nor, it seemed, did expectation. He was like a train with infinite stations on its line but no terminus.

Moses had reached the door of his new local. A jaded murky place. Crawling with small-time ruffians and drunks. He ordered a pint of draught Guinness, and retired to a deserted corner.

Yes, it was astonishing how little Eddie held on to, how much he left behind. Sometimes, when Moses couldn't sleep, he ran through the list of Eddie's lovers – the ones he knew of, anyway. They were more interesting than sheep, though not so very different, perhaps, not if you saw them from Eddie's point of view. Did he distinguish between the different girls at all? Did he remember Beryl, the mud wrestler, for instance? Did he remember Sister Theresa? Did he remember *anything*?

The door swung open. Eddie walked in, accompanied by a girl Moses had never seen before. Surprise, surprise. He wondered what number she was. 500? 1,000? He had told Elliot that he had a friend who had slept with two thousand women, but he really didn't know. This one's name was Barbara.

Moses asked her what she did.

'Hostess,' she said.

He thought of the aeroplanes gliding past his bathroom window, then of jet-set parties next to swimming-pools, but he couldn't fit Barbara's bomber jacket and her disgruntled mouth into either category.

He must have looked puzzled because Barbara added, 'In a club.'

In a club. Moses's face acquired a look that was both interested and knowledgeable. He had just placed her. She was almost certainly the girl Eddie had referred to in a recent (and uncharacteristically anxious) phone-call. He remembered the conversation.

'Moses?'

'That's right.'

'Eddie here.'

Moses had waited.

'I was just wondering,' Eddie had said, 'whether you felt like coming round tonight?'

This isn't like Eddie, Moses had thought. Eddie never asked people round. How could he? He was never round to ask people round. Something must be up.

'You see, there's this girl I thought you'd like to meet.'

'Who is this girl,' Moses had sneered, 'that I'd like to meet?'

Eddie chuckled. 'She's a topless waitress. She's got tattoos.'

'Where?'

'Soho.'

'No, the tattoos. Where are the tattoos?'

'I don't know. I thought maybe you could find out.'

So that was it. Another of Eddie's games.

As he glanced across at Barbara, he remembered something else that Eddie had said.

'She's angry about something. I think she's going to attack me.'

No sympathy from Moses. And certainly, with that sour twisted mouth, Barbara looked capable of violence.

'So.' Eddie smiled. 'What's happening?'

'There's a party coming up,' Moses said. 'Louise told me about it. If you want to bring Barbara along, I'm sure it'd be OK.'

Eddie made a face behind her back.

Moses grinned. 'That's settled then.'

Eddie bought Barbara a Bacardi and Coke, then he sloped off to play pool at the back of the pub. She watched him go. There was reproach in the fractional hardening of her face.

'Where do you work?' Moses asked her.

'A place called Bosom Buddies,' she said.

Jesus, Moses thought. If that's anywhere near as bad as it sounds. (Actually, knowing Eddie, it was probably worse.)

'What do you have to do?'

Barbara scowled. 'Talk to strangers. Mostly people I can't stand.'

Cheapskate businessmen from out of town, apparently. Sweaty little creeps in crumpled suits. And the bag who ran the place. Lashings of mascara, hands like chicken-feet, tongue like a blunt ladies' razor. She gloated jealously from a red sofa in the corner. Barbara had seen her twist a girl's nipple once for upsetting a client. 'Really nice piece of work, she is.'

71

Moses had been trying to imagine Barbara topless and sociable. He'd failed. There was a long silence while they both looked elsewhere. Eddie, it seemed, was having a good run on the table.

Later she said, 'I'm sorry, I can't seem to talk to people socially any more. It's too much like work.'

Moses said he understood that. Her surly mouth and her hands stuck deep in her jacket pockets – she looked cold, but she had already told him that she wasn't – now made sense to him. He wondered what she was expecting from Eddie, if anything. He knew there was nothing she could do to make her fate any different from Eddie's last girl – number 999, or whatever number she had been. Especially after that phone-call. Soon she would be just another five words in Moses's mind as he tried to get to sleep. She would be even less to Eddie. He would be on to number 1,001 by then.

It was this feeling, the feeling that she was owed something, something she would never get from Eddie, not in a million years, and certainly not in the three days the relationship would last, that made him start talking again when silence would have suited him just as well. He wanted to cut the ropes on her heart so it could float free of Eddie. He wanted to see her face light up. Just once.

'See him over there?' Moses said to her. 'The one in the denim jacket?'

Barbara squinted along his outstretched arm. She might have been aiming a gun. At close range, Moses realised she was ugly. She pulled away and nodded.

'That's Billy,' Moses said. 'He's a thief.'

A week ago, he told her, he had dropped into the pub for a quick drink. He noticed Billy standing at the bar with an *A–Z*, his index-finger tracing a route through the intricate grey tangle of streets, like a kid learning to read. His air of intense concentration roused Moses's curiosity. He positioned himself at Billy's elbow.

'What are you up to, Billy?'

Billy jumped, swung round, flipped the *A–Z* over, all in a single movement. Wired-up wasn't the word. He threw a few suspicious glances, left, right, and over his shoulder, then he leaned towards Moses, narrowing the gap between them to about six inches.

'I got a job tonight.' He stared at the bottles on the back of the bar as he spoke. His voice was so quiet you could have heard the clicking of a combination.

'A job?' Moses said jovially. 'That's really good news, Billy. It's about time you got a job.' He slapped Billy on the back, and sent him staggering.

Billy adjusted his denim jacket and gave Moses a withering look. 'A job,' he hissed. 'You know. A *job*.'

'All right, Billy, all right. No need to tell the world.'

Billy was fuming, the air rushing noisily out of his nostrils. He stared into his drink as if he was furious with it.

'And you're just checking up,' Moses lowered his voice, 'to see exactly where this job is. Right?'

He studied Billy innocently, and with great interest. He had never met a real thief before. He could smell whisky, crumbling garden walls at midnight, cold feet. He wanted to know more.

But Billy clammed up. He knocked his whisky back and ordered another as if Moses wasn't there, knocked that back too, and checked his watch. Moses wondered who he had synchronised it with.

Billy left the pub at ten on the dot. He made so sure nobody saw him leave that everyone saw him leave. Only seconds later Maureen sidled up to Moses with her red furry slippers and her lopsided grin. She nudged him in the ribs with her skinny elbow.

'Billy's got a job tonight then.'

'Has he?'

'I'm telling you.'

'How do *you* know, Maureen?'

'He had his book with him, didn't he?' Her eyes wrinkled up with a natural cunning that she had inherited from her uncle who had a legal business in Waterford. 'His *A–Z*. It's the only book he's ever read.'

She dived into her pint of cider and surfaced gasping.

''Course, he doesn't understand it, does he? That's why he always screws up. Never make a criminal, that Billy.'

Maureen had been right.

The next night Billy had slunk into the pub at around eight, his face pasty and dishevelled, his arms dangling, out of order. He asked for his usual, but without his usual enthusiasm.

Moses walked up to him and leaned on the bar. 'Sorry about last night,' he said. 'I was rat-arsed.'

Billy looked at him, then looked back at his drink. 'Yeah,' he said.

'How did it go?' Moses was trying to be friendly.

'I'm going to get bloody killed,' Billy said.

He'd got lost, he said, and turned up at the wrong house, and his mate'd waited two hours, and in the rain as well, and now his mate was down with pneumonia or something, and he'd rung his mate up to see how he was, and his mate'd said, as soon as he was on his feet again, he was going to tear Billy's head off.

'How long does pneumonia last?' Billy had asked Moses.

'Pneumonia?' Moses had sucked in air. 'You can die of pneumonia, Billy.'

Billy had grinned. 'Fingers crossed, eh Moses?'

Barbara crushed her cigarette out. She nodded in Billy's direction. 'Looks like he got away with it.' He still had his head on was what she meant.

'So far,' Moses said.

He went to buy her another drink. When he returned, Barbara's face was jutting brutally over the table.

'Where's Eddie?' she asked him. She looked ugly for the second time. Uglier than the first time, actually. Violence in the offing.

Moses glanced round. 'I don't know. Maybe he's in the toilet or something.'

'The toilet's right behind you, I would've seen him go in,' Barbara snapped as if he was not only lying, but lying badly.

Moses crossed the pub to where he had last seen Eddie. Billy was playing now, slamming balls into pockets, dominating the table with a precision and authority he couldn't seem to bring to anything else he did.

Even as he asked the question, Moses knew what was coming.

'Seen Eddie?'

Billy jerked his head in the direction of the side-door without taking his eyes off the table. 'He left.'

Moses felt a lot like Billy's mate as he walked back to where Barbara was waiting. He was beginning to understand why there were so many headless statues in the world.

She had already guessed the truth, judging by the look on her face: it was stiff and pinched, and suspicion had killed the light in her eyes. She probably thought of him as an accomplice, some kind of decoy, what with all his ridiculous stories. He told her what Billy had said.

She scratched at a crack in the table-top with a blunt fingernail. 'Did Eddie say anything about me? You know, earlier on?'

Yes, he did, Moses thought, remembering a brief exchange with Eddie at the bar. He said, *How the fuck'm I going to get rid of Barbara?*

'No,' Moses said. 'Not that I can remember.'

Perhaps she believed the lie. She still hadn't looked up from the table. The silence stretching between them finally came to an end when she snapped her handbag shut. 'Where can I get a taxi?'

'I'll show you.'

They left the pub and crossed the main road. He flagged down a cab for her. As she climbed in, he said something about seeing her at the party maybe. She didn't reply. She pulled the door shut, leaned back against the seat, closed her eyes. Her eyelids collected light from the neon fish and chip shop sign across the road, glowed a supernatural white. She looked blind.

The taxi did a U-turn and headed north.

Goodbye 1,000, he thought. Or whatever number you are.

*

First to see the fourth floor of The Bunker was Jackson.

'I'll bring something to drink,' Jackson said. 'We'll christen the place.'

He was full of gestures like that, tense and generous.

Moses opened all the windows that evening. Lingering indoor smells of bleach and disinfectant blended with exhaust- and curry-fumes and the unlikely scent of blossom from outside. It was May now. Air you could almost wear. A breeze so light that, had it suddenly been made visible, it would, he imagined, have looked like lengths of pale floating muslin. A warm red hem to the buildings. A thin veil of pink beyond, on the horizon.

Moses sat on the window-ledge and waited for Jackson. He was thinking of nothing, content simply to gaze out over the city as it accelerated towards the hours of darkness. When the bell rang, he didn't move at first. Then he seemed to unwind, to gather himself. His eyes clicked over into focus like the fruit in a fruit machine. Peering down, he saw Jackson's tangle of hair four floors below. He kicked off his left shoe, and peeled off his sock. He dropped his door-keys into the sock, rolled it into a tight ball, and threw it out of the window. It bounced off the pavement and into the gutter, missing Jackson by about six feet. Jackson, being Jackson, flinched.

'The keys,' Moses shouted.

Jackson cowered below, his face a pale area of nervousness.

'The sock,' Moses shouted. 'The keys are in the sock.'

He sat down again. He had just finished rolling the first christening joint when Jackson appeared at the top of the stairs. Jackson was wearing a beige raincoat with a wide sash belt and floppy lapels. It was an awful raincoat. Not for nothing had Jackson once been known as Columbo.

'You ought to be careful with those keys,' Jackson said. 'You could kill somebody with those keys.'

'I need more practice,' Moses said. 'You'll have to come round again.'

Jackson looked at Moses's bare left foot, then at the grey sock in his own right hand. He nodded to himself. There was a methodical deductive streak in Jackson. He thought first, asked questions afterwards. Two years back –

it must have been during Jackson's Columbo era – Moses had tried to persuade his friend to become a private detective.

'Well, the rain seems to be holding off,' Jackson observed, in silhouette against the perfect sunset. He cast around for somewhere to put his tightly furled umbrella.

'*Rain?* You forecast *rain* this evening?'

Jackson nodded, winced. 'A severe depression moving south-east across the country. Scattered showers followed by outbreaks of heavier rain during the night.'

Moses suppressed a grin.

Jackson handed Moses a plastic bag containing a bottle of Jack Daniel's. When Moses looked at him, not only with gratitude, but with a degree of curiosity, he explained, 'I thought it was going to be cold, you see.'

Moses couldn't help smiling now. He was glad that Jackson hadn't taken his advice about becoming a private detective. He now knew that Jackson, after a great deal of intense and detailed investigation, would always come up with the wrong murderer.

He also suspected that Jackson's constant reference to the weather was some kind of front. As if Jackson had inside him a device that took what he wanted to say and scrambled it. Moses doubted he would ever crack the code.

'Well,' and Jackson clapped his hands together in an attempt to convey the enthusiasm he quite genuinely felt, 'what about a tour?'

There was nothing much to see beyond the rooms themselves, but the rooms, bare and uncluttered, still seemed miraculous to Moses.

'You have to remember,' he said, 'that the whole place was three inches deep in pigeon shit.'

Rapid pecking movements of Jackson's head as he darted from one room to the next. He said little, but missed nothing. He noticed the skylight in the kitchen and the view of the Houses of Parliament. And when he saw the bath, he emitted a curious whooshing noise that sounded like red-hot metal being dipped in water. Moses took this for approval.

'So,' Moses said, when they reached the living-room again, 'what do you think?'

'I think it was time for you to move out of Eddie's.' A wily grin from Jackson, who never answered a question directly.

They cracked open the bottle of bourbon. Moses apologised for the absence of glasses. They drank out of jamjars instead.

'We're lucky,' he told Jackson. 'Bird has to drink out of a cake-tin.'

He sat down on the sofa and lit one of the joints. Jackson leaned against the windowsill. He was still wearing his galoshes. Things like that made him endearing.

Later, drunker, Jackson kept staring at Moses as if he suddenly found him quite fascinating. Moses shifted on the sofa. He tried passing the joint to Jackson. Perhaps that was what he wanted. Jackson accepted the joint, but the staring continued.

Eventually he had to ask, 'What is it, Jackson?'

Jackson's eyes slid sideways towards the door, then back to Moses again. 'Who was that?'

Moses looked confused. 'What?'

'Who was that woman?'

'Woman? What woman?'

'The woman you were talking to.'

'What are you talking about, Jackson? I wasn't talking to a woman.'

'Yes, you were. I saw you.'

Moses placed his right cheek in the palm of his hand and went back over the past few minutes with some thoroughness. 'I don't remember a woman,' he said finally.

'Didn't you see her?'

Moses shook his head. 'No, I don't think so.'

'How can you talk to somebody you can't see?' Jackson asked him.

'I don't know. I didn't even know I was talking to anybody.'

'She was sitting right next to you.'

'Was she?'

'Yes. There.' And Jackson pointed at the sofa.

'Where?'

'There. On the sofa. Next to you.'

Moses turned and studied the place where the woman he was supposed to have been talking to was supposed to have been sitting.

'What did she look like?' he asked.

'She was wearing a raincoat. A black raincoat. With a belt.'

Moses narrowed his eyes at Jackson. Whisky. A few joints. A devious intelligence. He wasn't convinced.

'It's true.' Jackson held his hands out in front of him as if he had an orange in each one. 'It's absolutely true.'

Moses examined his friend closely. 'All right then,' he said, 'what were we talking about?'

'I don't know. I couldn't hear. I was going to ask you when she left.'

'We must,' Moses said, 'have been talking very softly.'

'You were. You were sort of – *whispering* to each other.' Jackson gave the word a salacious twist.

77

'And she's left now, you say?' Moses asked, glancing again at the empty space beside him.

Jackson nodded. 'A couple of minutes ago.'

'Hmm.'

Moses sat quietly on the sofa absorbing this strange information. Then he thought of something.

He reached down with his right hand and touched the cushion next to him. And the funny thing was, it felt warm.

*

The following morning Moses went to see Elliot. Elliot was on the phone, so Moses waited in the doorway. He noticed how brooding, how oppressive, the office looked in the daytime. All those sombre reds and greys. They soaked up light, gave nothing back. At night Elliot's desk withdrew into the shadows, but now it showed – a drab industrial plastic construction, its sterility broken only by a pair of soiled telephones and an overflowing Senior Service ashtray. Only the pool-table exploited the natural light, turning a green that was almost fluorescent as the sun played on its surface. The office had been designed with the small hours in mind: drawn curtains, low lighting, smoke.

Five minutes had gone by. Moses crossed the room and sat down on the radiator. He could see Elliot in profile now. It was a very one-sided phone-call. Elliot was staring out of the window almost as if he was just staring out of the window. The telephone seemed incidental. He had hardly said a word.

Finally he said OK twice and slammed down the receiver. His sigh carried his chest forward a few inches and back again. A well-built man, Elliot, under all those playboy suits and ties.

'Christ,' Elliot muttered. He pushed the phone to the far edge of the desk. As far away as possible.

'Hello,' Moses said.

'As if I haven't got enough trouble already. Now you. What's up, Moses?'

Moses hesitated. 'I've got a ghost.'

'A ghost?'

'Yeah, a ghost. It's upstairs. In my living-room. Do you know anything about it?'

Elliot looked at Moses to see if he was being serious. Sometimes it was difficult to tell. 'No,' he said, 'I don't know anything about a ghost. You going to tell me about it?' He lit a cigarette, then tossed the packet across the room to Moses. He leaned back in his chair, his hands behind his head. Christ, the entertainment business.

Moses took a cigarette, lit it, and threw the packet back. 'It's a she, actually,' he began carefully. 'Apparently she wears a black raincoat.'

'Apparently? What do you mean, apparently?'

'Well, I didn't actually see her. This friend of mine, he – '

'You didn't actually see her?'

'No, you see I was – '

'Hold on. Let me get this straight, right? You're worried about a ghost you can't see?'

'Yes, but you – '

'What, you mean if you could see it, it wouldn't worry you?'

'It's not that, Elliot. It's just – '

But Elliot wasn't listening any more. He was bent double in his executive chair, clutching his stomach. He was killing himself.

'Well,' Moses said, easing off the radiator and starting for the door, 'I just thought I'd tell you – '

'Hey, Moses.'

Moses turned.

Elliot was prancing up and down the office with his jacket draped over his head. 'Wooooo,' he was going. 'Wooooooooooooooo.'

Oh well, Moses thought. At least I cheer the bastard up.

*

One further development regarding the invisible ghost.

The next weekend, at around four in the afternoon, the bell rang on the fourth floor of The Bunker. Moses peered out of the window. It was Jackson. Moses was surprised to see him again so soon. Visits from Jackson were usually few and far between.

He leaned out of the window. 'Keys,' he shouted.

This time he aimed at least twenty feet to the left of Jackson's anxious upturned face. The sock bounced off a car roof and into the road. Jackson scuttled after it. Moses went out to the kitchen to put the kettle on. He returned in time to see Jackson walk in, close the door behind him, and produce a bradawl from his raincoat pocket (the weather was still fine). He watched as Jackson began to bore a hole in the door about two-thirds of the way up. Jackson made small grunting sounds as his elbow gouged the air. It was a hard wood.

Once he had bored the hole according to his own internal specifications, he plunged a hand into his raincoat pocket and pulled out a hook shaped like a gold question-mark. He screwed it into the hole with a series of deft energetic twists of his wrist, the tip of his tongue appearing from time to time in the corner of his mouth – a sign of intense concentration. Then he stepped back to admire his handiwork.

Moses handed Jackson a cup of tea, as you would any workman.

'That's very nice,' he said. 'But what's it for?'

'That,' Jackson explained, 'is for her to hang her coat on.'

Another time, perhaps a month later, Jackson appeared at the top of the stairs with an antique upholstered chair. He placed it carefully just inside the door.

'In case she's tired after all those stairs,' he said.

A very thoughtful person, Jackson.

*

The week of the ghost was also the week of Moses's twenty-fifth birthday. On the Thursday night Moses booked a table for four in a restaurant in Soho. He wanted to celebrate the occasion quietly, he said, with a few close friends.

Poor Chinese restaurant.

The celebration reached its climax shortly before midnight with the waiters' hands fluttering in delicate protest, like birds attempting flight, only to weaken, fall back, return to the relative safety of their white tunics, as Moses, who weighed more than three of them put together and had woken that morning to a bottle of champagne, a Thai-stick and two lines of coke (his birthday presents), began to spin the revolving table like some kind of giant roulette wheel.

'Place your bets,' he cried.

'What are we betting on?' asked Jackson, very dry. 'How long we can survive before they throw us out?'

Bowls of rice and seaweed, plates of mauled prawn toast, bottles of soy sauce and dishes loaded with the stripped skeletons of Peking ducks took to the air, swift and confident, as if they were trying to teach the waiters' hands how to fly. This demonstration was not appreciated. The manager came weaving through the barrage to insist, politely but firmly, that Mr Highness and his party leave the restaurant.

Out on the street the recriminations began.

'And on my birthday, too,' Moses said.

'It was *because* it was your birthday that it happened,' Jackson pointed out.

'It was your fault, Vince,' Moses said.

'*My* fault?' Vince seemed genuinely taken aback.

80

'We would never've been thrown out of that place,' Moses said, 'if you hadn't worn that waistcoat of yours.'

'It is a *very* unpleasant waistcoat,' Eddie agreed.

'Look, fuck off you two. If you,' and Vince shoved Moses into a lamp-post, 'hadn't covered me in rice – '

Moses couldn't help giggling as he remembered how Vince had lurched to his feet halfway through the meal only to lose his balance and topple across a neighbouring table, his waistcoat luridly stuffed with Special Fried Rice and soup that must have been either Chicken with Sweetcorn or Hot and Sour.

'Mind you,' he went on, ignoring Vince, 'Jackson didn't exactly set a very good example, did he?'

Drunk for the first time since the night he confessed his asexuality, Jackson had suddenly, and without warning, plummeted headfirst into a dish of Squid in Black Bean Sauce.

'I was embarrassed by your behaviour,' Jackson explained. 'I wanted to hide.' Like a monkey with fleas, he was still picking the black beans out of his hair.

'Maybe you'll actually have to wash it now,' Vince sneered.

'I don't see how you can talk, Vincent.' Jackson was primness itself. 'That waistcoat of yours must've put down roots by now.'

'All your fault, Vincent.' Moses was returning to his theme.

Vince hated being called Vincent. His mother called him Vincent. He told them all to get fucked, and stalked ahead.

'Anyway,' Jackson smiled, 'what about Eddie?'

'Yes,' Moses said. 'That was *really* disgusting.'

During one of the lulls in the meal Eddie had turned away from the table as if to sneeze. A jet of pink vomit had flown out of his perfectly sculptured mouth and crashlanded in the grove of yucca plants behind him. Afterwards, Moses seemed to remember, Eddie had gone on eating, as if nothing had happened. A bit of a Roman, Eddie.

'Why was it pink?' Eddie wondered.

Moses couldn't think.

Vince, curious, rejoined them. 'Why was what pink?'

'My sick,' Eddie said. 'Why was it pink? Did I eat anything pink?'

Vince offered an obscene suggestion as to what it might have been that Eddie had eaten.

'That's not pink,' Eddie said, 'though, of course, you probably wouldn't know.'

A pause while Eddie and Vince hit each other. Vince staggered backwards over a dustbin. Eddie danced away, smiling.

'I still think it was Vince's fault, though,' Moses said.

The following day, after only four hours' sleep, Moses boarded a bus (his car had broken down again) with a two-litre plastic bottle of water, a family-size pack of Paracetamol, and a hangover that was like people moving furniture in his head. He was on his way up north. His foster-parents, Uncle Stan and Auntie B, were expecting him for the weekend.

*

Auntie B opened the door in her French plastic apron. Her hands showered white flour. When she saw Moses, her face seemed to widen; her eyes narrowed and lengthened, her mouth stretched into a smile.

'Moses,' she cried. 'How are you? Happy birthday.'

They embraced. Moses kissed her on both cheeks. Her hands stuck out of his back like tiny wings because she didn't want to get flour on his clothes. He heard the scrape of Uncle Stan's chair on the parquet floor of the study. It had been six months.

The Poles would have described themselves as an ordinary couple – middle class, middle aged, middle income-bracket – but Moses had noticed them the first time they visited the orphanage. They seemed different somehow. Their smiles didn't look glassy or stuck-on. They didn't bury him in comics and cakes until he couldn't breathe. They turned the other people who visited into fakes.

Mr Pole wore prickly tweed jackets with leather ovals on the elbows. He carried his pipe bowl uppermost in his breast pocket like a chubby brown periscope, and the rituals of smoking had transformed his fingers into instruments, fidgety and deft. He grumbled a lot. His wife – B, as he called her – was round and peaceful. When you heard her voice you thought of a cat curling up in front of the fire. When you kissed her, your lips seemed to touch marshmallow. So soft and sweet and powdery.

He had always looked forward to their visits, so when Mrs Hood summoned him to her office one day and asked him whether he would like to go and live with Mr and Mrs Pole he didn't hesitate. Nor did he need Mrs Hood to tell him how lucky he was. He had been dreaming of a moment like this for as long as he could remember without ever having really believed that it would arrive.

The Poles moved north, and Moses moved with them. They had bought a detached Victorian house on the outskirts of Leicester. They gave him a room of his own on the second floor. The view from the window skimmed the tops of several fruit trees, cleared the garden wall, and came to rest in the peaceful green spaces of a municipal park. He inhaled the smell of apples and the silence.

They were consistently straight with him. There was no coyness or pretence about his origins. He was ten years old, after all – no baby. They told him to call them Uncle Stan and Auntie B; that neatly sidestepped the twin potholes of *mum* and *dad* and, besides, he had already become accustomed to the names during their many visits to the orphanage. They explained why his name was Highness and not Pole. His name, they said, was all that he had that was truly his (well, not quite all, but they didn't tell him that – not yet), and he should keep it. Out of the way they closed ranks and stood up for him whenever necessary came a sense of their own uniqueness and strength as a family and, over the years, he grew to love them – not as parents exactly (he couldn't imagine what that must feel like), but as people who had been kind to him. Saviours, if you like. Apart from anything else they had saved him from an awful nickname (the children had called him names like Jew and Judas and Rabbi for years but then, when they discovered that he couldn't *really* be Jewish because he hadn't been circumcised, they began to call him, of all things, *Foreskin*); he simply left it behind, along with the iron beds and the rising-bells, the walls painted two shades of green, and the constant echoey clang and clatter of the place, as if everything was happening inside a metal bucket. It had been such a luxury to move into that house in Leicester, and it was always a luxury to come back. A hushed and cushioned existence – except, that is, for the platoon of grandfather clocks that stood in the hall; a passion of Uncle Stan's, they ticked and creaked and wheezed and, once in a while, all chimed simultaneously, a chaotic orchestra of gongs and xylophones and bells led, in Moses's imagination, by a mad cook spanking the bottom of a saucepan with a spoon. The carpets were fingernail deep and deliciously soft if, in the middle of the night, half asleep and barefoot, you had to cross the landing to the upstairs lavatory. The air smelt of wood-polish, pot-pourris of rose leaves, and Uncle Stan's pipe-tobacco, and then, as you moved towards the kitchen, of warm pastry and freshly ground coffee.

Moses sat at the kitchen table as Auntie B put the finishing touches to the evening meal. Outside the lawn had turned blue, and birds clamoured from the webbed branches of the cedar tree. Uncle Stan stalked in and out of the room, ransacking cupboards for things of no importance.

'How was your journey up?' The floral print of Auntie B's dress tightened across her wide back as she stooped to check the oven.

'Not too bad. The trouble was, I went out with some friends last night, to celebrate, and I think I drank a bit too much.' Even now, Moses was conscious of having to imitate good humour.

'Well,' Auntie B said, 'it was your birthday, after all. People often get a bit tipsy on their birthdays, don't they?'

A bit tipsy. Moses smiled to himself. 'Anyway,' he said, 'I feel a bit better now.'

Auntie B twirled round, her eyebrows high on her forehead, her mouth the shape of a lozenge. 'Would you like a drink? Hair of the dog?'

It was as if she had learned this last phrase from some book without ever having been able to imagine how she could apply it to her own life but here, suddenly, was the chance, and she had taken it, and felt bright, naughty.

'No thanks, Auntie B. Coffee's perfect.' He drained his cup to prove it.

Auntie B hovered with the percolator. 'Another cup?'

'Yes, please.'

Uncle Stan bustled into the kitchen, eyebrows bristling. 'Where's that magazine?'

Auntie B turned the upper half of her body and, beautifully bland, watched Uncle Stan as he began to pull drawers open. 'What magazine?' she said.

'You know the one I mean,' said Uncle Stan, in some kind of agony.

'No, I don't.'

'Oh, come *on*, poppet.' In an excess of irritation, he finally looked at her.

The corners of Auntie B's mouth tucked neatly under her round cheeks. 'Don't look at me like that, Stanley. I don't know where your silly magazine is.'

Uncle Stan sighed dramatically and hurled himself from the room. Moses grinned at Auntie B.

'He's always *losing* things,' she said, one eye on the door.

Nothing had changed, Moses thought. Uncle Stan had to worry and pester. Auntie B needed somebody who she could gently scold, hold up to ridicule, and then later, Moses suspected, draw towards her white upholstered bosom.

Two comfortable days went by – birthday presents, meals, TV. Auntie B produced endless cups of tea and coffee, and was constantly inventing excuses to cook or eat. Uncle Stan griped about money, aches and pains, old age.

It wasn't until Sunday evening that they broached the subject that they had, in their own meandering way, been leading up to.

'Well, shall I go and get it then?' Joints cracking, Uncle Stan rose out of his armchair.

Auntie B scarcely glanced up from the news. 'Why are you asking me, Stanley?'

Uncle Stan let out a rasp of exasperation. Life could be such a bugger. He left the room and returned five minutes later with a suitcase. He placed the suitcase on the coffee-table.

'Now,' he said, 'this suitcase was left to you by your real parents, Moses. Don't know what's inside it. Haven't got an earthly. None of my business, really. All these years it's been up there in the attic, getting dustier and dustier, waiting for you to be twenty-five. Well, now you are, so you'd better have it.'

Moses listened carefully as Uncle Stan told him what little he knew about the suitcase. Strange how familiar it seemed to him, though he had probably never seen it before. He picked it up and turned it round in his hands. It was as if it had once occupied a space in his memory, only to fade with time until it became so dim as to be invisible. The blank space had remained, meaningless until solved, like a riddle. A space that the suitcase, reappearing again like this, fleshed out, filled in, fitted.

One foot six by two foot six. Old leather, black where scarred. Battered brass catches. No tags or stickers, though. No marks of identification. And dusty enough to write your name on. So he did. Moses, he wrote.

He didn't open it that night. He waited until he got back to The Bunker the next day. On the journey down he noticed how light it was, almost as though there was nothing inside. That would be funny, he thought.

He opened a bottle of wine and put some music on. He placed the suitcase on the sofa. He turned the tiny key in the locks, first the left, then the right, and snapped the catches open. He lifted the lid.

A smell drifted up – something like dusty roses. A scent, perhaps. But a scent that had been preserved, that had aged. He parted the tissue-paper.

The contents of the suitcase were as follows:

1 dress
1 pair of red shoes (child's size 2)
1 photograph album.

That was it.

UNFINISHED HISTORIES (1972)

It was after ten o'clock at night. Arms pinned behind his back, almost as if handcuffed, Chief Inspector Peach stood at his office window. The storm was building. Staggered flashes of lightning took pictures of his massive silhouette. The trees over the road heaved, strained, testing the strength of their roots. Rain hissed down through the light of a single street-lamp, fine as silver wire. In the intervals between thunderclaps a typewriter could be heard, scratching and clicking beyond the door like an insect.

Storms made Peach think. Their explosions loosened the order in his mind. Thoughts long buried came tumbling down. He turned away from the window and crossed the room to his desk, his boots deliberate on the wooden floor. The angle of his head, lowered in thought, blurred the line of his jaw; his double chin had, with the years, almost doubled again. He sank heavily into his chair.

There were times when he saw himself as a premier surrounded by dissidents, when he saw his office as the object of endless plots and conspiracies. Deep down, he knew this was nonsense, morbid nonsense, and an injustice both to himself and his colleagues, but then the sound of thunder came to him, unfurling miles away, rolling across the countryside, breaking against the glass of his window –

He still remembered – how could he forget? – the weeks in 1959 when that feeling had washed over him, sucked him down, when no amount of struggling could bring him back to the surface. Though he had trusted nobody, he had been forced to turn the running of the village over to three of his sergeants while he retired to bed – to rest, recuperate, re-think. And there had been moments when he doubted whether he would ever return.

The breakdown –

Sheets of glass, infinite and tough, between himself and everything else. Sheets of glass thickening, thickening. Until he couldn't hear anything any more, until he couldn't make himself heard. He didn't want to think about it. He had worked through it, that was the main thing. When the feeling came now, he took it for what it was – the accumulating weight of responsibility, a sign of fatigue, his mind telling him to ease off. He obeyed. At sixty-four, he couldn't afford to go through all that again. He might really never come back this time.

A knock on the door dropped into his thoughts. Gratefully, he watched them scatter and disperse. When he spoke, his voice had its usual authority, its usual depth of tone. So much so that it blended with the retreating thunder.

'Come in.'

Dolphin – now Sergeant Dolphin (Peach had promoted him in 1969) – steered his large face round the door. 'I was wondering, sir, what you wanted me to do with this.' And he shuffled backwards into the office dragging a curious structure that appeared to be made out of strips of corrugated cardboard. It was about six feet tall, four feet wide and two inches thick. It had been painted brown. Leather straps dangled from the underside.

Ah, Peach thought. Ah yes.

'Lean it up against the wall, Dolphin,' he said, 'then take a seat. I want to have a word with you.'

Dolphin manoeuvred the structure into the gap between the bookshelf and a large-scale wall-map of the village. Then he closed the door and sat down. Too eagerly, perhaps, for a spring twanged somewhere beneath him. He cringed, muttered an apology.

With his moments of embarrassment, his nail-bitten fingers and his rosy outdoor face, he sometimes reminded Peach of a giant schoolboy. Peach approved of his eagerness, though. It was one of the qualities he looked for in a police officer. That, physical presence, and a shrewd mind. And Dolphin, surprisingly, had all three. That blundering physique of his concealed a wealth of deftness and tact. But Dolphin was fidgeting, tugging at his collar and rearranging his legs, and Peach finally took pity.

'An extraordinary case, wouldn't you say?'

'Most unusual,' the sergeant said. 'Ingenious, really.'

Peach frowned. He didn't want obsequiousness. He wanted fresh opinions, new angles: feedback. He prompted Dolphin once again. 'Had you suspected him at all, the greengrocer?'

'Well, no. Not exactly.' Dolphin shifted in his chair, as if by finding a comfortable position he would also find the right words. 'Mind you,' he went on, 'I know he's thought of escape before. It's just that I never thought he'd have the – ' he faltered for a moment then, trampling his inhibitions, came out daringly with – 'balls.'

Peach's lower lip curved, became succulent. 'I must say,' he said, 'that it surprised me too, Dolphin.'

'Though, God knows, he spent enough time with Dinwoodie.' Dolphin plunged into the stream of his thoughts. 'I suppose I should've suspected something, really. I just thought he was all bark, that's all. You know, like Dinwoodie. I'm going to do this, I'm going to do that, but nothing ever comes of it. And all the time he was building that – ' but he couldn't find the word to describe the structure that was leaning against the wall, so he pointed instead – '*that*.'

A sudden flicker of lightning and the structure jumped out into the room. Peach waited for thunder, but none came.

'Yes, well,' he said, 'I think there's an important lesson to be learned there, Dolphin. We tend to overestimate ourselves sometimes. Get cocky. Complacent. That's the biggest mistake you can make. Vigilance at all times, Dolphin. I can't stress that strongly enough. Security must be watertight. Watertight. Not a drop of it must ever escape. Do you follow me?'

Dolphin bit down on his bottom lip. 'Yes, sir.'

The lecture over, Peach eased back. His voice became conversational again. 'An intriguing case, though. Quite intriguing.'

Only two nights before, the greengrocer had confessed everything. In the harsh light of the interrogation room, his robust pink features had seemed bulbous, coarse. His methodical demeanour had looked plain clumsy. A failed escape attempt – and, let's face it, what other kind was there? – rearranged both a person's appearance and their character. Made them ugly. Broke them. Peach had seen it happen half a dozen times during his long career, and the sight of the greengrocer slumped on that hard chair, mouth slack and hanging open, mud drying on his dishevelled clothes, had reminded him of those other triumphs.

He remembered asking the greengrocer how the idea had come to him.

On a glorious spring morning, the greengrocer replied. Through his shop window, he could see part of a field which at that particular time of year was in the process of being ploughed. He knew that, owing to its unusual shape (a long wedge tapering to a sharp point), this field stretched all the way to the village boundary, just visible as a line of trees in the distance. He saw the field every day and had become attached to it. In the spring it looked especially beautiful – the grain of the earth chiselled into furrows, the white gulls flapping in the air above the farmer's tractor, like washing hanging out to dry –

Though he was himself a staunch advocate of the beauty of New Egypt, Peach became impatient.

'That's enough poetry,' he said. 'What about a few facts?'

After a brief wounded silence, the greengrocer continued.

On one of those spring mornings he had been unpacking a fresh delivery of apples. Granny Smiths, they were – a lovely fruit, crisp and green. (A warning glance from Peach.) He was transferring them from their crates to the window display when he noticed something extraordinary. Slowly, very slowly, so as to see everything as it really was and no other way, he stared first at the corrugated cardboard that lined the bottom of the apple-crates, then at the ploughed field beyond the window. He did this several times. Then, even though it was only eleven in the morning, he closed his shop and went upstairs.

He had spent the next two years gathering and assembling his materials. He had to work sporadically, so as not to attract attention. And, in any case, it wasn't every day that a delivery of apples arrived, was it?

'Do you remember how I dropped the price of my apples, Chief Inspector?' For a moment the greengrocer had been his old self again, his head wobbling on his shoulders, a smug light in his eye. 'I had to get rid of them, you see. So I could order some more.'

Peach nodded. 'The cardboard.'

'Exactly.'

'Very clever.' Peach's voice was as crisp as any Granny Smiths, though sourer perhaps. 'Go on.'

The greengrocer had worked night after night in the dusty gloom of the cellar underneath his shop, hunched over strips of cardboard, pots of brown paint and tubes of industrial glue. It had taken ages. *Ages.* And even when he had finished he had to wait another nine months to put his plan into action. The time of year was important, of course – but so was the weather. A moon would have been dangerous. Rain too. Snow would have been fatal.

Then, one spring evening, the conditions seemed perfect and he made his bid for freedom. Disguised as a section of ploughed field. It was so simple, a stroke of genius, really, even if he said so himself. (Again that smug look; Peach had silently prescribed further humiliation.) All he had to do was strap the corrugated cardboard on to his back, flatten himself against the ground (making sure the ridges on his back corresponded to the ridges of the field), and crawl a distance of about a mile. And crawling wouldn't have been a problem. He had spent months working on his stomach muscles.

'How did you do that?' Peach asked, curious.

The greengrocer, unexpectedly, blushed. 'I'd rather not say.'

Now Peach really wanted to know. 'How?' he repeated.

The greengrocer began to lower himself into his clothes as if he thought he could escape the question that way.

But Peach was relentless. 'Come on, Mr Mustoe. How did you strengthen those stomach muscles of yours?'

'I can't,' the greengrocer writhed. 'It's embarrassing.'

Peach almost rubbed his hands together at the prospect. 'Joel,' he wheedled, 'we're all men here.'

Joel threw a desperate glance at the ceiling, but it rebounded from the severe grey plasterwork and landed awkwardly on the floor. His resistance crumpled.

'Well – ' he began.

Dolphin pounced. 'Well?'

A touch over-eager, perhaps. Peach motioned to his subordinate behind the greengrocer's back. *Not so fast.*

' – in bed,' the greengrocer muttered.

'In bed?' Peach's voice was dispassionate then, almost medical. 'How do you mean?'

'With the wife.'

'Ah,' Peach breathed. 'I see.'

And he persisted, because degradation was part of the process. The greengrocer admitted, under duress, that he had worked on his stomach muscles in bed at night, startling his wife with a revival of sexual passion that put anything they had got up to on their honeymoon completely in the shade.

'Is that so?' Peach murmured. Dolphin took copious notes, the leer on his face making him look more than ever like a schoolboy.

And so, muscles toned, homemade ploughed field strapped in position, the greengrocer began to crawl. Unfortunately, he had only covered a hundred yards when a policeman trod on him – entirely by accident. Unfortunately, too, it was Sergeant Dolphin who weighed eighteen stone on an empty stomach. One yelp of surprise as the breath was crushed out of him was enough to give the greengrocer away. He was immediately apprehended and taken down to the police station. In Peach's presence Dolphin had confirmed the basic details of the greengrocer's story. A statement was written and signed. The greengrocer was then led away to a cell to reflect on his failure before being allowed to return home. Peach celebrated by throwing a cocktail party in his library.

'So what are we going to do with it?' Dolphin asked, bringing Peach back to the present.

Peach folded his hands over his stomach. 'Put it in the museum,' he said.

'Of course. Good idea, sir.'

'Yes,' Peach said, 'I think it will look rather splendid hanging in the museum.'

He stood up, and walked over to the section of ploughed field so lovingly, so painstakingly, constructed by the greengrocer.

'Remarkable piece of work,' he said. 'Really remarkable.' Then, touching on a pet subject of his, 'You know, if we could only harness their determination, their creativity, somehow, if we could only persuade them to do something for the community – ' He sighed. It would never happen. Not in his lifetime, anyway.

'I say, Dolphin,' and Peach became enthusiastic, 'what about taking it over to the museum now?'

'It's raining, sir. Might ruin it.'

'Nonsense. It's only a few yards. Come on, give me a hand.'

Taking one corner each, they began to ease the unwieldy structure out of the office and down the corridor. They passed an open doorway. PC Hazard – cheekbones like knee-caps, chin the shape of a soap-dish – looked up from the report he was typing.

'Need any help, Chief?'

Peach shook his head. 'We can manage. If anyone calls, I'll be in the museum.'

'Right you are, Chief.' Hazard turned back to the typewriter, began to stab at the keys, one finger at a time. A good man, Hazard. A bit primitive, but a good man.

Peach held the ploughed field upright while Dolphin wedged open the door to the courtyard. The rain had slackened off. The wind, a vast physical presence, threw its weight against the trees, and the trees swirled, their leaves roaring like stones dragged by the sea. The two men stood there for a while, admiring the power of the night.

'By the way, Dolphin,' Peach said, placing a hand on the sergeant's arm, 'you did well to apprehend the greengrocer. Extremely well.'

Dolphin's face became foolish with modesty. 'It was nothing, really. A bit of luck, that's all.'

'No, not luck,' Peach said. 'Planning. *Timing*.'

'Planning?'

'Why do you think we have night patrols, Dolphin?'

Dolphin considered this. 'Perhaps I should be congratulating you, sir,' he said, 'rather than the other way round.'

Peach smiled into the wind. In exchanges like this, it could be seen that the two men shared a similar brand of natural cunning. At times Dolphin's instincts led him, almost blind, towards perceptions and discoveries that astonished him. Like treading on the greengrocer, for example. In time, Peach thought, Dolphin would learn to be less astonished, he would learn to see these perceptions and discoveries as his reward for years of apprenticeship, as his right, as valid and innate parts of himself. Exchanges like this explained why Dolphin was, to all intents and purposes (though it had never been formalised), Peach's deputy and, consequently, Peach's most likely successor.

As they chuckled together over Dolphin's remark, the wind hurled itself against the cardboard construction, threatening to whirl it away across the courtyard. Dolphin reacted with the speed of his relative youth and held it down.

'I think we'd better get it inside,' he yelled.

Peach nodded.

The two men struggled across the asphalt, round a tree, past a rack of rattling police bicycles. They stopped in front of a long low building with a curving corrugated-iron roof and no windows. It looked like an aircraft hangar. The New Egypt Police Museum.

Peach produced a bunch of keys, selected one, and unlocked the metal door. Once inside, he reached for the panel of light switches. Neon strips began to pop and fizzle overhead.

The museum had been founded *circa* 1899 by Chief Inspector Magnolia. It was a private museum, intended for the edification and amusement of the police alone. During the past fifteen years there had been moves on the part of several villagers to have the museum thrown open to *all* New Egyptians; it's history, they had argued, *our* history, and in that sense they were right, of course, since the museum was, in fact, a comprehensive record of all the escape attempts that had ever occurred (in living memory, at least). But, naturally, Peach had quashed every request, every petition. The idea was intolerable. The museum acted as a library of information, he said, the equivalent of police archives, and, as such, must remain confidential.

He moved among the rows of exhibits. Rain tapped on the metal roof like a thousand men working with delicate hammers. He liked the fact that there were no windows. The building felt hollow, secretive. A drum, a womb, a submarine.

He paused before a lifesize reconstruction of the accident that Tommy Dane had staged on the main road outside the village in 1945. There was the actual hayrick Tommy had used (generously donated by Farmer Hallam). There, too, was Mr Dane's bicycle, its mudguards dented, its wheel-rims sprinkled with rust. A dummy Tommy Dane, dressed in clothes that had been appropriated from his wardrobe following his death, lay on the ground in the position he had described during his confession, the head resting in a pool of simulated blood. An account of the escape attempt (written by Peach himself) hung from the roof, accompanied by detailed explanatory maps. Peach nodded as he skimmed through his own terse paragraphs.

He moved on, stopped again. Now he was looking down into a grave, a grave that contained a spotless gleaming coffin. Fashioned out of the finest cedar, the handles plated in silver and carved to resemble a family crest, the interior upholstered in a magenta silk quilt, it must have cost a small fortune. Likewise the tombstone. The tall slab of Italian marble supported an angel with outspread wings and uplifted hands. The names and dates had already been engraved:

LORD OSCAR NOBLE BATLEY
1859–1938

– a little prematurely, though. Peach couldn't help smiling.

He walked to the far end of the museum. Here were artefacts dating back to the first recorded escape attempt. In 1899 the village postman, a man by the name of Collingwood, had devised a system of lianas stretching from his house on the western edge of the village green to the boundary a mile away. From reading the report (couched in rather fine Edwardian prose), one gathered that New Egypt had boasted a much larger number of trees in those days; one also gathered that Collingwood was a man of somewhat unusual build, being 'exceptionally small and agile' and possessing 'arms of quite extraordinary length'. Collingwood had owed his downfall to the son of one of the village constables. The boy had loved climbing trees, as most boys do, and had discovered one of Collingwood's lianas. Collingwood had collided with the boy in mid-air. He lost his grip, fell, and died instantaneously of a broken neck. The boy escaped with minor cuts and bruises. Shaking his head at this curious tale, Peach turned and, circling an ancient leather harness that had been suspended in the air by half a dozen stuffed birds, walked back to join Dolphin who was still waiting by the door.

And now the greengrocer's ploughed field, he thought.

In his view, the museum was a gallery, housing a collection of uniquely creative acts; it represented the flowering of local genius. For, if the truth be known, he had more respect for a Collingwood or a Tommy Dane than for all the other villagers put together. They failed – their failures were inevitable and, in the end, rather pathetic – but at least, and in the face of overwhelming odds, they *tried*.

He rested a hand on the smooth worn shaft of the hayrick. His domain, this. The neatness, the order. Every single one of the men and women represented in the museum had been born in New Egypt and had died (or would die) in New Egypt. Birth and death closed like brackets round a single desperate theatrical escape attempt. And every attempt had been studied, documented, catalogued. Every attempt had become a case-history. It was perfection of a sort.

Suddenly something snagged on Peach's line of thought, jerked it out of true.

The toy dog.

Blast that toy dog.

Peach swung round, hands clenched. A sour juice flooded the troughs between his cheeks and his gums. The diagonal lines on his forehead tangled, knotted. He brushed past Dolphin.

'I want that hung from the centre beam,' he snapped. 'If you could arrange it, Dolphin.'

Dolphin stared at Peach without seeming to – a technique he frequently employed when on duty in the village. 'But what about the report, sir?'

Peach waved an irritable hand. 'Get someone to do it.'

The way Dolphin was staring at the ground, there might have been a wounded animal lying there.

Peach noticed and understood. 'In fact, no,' he said, gathering the remains of his former jovial mood. 'Why don't you do it yourself? You brought the greengrocer in. You were present at the interrogation. And it'll be your first report on an escape. Why don't you write this one up?'

Dolphin's face acquired a sudden radiance. 'Thank you, sir. I will.'

'And don't forget to lock the door,' Peach added, withdrawing into the darkness. 'We can't have just anybody walking in here, can we?'

Dolphin agreed that they couldn't.

A gale outside now. Wave on wave of wind washed through the court-yard. Something banged repeatedly in the rifle-range like an old-fashioned gun. A dustbin overturned, and birds made of newspaper whirled up into the loud black sky. One hand clutching his collar to his throat, Peach stood the dustbin upright and replaced the lid. The wind, swooping down, lifted his tunic at the back and with a whoop of delight investigated the Chief Inspector's buttocks. (Like most figures in a position of authority, Peach was the butt for many scurrilous jokes, often of an anatomical nature.) This mockery touched an already exposed nerve and Peach, normally the calmest of men, felt like lashing out. At what, though? The wind? The toy dog? That empty coffin buried in the cemetery?

He stamped indoors, slamming the door. His flesh vibrated with anger under his uniform. Where was Hazard?

'Hazard? *Hazard?*' His voice boomed down the silent green corridor.

But the stuttering of the typewriter had ceased. Hazard must have gone home.

'Skiver,' Peach muttered.

He burst into the kitchen, put the kettle on. Then waited for it to boil, hands fidgeting in his pockets. Nobody pulled the wool over *his* eyes. *Nobody.*

A shrill whistling brought him round. He poured the boiling water into the teapot and carried it, together with a bottle of milk and a white china mug, into his office. While the tea brewed, he opened his filing-cabinet and searched for the dossier.

Ah, there it was. Filed under H. H for Highness.

He opened the pink cover. MOSES GEORGE HIGHNESS. He sat down at his desk and, sipping the strong tea, scanned the first few pages to refresh his memory.

A description of the child. The circumstances of his disappearance. Transcripts of the interviews with the parents. Certain phrases leapt out, clarified by the passage of years. *Babies disappear all the time.* Barefaced. Almost confessional. How could he have been fooled, even for a moment?

He turned the page. The reports of the daily search-parties. The discovery of the toy dog. Pretty slim pickings. Then a piece of paper slipped out of the file and see-sawed through the air to the floor. Bending with difficulty – these days Peach had to ask his wife to cut his toenails for him – he scooped it up. It was a cutting from the local rag. One of the most dramatic headlines they had run for years: TRAGIC DEATH OF BABY, it said. A lie, of course. A cover-up. He knew that now.

Running his hand across the stubble of his cropped grey hair, Peach turned the page again. The new entry was dated October 10th 1969. Over thirteen years after the funeral. He began to re-read the notes he had made of a conversation that had taken place on the main road that day.

He had stopped a car, he remembered, a routine check, only to discover that the driver was a policeman himself, from a town less than thirty miles away. The policeman was on holiday. On his way down to the coast to join his wife, he said. A couple of children brawled in the back of the car.

'Fine children,' Peach had remarked.

'More trouble than they're worth,' the policeman said. 'Got any kids yourself?'

Peach regretted that he hadn't.

'Just as well. I wouldn't have any, if I was you.'

Peach, who couldn't, winced. 'Yes,' he said, 'you're probably right.' But how he longed for an heir. The things he could have taught a son, for instance. Why, he might even have taken over from his father as Chief Inspector! Peach felt the splinters of his shattered hopes lodge in his chest.

The policeman, in a brash holiday mood, didn't notice. 'People have 'em,' he was saying, 'don't realise how much work they are, then they don't want 'em any more. What do they do? They dump 'em, don't they?'

A gloomy Peach nodded. But the policeman's next sentence snapped him back, as if his fantasy had been attached to the real world by a length of elastic.

'Talking of kids – shut up a moment you two, will you? – did you ever hear about that case a few years ago? The baby they found on the river? Happened down our way. Strange story that was, and no – '

Peach jumped in sharply. 'What baby?'

'Didn't you hear about it? These two old dears found a baby floating down the river. They brought him in to us. In ever such a tizzy, they were.' His laughter gobbled obscenely like water running out of a bath. 'They didn't even – '

But Peach didn't want to hear about old women. 'This baby,' he interrupted. 'What was it like?'

'About eighteen months old. Had a funny name. Something from the Bible – '

'Moses?' Peach's voice remained calm, but his heart seemed to be pushing against the inside of his uniform.

'That's it. And he was only found by the river, wasn't he? Some sense of humour *his* parents must've had.' The policeman's mouth opened wide. His teeth were curiously pale and large, like ice-cubes.

Sense of humour? Peach was thinking. Don't talk to me about sense of humour.

Before the policeman drove on, Peach asked for the address of the police station that had taken the baby into custody. The policeman never thought to question Peach's interest in the case. A fool, Peach thought, and a complacent one at that. But perhaps he was being unfair. After all, the man was on holiday. And he had given Peach his first real lead in thirteen years.

Peach looked up from the file. Lightning bleached the windowpanes a faint cold blue. The thunder had moved away over the hill. He turned that autumn morning over in his head. The blades of grass plated with early frost. Hedgerows rusted by a month of rain. A random shaft of sun bringing out the ginger in Sergeant Caution's two-day growth of beard.

And when he watched that policeman's car disappear round a bend in the main road, how strongly he had felt the temptation to disappear himself. To verify the story. To know the truth about Moses.

Two considerations had held him back. One, his sense of responsibility (imagine a Chief Inspector defecting! the hypocrisy!). And two, the pointlessness of such a move. What good would it do? If the baby had got away, had grown up in the outside world (he would be sixteen now, Peach calculated), he would have no memories of New Egypt. He might have been born anywhere. Equally, very few of the villagers remembered Moses now, not without being prompted. He had drowned in the river, and that was that. From both points of view the case was closed. There was no foreseeable danger. Better then to forget. Let time and apathy bury the memory. Only he, Peach, would carry the burden of knowing what had really happened.

And George Highness, of course.

George Highness. Would *he* talk?

Somehow Peach doubted it. The man was private to the point of arrogance, and stubborn with it. Those characteristics would prevent him broadcasting what he had done, would nip any revolutionary instincts in the bud. It would be enough for George Highness to know that he had outsmarted the entire police department of New Egypt. Peach imagined that he must derive enormous satisfaction from that knowledge.

Once again he saw Highness during the closing moments of that funeral in 1956. When he walked over to offer his condolences, Highness had actually *smiled*. No more than a slight puckering at the corners of his mouth, but a smile none the less. The sheer brazen *impertinence* of it. Since then Peach had developed a theory about smiling. Why, only the other day he had delivered a lecture on the subject to a group of new recruits.

'Now if you see somebody smiling,' he had told them, 'it can mean one of two things. One, that the person in question is perfectly adjusted to life in the village. Anybody who is that well adjusted should be viewed as a potential threat. Can any of you tell me why?'

Peach's glance had swept along the row of recruits. Not one of the four had anything to offer. A pretty dull bunch. He sighed.

'The reason is this. The person who is that well adjusted to life in the village is an exception. That person has occupied an extreme position. They are, in that sense, unbalanced, volatile. They are capable, at any moment, of veering to the other extreme, one of despising life in the village, one of plotting to escape from the life they despise – '

Peach had seen the faces of his recruits light up in turn as the point became clear. One or two nodded seriously as if they had known all along and had simply been waiting to have their knowledge confirmed.

'Now,' Peach went on, 'who can tell me what the second meaning of a smile might be?'

Again his gaze had moved along a row of blank faces. For God's sake.

Then one of the recruits, Wragge by name, a poor specimen of a youth with a nose that dangled from his face and a pair of close-set colourless eyes, stuck his hand up in the air.

'Yes, Wragge?'

'Could it be because they're harbouring a plan to escape, sir?'

Well, well. There was hope yet. Perhaps he was even looking at a future Chief Inspector. *Harbouring*, too. The perfect word to use in that context. Peach had studied Wragge for a moment and tried to widen the gap between those eyes, tried to invest that drooping nose with a bit of dignity, a bit of gristle. If only Wragge looked as intelligent as he obviously was.

'Excellent, Wragge. That's perfectly correct.'

He saw Wragge's mouth expand a fraction. A smirk of complacency. Peach had decided there and then that he didn't care for Wragge. But he might be useful, of course.

'When you see somebody smiling they might be dreaming of, or planning, an escape. A smile is a danger sign, a warning, a lead. I cannot impress upon you too strongly that you should treat a smile with the utmost suspicion,' he had concluded. Or almost concluded, because he had then experienced a moment of inspiration – wild, vivid, lateral – the kind of inspiration that made him the kind of Chief Inspector he was. 'Think of it like this,' he had lowered his voice for effect, 'somebody smiling is like somebody pointing a gun. They need to be disarmed or they will cause injury, damage, loss of morale. Even, perhaps, loss of life. There are times when I think smiling should be made illegal, but obviously – ' and he had raised a hand in the air, fingertips uppermost like a waiter with an invisible tray, to demonstrate that he was exaggerating to make a point, that he was, in fact, joking. Then he had himself smiled. There had been laughter among the recruits, but it had been serious laughter. The message had hit home.

He leaned back, pushed knuckles into his eyes. He returned to his scrutiny of the file. He turned up a sheaf of loose letters. These were answers to the barrage of enquiries he had unleashed following his encounter with that policeman in October 1969. There was one, for instance, from the policeman's immediate superior:

Dear Chief Inspector Peach,

Thank you for your letter of October 20th. I regret to say that I do not personally recall the case to which you refer since I was only transferred to this constabulary three years ago. However, I have had recourse to our records and I can inform you that a baby was indeed admitted to this police station during June 1956. On June 16th, in fact. The baby was registered under the name Moses George Highness.

It would seem that the Detective Sergeant in charge of the case attempted to locate the baby's parents, but without success. The only lead he had to go on was the name Highness, a name so unusual that he assumed it was an alias, a bogus name, devised to throw whoever found the child off the scent. Following the failure of these investigations, the baby in question was remitted to an orphanage in Kent, the address of which you will find attached to this letter.

I hope this has been of some help to you, and I trust your research into this most tragic of human problems continues to go well.

Yours sincerely,
Detective Sergeant Hackshaw

This most tragic of human problems. Peach's own words, lifted from his own letter. He had written as a police officer with a social conscience, a police officer who was working on a book about missing children. Upon receiving this letter from Hackshaw, he had immediately written to the orphanage. He had received the following reply:

Dear Chief Inspector Peach,

It is not our custom to supply information regarding the children in our charge; however, in this case, given your official position and your serious interest, I have taken it upon myself to waive the regulations. Moses was admitted to the Rose Hill Orphanage on June 29th 1956. I myself personally supervised the admission. He spent nine years with us – nine very happy years, I believe – and on June 1st 1965 was adopted by a couple with whom he had formed an extremely satisfactory relationship during the year previous.

Mr and Mrs Pole, formerly of 14 Chester Row, Maidstone, Kent, have now moved to Leicester. I regret to say that I do not have their new address. However, with all the resources at your disposal, I am sure that you will be able to trace them without too much trouble.

Yours sincerely,
Beatrice Hood

A third far briefer letter from a sergeant in Leicester confirmed the information supplied by Mrs Hood. The Poles had moved to the outskirts of the city, a green suburb. The sergeant had been kind enough to provide Peach with the address. And there Peach had let the matter rest.

He lay back in his chair and listened to the rain. Three years had passed since then. Three passive years.

His eyes were drawn to the corner of his office. There, propped up on a shelf, stood the toy dog, visible only as a ghostly patch of white in the shadows. Some remote ray of light had caught the black and orange glass of its left eye, so it seemed to be winking at him, mocking him. Balancing on three legs, it lifted its fourth and urinated on his career. And yet he couldn't bring himself to throw it out. It was the only piece of evidence he had. It was a symbol of progress – what little he had made.

At least he was one up on George Highness, though. There was some solace in that. At least he knew Moses was alive. Highness could only *hope* he was. Perhaps he would be able to torture Highness with that knowledge. Yes, he might just be able to make the bastard squirm a little. To think that the fate of the village should have rested in that man's hands. It was monstrous. *Monstrous*. Highness would pay for that. Unquestionably he would pay.

Hands folded on his desk, Peach schemed for a while.

Then the phone rang.

He lifted the receiver. 'Peach.'

'I'm sorry to disturb you, dear – '

It was Peach's wife.

'Hilda. What is it?'

'It's just that it's getting very late. I was worried about you.'

Peach glanced at his watch. Good Christ, it was almost one o'clock. He hadn't realised.

'I'm sorry, Hilda. I had no idea it was so late. I'll be home in a few minutes.'

'I'll have some supper ready for you.'

His dear wife. 'Thank you, Hilda. I'll be there very soon.'

He replaced the receiver. Locking up his office, he walked out into the rain.

*

At the age of forty-five, George Highness already slept as old men do. He went to bed early, usually at around ten. He took a glass of water with him for the night and a Thermos of weak tea for the morning.

By five he was always awake again. Then he would doze with the radio on, floating halfway between consciousness and dreams. The voices of the news announcers, turned to the lowest volume, muttered distantly, drowsily, like traffic or waves. At seven he poured himself a cup of tea, and sipped it noisily, as privacy allows you to, his head propped on a heap of pillows. Sometimes he reached for his electric razor and, holding a circular mirror in his left hand, trimmed his beard.

Then he could delay no longer, even though the day offered him nothing. He levered his thin legs out of the bed and on to the floor. The opening moments of this routine never varied. On with his dressing-gown and slippers, across the landing, and into the lavatory.

On this particular morning, perhaps because of the storm that had kept him awake for half the night, he was still asleep when the phone rang in his bedroom at eight-thirty. The sound reached down into his dream like an excavator's mechanical arm and scooped him out of the rubble of his subconscious. He rolled over groaning, pulled the phone towards his ear.

'Hello?'

'Could I speak to Mr Highness, please?'

George thought he could place the voice. A man's voice – alert, efficient, nasal. If he had been asked to put a smell to it, he would have said toothpaste. The name eluded him, however.

'Speaking.'

'This is Doctor Frost from the Belmont Home. I'm sorry to be calling you so early – '

Frost. Of course. 'That's all right, doctor. I – '

'I'm afraid I have some rather bad news for you, Mr Highness. It's about your wife – ' The doctor paused.

Like one of those puzzles, George thought. Fill in the missing words. He had already guessed the answer, but he said nothing. He closed his eyes and saw blue crosses in the darkness. He listened to the doctor's hygienic silence. He had always suspected Frost of being a coward.

Eventually: 'She died at seven o'clock this morning.'

George opened his eyes again. The room a watercolour in grey. A coating of dust on the lampshade above his head. Through the window, the elm tree and a triangle of glassy sky. He turned on to his side and drew his knees towards his chest.

'Mr Highness?'

'Yes.'

'Somebody will be contacting you later today. About the forms. I'm sorry, Mr Highness.'

Doctor Frost hung up.

George could see him now, a pink man in a white coat. Those sparse white hairs, how obscene they looked against his raw pink skull. His quick prim steps as he strutted down the hospital corridor. Congratulating himself, no doubt. An unpleasant task, successfully accomplished. On with the day.

And Alice –

And Alice, worth five or ten of him, lying in a drawer somewhere, her mouth ajar, her eyes transfixed –

George pushed his face into the pillow. His love, dormant these twelve years, rose in his throat, acidic, scalding. He tried to swallow, couldn't. He closed his eyes again, curled up. His last thought before falling into a deep sleep concerned the telephone. He would disconnect it. He had only had it installed in the first place so he could speak to her, or be there if she needed him. Now there was nobody to speak to any more. Cut it off. Complete the isolation.

Its brash nagging woke him again just after ten. The medical secretary from the Belmont. Wanting to know whether Mr Highness would collect the death certificates in person or whether she should post them.

'Post them,' George snapped, and hung up.

As he reached for his tartan dressing-gown, his body began to shake.

*

Alice, Alice, Alice.

He tried to use the sound of her name to bring her back. It had been so long. He was in danger of losing his sense of her. It would be as if she had never been.

He tried to gather solid details. To give her death, in distance, substance.

That green-blonde hair, scraped back in a denial of its beauty. Her shoes scattered, often singly, throughout the house, the insteps cracked, the heels trodden down. The time when, pregnant, she walked naked down the stairs to breakfast. And later, in the winter, the tip of her tongue on her top lip as she trickled peanuts into the miniature wire cage in the garden so the birds wouldn't starve. And that blurred smile, almost tearful, flung his way like a handful of grain, breaking up as it arrived.

Her smiles always blurred, as if seen from a moving train.

Her eyes always creased at the edges by dreams of leaving.

And how he would come back sometimes to find the doors locked and the curtains drawn. How he had to break into his own house. And all the breakfast things still standing on the table. Immovable from hours of being there. Petrified.

The butter decomposing on a china dish.

Wasps suffocating in the marmalade.

Such padded silence.

It was summer, the hot summer of 1959, but she wouldn't have the windows open. When he asked her why – a stupid question, but he could think of no others – she turned her smudged and punished eyes on him and said, 'Go away.'

Him, the world, everything.

For hours, for days, she lay upstairs. Once he walked into her bedroom, sat down on the quilt. In the darkness he mistook her shoulder for her forehead. The bed shook with her crying.

'Why are you crying, Alice?' he asked her. 'Tell me why you're crying.'

'I don't know, I can't help it, it just happens, I don't know why, I'm happy really – ' It all came flooding out until she was crying so hard her words lost their shape, became unintelligible.

She was committed in 1960. She committed herself, really. She wanted it. That was one day he didn't have to search his memory for. Maroon ambulance, black mudguards. Big silver headlights. And Alice shuffling down the garden path, taller than the two nurses who supported her. Eyes rolling upwards in their sockets. Frightening white slits. Regal somehow. But mad. Or not mad, perhaps, but painfully, unbearably unhappy. Mauve smears on her white exhausted face. Channels worn by the passage of tears. He remembered thinking, Alice is escaping. For the Belmont Mental Home, ironically, stood some three miles beyond the village boundary.

She only came back to the house once. And talked about prisons constantly. And the prisons kept shrinking. First it was the village. Then it was their house on Caution Lane. In the end, of course, it was her own body.

Alice is escaping. Well, now she had.

Perhaps he shouldn't cry for her. He had read somewhere that tears are like ropes: they tie a person's soul to the earth. Now the prisons no longer existed for her she was free. And he should let her go.

He sat in the kitchen and reviewed the twelve years he had spent alone. He had sung in the choir, and his voice – a bass baritone – had performed respectably enough. He had given lectures in the church hall under the watchful eye of the Chief Inspector, lectures on the history of the region, the traditions and the crafts. He had never really socialised, but nor had he been rude when approached.

And then there had been his book.

He rose to his feet and walked into the front room. Selecting the smallest key from the bunch he kept in his pocket, he unlocked the lid of his writing-desk. He reached in and pulled out a bundle of paper. About a hundred typed pages. His secret manuscript. The title scrawled in spindly black capitals:

NEW EGYPT –

AN UNFINISHED HISTORY.

He weighed the book in his hands. Not much to show for almost a year's work, but then he had scrapped a good deal. Besides, it had served its purpose. It had got him through those first few months of living without Alice. Plunging into a personal history of the village, he had found that he lost track of time, that he could put his loneliness to good use, that he could exorcise the ghost that Alice had become. He remembered those hours, days, weeks at the writing-desk with a kind of grateful nostalgia.

Shifting a pile of old newspapers, George sank down on to the sofa. He loosened the red string that bound the manuscript and turned the title-page. He skimmed across the opening sentence with a wry smile (I was born in the most boring village in England). With Alice still in mind, he moved forwards to his chapter on escape and began to read.

Stories of escape-attempts, songs of resignation and disillusion, fantasies about the outside world abound in the village and form a unique body of local folklore. They divide into two distinct categories. On the one hand there are ballads, nursery rhymes and moral tales, all of which serve to remind people of their allegiance to the village and to persuade them, often insidiously, that the world outside is a hostile and lonely place. Great emphasis is laid on roots, the idea of a birthplace, the feeling of being among people you have grown up with. An example of this first category (which is, by the way, the official folklore of the village and is written, more often than not, by members of the police force) would be the story of the man who leaves the village in search of a better life. At the beginning he can scarcely contain his joy. The open road, the new earth beneath his feet – why, the very air smells of freedom!

Then the sky slowly darkens and rain begins to fall. The man suddenly realises that he has lost his way. The wide grey landscape is deserted. He is alone. I may be lost, he tells himself, but at least I'm free.

After walking for a while he happens across a country tavern. Soaked to the skin, he asks the landlord for shelter.

The landlord eyes him with suspicion. 'You're not from around here, are you?' he says.

'No,' the man says.

'Be off with you then,' the landlord says. 'We don't have any dealings with strangers.'

At nightfall the man reaches a small town. His feet ache. He is chilled to the bone. He turns into an alley in search of a cheap place to eat and is set upon by a gang of local youths. They beat him senseless and steal what little money he has. He sprawls among the dustbins, big round drops of rain landing on his closed eyelids like pennies thrown to a blind man. I'm still free, he mutters.

A car drives into the alley and two policemen climb out. They arrest the man on a charge of vagrancy. They call him names and lock him in a cell for the night. The man lies shivering under a single coarse blanket. He has no home, no money, no future. As day dawns he stares out through the bars. I'm free, he thinks.

George was becoming depressed. He put the manuscript aside and went out to the kitchen. When he returned five minutes later with a pot of tea and a packet of Butter Osbornes he skipped a few pages. Then he saw the name Batley, and it opened a drawer in his memory. The Batley Affair. So long ago now. His interest awakened, he began to read again.

Oscar Batley is descended from de Barthelay who came over with William the Conqueror in 1066. He is hereditary lord of the manor and lives on the outskirts of the village in a house called Stone Hall. A man of considerable breeding, wealth and ingenuity, he has a film-star's eternal black hair and cheeks the colour of rare roast sirloin. In 1938, at the age of seventy-nine, he tried to escape. He bribed the doctor to pronounce him dead. (He decided on a sudden and tragic heart attack; after a lifetime of rich food and vintage wines, this had the ring of plausibility.) He then bribed the undertaker, not only to co-operate in the provisions for his funeral, but to build a coffin with hidden ventilation-holes. Finally he bribed the sexton to delay filling in the grave until the day after the funeral.

Batley's plan hinged on the fact that, according to ancient custom, he was entitled to be buried in an ancestral plot of land adjacent to his estate, the western wall of which happened to serve as part of the village boundary. Once the ceremony was over, the coffin would be lowered into the grave, the mourners would disperse, and Batley would wait in air-conditioned comfort until night fell. Then he would ease off the lid, clamber out of the open grave, and make good his escape across the wooded country to the west. Since he had died, the police would not be looking out for him. So the logic, presumably, went. An ingenious plan, but flawed in one fatal respect.

Batley died successfully enough. Death certificates were drawn up by the doctor and filed with the police. The coffin had been prepared in accordance with Batley's detailed instructions. The sexton had agreed to play his part (his initial misgivings overcome by a twenty-five per cent increase in his pay-off). A marble headstone had even arrived, imported from Carrara in Italy. Everything might have gone smoothly had Peach not insisted on a grand funeral procession through the village. Batley was an important local figure, Peach argued, and should be treated as such.

Batley's Victorian phaeton was wheeled out of his stables. It was repaired, oiled, and given a new coat of paint. Farmer Hallam agreed to supply two black horses for the occasion. There was a problem, however, with the plumes.

George couldn't help smiling. He was thinking of Tabasco, the under-taker. Shortly before his death, Tabasco had sat George on his knee and told him about the week Lord Batley spent in his back parlour. Tabasco had considered Batley a snob and a fraud, and he had rather enjoyed the power that the peculiar situation had bestowed on him. How Tabasco had cackled as he recalled his whispered dialogues with Batley! One, George remembered, had gone something like this:

'What the devil's happening, Tabasco?' Batley sat in his coffin like a large disgruntled baby. 'Why all the delay?'

'They're going to have a special procession for you,' Tabasco told him, 'because you're so important.'

'Oh God,' Batley groaned and ran his hands through his black hair in which, to Tabasco's immense satisfaction, streaks of grey were beginning to show. (So it was true: the hair *was* dyed.) 'How long am I going to have to wait?'

'Your guess is as good as mine. A week at least. Maybe longer. You know what this place is like.'

'Why, for heaven's sake? What's holding us up?'

'The plumes.'

'*Plumes?* What plumes, man?'

'The black plumes, your lordship. For the horses' heads. You can't have a funeral procession without black plumes. Not for someone of your distinction. That wouldn't do at all, would it?'

'Oh, damn this bloody place to hell.'

'I think I'd better screw you down,' Tabasco said. 'I can hear somebody coming.'

Just an excuse, of course, to shut the bastard up.

Still smiling, George read on.

No black plumes could be found. Lord Batley grew restless in his coffin. He complained of headaches, cramps, disorientation. He moaned about the food. He cursed what he called Tabasco's 'inefficiency'.

Meanwhile, in Magnolia Close, Hilda Peach, the Chief Inspector's resourceful wife, was improvising a pair of black plumes out of two old straw brooms.

The day finally came. It was December 15th 1938 –

How clearly George remembered that day. He must have been eleven. Clouds the colour of lead. Searing cold. His gloved hands. Alice on the other side of the street, standing between her parents, the wide dish of her face tilted at the sky like radar. Then the clatter of carriage wheels on the cobblestones. And what happened next.

– and the weather was bitterly cold. The route which the funeral procession was to follow had been mapped out by Peach himself. Lord Batley would lie in state in an open coffin. The people of New Egypt would line the streets. They would be wearing black. It would be a solemn but memorable conclusion to the life of a distinguished local figurehead.

Things turned out differently.

As the carriage slowed to negotiate the sharp bend that led to the church, PC Fisher noticed clouds of white smoke rising from the coffin. He broke ranks and hurried discreetly to Peach's side. Peach was supporting the grief-stricken Lady Batley.

'Chief Inspector, sir,' Fisher clamoured. 'Lord Batley's on fire.'

'A dead man on fire?' Peach raised his eyebrows. 'A little unlikely, don't you think?' Glancing down at Lady Batley, he seemed to be addressing the question to her. Lady Batley's eyes floated like pale helpless fish on the surface of her face.

'I know it sounds unlikely, sir, but look. Smoke.'

Peach looked. 'That's not fire,' he said calmly, 'that's breath. The man is still alive.'

Lady Batley collapsed moaning against Peach's arm. He passed her unceremoniously to Fisher.

Lord Batley was removed from his coffin in full view of the villagers who had lined the streets in his honour, and escorted, under their disbelieving gaze, to the police station. His widow followed, still weeping – though for a different reason now. The funeral cortège was quietly disbanded. The villagers returned to their houses.

As a direct result of this episode, it has become much harder to die. Inhabitants of New Egypt are subjected to a series of rigorous tests before being allowed to rest in peace. Peach inspects each corpse in person. 'One Lazarus is enough,' he is supposed to have said in that winter of 1938.

But what of those who had taken bribes from Batley?

The doctor was carefully beaten up by PC Hazard prior to having his licence to practise removed. Tabasco died two months after the funeral – in place of Batley, perhaps. The sexton, meanwhile, was given a lecture on greed by Peach and forcibly retired on a meagre pension.

And Batley?

Batley is still alive and well and living in New Egypt. He is one hundred and three years old now and is believed by many to have lost the ability to die –

And here the manuscript ended. George had lost his momentum, lost interest. In that moment, the moment when he pushed his pen aside, he had realised that he was no different from any other New Egyptian. The apathy had taken hold. What better comment on the nature of the village than that its self-appointed historian had failed to complete his history of the place! How typical, how *archetypal* that was!

It had been ten years since he had touched the manuscript, and he now knew that he would never go back to it again. What was the point? Who could he give it to? When he died, it would fall into the hands of the police and end up in that fucking museum.

Not on your life.

He would destroy it first.

*

The following day, at three in the afternoon, a man with tangled grey hair stopped outside George's house. It was Dinwoodie, come to pay his respects.

Dinwoodie unlatched the gate. A screech of metal disturbed a silence of dripping leaves. The gate, it seemed, was rarely opened.

He paused again, and stared up at the front of the house. Another death in the family. *Another*, though? He wished he knew. Even after all these years. *Especially* after all these years.

The front door opened before he could pretend to be moving, and George Highness emerged, wrapped in a brown overcoat and a yellow scarf. In his hand, a bunch of flowers. Dinwoodie jumped backwards, as if he had been caught red-handed at something. Which, in a way, he had been. Trespassing not so much on property as on grief. He gulped a hello.

'Good afternoon, Dinwoodie,' George said. To Dinwoodie, his composure seemed unnatural, suspect.

'I – ' he began.

'You wanted to see me?'

'Yes,' Dinwoodie said. 'I was on my way to visit you.'

'And very nearly there, by the look of it.' With his free hand, George indicated Dinwoodie's feet which were planted on, if not rooted in, the garden path. 'I was on my way out,' he continued. 'As you see.'

Cool customer, Dinwoodie thought. He tried again.

'I wanted to offer you my condolences,' he said. And then, by way of explanation, 'The death of your wife. I'm very sorry.'

At last George looked surprised. He blinked and angled an embarrassed glance into the shrubbery that divided the path from the small front lawn. 'Thank you,' he said, 'but it seems a little like the death of someone who was already dead.' A smile leaked from his face. 'If you follow me.'

'Yes,' Dinwoodie said. 'Yes, I think I do.'

The two men were both shuffling on the path now. Their eyes darted here and there as if following minnows in a pond.

'If you're going out,' Dinwoodie ventured finally, 'perhaps I could join you?'

'All right,' George said, but it was not too grudging. 'I'm going to the cemetery to put these – ' he held the flowers up as if they were slightly ridiculous – 'on my son's grave.'

Dinwoodie murmured, bowed; he might have been giving permission.

Side by side, they walked up Caution Lane. When they reached Church Street they turned right and began to climb the hill. Spring was late this year. Rain hung in the trees like pieces of broken glass. The branches, grey, spindly, arthritic, seemed to be resisting growth. Dinwoodie could hear George's knees cracking in the silence.

'A lot of tragedies recently.' Dinwoodie threw out the remark, then turned eagerly to George as if he had lit a fuse that might cause George to explode with some kind of revelation.

But George had withdrawn into himself. 'Yes,' he said. He fitted the word between gasps for breath. It was a steep hill.

A dark horse, Dinwoodie thought. Really a very dark horse.

He increased the pressure marginally. 'Your wife, of course. And then

Joel – ' He scanned George's face, but George still seemed more interested in the surface of the road, so he added, a little unnecessarily, perhaps, 'The greengrocer.'

'I heard,' George said. And just as Dinwoodie was about to prompt him again, George added, 'An extravagant plan, but doomed. Doomed from the very beginning.'

Dinwoodie, the fire that he was, kindled. Fingers spread in a primitive comb, he dragged a hand through his tangle of hair.

'Too extravagant, you think?'

George settled for the conventional response. 'Nobody's ever escaped. Why should an extravagant idea be more likely to succeed than a simple one?'

'You may be right,' Dinwoodie said. George's gloom didn't dismay him too much; at least they were talking now. 'But a simple plan,' he went on, 'might stand a better chance, you think?'

George gave Dinwoodie a look that Dinwoodie couldn't decipher: he saw a gloating first, then condescension, then sadness – then all three merged until he couldn't be sure what he had seen. He decided to risk it anyway. 'I have a plan,' he said.

'Really? You surprise me. What is it this time, Dinwoodie?'

'There's no need to be sarcastic.'

George sighed. 'I'm sorry. I'm not myself at the moment.'

Crap, Dinwoodie thought. You're yourself all right. He gave the church-yard gate a shove. It banged against the wall. Two crows, scared, broke away from the top of a yew tree. Black shrapnel against a lowering grey sky. George followed Dinwoodie up the path. He held his flowers upright in his hand and level with his face, the way you might hold an umbrella. As they climbed up through the cemetery, Dinwoodie's head rang with unvoiced arguments. He wanted to believe that it was only a matter of time before George heard. But they reached the grave in silence, with Dinwoodie still uncertain how to reopen the subject. He read the inscription on the stone.

MOSES GEORGE HIGHNESS
ONLY SON OF GEORGE AND ALICE
BORN MAY 22ND 1955
DIED JULY 14TH 1956
HE LIVES IN OUR THOUGHTS

Lines of scepticism showed on either side of Dinwoodie's mouth. It was a charade. He knew, he just *knew* that George had pulled it off somehow. Patience failing, he struck out.

'Your wife's dead,' he said, and then, with a sly weakening of emphasis that George, he felt, would detect and understand, 'and so is your son. There's nothing to keep you here now, George. Why don't we join forces, collaborate, and get out of this place? What do you say?'

George squatted on his haunches, arranged the flowers in a small rusty urn. 'On the contrary,' he said. 'Now they're,' and he didn't hesitate, 'both dead, there's everything to keep me here.'

'I don't understand. *What* is there to keep you here?' Dinwoodie's hand ransacked his hair for a reason.

'Memories, I suppose,' George said. 'These graves. The graves of the people I love.' It must have sounded sententious to him because he added, almost defiantly, 'Besides, what's out there, anyway?'

'Freedom,' escaped from Dinwoodie's lips before he knew it.

Still meddling with the flowers, George shook his head. 'Freedom isn't out there any more than it's in here.' He glanced round at the rows of damp tombstones.

'How do you know,' Dinwoodie cried, his hands clutching at the air, 'until you've tried?'

In a quiet voice George said, 'Dinwoodie, when are you going to grow up?'

Dinwoodie's face reddened as if he had been slapped on both cheeks. 'You know,' he said, trying to keep his voice under control, 'I used to think you had something, George. Guts, maybe. A bit of initiative. I don't know. That's what I thought. But you haven't. You haven't got anything. You're just a shell. I – I pity you.'

George rose to his feet. He stood at an angle to Dinwoodie. A remote smile on his face, he watched smoke drift from a chimney, fade into the sky. He had nothing to say, it seemed. Or if he had, he wasn't going to say it.

'Well, I'm going to try, anyway,' Dinwoodie said. 'And I'll do it alone if I have to.'

George looked Dinwoodie square in the face for the first time that afternoon. 'You haven't got a chance, Dinwoodie. You'll fail. You'll end up in that police museum.'

'Fuck you,' Dinwoodie said.

And he whirled away down the slope, trampling on the graves of his forefathers. His mouth, thin-lipped, chapped, set in a grim smile. It felt good to be walking on the dead.

Fuck him, he thought. Fuck them all. I'm not dying here.

He didn't look back at George Highness. They had parted in anger. He doubted they would ever speak to each other again.

*

At home that evening George couldn't settle. He kept seeing Dinwoodie's white impassioned face. He kept seeing Dinwoodie stride away across the graveyard, grey hair, grey raincoat flapping. With his gaunt frame and his square shoulders lifted, he had made George think of a cross. He knew in his heart, in his bones (wherever it is that you truly know), that Dinwoodie was dead.

As dusk fell, he left his house for the second time that day. Unprecedented, this. But perhaps he had some dim foreknowledge of the consequences and courted them as expiation for the way he had treated Dinwoodie. In any case, he could no longer stay indoors.

Where they had turned left out of the garden gate, he turned right and walked towards Peach Street. He could have given Dinwoodie some encouragement, he was thinking. He could have explained his theories about escape. He could even have told him about Moses. But George had kept the secret for so long that secrecy had become a habit. He saw secrecy as his plan's foundation, its strength, a guarantee, if you like, of its success. Superstitious of him, true, but impossible now to shake off. So he had been harsh with Dinwoodie, as you might be harsh with a pestering child. And in many ways Dinwoodie *was* a child. His tantrums, his enthusiasms, marked him out – even from a Tommy Dane or a Joel Mustoe. Tommy Dane's escape-attempt had been an act of violence, thoroughly in character, an integral part of his fight against authority. Joel's, on the other hand, had been a sly private affair; the greengrocer had turned to escape, George felt, because he sought tangible proof of his superiority – out of arrogance, in other words. Only Dinwoodie had pure motives. He had said it himself. He wanted freedom. Simple as that. It would have been noble if it hadn't been so naïve.

As George waited to cross Peach Street, a truck swept past trailing yards of blue smoke. Stacked upright behind the tailboard and lashed into position with ropes stood an entire platoon of dummy policemen. These were not the dummies he was used to (blue uniforms stuffed with old rags, foam rubber or straw). These were professional dummies, the kind you see in shop windows. They had eyes, noses, hands, hair. They were uncannily lifelike. Even at a distance he recognised a Peach, two Hazards and a

Dolphin. He shuddered. Alice's words came back to him like a prophecy. *Look at their faces!*

He stumbled across the road and climbed over a stile into the allotments. He sank on to a bench, breathed in the bitter fleshy smell of cabbages. Ranks of bean-canes sharp as lances. A guarded peace. Over by the tin shed where the gardening tools were housed he could make out the squat figure of Mrs Latter, the woman who ran the post office and a keen grower of marrows. He raised a hand to her, a salute rather than a wave, but she didn't respond. Perhaps she hadn't noticed him. He slid his hand back into his coat pocket like a useless weapon.

After picking his way through the rows of vegetables, he crossed the road again and set out across the village green. Passing the pond on his right (a squabbling of ducks, the plop of a frog), he turned left into Magnolia Close. The church rose at the end of the street, an obstacle, solid, adamant. George suddenly realised that the route he had chosen would lead him past the Chief Inspector's house. Normally he steered clear of Magnolia Close, but, then again, normally he didn't go out twice in a single day. He considered turning round, but his feet ached, and if he carried on past the church he would be home in five minutes.

Peach's house stood at right-angles to the church on the corner of the village green. It had once been the vicarage. Peach had evicted the priest shortly after the war claiming that, as Chief Inspector, he needed the house because it had such a commanding view of the village. (It also had an eighteenth-century wood-panelled staircase and an unusual parterre with triangular flower-beds enclosed by low box hedges, not to mention a topiary in yew dating, supposedly, from 1841. Enthusiasts would sometimes stop outside the house and enquire if they might look over the gardens. Mrs Peach was always most gracious.) But he hadn't won the house without a fight.

'What about the spiritual welfare of the village?' the then priest had argued. 'Is not my rightful place at the heart of the community?'

'It'll take you precisely three minutes to walk from the church to your new house,' Peach told him. 'I've timed it myself.'

'But *symbolically?*' the priest persisted.

No mean philosopher himself and as brutally secular as any medieval emperor, Peach had quashed the priest's arguments. Truth to tell, with his army of policemen behind him, his victory had never been in doubt. What did the hapless priest have to call upon but the assistance of his sexton (a widower with cataracts) and the wrath of God?

'But I *need* a big house – my *family* – ' he had pleaded, honest at last, and grovelling too.

Peach had quoted Colossians. 'Set your affection on things above, not on things of the earth.'

Touché, priest.

'My children,' the priest whimpered, 'I have to provide for my children.'

'And what makes you think that I'm not going to have children?' Peach had countered. 'I'm only thirty-six.'

The priest could hardly tell Peach that he had it on very good authority (from the doctor himself, in fact) that the Chief Inspector's wife was incapable of having children. He gave way, and was moved (the police transported his furniture) to a pleasant if characterless house on the far side of the village green. The roles of church and state were set for Peach's reign.

George had slackened his pace. He now stood at the entrance of Peach's driveway. Lights showed in all the windows. A murmur of voices reached George's ears. Some kind of party, it seemed, was in progress.

In order to peer through the living-room window, George had to part the sticky tentacles of a rose-bush and clamber up on to an ornamental stone mushroom. Inch by inch, he raised his face to the level of the sill.

The entire police force of New Egypt had assembled inside the room. Peach stood with his back to a log fire, his lower lip glistening, possibly with sherry. His wife moved among the officers with a tray of cocktail sausages and canapés. Firelight flickered on thick blue cloth. As George watched, Peach raised a hand.

'Gentlemen, your attention, please.' He took a pace forwards, hands clasped behind his back. 'Before we proceed any further, I'd like to make sure that we're all here. Sergeant Dolphin?'

Dolphin, with his schoolboy's face and his bully's torso, flush from his recent triumph over the greengrocer, took up position beside Peach and produced a clipboard and pen. He began to call out names, the names George knew off by heart.

'Arson?'

'Present.'

'Blashford?'

'Yes.'

'Caution?'

'On duty,' somebody said. 'In the station.'

Dolphin noted the information down. Then he proceeded. 'Damage?'

'Here, sergeant.'

George was gazing, mesmerised. He had never suspected Peach of using roll-calls. A small detail, granted, but one that might have found its way into the book, had he known about it.

Dolphin, meanwhile, had reached F.

'Fisher?'

'Night patrol,' a voice called out.

'Fox?'

'Present.'

Now laughter erupted as PC Grape said, 'Here, sergeant,' before Dolphin had time to call his name. Grape had something of Peach about him. He was reputed to possess a sixth sense that meant he could hear what people were thinking. George had the feeling that Grape would one day play an important part in thwarting some poor villager's dream of escape.

'Hawk-Sniper?'

'Yes.'

'Hazard?'

'Here.'

The collar of George's coat suddenly lifted in the wind. He glanced over his shoulder. He hoped to God that he couldn't be seen from the road.

Dolphin's voice droned on. 'Marlpit?'

' – esh. I mean, yes, sergeant.'

George whinnied. Marlpit had been caught with a mouthful of sausage.

'Peach?'

'I'm here, sergeant.'

A ripple of amusement. Sycophants, George thought.

'Pork?'

'Yes.'

'Savage?'

'He's still sick, sergeant,' Marlpit said, his mouth now cleared of sausage.

Furtive grins. Savage had shot himself in the foot during rifle-practice earlier in the week.

'Twinn, C?'

'Present.'

'Twinn, D?'

'He's on night patrol,' came the nasal whine of Colin, Twinn D's brother.

'Thank you, Twinn. Ulcer?'

'Yes.'

'Vassall?'

'Here, sergeant.'

'Voltage?'

'Here.'

In listening to this roll-call, George began to realise just how many police officers New Egypt employed. Of course, he *knew*. But it was the difference between knowing there's a lot of sand on the beach and counting the individual grains one by one. So far there had been six absentees and still the room heaved with blue cloth. A claustrophobia of truncheons and boots. And the names seemed to go on for ever.

'Wilmott?'

'Yes, sergeant.'

'Wragge?'

'Night patrol,' somebody called out.

Dolphin tucked his clipboard under his arm. Thanking his second-in-command, Peach moved forward again. He pushed his lower lip out and back, a signal that he was about to speak.

'We're here, as you know, to celebrate the arrival of a consignment of new APRs,* one of which,' and he stepped across to the shrouded figure by the bookcase and with a conjuror's flourish snatched off the dustsheet, 'we're lucky enough to have with us tonight.'

A muted roar of surprise and approval, for the figure was an exact replica of the Chief Inspector. Right down to the drooping eyelids and the jutting lower lip.

Peach laid a fond hand on his double's shoulder. 'I thought we'd put him outside the priest's bedroom window.'

A burst of raucous laughter. Everybody knew that the priest was terrified of Peach.

'Now, as I said,' Peach moved on, 'we have something to celebrate here tonight. And celebrate we will. But first, if you'll bear with me, there are one or two – '

George suddenly found himself lying on his back in the flower-bed. An undignified position, and one that he was, for a moment, at a loss to explain. Then he looked up and saw four policemen outlined against a sky of weak and distant stars. The night patrol. Fisher, Twinn (Daniel), Hack and, closer than the rest, the sickly leering face of Wragge.

'Well, well.' Wragge drew his pale ridged lips back over his teeth. They looked like anchovies, his lips. His breath, as if by association, stank of fish. 'Mr Highness.'

George lay motionless, the wind knocked out of his body. His cheek stung where it had torn on a rose-bush as he fell. Wragge removed his foot from George's wrist and, stepping backwards, jerked his head. George, shakily, stood up.

They led him, arms pinioned, through the front door, past Mrs Peach's fluttering hands, and into the room where her husband was making his speech. George would never forget the quality of the silence that greeted

* Artificial Police Representative

him. The silence of policemen. Wall to wall. Tight as a rack.

'Mr Highness, sir,' Wragge announced. 'We found him spying.'

Peach lifted his heavy eyelids. 'Spying, Wragge?'

'Looking through the window, sir.'

The silence tightened a notch. George hung his head. A tic pulsed in the delicate skin under his left eye.

Something quieter than outrage or contempt had taken possession of Peach's features. Something quieter, but equally threatening.

'I think, Mr Highness,' he said, 'that you had better come to my study.'

A snigger from Hazard.

'If you'll excuse me.' Peach was addressing his officers now. 'This won't take long.'

'I ought to be getting home,' George said. His voice cracked in mid-sentence; it had broken by the end.

Soft exhalations from many of the policemen moved like a draught through the warm room.

'Not just yet,' Peach said, almost kindly. Pressing a firm hand into the small of George's back, he guided him towards the door.

George had never set foot in the Chief Inspector's house before – it was a privilege usually reserved for police officers – but in his utter humiliation he noticed nothing.

Peach closed the study door behind them. 'The police are very excited,' he remarked.

George touched his cheek with the sleeve of his coat. 'Naturally,' he said. 'New security measures.'

Peach beamed. Taking the leather armchair on the left of the fireplace, he waved George to the one on the right.

'Yes, well,' he said, 'it's an important occasion. A milestone of sorts. I thought I'd give a small party. There's nothing like a party to lift morale – '

George let him talk. His mind drifted.

When he began to listen again, Peach's voice seemed to have moved closer, though the distance between them hadn't changed.

' – but one of the reasons I asked you in here was to say how sorry I was to hear the news. About your wife, I mean. Alice, wasn't it?'

George nodded. 'I suppose I'd been expecting it for years, really.' He touched his cheek again.

'You're bleeding,' Peach exclaimed. He offered George a clean handkerchief. George accepted it in silence.

Peach leaned back and crossed his legs. An inch of white and slightly dimpled ankle showed above his regulation grey sock.

George dabbed at the cut on his face, and waited.

Peach shifted his weight on to the other buttock. 'Even so,' he resumed, 'it must have come as something of a shock.'

George confirmed this, then added, 'But perhaps she'll be happier now.'

'Like your son?' Peach's voice had sharpened. He held it, like a knife, to George's throat.

'Yes,' George stammered, 'I suppose so.'

'By happier,' Peach pressed on, 'I take it you mean out of the village.'

'By happier,' George said, 'I mean dead.'

'But we don't know that, do we?'

'I beg your pardon?'

Peach slowed down, so George would miss none of his meaning. 'We don't know that your son is dead. Or do we?'

George blinked. 'We must presume so.'

He began to understand why Peach had insisted on the privacy of his study. But why now? After all these years?

'Or do we?' Peach repeated.

'I'm sorry, Chief Inspector. I don't know what you're driving at.'

'Don't put that act on with me,' Peach bellowed. Suddenly his teeth seemed very close to the front of his mouth.

Then his voice dropped into its lowest register. 'I'd like you to come clean with me, Mr Highness. Get the whole thing off your chest. Once and for all. You'll probably feel much better for it.'

Panic rose in George. The room swam.

'No,' he said. 'I can't.'

Peach braced his hands on his knees. He stood up. 'My handkerchief, please.'

'What?'

'My handkerchief.'

'Oh yes.' George opened his hand. The handkerchief lay crushed into a tight ball on his palm like a confession.

'Give it to me.'

George did as he was told.

'Now,' Peach said, 'stand up.'

George stood. And though he wanted to look away he couldn't. The Chief Inspector's face filled the field of his vision. He saw things he had never seen before: the tiny pinpricks in the wings of Peach's nose; the diagonal lines stretching from Peach's temples to the place where his eyebrows almost met; the figures-of-eight in the irises of Peach's cold grey eyes.

'You see,' Peach said, 'I know.'

The breath powering these words pushed into and across George's face. He smelt triumph in that breath. He smelt domination. Peach knew.

He knew whether Moses was alive or dead. He knew the truth. And that meant that he, George, would never know. Peach would never tell him. Peach would only taunt him, torment him. Play on his uncertainty. The fragility of his hopes.

He let his eyes close.

Peach had won.

*

George took to his bed, partly to rest his twisted ankle (sustained when Wragge pulled him backwards off the stone mushroom) and partly out of a deep sense of demoralisation.

He didn't answer the doorbell when it rang. From his bedroom window, he watched the priest creep away down the garden path, his curved back sheathed in the black shell of his cassock. Another of the crushed ones.

Nor did he attend Alice's funeral. *Too upset* was the story that went round – initiated by Peach, no doubt. Well, it was as good a story as any other.

During his second week in bed he wrote a poem. The first and last poem that he would ever write. He called it 'Epitaph'.

I lie in bed
I lie in bed
I lie in bed all day
'Cause maybe then
'Cause maybe then
My life will go away.

I do not move
I do not move
I do not move one bit
Life's too greedy
Life's too sad
I want no part of it.

See, I'm no good
I'm just no good
At anything at all
I'd rather lie
In bed than bang
My head against the wall.

So why am I
So why am I
So why am I alive?
That's the question
I'll be asking
Till the day I die.

Meanwhile I'll lie
I'll lie in bed
I'll lie in bed all day
'Cause maybe then
Eventually
My life will go away.

Self-pitying?
Yes.
Defeatist?
Yes.
Morbid?
Yes, yes, yes.
Had he stood accused of any or all of these charges, he would readily
have pleaded guilty.
What else was there to look forward to now except death?
The final – the only – escape.

THE BOND STREET MANDARIN

It was one of those terraced houses in Holland Park, white as icing and set back at a discreet distance from the road. The façade showed only as a few luminous holes in a high black screen of trees. The front garden had been allowed to run wild; a mass of shrubs and bushes, it sloped down to the railings which, like a row of policemen, held it back from the pavement. Gloria led the way up the flagstone path, chipped, uneven, lethal in the dark. One of her stiletto heels stuck in a crack and she nearly fell.

'Bit early for that,' Louise laughed, catching her from behind.

Gloria made a face. They were in different moods tonight, but maybe the party would even things out. The front door stood ajar. Music pulsed out of the gap. She paused on the bottom step.

'What're you doing?' Louise's blonde hair was a magnet for what little light there was.

'Cigarette,' Gloria said.

She fumbled in her bag. They both lit cigarettes. Just then the gate at the end of the garden creaked. More people arriving.

'Come on,' Louise said, taking Gloria's arm. 'Let's give it half an hour and then make off with the silver.'

Gloria smiled faintly. They ran up the steps and pushed through the door. They had to wait inside the hallway because two men were trying to manoeuvre an upright piano into one of the downstairs rooms. One of the men wore a winged superhero cap. The other was pissed and giggling. It was taking for ever and it wasn't funny.

'Maybe you'd better come back later,' the man in the cap grinned, meaning, Gloria suspected, *Stay, I fancy you.*

'Maybe I won't bother,' she said. She wondered why she had come in the first place. She felt jaded, highly strung, unlike herself. *Parties.* Just a lot of fucking babble. And there was always some jerk with a chainsaw laugh that sliced through all the other voices and set your teeth on edge. Christ, she thought, I *am* in a bad mood.

'Gloria?'

Gloria turned. It was Amy. Amy wore a pink designer cocktail dress. Her smile was a strip of white neon in the gloom of the hall. She held a piece of cake and a lit cigarette in one hand, and a glass of champagne and a toy revolver in the other. Embracing would be difficult.

Amy aimed her gun at Gloria. 'Peeow,' she went. Some people said Amy was a scream.

'Amy! What're you doing here?' Gloria had to heave the words into her mouth. They felt like too much luggage.

Amy took a step backwards, mimed astonishment. 'It's *my party*, Gloria.'

Christ, so it was. Gloria had forgotten. She shook her head at Amy, attempted a grin. 'My memory sometimes,' she said.

'So anyway,' Amy swept on, 'how've you been?'

'Oh, you know. OK.'

'Still singing?'

'When I can be bothered to open my mouth.' Gloria turned to Louise. 'This is Louise. Friend of mine.'

Amy acknowledged Louise with a wave of her hand. The smoke from her cigarette did something Chinese in the air.

'What's the piano for?' Gloria asked.

'Somebody's playing later on. Marvin Gaye's brother or something.' Amy's hand moved through the air again, suggesting mysterious and glamorous events. Her champagne glass tilted, anointing a white tuxedo as it went past. Not that Amy noticed.

'Is he any good?' Louise asked.

Amy's mouth hung open for a moment, and Gloria wondered why it seemed so dark in the hallway all of a sudden. Then she realised. Amy wasn't smiling any more.

The doorbell rang and Amy went to answer it. Gloria and Louise seized their opportunity and slipped upstairs.

'Jesus, someone should pull her plug out,' Louise said. 'Did you see the way she chucked champagne all down that guy's back?'

Gloria turned on the stairs and flung her arms out wide. 'Marvin Gaye's brother,' she proclaimed grandly.

They collapsed on each other laughing, then both thought the same thought and looked round. They didn't want to offend Marvin Gaye's brother and for all they knew he could have been standing right behind them.

*

Moses and Eddie arrived late. They had been delayed by two litres of Italian red wine and a *Hawaii Five-O* video. Moses hummed the theme tune all the way from Vauxhall Bridge to Holland Park. Eddie wrestled with the car radio, but couldn't shake the interference. A joint crackled in his fingers.

'Music,' he muttered. 'Where's the music?'

The party proved easier to find. Moses parked fifty yards down the road and they walked back. A girl with pale skin and black lips opened the door and draped herself along the leading edge. She was gazing at Moses and Eddie, but they seemed to have no more significance for her than the bushes or the garden path. Either she was very cool or she was very fucked in the head. Moses didn't know which, and hesitated.

Eddie moved in front of him and explained that they were very old friends of the people who were throwing the party. The girl's see-through eyes fixed on Eddie's face. She let the door swing open.

'You're so predictable,' Moses told him.

Eddie smirked. 'I got you in, didn't I?'

'I didn't need to "get in",' Moses said. 'I was invited.'

They rifled the kitchen for something more vicious than Cinzano Bianco. Five minutes of frustration and contempt, then joy as Moses turned up half a bottle of brandy under the sink. Somebody had obviously hidden it there for later on. But, as Eddie said, later had a way of turning into never.

Moses poured them both a glassful and tucked the bottle inside his jacket. They wandered out into the corridor. Moses noticed a girl standing alone at the foot of the stairs.

'Promise me one thing, Eddie,' he said.

'What's that?'

'Don't do another Barbara on me tonight, OK?'

'I wouldn't do that, Moses.'

'I mean it, Eddie. I don't want any more of your bloody messes to clear up.'

Eddie shrugged, smiled. A girl in red approached. Her eyes seemed to stick to Eddie, pulling her head round as she passed by. With Eddie there would always be messes.

'I'm going to look for Louise,' Moses said. 'See you later.'

The house distracted him, though, with floor after floor of lavish rooms. Beyond a pair of locked French windows a conservatory glimmered, its glass solarised by moonlight, its plants in jagged silhouette. Chandeliers of crystal chinked and glittered overhead. Two dozen bottles of champagne littered the top of a grand piano. A lot of people stood about – plastered, but ornately, like the ceilings. He was drawn into a few desultory conversations. He gave facetious answers to predictable questions. What did he do? He was a missionary, he sold insurance, he worked in a factory that made disposable rubber-gloves. Where did he live? Worthing (he was older than he looked). The brandy dwindled.

Emerging from the second-floor toilet, he was trapped by a man with a beard, glasses and a tartan shirt. The man smoked roll-ups (as a matter of principle, no doubt) and measured out his words like little parcels of brown rice.

'A pink nightclub? Interesting. Now tell me. How did that come about?'

Moses began to explain, then lost interest. Left a sentence dangling. The man was lighting another of his cigarettes. The wisps of stray tobacco glowed red like filaments. Moses suddenly felt like snatching the cigarette out of the man's mouth and hitting him. Thok! Right in the middle of that earnest political face of his.

The man blew his match out, looked up. 'You haven't finished your story.'

'No,' Moses said.

*

At one in the morning he was leaning against a wall on the third-floor landing. He was drinking red wine again. An open bottle stood at his feet. He felt relaxed, awake. The wall he was leaning against was a good wall.

There was still no sign of Louise. He asked Eddie if he had seen her. Eddie said he hadn't.

'Let's go downstairs,' Eddie said, 'and talk to people.'

'What people? I like it standing here. I don't want to talk to people.'

But life has things up its sleeve that it can produce at a moment's notice. Life is a great magician. Look:

'Who's that girl with the eyebrows?' Moses asked suddenly.

'Which girl with the eyebrows?'

'*That* girl with the eyebrows.'

Eddie turned and stared into a room across the landing. It contained about twenty people. At least half of them were girls. And, so far as he could see, all the girls had eyebrows.

'They've all got eyebrows,' he said.

'Sometimes, Eddie,' Moses said, 'just sometimes, I think you do it on purpose,' and with a kind of weary strength he seized Eddie by his jacket lapels, hoisted him, and pinned him to the wall like the social butterfly he was.

'All right then,' Moses said, 'let's try again. Who's that girl with the earrings? The *diamanté* earrings.'

Eddie studied the open doorway very hard.

'I can see two of those,' he said finally, grinning at Moses.

'No kidding. One in each ear?'

'No. Two girls, I mean. With *diamanté* earrings. Two girls. Four earrings. All *diamanté*.'

Moses let Eddie go. It was useless. It really was.

He shook his head and sank down on to the top step, his face in his hands. Even with his eyes covered over he could see her. And it *had* been her eyebrows that he had noticed first. They were pencil-straight, charcoal-dark, and they slanted at an angle to one another like the hands on a clock. When he first saw her, they said quarter to two. And it was. He would always remember that, and would be able to pinpoint their anniversaries exactly, to within the minute. She would like that, he thought.

He was still sitting there in his own personal darkness wondering whether she would ever have time for him when he heard Eddie's voice whisper in his ear.

'Her name's Gloria.'

Moses squinted through his fingers. 'How do you know?'

'I asked her.'

Gloria? He had never met anyone called Gloria before, and he wasn't sure he wanted to now. He was happy with his small life. There had been girls in the past – a week here, six weeks there, months in between sometimes – but the affairs, if that wasn't too pretentious a word for them, had always tailed off somehow. Things began in a heightened state – sex on coke, something like that – then rapidly went downhill. The more you got to know someone, the less you actually liked them. Nothing in the cupboard except skeletons. Something had been knocked together, impro-vised, *faked* really, so it wasn't long before cracks showed. How terrible that felt. To look at someone and suddenly realise the two of you had fuck all in common, nothing except the day of the week and the sheet you were lying on. Girls thought him nice, funny, strange at first. They ended up accusing him of vagueness and indifference. They shouted things like, *You're incapable of having a relationship.* He agreed with them, not knowing any other answer, not wanting to make excuses. Their anger, his sadness. And that was it.

He was no Eddie, though. He could have counted his previous lovers on the fingers of one hand. Well, two maybe. Just.

But now there was this Gloria. The same old pattern reared its ugly head. He felt painfully divided into areas of fascination and dread. Gloria. What kind of name was that, anyway?

Shit, he thought. Not all that again. You expect some things at a party. You expect a certain amount of drinking. Yeah, drinking's definitely involved. Drugs too, usually. You expect a bit of idle gossip, bullshit, repartee. And there's usually a guy in a tartan shirt and a beard who you have to try and avoid. What else? Well, there's always the chance of a fight or a brush with the law. You might throw up too. Blackout, even. Tailspin.

Head down the bowl. All that. But – he looked up and yes, she was still there and yes, she was still beautiful – someone called Gloria, someone with extraordinary eyebrows called Gloria, you didn't expect that. No, you didn't expect that at all.

And what if she was interesting too? He watched disconsolately as she said something and the two men she was with bent double laughing.

He moaned. He sat on the top step. People kept squeezing past him and saying sorry, and jogging his shoulder with their knees. He sat there, his face propped in hands that would probably never touch the girl with the eyebrows.

'What's wrong?'

Eddie was back again. In the dim greenish light of the landing, he definitely looked too good-looking to have been born in Basingstoke. Moses sighed. All the demons were coming out tonight.

'Gloria,' he said.

'What about her?'

'She's beautiful, I think.'

Eddie nodded.

'And interesting.'

'She's a singer,' Eddie said.

'How do you know?'

'She told me.'

Well, that's it, Moses thought. He reached for his wine with a distant smile. Either Gloria was unattainable or she was Eddie's, it didn't really matter which. She was already moving out of reach, he saw, turning her back on him, walking away into the room.

Gloria. What kind of name was that, anyway?

*

Sitting on the stairs, he remembered an incident that had occurred the year before on Bond Street. He had been on his way to some job interview. The discomfort came back to him. A humid grey morning. He was late, sweating, his open coat tugging at his legs. It had been like walking in water. He hadn't really noticed the two girls coming towards him, but, just as he stepped into the gutter to let them by, one of them shot a hand out with something orange in it. He stopped dead, stared, drew back – all in one fluid instinctive movement.

'Would you like a mandarin?' the girl said.

Moses was momentarily stunned, paralysed by the bizarre simplicity of this. A mandarin. On Bond Street. He gazed at the surprising fruit, then at the girl whose palm it nestled in. She looked eager and harmless.

'No,' he said, 'no thanks,' and hurried away, as if from a threat, a piece of unpleasantness.

The girl shrugged. Shadows entered the open pores in the skin of her face. She looked injured somehow.

He didn't get the job.

Afterwards he thought about the mandarin. He saw it again, resting solidly, like an orb, in the cupped palm of the girl's hand. It looked complete, sure of itself. It seemed, in retrospect, to be glowing, like something invested with real magic powers. And he had turned it down. He had said no to the mandarin.

He was certain now that he had failed some kind of test on Bond Street that morning.

But there was another way of looking at it too. In the end, of course, it was just a mandarin, a pleasantly refreshing citrus fruit, and why hadn't he accepted it for what it was? It wasn't poisonous, was it? It wouldn't bite. I mean, for Christ's sake, he even LIKED mandarins.

But he had said no.

Similarly now. He could ignore this – he checked again: yes – beautiful girl who he now knew was called Gloria. Simply pretend she wasn't there. But he knew what would happen. This Gloria, she was another mandarin. And she would glow in his memory, glow and glow, taunting, unforgettable.

A big blue satin bow appeared in front of Moses's eyes. It was attached to a blue dress and, inside the dress, was a girl. She was standing two steps below him, holding two glasses of wine.

'Would you like a drink?' she asked him.

'Yes,' he said. 'Yes, I would. Definitely. Thank you. Thank you very much indeed.'

*

After that things happened very fast and in a way that seemed surprising and confusing at the time but entirely logical in retrospect. Moses was standing on the landing with his new drink when Eddie edged out of a nearby room. Moses heard a soft groan come from somewhere behind him. He turned just in time to see a blonde girl crumple vertically, in slow motion, like one of those old brick chimneys being dynamited.

'Louise!' Moses cried.

He reacted quickly, catching her before she hit the floor. He whipped the brandy out and moistened her lips with the few drops that remained.

'What are you doing?' came a voice from the stairs.

Moses swung round in a kind of frozen tango position, Louise flung over his arms, head back, eyes closed. It was Gloria. He almost dropped everything and ran.

'It's – it's brandy,' he stammered.

'What happened?' Gloria asked.

'What happened?' Louise murmured, eyelids flickering.

Moses spoke to Louise. 'You fainted.'

He lowered her gently until she was sitting on the carpet with her back against the wall. Gloria knelt down, brushed the damp hair out of Louise's eyes.

'What happened?' she asked again.

'It was a friend of mine,' Moses explained. He knew this was going to sound implausible, but he decided it would be better to tell the truth. 'He's got these strange powers, you see. He can walk into a room and everybody stops what they're doing and turns round and stares. The whole room sort of freezes. It's some kind of chemical thing, I think. Sometimes people forget what they're doing completely, or pass out like Louise just did. He was here a minute ago, so I think that's probably what happened.'

'You know Louise?' Gloria asked.

'I'm a friend. We work in the same place. Well, sort of work. Me, I mean.'

Gloria smiled. 'You must be Moses.'

Her voice was menthol-cool, slightly husky, amused. Her lips moved like two halves of a dream that makes you feel good all day. Her eyebrows said ten past nine.

'Hello, Gloria,' he said.

*

'How did you know my name?' she asked.

He didn't answer. He just sat on the carpet next to Louise, and smiled. A boldness had descended on him like a black cloak with a scarlet lining. He suddenly felt a bit like Dracula – sinister, magnetic, predatory.

'I think Louise could use some air,' he said.

Gloria suggested the garden. Moses guided Louise down the stairs. They followed Gloria into the kitchen, through a sunroom, and out on to a wide paved verandah.

It was a cold still night. The remains of the rain that had fallen earlier dripped from the trees. A stone balustrade, upholstered in moss and topped with giant carved urns, ran the length of the back of the house. Gloria led Moses and Louise down a flight of steps. They crossed a lawn. A high hedge loomed. They passed under an archway and into a miniature formal garden. Now and then somebody laughed or screamed inside the house, but otherwise they only heard the party remotely, like a TV three rooms away.

'It's good to be outside,' Moses said.

Gloria took a deep breath, a form of agreement perhaps.

'I feel better already,' Louise said, and promptly stumbled on a loose slab of stone and almost toppled into the ornamental pond.

'I give up with you,' Moses said.

'Bloody footpath,' Louise said. 'Jesus.'

'Honestly,' Gloria said, 'fancy leaving a footpath there like that. Somebody could hurt themselves.'

Moses laughed.

'What are you in such a good mood for, Gloria?' Louise said. 'I thought you hated this party. I thought you were leaving.'

'Changed my mind.'

The two girls sat down at opposite ends of a stone bench. There would have been room for Moses between them – just – but Moses, imagining that nearness to Gloria as a kind of heat and not wanting to be burned, stood by the pond instead.

Silence. The city's parody of silence. Murmuring voices, a hiss of distant cars on wet roads, the hum of a million lit buildings. Something moved in the pond. Moses bent down.

'Hey, there are real goldfish in here.' He could see a whole shoal of them gliding through the water. Fat gold missiles fired into the darkness at the end of the pond.

'*Real goldfish.*' Gloria's voice mocked him slightly.

He looked over his shoulder, tried to read something more than mockery into that, but her face, backlit by the bright windows of the house, was illegible.

'Well, you know,' he said, 'in a house like this I thought they'd be motorised or something.'

There he was trying to explain himself and they were laughing at him. I'm making her laugh, he realised. And the thought soared in his head like an anthem.

*

Gloria left Louise sitting on the bench and walked across the grass. She paused some distance away. She seemed to be examining a statue of an angel. Moses waited a few moments, then followed her.

128

When he reached her he didn't give himself time to think or reconsider. 'I'd like you to come away with me,' he said.

'Now?' She kept her voice light, detached. Almost visible, it floated through the air towards him.

'No, not now. Well – maybe. But that's not what I meant.'

'What did you mean then?'

'I meant,' and he paused, this was sounding dreadful, 'some weekend.'

'I don't even know who you are.'

He swallowed. 'I'm not dangerous. Really I'm not.'

She tilted her face towards his. He saw a quizzical smile, the fire of curiosity beginning to burn. 'No,' she said, 'I don't think you are. But I really can't afford anything like that at the moment. I'm not working, you see.'

'I thought you sang,' Moses said, remembering.

She smiled. 'Not often enough.'

A pause.

'Tell you what,' Moses said. 'I got £80 the other day. For sheets and things. We could use that.'

'Sheets? What sheets?'

'Sheets. A man from the DHSS came round to see me. He told me I could claim for lots of things that I wasn't claiming for. "Like what?" I said. "Like sheets," he said. So I claimed for sheets and a couple of days ago I got a cheque in the post. £80.'

Gloria was laughing. 'You're making this up.'

'I'm not. I got it yesterday. No, the day before. Really.'

'Hold on,' Gloria said. 'What if this man comes round again and wants to see your new sheets?'

'Shit. I hadn't thought of that.'

'Well,' Gloria said, 'he probably won't.'

'He might, though.' Moses, worried now, clutched at his hair. 'I mean, that's just the kind of thing they do, isn't it?'

'Moses, I'm sorry I said that. I'm sure he won't come back.'

'He will. I bet he will, the bastard. You know what they're like. They've got clipboards and pencils attached to them with grubby little bits of string. They wear those pullovers. They make you feel guilty even when you haven't done anything – '

Gloria touched his arm. 'There's got to be a way round it.'

Moses looked down at her hand. 'You're right,' he said.

Gloria smiled as she saw the anxiety lift and a look of deep reflection take its place.

'I know,' he cried, 'I'll borrow some sheets from Eddie.'

'Who's Eddie?'

'Eddie's the man who made Louise faint.'

Gloria began to laugh again. 'I don't believe any of this.'

'People never believe me,' Moses said, 'but it's all true.'

'He's lying,' Louise said, walking towards them. 'He's always lying.'

Moses swung round. 'What do you know, Louise? All you can do is fall over at parties – '

'I didn't fall over – '

' – because you've drunk too much – '

'I *didn't* drink – '

' – and then,' Moses said, grinning, 'and *then* you go and sleep with people like *Elliot* – ' He wrinkled his face up in disgust. 'I just *don't understand* how you can – '

'You *bastard*, Moses.'

'Who's Elliot?' Gloria asked.

'A very good friend of Louise's,' Moses told her behind his hand. 'You know.'

Louise advanced on Moses.

'Look, if you're feeling better, Louise,' Moses said, backing towards the house, 'maybe we should go back inside and look for Marvin Gaye's brother. I've always wanted to meet Marvin Gaye's brother. Apparently he's *much* more interesting than Marvin – Ow! – Louise! – '

*

'Tell you the truth,' Louise said, when she had done with Moses and they were inside again, 'I don't give a fuck about Marvin Gaye's brother. I'm going to look for the toilet instead.' She left Moses and Gloria at the foot of the stairs.

'That girl.' Moses shook his head. 'Where did you meet her?'

'I've known her practically all my life,' Gloria told him. 'My parents play tennis with her parents. You know how it is.'

Moses didn't, but he was willing to learn.

In the meantime, they had climbed to the second floor. They timed it badly. They were just passing a room where fifty people were dancing to salsa when Amy blundered out. Three beads of sweat trickled from her hairline. Noticing Gloria, she stopped blundering and began, miraculously, to float. Moses recognised her because she was still wearing that awful blue satin bow. Gloria recognised her because she had no choice.

'Darling,' Amy oozed. A fourth bead of sweat appeared. Any more of those, Moses thought, and she'll have a tiara.

'Amy, this is Moses,' Gloria said. 'Moses, Amy.'

Amy studied Moses, her entire face twisting away from the cigarette that she was holding to the corner of her mouth. 'We've met,' she declared, swaying a little from the waist.

'That's right,' Moses said. 'You had two glasses of wine and you suddenly felt greedy so you gave one to me.'

'I felt *sorry* for you, darling. Sitting on the stairs all alone like that. What were you doing?'

'I was thinking about fruit,' Moses said. 'Mandarins, actually.'

Amy arched her left eyebrow, smiled out of the side of her mouth, then drew hard on her cigarette. These were separately machined actions. 'I like that,' she said.

'Thank you,' Moses said.

'Tell me – ' and Amy turned to Gloria – 'is this man anything to do with you?' Her lips chopped the smoke from her cigarette into signals that were very obvious.

Gloria considered Moses for a moment. Amy waited, eyelashes clashing. Moses thought of insect-feelers and shuddered.

'Not yet,' Gloria said finally, smiling.

'Oh well, in *that* case,' Amy said, and stalked off, all haughty angles.

'Thank Christ she's gone,' Moses said.

'You shouldn't have flirted with her.' Gloria's eyes were glittering with pieces of white light.

'*Flirted* with her?'

'Yes,' Gloria said. 'You were flirting with her.'

'Was I?' Moses was genuinely shocked. 'I wasn't.'

But Gloria just smiled at him. 'You know what?' she said. 'I've just remembered where we might find Marvin Gaye's brother.'

She led him back downstairs to a room by the front door. 'In there,' she said.

The door stood ajar, and they could hear somebody playing the piano inside, soft disconnected notes. Moses pushed the door open. They paused on the threshold.

The man sitting at the piano was black. He wore a blue suit and a mustard roll-neck sweater. Did he look like Marvin Gaye? What did Marvin Gaye look like? Moses couldn't remember. Anyway, the man was alone. There was nobody else in the room. Moses felt awkward, guilty somehow, as if they had stumbled into someone's private grief. He examined the room carefully. Yes, the man was alone all right. Nobody was listening to Marvin Gaye's brother playing the piano. Moses tugged nervously on Gloria's arm. He was fucked if he was going to hang around in a room full of nobody listening to a famous person's brother play the piano. Too embarrassing.

'Let's go,' he whispered. 'Quick, before he sees us.'

As they backed away, on tiptoe, the pianist turned round. He didn't look surprised or hurt or angry. Not a bit. In fact, he seemed very relaxed. He was even smiling.

'Can I help you people?'

'Well, OK,' Moses said. 'Are you by any chance Marvin Gaye's brother?'

'No,' the pianist said. 'Are you?'

Moses laughed. 'Somebody told us that Marvin Gaye's brother was going to play the piano tonight.'

The pianist scratched his head with one long humorous finger. 'I didn't know he had a brother.'

'I bet he hasn't got a brother,' Moses said.

Gloria summed up. 'Amy's always been full of shit.'

*

They found an unopened bottle of Chianti in the kitchen – the way the wine was lasting, anyone would think Jesus was going to play the piano – and wandered back upstairs to look for Louise. They came across Eddie in the Chinese room.

'Look who it is,' Eddie said.

'What've you been up to?' Moses asked him.

Eddie eyed Gloria. 'I could ask you the same question.'

'Oh, *you're* Eddie,' Gloria said. 'The one with the special powers. How exciting. To have special powers.'

Eddie seemed amused. 'Highness has a vivid imagination,' he told her.

'Highness?'

'Some people call him Highness.'

'Some people are drunk,' Moses said. 'I'm thinking of leaving. What are you doing?'

Eddie grinned. 'I'm thinking of leaving.'

'Alone?'

'No.' Eddie turned to a shy girl in tight jeans who had, until now, been attached to the back of his shirt. 'This is Dawn,' he said. Or it could have been Diane. Or Doreen. Moses didn't quite catch the name.

Dawn/Diane/Doreen smiled hello. A red ribbon blushed in her black hair like a moment of embarrassment.

'Where's Louise?' Gloria asked.

'I don't know,' Moses said.

'Police,' somebody announced calmly.

Later Moses wondered how this had carried above the soundtrack of the party. Some words had more punch, perhaps.

'It's a raid,' came the same calm voice.

There was a general furtive surge in the direction of the door, as if people were pretending that they weren't really leaving. Out on the stairs, the urgency increased and Moses was swept along, Gloria in front of him, Eddie and D/D/D somewhere behind.

Two officers with flat hats and glistening moustaches flanked the front door. One of them tipped his face at Moses.

'Not driving tonight, are we, sir?'

'Beep beep,' came a voice from the stairs.

Everybody laughed.

'I don't – ' Moses began, but the policeman, scowling, waved him through.

At the bottom of the steps Moses put his arm round Gloria. She leaned into him a fraction, just enough to tell him that she had been waiting for that. He felt her ribs tremble under his fingers. She glanced up, lips parted. He bent over her. His tongue brushed her teeth. Bedtime.

Louise's face floated into the corner of his eye. 'Somebody chucked a brick through the window,' she was saying.

They reached the pavement. Everybody had left the party at the same time, and small groups of people stood about looking out of context. Two panda cars nuzzled the kerb. Their blue disco-lights were flashing, but nobody was dancing. D/D/D shrank against a tree, her coat thrown over her shoulders.

'Where's Eddie?' Moses asked her.

She shrugged. She looked puzzled, derelict, cold.

Oh Christ, he thought.

'We've lost Eddie,' he told the other three. 'I'm just going to go and have a look for him. Wait for me, won't you?'

Gloria sent a queer little smile through the darkness towards him. He hesitated, self-conscious suddenly. 'I won't be long,' he said.

Inside the house a few people lay against the walls. Too smashed to move, react or care. Moses stepped over bodies, bottles, ashtrays – the rubble of a party. Music was still playing in the evacuated rooms, loud abrasive music, someone's expression of defiance. He asked one girl whether she had seen a man who looked like a statue. She stared right through him. It was a conspiracy, he decided. A conspiracy of statues.

After about five minutes he gave up. He almost broke his ankle on the way downstairs, but it was less out of drunkenness than out of impatience to be with Gloria again. He cursed Eddie as he rubbed the ankle where it had turned over. What was the point of all these escape-acts anyway? Who did he think he was? The Houdini of love? Fuck him.

He limped out through the door and down the steps. Long splinters of glass from the shattered window made Egyptian shapes on the footpath: pyramids, sabres, crescent moons. The trees creaked overhead, shone black, dripped moisture. Three figures waited by the gate with questions on their faces.

'No luck, I'm afraid,' he told them.

They stood there for a moment longer, shoulders hunched against the chill, all staring in different directions.

Moses leaned on the railings. He watched the road curve out of sight, dissolve into the mist. Someone had bought hundreds of aerosols of fine rain and sprayed them into the orange air that hung around the street-lamps.

Then Gloria came up, touched his arm. 'Where did you leave the car?' she asked, her face a mask of black and silver.

*

Moses dropped Louise and D/D/D in Victoria and now he was driving south down Vauxhall Bridge Road, alone with Gloria. They hadn't needed to discuss anything. It was one of those tacit agreements, after a party, three in the morning. Things like this didn't happen to Moses very often and when they did he was usually too drunk to notice. He was drunk now, but he was noticing.

'Does he always do that?' Gloria asked. 'Disappear like that?'

She huddled down in the passenger seat, her feet tucked into the glove compartment.

Moses chuckled. 'Yes, he does. I don't know what it is. Maybe he gets bored. Maybe it's all too easy for him. I don't know.'

Gloria wound the window down an inch or two and lit a joint. The slipstream took the smoke from her lips and bent it out into the night air – a silk scarf from a magician's sleeve. She seemed to be thinking over what he had just said.

'Bastard,' she said eventually. It was the last carriage in a long train of thought.

Moses glanced across at her and smiled. They kept turning towards each other at the same time as if there were magnetic forces attracting his face to hers and hers to his.

'Are you going to stay?' Moses asked, as he accelerated over the bridge. 'Tonight, I mean.'

Gloria snuggled deeper in her seat. 'Why? Have I still got time to change my mind?'

'You've got about three minutes.'

Three minutes isn't a long time and nothing had changed at the end of it except the name of the road. Suddenly they were home and in the silence as the engine died they kissed for the first time.

Moses locked the car door and stood, motionless but swaying, looking beyond the unlit windows of his flat. The world whirled. That last joint on the drive back. He could see no stars, only the racing-colours of the city sky, orange and grey. The street, high-sided, gorgelike, channelled the power of the wind. He felt as though he was being tested for aerodynamic styling, a test he would almost certainly have failed. A fine rain performed subtle acupuncture on his upturned face. He shivered. It was cold. He was out of his head. He could no longer remember how they had got there.

'Over here,' came a cry, blown in his direction by the wind.

Gloria was waving to him from the street-corner.

'See this?' she said, when he reached her. She was pointing at a poster on the door of The Bunker. It advertised an evening of jazz-funk with somebody called Jet Washington.

'That was yesterday,' Moses said.

'I know that. What I mean is – '

'He was terrible.'

'That's not what I – '

'People threw glasses at him.' Moses shook his head at the memory. The look of outrage on Jet's face when a plastic glass bounced off his shoulder. The impotence. The tearful slope-shouldered way he left the stage halfway through his set.

'Moses, will you – '

'*Jet Washington*,' Moses said. The side of his mouth twisted to signify disdain.

He looked down in surprise as Gloria began to pummel him in the stomach with her tiny gloved fists. 'Why are you doing that?' he asked her.

'I'm trying to get you to listen to me.'

'I am listening.'

'What I was trying to say was, do you think it would be possible for me to sing here?'

'Are you a singer?'

'You *know* that, Moses.'

'You're really a singer?'

'Yes.' Gloria leaned against the wall, the black plastic of her raincoat catching hundreds of slivers of silver light that twitched and shivered as she moved like broken-off pieces of Moses's amazement. She now seemed a lot less drunk than he was.

'What time is it?' he asked her. (Her eyebrows said about ten to four.)

Gloria held her watch up to the light. The action was beautiful because it was so serious.

'Five past three,' she said.

Moses shook with laughter and almost buried her entirely in his arms.

*

Why had he come to this foreign country? he wondered, cursing himself over and over again, though it was too late now, of course. The stupidity of it. But words were talismans, there was protection in their syllables, their sounds could stop the bad thing happening. Keep talking, he told himself, because talking can save you. Keep talking. All the time dragging himself across the sand towards the cover of the trees. All the time looking over his shoulder. Looking was important too. Never turn your back.

The animal crouched twenty feet away, its striped sides rigid, its breathing invisible. There are no tigers in the desert, he told himself. But it was there all right. He could hear the rage vibrating in its chest. It trembled for a moment – power that could be held no longer – drew back, sprang. He saw the teeth, yellow, filmed over with saliva, curving down like raised knives –

Something sharp dug into his naked shoulder, and he cried out.

'Moses,' Gloria whispered, tugging at him.

He jack-knifed upright. A bright blue light revolved in the room. 'What's happening?'

'I don't know. I was just going to find out.' Gloria put on one of his shirts and padded to the window.

Moses leaned on one elbow, still half asleep, bewildered. The dream lingered, mingled with the memory of recent sex. He couldn't work out how much of the sex he remembered was real and how much dreamt. They had pulled each other's clothes off. She had pressed her body to his.

The icy air.

Her nipples in silhouette, tiny minarets, and his hand moving over the smooth drifted dunes of her ribs, moving across the soft desert of her belly, moving down, down to the oasis. And her hand, too, had moved, following a trail of hair, discovering his scrotum, shrivelled like a dried fig with the cold, and she had bitten into it, and he had gasped a little, less out of pain than surprise, then she had lifted her head, her face invisible, and the whole thing linked with his dream because she had said something about Arabia –

'Moses. Come here. Quick.'

He eased out of the warm bed and slipped into his coat. Gloria stood at the window. On tiptoe, her heels off the ground. His shirt-tails reaching the backs of her knees. He wanted to say something, but the feeling wouldn't translate. He went and stood beside her.

Other people had opened their windows too, sensing tragedy as people do, intrigued because it wasn't theirs. An ambulance had drawn up below. It stood at a curious angle to the pavement; it looked casual, abandoned. As they watched, two men in dark uniforms wheeled a stretcher out of one of the houses opposite. A black nylon shroud hid the body. It had been stretched so taut that the feet made no hill. The two men slid the stretcher into the back of the ambulance, closed the doors, and exchanged a few words. All this without glancing up once. The revolving blue light accelerated away down the road, turned left at the junction. The night became orange and grey, ordinary again. People closed their windows, went back to bed. Moses and Gloria stared down into the empty street.

It was Moses who pulled away first. He walked into the kitchen, put the kettle on. He heard Gloria shut the window.

'I don't feel like sleeping any more,' she said from the doorway. 'If I go to sleep, men in black uniforms might come and take me away.'

'I wouldn't let them,' he said.

She was looking at the floor, one hand toying with the shirt's top button.

'I'm making some coffee,' he told her.

'That's good.'

'Lucky this didn't happen last weekend.'

'Why?'

'Last weekend I didn't have a kettle.'

Gloria laughed softly. Reaching up, she ruffled his hair. Then she left the kitchen, and he heard her moving about in the bedroom. When she returned she was dressed. She bounced her earrings up and down in her hand. They clicked like dice. He wondered if she was going to leave.

He unscrewed the lid on the coffee-jar, spooned the granules into two matching cups (they were new too), poured the boiling water on to the granules, added milk from a carton, and stirred, enjoying doing the small things slowly.

Gloria had folded her arms. She began to twist one strand of hair around her finger. 'I wonder what happened,' she said.

'I don't know.' He handed her a cup. 'There are a lot of old people living round here. They live here all their lives. Die here too. They never move. Some of them haven't even been north of the river. They'll look at you when you tell them you have and say something like, Nice up there, is it? Like it's a foreign country or something. Well, I suppose it is for them.' He paused. 'We all have our foreign countries, I suppose.'

Gloria smiled at him, then, as if that movement of her lips had set her body in motion, as if one was the natural extension of the other, walked towards him, met his mouth with hers.

*

It was still dark in the living-room, so Moses switched on the lamp. It shed a soft-edged glow. He arranged a few cushions on the floor. Then he knelt down, lit the gas-heater. It sighed like the inside of a seashell.

Gloria walked over to the window again. She stared out, thinking, perhaps, of her own body wrapped in that taut cloth, of a blue light revolving in the street for her.

Without turning round, she said, 'I wonder if that person was dead.'

'Probably,' Moses said. 'They covered the face.'

He stood behind her. Over her shoulder he saw somebody drive past in a white car.

'I still don't know you, really, do I?' she said. She turned to look at him, but couldn't. He was standing too close.

'No,' he said.

She let herself lean back against him. 'Too many blue lights this evening,' she said. 'Fucks me up, you see.'

He smiled at the way she'd said evening. It was almost morning now.

She pulled away from him again. He felt she had trusted him in that brief moment, had entrusted him with some sacred part of herself, and was now detaching herself, confident about what she had done, knowing she had left something behind. He watched her cross the room. She bent down next to his record collection. She flicked through, found Charlie Parker. She put him on. Humming the first few bars of 'Cherokee', she began to rummage in her bag. She held up a tiny white envelope.

'Since we're going to stay awake,' she said.

He smiled.

She chopped the coke on her own mirror, her legs folded beneath her, her body in a loose Z-shape.

'Two for you, two for me, two for later,' she said.

She took her two and handed him the mirror. When he handed it back, she was brushing the tip of her nose with the back of her finger and he

noticed a fine groove running between her nostrils and thought of Blue
Rooms on south-coast piers (holidays with Uncle Stan and Auntie B) and
penny-in-the-slot machines and smiled.

'What's so funny, Moses?'

'Your nose. It's like a slot-machine.'

'No more for you then.' She ran her finger across the dusty glass and
licked it.

The lamplight was diluting fast in the greyness of daybreak. Traffic grew
heavier on the main road. The record crackled to a finish.

Gloria sprang to her feet. 'Let's go out somewhere.'

She kept changing, landing abruptly in a new mood like a needle jumping
on a record and skipping whole tracks. She was a mystery-tour of a girl.
Constantly wrongfooting him. She'll go right here, he would think (an
instinct, this), she'll definitely go right. And she'd go left. Wonderful. He
delighted in being unable to predict her.

'Let's go and have breakfast,' she was saying. 'In a hotel. In Mayfair.'

She inhaled the smoke from her latest cigarette impatiently. Her eyes
had the glint of solid silver cutlery. 'What do you think, Moses?' Standing
over him now.

A smile of collaboration spread across his face like a fresh white tablecloth. He could almost feel the hands of an experienced waitress smoothing
it down at the corners.

Gloria swung down on to his lap. 'Some of those hotels have dress
restrictions so we'd better ring first.'

'OK,' and Moses was just reaching for the phone when he realised that
he didn't have one. That, in fact, he had never had one. That he ought to
have one. (He would have to speak to Elliot.)

More laughter. Another line each. The first side of Charlie Parker again
(for the third time).

During the next twenty minutes they ruled out The Ritz, The Savoy,
and Claridge's. Gloria said you couldn't eat breakfast in any of those places
without wearing jackets and ties and shit like that. They decided to take a
chance on Brown's in Dover Street.

Moses switched off the (by now) invisible light, and picked up his car
keys. Night was over.

*

Moses swept past reception in his leather jacket, his slipstream turning
several pages of the hotel register. He parted the glass doors of the breakfast

room and manoeuvred his large unshaven face into the head-waiter's line
of vision.

'We'd like a table, please.'

'For two, sir?'

Moses gave this a moment's thought. 'No,' he said. 'For four.'

'Certainly, sir. If you'll just follow me.'

The head-waiter, a narrow man with silver hair, threaded his way neatly
to the centre of the room. Moses and Gloria followed. Somewhat less
neatly.

'Why four?' Gloria hissed.

'Because you get a better table that way,' Moses hissed back.

It was five to eight. Moses surveyed the room with the superiority of
somebody who hasn't slept for thirty-six hours. There were one or two
businessmen dressed like seals in sleek grey suits, their hair slicked back,
still damp from the shower. An elderly couple, impeccable in cashmere
and tweed, exchanged crisp pieces of information. Their limbs creaked and
rustled like newspaper being folded as they shifted in their cane chairs.
The light in the room, tinged with pink, felt soothing. The air smelt of
coffee and oranges. It could have been summer outside. It almost was.

'Tell you the truth,' Moses said, after studying the menu for a while,
'I'm not all that hungry.'

'Neither am I.' Gloria lit a cigarette. Smoke trickled professionally out
of her nose. 'What about some champagne then? Lanot's only £17.'

Moses began to sweat. 'Fine,' he said.

Half a dozen waiters were hovering around their table in maroon and
black like clumsy humming-birds. Moses signalled one over. He broke his
flight pattern and stooped with a fat white pad. Moses ordered champagne,
coffee, orange juice – and two fresh grapefruits.

'Are you OK for money?' Gloria whispered when he had left.

Moses smiled. 'No, not really.'

'What about the £80 you got for sheets?'

'That's not for breakfast. That's for this special weekend that I want
you to come on.'

'You're not going to tell me anything about it?'

'No. You'll just have to trust me.'

Gloria smiled as she crushed out her cigarette. 'All right. I'll pay for
breakfast, you pay for the weekend. OK?'

Their waiter arrived with the champagne. As Moses watched him wave
his wrists in the air, address himself to the bottle, and, teeth clamped to
his bottom lip, ease the cork into his immaculate white cloth, Gloria's
words sank in.

'You mean you'll come?'

She nodded. 'I'll come.'

'It may not be for a couple of weeks, you know.'

'Do you think we'll last that long?'

Moses's laughter bounced around the room like a number of thrown balls. Knives and forks paused in mid-air. Eyes peered through eyebrows, over papers. Voices went underground, risking only whispers. Then one of the seals coughed, and the breakfast sounds pieced themselves together again into that familiar jigsaw where the sky is always at the top of the picture and children always look happy.

'Moses,' Gloria said, 'nobody laughs at breakfast-time.'

It had the ring of an old Chinese proverb so they raised their glasses and drank to it, discovering, as they did so, that they were laughing again and that the proverb had, buried within it, the power of proving itself wrong – infinitely.

Something occurred to Moses.

'Did we get any sleep last night?'

'About an hour.'

'What I mean is, did we have sex of any kind?'

Gloria touched her napkin to her mouth and surveyed him, the relic of a smile preserved on her face. 'Do you know what I thought when I first saw you?'

Moses couldn't guess.

'It was the size of you, you see. Relative to me, I mean.'

'What about it?'

'I thought, If I go to bed with this man, am I going to get crushed?'

Moses looked shocked. 'You didn't.'

'I did. I was really worried.'

Moses glanced down at himself, as if assessing his potential as an instrument of violence.

'And?' he said.

Gloria smiled. 'You were very gentle.'

*

They had parted at Green Park. Moses's heart pumping fast. The coke lasting. Or emotion, perhaps. Or some amalgamation of the two.

'I've got to get some sleep,' Gloria said. 'I'm supposed to be singing tonight.' She scribbled a few words on the back of a Marlboro packet. 'That's in case you want to come.'

'Of course I want to come,' he shouted after her as she ran away from their last kiss and down the steps into the tube station.

'Why?' she called back over her shoulder. 'Do you like jazz?'

'No,' he shouted. Which made her laugh. And her laughter hung on in the musty tunnel long after she had gone.

'Jazz,' he said to himself as he walked to his car. He thought of people with names like Rubberlegs and Dizzy – funny names, made-up names, names like his. He saw trumpet-players' cheeks blown up like bubble-gum. He saw sweat scattering like hot rain and the fingers of singers twisting round dented silver microphones and false ceilings built of smoke. He tried to fit Gloria into that.

Then it was evening and he was driving over Vauxhall Bridge. A dense fierce rain slammed into the left side of the car. On the north bank of the river the lights ran. Flood warnings on the radio. His life had been derailed by the night with Gloria. The whole thing already seemed unreal, as unreal as the tiger dream. He was thankful they had arranged to meet again so soon otherwise he might have begun to doubt whether any of it had actually happened.

'Gloria,' Moses said out loud.

He stamped on the accelerator and flicked into overdrive. In less than fifteen minutes he was there. The rain drenched him as he ran across the pavement. Downstairs he had to wait in a queue. Scarlet light discoloured one side of the doorman's face the way a birthmark does. From inside came the erratic fluttering heartbeat of a double-bass. He was close to her now.

But the first person he saw in the crowded bar was Eddie.

'You're late,' Eddie told him.

'What're *you* doing here?'

'I came to see your girlfriend sing.'

'How did you know she was singing?'

'She told me. At the party.'

Moses shook off his coat. He pulled up a chair and helped himself to some of Eddie's wine.

Eddie leaned across the table. 'Did you have a good night?'

'None of your business.'

'Well, anyway, you're late. She's been on once already.'

'What's wrong with you? Are you speeding or something?'

Eddie chuckled.

'So where were you?' Moses asked.

'What do you mean?'

'Where were you hiding?'

Eddie leaned back. 'In the broom cupboard,' he said. 'I think it was a broom cupboard. There was a broom in it.'

Moses had to smile. 'The broom cupboard. Of course. Next time I'll look in the broom cupboard. Anyway, listen. I dropped Doreen off for you.'

'Dawn.'

'What?'

'Dawn. Her name was Dawn.'

'I'm surprised you remember.'

'I found a bit of paper in my pocket this morning. It had Dawn written on it and a number. I rang the number to find out who she was.'

'And?'

'She said she never wanted to see me again.'

'Incredible.'

Eddie shrugged.

A hand reached down in front of Moses, snatched up his glass, and replaced it seconds later, empty. Before he had time to say 'Hello Gloria' or 'That's my wine' or 'What did you invite *him* for?' she was up on stage introducing herself.

'Good evening, folks,' she said, hands behind her back. 'This is Holly again – '

Whistles. Applause.

'Second set,' Eddie said. 'You see? I told you.'

But Moses was thinking, *Who?*

'That's her stage name,' Eddie whispered.

How come he knows so much? Moses wondered.

' – and this is the band who haven't got a name yet – '

More whistles. More applause.

Holly? Why *Holly?*

'Her surname's Wood,' Eddie told him. 'Her real surname, I mean.'

' – and we're going to do a few songs for you – not too loud, though, because they're trying to sleep upstairs – '

Jeering.

' – it's an old people's home or something – '

Laughter.

' – anyway, this is the first one – it's called "Ain't Nobody's Business If I Do" – '

Gloria swung away from the microphone and the band launched into the intro. Remote smiles played on their faces. The drummer was using brushes. He looked a bit like Teddy Kennedy. It was a slowed-down slurry version of the song.

' – oh and thanks for coming – ' Gloria was looking directly at Moses – 'don't think I hadn't noticed – '

Moses settled deeper in his chair, almost blushing. Eddie nudged him in the ribs, half-rose out of his chair, and, looking round as if Moses was somebody famous, clapped loudly.

For Christ's sake, Moses thought.

They had just finished their second bottle of wine, some French stuff, nineteen seventy-something. Now Eddie was ordering champagne. It wasn't that he was ostentatious. It was just that if money began to pile up in his bank accounts (and he had at least three) he felt as if he had slipped up somewhere, as if he wasn't really living. So he spent money like water and the water turned into wine and Moses drank it.

Moses turned back to Gloria. He quickly realised that he wasn't going to have to lie to her about how good she was. She didn't let the music dominate her. She used its rhythms, its momentum, and rode on them, always balanced, always in control. She could be as agile as the song demanded. She could wrongfoot you just when you thought you knew where her voice was going, leaping seemingly into a void, landing in places you hadn't even known were there. What a relief, Moses thought, not to have to lie to her.

He had been thinking about her off and on all day, going over remembered ground – incidents, gestures, fragments of conversation – going over and over them in his mind as waves go over stones, polishing them until they shone, felt smooth against his skin, had value. Something went through him, sideways and upwards, as he watched her performing on stage in her charcoal-grey forties' suit and her *diamanté* earrings and her diaphanous black scarf that she wore looped loosely about her neck, something made up of so many feelings, half-feelings and fractions of feelings that he felt like a whole audience – generous, expansive, irrepressible. The song finished and he was clapping, using every square millimetre of his massive hands.

Towards the end of 'Stormy Weather' Vince showed up. He dropped into the chair next to Moses, his hands wedged into his pockets, his waistcoat slippery with grease and oil and spilt drinks. His face had the dampness, the pallor, of a sponge. Stubble littered his chin. Moses could sense his knees jiggling up and down beneath the table.

Vince scowled. 'I feel like shit.'

Eddie grinned. 'I was just going to say. You look like shit, Vince.'

'How did you get in with that waistcoat on, Vince?' Moses asked. He poured Vince a glass of wine.

Vince downed it in one and slumped back in his chair. 'I haven't slept for three days.' He stared morosely at his empty glass. 'Took some smack on Wednesday night. Fucked me up completely.'

Moses and Eddie exchanged looks of resignation. Vince being histrionic again. Nothing unusual about that.

'I thought you'd stopped that,' Moses said.

'How many times do I have to tell you, Vincent?' said Eddie.

'Screw you.' Vince turned to Moses. 'You got any downers, sleeping-pills, anything like that?'

'Why would I have anything like that?' Moses said. 'I'm in love.'

Vince grimaced.

'I haven't seen you for ages,' Moses said. 'What've you been up to?'

'Not much,' Vince said. 'Staying home, mostly. Getting out of it.'

'With Debra,' he added as an afterthought. He held his glass out for a refill. Moses poured.

'Debra?' Eddie said, as if the name meant something to him.

'You don't know her,' Vince said. 'She must be one of the few women you don't know.'

'I wouldn't bet on that.' Eddie smiled.

'You don't know her,' Vince repeated.

Eddie looked pensive. 'Did she used to work in that café in Victoria Station?'

'No, she didn't.'

'She hasn't got blonde hair, has she?'

Vince looked at the ceiling. 'No, she hasn't.'

'Does she come from Hampshire?'

'No,' Vince said. 'Liverpool.'

'Was she at that – '

'Look, fuck off, Eddie,' Vince said. 'You *don't know* her. *O K?*'

'Well,' Eddie grinned lasciviously, 'I suppose there's still time.'

Vince picked up his glass of wine and threw the contents in Eddie's face. Vince smiled for the first time since he walked in. He was beginning to enjoy himself. Eddie wiped his shirt-front with one hand and smiled back.

'Why did you do that, Vince?' he said quietly.

'I got bored with the shit you were talking.'

'Was I talking shit?' Eddie asked, still dabbing at his clothes.

'Yes.'

The champagne arrived like a change of subject.

'Seen Alison recently?' Moses asked Vince.

'That fucking bitch,' Vince snarled. 'I haven't seen her since she went back home to mummy. I don't need any of that shit.'

'She rang me last week,' Moses said. 'Asked me to Sunday lunch.'

'Sunday lunch.' Vince's face screwed up in a paroxysm of scorn and disgust. 'Sunday fucking lunch. I've been to a few of those.'

'What about them?'

'It's her mother. She floats around like some kind of fucking wood-nymph. She talks a pile of crap.'

'What?' Eddie laughed. 'Like me?'

'Yes,' Vince said. 'Like you.'

'I can't go anyway,' Moses said. 'I've got something else planned.'

Eddie leaned forwards. 'With this Gloria of yours, I suppose?'

Vince leered.

'It'd be a shame,' Moses said, 'if any more of this nice champagne got spilled, wouldn't it?' and reaching for the bottle helped himself to another glass.

Eddie drew back, swallowed a thoughtful mouthful of champagne, and left the table to get some cigarettes.

'Sorry about this,' Gloria was saying over the microphone, 'but there've been some more complaints and apparently we've got to stop – '

Whistles of disapproval. Two or three people stood up in protest. Vince began to pound the table with his fist.

Gloria lifted her arms away from her sides. Nothing she could do. She glanced at the manager of the place. He stood by the bar looking uncomfortable. She asked him whether they couldn't end with a quiet number. After a moment's hesitation, he nodded, pressing the air down with one hand. Gloria turned back to her audience.

'OK, people, one more it is. A quiet one. So quiet that you'll hardly hear it.' She smiled to herself. 'This song was made famous by Billie Holiday. It's called "Strange Fruit" – '

Accompanied by the piano and the drummer's brushes, Gloria sang the song with a chilling stillness, staring straight ahead of her, seeing no one. The stillness spread, filled each member of the audience as if they were empty glasses and the stillness was water. When the song died away she didn't move. She let the applause rush at her, shake her, bring her back to life. She seemed surprised for a moment to find that she wasn't alone.

'Thank you,' she said, 'and goodnight.'

And then, peering at the ceiling, 'Happy dreams up there.'

*

'You were good,' Moses said.

Gloria wrinkled her nose, said nothing.

'I mean it. You were really good.' He pushed a chair out for her, but she stayed standing.

'Thank you, Moses,' she sighed.

'No, really,' he said, touching her arm. 'You sounded like a proper person on a record.'

'Did I?' Gloria smiled faintly. 'Give me a cigarette, would you?'

Moses handed her the packet. She took one, lit it, and inhaled deeply, her hand supporting her elbow. She stared away into the room. Moses had a sudden sense of awkwardness, of not knowing her at all. As if the previous night had happened in another dimension and needed to be re-established in this one.

The ordinary lights had come on. People looked pale, shifty, guilty of small crimes. The door to the street stood open, and a bitter draught ran through the bar.

'Come on, folks,' the manager called out, rubbing his hands together. 'We're closing now.' He seemed anxious to put an end to what had obviously been an awkward evening.

Gloria crossed the room to speak to him. She returned a moment later muttering, 'Fuck that for a laugh.'

They all walked up the stairs and round the corner to an Indian restaurant which, according to Eddie, served drinks until two in the morning. On the street Gloria took Moses's arm.

'I'm really glad you came,' she said. 'I'm just sorry it wasn't better.'

'You were good,' Moses told her. 'I meant what I said.'

Gloria shook her head. 'Anyway, that's the last time I sing in that place.'

In the restaurant Eddie was preoccupied with Danielle, a friend of Gloria's. Danielle had muscular tanned arms and eyes so green they made you think of envy. She may or may not have been about to become only the third lesbian ever to sleep with Eddie. Moses was preoccupied with Gloria, who really was a jazz-singer and who would almost certainly be spending the night with him, an event that he might or might not remember, depending on how much more he drank. Vince, who hadn't slept for three days, was preoccupied with the tablecloth. He hadn't said a word to anyone for hours. He seemed fascinated by the tablecloth, and touched it carefully with his fingertips at regular intervals. Eventually he spoke.

'I've got to go.'

Everybody else exchanged glances as people always did when Vince emerged from one of his long silences.

'OK, Vince,' Moses said.

'I'm going now.' Vince didn't move.

'OK, Vince,' Moses said.

'Goodbye, Vince,' Eddie said.

Still looking at the tablecloth, Vince rose to his feet, slowly, as if there was more gravity around than usual. His mouth tightened with the effort involved. He moved away across the restaurant like somebody walking on the sea-bed. The door opened and closed. A blast of wind. He was gone.

'He ought to be in the movies,' Danielle said.

Eddie agreed. 'Frankenstein.'

They carried on drinking bottles of wine which Eddie, with typical abandon, was now ordering in pairs. They were the last people in the restaurant. They hardly looked at the tablecloth at all.

Ten or fifteen minutes passed. Then, to everyone's surprise, somebody sat down in Vince's vacant seat.

It was Vince.

They all turned to him with questioning looks. Vince's eyes travelled across the smooth white wastes of the tablecloth. Finally he took a deep breath.

'I wasn't drunk enough,' he said.

*

Moses pulled up outside The Bunker. He cut the engine. Rain scratched at the windscreen.

'Listen,' he said. 'Can you hear it?'

The music, he meant. Dub tonight. Shuddering across the street. Bass notes that made the surfaces of puddles shake.

'No noise restrictions here,' he said.

'So will you try and arrange it for me?' Gloria said. 'You know, some-time.'

'If we're still together.'

Gloria smiled. 'You're stealing my lines.'

Upstairs, she flung her coat on to the chair by the door.

'Oh,' Moses said.

'What is it?'

'It's just that my ghost might be sitting there.'

'Your ghost?'

'Yes. She sits there sometimes, I think. It's her chair.'

'You've got a ghost in here?'

'Yes. Well, Jackson thinks so, anyway. I've never seen her.' Moses was smiling. He was imagining the ghost sitting on the chair with Gloria's coat over her head. Will somebody *please* get this coat off my head? 'She's harmless, though,' he went on. 'Sometimes I talk to her without even knowing it. I think we get on quite well, really. Jackson would've told me if we didn't.'

Gloria shook her head. 'I never know what to believe with you. Tell you one thing, though. You're right about the music. It's – it's everywhere.'

She wasn't exaggerating.

There was music in the floorboards, music in the walls, music in the windows, music in her earrings, music in the black mass of her hair, music in her eyebrows, music in the way Moses was looking at her, music in his voice as he said, 'Let's go to bed', music in her passage across the room towards him, music in the hinges of the bedroom door, music in their first quick kiss, more music in their second slower one, music in their undressing, music in his hands running over her skin, music in hers as they guided him in, music in the opening and closing gaps between their bodies, music in her orgasm, music in his, music as he turned, like the page of a score, away from her, music in their breathing as it slowed down, deepened, music in their sleeping, music in their dreams –

And music in Gloria's coat, it seemed, as it slid slowly from the chair on to the floor.

*

On the following Saturday morning Moses picked Gloria up from her flat in Victoria. He had cashed the sheet-money and filled his car with petrol. They were going away for the weekend. The weekend he had promised her.

It wasn't until they were driving up Maida Vale that Gloria happened to glance over her shoulder and see the two suitcases on the back seat.

Why two? she wondered.

She twisted round in her seat. One of the suitcases was compact – the kind of overnight bag that she herself had brought along. The other, though no larger, looked older, sturdier. Two leather straps held it fast, buckling at the front like belts. The locks were shaped like arrowheads, and halfway between them two words had been discreetly embossed in gold: REAL COWHIDE. At one end, where the hinges were, the leather had darkened as if it had been left standing in water. The most surprising thing about it, though, was the fact that it was there at all. They were only going to be away for two nights. Her mouth framed a question, but never asked it. The weekend had been Moses's idea. He would tell her in his own good time.

She settled back in her seat again and glanced secretly at his profile, what she called his driving face, as it rushed motionless across a landscape of white houses. But surely it couldn't just be clothes, she found herself thinking. Before her mind could start inventing possible contents, she shut it off. She didn't want to guess. It would ruin things. It was curiously reassuring, comforting almost, to know that, sometime in the future, the mystery would be explained. That was what knowing people was all about, wasn't it? In fact, the more she thought about the suitcase (in the abstract, that is), the more at ease she felt. It seemed to epitomise their relationship. Anticipation, excitement, surprises.

She leaned her head against the back of the seat and watched the trees flick by. Tree after tree after tree lining the main road. All the same make, all identical in age. All their intervening distances measured and exact.

Complete opposite of the suitcase, really.

*

Country and western music on the radio.

Moses often listened to country and western music because he didn't like it. If you listened to music you liked all the time, he had told Gloria, then pretty soon you didn't like it any more. That was what had happened with country and western music. Once he had really liked it. But he had listened to it all the time. And now he didn't like it any more. So he could listen to it all the time without worrying.

Gloria didn't have strong feelings one way or the other. She sang along, inventing words and making Moses smile. The day warmed up, and a dull haze accompanied their drive north, hanging over the monotonous deserted landscape, denying it greenness. The exit after Leicester, Moses turned off the motorway and it wasn't long before the road narrowed, acquiring ditches and hedges, and a high stone wall loomed up on the left, dusty and crumbling, the texture of stale cake, with overhanging cedars, their great flat branches reaching out like plates.

'This is it,' Moses announced, 'by the look of it.'

He swung the car into a gravel driveway. Stone dogs sat on the gateposts, their ears pricked, their eyes blind. Gloria peered through the windscreen for a glimpse of the hotel, but the driveway denied her that, winding first through trees – pines planted close together, gloom gathering between their tall red trunks – then through giant clumps of rhododendrons and hydrangeas. Gradually, on the left-hand side, the shrubbery thinned out, and Gloria caught flashes of a green lawn slick with recent rain. Beyond it lay a boating lake. A jetty crouched over the water on dark rotting stilts. A few conifers, almost black, clustered round the edge like mourners.

'Yes, this is it.' Moses nodded to himself. 'I recognise it from the postcard.'

'What postcard?' Gloria asked.

'You'll see.'

Moses parked in front of the hotel. They both got out.

Standing beside the car with her coat over one arm and her case in her hand, Gloria stared up at the façade. The name – DOGWOOD HALL – in white foot-high letters. Ivy trimmed close to the pale yellow stone. Blank windows. Neat, well-groomed, oppressive. Even the gravel at her feet looked arranged.

She noticed a bare patch where Moses must have skidded when he turned the car round. We've messed up their drive, she thought. And then, Why did he bring me here?

'Are you coming?' Moses called out from the porch.

Gloria looked up, smiled weakly. 'Yes,' she said. But first she covered the bare patch over, using the toe of her shoe.

*

Moses strode towards the reception desk. He felt powerful, executive. A man with a mission. Moses, he said to himself. Moses Highness.

He put his two suitcases down, leaned on the counter, and waited while the receptionist finished shuffling his papers. The receptionist was superbly bald, his head a pale yellow dome of polished marble. It had the allure of a piece of sculpture and, for one awful moment, when the man bent down to pick up a sheet of paper disturbed by the wind from the open door, Moses thought he was going to reach over and stroke it, which was what he always did with sculpture. Fortunately the receptionist straightened again quickly, as if he had had some kind of premonition.

'Can I help you?' he enquired.

'Yes,' Moses said. 'I'd like a double room, please.'

'A double room.' The receptionist blew a little stale air out of his wrinkled sphincter of a mouth and opened the hotel register. 'Can I have your name, sir?'

'Highness. Moses Highness.'

The receptionist's head began to wobble violently on his narrow shoulders. He stood behind his counter and stared at Moses, his mouth a widening rift in the lower half of his face. It was like watching an earthquake in an art gallery. What if the head toppled? Moses thought. Would his reflexes be quick enough to catch it before it hit the floor and shattered into a thousand pieces? He couldn't bear the idea of looking down and seeing one baleful eye looking up at him.

At that instant, Gloria appeared in the doorway, clasping her overnight bag in front of her with both hands.

'And this,' Moses said, unable to restrain himself, 'is Mrs Highness.'

'One moment.' The receptionist stepped backwards through a red curtain into some inner sanctum.

'He's extraordinary,' Moses whispered to Gloria.

Gloria clutched his arm.

Her grip tightened as the red curtain parted again. During his absence the receptionist had managed to regain absolute control of his head. Whether he had some surgical machine or device behind the curtain or whether he had simply applied a soothing lotion they would never know, but, whatever the remedy, his head was as firm as yours or mine as he asked Moses to sign the register.

'I hope you don't mind me asking,' Moses said, 'but have you been working here a long time?'

'Yes,' the receptionist said, staring at Moses with his lidless eyes. 'Yes, you could say that.'

'By a long time, I mean thirty years. Have you been here that long?'

'Yes, I've been here about thirty years.'

Moses leaned closer. 'I'm only asking because I think my parents stayed here, probably during the fifties, and I was wondering if, by any chance, you remembered them.'

The receptionist tilted his head sideways (Careful! Moses thought) and read the name in the register. 'No, I don't think so. I would have remembered a name like that.' And his upper lip lifted, raising the lid on a keyboard of discoloured teeth. It was a ghastly smile.

Moses drew back, disappointed. 'Well,' he sighed. 'I suppose it was worth a try.'

The receptionist laid the key of room number 5 beside the register. 'I'm sorry I couldn't help you, sir. How long will you be staying?'

'We're just here for the weekend.'

'It's not often we have young people here,' and the receptionist's head began to wobble again. 'I hope you enjoy your stay.'

Moses thanked him.

'Second on the left at the top of the stairs,' the receptionist said, and disappeared behind his red curtain again.

*

Gloria climbed the stairs ahead of Moses and waited for him at the top. There was a surprising delicacy, even tenderness, about the way he handled the older of the two suitcases. It looked like a child in his grasp, she thought. A child clutching its father's hand.

'That man gives me the creeps,' she said as Moses reached her.

He chuckled. 'What did his head remind you of?'

Gloria shuddered. 'I don't know.'

'Do you know what I thought?'

She shook her head.

'Taj Mahal.'

Gloria had to laugh. His face sometimes.

Moses unlocked the door of their room. It seemed cold inside because everything was green. Counterpane, curtains, carpet, wallpaper, lamp-shades, telephone. Everything. A few ungainly pieces of furniture stood against the walls. A tallboy. A wardrobe. A sideboard, its marble top veined like Gorgonzola. The bathroom had a chessboard tile floor. A jungle of silver pipes and fittings grew out of the back of the lavatory and up the wall. The taps on the basin said HOT and COLD. The wooden handle on the end of the lavatory chain was the shape of a slim pear. Gloria knocked it with her hand so it swung. Then she leaned over the bath and twisted the hot tap. Scalding water gushed.

'I'm going to have a bath,' she called out, 'then you can tell me all about these mysterious parents of yours.'

Moses smiled at her through the gathering steam, then withdrew into the room. He walked to the window. A lawn lay below, spread like a cloth of alternating pale-green and dark-green stripes, and stapled to the ground by croquet-hoops. Beyond the lawn, maybe a hundred yards away, the tarnished metal of a lake, fenced on its far side by a line of poplars that looked mauve, French somehow, as mist stole in behind them to remove the view.

The first weekend in June. Somewhere north of Leicester. He wondered why he had come all this way. Those questions he had put to Taj Mahal, had he really expected any answers, any joy? It had been too much to hope for. Still, he clung to the fantasy that his parents might once have stayed at the hotel, might have been happy there. Yes, maybe there was sufficient justification in that. Some kind of logic, at least. His homage to that secret world between the names. A message spirited across the years. Standing in their footprints.

He turned away from the window. He took a book out of his suitcase, tried to read, but found he couldn't concentrate. He could hear Gloria swirling water around. He walked towards the bathroom door.

'Hey, Gloria,' he called out. 'Any room for me in there?'
She laughed. 'You must be joking.'

*

After their bath they climbed into bed, their bodies warm and damp
between the crisp sheets. They made love quietly, as if someone was
listening. When they finally looked away from one another, dusk had inked
the windows in, like the o's in sch●●l textb●●ks. They lay there, not
talking.

Gloria felt relaxed, drowsy. Moses had rolled over on his side, his back
to her, his breathing soft and regular. She closed her eyes and her mind
drifted loose, drawing pictures, spinning riddles. It was one of those dreams
you seem to have under control, *seem* to, but the dream is strong, it strains
at the leash, it knows pretty much where it wants to go; you think you're
leading it and it ends up taking you for a walk. It began with a conscious
thought or a spoken phrase, she couldn't tell which. It sounded in her head
so clearly that she wasn't certain whether she had said it out loud or to
herself: *I know what's going to happen –*

She was standing by the door facing into the room, her arms behind her
back, the palms of her hands against the panelled wood as if she was
holding it shut. The tall window in front of her was blue-black, a syringe
glutted with blood.

What a mess it would make, she was thinking, if I opened it.

And, glancing down at her cotton summer frock, her bare legs, her little
girl's white socks, she shuddered; the feeling was like opening the fridge
on a hot day and standing in front of it with nothing on.

Moses was in the room too, she noticed. Over by the bed. There was a
suitcase on the floor beside him, and he hunched over it, fumbling with
the locks. He turned and looked in her direction several times, but didn't
seem to see her. He acted as if she wasn't there at all. This was such a
strong impression that she thought, Maybe I'm not.

At last he got it open. The inside, she saw, was lined with blue velvet
and moulded into holes and slots of differing shapes and sizes, each one
snugly filled by a piece of polished black metal.

Moses sat down on the bed facing her and slowly but professionally
assembled the gun. This took time. It was a complicated thing. The only
sounds in the room for a while were the clicks and squeaks of its interlocking
sections and appendages.

She was going to ask Moses a question, but thought better of it. He
seemed so removed. An automaton.

Finally he stood up and walked to the window. He opened it. All the blood, she noticed, stayed outside. She looked over his shoulder as he squatted down and, resting the gun on the windowsill, squinted along its gleaming barrel.

She saw herself walking across the tennis court in the garden below, trailing a black headscarf along the grass. (She recognised the scarf; it was the silk one, her favourite.) She was wearing a white summery dress fastened at the waist by a wide mauve ribbon. She didn't seem to be going anywhere in particular. Just walking.

The barrel of the gun tracked across until her head appeared in the centre of that tiny stylised spider's web. She chose that moment to glance up at the window, her eyes and mouth no more than dark smudges in the flat paleness of her face. Moses's finger tightened, squeezed the trigger. A thin jet of water spurted from the barrel.

She was standing by the door as before.

'*Look* at me,' she was saying. 'I'm *soaked*.'

She glanced down at herself. Her summer dress, her legs, her socks, were drenched. With blood, she noticed, quite casually.

'I'm sorry,' Moses said, sitting by the window, cradling the gun in his elbow. 'It was only a joke.'

He smiled. It was such a distant smile. It was like watching someone smiling on Mars.

Gloria woke convinced that she had been awake the whole time, that it had been a daydream. It was only when she looked at her watch that she realised that she had been asleep for over an hour. Moses was still fast asleep, facing her now, one arm reaching out towards her from under his cheek. She wondered if *he* realised he was asleep. She thought it was funny that she hadn't been lying in bed with him in the dream because the room she had dreamt about was the room they were in now. The dream had used such recent, present things. She shivered, remembering the innocent way she had looked at the blood on her dress and her legs; she hadn't really known what it was. She hadn't been frightened, though, she remembered, and was surprised by that. And that smile on his face at the end, a slight variation on his usual smile, but not so different, really, now she thought about it. She looked down at him. The smile was on his face now, she saw. She shook her head. He was the only man she had ever known who actually slept with a smile on his face.

Without waking him, she got out of bed, walked into the bathroom and stood in front of the mirror. She looked at the mirror rather than at herself. Tiny brown marks round the edge like liver spots. Old mirror. She picked up a glass from the shelf, filled it with cold water, and gulped it down.

Then she ran another bath, colder this time. Another bath? she thought. What's got into me?

She had already decided not to tell Moses about her dream, but one of the first things he said when he shuffled into the bathroom with one red cheek from where it had pressed against his arm was, 'Do you want to know what I've got in my suitcase?'

Gloria studied her feet. They didn't reach the end of the bath. Nowhere near.

'Have you been reading my thoughts?' she said.

'I never read people's thoughts. They're private.' He grinned, sat down on the toilet seat. 'You know, I've got the feeling you're going to like what I've got in that suitcase.'

So, Gloria thought. Probably not a shotgun kit then.

Moses tilted his head, narrowed his eyes. 'Is that your second bath in two hours or did I dream we went to bed together?'

'It wasn't a dream,' Gloria said.

*

Still drying herself, Gloria watched from the bathroom as Moses knelt down on the carpet and snapped the locks open. He lifted the real cowhide lid to reveal a mass of noisy tissue-paper. As he removed the layers, Gloria padded into the room on her bare feet, one towel twisted into a turban for her hair, another wrapped round her slender body almost twice. She stood behind him, one hand resting on his shoulder.

'It's a dress,' was all she could, rather obviously, say.

'Yes, it's a dress,' Moses said. 'I think it must've belonged to my mother.'

Gloria was uncertain how to react. Standing behind him, she could only guess at his face. He had told her nothing about his parents, not a single word, but the act of opening the suitcase seemed to have dimmed the lights in the room, lit candles, started something. The dress rustled like a chasuble as he unfolded it, releasing an incense that was fragile with age and storage. He held it up for her to see.

The style was early fifties, she guessed. A tight, shaped bodice, a narrow waist with a white plastic belt, and a layered, frothy skirt, just below knee-length, which, if danced in, would whirl out horizontally, spinning and billowing. The colour was a soft damask pink with white polka-dots. A real dancing dress.

'I'm not sure, though,' Moses said, 'not really.'

'I don't understand,' Gloria said. 'What do you mean?'

'It's difficult.'

Gloria moved on to the bed. She undid the turban and began to dry her hair. She watched Moses at the same time.

'I don't know who my mother is,' Moses said. 'Until I saw the photographs, I didn't even know what she looked like.'

'What photographs, Moses?'

'You don't know anything, do you?' He laughed to himself. 'Well, neither do I, really.'

He laid the dress across the foot of the bed. Then he rummaged in among the tissue-paper and pulled out a photograph album.

'These are the photos,' he said. Head bowed, the album unopened on his knee, he was wondering where to begin.

'I haven't told anyone before,' he said.

'Just start,' Gloria said. She rearranged the pillows on the bed and leaned back.

'Well,' he began, 'I'm an orphan, you see. Parents unknown. I can't remember them.'

Gloria nodded.

'The first thing I can remember,' he went on, 'is the sound of water. I'm lying on my back and it's like there's a roof over my head but there are holes in the roof and the light's coming through. I remember that so clearly. That darkness with pinpricks of light in it. That and the sound of running water. After that the next thing I remember is the orphanage – '

He gave her a picture of his life at Mrs Hood's establishment. The noise. The smells. The nicknames. He told her how a rumour had spread among the children, a rumour about him having been found by a river. Moses. Found by a river. *Very* funny. He had been convinced that the whole thing was just another joke about his name – the result, no doubt, of too many hours of Religious Knowledge. He had denied it fiercely. (He had had the only fight of his life about it, with a boy called David. After that, they called him Goliath. He couldn't win.) Later, though, he felt uneasy. Especially when he put the rumour alongside that primal memory of his. They had the sound of running water in common. Was that merely a coincidence?

Nobody enlightened him – perhaps nobody could – and he had learned to accept the darkness of not knowing. The mystery surrounding his origins had remained and endured.

'Then, a couple of months ago,' he said, 'just before I met you, in fact, it was my twenty-fifth birthday. Uncle Stan and Auntie B – they're my foster-parents – asked me if I'd like to come up for the weekend. Nothing much was happening in London, so I went. On the Sunday night they brought this suitcase down from their attic. "We've been looking after this for years," they said, "ever since we adopted you, but now you're twenty-five, it's legally yours. It's from your parents – "'

'God,' was all Gloria could say.

'You see, apparently, when I was abandoned by my parents, this suitcase was left with me. Mrs Hood stored it away until I was adopted. Then my foster-parents looked after it –

'Anyway, I couldn't believe it. I mean, imagine. I'd forgotten all about my real parents. I hardly ever thought of them because I'd never known them. I'd learned to live with that. Then suddenly, after all those years, they go and remind me of their existence again.'

Moses shook his head. He picked up the album of photographs, then put it down again. 'It's very strange. I've looked at these photos, and I've tried to remember being there, I've tried to recognise the faces, but it's like trying to remember places you've never been, it's like trying to recognise complete strangers. It's ridiculous. There are a few pictures of a baby in there, and I suppose it's meant to be me, but I don't recognise that either. Christ, I don't even recognise *myself*. But I'm staring so hard, you see, I'm trying so *hard* to remember that sometimes, just sometimes, I fool myself into thinking that I do remember. It's crazy, but I can't tell the difference. I don't know whether the memories are real or not –

'And what about this dress?' He reached out and touched the hem. 'When I first opened the suitcase, I thought I remembered it. It was like a flash. A gut-reaction. Very sudden. I remembered my mother, my real mother, bending over me, wearing that dress. But the more I thought about it, the more I realised that all I could really see in my memory was the dress. Just the dress bending over me. Nobody inside it.'

He paused.

'Nobody inside it,' he repeated softly, almost to himself. 'So you see, I can't *really* remember *anything* – '

Silence had filled the green room with water, slowing every sentence, every movement down. When he turned and looked at Gloria he saw that she had been crying. He moved on to the bed and dried her face with his hands.

'I'm sorry,' he said. 'I didn't mean to go into all that.'

She wiped her eyes with her wrists. 'That's all right.'

'It's me who should be crying really.'

'I know.'

*

They suddenly noticed that it was getting late and that if they were going to get drunk that evening (something they had promised themselves on the drive up) they would have to hurry. They opened their suitcases, pulled out clothes, began to dress each other. It was like a sex-scene in reverse and Moses kept wondering, as Gloria buttoned his trousers and his shirt, whether the film would start winding forwards again, towards nakedness. It didn't, though. Passively, he watched his body disappearing. Then Gloria stood in front of the mirror and aimed a hairdryer at her head while Moses dusted every inch of her slight body with special talcum powder, from the pale shell-like gaps between her toes to the Turkish Delight of her nipples. She passed the hairdryer from one hand to the other so he could slip her arms into the sleeves of her white silk blouse. He fastened buttons with huge fumbling fingers. He held a pair of black knickers at floor-level for her to step into, one foot at a time, then drew them past her knees, up her thighs and over her soft and unusually straight pubic hair (which had been aged dramatically by the powder). He zipped up her skirt, chose shoes, clipped on earrings. In ten minutes they appeared in the doorway, scented, presentable, and separating from a kiss (the film still running backwards, it seemed).

The downstairs bar was a riot of chintz and ormolu. Not a soul in sight. Even the barman was only half there. It took a few seconds of wild gesticulation to alert him to their presence. To make up for lost time they downed six gin fizzes between them in slightly less than half an hour.

'It's the crying,' Moses explained to Gloria. 'You have to replace the tears, you see.'

Gloria speared a green olive. 'Something that occurred to me,' she said. 'If you don't know where your parents live, or even who they are, what made you think they came here?'

'Yes, that was strange,' Moses said. 'When I opened the suitcase, there was this postcard lying in the bottom. I think it must've fallen out of the album. Anyway, it was a picture of this place, and it had a name on the back of it. Dogwood Hall. I looked it up in the phone book, found out it was a hotel, and here we are.' He scooped up a handful of peanuts. 'The album seems to cover a period of about four or five years. Two or three years of courtship and two years of marriage. Since the postcard probably fell out of the album, I thought they must've stayed here during that time. Who knows, I might even've been conceived here.'

'It's a pretty strange story, Moses,' Gloria said.

His eyes dropped from the wedding-cake ceiling to her face. Now he understood why he had brought Gloria along, why he had told her rather than Jackson, say, or Eddie. They would never have believed him. She did.

Gloria stirred the remains of her third drink with her finger. She was trying to imagine a life without parents. She found it almost impossible. Everything had revolved around her parents – or rather her parents had made everything revolve around her. She had been an only child and she had never doubted that they doted on her. Her every move had been recorded and cherished. She knew when she was born, she knew what her first joke was, she knew who had come to her first birthday party (she even had a movie of it). Her parents had given her everything – a swing in a rose-arbour when she was six, a thoroughbred pony when she was ten, a sports car (now written off) when she was seventeen, and a home throughout, for Christ's sake, a stable home. She felt unbelievably lucky all of a sudden, lucky and guilty. She remembered a line that she sometimes used at parties. 'I was a spoilt child.' Pause. 'Spoilt but not ruined.'

A waitress appeared in the doorway. 'Mr and Mrs Highness? Your table's ready.'

*

It was quarter past eleven when they staggered out of the dining-room. They hardly recognised the hallway. Vases loomed and undulated, portraits leered, walls curved away, carpets suddenly had gradients, and the corridor turned corners far too soon. Somewhere at the end of all this was room number 5.

Gloria, marginally the steadier of the two, played safe and stuck to the banisters. Moses, veering wildly, mowed down a suit of armour which had stepped out in front of him. The helmet crashed to the floor. Taj Mahal, already tucked up in bed with a history of the British Empire, heard the clatter of metal and thought: saucepans.

Back in the hallway, Moses, startled by the suit of armour, lurched sideways, collided with a table, and fell full-length on the carpet. A vase of lilies rocked and toppled over.

'It's the first time I've ever stayed in a hotel, you see,' he mumbled. 'I'm not used to it.'

Gloria was still clutching the banisters. Her stomach ached with laughter. 'You poor orphan,' she said.

Water began to drip on to Moses's neck from the overturned vase.

'Gloria,' he said. 'I think it's raining.'

He climbed to his feet, then stooped to retrieve the helmet, but kicked it with his size 12 foot before his hand could reach it. The helmet rolled under the table. Still stooping, he peered into the darkness between the legs of the table and began to call the helmet terrible names.

'Moses. Quick.' Gloria waved at him from the stairs. Frantic spastic agitations of her left hand. '*Quick*. Before somebody comes.'

She left the safety of the banisters and stood the vase upright. Then she tugged on one of Moses's arms. He responded, straightened up too fast, overbalanced, and fell backwards against the staircase, taking Gloria with him. The hallway shook. An oil painting slid sideways on the wall.

'Look,' he said. 'Poltergeist.'

They sprawled in a heap at the foot of the stairs. Hysterical. Incapable of movement.

Amazingly, nobody came.

*

Some time later they reached the landing. They began the search for their room-key. Moses had had it last, of that they were convinced. An excuse for Gloria to fumble around in various parts of his body. She found it accidentally in his trouser pocket while looking for something else. They missed the lock with it four times each.

'I've had men like this,' Gloria said.

She succeeded with her fifth attempt and they both fell into the room. They began to undress instinctively. Then Moses froze, one leg in and one leg out of his trousers. He had had a thought that was cold, green, and explosive.

'Champagne,' he cried. He toppled sideways, arms flailing, and knocked the lamp off the bedside table. The bulb blew with a soft contemptuous pop.

'Yes,' came Gloria's voice from somewhere.

Moses peered over the bed. She was lying on the floor in her blouse and tights, her head under the table, her legs askew. One of her shoes was in the bathroom, the other was in the waste-paper basket. She looked like a car-accident.

He clambered to his feet, crossed the room, and stood over her, swaying dangerously. 'Your eyebrows say quarter to two,' he said. 'It must be our anniversary.'

'Already?' Gloria murmured.

'I'm going downstairs,' he said, 'to find a bottle of champagne.'

Opening the door, he began to look for a way round the outside edge. Gloria crawled towards him, one hand outstretched, pointing.

'Trousers,' she said.

'What?'

She touched his bare thigh. 'Trousers.'

'Don't touch me,' he screamed. 'Otherwise something terrible could happen.' An erection now, he was thinking, would make it much harder to leave the room.

He returned some twenty minutes later covered in mud. The first thing he saw when he opened the door was Gloria wearing the pink dress. She held her arms away from her sides and twirled once, unsteadily. The skirt whirled out into the air. The sound of lightly falling rain.

'I knew it.' He leaned back against the door. 'I fucking knew it.'

'What?' Gloria said. She had tried the dress on without thinking, simply because it had been lying there on the bed, but once it was on she had kept it on because it fitted so well that it felt as if it belonged to her.

'You in that dress,' he said. 'It's perfect for you. You ought to keep it.'

'I couldn't possibly. It's your mother's.'

'Keep it.' Moses waved his arms about for emphasis. 'What do I want with a dress?'

He smelt almost sober as he kissed her because she had taken his breath away. He reached behind her and began to unfasten the dress. The rasp of the ancient zip was followed by a sharp knock on the door. If you could hear an exclamation mark, he thought, that's what it would sound like.

'Come in,' he called out.

A waitress wheeled in their champagne on a silver trolley. Then she smiled and withdrew.

'What's all that mud?' Gloria asked.

'I got lost,' Moses explained. 'I opened what I thought was the door to the bar and suddenly found myself outside. At first I didn't believe it. I thought they'd just turned the lights off or something. Then I tripped over a cauliflower. That's when I realised I wasn't in the bar – '

'Well,' Gloria was pouring the champagne, 'you got there in the end.'

'I always do. It's just that the middle can sometimes take a very long time.'

'Which can be a good thing,' Gloria said, 'in certain circumstances.' She slipped her clothes off, slipped into bed.

'I think I follow you,' Moses said. And did.

He turned out the one light they hadn't broken.

Gloria had draped the pink dress over a high-backed chair. In the moonlight the chair disappeared. It looked to Moses as if somebody was wearing the dress, somebody invisible, leaning towards him, bending over him, saying goodnight –

*

Gloria had opened the window. It was late. She leaned on the sill and blew smoke out into the night. It was so quiet after London, so quiet she could hear the blood hissing in her ears. She didn't feel tired any more, or drunk. If anything, the champagne had straightened her out. No tennis court lay below her, only a lawn, but she shivered as she remembered her dream.

'Moses? Are you awake?'

'Yes.' He sounded comfortable over there in the bed.

'Moses, I'd like to go rowing. What do you think?'

He sat up. '*Rowing?*'

Gloria faced into the room and made her hands into fists. She held them out in front of her and pulled them towards her chest several times, energetically.

'Ah,' Moses said. 'Rowing.'

'There's a boat on the lake,' Gloria said. 'I saw it when we arrived this afternoon.'

She could just make out the shape of Moses putting his feet on the floor.

'So,' he said. 'Rowing, is it?'

There was nobody about downstairs. The grandfather-clock in the hallway made them jump and cling to one another as it struck quarter past two. They walked over the blue-grey lawn, their feet soundless on the grass. The lake looked bright and black and waterproof. It could have been a giant tarpaulin spread out on the ground.

They found a boat complete with oars moored to the jetty. Gloria stepped in first, then Moses cast off and jumped on board. They almost capsized. The water made fleshy noises as it slopped against the sides.

'This is like being drunk,' Moses said.

Gloria laughed. 'You *are* drunk.'

She sat in the stern, hugging her knees, and watched Moses steer away from the jetty, noting the slight frown of concentration as he manipulated the oars, his head moving this way and that, judging distances seriously. Tiny creases appeared in the place that was made for creases in between her eyebrows. They signified emotion of the deepest kind.

'Moses,' she said in a voice that rose into the night sky like a full moon, 'I think, in a curious way, I love you.'

Moses pulled on the oars, and pulled with such vigour that the boat was halfway round the lake (and Gloria was flat on her back in the stern with her legs in the air) before he replied.

'That,' he said, 'is a very exciting thought.'

*

They were late for breakfast.

The hotel guests stared. Perhaps they had been woken in the night by the crash of falling armour, perhaps they had heard a boat on the lake in their dreams, or perhaps they were just senile, staring but seeing nothing. Most of them seemed to be approaching the end of their meals and would soon be gone. For breakfast read life, Moses thought.

The young couple (as they were probably now being called) sat at their table for ages, talking and smoking and drinking coffee. There was no rush; the sky showed blue at the top of the window and a 22-carat sun gilded the trees with layers of gold leaf. They knew the fine weather was going to last because Jackson had forecast rain. He had advised Moses to take along plenty of waterproof clothing. Foolish well-meaning Jackson.

On their way to the gardens at midday they passed the suit of armour in the hall and noticed that the helmet had been returned to its proper place.

'Did I really?' Moses said.

'You know you did,' said Gloria.

Moses paused on the front steps, his spirits lifted by the warmth of the morning and the light breeze that was carrying, as if on a silver tray, the unexpected smell of wild strawberries. Gloria looked stunning, almost edible, in her pink angora cardigan and her flaring yellow skirt and her sunglasses (for her hangover, she said). Moses had dressed all in white. Shirtsleeves rolled back along his forearms and a pair of loose-fitting cricket-flannels. Standing together in front of the hotel, they might have been posing for a photograph.

The path they took reproduced, in miniature, the twists and turns of the nearby river. It led away from the hotel, then doubled back and worked its way round to the old stables and outhouses. Trees arched overhead, meshed in a green ceiling, allowed only random shafts of sunlight through. Gloria walked in front, swinging her bare legs, turning every now and then to say something, patches of light illuminating different parts of her in turn – the hem of her skirt, one half of her face, the back of a knee – as if she had been invested with the memory that he had shared with her the previous night.

After twenty minutes or so they reached a point where the path veered away from the river and the trees thinned out. Gloria lifted a hand and pointed to a green door in an old brick wall.

'What's that?'

'Let's look.'

The green door wasn't locked. They pushed it open, the paint flaking away under their fingers, and found themselves in a vegetable garden.

There was an inert humid weight to the air as if it had been trapped inside those old brick walls for centuries, but there was a peace too, a lush sense of peace, as if it was content with its imprisonment. Countless passageways ran between head-high rows of sweet-peas, broad-beans and fruit-bushes. It would be the perfect place, Gloria was thinking, to sleep for a hundred years, like in the fairy-tales.

'Let's have a look in here,' she said. She took Moses by the hand and pulled him towards a ramshackle greenhouse. It must have been at least fifty foot long. Four steps of broken brick led down to the door.

Moses shoved the door open, jarring the loose panes of glass. A dense sweet heat enveloped his face.

Tomatoes. Thousands of them.

He led Gloria down the aisle that ran between the raised flower-beds, marvelling at the abundance of tomato-plants, marvelling too at the ancient lead irrigation-pipes and the massive sticky cobwebs slung across the winch-handles for the windows overhead. At the far end, and solid as an altar, was a stone sink. The priest was a rake.

It was sweltering in there. Drawing breath was like lifting a weight inside your body. Gloria removed her cardigan. Her white silk top caught on her nipples, then fell sheer, away from her rib-cage and her smooth flat belly.

'There is something about the smell of things growing,' Moses said, running the tip of his tongue up the side of her neck.

Things grew.

Gloria turned hard against him, and there was the taste of salt in their kiss. Moses began to undo his trousers.

'Moses,' Gloria whispered, pulling away and swatting his flies with the sleeve of her cardigan. 'In the *greenhouse?*'

'Your idea,' Moses said.

His hands slid under her skirt and inside her pants, pulling her towards him. He took her buttocks in both hands and lifted her slightly, then he was inside her, Gloria clinging to him, both arms round his neck, her heels locked behind his knees, her pants dangling from her left ankle.

Then:

Moses couldn't be certain, but he thought he saw the green door move. Yes, it had. Slowly it eased open and a bald man in a brown jacket came into view.

'Jesus,' Moses said. 'Taj Mahal.'

Gloria, thinking this was some new description of bliss, murmured agreement.

'The man in reception,' Moses hissed. 'Look. Over there.'

Gloria opened her eyes. 'Oh Christ.'

Moses staggered behind a large water-can with Gloria still attached, but this sudden movement, coupled with the shock of Taj Mahal's appearance, proved too much for him: he came.

'Oh *no*,' he groaned.

Still supporting her, he lowered her down on to her haunches, came out of her, and placed a hand over her cunt. Gloria squeezed her legs together, her eyes liquid.

'Sorry,' he said.

'It's all right.'

'It was that Indian bastard. Where is he now?'

Gloria raised herself a fraction, peeped through the tangle of tomato-plants. 'He's over by the cabbages.'

'I hope he hates tomatoes,' Moses whispered. 'I hope he's allergic.'

They both watched, breath held, fingers crossed, as Taj Mahal scrabbled about in the earth on the far side of the garden. It was stifling now – the sun beating down through the glass roof, the suspense. Moses pushed Gloria's hair back from her forehead and licked a bead of sweat from between her moist breasts. He kept his hand pressed to her cunt, catching the stuff as it came out of her. He liked the feeling of having the whole of that part of her in one hand.

Five minutes later, to their great relief, Taj Mahal left the garden, a small bunch of root vegetables in his hand. Moses and Gloria looked at each other, their flushed faces, their dishevelment, and started laughing.

'He would've died,' Gloria said.

*

Back in the room that afternoon, Moses opened the suitcase and took out the album. Its blue cardboard cover had been printed to resemble crocodile skin, and the word *Photographs* had been engraved across the bottom right-hand corner in an elegant gold script; a blue tasselled cord bound the pages together. Moses sat down next to Gloria on the bed and began to show her the pictures.

The first few were landscapes. They all had titles (written in a white chalk pencil because the pages were black) – titles like *Grape Meadow* and *Hazard Copse*. Then came several views of a country village entitled, simply, *Our Village*: a sunlit street, a row of shops (was that a greengrocer's?), a policeman on a bicycle.

Gloria frowned. 'This could be anywhere.'

'I know,' Moses said. 'But look.' He pointed at a picture of the village church. In the background, in the distance, something had caught the light, showed silver through the dark grey trees. 'Isn't that a river?'

'So?'

'Well, you remember what I said about the sound of running water?'

'But Moses,' Gloria said, 'that could've been anything. It could've been your father having a bath.'

'Maybe.' Moses didn't sound convinced.

As they went through the album, Gloria could see a story emerging – a rural setting, a man, a woman, courtship, marriage, a house, a baby – a story that would have struck her as romantic and touching, but perfectly ordinary, had it not been for the air of profound despondency that all the pictures seemed to breathe, release into the room around her. It was nothing she could put her finger on, just the sense that something was being held back. She tried to explain this to Moses.

'Jesus, I think you're right,' Moses said. 'I'd never really seen it that way before, but you're right. There's no real joy there, is there?'

Gloria turned back a few pages. 'Especially your mother,' she said.

The photographs showed a woman in her twenties. Tall, almost statuesque, yet ill at ease. She seemed always to be shying away from the camera. Her smile looked awkward, unconvincing, as if she had been told to smile when, in reality, she was feeling something else, as if smiling was a skill which she had still to master. *Alice, Summer 1953*, for example, where she was crouching on a white garden chair, her back curved, a cup in her left hand. A straw hat with a huge floppy brim shielded her eyes from the glare. She shrank back into the shadow it afforded her, surprised – no, more than that: alarmed. Or *The Boundary 1949*. In this one she wore a white blouse and a floral skirt, but the vivacious clothes clashed with her mood. She stood pressed against a tree, almost pinned to the bark, her hands in front of her, one clasping the other. There was always that sense of straining for effect. There was always that false note.

'What boundary, I wonder?' Gloria said.

Moses didn't know. But her question had made an important point. They could guess, they could speculate, they could fantasise. Further than that they couldn't go.

Moses's father, on the other hand, appeared confident, resourceful even. Moses turned to his favourite picture, *Birdwatching 1955*. His father stood in heroic semi-profile, a tall square-shouldered man with unruly black hair and kind eyes, remarkably similar in build, funnily enough, to Uncle Stan. He had dressed with a certain amount of panache: a Paisley scarf folded across his chest and tucked into a high-buttoning check jacket, a triangle of patterned handkerchief showing in his breast pocket, a shooting-stick under one arm, a newspaper (*Sporting Life*?) under the other. In his right hand he held a pair of binoculars. Hence the caption.

'Maybe he was just a better actor than your mother,' Gloria said.

Moses thought she was exaggerating.

Gloria shrugged. 'OK, what about this one then?' She was pointing at a picture that was titled *Our Ambition 1954*. 'How do you explain that?'

A country road stretched along the bottom of the picture. Beyond it lay a grass bank and a row of peeling silver birches. Beyond them, a gypsy caravan with big spoked wheels and a chimney that looked like a crooked toadstool growing out of the roof.

Gloria answered her own question. 'It looks to me as if they just wanted to get away from everything. And I'm not surprised, really. Look at the house. It looks really depressing.'

True, Moses thought. Despite the open windows and the parasol planted at a jaunty angle in the lawn (it must have been summer), the house looked withdrawn, lifeless, blind. The attempts at gaiety had fallen flat. The house where they had (presumably) lived together. The house where he had (presumably) been born.

The mood only lightened towards the end of the album.

'Oh look,' Gloria cried. 'It's you.'

Moses in woolly boots and mittens, cradled in his mother's arms (*Three Months Old*). Moses sitting upright in his pram, one arm in the air (*Conducting 1955*). Moses wearing his father's cap (*Just Like Dad 1956*).

'Is it really me?' Moses said. 'Are you sure?'

'That's you all right.'

'How can you tell?'

'How can I tell? Look at the size of you!'

'That's a normal size for a baby, isn't it?'

'That,' and Gloria tapped one of the pictures of Moses, 'is not a normal size for a baby. Believe me.'

'I don't know,' Moses said. 'I don't really know very much about babies.'

'Look at that picture of you wearing your dad's cap.'

'What about it?'

'Well, I mean, it *fits*, for Christ's sake. And you're only a few months old.'

Moses laughed. 'I suppose so.'

Gloria picked the album up and studied the picture still more closely. 'They loved you, though,' she said. 'I can see that.'

'Why did they get rid of me then?'

That was one question Gloria didn't have the answer to.

*

'I'm going down to the snooker-room,' Moses said. 'Coming?'

He was wearing nothing except a towel and a pair of socks. It was half past twelve on Sunday night.

'What?' Gloria said. 'Now?'

Moses nodded.

Gloria could see that he had some clearly defined idea in mind, but she couldn't guess what it was. She slipped her coat on and followed him downstairs.

By the time she reached the snooker-room Moses was beginning to undo his towel. When he was entirely naked he climbed on to the green baize and lay there, full length, on his back.

Smiling, she kicked off her shoes.

The cues lay stiff and silent in their brass racks over by the far wall.

The coloured balls glowed significantly in the woven string sacks under each pocket.

The scoreboard said 1 – 1.

One of the windows was open, and a breeze disturbed the heavy velvet curtains.

It was a warm night in Leicestershire.

*

Ice-cream van? Fire-alarm? Doorbell?

Moses had woken in a sweat, heart thumping, shocked into consciousness by the bright jarring sound.

Telephone.

His arm flailed out in the rough direction of the bedside table. His movements had the slow panic of someone sinking into quicksand. He found the receiver, picked it up, brought it over to where his head was.

'This is your early morning call,' came a woman's voice. 'It's six o'clock.' She sounded as though she had been up for hours.

'Six o'clock?' Moses groaned.

'You asked to be woken at six, Mr Highness.'

He lay there wondering why, then he remembered that Gloria had an audition in London at eleven.

'Thank you,' he said, and hung up.

He sat up, ruffled his hair, switched the bedside light on. Gloria was still asleep, he saw, now that his eyes were open (he wished they weren't; they stung).

Monday morning. The end of the weekend. The window an empty soulless slate-grey. He hated early mornings, especially early Monday mornings. They seemed to marshal all his anxieties, all his reasons for depression – troops of occupation that stamped about, brutalising everything, while he looked on, lost, weak, broken-willed. Looking at Gloria (one shoulder bare, a shield of dark hair, pouting mouth), he had the feeling that their best times together were already over.

He touched her shoulder. 'Gloria?'

'Mer.' The foreign language of dawn.

Without opening her eyes, she did a kind of somersault, fetching up against him, facing him, fitting neatly, like a spoon.

'Don't want to,' she said.

He smiled down at her, the kind of smile she would like to have seen. A sad fond smile. Nor do I, he thought. Nor do I.

They were similar in the mornings: dopey, laconic, functioning on automatic pilot. They washed, dressed, packed. They ate a quick breakfast. While Moses took the cases down, Gloria checked the room for anything they might have forgotten. Moses asked Taj Mahal for their bill and paid by cheque. Gloria handed the key over.

'Thank you,' she said. And then, at the door, 'Goodbye, Taj Mahal.'

The receptionist turned towards her, his head catching the light, and smiled almost pleasantly. Taj Mahal at daybreak. The best time to see it, so they say.

In fifteen minutes they were back on the motorway and settled into their separate silences. Moses became absorbed in the road, its surface the colour of a Siamese cat. Turn-off points for towns he would never see flicked by.

He glanced across at Gloria. She lay in her seat as usual, arms folded, feet in the glove compartment. She was singing snatches of 'Twenty-Four Hours From Tulsa'.

'Every car should have one of you installed,' he said, smiling.

'Every car should be so lucky.'

He had to agree with that.

'You know what you did,' he said moments later, suddenly remembering. 'No. What?'

'You called him Taj Mahal. You said, "Goodbye Taj Mahal."'

'I didn't.' Gloria seemed genuinely surprised.

'You did. And you know what else? I think he liked it.'

Gloria shook her head, laughed softly to herself. 'Old Taj Mahal.'

'Yeah,' Moses said. 'He looked at you and smiled.'

The sun was visible now through layers of cloud and mist. It looked like a beautiful woman trying on a négligé.

Cows tugged at the damp glistening turf.

The fields, rumpled at first, gradually began to flatten themselves against the ground, pretending they weren't there at all.

The sun tried on grey, then white, and finally it walked out of the shop naked. It reminded him of Gloria, also naked, packing the pink dress earlier that morning.

'Are you sure about this?' she had asked him.

'Yes,' but irritably, 'yes, I'm sure.'

She hadn't detected the uncertainty, the resentment, in his voice. It had been like a failure of perception on her part. She had packed the dress.

The road had changed colour. It was black now. The outskirts of London lay like a pile of ashes and clinker on the horizon.

'Where do you want to be dropped off?' he asked her.

She looked out of the window at the drab motorway landscape then across at Moses. 'In London, preferably,' she said.

'Sorry,' and Moses smiled, 'that came out wrong.'

An hour later he let her out in Victoria and waited long enough to see her swallowed up by the flow of the crowd down into the tube station, then he pulled out into the heavy Monday morning traffic.

PEACH INCOGNITO (1980)

He had told everybody the same story.

First Hilda. On the Sunday. At breakfast. The table smelling of flowers and polish, rich and waxy, tampering with the sharp aroma of his grilled herring. Light from the garden skidding off mahogany.

'I'm going to disappear for twenty-four hours,' he announced, as he buttered a slice of toast.

Hilda lifted a head of fading dehydrated curls. When questioning something, she displayed her infinite tact. She said nothing; she merely waited.

'I have some extremely important research to do,' he said. 'In the museum.'

'All right, dear.' Hilda bit delicately into the triangle of toast poised between her finger and thumb.

'It will probably be happening next weekend.' He spoke through the clinking of china. It made his words seem less naked. It seemed to clothe his deceit. 'Friday and Saturday, I should think. So don't expect me home on Friday night.'

Torn between amusement and concern, Hilda abandoned her usual discretion. 'You're not going to *sleep* in the museum, are you?' Her eccentric husband!

He was brisk, imperious. 'Either that or I'll use one of the beds in the station. It depends how things go. In any case, don't worry about me. I'll be all right.'

Hilda touched the handle of her tea-cup, traced its outline with a single lingering finger. 'And when will you be back, do you think?'

'Saturday night. Midnight. No later than that.'

Hilda nodded.

Watching her through the arms of the candelabra, he felt that she had taken the news too casually. He had to impress her with the gravity of the matter. He wanted it branded on her mind.

'I don't want to be disturbed, Hilda. Not by *anyone*. Is that understood?'

Hilda pressed a fingertip to one of the crumbs on her plate. Her bottom teeth gripped her upper lip. Now he had upset her.

'It's very important,' he explained, more gently. 'It's only for twenty-four hours.'

'I know, dear.' She faced him across the table, and her slightly lifted chin suggested a quaint bravery. 'I'll make you some sandwiches and a Thermos of hot soup.'

He didn't want bloody soup, but he said, 'That would be very nice.'

For the remainder of the meal, they discussed less controversial subjects: trimming the box hedges, revarnishing the table in the hall.

The conversation with Sergeant Dolphin had necessarily taken a somewhat different course.

'I'm going to be out of circulation for about twenty-four hours,' he told Dolphin on the Monday morning, 'and I want you to take over the running of the village.'

'Take over the running of the village, sir?'

Peach turned towards his office window, so as to hide his smile. The second half of his announcement had distracted Dolphin from too close or too immediate an examination of the first half. As he had known it would.

He swung round again, hearty, irrepressible. 'Be Chief Inspector,' he said. 'It'll be valuable experience for you, Dolphin. Stand you in good stead for the future.' He felt so expansive that he almost winked. 'It's high time you had the feel of the reins in your hands. The reins of power, Dolphin. I won't be here for ever, you know.'

In his eloquence Peach had ridden over the poor sergeant. He had, in fact, been quite carried away by his own oratory. 'Yes, sir,' were the only words Dolphin managed to get in – and those edgeways.

'I'm going to be working on a project in the museum. It's very confidential and I need absolute privacy. Under no circumstances do I want to be disturbed. *Under no circumstances*. Do I make myself clear, Dolphin?'

'Very clear.'

'I want you to pretend that I'm not here.'

'Yes, sir.'

'Pretend that I don't exist. Imagine, if you like, that I'm dead.'

He saw alarm go off in Dolphin's face. Well, perhaps that had been going a bit far. Still, it was gratifying to know that you were going to be missed. And the point, though exaggerated, was a valid one.

'Seriously,' he ran on, 'it'll make things more realistic. If a crisis occurs you won't be tempted to consult me. You'll be on your own, Dolphin. Just for those twenty-four hours. I've got a great deal of faith in you. I wouldn't be giving you this assignment if I didn't. But I'm sure you understand that.'

'Yes, sir.'

Well, Peach had certainly given Dolphin something to think about. And first thing on Monday morning too, the sergeant's eyes still foolish with sleep.

'I'll be briefing you on the exact timing later in the week,' he concluded.

'All right, sir.' Dolphin scraped at the floor with the rim of his boot, then he looked up. 'I appreciate the opportunity, sir. I'll be looking forward to it.'

That's my Dolphin, Peach thought.

*

It had all been so easy. On Friday of that week he organised the day patrols so that, for a period of precisely twenty minutes, the road that led south-west towards the village of Bunt would be left unmanned. Everything went as planned. At 6.30 on Friday evening he rode out of New Egypt on his bicycle. When he crossed the boundary he felt nothing. No hallucinations, no rush of adrenalin, not even a quickening of the pulse. Nothing. His feet pumped the pedals as before, the bicycle sped onwards. Once or twice he glanced from side to side as if the feelings he had heard about from previous escapees might be lurking in the hedgerow, waiting to spring out, infiltrate, be felt. He rode on. Still nothing happened. It was a pleasant evening in June.

Half an hour later he arrived at a small country railway station some eight miles west of New Egypt. He pedalled across the deserted car-park, his tyres silent on the tarmac. He dismounted behind a van with a shattered windscreen, and wheeled his bicycle through some bushes and down a crumbling mud bank into the copse that bordered the railway tracks. There, in the green gloom, among bleached cans of hairspray and the skeletons of motorbikes, he changed into civilian clothes. He folded his uniform and crammed it into his saddlebag. He locked the saddlebag. Then he dragged the bicycle behind a bush and camouflaged it with dead wood, brambles and leaves.

He walked into the Gents (hissing copper pipes, smells of pine and piss commingling) to check his appearance. When he saw himself in the mirror above the washbasins he thought how suspicious, how like a *criminal*, he looked. Partly the way he was dressed, he supposed. (He was wearing a beige check sports jacket, a green shirt, and a dark red tie which Hilda had given him for his birthday. His cavalry twill trousers had come out of a Christmas catalogue. On his feet, a pair of brogues. Respectable if somewhat characterless clothes. Deliberately so.) And partly the clandestine nature of what he was doing. His grey eyes watched him watching from beneath their heavy lids. His grey hair bristled like a bed of nails. The green shirt gave his face an unhealthy, slightly chilling pallor.

Still, he looked pretty vigorous for a man of his age.

*

If I were to die now, Peach wrote in a slightly unsteady hand, what would happen?

He sat back and considered the question. It would be a nightmare for Dolphin, of course. Though Dolphin wouldn't think of it as a death. Not right away. He would probably call it a *disappearance*. Still, that was serious enough. Nobody disappeared in New Egypt. Least of all a Chief Inspector. What would he do? Check the museum first. His only lead. But he would find no trace of Peach. Not a single clue.

Absolute nightmare.

It wouldn't be long before Dolphin began to suspect foul play. A kidnapping, for instance. Even, perhaps, a murder. (Peach's forty-year reign as Chief Inspector, his merciless grip on the community, had always made that a possibility – though who would dare?) He would have to lift the news blackout. He would have to inform the village. And then? Instant pandemonium.

Would anyone suspect that he had (a) *left* the village and (b) left it *of his own accord*? Only the more cynical of the villagers. Highness, for instance (he could see that sardonic twisted smile). The greengrocer, too, perhaps (those puffy knowing eyes).

In the end, after the obligatory month of search-parties and questionings, Dolphin would be forced to pronounce Peach dead. He would have to fake the evidence, concoct a foolproof story, produce a satisfactory corpse.

Some, Peach supposed (and this hurt slightly), would celebrate. He could imagine Dinwoodie dancing a solitary and hysterical jig in his garage. He shook his head. Poor Dinwoodie.

Others would mourn. He pictured a fragile and ghostly Hilda huddled in a room of dark furniture. He could hear the sound of uncontrollable mass weeping issuing from the windows of the police station on the hill.

And then the funeral.

Would there be a procession through the village as there had been for Lord Batley? Would they 'bury' him in an empty coffin? What a vicious irony that would be. So vicious that he almost resorted to prayer right there and then, but the priest's face rose before his eyes at the crucial moment (that pitiful jittery face, its faith built not on strength but terror) and he rapidly abandoned the idea.

He closed his notebook and tucked his pen into his breast pocket.

He would not die.

He leaned forwards, pressed his face to the window. The world beyond the streaked glass looked peaceful, almost familiar. Sunset an hour away. Evening light. The last rays reaching down through the woods, slender pale-gold arms emerging from the ruffled sleeves of clouds. Only the motion, the constant slippage of the landscape from right to left, seemed strange. A grass bank grew and grew until it hid the view. He watched as children do: as if the world was moving and he was still.

He was seventy-two years old, and it was his first time on a train.

*

Now they were swinging north into a long stretch of curved track and, simply by turning his head from right to left, he could see first the front then the back of the train. He suddenly became aware of how limited his knowledge was. From the window he had seen details of the village echoed, reproduced, enlarged – a boy spilling off his bicycle, a woman taking washing in, a flock of sheep wedged into a lane – but nothing could prepare him for the city that lay ahead. His wisdom, undisputed in the village, dissipated in this seemingly boundless world. It began and ended with the train he was travelling on. No, not even that. With the carriage he was sitting in. That was the sum of all he knew. It was daunting. He realised that he would have to rely on the qualities that had elevated him to the rank of Chief Inspector at such a comparatively tender age: vigilance, ruthlessness, intuition.

He began to see things that he had never seen before – at least not in real life: a viaduct; a white horse carved into the chalk of a hillside; an aeroplane, curiously silent and majestic, floating down over the train, almost grazing the tops of trees, its underbelly plump and vulnerable. A highly irregular thought occurred to him. Supposing he had left the village before now. Supposing he had left when he was younger, more receptive, more energetic, and returned armed with vivid first-hand experience of the outside world. Then he would really have known what he was talking about. Then he would have understood exactly what he was legislating *against*. And he would have been able to dispense his knowledge in tantalising fragments like some kind of oracle. A knowledge that only he (miraculously) possessed. How wise he would have seemed. Imagine the increase in prestige and credibility. Who knows, perhaps even the break-down could have been avoided. An interesting idea, in any case. Something to mull over. He jotted a few words down in his notebook: *The relationship of hypocrisy to the exercise of power*. He wondered if the idea had occurred to any of his predecessors. He doubted it, somehow. After all, it had only occurred to him once he had *already left* the village. Surely such an idea would have been unthinkable, quite literally unthinkable, while you were actually living there? Only this extraordinary detachment, this sense of removal, made it possible. It was as if he had risen out of his body and was looking back down at himself. He could see things in a way that he couldn't have seen them before.

The train chattered over the rails. You'll-never-go-back, it seemed to be saying. You'll-*never*-go-back-you'll-*never*-go-back.

Nonsense. Of course he would. He had to. He even *wanted* to.

He had allowed himself a maximum of twenty-four hours. Deadline Saturday 2100 hours. If he hadn't located Moses Highness by then, too bad. He had to be back in New Egypt by midnight. Otherwise his cover would be blown.

Once again he was struck by the enormity of the risk he was taking. Still, there was nothing for it now. Here he was, thirty miles out of the village, and moving further away with every minute that passed.

The train hurtled on towards the city, beating complicated rhythms now. Beneath the smeared glass, the landscape flowed like green weeds through water. He had never imagined such fluid speed. The percussion of wheels on rails. The flick-flick-flick of telegraph poles. Lulled him. He leaned his head back against the seat.

*

Where was he?

His eyes took in the blue and green check upholstery, the silver luggage-racks, the discarded newspaper, his own face in the window's mirror. A blonde girl sitting across the aisle returned his glance of confusion with a smile. She hadn't been there before.

Through the window he watched the march of strange buildings. Three tower-blocks, an office of reflecting glass, a multi-storey car-park. Semi-detached houses in a row like vertebrae. He was on the train. But where was the train?

As if to answer his question, the train lurched, throwing him forwards. It was slowing down. For a station, presumably. But which station?

'Is this London?' he asked the blonde girl.

'No, this is East Croydon,' she said. 'London's next.'

He thanked her.

So. He must have dozed off. He wondered how long he had slept. Fifteen minutes, twenty minutes – not much more. That girl must have joined the train at Three Bridges. Everything under control again, he began to move his mind into the immediate future. They were due in at 8.23. By the time he found a hotel and registered, it would be close to ten. He doubted whether he could accomplish much that night. He had a phone-call to make, but he could do that from his room. All right, then. An early night. An early start in the morning.

The white signs of suburban stations flashed by, almost too fast to read. West something. Something Common. Clapham Junction. Houses rushed up to the railway line. He saw a woman washing her hair, the bathroom lit by one naked bulb. It embarrassed him, this glimpse into her privacy. Then he saw two people standing in a yellow kitchen. Then an empty room with the TV on. Window after window. Life after life on display. He found himself thinking of the police museum.

As the train rattled over a bridge, he looked down. Though rush-hour was over, the street pulsed with the red tail-lights of cars. Glowing, dimming, glowing again as feet touched brakes. All those cars, all those lights. He sensed a surge of electricity. Friday night. The city charged up for the weekend. Perhaps the fascination showed on his face because the blonde girl chose that moment to speak to him:

'I love this place, don't you?'

He turned to look at her. The thrill in her voice, the ingenuous warmth of her smile, drew him in, persuaded him to tell the truth. There was nothing to fear from her.

'It's the first time I've been here,' he confessed.

'The first time?' Her voice lifted in disbelief. It was a musical voice. It resonated. It would be capable, he imagined, of wonderful laughter. 'Where have you been hiding?'

He instantly forgave her the slight impertinence of her question. She was an attractive girl – in her early twenties, he guessed – and some part of him was charmed by her forwardness.

'I live a very quiet life. In the country.' He sounded appropriately sedate.

'Oh, I'm just coming back from a week in the country – ' the girl began.

How easily these people speak of coming and going, he thought. As if it was the most natural thing in the world.

' – but what brings you to London,' she was asking him, 'for the first time?'

The phrase had become their theme, linking them privately. When she got home she would tell her mother, or her boyfriend, or whoever she lived with, that she had met a man on the train who had never been to London before. It was his *first time*, she would say. Can you *imagine*?

While they had been talking, the train had crossed another bridge, over the Thames this time (he caught a glimpse of the water, glinting black, sluggish as oil), and everybody was standing up, pulling on coats, hauling down cases. All this gave him time to frame a suitably vague answer to what had been, potentially at least, a rather awkward question.

'Business,' he said. 'I'm here on business.'

The girl, adjusting the belt on her raincoat, gave him a quick smile. Brisk rituals of arrival were beginning to override their conversation. Soon they were walking side by side down the platform. Gritty irritable light. The station, with its high arching roof, hollow and draughty, echoed with footsteps, voices, the whisper of clothes. Somehow the sound reminded him of birds – thousands of birds folding their wings. Once they had passed through the ticket barrier, the girl swung away from him.

'Well,' she said, 'I hope your business goes well.'

Her tiny downward smile intrigued him, as the beginning of a story does, but this, he realised, was already the end.

'Thank you,' he said. 'Good luck to you, too.'

'It's been nice talking to you. Goodbye.'

'Goodbye.'

He watched her walk away. She walked energetically. Her blonde hair rose and fell with the energy of her walking. He put his case down. He was acting very strangely. Really very strangely indeed. What on earth had prompted him to wish her good luck like that? He went back over the encounter in some detail and shook his head. He almost didn't recognise himself.

Suddenly a crowd of people spilled towards him across the concourse. Though startled, he stood his ground. They flowed round him as if he was part of the station. He had never seen so many people in one place. And every face lifted anxiously to the departures board as if they expected to read the news of some personal tragedy there. So many people and yet they all had different noses, eyes, hair. It seemed extraordinary to him that no two people looked the same. And another thing. He didn't *recognise* anyone. He had never seen so many *strangers*. For a moment he, too, looked anxious. Then he became exhilarated. The turmoil. The din. The *anonymity*. He could blend with the crowds, he could move about unobserved, no eyebrows raised, no questions asked. It suited him perfectly.

Outside the station he flagged down a taxi. The driver took him to a dark street lined with stunted trees. Somewhere between Queensway and Notting Hill Gate, it was (Peach had been following the route in his *A–Z*). He paid the driver, and the taxi rattled away again towards the main road. He stood on the pavement, his suitcase in his hand. He looked up. The Hotel Ravello. *It's not exactly The Ritz*, the driver had told him, but Peach had imagined worse places.

He climbed the steps and pushed the door open. A bell tingled. He found himself in a narrow hallway. A rectangle of plastic-coated card had been tacked to the wall. RECEPTION, it said. The arrow underneath indicated a doorway to the left.

'Hello?' he called out.

He walked up a short passage and peered into an office. Beyond the office lay another, darker room, separated from the first by a frosted-glass partition.

'Hello?' he called out again.

An Arab appeared. He had the watery strained eyes of somebody who watches too much television. His complexion was yellow on the surface, grey underneath. A few buttons on his shirt had popped undone, revealing the wrinkled socket of his navel.

'Yes?'

'I would like a single room,' Peach said.

'How many night?' The Arab spoke in a monotone. The words came automatically. He probably said them in his sleep.

'Just the one.'

The Arab produced a register. 'Sign here.'

Peach stooped and wrote *George Highness* in a confident scrawl. A merciless smile passed over his lips. That's the closest *he* will ever get to leaving the village, he thought.

He pushed the register back across the counter, received a key in exchange.

'Third floor,' the Arab said. 'Check out before midday.'

Peach nodded. He would be gone long before then.

As he climbed the stairs the décor deteriorated. Handprints on the walls. Scratches, patches of damp, graffiti. It certainly wasn't The Ritz.

His room had a flimsy hardboard door. The number, chipped gilt, dangled on a single screw. He turned the handle and walked in. Green carpet. Faded orange bedspread. Massive dark wardrobe. Chair. Gas-ring. Ashtray. He closed the door, put his case on the bed, and walked into the bathroom. He ran the cold tap and splashed some water on to his face. He dried on a threadbare towel that said, incongruously, GOOD MORNING. Stepping back into the bedroom, he took off his jacket, loosened his tie, and unlocked his case. He was travelling light: a pair of striped pyjamas, a washing-bag, a diary, a bus-map, binoculars, a Thermos of Hilda's homemade minestrone soup and half a dozen ham sandwiches wrapped in tinfoil. He crossed to the window and raised the sash. Then he settled on the chair and ate four of the sandwiches one after another. Even though the sandwiches were very good indeed (nobody made ham sandwiches like Hilda), his face registered nothing. He was thinking. The city made a sound like distant applause.

After gulping down a cup of minestrone, he reached for his diary. He thumbed through the pages until he found the number he was looking for. He moved to the bed and picked up the telephone. He dialled with nimble precise rotations of his index-finger. The number began to ring.

Somebody answered. A voice said, 'Eddie here.'

Peach blinked once, iguana-like. His lidded eyes fixed on the wall opposite. 'Eddie, this is Mr Pole speaking. Moses's foster-father.'

'Mr Pole. What can I do for you?'

What indeed, Peach gloated. He wiped the corner of his mouth with the back of his hand. An orange smear: minestrone.

'I'm sorry to bother you, Eddie, but I seem to have mislaid Moses's new address. I wondered if you could possibly – '

'No problem, Mr Pole. Hang on a moment.'

Because, until today, the world had always been inaccessible, Peach had always listened to telephone voices very carefully. He found he could often construct a picture of the person he was talking to. Sometimes a face. Sometimes a body too. Sometimes the room they happened to be in. He tried to picture Eddie now, but saw a dog instead. A white toy dog. He gritted his teeth.

'Mr Pole?'

'Yes?'

'You can reach him on 735–8020.'

Peach pulled his pen out of his breast pocket. '735 – '

'8020,' Eddie said.

'I see. And do you have his address by any chance?'

'I don't know his proper address, but the name of the club where he lives is The Bunker. He probably told you that, didn't he?'

'The Bunker. That's right, I remember now,' Peach lied.

'If you address a letter to The Bunker, Kennington Road, London SE11, I'm sure it'll get there.'

Peach scribbled frantically.

'OK, Mr Pole?'

'Thank you very much, Eddie,' Peach oozed, as only Peach could. 'You've been extremely helpful.'

Good old Eddie, he sneered as he rang off. What a fool. What a *dupe*.

He walked to the window. Anticipation started the motor in his lower lip. It began to slide in and out, a smooth action, almost hydraulic. This city was putty in his hands. He could shape it at will.

He was developing a knack for these phone-calls. Only a few weeks before, he had called the Poles in Leicestershire. A woman had answered.

'Yes?' Her voice had stretched the word out, making it sag comfortably in the middle like a hammock. He saw a plump woman with fussy hands. A roast in the oven. A couple of spoilt cats.

'My name's John,' he had said. 'I'm an old friend of Moses's. I haven't seen him for years, and I've been trying to track him down.' A bit of truth makes a better lie.

'Well – ' and Mrs Pole had given the word two syllables when one would have sufficed – 'the last *we* heard he was moving to some sort of *discothèque*, but I'm afraid he hasn't given us the exact address yet. I'm terribly sorry.'

Faced with her vagueness, he had become doubly precise. 'Could you tell me where Moses was living before? Perhaps they'll know.'

'That's right,' Mrs Pole had said, as if he was participating in a quiz-game of which she was the mindless compère.

Eventually she had given Peach Eddie's address and telephone number. She explained who Eddie was. A nice boy, she called him, even though she had only spoken to him once. The woman was plainly a nincompoop.

'I do hope you find Moses,' she had finished up. 'An old friend, are you?'

'Mmm.'

'Well – goodbye, John.'

'Goodbye, Mrs Pole.' And good riddance.

He unscrewed the Thermos and poured himself a second cup of mine-strone. Then he reached for another ham sandwich. He checked his watch. 10.15. Too late to make any further progress tonight. By 10.30 he was lying in bed, his *A–Z* propped on the mound of his stomach, half-moon spectacles resting on his fleshy belligerent nose. Shortly afterwards he leaned over and switched off the light.

One thought creeping up on him in the darkness threatened to sabotage his hopes of sleep. Suppose Highness had sent his son into the outside world with precisely this aim in mind: to tempt Peach to leave the village, to tempt him into a betrayal of everything he stood for. Suppose Highness now planned to exploit his absence. To expose him. To start an insurrection. This thought was so unpleasant that sweat began to accumulate behind Peach's knees.

But surely it was too fantastic, too far-fetched. Highness could never plan anything so complex, so ingenious. Not that moocher, that drone, that bonehead. Only he, Peach, could produce ideas of that calibre. He could run rings round that bloody layabout. He had covered every angle. He was the Chief Inspector.

He slept.

*

You can never be certain what it is that wakes you in the middle of the night.

When Peach woke, he heard shouting in the corridor outside his room. He tried to pick out words, but the language meant nothing to him.

He had been dreaming.

The dream hung eerily in his head like the hush after a bomb's dropped. He had been enveloped in darkness, a darkness that stretched infinitely in all directions. A sort of outer space. He had been surrounded on all four sides by bright orange ropes. He could see nothing but the darkness and the ropes. It was as if he was standing in a boxing-ring. A boxing-ring in outer space.

Not so much standing, perhaps, as floundering. He couldn't see a floor beneath his feet. At times whatever was supporting him seemed firm. At other times it tilted sharply, slid out from under him, gave way. And he would lunge for the ropes, wanting something solid, something tangible, to cling to. But his hands kept passing straight through the ropes as if the ropes weren't there. And he would try again and watch in astonishment, despairing, as the same thing happened.

There had been voices in the dream. Murmurings. Invisible spectators. They hadn't taken sides. They were neither for nor against him. They were simply there. Watching.

Then he had woken in the badly-sprung bed, his pyjamas damp, the darkness tinted orange by the street-lights, and he had heard voices in the corridor. Real voices.

Now somebody was running past his room. A door slammed. That foreign language again. What the *devil* was going on? He switched on the light and peered at his watch. 3.28. He got out of bed. As he pulled his beige jacket on over his pyjamas, some instinct persuaded him to slip his police badge into the pocket. He opened the door of his room just in time to see the door of the room opposite slam shut. He crossed the corridor and knocked.

He knocked again.

The door opened a few inches. A face appeared in the gap. Jet-black hair, olive skin, the pencil-shading of a moustache. An adolescent. Indian or Pakistani. Stale cigarette smoke in the room. The rustling of bedclothes.

'You're making an incredible amount of noise,' Peach said.

The boy offered him a blank face. Peach read a single word there. Stupidity.

'It is very late – ' he pronounced each word distinctly and gestured with his watch – 'and I want to sleep.'

The boy shrugged. Perhaps he really didn't understand. But Peach thought he detected a sly mockery in that blank face. He felt like seizing the boy by his stringy chicken neck and –

He checked himself. He wasn't in New Egypt now. All right, he thought.

'I am a policeman,' he said. And, reaching into his jacket pocket, pulled out his badge. Held it up next to his face like a third eye. 'Po-lice-man. Understand?'

The boy's eyes scattered. He poured some anxious language over his shoulder into the room. A girl's voice answered. She seemed to be giving the boy advice.

The boy turned back. 'Sorry,' he said. 'Very sorry.'

'Just shut up and go to sleep,' Peach snapped.

He stamped back into his room and closed the door. Instead of going to bed, he sat by the window. There was no darkness to speak of in this city. All night long a gaseous orange glow hung over the buildings. An ominous light. Like an emergency, a war, the end of something. No wonder people ran up and down corridors. How could you sleep with that fire burning in the sky?

He had only been gone a few hours, but he already longed for the muffled black night of the village, the air of secrecy, the cover of darkness. He didn't sleep for almost an hour and his sleep, when it took him, proved fitful and thin, disrupted by sirens, cat-fights, and the dreadful silence of orange ropes.

*

He was awake again at 6.30. The orange night had withdrawn. Through a window fogged with dust and fumes and breath, the sky glittered silver-grey. Sheer, streamlined, a colossal machine.

He threw the covers aside and with them all his paralysing thoughts of the night before. Wearing only his twill trousers, he shaped up in front of the mirror like a boxer. He lowered his head and shuffled his feet. He threw a few right jabs. Fff, fff. It felt good.

Even his face – heavy, collapsing, punished by time – couldn't dismay him this morning. He surveyed the folds and creases, the bulging, the sagging, almost with satisfaction. How perfectly they disguised those agile wits of his! He was conscious that he was approaching the day the way he approached a day in the village: optimistic, determined, supremely confident.

By 7.15 he had paid the bill (exorbitant! that was the last time *he* would ever leave the village!) and was making for Queensway on foot. He decided to breakfast at the Blue Sky Café, blue being a colour of which he was particularly fond. He found a table by the window, took in his surroundings. Teak veneer panelling to shoulder height. Matt yellow paint beyond. Sticky-looking ventilation-grilles. Cacti on the mantelpiece. He watched the door opening and closing on a succession of workmen who wanted cups of tea and bacon sandwiches. When he ordered, the waitress called him love.

Smiling, he arranged his *A–Z*, his bus-map and his diary on the table in front of him. He began to outline a strategy for his assault on The Bunker. The military side – reconnaissance, briefing, manoeuvres – appealed to him. In his mind, he wore a uniform.

'Excuse me.'

He looked up and saw an old woman sitting at the next table. He could tell from her accent that she wasn't English. Something about her face, too, didn't belong. Not another bloody foreigner. He sighed visibly.

'Were you addressing me, madam?'

The old woman reached across and touched him on the shoulder. Her hand descended so lightly that it might have reflected either awe on her part or fragility on his. The former seemed more likely.

'You're a man of great power,' she said. 'I can feel it.'

He glanced round. Nobody had noticed. The last thing he wanted, even this far from The Bunker, was to start attracting attention. He faced the old woman again. Her smile, almost coquettish, somehow avoided being grotesque. But he was brisk this morning, not easily charmed. He was too conscious of the ground he had to cover, of the red second-hand on the clock above the glass display-case of rolls and buns. His first thought translated rapidly into speech.

'What do you want?'

The woman placed the same light yet curiously restraining hand on his arm. 'What do *you* want, sir?'

Really, this was an impossible conversation. Quite impossible. He began to gather up his maps and notebooks. 'If you'll excuse me, I have some rather important business to – '

The woman's face broke up into a network of creases and lines in whose intricate web he suddenly, and unaccountably, felt himself to be a fly.

'Don't be frightened,' she said.

Frightened? Him? Outrageous. And yet –

This world. So very different. The cloth of the night dyed orange, embroidered with voices, torn by screams and the screech of brakes – had it frightened him?

The woman's words pricked his skin like needles. Doubts began to run in his bloodstream.

'You're not comfortable,' she was telling him. 'You're a long way from home, maybe that's the reason. Yes, I think that's the reason.'

Her voice scraped like dry leaves blowing over the surface of a road. Her dark eyes turned up stones. His scrambled eggs arrived, but he watched them congeal on the plate.

'Give me your hand,' she said.

He held out his hand, and she wrapped it in her cool papery fingers. She began to murmur to herself. This seemed to be taking place in a vacuum. Or not taking place at all. He was thankful nobody in the village could see him now. He observed his own submissiveness as if it was happening to somebody else.

'Who are you exactly?' he asked her.

'Oh, you can speak!' she exclaimed. 'I thought maybe you lost your voice. My name is Madame Zola. I'm a clairvoyant. Famous clairvoyant.'

He stared at his hand lying in hers.

'I can see,' she said, 'that you are, how shall I say, curious.'

He recovered. 'Where can you see that? On the palm of my hand?' But his sarcasm drifted past her. She seemed not to have noticed it. Beneath notice, perhaps. 'I am an old man,' he began again. 'One thing I'm not particularly curious about is the future.'

'You're also human.'

He didn't follow.

'You may be old,' Madame Zola said, 'but I'm older and I have to tell you one thing that maybe you don't know. People are always curious about the future. It's human character. They can be on the death bed. Still they have to know. Will I die? Will I live? How long will I live? What will happen when I die? All these questions. Always questions. Don't tell me you're not curious about the future.' She waggled a hand, almost in admonition, under Peach's nose. 'And that – ' one of her fingers stabbed the air triumphantly before curling up and rejoining the others – 'is why I'll never, *never* go out of business.'

Peach was thinking about Lord Batley. Batley had tried to escape at the age of seventy-nine. He had obviously believed in some kind of future. And wasn't he, Peach, desperately curious as to what the outcome of today's investigations would be?

Sighing, he admitted, 'You're right.'

'I know I'm right.' Her mouth curved downwards. 'Do you want to know what I see in your hand?'

'Yes.'

'Ah, you become simple now, you see? That's my effect. I see it happen. Everywhere I see it.' She waved a hand to include not just the café, but the city, the country too, the earth even, and the planets in attendance. 'That's *my* power.'

Her eyes drifted away from his, drifted beyond the yellow café walls and the steamy plate-glass, into a world that he couldn't imagine. A smile spread like water through all the cracks and crevices in her face until it was irrigated with a look of pure contentment.

'You're going on a journey,' she told him. 'An important journey. A difficult journey. It will happen very soon, this journey.'

'I know.'

'I'm right?'

'Yes.'

Her eyes misted over again. 'You're looking for something.'

He stared at her. She spoke in clichés, but the clichés were true. Her simple, almost facile, statements lodged under the mind's skin.

'But you feel lost,' she was saying. 'Among strangers. Alone.'

Her eyes refocused, seeking confirmation. He gave it to her.

'There's some danger – '

He remained calm. 'What danger?'

'That I cannot see.'

He glanced down at his untouched plate.

'You must forgive me, I didn't wish to stop you eating,' Madame Zola said (she had a foot in both worlds, it seemed, and could move from one to the other like someone playing two games of chess at the same time), 'but sometimes I feel something and when I feel something I cannot keep it inside. It has to come out. If I keep it inside I burst. Pif. Like a balloon.'

Peach suddenly found that he was hungry. He slid a forkload of cold scrambled egg into his mouth, then reached for a slice of toast. The butter had melted clean through. The toast sagged in his hand. He shrugged, ate it anyway.

'Anything else?' His briskness had returned with his appetite. They might both have been restored to him by Madame Zola.

She examined his left hand again. With his right, he gulped cold milky tea.

'I see only your strength, your power. You remember I said that you have power?'

'I thought you meant a different kind of power.'

'You have both,' and her smile, like a fishing-net, caught all possible meanings.

He withdrew his hand and wiped his mouth on a paper napkin. He began to gather his possessions together.

'You have to go now,' Madame Zola said. As if it was her idea, as if she was dismissing him.

'If you'll forgive me. I have an extremely testing day ahead of me.'

'I think I'll stay here a little longer.' She indicated the unfinished cup of tea in front of her. 'I wish you luck with your – ' and she paused, dark eyes glittering – '*business*.'

'Thank you, Madame Zola.' Peach even bowed slightly.

He paid the waitress and left the café. It was 8.45. The sun pressed against the inside of a thin layer of cloud. He unbuttoned his jacket as he hurried down Queensway. His mind, unleashed, sprang forwards.

That woman had slowed him down with her mumbo-jumbo. *You're looking for something*, she had said. But they all said things like that, didn't they, fortune-tellers? She couldn't have told him *what* he was looking for or whether he was going to *find* it, could she? Of course she couldn't.

Free of the Blue Sky Café, out in the open air, he welcomed his scepticism back like a friend whom he hadn't seen for a long time.

*

By the time he reached Bayswater Road the sun had broken through. It landed in a million places at once: a car windscreen, the catches of a briefcase, a man's gold tooth. He watched the city organise itself around him. He had his bearings now. Marble Arch stood to his left, half a mile away, solid as muscle. Hyde Park lay in front of him, a stretch of green beyond severe black railings. And somewhere to the south, approximately seven miles away, The Bunker waited. He leaned against the bus-shelter, his jacket draped over his arm.

After ten minutes the bus came. It dropped him at Oxford Circus. He caught another going south on Regent Street. The route he had selected took him past many of the famous sights of the city – the statue of Eros, Trafalgar Square, Downing Street, Westminster Abbey, the Houses of Parliament – but he only absorbed them subliminally. It was the action that interested him, not the scenery. His mind moved in another dimension, juggling possibilities, shaping initiatives. He wasn't a tourist. He was a policeman.

The bus swung left over a bridge and he knew, without looking at the map, which bridge it was. A barge loaded with machinery forged downriver, shouldering the water aside. Gulls fluttered above. They reminded him of the greengrocer's story. The gulls in the air above the ploughed field: symbols of freedom. How far he seemed from that closed world. How far he was.

When the bus turned into Kennington Road, he stepped out. His head swivelled. He used the gleaming dome of the Imperial War Museum (how appropriate, he thought) to orientate himself. One problem. Kennington Road ran north and south from the crossroads where he was standing. Which way should he go?

A police car pulled up at the lights. Peach approached the window on the passenger's side.

'Excuse me,' he said, 'but I wonder if you could tell me where The Bunker is?'

The policeman he was talking to had an unusually pale face. It was so pale that it was almost transparent. Even the policeman's eyelashes were pale. Peach's first albino.

'Never heard of it.' Not only an albino, but arrogant with it.

'It's a nightclub,' Peach explained.

The policeman pushed his hat back on his head, revealing a strand of colourless hair. 'Don't know it.'

His colleague, the driver, was muttering something.

'Try down there.' The policeman pointed south with his chin. 'Can't help you otherwise, mate.'

'Much obliged,' Peach said. 'Thanks very much.'

Mate, he thought. Bloody albino. Take his uniform away and he'd probably disappear altogether.

He set off down the road. The traffic lights had already changed, but several seconds passed before he heard the police car move away. He understood. If he had been approached by an old man in a sports jacket who was looking for a nightclub, he would have been suspicious too. Especially if he happened to be an albino. Axe to grind. Revenge on the world. He didn't look back, though. He kept walking. Basic psychology. Only the guilty look back. The guilty and the stupid.

He walked for five or ten minutes and saw nothing that even remotely resembled a nightclub (not that he was any too sure what nightclubs looked like in the daylight). Kennington Road ran south into a glitter of bicycle-shops and pub-signs. Council-blocks the colour of dog-meat. A green and white striped bingo-hall. Trees so dusty that their leaves looked plastic. He began to have doubts. What if Eddie had lied? Could Moses have covered his tracks?

He sat down on a bench and mopped his forehead and the back of his neck with a large white handkerchief. He opened his suitcase and examined his notes. He took those anxious questions of his and crumpled them like so much waste-paper. He began again, with a fresh blank sheet, as it were. Outlined his mission to himself. Stated the priorities.

1) Establish the exact whereabouts of the nightclub.
2) Establish whether or not Moses Highness is living at said nightclub.
3) If so, establish visual contact.
4) If not, start again – with Eddie.

Incisive now, Peach walked across the pavement and into a newsagent's. He asked the Indian behind the counter whether he knew of a place called The Bunker. The Indian didn't.

He asked a teenager at a bus-stop. The teenager didn't know either.

Peach walked on, undeterred, a pear-shaped man with a jutting lower lip. Sooner or later, he thought. Sooner or later.

Reaching another set of traffic lights, he noticed a pub on the corner. They would know. Surely. He consulted his watch. Half an hour to opening-time. He sat down on a low brick wall. And waited.

As soon as the bolts were drawn (11.32), he was through the double-doors.

'You must be desperate,' the landlord said. 'You nearly knocked the place over.' His eyes creased at the corners; he was making a joke, but the joke included as one of its ingredients a sense of wariness.

Peach eased himself on to a stool and leaned his forearms on the bar. 'Today,' he said, 'has not exactly been the easiest of days.'

The landlord tipped his head back, narrowed his eyes, nodded.

Peach didn't usually drink at lunch-time, but usually was a word that didn't apply. Not today. 'I'll have a pint of bitter,' he said. 'Anything for yourself?'

'That's very kind of you, sir. I'll have a lager.' The landlord pulled Peach's bitter first, then the lager. 'Your good health, sir.'

Peach raised his glass to his lips. 'Cheers.'

When he spoke again he had almost drained it dry. 'I was wondering,' he said, 'whether you could help me.'

'Do my best, sir,' the landlord said.

'I'm looking for a place called The Bunker. It's a nightclub. Somebody told me that it's on this road.'

The landlord shook a cigarette out of a squashed packet of Benson's. He ran the tip of his tongue along his sparse moustache, pressed his lips together, and nodded (Peach's intuition told him this happened a lot). 'I know the place,' he said. 'It's been open less than a year. Run by a coloured chap. Bit shady by all accounts.' He sniffed. 'No pun intended.' He struck a match and lit his cigarette. He put the match out by shaking it, the way a nurse shakes a thermometer.

Peach swallowed some more beer. 'Where is it?'

'Just down the road.'

'Where exactly?'

'About a hundred yards down. Right-hand side. You can't miss it.' The landlord smiled. 'It's pink.'

'Pink?'

'That's right.'

They looked at each other and shook their heads in the manner of men who have seen all kinds of things come and go. There was a certain intimacy about the moment.

'I don't suppose,' Peach ventured, 'you know whether a young man by the name of Moses is living there, do you?'

The landlord arranged his features in a position of deep thought. 'Moses? No. I don't know anyone called Moses.'

Ah well, Peach thought. Worth a try.

'Friend of yours?' the landlord enquired.

'Not exactly a friend,' Peach said, 'though we do go back a long way,' and, turning aside, he strolled through the arcade of his own amusement.

The landlord nodded once or twice. Smoke from his cigarette rose up through blades of sunlight. Traffic sighed beyond the frosted glass. A clock ticked on the wall. It was a pleasant pub.

Peach drained his glass.

'Another?' the landlord said.

'No, I don't think so.'

'It's on me.'

Peach hesitated. 'I really ought to be getting on, but,' and he consulted his watch, 'well, all right. Just a half, mind. Thank you very much.'

When he emerged from the pub some twenty minutes later, his head seemed to be floating on his neck as a ball floats on water. It was an unfamiliar though not unpleasing sensation. He paused outside a launderette and took out his notebook. *In the pool of the village*, he wrote, *you know where the water ends and the land begins. In the ocean of the world, you drift beyond the sight of any shore.* He read it through to himself and nodded several times. He was quite pleased with it. Really quite pleased. It had an oriental, no, a *universal* ring to it. Perhaps he would try it out in one of his pep-talks. He moved off down the road again. His lower lip slid in and out as he walked. He passed an Indian restaurant, a delicatessen, a vet's. Then suddenly, on the other side of the road, he saw the building that Terence, the landlord, had described. It was pink all right. It was very pink. And Peach was grateful for its pinkness. If it hadn't been so pink, he would probably have walked right past it.

He crossed the road. At last, he thought. The Bunker! He tried to peer in through one of the ground-floor windows, but he could see nothing.

Effective stuff, smoked-glass. He tested the double-doors. Locked. He wished he knew more about nightclubs: how they operated, when they opened, what the routine was. The smoked-glass windows confronted him with his own ignorance.

He stepped back to the kerb so as to get a better view of the rest of the building. On the second floor, he could see a pair of red curtains, a red lampshade hanging from the ceiling. The next floor up looked derelict: grimy windows, one pane missing. He would have assumed that the fourth floor was unoccupied too, had he not noticed a piece of black cloth covering one of the windows. He instinctively felt that this was where Moses lived. He walked round to the side of the building. Another door, also locked. Further along he found a metal gate about the width of a truck. Sharp green spikes lined the top to stop people climbing over. The padlock securing the gate was as big as his fist. He put his eye to the crack between the upper and the lower hinges. He saw a cobbled yard, a few dustbins, a stack of yellow beer-crates. Nobody had bothered to paint the back of The Bunker pink. Only the façade mattered, it seemed.

He stood back. He dismissed any thought of trying to break in. He would be running too many risks. Besides, the place looked impregnable. Especially to a man who couldn't even cut his own toenails any more. He would have to wait.

He looked round, noticed a café on the other side of the main road. Positioned directly opposite The Bunker, it commanded views of both entrances. He crossed the road and pushed the glass door open. No foreigners, he was relieved to see. Nobody at all, in fact. He took the table by the window and ordered a coffee.

The nightclub stood on the junction, flamboyant, still.

It was 12.52.

*

By 3.15 he had severe indigestion. He had eaten a sausage sandwich, a ham roll, two cheese rolls with pickle, a bowl of oxtail soup, and a slice of cheesecake, and he had drunk three cups of coffee and two cups of tea. And nothing had happened. He decided to go for a walk.

He paid the bill and left the café. The door jangled shut behind him. He set off down the road. He resisted the urge to glance back over his shoulder at the pink building. A truck slammed past him, flinging his shirt against his back. He followed the curve of a high brick wall and Kennington Park came into view. A nylon banner slung between two oak trees announced the opening of a fun-fair that evening. He crossed the road to investigate.

A green generator hummed in the north-east corner of the park. Long red trucks huddled under the dusty foliage. He picked his way through fierce pieces of machinery. They lay about in the grass, dismembered, sticky with grease. Parts of something called an Octopus, apparently. He couldn't imagine how they would look when assembled. Men with hands like wrenches were tightening nuts and bolts, shouting to each other in accents he could hardly understand. He moved through smells of beer and oil and sweat. Disco music crashed out of a gaudy wooden cabin at the foot of the Big Wheel. He winced. A man in fraying denims, hair tied back in a ponytail, gave him a hard still look as he passed – a look that seemed to freeze time and silence the music. Peach avoided the man's eyes. He didn't want any trouble. Leaving the clutter, the noise, the knots of fascinated boys behind, he wandered off across the grass.

The next half-hour passed uneventfully. He watched a woman push a crying child on a swing. The higher the child went, the more it cried. The woman looked away, smoking. Two black youths loped past in track-suits. They shouted something at him, but again he didn't understand. It would take a lifetime, and he only had twenty-four hours. He saw a man asleep on a bench, a pair of training-shoes for a pillow, a scar on his bald head like the lace on a football. Mostly there was nothing to look at. It was a drab park, and that beer he had drunk at lunch-time had taken the edge off things.

Then the nightclub slid into his mind – pink, triangular, a vessel carrying a cargo of mysteries – and he imagined the black cloth parting and a face appearing at the window. While he walked aimlessly in the park, the young man whose face he didn't know left by the side-door. Slipped the net. Escaped again. Time to get back, he thought. And almost ran back up the main road.

But nothing had changed. The black cloth hanging in the fourth-floor window as before. The same cars parked on the street outside. He walked into the café and sat down at his table.

The owner shuffled over in carpet-slippers. 'Twice in one day,' he said. 'You must really like it here.' He let out a dry sarcastic chuckle.

Peach ignored him. He ordered lasagne, a side salad, vanilla ice-cream, and a cup of black coffee. 'And make it slow,' he said.

'And what?'

'And make it slow.'

The man backed away, scratching his head.

He returned half an hour later. 'Slow enough for you?'

Peach nodded.

His lasagne stood on its plate like the model of a block of flats. The salad? A few dog-eared leaves of lettuce and a pile of carrot-shavings. He ate with no appetite, one eye on the window. He sometimes paused for minutes between mouthfuls. He was beginning to hate the pink building. He knew it off by heart, in minute detail, from the fringe of yellow weeds on the roof to the Y-shaped crack beneath one of the ground-floor windows. The pink façade had burned itself into his subconscious and would recur on sleepless nights. His eyes itched with the pinkness of it. He never wanted to look at anything pink again. Never.

Then it was 6.56. A black Rover – a Rover 90, registration PYX 520 – turned into the street that ran down the left-hand side of The Bunker. It parked. The door on the driver's side opened. A man got out. Early to middle twenties. Leather jacket. White T-shirt. Black jeans. Tall. 6′5″, 6′6″. Big too. 220 lbs, perhaps. Maybe more. The man was alone.

Peach had long since stopped eating. His two scoops of vanilla ice-cream subsided in their clear glass bowl. He watched the young man cross the pavement, unlock the black side-door, and vanish into the building. A minute or two later a hand parted the black cloth in the fourth-floor window. Peach's lower lip slid out and back. Once.

While his eyes were scouring the top of the building for further developments, a white Mercedes drew up on the street below. A West Indian climbed out. *Coloured chap. Bit shady by all accounts.* Could this be the owner?

The West Indian looked right and left as he locked the car door. A routine scan. Then he turned and walked towards The Bunker, lifting his shoulders a couple times, dropping his chin, the moves a boxer makes as he approaches the ring. He opened the double-doors and disappeared inside. Lights came on in a second-floor window. The owner, then.

Peach stirred the thick puddle his ice-cream had become. Part of him wanted to believe, despite all the evidence to the contrary, that Moses Highness had drowned in the river, that nobody had ever escaped from the village, that the hundred per cent record was still intact. But now he had proof of his suspicions – the proof that he had, in a way, been dreading. The young man in the leather jacket was no carbon-copy of George Highness – they shared certain basic characteristics: above-average height, similar hair-colour – and yet Peach knew he had seen Moses. It shook him. To know, after twenty-four years, that the baby had survived, escaped, grown up. *In the outside world.* Anathema to Peach. Anathema and nightmare. He stirred and stirred at his ice-cream. The man in the carpet-slippers asked him if he had finished. 'No,' he said.

He had seen what he had come to see and yet he couldn't leave. Some part of him still needed convincing. He had made inroads. He felt he understood the territory now. He might almost have been on home ground. And he had time to spare. So he waited.

After about fifteen minutes the double-doors swung open again. The West Indian appeared. He wore a dark suit (black? navy? maroon? from this distance it was difficult to tell) and a white tie. He lit a cigarette with a gold lighter and leaned against the wall. He smoked. His head moved, following cars, but he didn't seem to be waiting for anybody, just passing the time of day. He flicked his cigarette into the road. A shower of sparks.

The black curtain still open on the fourth floor. The light still on.

Dusk came down. Lights in the café now.

Peach suddenly realised how visible he was. A fat man in a lit window. His watching had become conspicuous. He should leave. Move closer. Adopt a more strategic position.

As he paid the bill he noticed the weight of the case in his hand. An inconvenience. Removing his diary and his binoculars, he asked the owner of the café if he would mind looking after the case, just for half an hour or so. The owner said he closed at nine. 'Fine,' Peach said.

Outside the café he paused just to one side of the window and hung his binoculars round his neck. When the West Indian was looking the other way, he walked off down the road. He crossed about two hundred yards below the nightclub and began to work his way back. Facing the nightclub, on the same side of the road, stood a fish and chip shop. Wood-veneer tables, red plastic chairs with spindly black legs, white neon lighting that showed every crease and vein in your face. No cover there. But just this side of the fish and chip shop window, Peach found a garage doorway. A low brick wall reaching out across the pavement hid him from the waist down. Shadow did the rest.

He now stood less than forty feet from the West Indian. Even without his binoculars, he could see the built-up heels of the man's boots. He could also see the side-door of the nightclub – Moses's front door, in effect. It was ideal.

He checked his watch. Exactly 7.30.

He took his diary out and turned to the page where he had jotted down the times of trains. Trains left Victoria for Haywards Heath at twenty-three minutes past the hour. He had to connect with the local train which would take him to within eight miles of New Egypt. The last local train left Haywards Heath at 10.35. If he caught the 9.23 from Victoria, he would get into Haywards Heath at 10.16. The 9.23, then, was the last train he could catch. A taxi to Victoria would take half an hour, perhaps less.

That left him with just under an hour and a half. It ought to be enough. It would have to be.

Twenty minutes passed.

Then the black door opened and Moses appeared. He had changed into a dark suit. Light slid off his wet hair. As he started towards his car, the West Indian called out. Moses paused, turned, walked over. The two men seemed to know each other well. They compared jackets and ties, pushed each other around. They both tilted their heads back when they laughed. They lit cigarettes, and smoke poured from their fingers like slow water. The damaged neon sign above their heads − FLOR AN'S − lit them both in the sharpest detail.

Peach raised his binoculars and focused on Moses. Neither the eyes (hooded, grey) nor the nose (long, slightly crooked) seemed familiar. The mouth, though. The smile that kept forming there. A smile he had seen too often in the past. It belonged to George Highness. The son had inherited his father's smile.

Now the two men were separating. But when Moses had almost reached his car, he turned, ran back, embraced, smothered, all but crushed the West Indian. Peach lowered his binoculars. Curious behaviour.

Moses returned to his car. He got in, slammed the door. He turned the ignition and the Rover fired first time, engine shuddering. He roared away in a cloud of blue exhaust. Two blasts on the horn. The West Indian shook his head. He straightened his clothes, retouched his hair. Then he settled back against the wall and lit another cigarette. He seemed to be smiling to himself.

And there Peach should have left it, he realised afterwards. That smile had clinched it. No question as to the young man's identity now. And yet he couldn't tear himself away. He still had an hour or so and he wanted to exploit this opportunity to the full. After all, he wouldn't have another. He left the shadows and crossed the side-street. He walked up to the West Indian.

'Nice evening,' he said.

The West Indian flicked his cigarette into the gutter. He dusted his jacket with a casual right hand. When he said, 'Yeah,' he was looking not at Peach but at his own lapel.

Peach slid his hands into his pockets, leaned back on his heels. 'I thought you might be able to help me.'

The West Indian looked along his cheekbones at Peach. 'Don't know about that.'

Peach studied the tight black curls on the man's head, sparkling and dense, he looked into the slightly yellow whites of his eyes, he noted the hint of red in the pigmentation of his skin, he saw his lips, ridged like shells, peel back to reveal gums that were pink and grey. Perhaps he stared just a fraction too long, or just a fraction too closely.

'What're *you* looking at?' The gap between the West Indian's two front teeth looked dangerous. Like the barrel of a gun.

'I'm looking for a friend of mine,' Peach began. 'His name is Moses. Do you know him?'

'Who are you?'

'Me?' jocular now, 'I'm an old friend of the family.'

The West Indian's top lip rolled back over his teeth. He glanced down at his hand. It curled, uncurled, against his thigh.

'You know what I smell?' he said.

'No.'

'Pig.' The West Indian smiled into Peach's eyes. 'I smell pig.'

Peach didn't understand. Not right away.

'And that's not a smell I particularly like, you know?'

Peach could feel the evidence, his badge, cold and heavy in his shirt pocket. Still he insisted: 'I'm a friend of the family, that's all.'

'Yeah,' said the West Indian, pointing at the binoculars, 'and those are for birdwatching.'

'Moses lives here,' Peach said, 'doesn't he?'

The West Indian lit another cigarette. Dunhill King Size. New York Paris London. The gold lighter snapped shut. 'Does he?'

'I'm asking you.'

'I should clear off if I was you.'

'Listen,' Peach said, 'I'm not being unreasonable. All I want to know is if Moses lives here or not.'

'You heard what I said.'

'Just tell me,' Peach said. He was sounding, he realised, less and less like an old friend of the family and more and more like a policeman. Only a policeman would persist like this. And the West Indian knew it.

'If you don't fuck off right now,' the West Indian said, 'I'm going to have to mess up that nice fat face of yours – '

Peach hit him hard in the solar plexus. It was a precision punch. It came out of nowhere. It even surprised Peach. He hadn't hit anybody for five years. The West Indian went down gasping.

Peach looked round for a taxi. There weren't any. He swore viciously. He only had a few seconds before the West Indian was up again and pulling a knife on him or something. He hastened off down the road. When he was fifty yards away he turned and saw the West Indian climbing to his feet. Peach began to run. In his youth he had been an exceptional dancer.

He and Hilda had won the New Egypt Dancing Trophy six years in a row. The rumba, the polka, the foxtrot – they had mastered them all. And even now, at the age of seventy-two, he could still show a remarkable lightness of foot.

As he rounded the curve in the road he heard uncanny jangling music. Not one music, but many, all mixed up, mingling. The lights of the fun-fair came into view.

The fun-fair. Crowds. Safety in numbers.

He crossed the main road and plunged into the park.

Saturday night. It was packed. Children brandished candy-floss and balloons. Strings of naked light-bulbs looped from tree to tree. The Big Wheel soared overhead. A girl's shoe landed with a slap at his feet, the strap still fastened. He looked up. Hair flew. Screams. The glint of teeth. He pushed on into the crowd.

He stopped outside a yellow tent. A crude picture of a dwarf in a jester's cap and bells had been painted on to the canvas. Bold red letters bellowed: THE WORLD'S SMALLEST MAN! ONLY THREE FEET TALL! THE MOST AMAZING AND UNIQUE EXPERIENCE! BRING A MAGNIFYING GLASS! Somewhere to hide while he got his breath back, collected his thoughts. He paid his 50p and ducked under the canvas flap.

The world's smallest man was watching *Star Trek* on TV. He was sitting in his own specially constructed lounge. All the furniture and fittings had been built to scale: a miniature sofa, a miniature lamp, a miniature clock – even the TV was miniature. Nothing separated him from his visitors – no bars, no sheets of toughened glass – and yet he didn't seem to be aware of them. He sat in his miniature armchair with his legs crossed, watched his programme on his miniature TV, and drank from a miniature tea-cup which he replaced, gently and precisely, on its miniature saucer after each mouthful.

For a moment Peach lost touch with his surroundings. Staring down at this little man (he really was *very* small), he felt neither shock nor pity, only a kind of recognition. The world's smallest man must, from time to time, have thought about escape. Perhaps he had even succeeded in escaping. But then, Peach's fantasy ran on, he found himself in a world in which he had no place. A world that overlooked him, trampled him. A world that couldn't help mistreating him because it was so big and he was so small. So he returned to his yellow tent and his miniature lounge. It wasn't exactly private, but if he concentrated he could imagine that he was alone. He could train himself to ignore those prying eyes, those personal remarks. It was a life.

Peach checked his watch. 8.24. If he wasn't in a taxi in twenty minutes he'd be done for. He used a buxom middle-aged couple to cover his exit from the tent and darted into the shadows beside the rifle-range. He saw the West Indian standing on the steps of the merry-go-round, white tie loosened, hands on hips, eyes scanning faces. He shrank against the damp green canvas. The *whang!* of pellets hitting metal ducks resounded in his ears. Sweat registered on his body as a series of cold patches.

He peered out again, watched the West Indian pass his fingertips almost absent-mindedly across his stomach. He smiled from his hiding-place. It had been a textbook punch. Nine inches. Pure Joe Louis. And fast, so fast the West Indian hadn't even seen it coming. Not bad for an old man.

He began to work his way round the back of the rifle-range towards the road. As if on a parallel track, the West Indian also moved north. The next time Peach looked for him, he saw him leaning against a yellow fence, his scowling face switched on and off by sparks from the dodgems. A second man stood next to him. This second man wore a parka adorned with various military insignia. He must have been seven feet tall. His face a wasteland and cold, so cold, despite the light bleeding from a string of red bulbs above his head. Peach shivered.

8.47.

Only fifty yards now separated him from the metal fence. Beyond the fence, the road. He waited for the two men to turn away, then he lowered his head and ran. The music, the screaming, the gunfire, dwindled. He heard only the rasp of his own breathing as he struggled through the clutter of machinery and cables. Trees added to the confusion. Once he gashed his shin on the jagged head of a tent-peg, but he didn't falter. He scaled the fence, cleared the pavement, teetered on the kerb. A truck lurched forwards with a vicious hiss as its air-brakes eased. He saw a yellow light and waved frantically. He didn't dare look round.

The taxi curved towards him through the traffic. He scrambled in and slammed the door. 'Victoria,' he gasped. 'Quick.'

The driver accelerated away. 'In a hurry, are we?'

8.58.

The taxi turned north at the traffic lights, and Peach glanced behind him for the first time. No sign of the giant or the West Indian. He leaned back against the seat. His leg hurt. He could feel the blood trickling down into his sock.

Orange lights splashed over his face. 'Never again,' he murmured. 'Never again.'

He wound the window down.

Air.

Every time the taxi stopped at a set of traffic lights, the driver pulled out a harmonica and began to play tunes that Peach remembered from the thirties and forties. Peach was suddenly overwhelmed by the sense of being somewhere strange, somewhere foreign yet magical, somewhere utterly incongruous. In his exhaustion he had become a tourist.

The driver caught his eye in the rear-view mirror. 'Don't mind, do you, guv?'

'Not at all,' Peach said. 'It's delightful. Very soothing.'

'*Soothing?*' The driver squinted over his shoulder. 'First time anyone's ever called it that.'

They both laughed.

The taxi rattled up on to the dreary skeleton of Vauxhall Bridge. It was only then that Peach realised he had left his case in that café on Kennington Road.

*

9.09.

Too late to turn round and go back. Too late, too dangerous. He took a swift inventory of the contents. Pyjamas, washing-bag, *A–Z*, a Thermos flask, one stale ham sandwich. Nothing that couldn't be replaced. And, more to the point, nothing that betrayed his identity. After all, it could easily fall into the wrong hands (the West Indian's, for instance). Thank God he had transferred his diary to his jacket pocket.

The taxi pulled up in front of Victoria Station at 9.21. Peach handed the driver a handsome tip.

'That's for getting me here on time,' he said, 'and for the music.' And for saving my life, he added silently.

'Cheers, guv.' The driver leaned across and looked up at Peach. Light skated off the thick lenses of his glasses. His teeth angled back into his mouth like a shark's. 'You ought to slow down a bit, man your age. You'll kill yourself. Take my word for it.'

Peach promised to take things easier in the future. It was a promise he intended to keep.

He caught the train with two minutes to spare.

He shared the carriage with a soldier, unshaven, hollow-cheeked, smoking. Just the two of them. Saturday night, Peach remembered. Not many people left the city on Saturday night.

The train shifted tracks on its way out of the station. A sound like knives being ground. Once over the bridge it gathered speed, shedding the lights of the city the way a meteor sheds sparks. The soldier slept, using his kit-bag as a pillow.

At Haywards Heath Peach climbed out. He had to wait twenty-five minutes on the draughty platform.

He sat on a bench and gazed at the initials, the messages, the obscenities, that had been carved into the thick green paint.

He stared into the darkness where the silver rails met. Sometimes the coloured lights of the fun-fair whirled through his mind like bright cars in a nightmare.

The local train stopped at every station on the line. This time he was alone in the carriage.

At 11.22 he handed his ticket to a yawning guard and walked down a long flight of wooden steps to the car-park. A breeze lifted and dropped the leaves of a tree, and he thought of the girl with the blonde hair. His bicycle lay where he had left it. He hauled it back up the mud bank, a twig twanging in the spokes. He switched on the front and rear lights, swung himself on to the saddle, and rode away.

Trees built a dark cathedral over the road. The moon slid out from behind a cloud and the gaps between branches turned into windows. Hedges rustled like a priest's vestments. Birds mumbled in the undergrowth. The air was cool, peaceful, sharp with sap. Peach pedalled slowly, his left leg aching. It was almost as if the day had never happened. He was conscious of moving from a garish dream into calm familiar reality.

He approached the village from the south-west. He caught a glimpse of the lights of Bunt across the fields to the right. He passed the phone-box the brigadier had used in 1945 after Tommy Dane's bomb blew up. Shortly after crossing the boundary into New Egypt he was blinded by the beam of a torch.

'Oh, sorry, Chief Inspector,' came a woman's voice. 'I didn't realise it was you.'

When his eyes readjusted Peach recognised PC Wilmott and, behind her, helmet askew, the excitable Marlpit.

'Not at all,' he said, dismounting, 'not at all. Very glad to see you operating with such efficiency at this time of night.'

Wilmott, a modest woman, ducked her head. Marlpit sucked in a string of saliva.

Peach smiled down. 'Anything to report?'

'Nothing, sir.' Wilmott tilted the shallow dish of her face so that it filled with moonlight. 'A very quiet night.'

Peach inhaled a deep lungful of village air. 'A glorious night too, if I may say so.'

The two constables murmured their agreement.

'Well,' and Peach climbed astride his bicycle, 'I should be off home.

Mrs Peach will be getting worried, no doubt.' He smiled again. 'Good night to you both.'

'Good night,' the constables chorused.

Peach had hoped to slip back into the village unseen, but now he thought about it he realised it really didn't matter. As Chief Inspector he was above the law, beyond suspicion. He explained his movements to no one. Like God he moved in mysterious ways. There were any number of reasons why he might have been riding a bicycle along the boundary at midnight. He might have been putting in a surprise appearance, as generals do, to boost morale. He might have been testing the alertness of his night patrols. He might simply have been taking the air. Rather pleased with his improvisations, he rode on into New Egypt. He forked right at the village green and in less than five minutes he was opening the front door of the old vicarage.

'Hilda, I'm home.'

There was no reply.

'Hilda?'

He walked into the lounge and found his wife asleep in front of a flickering television. He rested a hand on her shoulder. 'I'm back.'

Hilda's eyelids slid upwards as if she had only pretended to be dozing. 'I was worried about you,' she said.

'There's nothing to worry about.'

'But your trousers – '

He glanced down. His trouser-leg had torn just below the knee. Blood had soaked through. 'Oh, yes. I fell off my bicycle. Stupid of me.' He looked appropriately sheepish.

'Oh, John. But how did everything go?'

'Very well. Very well indeed, actually. I'm feeling rather tired, though.'

'Poor dear. I don't know why you take it into your head to do these things. It's quite unnecessary, I'm sure. And you know it only exhausts you.' In humouring her husband without ever quite understanding him, in her light-hearted approach to his incomprehensibility, in her ignorance, Hilda sometimes touched on the truth.

He smiled down at her. He wished he could describe his adventures to her – the cafés and hotels, the trains, the famous buildings. He wished he could tell her about Madame Zola, the world's smallest man, the Asian boy, the blonde girl (on second thoughts, no, not the blonde girl), Terence the landlord, the black nightclub-owner and his seven-foot sidekick. But these were stories he could share with no one. Not even his wife.

'You're right,' he sighed. 'I'm going to have a hot bath and go straight to bed.'

PEACH INCOGNITO (1980)

He kissed the top of her head where the grey curls were beginning to wear thin, then limped across the room, pausing by the door to say, 'It's nice to be home, dear.'

INJURY TIME

The shot orange of the street-lamps bled through the fog, stained the rain on the pavement, died in the white neon arms that reached out from the nightclub as Moses walked up, but the size of the man blocking the open doorway was no trick of the light. The man had rolled the sleeves of his white shirt back to his elbows, and skulls and anacondas tangled on his forearms. Moses had never seen such big tattoos, mainly because he had never seen such big arms. And the face. Its swollen pallor stopped him cold. The man had drinker's eyelids, puffy and hard, as if pumped full of silicon; they reduced the eyes beneath to mean glittery slits. His hair, scraped back from his forehead, slithered down over his collar in dark greasy coils. His sideburns bristled like wire wool. A giant gold hoop earring about three inches in diameter swung from his left ear. It was his one visible affectation. Moses thought it very unlikely that anyone had ever teased him about his earring. He knew from his own experience that big people sometimes get picked on by smaller people who want to prove something, but big was too small a word for this man, and nobody in their right mind would have picked on him. He was so big that there wasn't a word big enough to describe how big he was. So when he told Moses to hold it, Moses held it.

'I'm,' he gulped, 'I'm looking for Elliot. I'm a friend of his. I live up there.'

He pointed to his kitchen window on the fourth floor, but the man just stared at his hand.

Disconcerting.

After a long moment, the man's stare shifted from his hand to his face. So heavy, this stare, that it almost had to be winched. Then the massive head tipped sideways and he bellowed, 'Mr Frazer?'

So that was Elliot's surname. Probably an alias, though, knowing (not knowing) Elliot. Elliot appeared in the doorway. His head barely reached the man's shoulder.

'Can I see you about something?' Moses asked.

'It's all right, Ridley,' Elliot said. Then, to Moses, 'I've fired Belsen. This is his replacement, Ridley. Ridley, meet Moses.'

Ridley nodded.

Moses did likewise, glad to get out of shaking hands. He had already taken a look at Ridley's hands. They were chipped and grazed and scarred, and every scar told the story of someone else's pain.

'What's he doing here?' he whispered, as he climbed the stairs behind Elliot.

Elliot looked cryptic. 'We've been getting phone-calls. That's what he's doing here.'

'A kind of receptionist?' Moses ventured.

Elliot didn't laugh. 'You could say that.'

He sat down in his red chair, propped his feet on the desk, and lit a cigarette. He didn't usually come in on Mondays, but Moses had seen the white Mercedes float into the mist below his window. Signs of stress littered the office: screwed-up paper on the floor, an almost empty bottle of brandy by the phone, a crowd of Dunhill butts wedged upright in the ashtray like people in a Hong Kong swimming-pool.

'What are these phone-calls then?' Moses asked.

Elliot flicked ash, ran his tongue along his teeth; for a moment, Moses thought he wasn't going to answer. 'Bad phone-calls,' he said eventually. 'Old ghosts from the past, you know?'

'I thought you didn't believe in ghosts.'

'Yeah, well,' and Elliot allowed himself a wry grin, 'these ones I believe in.'

Moses crossed the room and fitted his cigarette into the ashtray. On his way back to the sofa his foot caught a pool-cue that had been resting against the wall. The cue clattered to the floor.

A door opened somewhere downstairs.

'Everything all right up there, Mr Frazer?' The voice was huge and violent and had tattoos all over it.

Moses stooped, clipped the cue into its wooden wall-rack, and stood back.

'Everything's fine,' Elliot called out. He looked across at Moses and almost grinned for the first time that evening. 'That's what he's doing here,' he said.

He stood up, stretched, strolled over to the pool-table. 'James Ridley. He was a wrestler for a while. Had to stop. Killed someone, apparently.'

'I believe that,' Moses said.

'They used to call him The Human Mangle.' Elliot bounced the white ball on his palm, then sent it rolling up the table. 'He used to sort of tear people apart and scatter the pieces around. That's what I heard. Fancy a game?'

Moses began to set the balls up. 'Could be you've got the right man for the job, Elliot.'

'Yeah, could be.' Elliot emptied the remains of the brandy into two tumblers. 'You were going to ask me something.'

Moses broke first and put a stripe down. As he played he told Elliot about Gloria: who she'd worked with, where she'd sung, and so on.

Elliot interrupted him. 'I know what's coming.'

'Well?' Moses said. 'Could it be arranged, do you think?'

'Leave it with me.'

When Moses walked downstairs an hour later he heard whistling. Clear repeating notes that seemed to reach from the past and expect no reply. Like a prehistoric bird, perhaps. Something exotic, no longer alive. He passed Ridley on the way out.

'That whistling,' he said. 'Did you hear it?'

Ridley tilted the great rock of his face at Moses. 'Yeah. It was me.'

His words weighed more than other people's. Boulders crashing down a mountain-side. Moses in their path.

Moses framed a silent oh and hurried away. Ridley could whistle like the ghost of a bird long since extinct and tear people into pieces as if they were paper. Ridley was dangerous. Very dangerous.

Definitely the right man for the job.

*

Moses woke to the sound of cheerful men delivering beer. He loved the clanking the metal barrels made as they rolled across the cobbled yard below. Sometimes the men whistled (tuneless whistling, nothing like Ridley's), sometimes they cracked jokes. This morning he could hear them swearing at each other. Short pungent phrases rose into the air like the smell of fresh bread.

From his bed he could see his new red telephone, installed by Elliot 'for security reasons', and the previous night he had received his first incoming call. From Gloria, appropriately enough. She had invited him to a drinks party at her parents' place in Hampstead. Seven o'clock, she said. It was a long time since he had been to a drinks party (and he had never been to a drinks party in Hampstead), so he was looking forward to the evening.

He eased out of bed and leaned on the windowsill. The north side of the building stood in cool shadow. In the distance the Houses of Parliament lay wrapped in a blue haze like presents that were no fun because you could guess what was inside. It was going to be a hot day. One of those days when the city smells of dusty vegetation, when the roads glitter with the chrome and glass of passing cars, when businessmen sling their jackets casually over their shoulders and secretaries lie on the grass in public parks. He moved towards the kitchen. He lit the gas and put the kettle on. Then he walked into the bathroom. A warm breeze drifted through the open window, tickled the hair under his arms, dropped a cellophane wrapper on the floor. He smeared his face with shaving-foam and reached for a razor.

And it was then that the pigeon landed on the window-ledge.

It immediately began to strut up and down as if it owned the place. Maybe it had once. Maybe it was one of the pigeons he had thrown out in April. Or maybe it was some kind of tourist pigeon who had got wind of that event and flown down from Trafalgar Square to do a bit of sightseeing. A snarl twisted his foam-bearded face. He put down the razor and picked up a bar of soap. He flung it at the pigeon. The soap grew wings and flew out of the window. The pigeon seemed to smile. Conspiracy of pigeon and soap.

'Bird,' he shouted. 'Bird, I need you.'

But Bird was probably far away. Sometimes he disappeared for weeks at a time. He was a free agent, no strings attached. He knew the city from rooftop to sewer, he knew its ins and outs, its ups and downs, he knew its fire-escapes, its skylights, its manholes. He stalked flocks of scavengers on the mud banks of the river, he raided the plush dustbins of Kensington and Chelsea, he slept in the warm air-vents of the West End. He would return with his ear torn and bleeding or a seagull's wing wedged between his blunt jaws, and Moses loved him for his nonchalance, his self-sufficiency. Yes, Bird was probably far, far away. Moses would have to deal with this alone.

He reached for the scrubbing-brush. Took careful aim. Let fly.

An explosion, a splash. The pigeon nodded, chuckled, casually took wing. A triangle of glass lay on the floor, reflecting the window it had once belonged to. The scrubbing-brush floated serenely in the toilet-bowl.

Moses examined the window. Only one pane broken. Well, he muttered to himself, at least it's summer, and began to sweep up the glass. He wondered whether he could get Jackson to invent some kind of pigeon deterrent, something that would blast the fuck out of them once and for all. He smiled as he finished shaving, dreaming of pigeon carnage.

The kettle boiled and he poured the water into his cracked brown pot. While he waited for the tea to brew, he went over to the phone. It was around ten. If he phoned Vince now, he might just catch him before he got out of his head. Vince didn't waste much time. Especially at weekends. He dialled the number. Somebody groaned at the other end.

'Vince,' Moses cried. 'It's a beautiful day.'

'You bastard.'

Moses smiled. Even Vince's language seemed benign this morning.

'Vince, part those filthy bits of cloth you call curtains and feel the sun beating on your face.'

'I'll give you beating on your face, you cunt. You woke me up.'
Oh, sacrilege.
'But Vince, you have to smell the morning air.'
'Fuck the morning air.'
'Well, all right. I just thought we could go out for a drink, that's all.'
'Where?'
Give Vince credit. He could sort the wood out from the trees.
'That pub next to you,' Moses said.
'About twelve, OK?'
'Yeah, but Vince, why don't – '
'If you say another word about the weather, I'm going to bloody kill you.'

Moses smiled again. Vince's threats were always idle. Now if that had come from James 'The Human Mangle' Ridley –

*

Vince was already standing outside the pub when Moses turned up a few minutes after midday. Both Vince's arms were bandaged from the base of his fingers to the crook of his elbow. He was struggling to light a cigarette. Eddie lounged against a nearby wall. He was wearing a three-piece suit and a pair of sunglasses. He was doing nothing to help. When he saw Moses he pointed to a bottle of Pils on the table.

'I got you a drink.'

'Cheers, Eddie.' Moses's throat was dry and he swallowed half the bottle before he put it down. He looked round for the inevitable girl. 'Not alone, surely?'

Eddie nodded, lit a Rothman's. Moses raised an eyebrow. They both drank.

'Nice suit,' Moses said.

'I'm working today,' Eddie explained. 'Got to be back by three.'

'That's rough.' Moses jerked his head in Vince's direction. 'What happened to him?'

'Usual story.' Eddie flicked ash. 'He got into a fight with a couple of windows.'

Moses sighed.

Vince moved closer, held his arms out for inspection. His fingers shook. They were stained bright yellow from the iodine. Blood had dried under his nails and embedded itself in the criss-cross creases on his knuckles.

'Did it hurt?' Moses asked.

'No,' Vince said. 'Glass doesn't hurt.'

Moses hadn't realised that.

'Not until afterwards,' Vince added, on reflection.

They laughed at that. Acts of self-destruction seemed to mellow Vince out. Afterwards he became tolerable, almost human. For a few days, anyway.

'I had to take him to the hospital,' Eddie said. 'It was two nights ago. I got back from Soho about half three. Cab dropped me off. When I walked up to the front door I saw it was open. Thought I'd been broken into. I went in and turned the light on. Everything looked normal. TV was still there. Nothing missing at all. Then I went into the bedroom. Vince was lying on my bed. Blood everywhere.'

Vince grinned at the ground. He was nodding as if to say, Yeah, it's all true.

'He was a right fucking mess. Out of his head completely. Skin hanging off his arms in flaps. I had to phone a cab, take him to St Stephen's. Didn't want him bleeding to death in my flat.'

'How did he get in?' Moses asked.

'I bust the door down,' Vince said.

'I'm going to get one of those metal doors,' Eddie said. 'You know, like they have in New York. Next time he's going to have to find somewhere else to bleed.'

'I'll smash the window,' Vince said.

Eddie gave him a steady look. 'I'll move.'

'I'll find you.'

'I'll move so far away you'll bleed to death before you get there.' Eddie smiled and went inside to buy another round. The drinks were on expenses, he had already told them.

Moses looked Vince over, sighed again.

'All this is mine,' Vince said. He pointed at the ground. The pavement around his feet was spattered with drops of blood, all the same shape but all different sizes, like money or rain. Some of them still looked fresh, a rich red; others had dried in the sun, turned black.

'You must've been here a while,' Moses said, bending down. 'Some of this blood's dry already.'

Vince grinned. 'Sherlock fucking Moses. I was here last night.'

Moses straightened up again. 'How many stitches did they give you?'

'That's nineteenth-century stuff. They don't use stitches any more. They use tape.'

'Tape?'

'They tape the flaps of skin together. It's better than stitches. Doesn't leave a scar.'

Vince liked to be thought of as an authority. He took a pride in knowing things that most people weren't fucked up enough to know. He was like a veteran returning from a war that nobody had ever heard of. He told stories of action he had seen, he showed off his wounds, but if you asked the wrong questions he retreated into sullen silence. With Vince there was always some kind of war going on. Whenever he got angry or depressed, bored even, he would hit himself with some lethal mix of drugs and alcohol, and then he would go out and try and beat shit out of a brick wall or a truck or a football crowd, anything so long as the odds were impossible. He always came off worst, he always suffered. His wars were all lost wars. But he never surrendered. That was where the pride came in.

Eddie returned with the drinks. He had taken his sunglasses off, and Moses now saw the swelling around Eddie's left eye. The skin had a singed look: yellow shading into brown.

'Christ,' Moses said. 'Not you as well.'

Eddie put his sunglasses back on. 'Somebody hit me.'

'Why?'

'He thought I was stealing his wife.'

'And you weren't?'

'I was just talking to her.'

'Just talking to her,' Moses scoffed. Eddie never *just talked* to women.

'All right, she read my palm.'

'The love-line,' Vince leered from the shadows.

'So you were holding hands,' Moses said. 'What else?'

'She asked me to dance.'

'How could you refuse?' Vince said.

'So we danced. I tried to, you know, maintain the proper distance, but – '

Moses snorted.

' – but she held me close.'

'And her husband didn't like it,' Moses said.

Eddie sighed. 'Her husband was a rugby player.'

Smiles all round. The conversation drifted, becalmed in the heat, the stillness outside the pub. At quarter to three Eddie said he had to go. 'What are you two going to do?'

'Drink,' Vince said. 'You got any money, Moses?'

Moses swapped a look with Eddie.

'Just asking,' Vince added quickly, but not quickly enough.

He had just taken Moses and Eddie back to an afternoon about a year before. In Moses's memory it felt like a Sunday. They had been at a party all night. They had slept late, got up wasted. Bleak windows, grey faces.

A pall hanging over everything. Intermission, Moses called it. One thing's over and the next thing hasn't started yet. So you wait, smoke, don't talk much. Greyness invading, the tap of rain.

Shifting Vince's coat, Moses noticed a name-tag sewn on to the collar. Vincent O. Brown, the red cotton handwriting said.

'Vincent O. Brown.' Moses's voice broke a silence of several minutes. 'Any guesses as to what the O might stand for?'

No response.

'What about Organ?' he said.

'Offal,' Eddie suggested from his armchair.

'You two can fuck right off,' Vince said.

'Oedipus.' Alison joined in, drawing on her personal experience of Vince, it seemed.

Vince slung a cushion at her. 'That goes for you too.'

She ducked and said, 'Ovary.'

The room suddenly came alive.

'Orifice.'

'Oswald.'

'Olive.'

'Orgasm.'

'Oaf.'

'Object.'

'That's *enough*,' Vince screamed.

'Hey,' Moses said. 'What about Onassis?'

Everybody started shaking with uncontrollable laughter. Vince was always complaining about how poor he was. In pubs he could never afford a drink, so people always had to pay for him. In restaurants he never ordered anything; he just waited until people had finished, then devoured their leftovers. He sponged compulsively, especially from Eddie. Skint was his favourite word. Broke came a close second. Onassis was the perfect name for him.

'You *bastards*,' Vince shrieked. He stood in the middle of the room, teeth clenched, knuckles white, then whirled round and stormed out, slamming the door behind him.

For a month or two he got real hell. Talk about taking the piss. The name really took off. Everybody began to call him Onassis, even people who hardly knew him. When he was hungry, they took him to Greek restaurants. When they dropped in to see him they did that ridiculous Zorba dance as they came through the door. They even dragged him off to see *The Greek Tycoon* (Anthony Quinn played Vince), lashing him to the seat so he couldn't leave until it was over.

One evening they went out for a meal together – Eddie, Moses, Vince and Alison – and Vince, drunk again, started smashing plates.

'Vince, this is an *Indian* restaurant,' Alison gently reminded him.

Vince didn't hesitate. 'When you're Onassis,' he declared, 'all restaurants are Greek.' He carried on smashing plates until they were all thrown out.

Then, just as Vince was becoming accustomed to his new role, even beginning to enjoy it, they dropped the name completely. Vince went from being Onassis to being anonymous again. All restaurants were no longer Greek. Alison stopped calling herself Jackie. Vince sulked for weeks, but ever since that time he had been very careful to avoid any allusions to money.

A Capri took the curve outside the pub too fast, bumped the kerb, then swerved away, tyres spinning, in the direction of World's End.

'Arsehole,' someone jeered.

Moses turned back to Vince and Eddie.

'Look,' Vince was saying, holding out his bandaged arms, his fingers curling up, 'I really *haven't* got any money. I spent it all on drugs.'

'Tightwad,' Eddie said. 'Skinflint.' He signalled a passing cab and climbed in. He wound the window down and leaned out, grinning. 'Bloody Greek.'

Moses watched Vince glaring at the taxi as it pulled away; Vince's fingers trembled with frustration now as well as pain. 'Don't worry about it, Vince,' he said. 'I've got a bit of money.'

Vince spat on the pavement. 'That *cunt*.'

Strange how Eddie always seemed to get under Vince's skin, Moses thought. And when Vince tried to retaliate, Eddie simply produced that smile of his, that infuriating smile which, like a joker, always won him the game. Moses could understand why Eddie got hit. What he couldn't understand was why it didn't happen more often.

'All right,' Vince said. 'You get the wine, I'll supply the drugs.'

Moses bought a two-litre bottle of Italian red from the off-licence across the road. That just about cleaned him out. Then they walked back to Vince's place.

Home for Vince, as he was fond of telling people, was the old Chelsea police station, and for once this wasn't bullshit. The building had been abandoned by the police three or four years before. Since then the pale-yellow brick façade had darkened to grey and the front door had surrendered most of its white paint to the repeated attacks of drunks from over the road. Vince shared the squat with about ten others, but he could never keep track of their names. *Turnover's too high*, he would say. Once Moses had walked into one of the rooms on the top floor and found a girl lying on a bed with her legs spread wide and a bloke slumped in the corner smoking a joint through a gas-mask. *Nutters,* Vince informed him. *From Australia.* That was all he knew. A few weeks later one of the nutters fell off the roof and died (people didn't last long in the old Chelsea police station). *Typical bloody Australians,* was Vince's only comment. He saw the death as an inconvenience: there had been investigations by the police, and he had received an eviction order as a result. He had ignored it, of course. Still, it made life difficult. He had been living in the building longer than anyone. Perhaps he was a survivor after all, Moses sometimes thought.

Vince selected a long spindly key from the bunch that he wore, like a jailer, on his belt. His fingers seemed to be shaking less, but it still took him a while to open the door. It was gloomy inside, twenty degrees cooler, and it smelt of ancient wood, greasy and dark from years of being touched and brushed against. It had the quietness of a place that wasn't used to quietness. It felt the way schools feel during the holidays. Traffic-sounds didn't penetrate. Only the clinking of Vince's keys as he slouched down the corridor and a radio muttering somewhere above.

The police had done a pretty thorough job of moving out. They had taken everything except an old grey filing-cabinet (no files inside), a few busted chairs and some posters, one of which (it described a wanted terrorist) Vince had taped to the wall over his bed. More recent tenants had left debris of a different kind: whisky-bottles coated with dust; fag-ends stamped flat; a buckled bicycle-wheel; articles of clothing with unknown histories – a pair of khaki shorts, an armless leather jacket, one blue high-heeled shoe. In the biggest room (once a lecture-hall) somebody had painted a series of pictures on the walls: a smiling cow in a lush green meadow, a funeral procession on a tropical beach, a man asleep in a wheelchair. Each picture had its own baroque gold frame, its own cir-cumflex of picture-wire, its own nail to hang on. Not real, but painted. And all with their own individual and realistic shadows, also painted. Moses had never regretted turning down Vince's offer of a room in the old Chelsea police station. If he had lived there he would probably have ended up painting pictures and frames and wire and nails and shadows too. Either that or he would have fallen off the roof. There were environments and there were environments.

Vince unlocked the door of his room and shoved it open. 'I'll get the drugs,' he said, 'then we'll go up on the roof.'

Moses waited in the doorway. Vince had masked the frosted-glass windows with off-cuts of dark-blue cloth, so the light that strained into the room was dingy, subterranean. He had few possessions. A single mattress, a ghetto-blaster, one or two books (*The Collected Works of Oscar Wilde* sprawled on his pillow), and a 2,000-piece jigsaw of one of Jackson Pollock's paintings. Pieces of the jigsaw lay scattered round the room, mingling with ashtrays, crumpled clothes, hard-drug paraphernalia and balls of dust. All the pieces looked identical: black and white with trickling yellow lines. It had been a present from Alison during happier times. *Bet you'll never finish that*, Moses remembered her saying. Vince never had – but he had never given up either. He was stubborn like that. One day that jigsaw would probably drive him mad.

Moses's eyes came to rest on the clothes rail in the corner of the room. Alison usually kept half a dozen dresses there. Now it stood empty, naked and angular, like the skeleton of some prehistoric animal. Relationship extinct.

Vince moved towards the door.

'That's everything,' he said. 'Let's go.'

*

After the coolness of the interior, the roof was like an oven door thrown open in their faces. Rows of chimney-stacks and steep slopes of grey slate trapped the heat in a flat area about twenty feet square. They sat on the low brick wall that acted as a barrier between the rooftop and a sheer drop to the courtyard sixty feet below. They took off their shirts. The smell of creosote rose into their nostrils. Moses opened the bottle. He poured the wine into two glasses that Vince had stolen from the pub across the road.

Vince produced a small white packet from the pocket of his waistcoat. One corner of his mouth curved upwards. 'Want some?'

'What is it?'

'Only sulphate.'

Moses nodded.

It was so still up there on the roof that Vince cut the stuff on the wall and not a single particle moved. Saturday afternoon clamour drifted up from the street. It sounded like music played backwards. They sat in the hot sun and waited for the bitterness to hit the back of their throats.

'Alison's left me for good this time,' Vince said suddenly, in the tone of voice you might use if you were discussing the weather or the price of cigarettes – disenchanted, but routinely so. It was unlike Vince to volunteer information of this kind, and when he did he usually spat it out, like phlegm, but this was a new Vince, a philosophical Vince.

Moses answered in a similar tone. 'I thought so.'

Vince tensed. 'How come?'

'Her clothes weren't there.'

Vince ground his cigarette out with the heel of his boot. 'Yeah, she came round the other day to pick up the rest of her things. You know what she said? She looked round the room and said, "I don't know how I could've lived here so long."'

Moses pushed a bit of air out of his mouth to show Vince that he too would have been pretty pissed off with a comment like that.

'*So long.*' Vince snorted in contempt. 'She was only here for two months. Two fucking months.'

'Actually,' Moses said, 'I'm surprised it lasted that long.'

'What're you on about?'

'Her living with you.'

'Yeah, I know, but what d'you mean surprised?'

'You and her,' Moses said. 'You didn't go together.'

A jet fighter, miles above, released a single trail of vapour. It was so straight that it looked as if it had been drawn with a ruler. It seemed to underline his words.

Vince shifted on the wall, looked over the edge. His eyes moved thoughtfully across the jumble of padlocked sheds below.

'You know what I said?' he said after a while. 'I said she'd better make bloody sure she'd got everything she wanted because she wouldn't want to come back again, not if that was the way she felt, not to this fucking hole.'

Moses couldn't help grinning. It *was* a fucking hole.

'Then she told me not to be so sarcastic.'

Moses poured them both another tumbler of wine. 'Yeah,' he said, 'I can almost hear her saying that.'

'Well,' Vince said, and reached for his rolling-papers. During the silence that followed, he built one of his specials. B-52s, he called them. Three joints in one. Malawi in the fuselage, Lebanese red in the wings. B-52s weren't lightly named. They wreaked destruction. Large-scale destruction. They wrapped people round toilet-bowls and made them wish they were dead.

Vince lit the nose and the two wingtips. He inhaled, bared his teeth, leaned back against the wall. When all three ends were burning fiercely, he passed the lethal plane to Moses with a smile. Vince was happy now. One of his greatest joys in life was making people wish they were dead.

He got up, paced round the rooftop, his badges glinting in the sun, his bandaged arms held parallel to the ground. 'Well,' he said, 'there'll be no more windows broken over Alison, that's for sure.'

Moses considered this. 'Yeah,' he said eventually. 'There've got to be better reasons than that.'

'Fuck off and die,' Vince said.

Moses left about half an hour later, before it became too late to leave at all. Vince said he was going to carry on. He flipped open the lid on a tin of capsules. 'Painkillers,' he grinned. 'For my arms.'

Moses lowered himself backwards through the skylight. 'Any excuse,' he said.

*

Ground level.

Moses shaded his eyes. There was a big bucket in the sky at the end of the King's Road. This bucket was overflowing with molten gold light. The light was called sunset, and this is how it worked. The bucket slowly emptied of light. As the bucket emptied, the light slowly darkened – gold to orange, orange to red, red to purple – until, after hours of pouring, only the sediment remained: black light or, in other words, night.

Moses began to walk east. It was around six. At this point the light was still gold and the supply seemed endless. The people coming towards him had gold faces, gold hands, gold fingers, gold rings. They looked as if they had just stepped off planes from somewhere exotic. He wondered if he looked as if he had just stepped off a plane. He felt as if he was still on one. That old B-52. Where was his car?

There it was.

He slid into the front seat, basked for a moment in the aroma of hot leather. Ahhh, Bisto.

Jesus, he was driving already.

He plugged a cassette in, top volume. One of Gloria's. Cuban stuff. What the hell.

He was heading riverwards. The road seemed calm enough. His Rover floated on a purring cushion of air.

He watched a supersite poster glide past. It was a picture of a man sitting in a desert. The man had clean-cut features, neat black hair and a firm jaw. He was wearing a dinner jacket. He was smiling. It was nice in the advert.

Moses smiled back. He knew how the man felt. He was in an advert too.

*

Certain items of clothing struck him immediately as being inappropriate for a drinks party in Hampstead. The plus-fours, for example. The kilt. The straitjacket (a twenty-first birthday present from Jackson). He flicked through his wardrobe. He was proud of his wardrobe. As part of a new drive to inject system and discipline into his life, he had spent a whole day alphabetising his clothes. From A for Anorak to Z for Zoot Suit. Shirts were all ranged under S, but they also had a strict internal order of their own: Hawaiian, for instance, came before Psychedelic but after Bowling. Those shirts that had no obvious style or function were classified according to colour: Amber, Beige, Charcoal, Damson, and so on. It was some time before he reached his sharkskin suit, but when he did he realised that he need look no further. That was it. Suit: Sharkskin.

He had bought it from a charity organisation that operated out of a basement flat in Notting Hill Gate. A woman of about fifty had answered the door. She wore a necklace of wooden beads, a tweed skirt, and a pair of stout brown shoes. She seemed vigorous but absent-minded at the same time.

'Oh dear,' she said, when she saw him. 'Oh dear.' And then, turning back inside, 'Sorry. Do come in.'

Moses had fallen in love with the suit at first sight. It had a double-breasted jacket, a pocket that slanted rakishly over the heart, and a grey watered-silk lining with triangular flaps sewn into the armpits to soak up sweat (a task which, thankfully, they had never had to perform). The trousers, high-waisted, roomy, pleated, tapered nicely to a half-inch turn-up at the ankle; they were the kind of trousers that Robert Mitchum used to wear in those movies he made in the forties. The colour of the suit? Well, at first glance it looked grey, a sober darkish grey, but when you examined it closely you could see that the cloth was shot through with tiny flecks of blue and orange. In sunlight it would come alive. Perhaps the best thing about the suit, though, was the label inside. PURE SHARKSKIN, it said, and gave an address in St James's. Moses didn't know what sharkskin was, but he certainly liked the sound of it. He tried the suit on behind a purple velvet curtain and it fitted perfectly. It might almost have been tailored to his measurements. A miracle. He marched straight up to the woman at the counter.

'This is a wonderful suit. I'll take it.'

'How strange that you should choose that one.' The woman's eyes settled cautiously on his face. 'It only came in yesterday.'

'I was lucky then.'

'I shouldn't really tell you, I suppose, but the man who it belonged to only died last week.' The beads of her wooden necklace clicked between her fingers. A rosary of sorts.

He couldn't think of anything that wasn't tactless.

He finally broke the silence with the words, 'He must have been a big man.'

'Yes. He was. He used to row.' And the woman stared Moses straight in the eye as if he had accused her of lying.

'You knew him then?'

'Yes, I knew him.' She sighed. 'I knew him.'

'Oh,' Moses said. 'I'm sorry.'

'That'll be four pounds.' She had already folded the suit and tucked it out of sight in a brown paper bag.

Afterwards he couldn't help wondering why she had said *Oh dear* when she saw him standing in the doorway. Did he resemble the man who had died the week before? Had she loved that man, perhaps? Had she thought of Moses as some kind of ghost? And, if so, had he then upset her further by selecting, as it were, *his own sharkskin suit?*

He would never know, of course, but the incident gave him a peculiar feeling: the feeling that all happiness was rooted in grief, the one evolving naturally, organically, from the other, like flowers from earth.

*

Shit, seven-thirty already. He should have been in Hampstead by now. Drinking. And he was still in Lambeth. Naked. It was the speed, the dope. They had reversed him into his memory.

He dressed, checked his face in the mirror, ran some gel through his hair, snatched up keys and cigarettes, and took the stairs, three at a time.

'Hey, Abraham! What's up?'

It was Elliot. He was standing on the corner, hands in his pockets. Only his shoulderblades touched the wall. That cool. He was wearing his maroon suit. A white tie glowed softly against the backcloth of a black shirt. He looked beautiful.

Moses walked over. He forgot the rush he was in. It was good knowing people who smiled when they saw you. It could make you forget anything.

'What's with the tie, Elliot?'

Elliot looked down at his tie as if he was seeing it for the first time. 'You like it?'

'Not bad. What's it made of?'

'Silk, man. Hundred per cent.'

'Really?'

Elliot held the tie out on the palm of his hand. 'Feel it.'

Moses bent over the tie, studied it closely, tested it between two fingers. Silk. You could feel that. He turned it over and held the label up to the light. SILK. 100%. He nodded, looked impressed. 'That's a great tie.'

Elliot tucked the tie back inside his jacket.

'Mine's terylene,' Moses said. 'Hundred per cent.' He waved his tie in Elliot's face.

Elliot looked pained. 'Terylene's shit, Moses. If you're going to live here, you better smarten up.'

'What about this then?' Moses opened his jacket and tapped the label. 'Pure sharkskin, this is.'

'Don't give me no fish talk, Moses.'

'All right,' and laughing, Moses lunged at Elliot's jacket. 'What's yours? Polyester?'

'If you touch me,' Elliot said, 'I might have to call Ridley.'

Moses backed away with his hands in the air. 'OK, Elliot. You win.' He felt for his keys and walked towards his car.

'Hey, Moses, about your friend, the singer,' Elliot called out. 'She's on. Thursday. Happy now?'

Moses turned round, rushed over to Elliot, and hugged him. Smothered him in grateful sharkskin and terylene. 'That's great, Elliot. That's really great. I'll tell her tonight.'

'Jesus, Moses,' Elliot gasped when Moses finally released him, 'you nearly fucking killed me there.' He straightened his jacket and tie, hitched his trousers up, patted his hair. 'Jesus,' he muttered.

But Moses was already turning the key in his ignition. Two blasts on the horn and he vanished round the corner in a cloud of blue exhaust.

Nothing special happened on the way to Hampstead. He drove fast and learned quite a lot about Aztec rituals from some programme on Radio 4.

*

He turned into a street that ran along the southern edge of Hampstead Heath. Narrow, fastidious, a clutter of expensive parked cars. He noticed blue plaques on the walls of houses, the slanting roof of a conservatory, a cello in an upstairs window. Then the street widened, wound north. Double electric garages now. Serious children with golden hair. The burglar alarms alone looked worth stealing. When he reached the number that Gloria had given him he had to stop the car and double-check the address. It was the right house.

He didn't honestly think he'd ever seen anything like it. Sweeping expanses of white façade that looked as cold and slippery as ice-rinks. Sheer stretches of glass (sometimes reflecting his shadowy figure, for he had parked the car and was now walking round the outside). The building seemed to absorb colour from its immediate surroundings – deep blue from the shadows, silver from the moon – and yet a grey day, he imagined,

219

would only serve to heighten its intrinsic whiteness. No garden to speak of. No plants or flower-beds. Only a functional patio and a two-tier lawn. Trees and shrubbery shielded the house on three sides. On the fourth, a view of the heath. The effect was one of spartan luxury, a sort of inverted flamboyance. Gloria's roots, he thought. And smiled, thinking of his own.

He circled the house for the second time. The lawn looked so modelled, so planed, that it seemed as if the house had just landed and would shortly be taking off again, leaving no memory or proof of its existence except, perhaps, for a few indentations in the grass that would be gone by morning; it didn't seem to grow, or even belong there. When he returned to the staircase again – this was semi-circular, and broke up the relentless linear mood of the building – the door opened and a slice of white light fell across the lawn. A woman in a white knee-length dress appeared, her backlit hair a platinum-blonde, her figure youthful. From a distance she looked perfect, alien. This did nothing to rid Moses of his initial impression that the house had just fallen out of the sky. He approached the steps.

'Good evening,' he called up.

She must have noticed him already because there was no trace of surprise in her voice. 'You must be Moses,' she said.

'And you,' he said, reaching her and extending a hand, 'must be Mrs Wood.'

'Heather.'

Her name was like her voice – springy, fragrant, open-air somehow – and he told her so.

And Heather laughed, so he laughed too, and they stood there in the doorway still shaking, or rather, by now, merely holding hands.

'Am I late?' he asked her.

'Late? No. We've only just opened the first bottle of champagne. I call that perfect timing.'

She ushered him into the house ahead of her, but he paused just inside the door, needing a moment or two to take things in. The living-area that spread out below him was thirty or forty feet long and furnished in a style that could, perhaps, have been called cubic chic. Blocks of white fibreglass or plastic, upholstered in white leather, acted as armchairs and sofas. An original Picasso drawing hung in a spotlit alcove. The floor was a stretch of pale natural wood, lacquered like a dance-floor and lavished with a profusion of white scatter-rugs. Six-foot Yucca palms and other, taller exotic plants led his eye towards the ceiling high above, a slanting amalgamation of mirrors, pipes and glass through which he could see, at certain points, a few rectilinear sections of starless night sky. Almost giddy, he dropped his gaze to the centre of the room. A long low coffee-table (also white, also cubic) dominated; arranged on its perfect surface, two bottles of champagne in a silver ice-bucket, a pair of mother-of-pearl opera-glasses (to see people on the other side of the room?), a vase of wild grasses and an Indian conch.

Moses took a deep breath. 'Nice,' he said.

Heather smiled. 'Introductions,' she said and, taking him gently by the arm, guided him down the steps. Her hand was elegant, tanned, and uncluttered by rings, except for the one that bound her, presumably, to Mr Wood.

Thirty or forty people stood about in different parts of the room. Heather steered Moses from one clique to another, supplying him with names and, where appropriate, pieces of information, gossip or scandal to fix the names in his mind. She was an accomplished hostess, but Moses's mind, bombarded by an afternoon of Vince, took in less than it might have done.

He remembered meeting a barrister called John Dream, though, because John Dream looked exactly like Bernard Levin. Heather, laughingly, agreed.

He remembered 'Prince' Hudson Oleander too. 'Prince' Hudson Oleander was a tennis pro from Famoso, California. He had a lecherous sunburnt face with cracks in it, like wood. Apparently he had won the title 'Prince' at a tournament in Forest Hills on account of his extraordinary graciousness on court. 'Apparently,' Heather whispered behind her hand, 'it's the only title he's ever won.'

Then there was Hermann von Weltraum and his wife, Lottie. ('Astrologers,' Heather explained, 'from Munich.' Moses thought momentarily, almost wistfully, of Madame Zola, Famous Clairvoyant. He wondered if the Germans were Famous Astrologers. Looking at Hermann's prissy pink face he doubted it somehow.) And Romeo Pelz, a clothes designer, and his male assistant, Derek. ('Romeo,' Heather lowered her eyes, 'lives up to his name.') And Christian Persson, a member of the Swedish delegation for human rights and a man, Moses saw, with absolutely no sense of humour. Christian Persson introduced Moses to the Very Reverend William Cloth, vicar of the parish. Heather moved away to fetch Moses a drink. He would need one, the glimmer in her eyes seemed to say.

The religious atmosphere of the group was quickly dispelled by the apparition of a short muscular woman with glazed brown eyes. She had dark curly hair and wore a caftan. If she had had a beard as well as a moustache, she could have passed for Demis Roussos. She was, in fact, Margaux Kampf, an actress.

'I'm Margaux,' she purred. 'With an x.'

Moses looked puzzled. 'I didn't hear an x. Did you hear an x, Mr Persson?'

The Swede's pale-blue eyes opened wide. 'I'm sorry. I don't understand.'

'It's on the end, lovey,' Margaux growled. 'It's a silent one.'

Jesus, Moses thought. He looked across at the Reverend. The Reverend was also thinking Jesus, by the look of it.

'I'm Moses,' Moses said. 'No x.'

'That's cute,' said Margaux. 'What do you do?'

'I'm an escape-artist,' Moses said. 'Watch.' And he turned round and walked away.

Heather moved towards him with a glass of champagne. 'Is this all right, Moses? Or would you prefer something stronger?'

Moses assured her that champagne was quite strong enough for him.

Heather smiled past him. 'Here's someone I don't need to introduce you to.'

'Champagne's quite strong enough for me.' Gloria was mimicking him. 'What're you up to, Moses?'

She was all lit up tonight with the thrill of being on her own ground. She wore a bottle-green turtleneck, a black moiré skirt, black tights. Jet earrings swung against her pale neck. Her dark eyes trained on his face like search-lights, scanning him for signs of misbehaviour.

He smiled. 'I'm trying to make a good impression.'

'You're full of shit, Moses,' she said.

He held up a finger. 'Not completely. I've got some news for you. You're singing at The Bunker. I've fixed it up with Elliot.'

'I take back everything I said.' She took his face between her hands and kissed the tip of his nose. Then pulled away laughing. 'I know what you've been doing. You've been taking speed.'

'How do you know that?'

'I just tasted it. On the end of your nose.'

They were still laughing when a man in a pale grey suit appeared at Gloria's elbow. 'May I be introduced?'

'Dad,' Gloria said, 'I'd like you to meet Moses. Moses, this is my father.'

The two men shook hands.

Mr Wood had a way of looking at you from under his eyelids that made you feel as if you were testing his patience. He doesn't like me, Moses thought. He watched Gloria move away, and it seemed as if she was taking his joy and spontaneity with her. He didn't want to be left alone with Mr Wood. There was only one way to talk to this manicured man, he sensed, and that was politely. The prospect of having to be polite depressed him.

'This house is amazing,' he blurted out and instantly regretted it; Mr

Wood looked like the kind of man who expected precision not superlatives.

'I suppose a lot of people say that,' he added, trying to salvage something from the wreckage of his opening remark.

The ice squeaked in Mr Wood's glass, but didn't quite break. Moses felt like the *Titanic*. Sinking fast.

'Yes,' Mr Wood said. 'Most people say that.'

Perhaps he felt, during the brief silence that followed, that he had been a little too abrupt or uncharitable because he then offered to show Moses the plans of the house, if he was interested, that is.

Moses said he was. I suppose most people say that, he thought.

Mr Wood took him over to the far side of the room. He unrolled a giant scroll of paper, spread it flat on the table, and pinned the corners down with glass weights. Then he began to talk quietly about the juxtaposition of planes, the distribution of space, and so on. Moses now remembered Gloria mentioning her father and architecture in the same breath, and suddenly all the pieces fell into place.

'So you designed this house yourself?'

'That's right,' Mr Wood said, as if Moses had finally found the answer to an extremely simple riddle, as if Moses's surprise was, in itself, surprising.

Mr Wood was an attractive man. Very attractive. He was one of those people who look ten years younger than their age, even though you don't know how old they are. But Moses had one problem with him. He behaved like one of his own technical drawings. He was what he did. He was too *designed*. The neatness of his features and his suit. The efficiency of his gestures. The measured way he used words – the way you might use bricks. And his smile, a ruled line across his face that, even now, seemed to be disclaiming any beauty the building might have achieved over and above its functional perfection. That's all very well, Moses thought, but where does *Mrs* Wood fit in? He had instantly picked up on the playful streak in her, yet the only thing he had noticed in the house so far that in any way resembled her or might be seen as her doing was the vase of wild grasses on the coffee-table. And there couldn't be much room in a technical drawing, he imagined, for a vase of wild grasses. He suddenly felt the urge to rescue her from all this. To ride into the white house on a black horse. To snatch her up from under her husband's perfect nose. To save her from sterility, these expensive chains, this rich death. A rustling distracted him. Mr Wood was rolling up his plans with brisk dry movements of his hands.

*

Moses subsided on to a settee with a fresh glass of champagne. He had wanted to speak to Gloria, but she was tied up with friends of her mother's.

Disconsolate, he faced into the room, watched the guests manoeuvring.

Romeo Pelz, for instance, whose eyes were black except for one tiny silver point at the centre of each pupil, had his arm round Derek's narrow shoulders and was extracting, by the look of it, some kind of promise or assurance. Derek listened, eyes half-closed, mouth widened like a cat's, and revolved his head, first clockwise, then anti-clockwise.

Mrs Violet de Light, a shivery woman of forty-fivish with a bell of grey hair and darting eyes (her husband was a publisher, Moses remembered Heather telling him, and she worked on several committees), leaned against the wall in the space between two paintings, her scrawny body twisting sideways and upwards towards Christian Persson like a lightning-struck tree, her ear no more than an inch from his blond Don Quixote beard and his mauve lips as he told her that, no, it wasn't so much religion that mattered in his work as *morality*. Mrs de Light quivered with fascination at the word.

Ronald, a journalist, stood by the bookcase. He was gulping neat vodka and casting long shadowy glances in the direction of a girl called Phoebe (whose *professional* name, Moses had heard someone bitch earlier on, was *Dolores*). Phoebe was being clutched from behind by the tanned Prince Oleander. His rugged face nuzzled her neck. One of his hands steadied her hip; the other gripped her wrist and guided it smoothly this way and that. Some kind of impromptu tennis-lesson, presumably. A backhand pass. Prince Oleander was having trouble keeping his eye on the imaginary ball. He seemed more interested in the way Phoebe's breasts were plunging against the two flimsy strips of pink material that made up the top half of her dress. Moses saw Ronald's grey face sag. This was one game the journalist would never win.

John Dream, meanwhile, was leafing through a book in the comfort of an armchair. He occasionally lifted a hand to pat the crinkly greying waves of his hair. He patted them very carefully as if they were priceless or easily frightened.

The Very Reverend Cloth stood in the middle of the room, transferring his vacant pulpit gaze from one passing guest to the next. Nobody stopped to talk to him, with the exception of Heather who might have been a puppeteer the way she brought sudden jittery life to those rather wooden limbs.

Now and then Moses caught a glimpse of Gloria threading her way through the gathering, as sharp and bright as a needle. He saw her walk up to a young American who looked like Paul Newman. He watched Gloria listen to Paul Newman talking. She seemed to be listening with her whole body. She radiated interest like light. Paul Newman slipped an arm round her shoulders and slid a few droll words out of the corner of his mouth. They both laughed. Those few moments hauled him back to the first time he ever saw her, talking to those two men at the party in Holland Park, and suddenly it was as if the gap between them – there then, there now – had never closed, as if that first impression had stained the way he looked at her, stained it with some bitter resin that nothing they ever did together, no amount of closeness, could remove, and suddenly he wanted to be John Dream, buried in the pages of a book, oblivious, content, or home alone, pouring milk into a dish for Bird – anything but this. And Gloria chose that moment to notice him. She detached herself from the American – rather too abruptly, Moses thought – and moved towards him through the crowd. The smile she was carrying looked forced somehow, artificial. It was like watching an air stewardess moving from first class to economy, her pleasantness no longer natural but obligatory. It was like being back at the orphanage. He felt condescended to.

She sat down next to him.

'Are you all right?' she said.

She touched his arm. An afterthought.

He didn't look at her.

She tightened her grip on his arm. 'What's wrong, Moses?'

'Nothing,' he said.

His arm felt pressurised. He moved it away from her.

'You were having a better time over there,' he said. 'Maybe you'd better go back.'

He wanted her to understand this simple unreasonable jealousy of his, but when he lifted his eyes to meet hers, he saw that she had taken a different turning somewhere. Suddenly they were miles apart and travelling in opposite directions.

'Is that what you want?' she said.

He shrugged.

She got up and walked away.

He didn't watch her go.

Herr and Frau von Weltraum, the German astrologers, took her place on the settee.

'Do you, by any chance, speak German?' Hermann asked, pushing his spectacles a little higher on his inquisitive pink nose.

'*Nein*,' Moses said.

Hermann found this tremendously funny, and turned to relate it to his wife. His wife leaned forwards so as to smile at the humorous Englishman.

But the humorous Englishman had left.

*

Out on the patio Moses almost tripped over Ronald the journalist. Ronald lay against the wall, legs splayed, hair plastered over his forehead.

'What are you doing down there?' Moses asked.

'Drinking.'

'What are you drinking?'

A bottle rose into the air. Moonlight silvered the transparent glass. 'Vodka. Have some.'

'Thank you.' Moses swallowed a mouthful and handed the bottle back.

'I'm Ronald,' Ronald said. 'Who are you?'

'Moses.'

'Christ.'

'Yeah, I know.' Moses studied the journalist with some curiosity. 'So what are you really doing out here?'

Ronald mauled his face with his free hand. 'I'm pissed off. Bloody pissed off.'

He had been looking for Phoebe, he explained. You know, *Phoebe*. The girl with the incredible tits. He had looked all over the house. No dice. So he tried the garden, didn't he. He was just crossing the lawn when he heard this moan. Coming from the shrubbery, it was. He got down on his hands and knees and crawled the last few yards. And there she was, kneeling in the bushes, her dress pushed down to her waist, her fat breasts erotically tattooed in light and shade. Bloody marvellous sight. Except she wasn't alone, of course. How did he know? He saw this pair of hands appear on her shoulders, didn't he. He watched them sort of slide downwards until they were – oh Christ –

'Prince Oleander,' Moses said. 'Giving her another tennis lesson.'

The journalist's head slumped on to his chest. Then he lifted the bottle to his mouth and swallowed twice, fiercely. He had *watched*, he told Moses. He hadn't *wanted* to. He just *had* to. He had watched them fucking in the shrubbery. Shuddering rubbery fucking in the shrubbery. He had watched them for ever. Well, until Phoebe started coming, anyway. *That* he couldn't take. So he had dragged himself back to the patio and hit the bottle. He wanted to get shit-faced. Best way to be.

'Are they still out there?' Moses asked, cocking an ear.

'I don't know. Don't fucking care. Thought I was in with a chance, you see. But I don't come from Calibloodyfornia, do I.'

The vodka bottle lunged at Moses again. He shook his head this time.

'Californication,' Ronald said. He laughed bitterly.

Moses climbed to his feet. 'Thanks for the drink.'

'You going?'

Moses nodded. 'Got to find someone.'
'Fucking women,' Ronald said.

*

The day was catching up on Moses. Moving back indoors, shaky now, a little brittle too, he suddenly understood that the setting for the party, though extravagant and dreamlike, was at the same time perfectly stable. Cushioned on the surface, rock-solid underneath. Everything running along preordained and well-oiled lines. Crossing the living area, he saw the discreet glances of shared amusement that passed between Mr and Mrs Wood, he saw their confidence in each other, the strength of their attachment. They could invite strangers, frauds, drunks, vicars, tarts – all potential spanners in the works – to their parties, they could mix them together like some giant human cocktail, they could flirt with other people's chaos because they knew it would never happen to them. The spanners in the works might make a pleasant tinkling sound, but they would never damage the machinery. How could he, Moses, match a performance like theirs?

As was happening more and more these days (ever since the arrival of the suitcase, in fact), Moses's thoughts turned to his own background, setting against this brilliant suburban machinery, against this concentration of dazzle, a darkness illuminated only by a few photos in an old album and a dress that he had given to Gloria (who probably had hundreds more upstairs), and a sudden panic washed over him, the feeling that he had been squandering valuable time, that he should have been buying torches, lighting fires, calling electricians, anything to lift the darkness a little, to reveal *his* machinery.

Where *was* his machinery? Perhaps *he* had been the spanner in those particular works. Too big a spanner. Perhaps that explained everything.

Perhaps.

But he wanted to *know*.

*

Somebody had turned up the volume of the conversation. Fred Astaire was trying to make himself heard with his own version of the Cole Porter classic 'Anything Goes'. How apt, Moses thought. Unable to find Gloria, he ended up in a lamplit corner next to Paul Newman. Next to Paul Newman stood the awful Margaux.

'Moses!' she cried. 'Moses with no x! Come and talk to us!'

Moses groaned inside.

'Have you two met?' Margaux asked.

'I don't believe I've had the pleasure,' Paul Newman said.

I don't believe you ever will, you bastard, Moses thought. The American had a pleasant transatlantic drawl and, for a moment, Moses wished he had brought Vince along. He would have enjoyed watching Vince toss a glass of champagne in that pleasant American face.

'This is Moses,' Margaux was saying. 'Moses, this is Tarquin.'

Tarquin? Jesus.

'Have you seen Gloria?' Moses asked.

Neither of them had. Not recently, anyway.

'It's very important.' He looked round, as much to avoid further conversation as anything else.

Ronald stumbled past, ash on his tie, flies undone. He had stuck the vodka bottle in his trouser pocket. It swung against his hip like a six-gun with no bullets in the chamber. Phoebe and Prince Oleander still hadn't reappeared. They were probably still fucking in the shrubbery (one day my prince will come). Violet de Light, who had seen her husband stroking Margaux's hand on the patio, had captured Romeo and was pawing him in a desperate last-ditch attempt to arouse her husband's jealousy. Raphael de Light, the publisher, knew Romeo was gay. He wriggled with amusement in the kitchen doorway. John Dream was quietly taking his leave of Heather who, turning back into the room, caught Moses's roving eye and came towards him.

'Moses, are you enjoying yourself?'

'It's a wonderful party. Tell me. Have you seen Gloria anywhere?'

'The poor boy's desperate,' Margaux said.

You cunt, Moses thought, and smiled pleasantly. He began to look round the room again. For a blunt instrument this time. Margaux drifted serenely out of range.

' – I don't know where she is,' Heather was saying. She pushed her hair back from her forehead with spread fingers. An expensive smell circled her left wrist like a bracelet.

Moses felt a wave of nausea well up inside him. His body started moving up and down, up and down, a smooth well-oiled movement, almost pistonlike. The sweep of Heather's hair became a part of this. The smell of her perfume too. He didn't dare look at her.

' – she could be anywhere – '

He heard her voice through a buzz of interference. The air between them had broken up into patches of black and white. He hoped to Christ he wasn't going to pass out. Not in Hampstead. He hoped with a desperation which, if anything, made it seem more likely to happen.

'Got to go to the bathroom.' Hardly able to move his lips. Mouth heavy, hydraulic. And he could see the sound waves his voice made looping out towards her. Loch Ness monsters made of words, of frequencies. There was a look of concern on her face, he thought, but it was like a bad television picture. All snow. No, bigger than snow. Black gaps between the flakes.

' – first on the right at the top of the stairs – '

He thanked her.

All the way to the bathroom he seemed to be falling. He locked the door and dropped to the floor.

*

Time passed.

Slowly – reluctantly, it seemed to Moses – the nausea withdrew, the pistons ceased. He lifted his head. Marble surfaces. Gold fittings. Plants. In the centre of the room, a sunken bath. Roman-style. He reached over, turned on the taps. There was great wealth in their smooth tooled action, in the instant power they released. He listened to the crash of water on enamel as Chinese philosophers once listened to crickets. He drifted into calm stretches of contemplation. Mr and Mrs Wood must have extraordinary problems, he thought, to own a bathroom as magnificent as this. He would write a book one day. He would call it *The Bath – A Definitive Study*. Something serious like that. There would be glossy colour plates shot by you-know-who and an introduction written by somebody distinguished. He could already see the press reviews:

– It is not easy to find words to describe the joy, the delight, the passion which Mr Highness evokes – *Publisher's Weekly*

– I was held spellbound. Mr Highness is clever, very clever, and immensely entertaining – *Sunday Telegraph*

– Memories came flooding back. Enthralling – *Woman*

– Exhibits a wonderfully dry sense of humour throughout – *Times Literary Supplement*.

Fame beckoned. Fan-mail. Royalties. He would have enough money to fly to America and look for another Highness. He might even appear on the Michael Parkinson show.

As he left the bathroom he heard a sigh of ecstasy and, turning round, saw Margaux and Mr de Light (his future publisher maybe!) breaking from a surreptitious drunken clinch.

'My Raphael,' Margaux murmured. 'My priceless Raphael.'

'Mein Kampf,' whispered Mr de Light, erudite even in desire.

Moses didn't know how long he had spent on the bathroom floor, but the party, he was glad to see, was obviously still in full swing.

Moses slipped across the landing and down the stairs. There had been a few departures, he learned. Violet de Light had stalked off in a huff. Christian Persson had gone to Heaven (he wanted to check out London nightlife). Phoebe and her tanned tennis-player had taken leave of the Woods (and the bushes) and sped off in a white Golf GTI convertible. Ronald had departed too, but only into unconsciousness. He lay in the garden, his face a mask of masochistic agony, the casualty of too much jealousy and vodka. Alcohol had also transformed the Very Reverend Cloth. He towered over Lottie von Weltraum, two fingers raised, the other two tucked into the palm of his hand, like the pope. He was telling her that he would like to talk to Derek about unnatural acts. But Derek was in the bathroom with Romeo, performing one. Moses knew. He had watched them go in together. Then, finally, he saw Gloria. She was standing in the Picasso alcove. Talking to Paul Newman. Moses walked over.

'Hello, Gloria.'

'Hello.' Without actually moving at all, she seemed to shrink from him. Perhaps to fill the silence, she said, 'Have you met Tarquin?'

'Yes,' he said. 'Where've you been? I've been looking for you everywhere.'

'Is that what you were doing in the bathroom for an hour? Looking for me?'

Moses stared at her.

'Are you all right now, Moses?' Tarquin asked.

Moses swung round. 'None of your business, Paul.'

The American smiled. 'My name's Tarquin.'

'Well, you look like a Paul to me.'

Gloria pushed Moses away into the corner. 'Why are you being so weird tonight?'

'I'm not being weird. This is weird.' He waved a hand in the air to indicate the room, the house, the party. 'You're from a different world, Gloria. I don't know where I'm from, but I don't think it's somewhere like this. In fact, I know it isn't.'

'What's that supposed to mean?'

Moses pressed his fingers into his eyes. 'I don't know.'

Things had begun to drift away from him again. He was travelling backwards on a slow roller-coaster. Voices sounded distant and cramped, like voices on the telephone, and even his dislike for Paul Newman was being sucked back into a past that was vague, gelatinous, irrelevant.

He looked down at Gloria. Her eyebrows told him that it was time to go home.

'I ought to be going,' he murmured.

She nodded.

They found Mrs Wood adjusting her hair in the full-length mirror by the door.

'Thank you for the wonderful party,' Moses said. He took her hand in his, bent over it, and touched it with his lips. For one awful moment he thought he was going to be sick on it, but the spasm passed and he straightened up again, pale but undisgraced.

'Lovely to meet you,' she said. 'I hope we'll see you again.'

'I like you,' Moses said.

She smiled. 'I like you too, Moses.'

'I'll see you out,' Gloria said.

In the night air Moses felt better. 'Did I really kiss your mother's hand?' he asked Gloria.

'Only just,' she said. 'I mean, you nearly missed.'

They both began to laugh. Softly, privately, for different reasons.

Moses leaned back against the voluptuous white curve of the staircase. 'You see, you never told me your parents lived in a spaceship.'

'Moses, you're very drunk.'

'And you, Gloria, are very beautiful.'

'Are you sure you can drive?'

'I'll be all right.'

'Maybe I should call you a cab.' She was trying very hard to be stern with him. 'Do you want a cab?'

'No, I'm all right. Really. My motor skills are unimpaired. Look.' And very carefully, like someone mounting a butterfly, he leaned over and placed a kiss on Gloria's lips.

It was nice, so he did it again. Doing it for longer didn't seem to make it any less nice. Though this time it was a little less like someone mounting a butterfly, perhaps.

He ran down the stairs and his voice hovered in the air behind him.

'Remember, you're singing. Thursday.'

*

The posters had been up since the beginning of the week – bold black letters on a dayglo orange background: HOLLY WOOD. THE BUNKER. THURSDAY JUNE 26 10 PM – and by nine-thirty on Thursday night many of the tables had been taken. Moses sat in a dark corner and glanced across at Gloria. She was discussing something with her pianist. It was extraordinary how interesting she made the dance-floor seem just by standing on it. He had wanted to wish her luck again, but by the time he had ordered another brandy and returned to his table she was already up on stage. She had her usual band. Only the saxophonist, Malone, was new; he stood to one side, facing away from the audience, wearing a brown coat that buttoned all the way from his ankles to his throat. Gloria had chosen a shimmery pink dress this evening – to go with the building, she had told Moses earlier. She had backcombed her hair into a mass of spun black candy-floss. A fringe hid the time her eyebrows were telling. One hand on the microphone, she turned, said something to the guitarist. Moses's heart did a swift drumroll. He still couldn't adjust to the sight of her performing. This public Gloria was always an apparition out of nowhere for him, some exotic derivation of the girl he knew, smiled at, slept with. It made him dizzy to feel himself slipping into the objectivity he saw in other people's eyes when they watched her sing.

But there she was, spotlit now, one hand shading her eyes.

'I'm going blind up here,' came her voice, husky, echoing above the hiss of the P A. 'Could someone do something?'

The lights dimmed. The buzz of the audience cut out as if a plug had been pulled.

'Thanks.' A quick smile, and then simply, 'My name's Holly and this one's for Moses – '

It was one of those songs where the voice sets out alone and the instruments creep in after a verse or two, discreetly, one by one, like people arriving late at a theatre. A brave way to open, Moses thought, still feeling the glow that her surprise dedication had given him. He had only heard her sing twice before, but it seemed to him that she was singing better than ever tonight. There was an edge to her voice, even when she softened it, that cut into the silence of the audience, left marks to prove it had been there. People would walk out talking about her.

As the first song faded into brushwork and random piano, applause flew towards the stage on great clattering wings. Moses suddenly imagined Gloria ducking, her hands thrown up around her ears. He was too pre-occupied with this vision of his to clap. Or to notice that Elliot had slipped into the vacant seat beside him.

*

'What's up, Judas?'

Moses jumped. 'Elliot. How long've you been there?'

'Not long.'

'Want a drink.'

'I've got one.'

'So what's new?' Moses had meant nothing by the question, but he watched it hook something big in Elliot.

Elliot's head lifted. 'Are you in any kind of trouble?'

Moses looked blank. 'Not so far as I know.'

'What I mean is, are you in any kind of trouble with the police?'

Moses grinned.

'I'm serious.' Elliot moved his shoulders inside his jacket. He tipped some brandy into his mouth, swallowed, and bared his teeth. 'Last Saturday I had a visitor. It was right after you drove off in your car. He wanted to know if you lived here. He knew your name.'

'Who was he?'

'I don't know. He was a big bastard. Wore one of those old check jackets that look like a dog's thrown up on it. I reckon he was a copper. Plain-clothes.'

'What makes you think that?'

Elliot leaned back, pushed his empty glass around on the table. 'You get to recognise the smell. Something about them. And *that* bloke, I smelt it on him right away.'

'So what did you tell him?'

'I didn't tell him nothing. I told him to fuck off. Then he hit me.'

Moses's eyes opened wide. 'What d'you mean he hit you?'

'He fucking hit me. Right in the guts. Took me by surprise, didn't he.' Elliot drained his glass.

Moses was up to the bar and back again with two brandies like a man on elastic.

'That was the other thing,' Elliot said. 'The way he hit me, right? One, blokes like that, they don't go around hitting people, not unless something's really getting on their tits. Two, he knew how to hit. I mean, he had a punch. There was muscle under that jacket. Technique too. He was a copper all right. No question.'

Elliot turned towards the stage. He registered no emotion or feeling of any kind. His mind had travelled somewhere else. It had left his face vacant, the bolts drawn, the power switched off at the mains. He was looking at Gloria, but he wasn't seeing her at all.

After a minute or two Moses said, 'So you don't know what this bloke wanted?'

'He wanted you,' Elliot said, without taking his eyes off the stage.

'It could've been a mistake. Why would anyone want me?'

Elliot touched his solar plexus. 'It didn't feel like a mistake.'

'You didn't tell him anything, though?'

233

'No,' and now Elliot turned back to look at Moses, 'but he knew.'

Fear flickered down through Moses's body. He swallowed the rest of his brandy. 'I wonder what he wants,' he said.

Elliot lit a Dunhill, tapped it on the edge of the ashtray. 'Me and Ridley, we went after him, but we lost him in the park. He just vanished.' He leaned his elbows on the table, held his cigarette close to his mouth as he talked. 'I tried to trace him, asked around, made a few phone-calls, but nobody knows anything. He just vanished, like he was never there. Real thin air job.'

He finished his drink and stood up. 'All I wanted to say was, watch yourself, all right? I don't know who that bloke was, but he was a tough old sod and he had something on you.' His hand moved across his stomach again like someone exploring a painful memory. 'If he turns up again I'm going to get Ridley to sort him out.'

Moses nodded. 'Thanks, Elliot. And thanks for telling me.'

As Elliot slipped away into the crowd, Gloria said, 'Thank you,' and slotted the microphone back on to its stand. She stepped down off the stage and walked over. She took one of Moses's cigarettes. He lit it for her.

'Well?' she said. 'How was I?'

'Brilliant. You're singing better than ever tonight.'

She eyed him curiously. 'Are you OK, Moses?'

'Yeah.' He hoisted himself a little higher in his chair and assembled a smile for her. 'Yeah, I'm fine. I was just thinking, that's all.'

'Did you hear Malone? Isn't he great?'

'I was too busy listening to you.'

Gloria laughed. 'Moses, you're a terrible liar.'

'I was,' Moses said. 'Honestly.'

She touched his shoulder, then his cheek, and slipped away with a rustle of pink silk. She had to talk to the band. Letting his eyes drift beyond her, Moses noticed the clandestine figure of Jackson standing by the bar. Jackson seemed to be talking to Louise. Moses stood up, walked over.

'Jackson,' he said. 'I didn't know you were here.'

Jackson looked startled then shifty. He pulled his jacket in towards his body like a bird folding its wings. 'I was just talking to Louise.'

'I can see that.' Moses turned to Louise. She was wearing a black T-shirt, black ski-pants with silver ankle-zips and black patent-leather pumps. It might have been The Bunker's uniform. 'I hear you're going away.'

'Holiday with my parents.' Louise wrinkled her short nose. 'Still, free sun, I suppose.'

'Can't be bad,' said Moses, who had never been abroad in his life.

'You don't know my parents.' Louise had an infectious chuckle, and Moses caught it. 'I was just telling Jackson. I'm having a beach party. Two weeks' time. You going to come?'

'Love to. Where?'

'Ask Gloria. She's got the details.'

'Oh Christ,' Jackson said. 'Look who it is.'

Moses turned to see Eddie steering his magnesium smile through the smoke.

Louise muttered, 'I ought to be getting back to work.'

Jackson dipped his head into his pint, but his eyes clung to Louise as she disappeared behind a pillar. This startled Moses. He had seen Jackson look at clouds that way before, but never women. But now Eddie had arrived and was slapping Jackson on the back. Jackson's beer slopped over.

'Thank you, Eddie,' Jackson said.

'Jackson,' Eddie said, 'I thought you never drank.'

Jackson twisted his head to one side and smiled craftily, looking more than ever like a bird, the kind that steals jewellery. 'Sometimes I go wild,' he said.

They sat at Moses's table in the corner. Eddie's new lover had a sleeping eye that made anything she said seem ironic. But were these fringed white cowboy boots of hers ironic? Moses doubted it somehow. He wondered what number she was. 1,000? 1,500? Eddie was just saying that he'd had a pretty hectic week. Maybe 2,000, then. The girl laughed, unaware of the significance of Eddie's remark.

In the meantime Gloria had climbed back on stage.

'Me again.' She held the mike in one hand and a glass of white wine in the other. 'Thanks for all your help this afternoon, Ridley. This one's for you.'

Moses glanced round, but he couldn't see the big man anywhere. Still, it was a nice gesture. Word would get back, and somewhere in that gigantic construction of muscle and bone, somewhere in that mobile pain-dispenser, there had to be a heart, a tattooed heart, no doubt, but a heart none the less.

He had been trying not to think about what Elliot had said, but the anonymous policeman kept bursting into his head regardless, as if his head was a house that was staging a party and all his usual thoughts were guests and the policeman was a policeman. 'It's a raid,' came a calm voice. 'Great party,' his thoughts said, 'really great, but I'm afraid we've got to be going now.' And, reaching for their coats, they all filed out at the same time, left him alone in the house. Alone with the policeman . . .

' – and Malone on tenor sax – '

Gloria was introducing the band. If he didn't listen to the saxophone this time, she'd murder him.

He only had to wait until halfway through the next song, then Malone unleashed a sixty-second solo, and played with such raw soaring power, assembled such an intricate structure of notes, that listening to him was like being led through some extraordinary abandoned mansion. It was as if Malone somehow knew of Moses's anxiety and was building a house specially for him, a different kind of house, a house where policemen would never appear at the door. The saxophone scaled the façade, dropped into an upstairs room, tiptoed across the landing, opened a door with rusty hinges, tripped, stumbled to the edge of a parapet, peered over, stepped sharply back, ran down flight after flight of stairs, through ballrooms peopled by the ghosts of dancers, through echoing cloisters and claustrophobic passageways, past windows with vistas and hushed rooms no longer used, tore through curtained doorways and out, finally, into the open air, paused to breathe the air, ran on through gardens with peacocks and fountains, along spacious landscaped avenues, past sudden explosions of plants from South America, and back down a sweeping gravel drive to the road where Gloria was waiting with the rest of the song.

'Malone,' she said, over the applause. 'We just borrowed him for the night. I wish he didn't have to go back – '

'Renew him,' Moses shouted. 'Renew him.'

Malone bowed majestically in his cylindrical brown coat.

Five minutes later Moses pushed his way through the crowd to buy another round of drinks. He swayed from side to side, collided with some people, rebounded off others, but he always did that when he was drunk, he meant nothing by it, so he was surprised when he heard somebody swear at him, surprised enough to turn and catch a glimpse of an unidentifiable object flying towards him at great speed.

At first he thought he was in bed because he was lying down and he felt strangely comfortable. But then he realised that the ceiling was the wrong colour and anyway, what would all these people be doing in his bedroom? They were bending over him and their heads looked like tulips, the hard conical shape of the buds before they open, and he wanted to laugh.

Gloria knelt beside him.

'Why aren't you singing?' he asked her.

She gazed down at him sadly, as if he was dying in a film. 'That's over,' she told him.

'I must've missed the last bit,' he said.

She nodded. 'Yes, you did.'

'Malone was good.'

She smiled and ran a cool hand through his hair. 'How do you feel?'

'What happened?'

'You got hit.'

Moses smiled faintly.

Now Ridley loomed above him. His one gold earring swung like something a hypnotist might use.

'Moses,' and Ridley held a finger up, 'how many fingers can you see?'

'One.'

Ridley held up two fingers. 'How many now?'

'That's not nice, Ridley.'

'He's all right,' Ridley told Gloria. 'Better get him upstairs, though.'

They helped him up to his flat and put him to bed with an ice-pack over his eye. Gloria said she would stay the night.

'That's very nice of you,' Moses mumbled, 'to look after me.'

'Don't be a prick,' she said.

He woke at midday, and this time he really was in bed. The right side of his face felt fragile and stiff, twice its normal size. He could hear Gloria singing somewhere. One of the songs from last night. She must be in the bathroom. He tried to open his eyes, but only the left one worked. There was a huge gold tiara outside the window. He closed the eye again.

'Gloria?' he called out.

He heard the floorboards creak as she walked into the bedroom.

'Gloria?'

'Yes?'

'Tell me something,' he said. 'Tell me what that gold tiara's doing outside the window.'

Now he heard her laughing.

He opened his left eye again. The empty gasholder gleamed in the afternoon sun. The sun is clever, he thought. It can turn buildings into jewellery.

Gloria went out to the kitchen to make some coffee. When she returned, Moses was sitting up in bed with both eyes open. Gloria screamed and threw his coffee all over the wall.

'What's wrong?' he asked.

'Your eye.'

'What about it?'

'Look in the mirror.'

He crawled across the bed until his face appeared in the mirror. 'Jesus,' he gasped.

The white part of his right eye had flooded with blood. The right side of his face had swollen too; sheets of pain, bright as aluminium, flashed across the inside of his head when he pressed his cheek.

'How did it happen?' he asked. 'I can't remember a thing.'

'Well, apparently you bumped into this guy and spilled beer all down him. It doesn't seem like a very good reason to hit someone but Ridley said he knew the guy from somewhere. He used to be a boxer and he's always looking for trouble.'

Moses groaned. 'A boxer? Trust me to get hit by a boxer.'

'Ridley threw him out. You should've seen it. He just picked him up by the scruff of the neck and chucked him in that skip. The guy was furious. I don't think I've ever seen anyone look so furious. But Ridley just stood there with his arms folded and said, "I don't want to see you again. Ever."' Gloria laughed and shook her head.

'I wish I'd seen it,' Moses said.

'You were lying on the floor. You must've been out cold for about two minutes.'

Moses touched his cheek. 'D'you think anything's broken?'

'I don't know. It might be an idea to check.'

'Have my head examined, you mean.' Moses grinned. 'Shit, it even hurts to grin.'

Gloria drove him to St Thomas's in Waterloo. The doctor, an urbane Pakistani, told him that he had sustained a hairline fracture of the right cheekbone. It would heal naturally, he said. As for the eye, that was just a broken bloodvessel. He wrote Moses a prescription. There didn't appear to be any concussion, he said, but he advised Moses to take things easy for a few days.

'If I was you,' he concluded, stroking his neck with an elegant tapering finger, 'I should try not to get into any more fights with boxers.'

Moses promised to avoid anyone who looked even remotely like a boxer.

On the way back to The Bunker Gloria turned to him. 'You know something else that happened last night? After I'd finished singing, Ridley came up to me. Oh shit, I thought, what've I done now? But he just put his hand on my shoulder and smiled and said, "That was fucking diamond."'

ROCKETS IN JULY

The Rover touched fifty-five as an art collector touches his own private Rodin. Moses loved his old car. Gloria had wanted to hire a Porsche to drive down to Louise's party in (these girls with parents in Hampstead!), but a Porsche, they found out, cost about £130 a day and neither of them had that kind of money. Gloria capitulated gracefully. She settled for half a Porsche which, when commuted into powders and liquids, turned out to be a gram of coke and a Thermos of Smirnoff and crushed ice. Much more sensible.

'So where is the party exactly?' Moses asked her.

Gloria, navigator for the trip, snuggled down in her seat. 'A place called Star Gap,' she said. 'It's somewhere on the south coast. Don't worry. We'll find it.'

Moses nodded.

They had left the rain behind in Purley (where rain belongs) and as the car swung away from a roundabout and climbed up through the trees towards Godstone the sun broke through, beat like a sudden drum rhythm in his blood. He wound the window down, listened to the cymbal hiss of tyres on the wet road. Gloria put sunglasses on and pretended to be an Italian movie-star. Smiles journeyed between them. So did the Thermos of vodka.

They had been driving for an hour when Gloria sat up.

'What about a deviation?' she suggested.

Moses narrowed his eyes. 'In what sense of the word?'

'I thought that, on this occasion,' she said, in a voice that left him in no doubt, 'the two senses of the word might be combined in a single act.'

Moses smiled.

'It'll be the first time, you see. Outdoors, I mean. We can't really count that greenhouse in Leicestershire, can we?'

Moses agreed that they couldn't really count the greenhouse in Leicestershire.

Gloria consulted the map. 'Now, let's see. We'll be passing through a big patch of light green soon and, according to this, light green means either forest, woodland, or an area of outstanding natural beauty, so what I – '

'That means that if you were on the map,' Moses interrupted, 'you'd be light green.'

'That's very nice of you, Moses,' Gloria said, colouring slightly (though

239

not light green). 'Anyway,' she went on, after they had kissed dangerously (Moses always closed his eyes when he kissed), 'what I was going to say was, why don't we deviate somewhere in this area of forest, woodland or outstanding natural beauty?'

'Exactly what I was thinking. How far is it?'

'About seven miles.'

Moses stamped on the accelerator. The needle on the speedometer swung wildly between fifty-eight and sixty-five mph.

Porsche indeed. Who needs a Porsche?

*

They parked on a scenic bank of leaf-mould about half a mile up a lane that led eventually, so Gloria maintained, to a village called Balls Green. Gloria was so taken with the name that she was all for checking it out right away until Moses leaned over and, resting a hand on her wrist, gently reminded her that their departure from the main road (deviation in the first sense) had a specific purpose (deviation in the second sense) and Gloria was so overwhelmed by his logic and his singlemindedness that she instantly put all other thoughts out of her head.

They had a line of coke each in the car. Gloria began to slip out of her shorts.

'In here?' Moses looked surprised.

Gloria laughed. 'No. I'm just changing.'

From surprise to bewilderment. '*Changing?*'

'You'll see.'

Outside the clouds parted to reveal a sky of almost transparent blue. Trees shifted their leaves and branches like people exercising. The air had warmed up.

Moses stood a little way from the car and let the sun move over his face.

Then Gloria was walking towards him in a long black skirt that she had fastened at the waist with a studded leather belt. She put an arm round him. 'You know what I think, Moses? I think this is an area of outstanding natural beauty.'

He looked down at her and said, 'Well, it is now, anyway.'

Hand in hand, they strolled up a mud track between massed banks of blackberry bushes and old man's beard. Gloria noticed a stile set back in the hedgerow and a field beyond.

'What about in there?' she said.

They surveyed the field together. Lining one side, a row of silver birches, their bark scalloped, edged in black, catching the sun like the scales on fish. Tough springy grass sloped up to a copse at the far end. No sign of any livestock.

'A perfect field,' Moses said.

He vaulted over the stile. Gloria handed him the Thermos and followed, pinching her skirt between finger and thumb, as ladies descending staircases in ballgowns do. Moses, waiting below, ran a hand up her thigh. It encountered nothing but warm bare skin. Gloria smiled. Moses began to understand the full significance of the skirt.

They sat side by side on the grass. They drank vodka and breathed the lush agricultural air. Gloria said she could smell magnolia and Moses agreed, even though he couldn't really think what magnolia smelt like. It was that kind of field.

Soon she was arranging herself on top of him, and it wasn't long before he was inside her in a way that she had engineered and he was very happy with. Her skirt hid their four legs and far more besides.

'You're cunning,' Moses said. The skirt, he meant.

Gloria smiled. 'Someone's got to think ahead.'

They fell silent, moved together. For a while it seemed as if Sussex might prove to be more accommodating than Leicestershire. Gloria could have been a tree doing its exercises. Sometimes her body shuddered as if a gust of wind had caught it, and one arm rose into the air beside her ear, the hand clenching and unclenching. Her eyelids trembled like leaves. Moses grasped her by the waist with both hands, twisted his face sideways into the grass. He closed his eyes. No sky any more. Only this green smell and the arching of his back. It was extraordinary how quickly she could move him from humour to ecstasy.

Then he heard the cough.

'I don't believe it,' he came back to say.

But they had both heard it. A harsh bronchial cough, such as belonged in a doctor's waiting-room rather than in an area of outstanding natural beauty, if not for its own sake, for theirs. Gloria had the presence of mind to leave her body exactly where it was.

'Pretend we're having a fight,' she whispered. 'I'll do the talking.'

Moses began to struggle, though not too hard, for fear of displacing the skirt.

A man leaned over the stile. He wore a flat cap and a pair of shabby corduroys. A burlap sack bulged on his back. His tiny eyes circled the field, moving jerkily as flies, then settled on the young couple in the grass below.

'That's a private field, that is,' he observed.

Gloria launched into a complicated story about how they were driving down to visit friends on the south coast and how they had stopped to stretch their legs and how they had then got into an argument and how they were now sorting out their differences and how they would soon be on their way because they were already late for lunch.

The man said, 'Ah.'

Gloria assured him that it would only be a matter of a few minutes and that they would leave the field exactly as they had found it because they both had a great respect for the countryside, in fact they adored it, and what they were supposed to be doing this weekend, actually, was looking for a house, the house they would live in after they had got married, though, after today, she was having second thoughts about the whole thing.

The man eyed them with suspicion, a look that seemed to reflect, more than anything else, the immense gap between their lives and his, a look that had a gloating lascivious edge to it that made them both uneasy. They were relieved when he hoisted his sack higher on his shoulder and took a step backwards. But there he paused again.

'All right,' he said, 'but don't think I don't know what you're really up to.' He nodded, coughed, spat twice, and, turning away, disappeared up the track.

'Well, we've tried Sussex and we've tried Leicestershire,' Gloria said, as they walked back to the car. 'How many counties does that leave?'

Moses didn't know.

'What a country,' Gloria sighed. 'We'll just have to keep trying, I suppose. One day, somewhere, it'll happen.'

Moses agreed that this was a desirable goal and one that would prove most satisfying, he thought, when accomplished.

They climbed back into the car. Moses started the engine. They looked at each other and sighed again.

'Coitus interruptus,' Moses said.

They drove away.

*

Fifteen minutes later they were passing through a village when Moses said he had to stop for a piss.

'Can't you wait until we get out into the country?' Gloria asked him.

Moses swung the car on to a grass verge. 'Oh, this'll do.'

They had stopped outside the last house in the village. A simple red-brick house with a glass porch, white windows, and a blue front door. A framed notice, protected by a sheet of glass and mounted on two wooden posts, grew out of the low privet hedge that separated the front garden from a narrow strip of asphalt pavement. Moses, squinting, could only read the word POLICE. That's a funny place for a police notice, he thought.

Gloria got out and, leaving her door open, eased up on to the bonnet, wincing as the heat from the engine seeped through the thin fabric of her skirt. Moses crossed the road. He scaled a ditch and stood facing away from the car.

'Carthorse,' Gloria jeered.

Moses turned and grinned at her over his shoulder. He was about to say something when a movement behind her distracted him. The blue front door was opening. A policeman emerged.

Moses's heart plummeted down through his body like a lift with the cables cut. He clutched, one-handed, at the place where it had once been. He had just remembered the Thermos of vodka on the floor of the car. And the coke in the glove compartment. And Gloria had mentioned something about having some grass on her. He tried to warn her by making a serious face but all she did was make faces back. He watched helplessly as the policeman came up behind her.

'Good afternoon, miss,' the policeman said.

Gloria leapt off the bonnet.

'I'm sorry,' the policeman said. 'I didn't mean to startle you.'

'I didn't hear you,' Gloria said.

The policeman smiled remotely. 'People in the village say I have a very soft tread.'

By now Moses was standing next to Gloria. Tiny wet spots spattering the front of his trousers testified to the haste with which he had finished his business on the other side of the road.

'Good afternoon, officer,' he said. He hoped it sounded brisk enough. But co-operative at the same time.

'You know, for a moment,' the policeman said, transferring his gaze from Gloria's face to Moses's, 'I thought you were going to piss all over *my* hedge.'

Moses and Gloria both laughed – rather too abruptly, perhaps. The policeman waited until they had stopped and then smiled unnervingly as if he knew something which they were only pretending to know.

As he turned his attention to the car, however, a change came over him. He became more enervated, less sinister. He seemed to find the number-plates particularly interesting.

'This your car, is it?' he asked, managing to translate his mounting excitement into an official question.

Moses said that it was.

'May I ask where you're coming from?'

'London.'

'London,' the policeman repeated in a voice that had thickened like soup. He rolled the word sensually on his tongue. He seemed to regret that there were only two syllables; Aberystwyth, for instance, would have been better. None the less, saliva was beginning to flood into the narrow troughs between his cheeks and his gums.

'But that,' he continued, indicating the number-plate with his boot, 'unless I'm much mistaken, is a Midlands number-plate, is it not? In fact, I'd go so far as to say it's a Leicester number-plate. Am I right?'

As he pronounced the word 'Leicester', a bright jet of saliva spurted from the side of his mouth. Moses watched it trickle down the car-door. What the *fuck* is going on here? he wondered.

He began to explain that, yes, they were Leicester number-plates because the car had originally come from Leicester. A friend of his, who had moved away from Leicester, up to Edinburgh, in fact, had sold it to him. But that was four years ago and he himself now lived in London.

This casual dropping of the names Leicester, Edinburgh and London in such rapid succession was proving too much for the policeman. He had unfurled an enormous white handkerchief, almost the size of a sailcloth, and was pressing it to his mouth. The handkerchief was drenched in seconds. Unwilling to risk speech again for hydrological reasons, his excitement now unquenchable, he seemed to be about to wave them on their way. And that, no doubt, would have been the end of the matter. But Gloria chose that moment to glance back down the road.

'What's *that*?' she cried.

The two men swung round. One of those old-fashioned motorised wheelchairs with a khaki canvas surround and plastic windows whined round the bend towards them. But there was something about this wheelchair, Moses was thinking, that wasn't quite right. As it drew level, he realised what had been troubling him. The wheelchair wasn't a *real* wheelchair; it was a motorbike *disguised* as a wheelchair.

'Good Christ,' the policeman exclaimed, allowing the handkerchief to drop away from his mouth (and hosing down one side of Moses's car as a result), 'that's old Dinwoodie!'

He raised his whistle to his lips and tried to blow a piercing blast, but all he succeeded in producing was a spray of furious white froth. As he looked on, foaming, impotent, the wheelchair accelerated with an unexpected surge of power and simultaneously jettisoned its entire outer shell to reveal a pre-war olive-green BSA. It was a quite extraordinary moment – like watching a rocket leaving the earth's atmosphere or a chrysalis releasing a butterfly. Old Dinwoodie vanished round a curve in the road with one arm raised in triumph, his grey hair flapping on his shoulders, blue smoke belching from his exhaust.

The policeman cried out, half in anguish, half in exhilaration. He turned and raced back into the house, spraying a cluster of rose-bushes as he went which, as it happened, were in dire need of water because it had been an unusually dry summer in the south-east.

'Emergency, poppet,' he slobbered.

Through the open door Moses saw the policeman brush his wife aside and begin to ransack a cupboard under the stairs. Moments later the policeman emerged again, brandishing a megaphone and a red-and-white-striped police-beacon, one of those plastic ones with a magnetic bottom. Ignoring his wife, he burst from the house, sprinted across the lawn, and hurdled the privet hedge, helmet askew, uniform marinating in the juices now flowing freely from his mouth.

'Quick!' he spluttered as he reached up and attached his beacon to the roof of Moses's car. '*Quick!* Before he gets away!'

Moses gazed at the policeman in utter stupefaction. He was beginning to think that the man was dangerously mad. He looked across at Gloria for guidance or advice. Gloria was giggling. He looked at the policeman again.

'I don't know what you mean,' he said.

'What are you waiting for?' the policeman shrieked. 'Follow that wheel-chair!'

It dawned on Moses that his car was about to be appropriated for police purposes. The policeman had already bundled Gloria into the back seat. Now he was in the process of clambering into the front himself. The Thermos of vodka rolled against his boots but he kicked it away without seeming to notice.

Moses walked round to the driver's side and climbed in. The policeman was sitting in the passenger seat, hunched over, rigid, mopping at his mouth. He was staring at the windscreen like somebody watching their favourite programme on TV. Moses started the engine. He didn't understand what was happening, he didn't know what kind of policeman this policeman was, but he had decided that it would be wisest to play along, for the time being at least. And besides, he thought, relaxing a fraction now it seemed that the car wasn't going to be searched after all, it isn't every day that a policeman tells you to follow a wheelchair, especially a wheelchair that isn't a wheelchair but a motorbike disguised as a wheelchair.

They had only been driving for two or three minutes when the motorbike came into view about half a mile ahead on the open road. Moses was disappointed. He had been looking forward to breaking the speed limit. Legally, for once.

'He isn't really trying,' he complained.

'Oh yes he is,' the policeman said. 'He's trying like absolute hell.'

He could imagine exactly what was going through old Dinwoodie's head, he told them. He had done his homework and he recognised the symptoms. That initial rush of adrenalin would even out into a feeling of euphoria, one hundred per cent euphoria, which, in turn, would give way to a sense of disconnection, creeping up gradually, stealthily, making everything seem unreal, paranormal, only distantly experienced.

Moses absorbed this curious information in silence.

When Gloria asked the policeman whether he had brought any handcuffs along, the policeman replied with a confidence that was almost patronising. 'Oh *no*,' he said. 'We shan't be needing anything like *that*.' He had his saliva under control at last which made it possible to pick up the tremor of exultation in his voice.

Meanwhile they were still gaining rapidly on old Dinwoodie. The policeman removed his helmet. Then he wound the window down and leaned out with his megaphone.

'Dinwoodie? This is Police Constable Marlpit. Please pull over to the side of the road immediately. I repeat, please pull over immediately.'

He shook his head and turned to Moses. There was a very good reason, he explained, why his words were having so little effect. Old Dinwoodie had just caught a glimpse of the South Downs for the first time in his life. They stretched away above the trees, they stretched into a distance he had dreamed about. Their modest green undulations, the copses nestling in their hollows like soft green explosions, like miniature puffs of smoke, brought tears to his eyes. They were more beautiful than he had ever imagined. And he was floating towards them, untouchable, part of everything. He was dissolving. He could no longer feel where his body ended and the air began. It flowed round him as the grain in a length of wood flows round a knot. Everything was warm and slow, and there were no sharp edges any more, no needs, no pain. His goggles were misting over. His grip on the throttle was relaxing.

During this monologue Moses couldn't, at certain points, be sure if Marlpit was talking about himself or about Dinwoodie. There seemed to be a temporary blurring of identities. As if Marlpit had inhabited, and could read, Dinwoodie's mind.

By the time Moses drew alongside the motorbike, his speed had dropped to fifteen miles an hour. 'This has got to be the slowest car-chase in history,' he muttered to himself.

PC Marlpit was bellowing through his megaphone again. Old Dinwoodie just didn't seem to hear.

'Jesus,' Moses said. 'He's driving with his eyes shut.'

Even as he spoke the motorbike slowly wandered off the road, slid sideways down a muddy bank, and folded in a ditch. Dinwoodie sat up in the long grass, dazed but unhurt, his goggles dangling from one ear. His eyes were open now. Tears were streaming down his face.

Moses pulled into the side of the road.

Marlpit climbed out. 'I shan't be needing you any more,' he said. He leaned his elbows on the window. 'However, I would like to thank you, on behalf of the village constabulary, for your patience and your co-operation.'

He fitted his helmet back on to his head and detached the beacon from the roof of the car.

'Excuse me, officer,' Moses said, 'but what did old Dinwoodie do exactly?'

'Oh,' Marlpit blustered, genial now, almost offhand, shaking his head at the improbability of events, 'he was just trying to escape, that's all.'

And before Moses could question him further, he about-faced and marched back up the road to where old Dinwoodie was sitting, hands draped over his knees.

'Escape?' Moses said, half to himself. 'Where from?'

A prison? An asylum? Certainly old Dinwoodie looked a bit mad, with his antique leather flying-helmet and his spaced-out teeth and his tears all caught up in the bristles on his cheeks — but what about Marlpit? That wasn't exactly normal behaviour for a policeman, was it?

Gloria made a face as she climbed back into the front seat. Marlpit's saliva had left a long dark stain on the tan leather. It bore a curious resemblance to a truncheon. She stared into the distance for a while, as if hypnotised. Then she turned to Moses.

'Did you see?' she said. 'He was crying.'

Moses nodded. He glanced in his rear-view mirror. He watched Marlpit bend down and begin to brush the mud and twigs off old Dinwoodie's trouser-legs. Dinwoodie stood in the ditch, as helpless as a child, wiping his face with the backs of his hands.

Moses shifted into gear and pulled away.

'Nobody's going to believe this,' he said.

*

Barely wide enough for two cars, the road bumped down towards the sea between fields of green wheat and treeless hillsides cropped by flocks of sheep. *Look for a white hotel*, Louise had said.

Gloria saw the building first. It sat on a sharp bend where the road veered away from the cliffs and ran inland again, as if frightened for its own safety. A gravel car-park lay to the right, bounded on one side by a pub and a café and on the other by a row of fishermen's cottages. The cliffs dropped downwards here, then sloped up again, forming a kind of shallow bowl against the sky. The sea filled the bottom of the bowl.

Moses stopped the car in front of the pub.

Star Gap.

The cliffs eroded as much as seven feet a year in some places, Louise had told them. One of the cottages had toppled on to the beach a while back. Now only one inside wall remained, flush with the cliff-edge. You could still see the patterned wallpaper, the outline of fireplaces, the empty squares where the ghosts of pictures hung.

Women in sheepskin coats walked their dogs along the beach at dawn and dusk. Pensioners ate ham sandwiches in their warm cars, tartan blankets draped over their knees. Fishermen still fished; their boats, drawn up in neat formation on the pebbles, foamed with orange netting. Foreign students turned up on bicycles, played guitars or radios, sunbathed topless. But none of this could dispel the forlorn doomed atmosphere of the place. You didn't have to be Madame Zola to see that it had no future to look forward to. The air, though bracing, harboured a curious smell of decay (seaweed? rotting fish? the mobile toilets?), and all the colours – the pastel blues, the pearly greys of the cottages, the lemon-yellow and peppermint-green of the café – had bleached over the years, were slowly becoming different shades of white. You could imagine a corpse being found there, months after the investigation, when everyone had given up hope, when it no longer meant anything. Then Moses remembered Louise telling him a story about how, in the early seventies, the police thought they had discovered Lord Lucan's body in the gorse bushes behind the pub. It had turned out to be someone far less important.

'Strange place for a party,' he said.

'Louise used to come down here a lot when she was a kid,' Gloria told him. 'Her parents've got a house a few miles inland.'

They took another couple of lines of coke each and walked to the cliff-edge. A makeshift staircase built out of scaffolding, splintery planks, and wire mesh led down to a wide pebble beach. The coastline curved away to the west, the chalk of the cliffs pocked like cheese and topped with a layer of grass as thin as rind. They leaned on the safety-rail. All the metal had turned brown and orange, and the colour rubbed off on their hands and sleeves.

It didn't matter.

The sun pressed their faces gently into the book of the day like flowers.

A rustling as Gloria's hands dived into her bag, did a miniature breaststroke through its contents, and surfaced again with a pair of sunglasses.

She could bring something to the most simple action – something that no one else could bring. It didn't have a name, this something that she brought. It just ran through her movements like a current and carried him away.

Her eyes invisible now behind the sunglasses, she smiled at him with her mouth as if she had guessed what he was thinking.

Then her mouth altered and she lifted an arm.

'That must be them. Over there.'

He turned.

About a hundred people clustered at the base of the cliffs. Some danced, others sunbathed.

Music blared, faded, blared on the shifting air.

'Yes, I can see Louise.'

Gloria pointed to a tiny figure in a blue bikini. They waved and shouted and the tiny figure in the blue bikini waved back. They ran down the steps and across the pebbles, their shoes crunching like a lot of people eating apples at the same time.

Louise looked great. The Spanish sun had bleached her hair white-blonde. Her deep tan turned them into ghosts.

'Look at you.' Gloria hugged her. 'How was it?'

'Costa del phoney,' Louise laughed. 'The beach wasn't even a real beach. Just a lot of stones and grit all ground up to look like sand, but it didn't look like sand, it looked more like grey dust. And it was *packed*. People lying about four deep like a mass grave or something. So we went up the mountain to this private swimming-club every day and lay around and drank and did absolutely fuck all.'

'I hate you,' Gloria said.

'You look wonderful,' Moses said. 'Elliot'll be all over you.'

Louise laughed. 'Same old Moses. How's the eye?'

Moses turned his head sideways and leaned towards her.

'Shame,' Louise said. 'I thought it had a bit of class, that eye. Like you were possessed or something.'

'I think maybe I was that night,' Moses said, remembering.

'Hey, Louise, you old tart.' Gloria flung her arms around her friend again. 'Happy birthday.'

'Twenty-one,' Louise groaned.

'Oh shut up,' Moses said.

'Well,' Louise said, 'the drink's over there, the sea's over there, and later

249

on – ' she pointed to a mountain of boxes, crates and driftwood – 'there's going to be a bonfire.'

'I'm going to go off and explore,' Moses said. 'You know, look for treasures. It's ages since I've been to the beach.'

The two girls grinned at each other.

He scrambled down a steep bank. The stones had been shored up in a smooth frozen copy of a wave. They rattled like metal chains as he dislodged them. When he reached the sand he took his shoes and socks off.

It was low tide. The sea had rolled back, exposing its seedy underworld: rocks, shells, rusty metal spars, clots of oil, rotting netting, seaweed, driftwood, jagged cans, plastic detergent bottles, bits of junk from Holland and France. There was something magical about these battered travelled objects, though. You never knew what might turn up at your feet. A piece of blue glass, for instance, polished to a jewel by the sea, as if the sea was a craftsman and each of its waves a skilful, practised movement of a hand. Real treasures. He stepped from one rock to the next, keeping his eyes fixed on his feet so as not to slip. When he looked up again, the party had shrunk to nothing. He was alone.

The sea lay flat – sluggish, almost greasy. Waves creased and uncreased lazily, folds in blue leather. An oil tanker sat on the horizon. He squatted on his haunches, skimmed a few stones. His thinking slowed, moved at a leisurely pace like a procession, each thought a carriage drawn by two patient horses. Some of the thoughts were linked, some seemed random and didn't belong, some repeated themselves over and over. He had put distance between himself and the party, and he now became aware that, in some mysterious deep-rooted way, he had been thinking about the same thing all along: old Dinwoodie. Suddenly the patient horses acquired plumes, the carriages turned black, the whole procession mourned what had happened to him. In that rare blue seaside air the incident began to crystallise. Two portraits. In the first the old man sat in tearful confusion, twigs and grass stuck to his jacket, badges of despair, his eyes containing nothing but the fragments of some broken dream. In the second the policeman gloated at the motorbike as it grew in the windscreen, his hands braced on his knees, drool on his uniform, in the grip, it seemed, of an exquisite tension or excitement. The old man's tears, the policeman's saliva. Misery and greed.

'Hey!'

He recognised the old man's feelings, knew them inside out. Nights in the orphanage. Awake in the darkness. Nineteen others sleeping. The rise and fall of their breathing. An empire of lost children. Sometimes imagining himself alone. Then it would seem as if the very air had come alive.

Frightened then. Turning the damp pillow. Pulling the coarse blankets over his head.

And then the day the Poles had come to take him away in their old Ford Anglia. The smell of those blue plastic seats as they drove north. The smell of freedom.

And I helped the policeman, he thought.

What had the policeman said? Something like, *Oh, he's just trying to escape, that's all.*

That's all.

And I helped the policeman.

'Hey! Moses!'

That wasn't one of his thoughts. That had come from somewhere behind him.

*

Looking round blinded him at first. The intense whiteness of those soaring walls of chalk. Then the shout came again, abrasive, familiar, redirecting him. Now he could see two figures sitting at the foot of the cliffs. Was that *Vince*? What was *he* doing here?

Moses started up the beach. It sloped sharply, and the pebbles ran out from beneath his feet. He felt like someone trying to go up an escalator that's going down. In the end he had to drop on to all fours.

Vince – for it was Vince – jeered from his vantage-point. He was leaning against a rock, his arm around a girl. Moses had to smile. Typical Vince to come to a party and then sit as far away from it as possible. He looked totally out of place in these natural surroundings. The sun lit every crease and crevice in his haggard face, and showed up all the stains on that infamous black waistcoat.

He handed Moses a bottle of brandy. 'You weren't expecting to see me, were you,' he said, as if that alone justified the trip down.

Moses swallowed a mouthful of brandy and handed it back. 'Thanks. No. So why are you here?'

'Eddie told me about it.' Vince passed the bottle to the girl. She held it to her lips and tipped her head back. Three gulps. It wasn't the first time she had drunk brandy out of a bottle.

'So Eddie's here too?' Moses said.

'Yeah. He gave us a lift down.'

'Christ, you're lucky to be alive.' Moses addressed this remark to the girl.

She twisted the bottle into the stones so it stood upright. She had fat

251

arms and a big awkward body, but when she smiled she looked like a madonna. It was a really beautiful face.

'You're not kidding,' she said. 'That Eddie, he drives like a fucking maniac.'

A madonna with a Liverpool accent.

'That's because he is a fucking maniac,' Moses said.

'Fucking right.' The word fucking sounded so much better coming out of her mouth. It might have been invented specially for girls from Liverpool. 'No way am I going back in that car. I'd rather walk.' She shook herself. 'He gives me the creeps, anyway. He a friend of yours?'

Vince looked at Moses.

'Sort of,' Moses said. 'We used to live together.'

The girl closed her eyes, offered her wide pale eyelids to the sun. Vince sifted stones with his dirty fingers.

'I knew there was something different about you,' Moses said. 'Your arms.'

'Yeah, they didn't do a bad job, did they?'

The bandages had come off. Thin red scars ran the length of his forearms where the glass had lifted flaps of skin away, but they were main roads on a map not the railway lines you get with stitches.

'So tape really does work,' Moses said. 'Three months and you'll be able to do it again.'

Vince grinned, leaned back against the rock. No rise out of him at all. No venom. For the first time ever Moses could imagine Vince living beyond thirty. Vince with a wife and kids. Vince with a mortgage, a food-processor, and a sense of responsibility. He put it down to the influence of this girl from Liverpool, whose name, Vince finally told him, was Debra. No o, no h.

'Don't think my parents knew how to spell it,' she said.

Most people called her Zebra, she told him, because she wore a lot of black and white, and at least that was spelt right. She took another long pull on the brandy, lit a Benson and Hedges, and stared out towards the sea.

'I've always been fat,' she said. 'Once I screwed up this weighing-machine in Blackpool. I was so heavy it thought I was a fucking man.' She chuckled. 'It called me sir. My mum nearly died.'

She tapped the end of her cigarette. The ash fell, invisible, against the grey pebbles. 'Once I got so depressed I almost did myself in.' A pause. Then her madonna smile. 'Didn't have the guts, did I.

'I'm pretty used to being fat now. Fuck it is what I think. It's me, isn't it. Fucked if I'm going to change. Like I like chips, right?'

'And alcohol,' Vince murmured.

'And alcohol. Fucked if I'm going to give them up just to please some git in a magazine.'

'I know,' Moses said. 'It's like someone telling me I ought to be shorter or something.'

Debra nodded. 'That's right.'

'I'm not supposed to be short and you're not supposed to be thin and – ' Moses glanced at Vince's arms – '*you're* not supposed to be alive.'

Debra smiled, but Vince ignored the remark. 'You're not fat, Zeb,' he said. 'You're more sort of voluptuous, really.'

'Fuck off, Vincent.' And before Vince could move, Debra was sitting on his chest.

Vince began to struggle. 'I'll beat shit out of you,' he warned her. 'I will.'

She just laughed. 'You couldn't beat shit out of a nappy.'

Moses watched her pin Vince's scarred arms to the ground; it was good to see Vince being treated with the respect he deserved. He wondered why she had told them all that stuff about herself. Maybe she had always been teased, he thought. And maybe, over the years, she had learned to get in first herself, to sound at home with her disadvantages, before people could start pointing fingers or cracking jokes. He liked her, he decided. She was someone else who didn't quite fit. The world would never be off the peg for either of them.

*

Half an hour later Moses said he really ought to be getting back to the party.

Vince and Debra, arm in arm and reconciled, told him they were staying put.

Moses motioned to the bottle of brandy, almost empty now. 'But aren't you going to run out pretty soon?'

Vince patted the carrier-bag beside him. A clink of glass answered Moses's question. He should have known that Vince would provide for his own oblivion.

The sun, coppery now, was dropping into a bank of grey cloud. Safe deposit for the night. The tide had turned. The sea, ruled into straight lines by the waves, was covered with the hieroglyphics of swimmers – black dots for heads, the pale flash of arms.

Walking back through the fading light, he stopped whenever he thought he saw something interesting. Most stones seemed to be grey (flint) or white (chalk). If he stared hard enough he found his eyes began to invent exceptions. But as soon as he crouched down, touched one with his hand, it turned ordinary again. This process repeated itself, as if it was a lesson he was supposed to be learning. Some stones, he noticed, were the strangest most luminous colours when wet, but if you picked them up and dried them off they lost their allure, looked just like a million other stones. He did find a few treasures, though: a meteorite, no bigger than a ping-pong ball, rust-brown, fissured as a brain; several smooth pieces of glass, white on the outside, blue, yellow or green on the inside, like boiled sweets dusted with sherbet; and a dull green stone the exact shape of a lady's automatic. He fitted this last stone into his palm and bounced his hand in the air a couple of times, as he had seen people do with guns, testing it for weight and balance. It felt good: small, compact – good. He raised his arm stiffly, aimed at the setting sun, and fired.

A red stain appeared in the sky away to the right. He must've missed. Hit a cloud by mistake.

He blew across the barrel of his new stone gun.

'Sorry about that,' he said.

*

Somebody had lit the bonfire. Scraps of paper floated upwards with the smoke, then dived and swooped, jittery as bats, glowed red until the black air blew them out. Sometimes a damp branch whined or popped, spat sparks, tiny flutes of steam, jets of green flame. It was a warm night, but the fire drew people in. Their disembodied faces hung in the darkness. In that leaping athletic light, they looked like caricatures of themselves – their noses pulled, their lips grimacing, their eyes coloured-in black. Moses recognised Alison, though. She looked more Pre-Raphaelite than ever with her wide tranquil forehead and her scorching red abundance of hair. He made his way round the fire towards her.

When she saw him she let out a little cry of surprise. She hadn't known he was coming, how was he, what had he been doing – her usual flurry of familiarities and exclamations.

'Have you seen Vince?' he asked her.

'Not for weeks,' came her reply. It was funny, but whenever you mentioned Vince's name these three lines appeared on her forehead like seagulls flying in formation.

'What I meant was, have you seen him here?' He tried to put his hands in his pockets, but he had crammed them too full of treasures. Ballast for his lightheadedness.

'What?' Alison cried. 'Is Vince here?' Dismay loosened the skin round her mouth.

Since Vince was their only common ground, they usually ended up treading all over him whenever they talked to each other. These days Alison trod warily. She didn't regret leaving Vince, not for a second, but one nagging fear remained: the fear that she wasn't free of him, that he was still attached to her, as if by a length of elastic, that he might spring back into her life at any moment. *I don't like emotional blackmail, and I certainly don't like being hit for failing to respond to it*, she had told Moses more than once. *I don't measure love in bruises*, she had said on another occasion — rather sententiously, Moses thought. Still, he could hardly disagree with the sentiment, and when he talked to her he often found himself having to reassure her or, more accurately, perhaps, having to listen to her reassure herself. She was tough, he still believed that, but Vince seemed to have touched a nerve in her, a nervousness, and brought it to the surface, put it on display. She felt the threat of his presence so acutely. Now she knew he had come to the party she kept glancing over her shoulder, probing the darkness around her. Vince was out there, she was thinking, plotting something malevolent against her. She was wrong. The only person that Vince was capable of plotting something malevolent against was himself.

'I wasn't expecting *him* to turn up,' she was saying. 'If I'd known that, I would've thought twice about coming.' She stabbed at some stones with the toe of her shoe. '*Shit*,' she broke out, bitterly. 'Everything was going so well.'

Vince might have planned the whole thing out of spite, purely to spoil her evening. A fourth seagull appeared on her forehead.

'I don't think it's as bad as you're making out,' Moses said. 'I don't think he even knows you're here.'

Alison said nothing.

'And even if he finds out I don't think he'll bother you.' He tried to put it tactfully. 'He didn't come alone, you see. He brought somebody with him.'

All four seagulls banked and vanished. They left only the faintest of after-images. It was so neat a reversal that Alison's face might have been a coin that somebody had just flipped over.

'Who's he with?'

'A girl called Debra.'

'Debra?' Alison looked thoughtful.

'You probably don't know her. I only met her today.'

'What's she like?'

Moses knew Alison well enough to have anticipated this: the is-she-good-looking bit.

'Look,' he said, 'I'm not taking sides.'

'I didn't ask you to take sides. I just asked you what she was like.'

Moses sighed. 'She comes from Liverpool. She's got a good sense of humour. She doesn't put up with any bullshit.'

Alison looked up sharply. 'What's she doing with Vince then?'

Moses had to laugh because he had just thought exactly the same thing. But he wasn't going to give Alison the satisfaction of knowing that. 'That's her problem,' he said. 'Why don't you forget about Vince? Pretend he isn't here. I mean, you probably won't see him anyway. The last time I saw him he was sitting about two miles away. Way over there, under the cliffs. "Fuck the party," he said. "I'm staying where I am." '

Alison picked up her drink, smiled into it sadly, almost fondly. 'Typical Vince,' she murmured.

Moses looked away from her.

The moon had floated up into the night sky. Someone had cut its string. Cut mine, he thought. That afternoon, after leaving the village behind, Gloria had said, *Let's change the mood.* She'd rolled a fat joint and they'd smoked it driving. It'd worked. Suddenly they were out of their heads and laughing, and Moses had spun off into fantasy. He'd imagined making drunk uninterrupted love to Gloria on a bed of sand, he'd imagined swimming afterwards with nothing on, he'd imagined moonlight on the surface of the water.

Well, at least the moon was playing its part. A stack of silver dishes reached from the shoreline to the horizon, swaying with the motion of the waves.

But where was Gloria? He hadn't seen her for ages.

Alison broke into his silence. 'I was just thinking, Moses. Why don't you come round to my parents' house next Sunday? We often have people round on Sundays. I think you'd enjoy it.'

Moses remembered talking to Alison's mother on the phone once. He remembered the allure in her voice. 'I'd love to,' he said. 'I'll call you next week, OK?'

Soon afterwards Alison drifted away to talk to somebody else.

Moses didn't mind in the least. You could overdose on Alison. Still, he would take her up on that invitation.

*

While he was rooting about among sausage-boxes and sacks of briquettes,

Moses looked up and saw Jackson skulking in the shadows of a recent rock-fall. Jackson was clutching a brown paper parcel in both hands and looking apprehensive, as if he was about to walk into an ambush; he kept advancing a few paces then stopping again, bending forwards from the waist and twisting his head this way and that.

'Jackson,' Moses called out.

Jackson started, turned round. He brought one hand up to shield his eyes against the glare of the fire.

'Oh, it's you, Moses.'

Jackson had travelled down alone by train. The parcel was a box of rockets, he explained. A birthday present for Louise.

He perched on a crate, the parcel on his lap. 'You've no idea how difficult it is,' he said, 'to find rockets in July.'

Moses suppressed a smile. Only Jackson would've thought of such a thing.

'In one of the shops the woman got really angry with me,' Jackson said. 'She told me I was four months early. "Four months early?" I said. "Why?" "November the fifth," she said.' He shook his head as he remembered.

He had been looking for Louise for hours. 'It's so dark,' he complained. 'I keep treading on people.'

Moses laughed. 'We'll find her together.'

Jackson hadn't thought of looking in the sea. They were walking along the shoreline when Moses saw her ten yards out.

'Louise,' he shouted. 'Here a moment.'

Clouds had hidden the moon. When Louise stood up, the water wrapped itself around her thighs, looked as if it didn't want to let her go. She stumbled as the undertow sucked pebbles past her feet, but struggled free and ran towards them smiling.

'Jackson,' she said. 'I didn't think you'd make it.' She snatched up a white towel and began to rub her hair, tilting her head first to one side then to the other.

'Here,' and Jackson held out the parcel, 'this is for you.'

Draping the towel round her shoulders, Louise accepted the parcel, examined it, all four sides of it, with her wet hands, left dark fingerprints on the brown paper. She held it to her ear and shook it gently, two dents of puzzlement between her eyebrows, but waves kept breaking behind her with a dull thump and foam came sliding round her ankles, drowning any other sound she might have heard. Jackson said nothing, content, it seemed, simply to watch her. She tore the brown paper off and pulled out an oblong box secured with Sellotape. She broke the Sellotape with her teeth and opened the lid. The rockets lay inside, tightly packed, two rows deep.

Bright red and yellow. Twisted blue-black touchpapers. Long blond launching-sticks.

'There's twenty-one of them,' Jackson explained, 'because that's how old you are.'

And then, when she still didn't say anything, he shifted from one foot to the other and added, 'You know, like the candles on a cake.'

When Louise lifted her eyes from the box of rockets to Jackson's anxious face, her deep tan and the slick blackness of the sea behind her gave her smile a new and unexpected dimension: for a moment she was an actress – famous, glamorous, spotlit for the cameras.

'They're beautiful.' She rested a hand on Jackson's shoulder and kissed him on the mouth. 'Thank you, Jackson.'

Jackson looked pleased, serious and uncomfortable. It was a speciality of his: he did it with equal measures of each.

Louise turned to Moses. 'Aren't they great?'

'Well,' and Moses thought of the coat-hook and the chair, 'Jackson's always had a way with presents.'

'You know what I'm going to do?' Louise said. 'I'm going to get some empty bottles and I'm going to line them up in one long line and I'm going to put rockets in them and then I'm going to let them off, one by one, like they do on royal birthdays or whenever it is.'

She ran off up the beach.

Moses and Jackson sat down on the stones to wait for her.

'Does she like them, do you think?' Jackson asked.

'*Jackson*,' Moses said. 'Didn't you see her face?'

Jackson chuckled to himself. 'You know, I thought it was going to rain tonight. I mean, really rain. A real downpour. And look what happens. This is probably one of the warmest nights of the year so far.'

The moon slid out from behind a cloud. Its movement was so smooth that it might have been running on greased tracks. Moses glanced down at his latest bottle of wine. Soon Louise would be able to stick a rocket in the end of it. He wondered where Gloria was, but only vaguely, and was surprised by the vagueness of the thought. He watched Jackson fold his raincoat and place it beside him on the beach.

'If you thought it was going to rain,' Moses said suddenly, 'how come you brought fireworks?'

Jackson grinned as if Moses had just fallen into a carefully-laid trap. 'Maybe I wanted her to feel sorry for me,' he said.

Moses smiled.

Louise returned, wearing a knee-length pink T-shirt. She was dragging a crate of empty bottles. Moses and Jackson helped her to wedge the bottles into the pebbles at intervals of ten feet so they formed a long line parallel with the sea. Then she borrowed Moses's lighter.

'Here goes,' she said.

She lit the first touchpaper and jumped back. The rocket seemed to hold its breath for a moment, to gather itself, then it fizzed out over the sea, a fierce arc of sparks, and fizzled out, dropping a cluster of silver stars into the darkness.

'One,' chanted the crowd of people now assembled at the water's edge.

Louise was lighting the second rocket when Moses felt a slight tugging on his sleeve.

'There you are,' Gloria said. She looked excited, dishevelled. He could see all the parties she had ever been to in her eyes. 'Where've you been?'

'Looking for you,' he said. 'Where've *you* been?'

She laughed. 'I must've been in all the places you didn't look.'

He stared at the sea beyond her. He saw the stack of silver dishes crash. It struck him that neither of them were telling the truth. He hadn't been looking for her, not for at least two hours. Not at all, really. It had just been something to say. But her lie, he felt, had nothing to do with what she had said. Her lie had something to do with what she *hadn't* said, though he didn't even have a glimmer of what that might be.

A rocket screamed out over the sea. It scored a ragged orange line in the night sky and self-destructed. The explosion rebounded off the cliffs behind them. He felt Gloria jump.

'Seven,' came the chant.

Gloria said something about going up to the car. He moved away with her towards the steps. The night seemed to darken then. He stumbled, almost fell. When he looked across at Gloria he saw that she was disappearing again.

'No,' he cried out.

But her body had already vanished, her body vanished first, and when he searched for her face some of her features (fringe, pupils, lips, eyebrows) instantly became invisible. Gloria and the night, they were made of the same stuff; she was turning into one small part of that immeasurably vast darkness. With a shiver he remembered Louise rising out of the sea, he remembered the reluctance of that black water to surrender her. He wanted to kiss Gloria, just lean across and kiss her, but he didn't know how to find her mouth, or what exactly he would be kissing if he did. They had reached the steps now. A swaying in his head. Panic or nausea, he couldn't tell which. He grasped a metal stanchion for support.

'Have you got a cigarette?' he said.

'In the car,' her voice came back from somewhere above him.

He reached the top just behind her. Only her hands, her cheekbones, the whites of her eyes, remained. She was going fast, dissolving in the night's black acid. If he let her go he would have to wait until daylight to look for her and she might be miles away by then, a corpse or as good as, lost to him for ever. Where was the nearest light? In the car, she had said. Yes, there was a light in the car. If he could get her there in time. He hardly dared to look at her. When he did, a splinter of white light in the corner of her eye, a fraction of her, returned his glance. Like a dream where you can't run fast enough, he started over the gravel, pulling her by an arm he couldn't see. She seemed to be resisting. Didn't she realise what was happening? Or was that what she wanted?

'Nineteen,' came a faint cry.

'What's the hurry?' She tripped, laughed as he caught her.

He half-carried, half-dragged her the last few yards. He unlocked the door, tore it open. The light came on. It was dim, but it was enough. A sickly pallor ran back into her face, rebuilding her features, filling in gaps. Her surprise became visible.

'What was all that about?'

'All what?'

'All that crazy rushing to the car.'

He slid into the driving-seat. His heart was banging like a stone in a tin can. He switched the radio on. Frank Sinatra was singing. 'Strangers in the Night', of all things.

'I thought you were going to disappear,' he said. 'I didn't want you to disappear.'

He watched her face in the light from the radio. She was hugging her legs as if cold or alone, her chin resting on her knees. Even though he could now see all of her he felt that some crucial part of her had eluded him. He had failed. She *had* disappeared.

> *It turned out so right*
> *For strangers in the night –*

Why does music always do that? he wondered.

'Shall we go?' he said.

'Where?'

'Back to London.'

'No,' she said. 'Not yet.'

A silence.

'No,' he sighed. 'I don't really want to either.'

She sat up, possessed of some new efficiency now, and opened the glove compartment. She undid the envelope that contained the coke. She tipped half the contents on to the cover of his logbook. Using her own razor-blade, she cut the stuff into four lines. She rolled a £5 note and, bending quickly, vacuumed up the two lines nearest her. Then she passed him the £5 note. He leaned over, his face almost touching her knee, and did the same.

'I'm going over to the pub for a brandy,' he said. 'Coming?'

She sniffed twice, once with each nostril. 'No, I think I'll go back down.'

He got out of the car, locked the doors.

'Moses?'

He looked up. She had reached the top of the steps. 'Yes?' he said.

'Thank you for not wanting me to disappear.'

'That's all right.' He had spoken quietly. He doubted whether his voice had carried to where she was standing.

They looked at each other across a distance for a moment, then she turned and started down the steps. He watched her until she disappeared below the level of the cliff-top.

*

'Nice place, isn't it?' Vince said.

Moses stopped short, a yard inside the door. He hadn't expected anything, but if he had, he wouldn't have expected anything like this. Vince was sitting in the shade of a life-size cardboard palm tree. Along one wall there were wooden booths with Wild West swing-doors. A chrome and purple jukebox in the corner. Pineapple ice-buckets on the bar. Red plastic diner-stools with silver legs. Green glass fishing-floats dangling from a mass of orange netting overhead. Hanging on the far wall, a Mexican poncho, three hunting-horns, a coolie hat, a sabre, a painting of a bullfight, and a stuffed swordfish. And all this at first glance. The way Vince was grinning, it might have been his doing.

'I thought I might find you in here,' Moses said.

'No, you didn't. It's a horrible surprise.' Vince's grin widened. 'Because now you're going to have to talk to me and buy me drinks.'

Moses stood by the door, one hand massaging his forehead. Not only Disneyland in here, but Vince. He could feel the stones in his pockets beginning to weigh him down, to drag him floorwards.

'Mine's a brandy,' Vince said.

Moses pushed towards the bar.

'Yes sir?' The landlord had dyed black hair and wore a vermilion shirt with silver metal collar-tips. There was nowhere to look.

'Two brandies,' Moses said. 'No ice.'

He watched the landlord press the glasses to a Hennessey optic. 'Quite a place you've got here.'

'You like it?' The landlord flashed him a smile. All crow's-feet and dentures.

Moses was fucked if he was going to say it again. Someone might think he was taking the piss and knock him out. That was all he needed. He paid quickly, smiled, and squeezed back to the safety of the palm tree.

Vince grabbed his drink and swallowed it whole.

'If you're going to drink them like that,' Moses said, 'it's hardly worth me sitting down.'

'Should've brought me a double then, shouldn't you.'

Moses shook his head. 'You would've drunk that twice as fast.' He leaned back against the fake teak panelling. 'What's wrong with everyone today? Everyone's acting so strange. Jackson turns up with a box of fireworks. Louise is all brown and goes swimming in the middle of the night. Gloria keeps disappearing. Eddie's pretending he isn't even here. And you.' He turned to face Vince. 'You sit there quietly, not breaking anything. What's going on, Vince?'

Vince shrugged.

Moses reached for his glass. 'And the seagulls. Did you notice the seagulls?'

Vince hadn't.

'What they do is, they sort of spread their wings and float upwards on the air-currents till they're level with the top of the cliff, then they slide sideways – ' Moses demonstrated with his hand – 'float all the way down again till they reach the bottom. Then they start all over again. Do exactly the same thing. Millions and millions of times. Why do they do that? Does it feel good?'

Vince didn't know.

'Everybody's up to something.' Moses stubbed his cigarette out in the tail of a pink china mermaid. 'Even the birds.'

'Have you got any of that left?'

Moses looked blank. 'Any of what?'

'Any of whatever you're on.'

'No.'

Vince knocked back the rest of Moses's drink and banged the empty glass down on the table.

'All right,' Moses said, 'but this is your last one.'

He returned to the bar.

The landlord winked. 'Two brandies. Right?'

'Right.'

'No rocks. Right?'

'Right.'

'Plenty of rocks on the beach. Right?' The landlord's mouth opened. A round dark hole. The shape of a railway tunnel. A long train of laughter came squeaking out. How about a drink yourself? Moses thought. Oil, for instance.

'You know,' the landlord rattled on, 'I've been here fifteen years now and I don't reckon I've been down to the beach more than half a dozen times.'

Oh, so it was the life-history now, was it?

'Too busy up here, I suppose,' Moses said. Collecting all this junk.

'I keep myself pretty busy.' The landlord picked up a white cloth, began to caress a glass. 'Going to invite me down there later on?'

'Sorry,' Moses said. 'Not my party.'

When he returned to the palm tree he decided it was time to start pestering Vince. Vince was acting too cocktail-party for his liking. He wanted the old blood-and-vomit Vincent back. The Suicide Kid. Onassis on acid. The dregs at the bottom of the King's Road.

He began with, 'Seen anything of Alison recently?'

Vince scowled. 'No. Why? Have you?'

'Oh, a little bit, you know.' Moses was airy. 'I'm seeing her next Sunday. She's asked me round for lunch.'

'Muswell Hill?'

Moses nodded.

'What d'you want to do that for?'

'I want to, that's all. Anyway, what d'you care?'

'I *don't* care. I don't give a fuck.'

It looked as if Vince still hadn't got Alison out of his system. He didn't know it, of course. There was too much other shit blocking his system for him to be able to find out.

The bell rang for last orders.

'Anyway,' Moses began again, 'I want to meet this woman you're always going on about. Alison's mother.'

Vince flared. 'What d'you mean always going on about her? I'm not always going on about her.'

'All right, you've only mentioned her once or twice,' and Moses leaned into Vince's face, 'but I want to meet her, I want to see what she's like.'

Vince pushed Moses away. 'She's a phoney.'

'You told me that. What else?'

Vince twisted away. His bloodshot eyes tracked a girl in black tights.

She almost took the whole conversation with her as she walked out of the door.

Moses nudged Vince. 'What else?'

'Christ, I don't know. She must be at least forty but she acts like time's stood still for twenty years. Fucking hippie's what she is.' Vince wiped his forehead with his sleeve. 'She floats round the house in an old velvet dress like some kind of fucking museum-piece. Chainsmokes through a cigarette-holder, shit like that. She can't do anything normally, you know? She sits in this green chair of hers and looks at you like she's sorry for you or something, like she *understands* you. She makes me fucking puke.'

Moses smiled to himself. This was more like it. And he rather liked the idea of somebody chainsmoking through a cigarette-holder. That kind of perversity appealed to him.

'She drinks a lot too,' Vince was saying. 'A fuck of a lot. There's always a bottle of vodka down the side of her chair. They all drink in that house. Alison's the only one who doesn't. She's probably seen her mother make a fool of herself too many times. No wonder she's thinking of moving out. If I had a mother like that, I would've moved out when I was fucking born.'

He stole one of Moses's cigarettes. He lit it, sucked the smoke deep down. Half the cigarette was gone before he spoke again.

'Yeah, she's always out of her head,' he sneered. 'You'll probably like her.'

*

Closing-time.

Somebody had wedged the door open, and Moses could see a triangle of lit gravel and a strip of dark-blue sky above the darker outline of the cliff. The landlord was shouting something about glasses. His vermilion shirt was shouting too. Moses couldn't understand either of them. He suddenly felt drunker than he had for ages. Movements kept breaking up into staggered versions of themselves. If he closed his eyes, his whole body began to lift and turn in one long slow backwards somersault. Like being inside a wave. What a terrible, terrible place to get this wrecked in. No rocks, right?

He got up and the world sat down. He couldn't look at Vince. He knew the upward curve of Vince's lips would make his stomach churn. He aimed for the rectangle of darkness where the breeze was coming from.

Then he was zig-zagging over stones. A single headlamp blinded him. Tyres spun viciously, kicked up dirt and gravel. He heard a girl's laughter submerge in the rough snarling of motorbike engines, submerge, surface, then submerge again, like someone drowning, like someone going down for the third time.

He had long since lost Vince.

He stumbled into something (lobster-pots?), cracked his shin, then found himself climbing, falling, scrambling down the steps, slamming into the scaffolding at the end of each flight, winding himself on the metal rails.

Once he looked for the fire. It had shrunk. It threw out orange starfish arms into the darkness.

When he reached the beach he thought he saw Gloria. An impish figure on a white rock. That way of sitting – arms hugging her legs, chin resting on her knees – seemed to belong to her. The next time he looked – lifting his head was so hard, like fighting the pull of a magnet – she had gone.

Halfway between the steps and the fire everything began to whirl about. This was the worst so far. It felt as if someone was stirring the night with a giant spoon, as if he was one grain of sugar in the bottom of a cup. He spun away to the base of the cliffs and collapsed on the pebbles. He retched and retched, but only bile and bitter froth came up.

He couldn't have guessed how long he spent there, his forehead pressed to a boulder, cooled by the damp chalk. An hour, maybe. Even two. His hair, wet through with sweat, gradually dried into stiff strands. He was shivering, but being cold made him feel better. He scooped up handfuls of shiny wet pebbles and rubbed them into his face.

Once he saw Gloria run past, light steps, light years away. He didn't call out, and she didn't see him.

He was glad about that.

*

Afterwards he couldn't remember exactly how the fight had started.

When he stood up, shaky but clear, he walked down to the sea to rinse his face. By the time he reached the fire it must have been late. Only a few people were still awake, talking in low voices. The evening had divided them into couples. He sat down next to Gloria.

'Where've you been?' Vince asked from the other side of the fire.

Moses smiled. 'Throwing up.'

Gloria murmured, 'Oh, Highness,' and rested her head against his shoulder.

Highness? he thought.

'I'm all right now,' he said.

He stared into the mass of collapsing red embers. Sometimes a flame leapt up, like something growing, only to wither, fall back, die out. Jackson said he was going to gather some more wood so the fire would last the night. Louise went with him. Then Moses felt hands on his shoulders and suddenly he was somersaulting backwards down a steep bank of stones. He lay still, not understanding what had happened. Then he looked up and saw Eddie standing over him. Eddie grinned.

Moses propped himself up on one arm. 'Hello, Eddie.'

Eddie kicked the arm out from under him. 'Come on, shithead. This is a fight.'

Moses laughed good-naturedly. A fight. What next. But as he tried to clamber to his feet Eddie pushed him over again and something competitive took hold. He shoved Eddie in the chest. Eddie staggered backwards down the beach.

Moses stood up. He was a head taller than Eddie and he had a seventy-pound weight advantage, but Eddie was muscular and his muscles were hard and supple from sleeping with at least fifteen hundred women and he was using his muscles with a frenzy Moses hadn't seen before.

Their struggle took them some distance from the fire and now they faced each other, panting, watching each other's eyes for the next move. Eddie was grinding his teeth together, his face contorted by a kind of predatory glee. He looks as if he wants to kill me, Moses thought. Why? he wondered.

He glanced sideways, brushed some chalk off his sleeve. 'Isn't that enough now, Eddie?'

'*Isn't that enough now?* So we've had enough, have we? Poor little Highness has had enough.' And, lowering his head, Eddie charged.

Moses stepped to one side and, using Eddie's momentum, sent him diving headfirst into the pebbles. It was too easy. Eddie picked himself up, slowly but automatically. He shook himself. He leered over his shoulder at Moses, his features stretched wide across his face. He was breathing through his open mouth like an animal.

He charged again. The same thing happened. Moses the matador. For once, though, Moses didn't see the funny side. He was tired. Bored too. But Eddie wouldn't let up. He charged a third time, arms extended like horns, fingers curved and spread. This time he caught Moses, clawed at his collar, clung on. They both crashed to the ground. Moses heard something rip. He rolled over, twisted free of Eddie's grip. He scrambled to his feet. Eddie lunged for his ankle, but Moses stepped out of reach. He noticed that one of his pockets was torn. All his treasures had fallen out.

'You bastard. Now I've lost all my stones.'

'Ahhh. Now he's lost all his stones.'

Moses looked at Eddie and saw fury running in his veins instead of blood. When Eddie rushed him again, he seized Eddie by the wrists.

'What do you want, Eddie?'

'*Nice* Highness.'

'Look, can we stop this now? I'm bored, OK?'

'You're so *nice*, *aren't* you, Highness? *Everybody* likes *Highness*. *Don't* they, Highness?'

Eddie was spitting the words out from a distance of six inches. Moses could feel the saliva hitting him in the face.

'What d'you want?' He shook Eddie by the wrists. 'D'you want to hit me? Is that what you want? All right. Hit me.' He flung Eddie's hands away from him. And waited.

Eddie swayed from the waist, almost lost balance. His laughter sounded like heavy breathing. Then his arm uncoiled through the air and the palm of his hand landed hard and flat on Moses's face.

'That'll teach you,' he hissed, 'you bloody martyr.'

Moses had forgotten about his fractured cheekbone, but as he felt the pain exploding inwards through his head, as he watched Eddie laughing at the surprise on his face, it seemed to him that Eddie had chosen that side of his face quite deliberately.

'You fucking shit,' he shouted.

Eddie's eyes lit up. 'Now, now,' he said. He began to run backwards, dance backwards on his toes, like a boxer, but when he stumbled on an empty bottle Moses jumped at him and landed a punch on the side of his head. They rolled down a slope towards the sea. Moses forced Eddie on to his stomach. He placed both his hands on the back of Eddie's head and, mustering all his strength, twisted Eddie's face into the beach. He heard Eddie laughing through a mouthful of stones.

Then he got to his feet and walked back to the fire.

*

The sea was breathing deeply like someone sound asleep, each wave a soft exhalation through its open mouth. In the silence between waves Moses could hear the softer breathing of the people all around him.

He had been trying to get to sleep himself, thinking that if he synchronised his breathing with the rhythm of the waves, if he harnessed himself to all that natural hypnotic power, then maybe he would drift off.

No such luck.

His eyes stung so much they wouldn't stay closed. The coldness of the stones soaked up into his hip. He looked around for the blanket Gloria had brought down from the car, but it had disappeared.

Jesus, he ached all over. Skinned knuckles on both hands. His left shin caked with blood. A jarring pain in his cheek. He rubbed the back of his neck and his hand came away sticky with tar.

He just hoped Eddie had come off worse.

The sky had diluted – black to grey. Instructions for the creation of dawn: just add water to the colour of the night. Not a hint of sunshine anywhere. It looked as if the weather had broken.

He glanced down at Gloria. She was still asleep, burrowed into the bay-shape he had made with his body when he lay down, her head resting in the hollow between his hip and his rib-cage. She had curled up very tight, like a fist. There was oil on the soles of her shoes, and on her neck, just below her ear, he saw two tiny moles that he had never noticed before. Dracula scars.

'Gloria?' He ruffled her hair. Her mouth twitched, but she didn't wake up.

'Gloria?'

She jack-knifed into a sitting position, her eyes wide open. 'I was dreaming,' she said.

'What were you dreaming about?' he asked her as they trudged across the beach.

She frowned. 'Someone had hidden my voice. Someone had stolen my voice while I was sleeping and hidden it somewhere.'

They walked up the steps, their heads bent, the wood creaking under their feet. The grey air flapped around them like damp canvas. Their clothes were stiff, sticky with salt.

'Why do I feel so cold?' Gloria spoke through mauve lips. 'I don't think I've ever been so cold.'

When they reached the top they paused, looked back down. It was high tide. Grey sky. Grey sea. There was no way of telling where the horizon was, nothing to suggest a division of any kind. A foghorn groaned in the distance. An explanation there, perhaps. Grey sea. Grey beach. At the base of the cliffs, a splash of colour, the only splash of colour visible. The reds, greens, blues of sleeping-bags. Sudden and out of place, like something spilt or dropped. An accident. The scattered pieces of a puzzle.

'Come on,' Moses said. 'It'll be warmer in the car.'

On their way across the car-park they passed Eddie's car. Moses peered in through the windscreen. He smiled at what he saw.

'Hey,' he called out. 'Come and look at this.'

Gloria stood ten yards away, her hands tucked into her armpits. 'What is it? I thought you said we could sleep.'

She trailed back to Eddie's car and looked through the window. Eddie,

Vince and Debra were sitting inside. All three sat perfectly upright in their seats with their eyes closed. They were all fast asleep.

'So?' Gloria said.

'What does it remind you of?'

Gloria shrugged. 'I don't know.'

'Old Dinwoodie.'

'Old who?'

Moses stared at her. 'Old Dinwoodie. You know. It was just before his bike went off the road. He was driving along with his eyes shut. Don't you remember?'

'I didn't see that.' Gloria turned away.

Moses's smile had narrowed, but a trace of it still lingered as he followed her to the car. Some part of him was immensely pleased that she had seen Eddie sitting there with his mouth open like that.

*

He ached into consciousness again, his forehead pressed against cold glass. He had lost all feeling in his right leg. He opened his mouth in the shape of a scream as he shifted and felt the life begin to crawl back through his skin. Christ, what a night.

He wiped the window with the less painful of his two hands. The mobile toilet door had swung open: it banged repeatedly on the tinny grey drum of its own side wall. Mist clung to the summit of the field beyond. Two or three dismal sheep grazed beside the wire fence. In front of the café, a few people in sweaters clutched white china mugs. They looked like the victims of some minor natural disaster. Nobody seemed to be talking. At least the café had opened. That was something.

He heard Gloria yawn from beneath her blanket on the back seat. He turned to look at her. Ouch: his neck. First her hair emerged, then an ear, and finally the rest of her face, exhausted, but still beautiful.

'Don't look at me,' she muttered.

He watched her in the mirror instead. Smeared mascara. Blue crescents under her eyes. She looked bruised.

'Moses,' came her small voice, 'd'you think there's any chance of a cup of coffee?'

He smiled. 'Yes, I think there's a chance.'

He got out of the car and stretched.

During the forties and fifties the café must have been quite safe. A place to take the family at weekends. A beauty spot of sorts. And even now, on a calm day, you could sit at one of those unsteady metal tables on the terrace and listen to the sea rustling over the pebbles below and believe that everything was all right. But what about the raw winter nights when storms blew in, and the waves hacked and munched at the base of the cliffs, and the black gap gaped and beckoned? There was fear in that old place as it watched the worn grass diminish year by year, as the sixty-foot drop edged nearer and nearer. He could almost hear the death-rattle of those loose sheets of glass, the teeth of the café chattering.

A few tables and chairs had taken up positions outdoors. They had been painted strange garish colours: mustard-yellow, hot-pink, lime-green. It was like an exhibition of freaks, a zoo of four-legged creatures with no heads. One of the tables was psychedelic mauve. It stood apart from the rest of the furniture as if embarrassed or shunned. Angled away from the sun-terrace and halfway to the cliff-edge, it gave the impression that, any moment now, it might break into an ungainly blundering run and hurl itself into the void.

Table kills itself.

On his way into the café, Moses passed Eddie. Eddie looked up, but nothing registered on his face. He had a split lip and a smear of oil on his forehead. His grazed hands dangled in his lap. He obviously wasn't going to explain what last night had been about.

Moses carried two cups of coffee out on to the grass and handed one to Gloria. She was sitting on the mauve table, elbows on her knees. He suddenly remembered the man with the dyed black hair and the vermilion shirt, the man who laughed like a train, and smiled to himself.

'I bet I know who painted this table,' he said.

Gloria held her cup close to her lips and stared at the horizon, her face in profile against the dull sky. Her mood had altered in the last five minutes. It was as if she had woken up without thinking and had now remembered something depressing.

He asked her if she was all right.

She nodded.

She found her cigarettes and lit one. She let the smoke drift out of her mouth without seeming to notice.

He asked her if she wanted to go.

She shrugged. It must have meant yes, though, because she threw her cigarette away and picked up her bag.

They searched half-heartedly for Louise. They couldn't find her any-where so Moses wrote a note. *Louise*, it said, *we were very tired and had to go. Thank you for the wonderful party. Lots of love, Moses and Gloria.* He left it with the woman who ran the café.

Vince had been watching Moses from his table on the sun-terrace. Now he came over and asked if he and Debra could have a lift back. Moses told him yes.

Eddie was sitting on a bench outside the café. He looked more than ever like a statue, not because of his classic features or his athlete's physique, but simply because he watched them leaving with blank eyes. He didn't even wave goodbye.

Moses and Gloria didn't talk on the way back – but then they never seemed to talk much on the way back from places. And this time, maybe because of the other two, Gloria didn't sing either. The only sound, apart from the hum of the engine, was a very soft sound, softer than a hundred tons of cotton wool, almost unidentifiably soft, and heard by Moses alone: it was the sound of Alison's mother chainsmoking cigarettes through a six-inch cigarette-holder. The only time anyone spoke was at the beginning of the journey when Debra asked Moses whether he could possibly drop her in Lewes.

'No problem,' he said.

It was only later that he realised, with a stab of disappointment, that this meant taking a different route and that they would not now be driving back through that strange village.

TALKING TO HORSES

During the last few days of July the temperature soared. Heat welded the end of one month to the beginning of the next, and hardly anybody noticed the join. A middle-aged man was arrested for jumping naked into the Serpentine. Summer at last.

The first Sunday in August Moses drove north-west across London, an *A–Z* open on his lap. He had been invited to Alison's parents' house for lunch. He was to drive to the Shirleys' house and back again so many times during the coming weeks that the route quickly stuck in his head, became automatic, second nature. Years later, driving a different car, going in a different direction, he would sometimes slip into one part of it by chance – only two or three streets, perhaps, but he would recognise the sequence – and he would wonder why it seemed so familiar. And sometimes he would remember, with a feeling that was like hunger or butterflies, the way it tightened his stomach, turned it over. With a feeling that was like homesickness.

He left The Bunker at noon. He hadn't thought to park in the shade (this was England, after all), and the air had massed inside his car, dense and sweltering, essence of leather. He wound all the windows down, rolled up his sleeves, and drove fast. One hand on the gearstick, one on the wheel. Eyes screened by sunglasses. And slowly the stubborn air broke up. The city looked evacuated, streets beaten flat by a high sun, the chill tunnels of tube stations gaping and empty. 82 degrees, the radio said. Unbelievable, this weather.

He arrived at the house to find the front door ajar. A cool hallway smelling of cinnamon and hyacinth and antique furniture. Dark-blue walls hung with charcoal drawings. Distant voices rooms away.

Nobody heard him knock.

He crossed the threshold, the sun pressing on his neck, his shoulder-blades. At the end of the hall a second door, also open, framed two girls in leotards practising handstands on a square of sunlit grass. New noises now. Laughter and jazz. The delicate percussion of glasses. The snap of cards.

He waited.

Then a woman with a shock of messy glossy black hair stepped backwards into the hall, talking to somebody he couldn't see. When she turned and noticed him, he flinched, moved forwards suddenly, as if she had caught him redhanded at something.

'Are you a burglar?' she asked him. She cocked an eyebrow, used only half her mouth to smile with.

'No,' he said. And, smiling back, he felt the heat issuing from her slightly bloodshot blue eyes. Her satin dress crumpled as she moved, like the air above a fire.

'In that case,' she said, 'how about a glass of white wine?'

The woman was Mary Shirley, of course, and though he couldn't fault Vince's savage rendering of detail – she wore black, carried a six-inch cigarette-holder between the first and second fingers of her left hand, talked like an old movie – he couldn't help feeling, at the same time, that there was something about her, a presence, perhaps, that Vince had chosen not to mention. As soon as he walked into that rundown red-brick house, as soon as he saw her in context, smoke curling like a blue creeper up her arm, he knew that Vince's words had become redundant, that he could leave them behind on the porch. It was strange ground for him, as it must once have been for Vince, but he felt no unease, only the pressure (almost sensual, this) of his own aroused curiosity.

'Yes,' he replied. 'That would be very nice.'

*

He watched Mary arrange herself on an upholstered cane chair in the garden. She folded her legs beneath her and stood a bottle of vodka upright against the backs of her knees. She lit one cigarette after another and dropped her ash on the lawn. In the sunlight her skin looked pale, almost soggy, but her eyes travelled lightly over everything, and she gave the impression, without speaking or moving, that she was orchestrating what went on around her, that she could steal the show at any moment she chose. Into one silence she inserted the following words:

'I've been having terrible dreams.'

She lifted her eyebrows, swirled the vodka in her glass. People began to listen.

'What dreams?' This was Rebecca, Mary's youngest.

'It was sunset,' Mary said, 'and I was standing on a footpath somewhere in the country. The sun was going down behind a ridge and the sky was green and orange, the colour you get when you burn copper. A row of spiky black figures were walking along the ridge. They were carrying sacks on their backs.'

She leaned sideways, tossed her cigarette into the nearest flower-bed.

'I was terrified, for some reason. I stood there, hoping desperately that they wouldn't notice me. But I knew how powerful their eyes were.

273

Distance and darkness were nothing to them. And the more I worried about whether or not they were going to notice me, the more real that danger became. It was almost as if they could hear me worrying.'

Moses, who knew that feeling, nodded to himself.

'Then, suddenly, I was in a small room. The walls of the room were solid with cages, and inside the cages were jackdaws, hundreds of them. The room was full of the sound of their wings thrashing. I remember thinking: This is what panic sounds like. The figures I had seen up on the ridge were in the room too. Silent hooded figures. And that's when I made the connection. Those sacks on their backs, they had been full of jackdaws.

'Then one of the figures stepped forward. He opened one of the cages and took hold of a jackdaw. The jackdaw struggled, cried out, but the man's hands were too strong. He held the jackdaw up to his face, bit off its beak, and spat it on the floor. Then he tore its throat out with his teeth and, raising the jackdaw in the air like a chalice, tilted his head back. Blood poured from the jackdaw's throat into the man's open mouth – '

'Oh, disgusting,' Rebecca cried.

'Mary, please,' Alison said.

'Then,' Mary said, 'he offered it to me – '

'Then what happened?' Rebecca said.

Mary leaned back. 'Nothing. That was the end. Now,' and her eyes scanned the members of her audience, 'who can tell me what *that* means?'

Moses saw the mischief in her smile as she spun the top off her private bottle with her thumb and poured herself another vodka. She wasn't beautiful, but she was, he had already decided, extraordinary.

*

Sometime during the afternoon he walked into the kitchen and found Mary standing by the draining-board.

'Would you like a drink?' she asked him. 'Is that what you're looking for?'

He said he would. He asked her what she was drinking.

'Vodka,' she said. 'I like vodka. It's tasteless.' And then grinned at him as if challenging him to contradict her. When he didn't, she said, 'I've forgotten your name. Or maybe I never knew it.'

'Moses.'

'That's a peculiar name.' She handed him a large neat vodka, then looked at him sideways-on. 'I suppose you've had problems with that.'

He ran through a few of the nicknames he had been given over the years. *Foreskin* made her laugh. He laughed with her.

'How terrible,' she said. 'How very demoralising.'

She kept him guessing as to how seriously she meant that. Up close her gaze was like light. Hard to look straight at.

'That dream,' he said. 'Was it real?'

She swallowed a mouthful of vodka before answering. 'What do you mean?'

'I mean, was it a real dream? Did you really dream it?'

'What a strange question. Yes, of course I did.'

'I just wondered. You seem like the kind of person who makes things up.'

'I seem like the kind of person who makes things up.' In repeating his words she had given them a sardonic edge.

'I didn't mean it like that.' He tried to explain that, although he didn't know her, she seemed like someone who was just naturally inventive, someone who could create events out of routine. He explained it badly, but he thought she could probably read the meaning beneath his clumsy words if she chose to. At the same time, he was beginning to realise that if there were two routes, a hard one and an easy one, Mary would always take the hard one.

'Oh, I am.' She lifted her shoulders, drew down the corners of her mouth. 'I'm a wonderful storyteller. I'm famous for it.'

'So famous,' Moses said, 'that even I'd heard of you.'

Mary walked to the window, swung round, and studied him over the rim of her glass as she drank. 'I don't know whether I like you,' she said.

'I don't know whether I like you either,' Moses said.

A rushed moment, as if an hour had passed in a few seconds, and suddenly they were both smiling. Afterwards he couldn't decide whether they had both started smiling at the same time or not and, if not, then which one of them had started smiling first. He could only say that it had felt like some kind of understanding, the way their smiles seemed to synchronise.

*

As he followed her back into the garden, a university professor broke off what he was saying to her husband Alan and, brushing her elbow lightly with his hand, steered her into their circle.

'Ah, Mary,' he exclaimed, 'perhaps you can tell us. What's the attraction of life in Muswell Hill?'

'I like Muswell Hill,' she said. 'I've got a dustman called Maurice.'

'Maurice?' the professor said. 'How charming.'

She had given the name its French pronunciation so perhaps he was imagining a pale tubercular dustman with manicured hands and a waxed moustache. Just a few words from Mary and the area acquired a new dimension, became exotic, fashionable even, and people began to wonder why they didn't live there too. She had that ability. She could make something fascinating simply by placing it under her own unique microscope.

'Oh no,' she was saying, 'he's not like that at all. He's very – ' she paused, put a thoughtful finger to her chin – '*long*. He looks a bit like Donald Sutherland.'

Alan snorted. 'He doesn't.'

'He does too. He's got the same ears. *And* eyes. And his hands are so big that if you put a cup of tea in them it disappears completely.'

She raised her cigarette-holder to her lips, released it again like a blown kiss. 'Me and Maurice. Sometimes, on Tuesday mornings when I'm not working, I ask him in for a cup of tea. We sit down at the kitchen table and we talk rubbish.'

A smile ran across her face, the way an urchin runs across a street: dodging cars, hooted at – the same cheek, the same delight.

'You know what he said to me once? He said, "I've never seen rubbish like your rubbish, Mrs Shirley." When I asked him what was so special about my rubbish, he said, "I've never seen so many bottles in one dustbin in my whole life. It was a real bugger to lift. Ted (Ted's his mate) nearly hernia'd himself." Really. He said that. Ted nearly hernia'd himself.' She rocked with laughter in her cane chair. 'He told me he could tell what people are like from their rubbish.' She slowed her voice down, made it sombre, fumbling. ' "If someone eats a lot of tuna fish I know it. You can't hide anything from a dustman. And I'm worried about you, Mrs Shirley." "Worried about me, Maurice?" I said. "I don't eat tuna fish." He shook his head, very serious and wise, and said, "There's too many bottles in that rubbish of yours, Mrs Shirley, and don't tell me they're lemonade bottles, because I know different." '

'What did you say to that?' The professor swayed back on his heels. Later he would drink himself into a flower-bed and fall asleep.

' "Some of them are probably lemonade bottles, Maurice," I said, "because that's what I put in my vodka sometimes." '

'Not if you can help it,' Alison scoffed.

'Sometimes, I said. And then – this was the best one – a few months ago Maurice was sitting at the kitchen table, blowing on his tea to cool it down, when I saw a thought move across his face. It actually moved across his face. I saw it. "You know, if there was a competition for the loudest rubbish, Mrs Shirley," he said, "yours'd win hands down." "Competition for the *what*, Maurice?" I said. "Competition for the loudest rubbish," he said.'

Mary loved that story, and Moses often heard her repeat it that summer. 'OK, so we drink a bit too much,' she would say with a swagger in her voice, 'but at least we've got the loudest rubbish in the area.'

'How do you know?' somebody new to the house would ask.

'Maurice says so,' she would say. 'Maurice is our dustman.'

'And it was true,' she went on, pouring herself another vodka, 'because I went out one day and listened. The noise was dreadful. Absolutely dreadful. So when his birthday came round I bought him a bottle of whisky to make up for it. When I gave it to him, he looked at it and then he looked at me and said, "You're a crafty one, Mrs Shirley." "Crafty?" I said. "Why?" I honestly couldn't see it. "Trying to turn me into an alcoholic too, are you?" he said. "I'm not an alcoholic, Maurice," I told him. "I just like to drink." "I'm not a dustman either," he said. "I just carry dustbins." '

She let smoke drift out of her mouth and across her face. It veiled her grin.

'No posing, no games, no voyeurism,' she said, glancing down at Moses. 'Just straight up, that's Maurice. A real breath of fresh air.'

She had already told Maurice that if they ever tried to take him off his route she would fire off letters of complaint, a salvo of letters, she said, to the council, to her local M P – to the Department of the Environment, if need be.

'I'd raise an enormous *stink*.' She nodded to herself, her chin tilted upwards as it always was when she threw down the gauntlet. And then burst out laughing when she realised what she had said.

*

Moments alone with Mary were rare in the beginning. Too many deflections, too much chaos. What she called *a full house*. A full house on Sundays meant they were winning, she said. Winning the fight against monotony and playing safe and death. Winning the fight against going through life too soberly. *When the chips are down, that's all this is*, she would cry, one hand clutching a bottle to her chest, the other sweeping, declamatory, all-embracing, round the garden. *A fight, a gamble, a throw of the dice.*

The house seemed a part of this. It drew life from her, held the same philosophy, and, like a magician's hat, conjured endless surprises: a fancy-dress party, a water-fight, a string quartet – even, once, a white rabbit sitting, like a hallucination, but perfectly content, on the bathroom floor (it belonged, Moses discovered later, to a schoolfriend of Rebecca's). Moses found himself constantly sidetracked, constantly in demand – most of all, curiously enough, by members of the family. Rebecca, skinny, mercurial, eight years old, took him firmly by the hand that afternoon and led him off to Highgate Cemetery. To pick blackberries, she said. (They didn't find any blackberries – it was too early, perhaps, or too late – so they picked flowers instead and drank chocolate milk in a sweet-shop and met a man with braces made of string and hands that shook even though, as Rebecca pointed out, it wasn't cold at all; they decided to be frightened of him and ran all the way home.) Sean, quieter, darker, thirteen, came and asked Moses to help him build a cage for his rat. Alan beat him at pool on the table in the attic (a secret bottle of malt whisky in the cue-rack, laughter rising up from the garden), and arranged a bicycle-ride through old Hampstead for the following weekend. (If you had been invited once, and the family took to you, there was no need, it seemed, for a second invitation; you were simply expected.) Even Alison, less precious on her own territory, had him admiring her latest textile designs. 'There's no peace in this house,' he sighed that evening, sinking into the nearest armchair. 'No peace,' Rebecca echoed, and jumped into his lap to prove the point.

The week trickled through his fingers like quicksand then it was Sunday again. One Sunday spilled over into the next, they blurred and formed a third, a switchback of events, an irresistible current that swept him along, that made him weightless as a piece of cork or an empty bottle. The moments he spent alone with Mary were islands he fetched up on by chance, explored, but soon left again because in that house there were always ships passing by, there was always smoke on the horizon. Though he didn't always want rescuing.

Was it that first afternoon or another Sunday later in the month that he discovered her, perched on the upturned water-tank at the bottom of the garden, apples crushed to sweep pulp at her feet, wasps droning invisible somewhere as if the air itself was dozing, and told her, drunk now, swaying above her, that she was different?

'Don't fool yourself, Moses,' she said, and some fatigue in her smile made him think for a moment that he was just another actor with the same lines, 'I'm an ordinary woman, a perfectly ordinary woman.'

But her voice denied it. Her voice had colour, substance, contours. On her lips each phrase became a view of hills, soft rounded hills fringed by woods, green with rain, veiled in mist. He could literally gaze at her speaking.

He remembered the time he'd heard her voice on the phone, months ago now, and how it had hung on in his head, painting pictures. Then that first Sunday in Muswell Hill, he'd watched her prepare the evening meal. A cookery book lay open in her hand. *Reduce the volume of the gravy*, she declared, only to burst out laughing at the absurdity of the language. At one moment she could turn the recipe into an address to the troops, the next she made it sound like a prayer – to which Mary, iconoclast that she was, would probably have said, *That's* exactly *what it is. A prayer* – but her voice always (and despite itself, perhaps) performed. So he couldn't help smiling to himself when she told him how ordinary she was, couldn't help smiling at the way her voice and her words, simultaneous phenomena, took different sides.

'Why is it so important for you to be ordinary?' he asked her.

'Why is it so important for you to prove I'm not?' she replied.

Most of the time she got the better of him like that.

*

Those Sundays of drinking into the small hours.

It was like a tree, Moses sometimes thought. As the night grew older, so the members of the family would detach themselves, first Rebecca, then Sean, then Alison, then Alan, until, finally, only Mary and Moses were left, clinging, very drunk, to their respective branches.

'That's beautiful,' Mary said, when he told her.

Alan must have thought so too. During the next few weeks he produced a series of drawings, primitive supernatural drawings, which he called *The Family Tree*. The tree had six leaves and each leaf was a face. On one of the leaves Moses saw his own face, and was touched to find himself so accepted. He liked the last drawing best of all. It showed the tree at five in the morning, its branches stripped and bare, all the fallen leaves lying curled up on the ground with their eyes closed (it must have represented one of the Sundays when Moses, too drunk to drive home, had stayed overnight in the guest-room because his face was there with all the others). Alan built frames for the drawings and hung them on the kitchen wall above the Swiss cheese plant. 'So we can look at them,' he said, 'while it's actually happening.'

Every now and then there were emergencies, times when the Shirleys, either through some oversight or simply because of their own excesses, ran out of alcohol. Moses loved to watch Mary then. The horror, the panic, the outrage, that flickered almost frame by frame across her face. The glint of resolution as she took charge. 'Listen,' she would say, hands on hips, 'I run a tight ship. This house cannot be dry.' There would be groans of, 'But we only looked last week and there was nothing then,' and Mary would say, 'Well, at least try.' And so a kind of alcoholic safari would begin. They would scour the house, all but tear it apart in a desperate search for a bottle of something – anything. In the end they often found bottles in the most obvious places – in Alan's briefcase, under Mary's pillow. 'You see,' Mary would gloat over those who had doubted her. 'You just have to believe.'

Once, though, she walked in through the back door brandishing an unopened bottle of Teacher's. Mud streaked the glass. A snail had camped on the label. 'Now where,' she said, 'do you suppose I found this?' Nobody sitting at the kitchen table knew. 'Under a rhubarb leaf at the bottom of the garden,' she said. The culprit was never found. Moses suspected Rebecca, who had never concealed her scorn for the way her parents drank. '*Alcohol*,' she would say, supremely disdainful in her glasses with their pale-blue rims, '*I* don't need *that*.'

Another time they ran out at five-thirty on a Sunday afternoon. Serious. One and a half hours until the off-licence opened. One football match, two LPs, three mindless game-shows between them and a drink. Mary rose to the challenge as usual. 'Oh, there'll be a bottle of something somewhere. The law of probability.' They searched the house room by room, cupboard by cupboard, drawer by drawer. Many secrets were discovered, many lost things found, but not a single bottle came to light, not unless you counted a flagon of Sean's homemade beer, dusty and opaque, and at least five years old. Not even Mary would touch that. They returned to the kitchen and sat down at the table. The clock said five past six. It began to drizzle outside. Despondency set in.

Mary sighed. 'This never used to happen.'

Alan was trying to balance a spoon across his forefinger. 'Think of it as a test,' he said.

'I'm not in the mood for tests,' Mary snapped.

Alan smiled.

Alison said, 'I'll make some tea.'

'*Tea*?' Mary made it sound like a four-letter word.

Moses had noticed before how Alison and Mary swapped roles. When Mary became impetuous or extreme, Alison humoured her, made sensible suggestions, as a parent would. The look that Mary gave Alison as Alison put the kettle on was one of pure truculence.

'My children.' She shook her head in disbelief. 'Where do they get all this virtue from? All this common sense? It's beyond me. Utterly beyond me.'

Moses had been doing some lateral thinking. Suddenly he hoisted himself upright. 'There's one place we didn't look.' He jumped to his feet. His chair crashed over backwards. He threw the kitchen door open and took the stairs in three giant bounds. The house shuddered at his enthusiasm. Alison rolled her eyes and sighed. Several people watched the kitchen ceiling as Moses tramped overhead.

Silence.

Then: 'Hold the tea.'

Moses appeared in the doorway like a champion, a bottle held aloft. 'Brandy!' he cried.

Applause from the people gathered round the table. A piercing two-fingered whistle from Mary.

'Where was it?' Alan asked.

'In the cistern.'

Rebecca wrinkled her nose in disgust.

'That would explain the missing label.' Alan turned the bottle in his hands as if he was an expert in the field of bottles found in cisterns.

'The cistern.' Alison's voice was edged in sarcasm. 'Of course.'

'Extraordinary,' Mary said. It was a word she rarely used. She looked very pleased with Moses.

After that incident they all became firm believers in the mysterious powers of alcohol.

*

As summer faded, moths invaded the city. Their sturdy furry bodies cannoned off lampshades and windowpanes. They were constantly flying into Mary's face as if she was the only source of light. When they died their wings crumbled into a fine bronze dust that nobody could remember seeing before.

One Sunday night, after everyone had left, Moses was drinking gin on the terrace with Alan and Mary when Rebecca appeared on the kitchen doorstep. She was holding a sheet of paper very carefully in both hands.

'I thought you were in bed,' Alan said.

'I was,' she answered, 'until I found this.'

In her white nightie, she looked like a tiny priestess as she advanced over the flagstones towards them, her eyes trained on the sheet of paper between her hands, her lips pressed together in concentration. On the paper lay the remains of a giant moth, two inches long, its soft grey fuselage still intact, its wings, almost gold, disintegrating.

'Look at this dust,' she said. 'It shines.'

'So it does,' Mary said. She fetched a mirror from the kitchen, then she began to smear the gold dust on to one of her eyelids with the tip of her little finger.

'What are you doing, Mum?' One hand gripping the arm of Mary's chair, standing on tiptoe so she could see, Rebecca was perfectly poised between horror and fascination.

Moses and Alan exchanged a faint smile.

When Mary had completed both eyelids she said, 'Well? How do I look?'

Rebecca stared at her mother. 'It looks like real make-up.'

'Of course it does. That's why the ugly god used it.'

'What ugly god?'

A very long time ago, Mary began, moths used to live for seventy years, just like human beings. In those days the gods who looked after the world were very decadent. They sat around in the sky, they drank a lot, they dressed up and went to parties. One day they decided to hold a ball. It would be the grandest ball ever.

On the evening of the ball one of the gods was sitting in front of his mirror. He was very miserable. He was in love with the queen of the gods who was the most beautiful and unattainable of women, but he was so ugly that she had never noticed him. 'I'm *so* ugly,' he moaned. 'If only I was beautiful too. Then perhaps she would notice me.'

At that moment a moth flew in through the open window. It fluttered and flapped around the room for a while, then it suddenly dropped on to the ugly god's dressing-table. The ugly god was somewhat startled. At first he thought the moth was just tired, but when he turned it over gently with his finger he realised that it was dead. First his ugliness and now this death. He was about to heave a long sigh when he noticed a deposit of fine dust on the end of his finger. A glittery coppery dust. A glamorous dust. Sitting up a little straighter in his chair, he touched the moth again with his finger. Then he touched the skin above his eye with the same finger, once, very delicately. He looked in the mirror and smiled at what he saw.

He caused quite a stir when he arrived at the ball that night. Several of his friends didn't even recognise him. Ladies bought him drinks and paid him compliments. The queen's suitors huddled in a corner, pointing and muttering, their eyes green with envy.

And then the trumpets sounded and the queen of the gods made her entrance. Surrounded by giant male bodyguards, she looked as beautiful and unattainable as ever. When she passed the ugly god, however, she paused.

'You're beautiful!' she cried. 'Who are you?'

The ugly god bowed low and told her his name.

'Come to my chamber tonight,' the queen commanded him, 'and we shall be lovers.' And with a rustle of silk and gossamer she was gone.

The ugly god was immediately mobbed by a host of jealous suitors.

'What's your secret?' one of them hissed. He wore the same lipstick as usual. Made from the juice of crushed rose petals. Very dreary.

The ugly god was still dazed, as much by the queen's beauty as by her invitation. 'A special powder,' he said.

'What powder?' hissed another. He had dyed his hair with a solution distilled from the bark of silver birches. Old hat.

The ugly god realised that he had already said too much. 'I cannot say,' he said. And smiled in a most infuriating way.

He spent an exquisite night with the queen, but by the next morning the powder of the wings of the moth had rubbed off and he was ugly again.

'Get out of my sight!' the queen cried when she awoke. '*God*, I must've been drunk last night!'

The ugly god was chased out of the palace in disgrace. On the street he met two of his friends. 'Hello, ugly,' they said. They were full of gossip about the mysterious stranger who had attended the ball and spent the night with the queen. 'Weren't you there?' they said. 'Didn't you see him?' But the ugly god was too sad to reply. He had lost the queen's love and he didn't know how to win it back.

When he reached home he sat down at his dressing-table. He had no powder left. He had used it all the previous night. That was the trouble. The powder of the wings of moths was a very rare substance.

And then he had a brainwave. He put on his divine robes, stood at the open window and, drawing himself up to his full height, raised his right hand. 'I hereby decree that from now on,' he said, 'moths will only live for one day.'

Back inside his room he could scarcely contain his delight. He jumped up and down and shook his fists in a very ungodlike manner. If moths died often enough then he would never run out of their magical powder. So he would always be beautiful. And the queen would love him for all eternity.

He returned to the palace wearing some of his new make-up. The queen embraced him. 'Oh, how beautiful you are! How could I have sent you away?' she cried. 'What a *terrible* hangover I must've had! You must come and live with me for ever! I command it!'

And so the ugly god moved into the palace and married the queen and lived happily ever after. Moths died more often than they used to, of course, but happiness is more important. And besides, nobody ever made the connection.

Rebecca was smiling. 'So that's why moths only live for such a short time.'

Mary nodded. 'Now off to bed with you or you'll look like an ugly god in the morning.'

Rebecca kissed everyone goodnight and disappeared upstairs.

The bottle of gin was empty, but another lay chilling in the freezer. They wouldn't be searching the house tonight. While Alan fetched the new bottle, Mary put some music on. She stood at the end of the terrace where the light from the house was swallowed by the darkness of the garden and sang along with Marlene Dietrich, a glass in her hand, her eyelids glistening a powdery gold.

> Men cluster to me
> Like moths around a flame
> And if their wings burn
> I know I'm not to blame –

And the moths fluttered out of the night, the words of the song mysteriously come to life.

'It suits you,' Moses said.

Mary looked up. 'The song?'

'The make-up.'

He settled deeper in his chair. The white roses on the back wall held out the tiny shiny bowls of their petals, collected all the moonlight from the sky. A grey cat tightropewalked along the fence; its tail curled up into the air like smoke. Somebody coughed two gardens away.

'You know, sometimes, moments like this,' he said, 'I feel as if I live here.'

'Why don't you?' came Mary's voice, light, provocative.

'I'm serious. I feel as if this is where I really live. Here in Muswell Hill. In this house. There's something about being here. I can't explain it – '

That morning he had been playing with Rebecca in the garden. He had gripped her by the wrists, a sailor's grip, and swung her round in the air. She had whirled out horizontally, making a sound like the wind or a ghost, her legs as slack as a rag doll's legs. He could still hear her crying 'Faster, faster,' he could still feel her never wanting it to end. When he had finally slowed down and set her on her feet again, she couldn't stand. She had staggered about like a drunkard, and he had copied her. It was part of the game to act dizzier than you really were, to act a bit crazy. They had ended up in the lavender bush, a tangle of legs and arms, helpless with laughter. At that moment he had glanced up at the house and noticed Mary standing in an upstairs window. She had been smiling, but not at him. Her smile seemed to precede his awareness of her. It seemed to relate to what had gone before – the game, the laughter. A strange thought had come to him: she wants another child, *my* child. Then she had seen him watching her and she had pulled back from the window, back into the shadows, as if frightened he might read her mind. But perhaps he already had.

'Mary?'

'Yes?'

'What were you smiling about this morning? You know, when I saw you in the window.'

Mary turned and walked away down the garden. He watched her go. He could see nothing of her, only the tip of her cigarette glowing as she paced up and down in front of the hedge. Then a red scratch on the darkness as she threw it away. The trees shivered as a breeze passed by.

Alan returned with the second bottle of gin. Shortly afterwards Alison joined Alan and Moses on the terrace. She sat down on the kitchen doorstep, her hair wrapped in a white towel. She smelt of cleanness, dampness, shampoo. She was drinking water.

'Moses,' she said, 'you're still here.'

'Moses is always here,' Mary said, appearing out of the darkness in her black dress, making them all jump. 'Moses is one of the family. Aren't you, Moses?'

Her smile rested on his face, and her hand touched his shoulder for a moment.

Her eyelids still dusty gold.

Queen of the gods.

*

The following Wednesday Moses's phone rang. It was Mary.

'Have you got any plans for lunch?' she said.

He laughed. 'What do you think I am? A businessman?'

'I've got a couple of bottles of white wine and a cold chicken,' she said. 'I thought we could have a picnic on Parliament Hill. Rebecca wants to fly her kite. Would you like to come?'

'I'd love to.'

'We'll meet by the bench at the top of the hill. Do you know the bench I mean?'

'I'll find it.'

'One o'clock then.' She hung up.

Moses smiled to himself. Mary always sounded so formal on the phone. It was because she hated them. 'How can you talk to someone when you can't see their face?' he remembered her saying. When he tried to argue the point, she closed him down. 'Telephones,' she said, and her voice registered the most profound disdain. 'They fake closeness. They pervert distance. Distance should be respected. I'd rather drive fifty miles to speak to someone in person than talk to them on the telephone. I only use them when I have to.' She spoke of telephones as if they had wounded her in the past.

When Moses arrived at the bench, they were waiting for him, Rebecca wearing black jeans and a pink sweater, Mary in a black dress, the usual *diamanté* brooch at her throat, the usual jet earrings.

'We would have driven down and picked you up,' Mary said, some of the formality lingering, 'but we thought you might be out.'

'Lying in a skip somewhere,' Rebecca said, squinting up at him.

'I don't lie in skips,' Moses said. 'Not on Wednesday mornings.'

'So we telephoned,' Mary said, 'instead.'

'I'm glad you did,' Moses said.

'Moses?' Rebecca said. 'Do you know anything about kites? Kites that look like dragons, I mean.'

'I know a bit about kites because I had one once. It was an aeroplane, though, not a dragon. Do you think that matters?'

'I don't know. The thing is, aeroplanes are supposed to fly. I'm not so sure about dragons.'

Moses squatted down and examined the dragon.

'And look,' Rebecca said, 'it's got holes in it.'

'Ah,' Moses said, 'but this is a Chinese flying dragon, and Chinese flying dragons fly *even better* than aeroplanes.'

'You're making it up,' Rebecca said. 'There's no such thing.' But she wanted there to be.

'And this – ' he glanced around – 'is perfect Chinese flying dragon weather.' He pointed at the sky. It bustled with huge white clouds which kept bumping into each other, but very lightly, as if they had been pumped full of air. If you pricked one it would burst, he told her, and later you would find pieces of shrivelled cloud scattered about on the ground. He drew her attention to the trees, which rustled like presents being unwrapped by the breeze. Then one final (and unexpected) piece of evidence: a Chinese man chose that moment to trot by, one hand on his pork-pie hat. 'You see?' Moses laughed. 'What did I tell you?'

Rebecca had to smile. 'All right, I believe you.'

And, in no time, the dragon was flying magnificently. Mary spread a rug on the grass. Moses sat next to her. They watched Rebecca as she skipped down the hill, the string clenched in her fist, her eyes fixed on the twisting gold tail in the air above.

'That was mine when I was her age,' Mary told him. 'When I was living in North Yorkshire. You didn't know I was a northerner, did you? You didn't know I came from a coal-mining family?'

Her revelations, he had often noticed, tended to coincide with moments of contentment, as if she felt she couldn't allow time to pass too comfortably. A coal-mining family? Perhaps that explained her coal-mine-coloured tights, her kohl-lined eyes, her attachment to black. He smiled to himself.

'I come from a small mining-town,' she went on. 'We moved away when I was nine. That's why I haven't got an accent any more.'

'Was your father a miner then?'

'No, he was a teacher. My grandfather was a miner, though. My grandfather – I remember him so vividly. Especially the back of his neck. He had these lines, hundreds of lines that criss-crossed, made diamond shapes. The lines were all ingrained with black. The coal-dust, I suppose. It gets into your skin. Becomes a second skin.

'I used to call them necklaces, those tiny strings of diamond shapes. Grandpa's necklaces. It used to make him chuckle. My mother tried to put a stop to it. "Men don't wear necklaces, Mary," she used to say. As if it was something I didn't know. She was a very stupid woman. Missed the point completely.

'Grandpa was special. He was a man and he wore necklaces. I thought that was absolutely wonderful, whatever my mother said. Sometimes he wore a scarf, for his bronchitis, and I would pester him until he took it off. "I want to see your necklaces, Grandpa," I used to say. "Show me your necklaces." And he would slowly loosen his scarf, making a game of it, chuckling his deep chuckle and shaking his head as if he had never heard anything like it.

'But I think it scared him in a way. I think he was always listening out for my mother. Ready to pretend nothing was happening if she came in. Why do parents do that? Why do they try to close you down like that?'

'Well, you don't, do you?' Moses said.

'Of course not.' Such vehemence in her voice. She might have been disagreeing with him. Sometimes she seemed to be correcting not *what* he said but *how* he said it. As if his emphasis had been all wrong.

Then she added, wistful now, 'I suppose I learned something.'

'What about your father?'

'He was a quiet man. No necklaces. He would do anything to avoid an argument, anything for a bit of peace and quiet. The only time I can remember him raising his voice was when he left the dinner-table once and stood in the doorway and shouted, "I'M NOT GOING TO ARGUE, MAEVE." Maeve was my mother.'

She was laughing, but Moses thought he detected a new brightness in her eyes: tears.

'Poor old Dad,' she said. 'I haven't thought about him for so long. She killed him, really.'

'Your mother?'

Mary nodded. 'She needed drama. She needed scenes. That's where her momentum came from. But he couldn't take it. One of them had to give. He used to think that she would run out of steam if he kept quiet, but silence made her hysterical. She would work herself up into a frenzy. It was frightening, like watching someone having a fit. And he would be sitting in his chair, waiting for it all to blow over. Looking so small. Scared. Not even daring to look up. He would just sit there, waiting for it to end so he could light his pipe and switch on the radio and draw rings round the names of horses in the back of the paper.'

She fell silent, one hand in the hair at the back of her neck. After staring at the grass for a while, she said, 'They never should've married.'

'Then you wouldn't be here,' Moses said, 'sitting on this hill with me and Rebecca. Then you would've missed all this.'

Mary smiled. 'I'd be somewhere. I would've forced my way into the world somehow.'

Her airy confidence annoyed him. 'Yes,' he persisted, 'but not *here*.'

'No,' she agreed, 'not here.' The distinction didn't seem to be important to her.

Then a familiar but anxious voice called from the bottom of the hill. 'Moses? What do I do when I want it to come down?'

They both laughed at the look of utter helplessness on Rebecca's face. Helplessness in the face of insurmountable odds.

That picnic on Parliament Hill set one or two new precedents. It shifted the scene away from the house in N10 and on to more neutral territory. It also disrupted the neat pattern of Sundays only. It meant that, in future, they could meet wherever they liked, with or without the children, and on weekdays too. Mary taught part-time, so she often had free mornings or afternoons. Moses, of course, was always free. They began to go on expeditions, locally at first, in Muswell Hill, then further afield, as if their courage was growing. They discovered some unusual places: a church in Epping Forest, a pub in Rotherhithe, a stretch of canal in Kensal Rise. Slowly they were building up common ground, creating, as it were, their own private frame of reference.

The impetus came mostly from Mary – an abrupt phone-call or a note, sometimes posted, sometimes delivered by hand, never more than a sentence long, and signed simply 'M'. Once or twice she even arranged trips over Sunday lunch. Everything was done naturally and openly, everything was above board and beyond suspicion. It was strange, but he often had to remind himself that, after all, they had absolutely nothing to hide. The conditions for guilt existed without the grounds for feeling guilty. Just occasionally he felt burdened somehow as if he had become the repository of a trust that he knew he was going to betray. He wondered how that had come about. Would come about. If it came about.

One fact stood out clearly enough. Some kind of bridge was being built. And he was walking over it as easily, as thoughtlessly as in a dream, simply because it was there.

*

One Thursday evening in September Moses arrived home to find a note slipped under his front door. *Feel like a drink? M*. He turned round to see Mary standing behind him.

'Well?' she grinned. 'Do you?'

They drove north in Mary's 1968 Volvo. The sky predicted thunder, black stormclouds edged in gold. Mary wore a tight black dress, black gloves to the elbow, red lipstick.

'Let's stop at the first pub we see,' she said, 'and sink a few Martinis.'

The first pub they saw was somewhere in Highgate: brown curtains, Skol beer-mats, nothing special. Mary walked up to the bar to order their drinks. Moses took a table by the window. He watched the bartender reach for a bottle of dry Martini.

'No, no, not that,' he heard Mary call out. '*Real* Martinis. You know. *American* Martinis.' She wasn't being high-handed or condescending; she just seemed amused at the misunderstanding.

The bartender (thin, whiskery, whisky-sour) stared, first at Mary, then at Moses, and Moses suddenly realised what he must be thinking. The age difference. The tight dress. The lipstick. Prostitute, he was thinking. And the word was making an ugly screeching sound in his mind. Nails on a blackboard. Painted nails.

Mary didn't seem to have noticed. She was giving the bartender instructions. 'Large gin. Dash of dry Martini. Just a dash, mind. A green olive, if you've got one. And no ice, of course.'

'Of course.' The bartender stared at her for a moment longer. He seemed to want her to know exactly what he thought of her. Then he began to put the drinks together. In his own sweet time. With infinite distaste.

Eventually he set the glasses down in front of her. One slopped over.

'Sorry, madam,' he smirked, 'but we don't usually get your type in here.'

And, turning his back on her, he busied himself with a couple of dirty glasses.

Moses felt anger well up inside him, hot and sudden, like blood from a deep cut.

'I know what he's thinking,' Mary said when she sat down, 'and I know what you're thinking. Don't let it get to you, Moses. If I can deal with it so can you.' She raised her glass. 'Cheers.'

He knew she was right, but he couldn't help himself: the bartender had crawled under his skin. He hated people who stood their weakness on a pedestal, who thought their small minds gave them the right to sit in judgment over others. His anger simmering, he ostentatiously lit a cigarette for Mary. The bartender was still polishing glasses. His eyes would swivel in their direction every now and then and slide away again whenever Moses looked up. A few locals sat on stools at the bar. Their eyes swivelled too.

Mary finished her drink. 'Not bad,' she said cheerfully, 'for somebody who's never made one before.'

Moses tried to smile.

'Would you like another?' she asked him.

'Somewhere else,' he said.

Instead of following her to the door, he walked up to the bar. The bartender, still polishing, pretended not to notice him.

'Listen you,' Moses said in a low voice, 'if you ever do anything like that again, I'm going to come in here and knock your fucking head off, all right?'

He waited long enough to see the bartender's face take on a certain rigidity, the rigidity of fear, then he turned away.

'That's assault,' Mary told him when he joined her outside.

'I didn't touch him.'

'You threatened him, though.'

Moses opened his mouth to say something, then changed his mind.

She linked her arm through his. 'Well,' she said, 'I don't suppose we'll ever go there again.'

'No,' he said.

A few yards short of the car, he stopped. Shaken, yet strangely ignited. 'You know,' he said, 'I've never done anything like that before.'

They told the story over lunch the following Sunday. It rapidly became spectacular. Mary hadn't left the pub at all, she had slouched against the wall, filing her nails, a gangster's moll, while Moses, mafioso, did terrible things to the whiskery bartender: he had shaken the bartender by the scruff of the neck until his false teeth flew out; he had cleaned Mary's shoes with the bartender's face; he had thrown whisky around and reached slowly for his lighter while the bartender gaped, grovelled, dribbled like a fire-hose in a drought. The story changed and grew with every telling; it became more vicious, more surreal, more *just*. It always went down well at lunches and parties. 'Oh Mary,' someone would clamour, 'tell them the one about Moses. You know, the time he blew up that pub in Highgate.' Before long the incident had distorted beyond all recognition. Even the memory blurred. Only the names remained the same.

*

Mary and Moses.

This intimacy grew, slowly as a plant or a face, its slowness old-fashioned (something Mary claimed to be herself). It was like the colour of a leaf changing. It used the slipping of summer into autumn as a metaphor to describe itself. One week it was green, the next it was orange, and the week after that it was red. Something had happened in between, some gradual yet tangible chemical development had taken place. She had spoken once of starting something that you can't control. He had forgotten the context, but remembered the words. They surfaced whenever he thought about her.

He returned again and again to the same point. It wasn't that she was beautiful. He never stood and looked at her and thought, as he might have done with Gloria: she's beautiful. It was an attraction of a different nature altogether. It transcended simple good looks. It almost transcended definition. He only knew that when he was with Mary he felt an affinity that was unthought-out, unforced, uncanny. He felt good. And he marvelled at how effortlessly that feeling had come into being. Only the thought of her marriage, her family, brought him back to earth, anchored him. And she talked about them regularly and passionately. Take Alan, for instance. She was still in love with him, she said. He was the only man in her life. He knocked everybody else into a cocked hat. She fought for Alan even though there was no fight going on. Hold on, Moses wanted to say to her sometimes, I *agree* with you. They were surrounded by natural obstacles: Alan, Alison, Sean, Rebecca – her love for them, his too. It was reassuring, in a way. It meant that nothing bad could happen.

Inevitably, perhaps, he saw less of Gloria. He called her less. And he was surprised to discover that he didn't miss her at all. Late one Sunday night (one of the nights he actually managed to make it back to The Bunker) she called him.

'I've been trying to get hold of you all day,' she said. 'Where've you been?'

She probably hadn't meant it to sound like that, but that was how it came out. He told her the truth. 'I went out to lunch. At the Shirleys'.'

'Who are they?'

'Alison's family. The Alison who used to be with Vince. I told you.'

'Oh yes.' Her voice sounded flat. As if all the lifeblood had been drained out of her.

'You sound strange,' he said. 'Are you OK?'

'I'm fine. Just tired, that's all. Anyway, look, what I wanted to ask you was, do you want to do something on Thursday night?'

Her voice had lifted, seeking brightness in his reply, but he didn't have to think very hard to remember that he had already arranged to meet Mary on Thursday. He carried the phone over to the window. No cars were waiting at the lights so when the lights changed nothing happened. Sunday night. Almost two o'clock. Dead time.

'Hello?' came Gloria's voice. 'Are you still there?'

'I'm sorry,' he said, 'I can't. I'm doing something on Thursday.'

A moment silence, then: 'That's what I thought.'

'What do you mean?'

'That's what the phone's been trying to tell me all day. When I called you this morning, it just rang and rang, and nobody answered. I didn't call you this afternoon because I thought, all those times I called in the morning and nobody answered, that was a good piece of advice. You're wasting your time, kind of thing. You might as well forget it, save yourself a lot of trouble. Looks like it was right, doesn't it? Shame I didn't listen.'

'You got through,' he said. Beginning to wish she hadn't.

'Yes. I got through.'

He had never heard her sound so low. 'Do you want me to come over?'

She hesitated. 'No, it's too late. And anyway, you don't want to, really.'

It was almost a question, it called for a denial. Moses didn't answer. He felt so tired. He wanted to go to bed alone. Not talk. Drift into sleep.

'All right. Look. See you around, OK?' Gloria said, staccato now. 'Bye.'

She hung up.

He listened to the buzzing for a while, then he put the phone down.

Two minutes later he was sitting on the bed unlacing his boots when the phone rang again. He had thought about ringing her back when she hung up like that, but he had decided against it. He didn't know what to say to her. Any conversation they had now would run round in vicious circles. Telephones solve nothing, he told himself. And he heard Mary's voice calling him an escapist. Now Gloria was calling him back and he would have to talk to her anyway. He didn't want to answer, but he had to, really. She knew he was there. He could hardly pretend to be asleep already. He walked back into the next room, his bootlaces trickling on the floor behind him. He picked up the receiver and looked at the ceiling. 'Hello?'

It wasn't Gloria.

A voice, high-pitched, sexless, ageless, chanted:

> *Humpty Dumpty sat on a wall*
> *Humpty Dumpty had a great fall*
> *All the king's horses and all the king's men*
> *Couldn't put Humpty together again –*

'Who's this?' Moses said.

Silence. Then, very faintly, the sound of breathing. Light and quick. Excitement, he thought. And imagined a child on the other end. But knew this was no child.

'Who are you?' he said.

'Don't you remember me?' the voice whispered. Then hung up.

Click. Buzz.

It took Moses a while to realise that the call had not been for him but for Elliot. Thinking about it, it had to have been for Elliot; it had the same eerie theatrical vindictiveness as the white arrows and the skinned pool-table. Even so, it chilled him. Suddenly he needed to talk to somebody. If he used the phone again he could erase the memory of that voice.

He picked up the phone and dialled Gloria's number. He let it ring twenty times before replacing the receiver. He wondered if she was asleep already or just not answering.

He went to bed and tried to read. The words jumped on the page. None of their meaning registered. After ten minutes he switched the light off. The darkness buzzed like a phone left off the hook.

There were no more calls.

The next day he told Elliot. Elliot shrugged. 'That's what I said. We've been getting phone-calls.'

Something had fastened on to Elliot during the past few days and sucked all the colour out of his face. He looked grey. Even his gold medallion looked grey.

'Everything all right, Elliot?' Moses asked.

Elliot jerked forward in his chair and stalled as if the clutch controlling him had slipped. 'None of your fucking business, all right?'

Moses stared at him. 'Well,' he said, 'I just thought I'd let you know, anyway,' and moved towards the door.

Elliot leaned back. He pushed the tip of his tongue between his front teeth, worked it in and out of the gap. 'Hey, Moses?' he called out. 'If there's any trouble at night, call this number.'

He slipped a piece of paper across the desk. Moses walked back and picked it up. Seven digits. A perfectly normal London number.

'Who's this?' he asked.

'Me,' Elliot said. 'Sometimes.'

He smiled craftily. But as far as Moses was concerned Elliot had just let him know that he was worried.

*

Thursday came. The sun was shining. Clouds lay in white clumps on the clean blue surface of the sky. When the doorbell rang at midday, Moses leaned out of his window and saw Mary below. Light showed as silver on the black gloss of her hair (she had dyed it again). A black skirt swirled around her pale calves. He called her name and she looked up. She didn't answer, though. She didn't approve of people shouting in the street. For somebody who had often been described as bohemian, eccentric even, she could be surprisingly conventional at times. But she used that. The two qualities ran alongside each other in her like trains running on parallel tracks, and she could switch at will. It was part of her struggle to resist classification. Two or three times he had heard her mention some scene from an old black and white movie. A man's talking to a woman. The man's so wrapped up in what he's saying that he doesn't notice that he's boring the woman. In the end the woman becomes so thoroughly bored that she leaves the room. The man carries on talking, utterly oblivious, utterly foolish. It's quite a while before he swings round to discover that he's alone, that he's been talking to an empty room. The moral? In Mary's words: *Nobody should ever take anybody else for granted.* The implication being, *least of all me.*

But Moses couldn't imagine anyone taking Mary for granted. Even her most mundane remarks seemed provocative somehow. Perhaps because you wouldn't have expected them to come from her. Sentiments expressed by millions of people every day. Sentiments like, 'I love my husband,' or, 'Nobody could ever take my children away from me' (yes, sometimes she sounded like a soap-opera). She stamped them as her own only by the blunt unadorned *categorical* way she spoke. When Mary talked of basic emotions she left no room for doubts or indecision. To Mary, this proved that she was a perfectly ordinary person. To Moses, it set her apart from just about everybody he had ever known.

He wanted to understand her more, especially when he was drunk, but she always turned his questions round. The answers, when they came, told him more about himself. He didn't want to hear about himself. So he persisted. And learned even less.

Only last Sunday he'd said, 'I want to know how you work. I want to know what goes on inside your head.'

Frowning, she'd replied, 'I'm not a machine, you know.'

'Maybe that's what it is about you. You're not set in your ways like – '

'Like other people my age?'

'I wasn't going to say that.'

'There's something you've got to understand, Moses. I'm not a bloody stone. I *change*. I'm changing right now. Right in front of your eyes.'

'Stones change too.'

'That's what I'm saying. Everything changes. Every*one* changes. I'm just the same as everyone else. Stop treating me like a freak.'

His patience had come apart then. 'You never admit anything, do you? You've always got to have the last word.'

She'd stared at him thoughtfully. 'You know, one day you'll realise I'm right about me and you're wrong and then you won't be honest about why you don't want to see me any more.'

He'd denied this, but she'd given him one of her knowing looks.

'You're going to have to have a lift installed,' Mary said.

He turned and saw her standing in the doorway. She didn't sound out of breath, not in the slightest. She must have rested halfway up. He smiled to himself at this little insight.

'A drink?' he said.

'Maybe just one,' she said. 'For the road.'

He poured two whiskies. It was the first time she had seen where he lived. While he hunted for money and keys, she explored, glass in hand, lips pressed together. She walked into the kitchen and the bathroom, then emerged again, crossed the lounge, and disappeared into the bedroom. He heard her pause inside the door, take two or three quick steps, and pause again.

When she returned she asked him, 'How often do you wash your sheets?'

'I don't know,' he stammered. 'Not very often, I suppose.'

'*How* often?'

'About once every three weeks.'

'You should leave them longer,' she said. 'They smell wonderful.'

He stared at her.

She gave him a radiant, brazen smile. 'So where are we going today?'

*

As they went through the cemetery gates they passed an old man in blue overalls. He was shovelling dead leaves on to a slow-burning fire. They said good afternoon to him. He scowled, grunted something. They walked on, stopped beneath the memorial to Karl Marx. Somebody had daubed his massive Humpty Dumpty head with red paint. Perhaps that explained the man's black mood. In the distance, through the trees, Moses could hear the laughter of children.

Mary was smiling. 'When I brought Rebecca here, two years ago, she stood in front of Marx and looked very puzzled. After a while she turned to me and said, "How come he got a big statue like that just for inventing a boring old shop?" She thought he was the Marks in Marks and Spencer's. It was one of her first jokes.'

Moses could picture Rebecca squinting up at Marx, he could picture the indignation, the disbelief, on her small face. He too smiled.

They turned down an overgrown path between two rows of uneven leaning gravestones. Grass sprang up, stiff and blond as straw. Brambles clung to Mary's stockings. They watched a squirrel steal a red carnation from a wreath and eat it in the shadow of a bush. The old man's fire shook slow blue smoke into the air like incense. Mary sat down at the foot of a tomb and lit a cigarette. Moses sat down next to her. As he read the inscription on the stone – In Memory Of Our Beloved Father – something came free in him. Words took shape.

'It's pretty strange,' he said, 'not knowing where your parents are.'

Mary glanced round at him. 'What do you mean?'

'If my parents were dead, properly dead, in graves with names on, then at least I'd know where they were, wouldn't I? As it is, I haven't really got proof of anything.'

He wrenched a few blades of grass out of the ground and twisted them until they were dark and wet. He had sounded so bitter, surprising even himself.

'I don't know what you're talking about, Moses,' Mary said. 'You've never told me anything about your parents.'

So he told her. The same story he had told Gloria in that hotel in Leicestershire. He recognised many of the phrases. He added where necessary, especially for Mary, and found himself believing his embellishments. It was *his* story – one of the things he only entrusted to the people closest to him. It sealed a friendship, a relationship. Sanctified it, almost. Yes, he had the feeling, this time above all others, of handling something priceless and fragile, like the bones of a saint, something that could easily break up, decay, crumble into dust.

When he came to the end, Mary gave him a long careful look.

'I'm going to say something and you're probably not going to like it.'

'What?' he said, uneasy now.

'I think that was a nice performance. Almost convincing.'

'But it's true.'

'I know it's true. That's not the point. You were performing, Moses. You performed the whole thing. That's not the first time you've told somebody, is it?'

He looked away from her. 'No,' he mumbled. His stomach twisted as if he had been caught cheating.

'I know,' she said. 'It shows. You've told it before. Quite a few times, I imagine. You're not really even thinking about your parents when you tell it. Not any more. You're just using them. You're using your own family, your own history, to pull emotions out of people. You didn't really feel anything when you told me all that stuff about the dress – except self-pity, maybe. It wasn't real, Moses. It didn't *feel* real. It was like something put on specially for tourists. Some kind of ritual disembowelling. Is that all I am to you? I don't want smiling natives and air-conditioning and cabaret. I want real stuff. You've reached the point where you've sanitised everything. You can't take it any further. You know it and I know it. So why do it?'

He couldn't answer.

Anger shook her to her feet. She walked away. He noticed the blades of dead grass stuck to the back of her skirt.

In the car, she said, 'You know something? You don't need us. It's not us you need – me and Alan and Rebecca and Sean and Alison. It's your parents. Your family. Your *real* family. So find them. Stop using us.'

'How am I supposed to do that?' he said.

'I don't know. But at least you could start trying.'

He dropped into a painful silence. It took him minutes to struggle out. 'I *do* need you.' He could hear a childish defiance in his voice.

'Find them, Moses. Then you can decide that.'

She left him outside The Bunker. He thanked her for the afternoon, but the words came out awkward, accusing. After she had driven away, he went through a bewildering variety of responses in a very short space of time – fear, guilt, anxiety, amusement, cynicism. None of them seemed to fit.

That feeling of not knowing what to say.

He had sat in the car, on the gravestone, tongue-tied, panic-stricken, his bowels churning. Part of him hated her for attacking him there, in the area of trust and confidences. Another part of him applauded her, told him she was justified. He liked to appear as the victim of mysterious and tragic circumstances, he liked to manipulate people, he liked the sound of his own voice. He liked being thought of as special. What had she said? Something about disembowelling for tourists. She was right. She had been hard with him in precisely those areas where Gloria, say, had been soft. She had been *accurate*. That thought startled him. Suddenly it seemed as though she had passed a test which he, unwittingly, had put her through.

*

The next Sunday the weather broke.

Moses woke to the sound of a roof-tile shattering on the street below. Thunder in the distance, constant thunder, as if the world was ill. Wrapped in his dressing-gown, he stood in his bleak kitchen, swallowing coffee and watching the rain come down. After what Mary had said, he had made a few enquiries regarding the whereabouts of his parents, but he had drawn a complete blank.

On Friday evening he had phoned Uncle Stan and Auntie B. Auntie B had answered.

'You know, I *thought* that suitcase would upset you, Moses,' she had said.

She was so straightforward about things, Moses thought. Mary would probably adore her.

'A bit of a funny idea, really,' she had gone on, 'leaving a suitcase like that.'

'You're absolutely sure there wasn't an address anywhere?' Moses had said. 'What about on that letter?'

'Oh no, there was nothing. Nothing at all. Only a "to whom it may concern". I don't think they wanted *anyone* to know who they were.'

Moses had asked her for the address of the orphanage where he had grown up. He phoned the orphanage on Saturday morning. He spoke to a Mr Parks (Mrs Hood had died, apparently).

'Even if we had that kind of information,' Mr Parks said, 'we couldn't possibly divulge it. Not to anyone.'

Divulge. Really, he said that.

'I'm not anyone,' Moses said. 'I'm the person involved.'

'I'm sorry. It's not our policy to – '

'I don't think you heard me, Mr Parks. It's my parents I'm looking for. My own parents.'

'I'm very sorry.' Mr Parks appeared to be gloating then. 'We can't help you.'

Moses slammed the phone down.

He resorted to directories, though without his usual enthusiasm. He spent most of Saturday afternoon in the Trafalgar Square post office. He thumbed through every directory he could lay his hands on. He came out with black fingers and a headache.

Perhaps his parents were ex-directory. Perhaps they didn't have a phone. Perhaps they had emigrated. Or died, like Mrs Hood. He was beginning to wonder whether in fact he had ever actually *had* any parents. Perhaps he was a miracle of science. Or perhaps he had been delivered by a giant stork.

The perhapses seemed to go on for ever.

He turned round to see smoke rising from the grill. His toast was on fire. The last of the bread too. He switched the grill off and blew the flames out. He waited for the toast to cool, then he scraped the burnt bits off. He tried to spread it with butter, but the butter had been in the fridge for too long. Suddenly there were fragments of toast shrapnel all over the kitchen floor.

After sweeping up his breakfast with a dustpan and brush, Moses went and stood by the window. Rain. Grey skies. Misery. He watched a woman walk towards the bus-stop, hunched under a green umbrella. She was probably just tucking her chin into her collar to keep from getting soaked, but to Moses it looked as if she was carrying the heaviest umbrella in the world.

*

He dressed slowly and drove north through the drenched empty streets. It was no longer a decision whether or not to go to Muswell Hill on Sundays. It had become imperative, automatic, like breathing.

Mary opened the front door. She was wearing a faded black dress fastened at the waist with one of Sean's studded leather belts. She had a scarf round her neck, wispy, cloud-grey, made of something diaphanous like chiffon. Her fairy-tale look. She eyed him suspiciously.

'I didn't think we'd see you again,' she said. 'Not for a while, anyway.'

He wiped the rain out of his eyes with the back of his hand. 'Why not?'

'After last Thursday I thought you'd probably stay away. Lick your wounds. I wouldn't have blamed you, actually.' She smiled faintly, and he smiled back, then looked away.

'You're not quite over it yet,' she said, 'are you?'

He breathed in deeply. 'No.'

She seemed to approve of this. She took a step backwards and looked at him again, afresh almost. 'Christ, you're soaked,' she laughed. 'Come on in and get some dry things. We're getting drunk as usual.'

He followed her straight upstairs. 'Who knows,' she joked over her shoulder, 'maybe I'll attack you again later on.'

'There's nothing left to attack.'

She stopped on the top step, smiled down at him. 'I wouldn't be too sure about that.'

Lunch was spaghetti bolognese, a tossed salad, and bottles of Chianti on the oak table in the kitchen. Moses drank quickly, with exhilaration. The glasses of wine were a series of weights. Suddenly the scales tipped and he was drunk again.

After the meal he washed up unsteadily. Broke a plate. Outside the rain sluiced off the roof, flooded the terrace.

Rebecca, drying, groaned. 'I wanted to go out.'

They left the saucepans to soak and played the rain game with Alan. The rain game is easy. All you have to do is say what the rain is coming down in.

Alan said, 'Buckets.'

Moses said, 'Ten-gallon hats.'

Rebecca said, 'Swimming-trunks.'

In theory the rain always stopped before you ran out of containers. Not on this particular afternoon. It went on raining using containers they had never even heard of.

It was still raining two hours later when, after a series of twists and turns, the conversation arrived at marriage.

'You're lucky,' Moses was telling Alan. 'Your marriage is the kind of marriage I'd want if I was married.' He was entering the third stage of drunkenness now: the earnest stage (the fourth was loss of memory and balance, the fifth was coma). He poured himself another glass of wine. Like the rain, it didn't look as if it would be running out in the near future.

'It's your sense of priorities,' he went on. 'I mean, you're each other's priority and because you know you're each other's priority you can act like you're not. You can go anywhere, do anything. Maybe sometimes it looks like you're putting other things first, but that doesn't matter because deep down you know, you see. If you're Alan you know that Mary's always there, and if you're Mary you know that Alan's always there – '

'And if you're Moses,' Mary interrupted from her green chair in the corner, 'you know that Alan *and* Mary are always there.'

'Yes,' he had to admit, 'that's probably true.'

'And if you're Alison,' came Sean's voice from the scullery, 'you know that Vince's always there.'

'*That* is *not* true,' Alison cried, though she knew it was.

Mary smiled down into her drink. 'Vince,' she murmured.

Moses set that smile against the things that Vince had said about her. And couldn't help himself. 'You know what he said about you, Mary?'

'Who? Vince?' Mary said. 'No. Tell me.'

'He said you act like time's stood still for twenty years.'

Mary's face lifted, lit up. 'That's right,' she said. 'My God, that's absolutely right. All this – ' and Moses took it that she meant this heady Muswell Hill air she breathed, the spirit of the house, her happiness – 'it hasn't changed in twenty years. How wonderful!'

He had to laugh because she looked so victorious, so fulfilled, as if she had just won a prize. He knew how much Vince would have hated him for telling Mary what he had said about her. But how much more Vince would have hated the fact that she had taken the insult as a compliment, that she had discovered a new truth in those bitter words. Outmanoeuvred again. Bitch.

And suddenly Moses saw her as some brilliant species of fish. She exploited to the full the privacy and depth and space of the element she moved in. One moment she tilted her scales to catch the light and masqueraded as a piece of reflected sky, or travelled incognito through the darkness of the ocean bed. The next she lay on the surface, all gall and nonchalance and dazzle. And when those crude hooks ploughed or wheedled their way through the water towards her, she slipped past them with infinite grace, infinite delight.

Fishwoman, he thought.

Some day he would tell her that and make her laugh.

In the meantime the rain was still falling, collecting in deep pools on the terrace, the perfect background to his thoughts.

*

Evening had fallen. Moses had fallen too, snapping the back off a kitchen chair (Alan had laughed and said, 'It's all right, I like stools'). Now he stretched out on the living-room floor, a tumbler of brandy in his hand. Alison sat crosslegged in front of the TV; there was a crackling as she drew a brush through the forest-fire of her hair. Sean was beating Alan at pool upstairs. Rebecca was in the bath. He wondered where Mary had disappeared to, and the thought lifted him effortlessly to his feet.

Outside the rain had stopped because everybody had forgotten about it. The eaves and drainpipes of the house creaked with the last of the downpour. A few pale clouds overlapped at a great height.

He found her sitting on the low brick wall separating the Shirleys' front garden from their next-door neighbours'. She wasn't wearing any shoes.

'Haven't you got cold feet?' he said.

She didn't react.

He tilted his head back until it was parallel with the sky. It was so dark up there. Giddy and unending. Stars staggered. One tripped and fell a million miles.

'What did you mean,' she said finally, 'by that little *monologue* about my marriage?'

'I meant what I said.'

'It sounded like a challenge.'

'To do what?'

'I think you know the answer to that. I also think you're playing games.' When he didn't respond, her eyes turned on him and her voice hardened. 'Playing games,' she said, 'with me.'

'What about you? Aren't you playing games?'

'That's not my style.'

'What do you call what you're doing then?'

'Fear. Risk. Confusion. Take your pick.'

'I don't see what the difference is.'

She reached out, placed a hand on the back of his head and drew his mouth towards hers. She kissed him with closed lips. As the first kiss merged into a second then into a third, her lips gave, parted under his. He tasted wine and through the wine he tasted her.

She leaned back against the wall, stared uphill into the sky. 'That's the difference, Moses. I really do it. You don't.'

He didn't say anything.

'You know, sometimes,' she said, 'you can hear the motorway from here.' It might have been a private joke, the way she smiled.

He couldn't hear the motorway. That breathy silence could have been anything. He was drunk, he was thinking, but not drunk enough. Panic.

Mary's head, resting on her knees, moved from side to side as if she was denying something. 'What am I doing?' she murmured. 'What am I doing? What are *you* doing?'

'Sitting on the wall,' he said.

'Sitting on the fence,' she came back instantly. And smiled at him sideways, through her hair, her lips shining like dark glass.

In that moment he felt her quickness could get them out of anything. He didn't believe what she said about confusion and fear and risk. This was Mary. She was extraordinary. They would be all right.

*

He woke early as he always did in strange beds. He had a headache and creases on his cheeks from sleeping face down. When he tiptoed downstairs through the quiet house he found Mary in the kitchen. She was making toast and coffee. The open window let birdsong and a suggestion of sunlight into the room.

'It's going to be a nice day,' she said. 'I thought perhaps we could go for a walk on Hampstead Heath.'

'Don't you have to work?'

Smiling, she handed him a piece of toast. 'I'm ill,' she said.

They left the house just after seven and drove to the Vale of Health. Mary parked the car next to a deserted fairground. She pointed at the dodgems rimmed with orange rust and standing at curious angles to one another. 'People at a party,' she said, and once again he saw that nothing was wasted on her. She could make the world more interesting just by looking at it.

They scaled a steep bank of bleached grass. At the top the woods began. Beech trees stood on the hard-packed mud, their trunks dusted with green, their leaves sapped of life, shot through with holes, ready to drop, their roots rising through the surface of the ground.

Moses bent down. 'They look like ribs,' he said, 'the ribs on starving horses.' He glanced up to see Mary watching him with a curious smile on her face. It made him feel as if he had been doing something slightly eccentric. He began to get a glimmer of the reason why she liked to be with him.

'Yes. Yes, they do,' she said.

He rejoined her on the path. 'When I was at school,' he said, 'I used to talk to horses.'

On Saturday afternoons, he told her, he sometimes had to play football. Matches were specially organised for the boys who were no good at games. For the spastics, as they were known. In his first year Highness MG was thirteen years old and just over six foot tall. Highness MG was a spastic.

On the one afternoon that stood for all the others in his memory a Welshman by the name of Davies took the game. Davies was an officious little bastard. He wore royal-blue track-suits and ran on the spot all the time. He was only 5'8". Highness MG had been put down to play right-back. A real spastic's position, right-back. So far as he could work out it meant staying at one end of the pitch, more or less out of the way, for forty-five minutes. Then, at half-time, he had to walk down to the other end of the pitch, to the area diagonally opposite, in fact, and stay there for *another* forty-five minutes. Unless there was injury time (what a terrible phrase; it sounded like everybody was officially supposed to hurt each other), in which case he would have to stand around for *even longer*. He arrived at the pitch that afternoon wearing his brand-new games jersey. The collar chafed his neck. The wind blew around his bare knees. It really was a very tedious and unpleasant business altogether.

Time went slowly. Sometimes the ball passed through his section of the pitch accompanied by rapid breathing, shouts, and the thudding of energetic boots (some spastics tried harder than others). He watched it go by like a rather dull carnival. Once the ball ran loose and rolled towards him. He lunged at it half-heartedly. The weight of his boot (size $9\frac{1}{2}$, suspiciously clean) carried his leg higher into the air than he had bargained for, causing a temporary, though not total, loss of balance. For those few moments he must have looked like a clumsy can-can dancer. The ball trickled under his raised leg and into touch.

'Oh, *Midget*,' everybody yelled. 'Come on, *Midget*.'

Mary interrupted him. 'Why Midget?'

'Because my initials are M G.' He winced. 'You know, in some ways, I think I hated that name even more than Foreskin.'

'That's because it's true,' Mary said. 'In some ways you *are* very small.' And when she saw the look on his face she added, 'I'm sorry, but I mean it.'

Moses went on with the story.

Because these matches featured spastics they always took place in the most remote corners of the school grounds. On this particular afternoon they were playing right up against the boundary fence. Beyond the fence lay an ordinary field. A field with no white lines on it. A field where footballs were meaningless and the Welshman's whistle had no power. A sensible field, in other words. At some point during the second half Midget got fed up with searching for insects in the long grass. He ached with cold and the inside of his thigh stung where the ball had struck it while he wasn't looking (he was convinced that Puddle had done it on purpose). He wandered casually to the edge of the pitch and crossed the touchline. Sacrilege. Heresy. Taboo. He half-expected alarms to sound, dogs to start barking, search-lights to track him down in the gloom of that November afternoon, but, strangely enough, nobody seemed to notice.

He leaned on the metal fence. There was a tree in the middle of the field. Two or three horses stood in the shadow of its branches.

'Hello, horses,' he said affectionately.

It seemed like the first time he had spoken in ages.

They were old and tired, these horses. They had obviously had hard lives and had been put out to grass. One of them, a roan with shaggy hooves and a bulging sack of a stomach, lifted its head and shambled over.

He moved his hand out slowly, stroked the soft puffing nose.

'What's it like in there then?' he said.

Then he heard the whistle screech and saw a blur of royal-blue in the corner of his eye. The horse's eyes rolled back. It shied away from the sudden rush of colour, thudded off into the sanity of its field.

'Goodbye, horses,' he said.

'What the blazes are you doing, Highness?' Davies shouted, jogging on the spot. His voice was going up and down too.

'Talking to the horses.'

'Talking to the horses, *sir*.'

'Talking to the horses, *sir*.' Feeling like a parrot, sir.

'And why, when you're supposed to be playing football, are you talking to horses, Highness?'

'They're more interesting. Sir.'

His reply was greeted by a burst of applause. Davies froze in stupefaction, one knee in the air, until he realised that it was the crowd three pitches away (who had just seen Darling S G B of the First X V go over for a try to put the school ahead of its local rivals).

'Davies never forgave me for that,' Moses said. 'You know what he wrote on my report? He wrote: *Highness seems totally uninterested in any form of physical exertion whatsoever.*'

'Nicely put,' Mary said, 'but no longer entirely true, I suspect.'

Moses laughed.

He had never been to Kenwood House before, but it seemed appropriate to be seeing it at eight o'clock on a Monday morning, as if that specific time and place had been reserved long in advance. He had the feeling that, although everything was unusual, everything was as it should be.

Mist dressed the trees in grey uniforms, confined the world to little more than the footpath they were walking along. They reached a ditch. He jumped over. Mary stooped to examine a dam of twigs and leaves. She almost lost her footing on the bank. She was no athlete either, he saw. She would probably have talked to horses too. He held a hand out to her and helped her across.

They sat down on the grass beside the lake, the house a suggestion of white in the mist behind them. Mary leaned back against him, her head resting on his stomach. It was strange, her lying against him like that. In a flashback he saw Gloria in the same position, that Sunday morning on the beach. That kind of duplication worried him; it was as if, sooner or later, all human contact fell into the same tired easy patterns. He wanted to establish a difference between the two. He bent over and kissed Mary's mouth. It was cool, closed; it didn't move under his.

The sun pressed through the mist, brought out a fluorescence in the grass, a pallor in her skin, then it withdrew again, turned back into an area of brightness in the sky. The pressure of her head on his body spread, ran through his blood until he was alive to every part of her: the veins on her hand, the gleam in her hair, the curve of her nearest breast whose shape he still didn't know. It was like being injected with some kind of slow drug that convinced him once again just how extraordinary she was – an injection she could quite reasonably deny all knowledge of, and would, knowing her.

It *was* a game, whatever she said. And, as in any game, there were rules. She laid down two rules that morning on the heath. The first after several minutes of silence. She levelled her chin at him suddenly, reminding him of a general, her profile in relief against a battalion of trees. 'Nothing is to be destroyed,' she said.

He said nothing.

You, me, him, us, them, he thought. A tall order, that. Like a tray stacked high with crockery. A cup slides towards one edge. You tilt the tray to try and save it. A plate falls off the other end. Crash. Nothing is to be destroyed, he repeated to himself. He looked at her and saw what they had together as a circus-act.

And the second?

'You must never let me fuck you,' she said. 'Never.' And when she saw him smiling, 'No, I'm perfectly serious, Moses. Even if I ask you to, you must never let me. Promise me that.'

Even then he had a presentiment of how erotic a rule like that could be. Was that the reason for it, though? He never knew with Mary. She experimented with herself. 'I put myself through things,' she had told him once, and he remembered thinking of lions and hoops of fire. Still smiling, he nodded. He promised.

'You see,' she said, 'I've never done this before,' and her eyes dilated, somewhere between triumph and fear.

'I don't understand. Never done what before?'

'I've only been with Alan. That's it. That's all I know.'

He found this almost impossible to believe. She had led him, he felt, to believe the opposite. And he had never kissed anyone who kissed so well. But then there was a certain innocence about her kiss that made him think: Well, perhaps she *is* telling the truth. An innocence that her experience, such as it was, had done nothing to corrupt or transform.

So they were agreed: their relationship was to continue as it had started – orally.

One question wouldn't go away, however. Mary had made the rules –

but was she going to stick to them? After all, everybody knows what rules are for. And Mary was perverse enough to do exactly that.

*

'That looks forbidden,' Mary said. 'Let's try it.'

She backed the Volvo on to the grass verge and switched off the engine.

It was October now. Leaves the colour of tobacco. Air you could smoke like a cigarette. One of those days you remember years later. You don't always remember the date or the place, sometimes you don't even remember who you were with, but you remember the way your mind emptied out like a sigh, you remember the ease of your body's moving, the feel of the air on your skin, the shape of a cloud, you remember a casual phrase, something somebody said without thinking, something that takes on significance purely through being remembered: *That looks forbidden. Let's try it.*

A path curved away ahead of them. On the left, beyond the metal cattle-fence, a meadow sloped up to a ridge whose cutting edge had been blunted by a row of trees. To the right a high brick wall allowed them teasing glimpses of a mansion set in the middle of a private park. Once Moses saw a deer glide through the smoky distance. They followed the path for about twenty minutes until it narrowed, ducked into a wood.

Mary stood still, inhaled. 'That's so erotic.'

All that mulch and mould, she meant. All that humus, bark and fungus. Matured, ripened, sweetened in the dark container of that wood. He remembered her smiling up at him, her face between his thighs. 'My God, how *good* that smells.' And so crestfallen when he told her that he had just washed his sheets for the first time in almost four weeks. 'Four weeks,' she had groaned. 'What a terrible waste. How could you do something like that, Moses? How could you throw it all away?' In mourning, almost. He had looked puzzled and amused. He had never thought of dirt like that before.

Now she was standing next to him, her eyes flecked with silver, saying, 'Jesus, you know what this is like? This is like having my face in your pants.'

They lay down on the noisy leaves, each sensing the other's body stirring under all the layers of clothing. One hand eventually discovering the warm pale flesh of her stomach made her gasp. She curled round, took him in her mouth so softly, so gradually, that he didn't have to will his orgasm; it rushed him from a distance, threw him backwards, shook him like a fit. She drank him, spilling nothing.

Afterwards she moved towards his mouth.

'Taste yourself,' she said.

The air lay cold against their faces, everywhere except their lips which it couldn't reach. The leaves crumbled into dust under their bodies.

He drew back so he could look at her.

'You don't seem so tall when we're lying down,' she said. 'Maybe we'll have to lie down more often in the future.'

He smiled.

'And that taste,' she said. 'That taste in the daytime. That too.'

He leaned above her watching the light, the white October light, run like acid into all the lines on her face, making them deeper, more pronounced. He traced one that curved through the thin mauve skin beneath her eye.

'You look older outdoors,' he said, meaning he liked the way she looked.

She lay back, looked up at him. It was her look. It came at you horizontally (vertically, in this case). Shrewd eyes, head cocked, mouth pushed forwards, almost pouting. It was amused, sceptical, challenging, but most of all it was enigmatic since she used it as shorthand and he could never gauge its meaning.

'I'm forty,' she said. 'Next year I'll be forty-one.'

He lay back, his head next to hers in the leaves. 'I was thinking,' he said. 'Does Alan know anything about this? I mean, if he knew, what would he think?'

Mary sighed. 'How should *I* know? I told you. I've never done this before. I have no idea.'

'You don't think he suspects?'

'Why should he? He trusts me. He hasn't *got* any suspicion.'

She saw Moses frown. 'I'll spell it out for you,' she said. 'I've been married for nineteen years. I know Alan and he knows me. It's close, you know? Even after all this time. And I would never leave him. Not for you. Not for anyone. And you know that too, if you're honest with yourself. That's why you're in this thing. It's safe.'

He realised that she was angry because she thought he was trying to put her marriage in a box, and nobody could do that to her marriage. He wasn't, though. He only wanted to know what it felt like to be in the middle.

'I'm sorry,' he said. 'Sometimes you don't understand what I'm trying to say.'

'If you can't be clear, that's your problem. I'm not an interpreter.'

Moses sat up, looked away from her.

'I'm a wife and a mother,' Mary said. 'Whatever else I am comes third.'

He knew that. At the same time he found that degree of clarity a bit suspect. 'How can you be so sure?' he asked her. 'How can it be so neat?'

'It's nineteen years of my life, Moses. If I wasn't sure about that, I wouldn't be sure about anything.'

'Maybe you just described me.'

'Maybe I did. But there's a big difference. I'm forty. I can't afford to be wrong.'

'Old woman,' he said. He knelt in front of her and put his hands on her shoulders.

'Yes,' she said, defiant now, leaves in her hair, 'I *am* old.'

'Kiss me,' he said.

She stared at him steadily for a moment, then her face relaxed. She kissed him.

*

The wall seemed to go on for ever. Everything was happening on the left and Mary, brighter now as if they had, between them, cleared the air, pointed, scrutinised, cried out:

'Look. A weir.'

The water, shaped like a comb, fell sheer into a still pool. She told him a story about a girl she had known when she was at college. The girl had drowned herself just below a weir. When they found her, she was floating, bound in weeds, like Ophelia. She had left a note behind in her room. *I would have done this months ago, but I had to wait for my hair to grow.*

Moses shivered.

'And I remember everybody telling her how much nicer she looked with her hair long,' Mary said.

Later they passed a bonfire.

'You know what Rebecca used to call those?' she said. 'Cloud factories.'

Then they saw a sofa overgrown with brambles, a jay (no more than a scribble of blue on the grey paper of the afternoon), and a moon rising above the trees, as see-through as a piece of dead skin. It was one of those days when everything you see has a story attached to it, when everything you see reminds you of something else.

But nothing happened on the right. They glimpsed the house at intervals, from a number of different angles, through gaps where the wall had tumbled down, through cracks in padlocked doors and, once, through the bars of an ornate wrought-iron gateway. There was something pornographic about the way the house revealed itself. It turned them into voyeurs.

After walking for almost two hours they reached the car again.

'How peculiar,' Mary said, 'to go all the way round the house like that, to go so *far*, without ever getting any nearer.'

It struck Moses that, on another day, they would probably have ignored the PRIVATE PROPERTY signs and scaled the wall and explored the grounds. But he said, 'Some things are better from a distance.'

'I hope that doesn't include me.'

He smiled. 'You know it doesn't.'

But she had come perilously close, it seemed, and knew it. For that walk round the wall, he thought, had summed up their entire relationship.

Never getting any nearer.

The rules still intact.

*

Gloria phoned again.

He didn't want to talk to her at all. He had nothing to say. He found himself feeling delayed by her call, as if he had something important to do, which he hadn't. She sounded cheerful which made him sound depressed. His mind drifted as she talked. He said yes, no – anything, really. He didn't care whether he gave himself away or not.

When she had finished answering the questions he hadn't asked her she began to ask him questions.

'Are you still seeing the Shirleys?'

'Yes. Weekends, mostly. Sometimes I stay there a couple of days.'

'Oh. That's nice.' She was trying to be big-hearted. Taking an interest in something that either upset or annoyed her. It made him want to rub her face in it. Would it be 'nice' then?

'What do you do there?'

'We get drunk, talk, go for walks – '

'Is she an alcoholic?'

'Who?'

'The mother. Mrs Shirley.'

'No. She just drinks a lot.'

A short laugh from Gloria, but he hadn't meant it as a joke. Then a pause. 'Are you all right?' she said. 'You sound a bit morose.'

'I'm fine,' he said, sounding morose.

'What is it then? Don't you want to talk to me?'

'I don't know,' he said. But really she was right. He didn't want to talk to her. He couldn't explain it to himself so there seemed little point in trying to explain it to her.

'Can I come round?' she was asking him now.

'When?' he said. Thinking tomorrow, the next day, something like that.
'Now.'

Jesus, he thought. Then he went blank. Looked at the clock even though he already knew what time it was.

'If you like,' he said finally.

'See you in about half an hour.'

He put the phone down and began to wait for her to arrive. He resented her presumption. Inviting herself round like that. But why, in that case, hadn't he simply said no? How was it she had acquired the power to rob him of initiative?

*

She hung her coat on the ghost's coat-hook even though he had told her a thousand times.

'I'm worried about you,' she said, moving across the room towards him.

He kissed her, then he turned away. 'Why?'

'I think you're getting in over your head.'

'Over my head?' He laughed, but there was no humour in his laugh. What right did she have to say that? 'How do you know?'

She sat down on the sofa and lit a cigarette. He could hear it crackle in the silence as she inhaled. 'Call it a hunch,' she said.

He looked over his shoulder at her. It was something Mary might have said. She phrased things that way.

'I mean, I don't care what you do with her.' Gloria was examining her shoes.

'And what if I told you we don't *do* anything?'

'I don't care. The thing is, you're not being straight with me. You keep everything to yourself. I don't know where I stand any more.' She paused, looked up from her shoes. 'That means something, don't you think?'

Moses turned back to the window and pressed his forehead against the cold glass. He felt sick, uncertain, found out. His mind was going blank with the division of things. Down in the street he could see three children sitting on a wall. They were laughing and swinging their legs. He wanted to sit on a wall. He wanted to laugh and swing his legs.

'Moses,' and Gloria's voice had softened now, 'just tell me where I stand.'

'It's a friendship,' he heard himself insisting.

She looked down at her hands. For the first time, he saw her as a nun, her smile limited and prim – superior. She was making him ridiculous. A *friendship*. How pompous. But what could he tell her? He tried again.

'I like them all. The whole family. That's why I go there. It's as simple as that. I can't see why you're making it into such a great drama.'

She came and stood next to him, her shoulder touching his upper arm. It was a forgiveness routine (for what?). He turned to look at her. She turned a moment later. They kissed. But the deeper their kiss became, the less he could see. It was all too close. He couldn't focus. Everything blurred and swam away.

*

Sleeping together didn't change anything. His body went through the motions – and not without a certain practised tenderness – but his mind floated free. His orgasm, when it came, seemed to happen somewhere else. It was like hearing an explosion in the distance as you walk down a quiet street: you pause for a second, listen, then walk on unaffected.

He lay on his back afterwards, one arm over his face, the other across his stomach. He wished the afternoon would accelerate into dusk so their faces became invisible. Gloria asked him what he was thinking about.

'Nothing,' he said.

When, actually, he was.

He was thinking about a picture he had seen while he was fucking her. Night-time. A street of ordinary houses. No lights in any of the houses, though. It had been raining in the picture. Even now the sound of a light drizzle came to his ears, scarcely audible, like the movements of insects. The street looked dark, empty, shiny. Halfway down on the left a pink sign flashed on and off . . . on and off . . . the only colour, the only life in the surrounding darkness. In neon script it said *Goodbye*. Just that one word. Staining the wet black tarmac pink. Nice picture. He could have watched it for a long time. It was so monotonous, so precise, so comforting. Very nice picture.

'Nothing,' he repeated.

*

The mood lingered.

That night, after Gloria left, he thought about Mary. He stared at the kitchen floor as he thought about her. A colour appeared: yellow. Texture followed and the yellow turned into sand. A silent wind blew and the sand drifted. Something showed through. A fragment of mosaic. He bent down, blew on it. The mosaic grew.

There could be an entire floor here, he thought. He began to remove

312

the grains of sand with a fine toothbrush so as not to damage anything that might be there.

This is ridiculous, he thought some time later, having cleared about forty square feet of mosaic with a toothbrush. There's probably a whole villa here. First he used a broom, then impatience gave him a shovel. His mind raced on ahead. It came back with the word city. He called in cranes, trucks, bulldozers. He supervised the excavations.

He stood back. So. A city. Well, he'd known it all along, really. Just hadn't dared believe in it. In case it disappointed him. In case it let him down. He was superstitious that way.

Now he walked through what he had unearthed without reaching its limits. He paused in courtyards, he followed streets, he crossed squares. He stood at crossroads. He felt like a tourist. Overawed. Bewildered. No mastery of history.

Inadequate.

He faltered at the word.

A sudden blur of colour took him by surprise. It sprinted along the very edge of his vision. The flicker of a lizard? The sun glancing off a stone? These were possibilities, but not convincing ones. He ran to the corner just in time to catch a glimpse of someone on a bicycle. The someone wore an orange anorak.

He would've known that orange anorak anywhere.

Alan.

Well, he supposed he should've been expecting that. Yes, he should've expected to run into Alan. He sank down on to one of the massive hewn blocks of stone that made up the kerb. No point chasing him, though. No point even calling out. What could he say?

After that it seemed to go dark in a second. Night descending. The weekend again. Traffic lights turned green on the main road below and strange people's feet pressed accelerators. Voices bumped against the kitchen window like balloons. Outside there was another city.

Three phone-calls happened in quick succession.

First Eddie wanted Moses to come to a party in Barons Court.

'No,' Moses said.

Then Jackson called from his aunt's in Cheltenham to ask Moses whether he had seen any sign of the cold front which ought to be moving towards London at that very moment.

'No,' Moses said.

And finally Louise rang, jaunty as ever (she called him honey), and asked him if he minded filling in for her at The Bunker because she had promised to take an old Spanish friend of hers to see Gloria sing.

'No,' Moses said. 'I don't mind.'

*

He sat in Louise's Perspex box that evening and sold tickets. People paying to get in were impressed by his expressionless face and his sullen monosyllables. All the best clubs hired people like that.

But nothing could lighten Moses's mood, not even Ridley's imitation of a bird of paradise. An Anti-Nowhere League single was running through his head:

> *I've been here and I've been there*
> *and I've been every-fucking-where*
> *so what, so what, you boring little cunt –*

The night dragged, joyless.

When the club closed at two, he left Ridley to lock up. He climbed the stairs, put some music on and stretched out on his sofa. He had a sense of the building falling silent under him.

He went to bed just before three.

He woke almost immediately, it seemed, but a glance at his clock told him it was four-fifteen. Bird stood on the windowsill, one paw raised. When he saw Moses he opened his blunt jaws and released one of his famous seagull cries. It rose from the bottom of the night, desolate but urgent, chilling – a warning.

'What is it, Bird?'

Then he heard a sound. It followed so closely on his words that it might have been surreal punctuation. Something like glass shattering, he thought. He lay still, propped up on one elbow, every muscle rigid.

Hearing nothing more, he eased out of bed, pulled on a T-shirt and jeans, and stepped into an old pair of desert-boots. His movements unusually light, he crossed the room and listened at the door. A truck shifted gears on the main road; a window vibrated somewhere, then the building quietened down again.

He crept downstairs until he reached the door that connected his stairs with the short corridor leading to Elliot's office. Here again he paused, heard nothing. He flung Elliot's door open with a crash and flicked the light on. The walls, the desk, the sofa, leapt out at him and froze. It occurred to him that if there was anyone in the building they would now know that they were not alone.

He moved back along the corridor towards the stairs that led down into the nightclub. His footsteps made no sound on the carpet. He began to

314

take the stairs. One by one, one hand on the wall. He stopped at the bottom of each flight. Listened. Before turning blind into the next flight. It was a gamble every time, a private dare. Sooner or later something would be there. It was like Russian roulette. There had to be a bullet in one of the chambers.

Then he had reached the bottom of the stairs and the dim expanse of the foyer lay ahead. To his left a glimmer of pale light showed him where the Perspex ticket-box was. To his right a wide corridor led to the bar.

He edged into the corridor. The darkness thickened, began to pulse. Then he remembered the policeman. And wanted to run or scream. Wanted to hurl himself to the floor and thrash about like an epileptic. Fear had him. Still he inched along the corridor. When the carpet turned to wood beneath his feet, he knew he was standing on the dance-floor. The darkness sang like an electric fence now. He could feel the hairs lifting on his bare forearms. A sudden draught of cool air brushed past him. Where had that come from? He sensed a movement to his left and turned. Something struck him where his neck joined his shoulder. The darkness was a night sky showering big flakes of snow. He hit out sideways and made contact with something that felt smooth and hard. A person's face, perhaps. He heard a noise like air escaping from a valve. Then he was lying on his back.

He couldn't have lost consciousness though, because he saw a shape slip away across the dance-floor. Or thought he did, anyway. He hauled himself to his feet. He had the feeling that he was coming last in some kind of bizarre race.

He found a broken window in the Ladies. The same toilet he had taken speed in all those months ago. He stood on the seat and put his face to the gap. Cold air touched his hair. He heard a car pull away in the side-street. He doubted that it was the person who had broken in. It seemed too convenient somehow. Besides it had taken him ages to cover the distance from the dance-floor to the toilet window. Whoever it was would probably be far away by now. Whoever it was.

He had a piss. An afterthought, really. So casual it made him laugh. He walked back into the club and turned all the lights on. No blood, no shit, no white arrows. He switched on the PA. Thump, hiss. For the next hour he played music. Bands like Crass, Siouxsie and the Banshees, The Pack, Crisis, The Fall. He even found the Anti-Nowhere League single that had been crashing through his head all evening. He played that too.

> so what, so what, you boring little cunt
> who cares, who cares what you do
> who cares, who cares about you

you
you, you, you —

At times he had the feeling that the person who had hit him was listening outside the broken toilet window. In a way he hoped so. Because the music was for him.

He shivered behind the DJ's Perspex shield until it began to get light. Only then did he switch the lights and the power off and climb back up the stairs to bed.

*

He woke at midday. His neck ached. The sky was grey and grit blew in the wind. Pigeons peeled off the windowsill across the street like plump aeroplanes, stumbled through the air in clumsy circles, and landed on the windowsill again. There were machine-guns in his mind.

He tried ringing Elliot on the internal extension. No reply. Great. He went out to buy some breakfast.

Dino took one look at Moses as he pushed through the door and his whole face expanded into a smile. 'Hello, Moses.' He pronounced it *Maoses*, as usual. 'You look terrible.'

'I didn't sleep too well.'

Dino was wearing a badge on his shapeless grey sweatshirt. *It's all Greek to me*, it said.

'That's a great badge, Dino,' Moses said.

'You like it?' Dino squinted down, his chin doubling. 'One of my mates gave it to me.'

'You know, I could use a badge like that.'

'Yeah, but you're not Greek, are you?' Dino cackled and vanished into the back of his shop.

When Moses got back to The Bunker he found a note under the door. *Dinner tonight? M.* He couldn't understand how they had missed each other. He had only been out for fifteen minutes at the most. He ran back to the main road and looked for the old blue Volvo. Not a sign. He shrugged his shoulders and, slipping the note into his pocket, walked slowly home.

*

He stayed in all afternoon waiting for Elliot. When he saw the white Mercedes glide into the side-street on the stroke of five he ran downstairs.

'Elliot – '

'Hey, Abraham! What's up?'

'Elliot, listen. We got broken into again last night.'

'Don't be funny.'

'It's true, Elliot.'

Upstairs in the office, he told Elliot the whole story in detail. He only left out the part where he had sat in the club until dawn playing records. He couldn't make any sense of that himself. When he had finished, Elliot propped his feet on the desk and blew some air out of his mouth.

'Shit. You all right, Moses?'

Moses nodded.

'You sure?'

'It was only a glancing blow,' Moses explained. 'I think he was aiming for my head, but it was dark and my head's much higher up than most people's, so he got my shoulder instead.'

'Lucky you're big, right?'

'Yeah,' Moses said. 'Lucky I'm big.'

Elliot drew his lips into his mouth and stared out of the window. 'You didn't get a look at him?'

Moses shook his head. 'Too dark.'

'OK, leave this with me. I appreciate what you did, you know, but next time, if you hear something, call me first. All right?'

Moses moved towards the door. 'I'll remember that.'

Elliot faced back into the room and, adjusting his gold bracelet, said casually, 'Just as a matter of interest, Moses, who was that woman coming out of your door the other day?'

'Woman? What woman?'

'Nice-looking, but getting on a bit. Had a black dress on.'

'Careful, Elliot,' Moses said. 'That's my mother you're talking about.'

'Your *mother*? Don't give me that – '

But Moses had already left the office.

Elliot, who had seen Moses kissing the woman on the street, looked puzzled. Sons don't kiss their mothers. Not like that. Not with tongues. Some of the stories Moses came out with. Like that one about a friend of his who had slept with two thousand women. That had to be some kind of record, that did. Elliot grinned, shook his head, whistled through the gap in his teeth. Then the grin faded, his face tightened, and he went back to hoping the phone wasn't going to ring.

*

'Christ, Moses,' Alison said, 'that's scary.'

He had just told the Shirleys what had happened the previous night. He glanced across at Mary. She was tilting her knife this way and that, catching light on the blade.

'Why don't you leave?' she said. 'If it's that dangerous, why not find somewhere else to live?'

'I can't,' he said.

'Why not?'

'I don't know. Elliot's a friend. I owe him.'

Her knife struck the table. 'When are you going to stop being other people's fool?' she snapped.

He had been smiling, but the smile stiffened on his face. The silence round the table had the tension of held breath.

'When are you going to stop being grateful, for fuck's sake? When are you going to stop letting people use you? Stop being grateful, Moses. Start standing up for yourself. You don't owe anybody anything, don't you see that? Jesus Christ, it makes me sick the way you sit there like a stuffed prick and say "I owe him". You *don't owe*. Got it?'

She stared at him, her face mottled, tight with anger, and he remembered the time he'd told her about Eddie. He'd tried to explain the way Eddie treated women. 'It's not intentional,' he'd said. 'He can't see it. He just does it.' She'd considered this, then she'd said, 'He sounds like a shit to me.' Of course he'd sometimes thought of Eddie as a shit. The time Eddie dumped that topless waitress on him, for instance. Or the night of the beach party. When it affected him personally, perhaps. And suddenly, in that moment, Mary's judgment had spread to cover everything that Eddie did. She's right, he'd found himself thinking. Eddie's just a shit. A shit from Basingstoke. Where shits come from. It all made sense. But later he'd remembered that she often seemed jealous of his friends, his 'other world', as she called it, and that she often put them down without giving them a chance, almost as a matter of principle. So he'd swayed back again. Eddie had become a statue once more. Mythical, unaccountable, creating his own laws.

Wasn't this new outburst of hers similar? Wasn't she just pulling The Bunker down because it didn't include her, because it was something she felt she had to compete against? Or was she really concerned about his safety?

When he looked across at her, she said sadly, 'When are you going to learn, Moses? When are you going to learn?'

'You're right,' he sighed. He wanted to learn from her. He really did.

But, at the same time, he knew that nothing she could say to him would ever make him leave The Bunker.

*

Later, drunker, they stood talking on the terrace. A light wind tugged at the edges of the shawl that she had wrapped around her shoulders. On a sudden impulse she leaned across to kiss him. He stepped back so abruptly that she almost lost her balance.

'Not now,' he said.

She glared at him. 'Why did you do that?'

'I don't want to do that now. Not here. It's too dangerous.'

'*Dangerous?*' Her lip curled. She seemed to find what he was saying utterly beyond belief, utterly contemptible. 'What do you mean *dangerous?*'

'You know what I mean, Mary.'

'No, I don't. I don't know what you mean. What's wrong with you today?'

When he didn't reply, she wrapped herself more tightly in her shawl and, backing away from him, said, 'Christ, sometimes you chill me to the bone.'

She almost trod on Alan's foot. Alan had been standing in the doorway. Moses hadn't noticed him either.

'What's going on out here?' Alan asked. Light-hearted though, not accusing. He obviously hadn't seen anything.

Mary pushed past him without answering.

Moses smiled. 'Just a little difference of opinion.'

'Ah yes.' Alan's eyes glittered behind his glasses. 'That happens in this house.'

Moses found Mary drinking brandy in the living-room. He told her he was sorry, but said they had to be more careful. Mary shook her head.

'It was the moment. You destroyed it.'

Moses said nothing.

'I thought we agreed about that,' she said. 'I thought we said no destruction.'

'That's crazy.'

'What's crazy?'

'Blowing it up into something so big.'

'You destroyed the moment, Moses,' she insisted, and that had the power to negate anything he said.

It unnerved him, the way everything was suddenly turning round, coming back on him like a wave. Mary had laid down laws about no destruction and no fucking and then she had handed them over to him to enforce while she, it seemed, was free to modify or challenge them whenever she pleased. It was as if, in suspecting him of wanting the relationship with her simply because there was no responsibility involved, she had created a sense of responsibility herself, given it to him, and claimed the role of devil's advocate for her own. At last he realised that if the rules were still intact it was purely his own doing. They could be broken any time he chose.

*

Perhaps that was why he got so drunk that night. It anaesthetised the fear. You just blundered about regardless, sorted out the wreckage in the morning.

At midnight he found Mary alone in the kitchen. She had just put on a record of Billie Holiday songs. She was drinking neat vodka. She held out a hand to him.

'Everybody's gone to bed,' she said. 'Let's dance.'

They danced.

Once, when he glanced towards the door, she whispered, 'Don't be frightened.'

'I'm not,' he said.

'You flinched. I felt it.'

'I don't remember flinching.' He pulled away, looked down at her. 'When did I flinch?'

She smiled and pressed her face into his shirt. 'Relax,' she said.

It wasn't dancing music, but they carried on dancing. In one of their closer moments, he let his hand rest against her right breast. One of her hands instantly flew up and knocked it away.

'Sorry,' he said. 'Didn't you want me to do that?'

'Accident,' she murmured. 'It was an accident.'

His hand returned.

Afterwards he couldn't remember the sequence of events that led from the kitchen to the guest-room. He only remembered that he couldn't stop touching her. Then he was lying next to her in the bed he always slept in when he stayed overnight. They were both naked. Two of his fingers were sliding the length of her cunt and she was moaning. Don't moan, he wanted to say, but that would probably be destruction again. Jesus.

He tried, as his fingers moved inside her, to work out who slept where and how thick the walls were and who would be likely to hear, but he was too drunk to arrive at any solutions. He travelled no further than the initial anxieties. Meanwhile Mary moaned. Non-stop.

Why's she moaning? he wondered. She had never moaned before. She hadn't moaned in the woods, for example.

Once the sound of a revving car stifled her. He longed for traffic-jams outside the bedroom window. How typical, he thought, that they lived at the end of a cul-de-sac.

Despite his anxiety, despite the rules, despite everything, he was just about to push his cock inside her when the door of the guest-room opened. Alan stood in the doorway wearing his pyjamas. His glasses picked up light from outside. Blank silver discs for eyes. Head cocked at an angle, poised insect. Silence.

Moses trembled. Mary lay still. The place where his knee pressed into the back of her thigh had turned sticky and cold. They both seemed to be waiting for Alan to do something.

Alan spoke to Mary. 'I think you've got a bit mixed up.' His voice held no trace of censure. Only a soothing calm. Perhaps it sounded a little as if he was talking to a wayward child.

Mary didn't move.

Alan came forwards and stood over them. 'Come to bed when you're ready,' he said. He ruffled Mary's hair, then Moses's. Then he left the room, closing the door softly behind him.

Mary left soon after without saying anything.

Gloria would've laughed, Moses thought, just before he fell asleep. How Gloria would've laughed.

A hangover dulled the panic he might otherwise have felt when he woke the next morning. He needn't have worried, though. They all ate breakfast as usual, in chaos, three people talking at once.

Nothing had changed.

*

A few days later Gloria rang up.

'Moses,' she said, 'I want to speak to you.'

'You are speaking to me.'

'Really speak to you. Not on the phone.'

The receiver felt twice its normal weight in his hand. It must be something serious. They agreed to meet at a pub they both knew in Battersea. A quiet place with a clientele of transvestites, pensioners and UB40s. London in a nutshell. Moses had been a regular there in 1979.

As he pushed through the door that evening, a woman with plasters on two of her fingers stuck her hand out. 'Fifty pence tonight, love.'

Of course. It was Tuesday night. And Tuesday night was Talent Night. Always had been.

Dolly stood at the bar knocking back the gins. One of the local stars, Dolly. Her copper bouffant hairdo told you that. She had a voice that poured liquid concrete into songs, made them strong and real so they lasted in your head. She was arguing with June, but not so hard that she couldn't wink at him as he squeezed by.

He winked back. 'All right, Dolly?'

'How are you, darling?'

They had an understanding, him and Dolly. They both thought June was a cow. (June thought she was Loretta Lynn.)

'You want to know what June looks like?' he had said to Dolly one night.

'Go on then.'

'Stand in front of the mirror. That's right. Now, put your finger in your mouth – '

Dolly had screamed with laughter. 'Did you hear that? Did you hear what he said?'

'Come on, Dolly. Put your finger in your mouth. No, it doesn't matter which one. That's it. Now, close your lips round your finger. Not too hard. Just so there's no gaps. Perfect. Now then. Take your finger out again, but don't move your lips. Carefully. There. Now look in the mirror. June, isn't it?'

It was true. June really did look like that. Dolly had almost pissed herself that night.

He pushed past a man who was wearing a black bra and a serious, almost scholarly expression, and ordered a Pils. The woman behind the bar remembered him too. They chatted for a moment, then he told her he was meeting someone and edged towards the back of the pub. He sat down in a corner beneath a framed picture of the Matterhorn. The mountain rose against a sky of faultless blue. Four blurred red flowers occupied the foreground. As good a place as any for a serious conversation.

He finished his first drink, started a second.

Then he saw her standing in the doorway, hair teased by the wind, eyebrows of miraculous precision. He couldn't call out because June was singing. June's voice had, in its time, cracked everything from glasses to safes. No competition then. He waved, but his wave was lost in the rough sea of couples dancing. Finally he stood up. Then she noticed him and smiled quickly. When she reached him, he bent down, kissed her cheek. He thought he smelt snow on her skin. The first sign of winter.

He bought her an orange juice. She removed her gloves. He said he was sorry, but he had forgotten it was Talent Night, he had thought it was going to be quiet, still, they might as well stay now, mightn't they?

She sipped at her orange juice, eyes lowered. She turned the glass in her white fingers. Her gloves on the table looked like hands praying. He could sense the words building up behind her closed lips.

When he stopped talking, she hesitated, then she said, 'There's something I've been meaning to tell you.'

He looked at her carefully. If his eyes had been hands, they would have been holding a wounded bird or a grenade or a piece of priceless china. That's how carefully he was looking at her.

'I've slept with Eddie.'

He leaned back. So have about two thousand other people, he thought. So what. It was an abstraction, a statistic. It had no real meaning of its own. He waited for her to go on.

'It started at that beach party. I didn't see you for hours. I couldn't find you anywhere.' Describing anxiety, her voice was calm.

He said, 'I didn't know where you were either.'

'He kept appearing next to me and standing there and looking. You know that look he's got.'

'Yes,' Moses said. 'I know.' He heard lift doors slide open and fifty sighs leave fifty pairs of lips in unison. Yes, he knew.

'I don't know why he chose me. It could've been anyone, probably. He's strange like that.' She paused to meditate on what she had just said.

'He waited until I got drunk,' she went on. 'We kissed and things. You didn't notice.'

'It was dark.'

'What?'

'It was dark. How could I notice?'

'You just went off somewhere. You weren't around. You didn't seem to care.' She lifted her eyes to his. 'You should've been around.'

'I remember climbing the steps the next morning,' he said. 'Those wooden steps to the top of the cliff. It was cold. You were shivering. You'd just had a dream about somebody stealing your voice. But if they had you wouldn't have been able to tell me about the dream.' He smiled. 'I remember putting my arm around you. It made climbing the steps even harder. But I wanted to. I remember that.'

She shook her head. 'You live in a world of your own.'

A drumroll rumbled over the end of her sentence. A cymbal crashed as her eyes drifted away from his, sideways and downwards. Two men in sequined evening gowns minced on to the stage, bulbous silver microphones in their fists.

'We're The Revelation Sisters,' hissed the one in red.

The name rang a bell with Moses. He stared absently over Gloria's shoulder at the two glittering gyrating men. Their dresses split to the tops of their muscular shaved thighs. He could see the tendons flexing in the backs of their knees.

'When I first knew you,' she was saying, 'you were so – oh, I don't know – *thoughtful*, I suppose. You thought of everything. You really tried. But these days – I don't think you ever think of me at all. You look at me and smile, but you're miles away. Thousands of miles away.' She laughed bitterly. 'It's like you're on another planet or something.'

The man in the blue dress (his name was Sheila, apparently) was licking the tip of his microphone. He had a long athletic tongue. Like an animal, it was. A blind pink animal.

'Anyway,' she went on, when Moses didn't reply, 'it wasn't until about two weeks later that we slept together. Sorry. I mean fucked.'

'You don't have to tell me all this, you know,' he said, but he knew the whole thing was going to come out anyway, all over the tawdry stained table-top, all over the red plastic ashtray, the two dirty glasses and the crumpled peanut packet. People had to talk Eddie out of their systems. The number of times he had been forced to sit through that. He sighed.

'He just came round – one Sunday, I think it was.' She aimed a glance at him, a glance that was tipped, he thought, with spite. 'He didn't ring beforehand or anything. He just turned up. A knock on the door and there he was. Grinning. "Hello, Gloria," he said. "Can I come in?"'

She let out a mocking laugh. The way she was telling it, she was rubbing salt in her own wound. And wasn't this supposed to be hurting him?

'Cheeky bugger,' the man in the red dress growled. He leaned down and playfully slapped one of the audience. It was the man in the bra. His scholarly expression played truant for a few seconds.

'You know, I never really noticed how beautiful he was before. He came in and we talked for a while, I can't remember what about. It wasn't important, really. After that we went to bed. He knew it was going to happen all along. He said he knew the moment I opened the door.' She traced a pattern in the spilt beer with her fingernail. 'I suppose I knew it too, really.'

A loud cheer turned her head. The man in the red dress had toppled off his high heels. He sprawled on the stage, legs wide apart. He had lost one of his false eyelashes.

Sheila covered his eyes with the back of his hand in a theatrical gesture of horror and despair. 'First chance she gets,' he said, 'she's on her back with her legs open.'

Gloria spoke through catcalls and raucous laughter. 'You haven't said anything, Moses.'

He stared at her. Something seemed different. Suddenly she had the distance of an acquaintance, suddenly he couldn't imagine ever having been close to her, and he didn't know why. He stared at her until her features began to come loose and revolve slowly, like twigs or leaves, on the pond of her face. What was it?

At last he realised. It was her eyebrows. They weren't telling the time any more. They were just eyebrows. Ordinary eyebrows. Even slightly curved! He couldn't remember this happening before. Not ever.

'Why are you staring at me?'

His eyes drifted away from her face to the stage behind her where a drummer with a crew-cut was juggling sticks. He was remembering how once, in the middle of 'God Bless the Child', her eyebrows had said, miraculously, and only for a split-second, four minutes to three.

'Say something, Moses. Please.'

He shrugged, smiled. 'I suppose it was bound to happen, really. But it's funny it never occurred to me. That's the strange thing.'

'I don't follow.'

'Everyone falls for Eddie. But it's all right. It doesn't mean anything.'

'What do you mean it doesn't mean anything?'

'It doesn't mean anything. To him.'

'How do *you* know?'

He didn't answer her this time. It was useless. He didn't want to have to start explaining how Eddie was some kind of statue, how he didn't have any time, how he had to live faster than other people, how *nobody* could mean anything to him, how he wouldn't *want* them to, how that would hold him back, make his eventual return to that pedestal (wherever it was) too difficult. And how could he tell her that he, Moses, had fallen in love with her eyebrows, but that now he didn't feel anything for them any more, and that, from now on, as far as he was concerned, they were eyebrows just like anybody else's?

He glanced up, as if for guidance, and saw the picture of the Matterhorn above her head. He nodded to himself. Yes, the way he felt, he might as well have been in Switzerland. Blank as those wastes of snow. Blurred as those red roses. Emotions frozen solid. He imagined Gloria walking towards him across thin ice. It cracked and squeaked under her feet. She wasn't going to make it. And he wasn't going to help her.

'Let's leave,' he said.

In the car she turned to him. 'So what happens now?'

'I don't know.' He concentrated on the road, noticed how smoothly he was driving. All the lights changed to green when he approached as if the gods were riding shotgun. That was funny.

She lit a cigarette. The match rasped, tore the darkness open. In those few seconds he quickly searched her face once more for some faint indication of the time. It told him nothing. The idea that her eyebrows had once been the hands of a clock, that her face had once been a clock-face, recording their time together, an eternity, perhaps, now seemed fanciful, absurd. Was this the end then?

'I don't know,' he repeated.

Nine Elms Lane: windswept, empty, no one at the bus-stop. Scaffolding imprisoning the fronts of buildings. Advertising hoardings hiding the truth of the river. Once he glimpsed a mud bank, pimply as a slug's back. He beat the lights, streamed left on to Vauxhall Bridge.

Gloria used her cigarette to fill the few minutes it took to reach her flat. She inhaled. She exhaled. She studied the filter. She flicked ash out of the window. Finally she threw the cigarette away, a handful of red sparks in the rear-view mirror.

'Are you coming in?'

'I ought to be getting back,' he said.

She nodded. 'Thanks for the lift.'

She began to walk away.

'Hold on,' he called out. 'What about Saturday?'

She looked over her shoulder, frowned. She had obviously forgotten.

'You're singing at The Blue Diamond. I was going to come along.' He smiled. Her memory was like a sieve. Only his unusual size had so far saved him from falling through.

She shrugged. 'If you want.'

It's strange, he thought, how sometimes you can watch somebody walk away from you and they can look ugly, even if you know they're beautiful.

*

Sitting next to Gloria he had been calm. Objective. Almost tranquillised. Alone again, he felt the irritation mount. Dig its spurs in. Draw prickly blood. Things chafed now: the damp air in his flat, the music shuddering up from below, his own clothes against his skin.

He walked over to the suitcase of memories. As he went to lift it from the windowsill, it slipped from his grasp and crashed to the floor. He lost his temper then, and kicked it away from him.

Moments later, regretting the outburst, he squatted on his haunches and snapped the catches open. Many of the photographs had come loose, fallen from the album. They lay jumbled in the bottom of the case. One had flipped over, showing the white of its reverse side. He looked closer. Something written there. The ink, once blue, had faded to a pale grey. He held it up to the light and made out the words: *14 Caution Lane, New Egypt.*

New Egypt? He turned the photograph over with nervous fingers. It was a picture of the house. His mother and father standing by the narrow wooden gate. Their hooded eyes, their awkwardness. It was a picture he had studied many times because it was the only one that showed them together. But he had never noticed those words on the back. So faded. Almost invisible.

New Egypt.

He jumped to his feet, snatched up the phone. He dialled Mary's number. Mary answered.

'Mary,' he rushed in, 'you'll never guess what.'

'Who is this, please?'

'It's me. Moses. Guess what's happened, Mary.'

'How am I supposed to do that, Moses?' she drawled, her voice at its drollest.

He laughed. 'All right, I'll tell you. I think I've got a lead. On where my real parents live.'

He told her how he had come home depressed, how he had knocked the suitcase over, how the whole thing had been a product of his own clumsiness and frustration.

'I mean, what a coincidence,' he said, 'that that one particular picture landed on top. I might never have seen it otherwise. And all the others are blank. I've checked them.'

'I don't believe in coincidence.'

'All right, luck then.'

'I don't believe in luck either.'

'I know, I know, you make your own. Like bread. Mary, listen. I'm scared. I mean, New Egypt. That must be the name of the village where they live, don't you think? And don't tell me you don't believe in fear.'

Mary laughed. 'I'm not surprised you're scared. Now you might have to get off your arse and do something.'

'Find them, you mean?'

'That's exactly what I mean.'

'What if I'm not ready?'

'Oh, you're ready, Moses. You've been ready for a long time.'

THE RETURN OF THE NATIVE

On the last Saturday in November Mary did something she had never done before. She arrived at The Bunker without telling Moses first. No note, no phone-call, no prior arrangement. She appeared at the top of the stairs in a black dress fastened at the throat with a *diamanté* brooch. She wore a black wool coat thrown over her shoulders like a cape. She brought cool air into the room with her.

He noticed the driving-gloves in her left hand. 'Are we going somewhere?' he asked her.

'Yes.' She seemed to weigh the silence before adding, lightly, 'We're going to see your parents.'

'*What?*'

'You heard me. We're going to see your parents.'

'Today?'

'Now.'

'But,' Moses panicked, 'but they don't know we're coming.'

'So what are you going to do? Call them up and say, "Hello, can I come and see you for the first time in twenty-five years?" '

'Twenty-four and a half, actually.'

'Or maybe you'd like to send them a quick telegram? Hi stop. My name's Moses stop. Remember me? stop.'

Moses grinned despite himself, then immediately looked worried again. 'But listen, Mary,' he said, 'how do we know they still live there?'

'How do we know they don't until we try?'

He paced up and down in front of the window, his right eye blinking as it always did when he was nervous. Mary watched him from the sofa, one leg tucked underneath her body, elegant, mischievous – determined.

Then he swung round, hands spread. 'There's no point just turning up. I mean, what if they're out?'

'What if they're having a garden party? What if they're having sex? What if they're horribly deformed?' Mary threw her hands up in exasperation and caught them again.

He frowned. 'I suppose so.' He was thinking hard now. 'But hold on,' he quickened, sensing a loophole he might wriggle through, 'we don't even know where this New Egypt is.'

'Don't we?'

'No, we don't. And I don't have a map either. Sorry about that.' He spread his hands again, grinning this time.

Mary grinned back, slid a hand into her bag. The hand emerged with a *Shell Road Atlas*. '*I've* got a map,' she said, '*and* I know where New Egypt is.'

'Shit.' There was no way out of this. 'Where is it then?'

But Mary wasn't telling. She handed him his coat instead, led him downstairs to the car and opened the door. 'Get in,' she said.

He obeyed. Reluctantly.

Soon they were leaving the southern suburbs of the city. Frost glazed the rooftops of the last few houses; net curtains, like another kind of frost, hid the windows. Then open country, a dual carriageway through brittle woods. A new roundabout, fat yellow bulldozers, mud the colour of rust. The sky cleared. The grey turned blue. Sun struck through the windscreen, bounced off Mary's *diamanté* brooch.

He turned to her with a puzzled look. 'You know, I think I recognise this road. Should I recognise it?'

Mary shrugged. 'I don't know.'

He studied the road in greater detail. Yes. There, for example. He remembered laughing at that signpost (PICNIC AREA I HARTFIELD 4) because it sounded like a football result.

'Are you sure we haven't driven down this road before?' he asked.

'I have, lots of times, but never with you. Oh,' and she smiled across at him, 'I almost forgot. Look behind your seat.'

He reached round and pulled out something he had no trouble recognising: a bottle of twelve-year-old malt whisky.

'It's for you,' she said. 'You can open it if you like.'

'For me? Why?'

'It's not every day you go and meet parents you've never seen before, is it?' she said.

*

It had been all right to begin with. The drive south. The sunshine. The whisky. But now he had the map on his knee and the village was less than an inch away and he was trembling. It was a feeling he hadn't known for years, this trepidation, and it made a child of him. He wanted a hand to cling to, a bed to hide under. He wanted to turn round and run off in the opposite direction.

What was he going to say to them, these parents?

He tried out a couple of approaches in his head.

Polite: 'Good afternoon. Mr and Mrs Highness?' No, they'd probably take him for a Mormon and slam the door in his face.

Tantalising: 'Mr and Mrs Highness? I've got some rather good news for you.' Then they'd think that they'd won the pools or something. What a let-down when they discovered the truth.

Direct, but awkward: 'Um, hello. My name's Moses. I'm your son, I think.' What would they do? Faint? Burst into tears? Pretend they didn't understand ('Moses?' A blank look – affable, but blank. 'Sorry, son. You must be confusing us with someone else.')

He just couldn't imagine it.

And now they were turning off the main road. A country lane took them up a steep hill in a series of tight curves. New Egypt appeared on a signpost for the first time (NEW EGYPT $2\frac{1}{4}$) but it didn't sound like a football result and he wasn't laughing. They began to descend. A sign loomed on the right-hand side. Two grey metal stanchions buried in tall grass and ragged ferns.

NEW EGYPT

He reached for the bottle again, now almost empty. He smiled fleetingly. Mary thought of everything. She was an expert in a crisis. She ought to be. She had caused enough of them herself. Look at her now. So serene. Whisky always did that to her. He hoped they didn't get stopped by the police. Unlikely, though. There wouldn't be many –

Police.

Suddenly everything connected.

'I *have*,' he cried out. 'I *knew* it.'

Mary stamped on the brakes. The car slewed into the hedge that lined the road. 'Moses,' she said, 'I wish you wouldn't shout like that.'

'I *have* been here before,' he said.

She switched the engine off and leaned back against her door. She lit a cigarette. 'So tell me about it.'

He told her the whole story of the drive down to the south coast in July. The bizarre slobbering policeman. The motorbike disguised as a wheelchair. Old Dinwoodie in his flying-helmet.

'How extraordinary,' she said when he had finished. 'Just think. That Dinwoodie might be a friend of your father's.'

Moses looked dubious. 'I don't know. He looked like he'd just escaped from a mental home or something.'

Mary threw her cigarette out of the window. She started the engine, shifted into gear and pulled back on to the road.

'I'm rather looking forward to this,' she said.

*

They approached the village along a street of identical red-brick houses. They saw nobody. No movement in the windows, no smoke rising from the chimneys.

They reached a crossroads and turned left up the high street. They circled the village green. One peeling sightscreen. A duck-pond brimming with sky. No ducks, though. The clock on the church tower had stopped at ten past seven. Moses wondered how long ago.

'I feel like the last person alive,' Mary said.

Moses nodded. She was speaking for both of them.

There seemed to be no centre to the village. After passing the post office for the second time, she stopped the car outside a pub.

'You might as well ask in there,' she said.

'Ask?'

'Yes, ask. Where your parents live. That's why we're here, Moses. Remember?'

He leaned out of the window. The pub, he saw, was called The Legs and Arms. On the sign hanging above the doorway a pair of legs and arms, both disembodied, engaged one another in a sort of clumsy pink swastika.

'Take a look at this place, Mary.'

'Are you going in or not?'

'The name, Mary. Did you see the name?'

She sighed. 'I suppose I'm going to have to do this myself.'

'No, it's all right. I'm going.' He opened his door and clambered out.

When he first pushed through the double-doors he thought the pub was empty. The silence. The gloom. The stale smells of peanuts, spilt beer, cheap cigars. Then he began to notice people. Half a dozen or so. All sitting on their own in different corners. Not a word from any of them. Only, now and then, the rustle of a coat, the clink of a glass, a sigh. He walked up to the bar. A man slumped on a stool with a pint of bitter and a whisky chaser. He wore a green anorak and a pork-pie hat. He had a boxer's face: dented in some places, swollen in others. Then Moses noticed the broken blood-vessels showing like red threads in the surface of the man's skin. Not a boxer's face. A drunk's.

'Excuse me,' he said.

331

The drunk's head rotated slowly, sideways and upwards. 'Hundred yards,' he said. A sluggish voice, blurred words. His eyes kept sliding away.

'Excuse me,' Moses said. 'I need some directions.'

'After all those years. Hundred yards then bam.' The drunk's elbow jerked. Beer slopped on to the bar, frothy as bile.

Moses nodded. He looked round casually for someone else.

'Tell us about your stomach muscles, they said. Tell us what you do with your missus.' The drunk's face twisted with sudden frenzy. 'Those filthy bastards.' He aimed a soiled and trembling finger at Moses's chest. 'I could've done it, though. I could've bloody done it.'

Loop-tape in his head, Moses thought. That's what happens in pubs. You get these weirdos. You come in halfway through and it sounds like gibberish. You wait an hour or two till they get round to the point where you first came in and you listen to the whole thing again. And sometimes it begins to make sense. Sometimes. But he didn't have an hour or two today.

He noticed an old lady over by the window. Sun poured through the glass. She sat in its cold transparent glow, spotlit, brittle, both hands clasped on the head of her cane. Her chin moved rhythmically, as if she was chewing something. He approached.

'Excuse me,' he said. 'I'm looking for Mr and Mrs Highness. I wondered if you – '

The old lady raised eyes of the palest blue. They seemed to look beyond him to a scene of utter horror.

'You had better ask my husband,' she said.

'Your husband?' Moses glanced round.

'Oh no. He isn't *here*. He's at home. On the manor, you see. Lord Batley never leaves the manor.' She shuddered. 'Never.'

'You're Lady Batley?'

The old lady lifted her chin an inch. Not pride exactly, but the memory of pride. 'Yes,' she said. 'I am.'

'Lady Batley – ' Moses was squatting beside her now – 'I'm trying to find Mr and Mrs – '

'I sometimes come here for a glass of white wine. I don't think there's any harm in that.' She smiled at him. Looking into her eyes was like looking down through fathoms of clear water to something lying on the ocean-bed. It gave him a kind of vertigo.

'Of course, I don't know what Oscar would say,' she quavered. 'Oscar doesn't like to see women drinking alone. He *disapproves*.' She lifted one dappled hand to her breastbone. 'He tried to die once, you know. I told him, I *told* him it was no good. He promised me that he would never do it again.'

'Never do what?' Moses asked.

Lady Batley stared at him. 'Die,' she said.

She sat there chewing in the cold light. He could see straight through her skin to the tangle of veins beneath. One coiled on her left temple as if squeezed from a tube of pale-blue oil-paint.

He stood up.

Walking back across the pub, he stopped to look at a picture on the wall. It was a drawing of a policeman. Cut from a magazine, by the look of it. Two darts pinned it to the flock wallpaper. One through each eye.

Moses frowned, looked around. A woman had just appeared behind the bar. She was washing glasses. A little routine, she had. Into the water, on to the brush, into the water and out. Nice rhythm. All right, he thought. One last attempt.

'Do you know where I could find Mr and Mrs Highness?' he asked her.

It was the drunk, surprisingly, who reacted. 'What about Highness?'

Moses held up a picture of his parents standing outside their house. 'Do Mr and Mrs Highness still live here?'

'Not exactly.'

'You mean they've moved?'

The drunk seemed to find this extremely funny. 'Moved? Did you hear that, Brenda? "Have they moved?" he says.'

The woman behind the bar allowed herself a sour smile.

'Where are they then?' Moses asked.

'Only one of them's moved.' The drunk released this information with a sly glance.

'Which one?'

'Mrs Highness.'

'So she's left her husband?'

The drunk cackled. 'In a way, yes.'

Suddenly Moses understood. 'She's dead?'

'Yeeaahh. Wa-hay.' The drunk banged the bar with his red hand. '*What a clever boy.* Yeah, died in the home, she did.'

'In the home?'

'The loony-bin, the nuthouse, the funny-farm. Where anyone with any sense round here ends up.' He sucked down the last of his beer. 'Are you a detective?'

Moses smiled. 'Not a detective, no.'

'Not a policeman, are you? Not a bloody copper?'

'No.'

'Thank Christ for that.' The drunk slung his glass across the bar. 'Give us another, Brenda.'

'You've had enough,' Brenda said. 'Time you went home, Joel.'

'Ah, come off it, Brenda. Give us a pint.'

Turning her back on him, Brenda reached up and rang a bell. 'Drink up, please. We're closing now.'

'Brenda, it's not even two o'clock yet,' Joel protested.

Brenda ignored him.

He rolled his eyes, shook his head. 'All right then, give us a half.'

Still Brenda said nothing.

Joel cuffed his empty glass aside and lurched towards the door.

'I'm sorry to bother you,' Moses said to Brenda, 'but could you just tell me where this house is?'

She took one look at the picture and gave him a set of simple directions. The house, she told him, was no more than two hundred yards away.

'Thank you,' he said. 'You've been very helpful.'

Brenda's hard face softened a touch. 'You don't come from around here, do you?'

He hesitated, then shook his head.

'Count your blessings,' she said. She rang the bell again. 'Come on, you lot. Let's have your glasses now.'

People began to rise from their chairs as if from the dead.

Outside the pub Moses bumped into the drunk, almost knocked him over.

'You're a bloody policeman, you are,' the drunk shouted. He grabbed at Moses's sleeve with a scaly hand. 'I know a policeman when I see one. You're a bloody policeman.'

Moses shook himself free. 'I don't know what you're talking about,' he said.

He turned and walked back to the car.

'Bloody policeman,' the drunk jeered after him.

Moses opened the door of the Volvo and climbed in. Mary was smoking. Blue veils swirled around her face. She watched him through them.

'Looks like you made a new friend,' she said.

*

She started the engine. 'You were ages. I thought you'd made a run for it.'

'I almost did,' he said.

They drove past the drunk. He was still standing on the pavement, waving his fist and shouting obscenities.

'Why's he calling you a policeman?' she asked.

Moses shrugged. 'Because I was asking questions, I suppose.'

'So what did you find out?' She slowed down, weaved in and out of the potholes in the road.

'My mother's dead. She died in a mental home or something. I couldn't really understand everything. Turn right here.'

They passed a row of terraced houses. Paint had dropped from the façades, lay on the ground like old leaves. Scrap metal sprawled on unmown lawns. A car with no wheels stood in a driveway. They saw no people. Not even any children.

'My father's still alive though,' he added. 'Apparently.'

He lit a cigarette, inhaled. The smoke came out with a sigh. 'It should be down here somewhere on the left. On the corner. That's what the woman said.'

'Are you all right?' Mary asked him.

He nodded. 'I think so.'

They both recognised the house at the same time.

It had aged since the photographs. The front lawn had lost grass as old men lose hair. Bleached grey wood showed through the paintwork round the windows. A section of guttering lay on the garden path. A shattered roof-tile too. No parasol, of course. When Moses peered through a downstairs window he saw a sofa with no cushions and a fireplace stuffed with crumpled newspaper, no real signs of life.

They stood on the porch. The doorbell didn't seem to work (Mary had listened through the letter-box), so they tried the brass knocker instead. Solid thuds echoed through the house like hammerblows. Nobody came.

'Doesn't look like there's anybody there.' Moses couldn't keep the relief out of his voice. Now they could drive back to London with clear consciences, he was thinking. At least they had tried.

'Let's go round the back,' Mary said.

He followed her, dread rising suddenly in him like floodwater.

Mildew grew on the side wall of the house. A drainpipe had come away; it stretched across the concrete path, a spindly fallen tree. The back door was green. Somebody had nailed a piece of hardboard over one of the glass panels.

'After you,' Mary said.

Moses turned the handle. The door grated open. He glanced over his shoulder at Mary, saw encouragement in her smile.

He found himself in a corridor. He picked his way over the scattered bones of a bicycle. Several massive cardboard boxes had been stacked against the wall. There was scarcely enough room to squeeze by. He tilted his head sideways to read one of the labels. THREE-PIECE SUITE, it said. ARMCHAIR. He moved on, passed an open doorway. The kitchen. A fridge gaped at him, nothing in its mouth. The house smelt unused, unlived-in. But a queer sourness hung around the edge of that smell, a sourness he couldn't quite identify: something like fish, something like sweat, something like margarine.

At the bottom of the stairs, he hesitated.

'Hello?' he called out.

But too softly. He cleared his throat.

'Is anybody there?'

Something shifted overhead. Something creaked.

'Bugger off,' came a hoarse voice. 'Bugger off and leave me alone.'

Moses stepped backwards.

Mary touched him lightly on the wrist. 'Go on,' she whispered. 'I'll be right behind you.'

He began to tiptoe up the stairs. The higher he went, the sourer the smell became. More like rotten fish now, old sweat, rancid margarine. And tinged with the reek of stale cigarettes. The fifth step from the top groaned under his weight.

'Bugger off I said,' came the voice again, still hoarse, but angrier. 'Get out of my house.'

Moses had reached the landing. He passed one closed door, then a second. A third, to his right, stood ajar. He pushed on the varnished wood and it gave. In the widening gap, he saw an old man on a double-bed.

The old man wore a pair of glasses, a pale collarless shirt and a green cardigan (whose smooth brown buttons looked like chocolates). Nicotine had stained the lenses of his glasses yellow and one of the arms had been mended with black insulating-tape. He had the most enormous beard. Three feet long and almost as wide. If you had walked down the street behind him, you would have been able to see it protruding from either side of his head. Once black, now threaded with minute white hairs, it spread down over his chest and tucked into the V of his cardigan. With his glasses and his beard he looked, Moses thought, like a man in disguise; it would have been difficult to describe his eyes, for instance, or his mouth.

A beige horse-blanket concealed the lower half of the old man's body. His hands rested on the outside. They were beautiful hands. Stained, like the glasses, but ascetic, tapering and permanently curved, as if made to bless the small round heads of children. One lay flat, palm down, beside his thigh. The other held a cigarette.

That the old man chainsmoked was obvious from a glance at the dented saucepan which served as his ashtray. It was piled high with cigarette-butts. The cigarette-butts had outgrown the saucepan, overflowed on to the bedside table, outgrown that too, and overflowed on to the floor. From there, of course, they could fall no further, so they had begun to pile up again. They behaved in exactly the same way as snow does. They might have fallen from the sky. Even as Moses stared, entranced, the old man squeezed the end of his latest cigarette between finger and thumb and tossed the new butt on to the mountainous heap of old ones. It tumbled from the saucepan on to the table, from the table on to the floor. It might have been a demonstration of how the system worked. The old man folded his hands on the blanket. He seemed to be waiting for Moses to speak.

'Mr Highness?'

The name sounded so strange in his mouth, felt as awkward as a stone. This was the confrontation he had dreamed of. All those hours in phone-boxes. Fingers black from thumbing through directories. The reek of urine in his nostrils, in his soul. Another Highness! How could he ever have imagined that it would happen not in America but in Sussex, not with a stranger but with his father?

'Who the bloody hell are you?' the old man said.

Moses didn't hesitate now. 'I'm your son. Moses.'

A new stillness seemed suspended in the room.

'I thought you were a policeman,' the old man said. 'Or the bloody priest.' He almost smiled.

'No.'

The old man shifted in bed, using an elbow to raise himself higher on his soiled stack of pillows. He lit a cigarette, dragged hard. When he spoke again, no smoke came out. He must have absorbed it all.

'Well,' he said, 'I suppose you had better sit down.' He indicated two simple wooden chairs by the far wall. 'Bring them over.'

Moses crossed the room and returned with the chairs. He placed them side by side next to the bed. He offered one to Mary. They both sat down. He couldn't help noticing the sheet that the old man was lying on. It started out white at the edge of the bed and, after moving through various shades of grey, turned almost black, a glossy black, as it slid beneath his body.

'I'm afraid I'm not used to entertaining.' The old man's smile of apology closely resembled pain. He lifted his cigarette to his lips and sucked smoke deep into his lungs. His eyes drifted from Moses to Mary for a moment.

'I'm sorry,' Moses said. 'This is Mary. She's a very close friend of mine.'

'George Highness,' the old man said.

They both leaned forwards and shook hands.

It was all so improbable. Moses became daring. 'You didn't expect me then?'

The old man took this seriously. He lowered his eyes. 'No, I never expected to see you again. Of course, I imagined you. Many times. I even imagined you sitting where you're sitting now. But they were all ghosts, different ghosts of you. The real you had gone.' He lifted his head. 'I could never imagine how you'd look. It's curious, but I think you look more like your mother, actually.'

'My mother?'

'She's dead,' the old man said quickly. 'She died eight years ago.'

'I know.'

'You know?' The old man seemed alarmed. 'How?'

'Somebody in the pub told me.'

'Who?'

'I don't know his name. He was wearing a green anorak. He was drunk.'

'Ah yes, the greengrocer.' The old man drifted on his bed for a while as if on a raft. 'But did I ever think that you'd come back?' He shook his head and his beard rustled against his shirt. 'No. Never. I never hoped for that.'

Half an inch of ash toppled off the end of his cigarette and landed in the lower extremities of his beard. He brushed it away with deft practised movements of his fingertips. It seemed to distract him from something he had been about to say. A silence fell.

Eventually he said, 'You must have a lot of questions.'

'My mother,' Moses said. 'She died in a mental home, didn't she?'

'He told you that too?'

Moses nodded.

'That bloody gossip, I could kill him.' The old man's head jerked fiercely towards the wall. 'Yes, she died in the mental home just outside the village. She had been in there for twelve years.'

'What was wrong with her?'

'Oh,' and he twirled his left hand in the air beside his ear, 'they had names for it. They called it manic depression. They said she had an avoidant personality. They had all kinds of fancy names. But the truth was far more simple, really. She was born in New Egypt. She was a New Egyptian. The world, even this tiny world, hurt her physically. It hurt her the way sun hurts people with fair skin. She wanted shade. She stayed in bed all the time. She drew the curtains on her life. She wanted to die. Nothing I could say to her made any impact whatsoever. I told her I loved her. I told her I needed her. She listened, but she didn't really hear. Her pain was so great, I suppose, that she couldn't even begin to imagine mine.

There was nothing I could say to her, nothing that would make the slightest difference. I couldn't tell her life was wonderful. It wasn't and she knew it wasn't. I couldn't paint a glowing picture of the future. We didn't have a future. She knew that too. She may have been disturbed or mentally ill or whatever you choose to call it, but she understood what life in this village meant. Means. It means boredom, loneliness and despair. And this, I suspect, touches on the question you must be longing to ask. Why did we get rid of you? That's the big question, isn't it? Am I right?'

Moses nodded.

'We got rid of you,' the old man said, 'because we didn't want you to turn out like us. We didn't want you to turn out like everybody else in this bloody village. We wanted you to have a better chance in life – '

'But what's so terrible about life in this village?' Moses interrupted.

The old man let out a high-pitched yelp and doubled up. His cigarette flew from between his fingers. His glasses clattered to the floor. Convulsions racked his entire body. Several seconds passed before Moses realised this was laughter, laughter that had developed into a coughing fit.

'Christ,' the old man wheezed. He leaned back against his soiled pillows, flushed and breathless. 'Christ, that was a good one. A bloody good one. Are you hungry?'

Mary wasn't.

'I could eat something,' Moses said.

'Go downstairs,' the old man said to Moses. 'You'll find some tins in the kitchen cupboard. Biscuits too, if I remember rightly. Bring them up here. And a couple of forks. This is going to take some time so I think we should eat first.'

Moses ran down the stairs. He edged round the gas-cooker and into the kitchen. The wallpaper (orange and yellow discs) hung limply from the corners of the room. Sheets of newspapers dated 1970 covered most of the brown lino floor. Grease had clogged the transparent plastic air-vent in the window above the sink. Somebody had hurled a stack of dirty washing-up into the rubbish-bin – and none too recently, by the look of it.

The kitchen cupboard had lost both its handles so he had to prise the twin doors open with a carving-knife. The contents of the cupboard were as follows:

The bottom shelf: seventy-seven tins of John West sardines in tomato sauce.

The middle shelf: thirty-nine packets of Embassy Number One filter cigarettes.

The top shelf: a screwdriver, a Christmas card, and one half-eaten packet of Butter Osborne biscuits.

Shaking his head, Moses selected four tins of sardines and lifted down the biscuits. He found two bent forks in the drawer under the sink. He couldn't see any plates (except for the ones in the rubbish-bin). That was the lot then. He hurried back upstairs.

The two of them were laughing when he walked in. The old man quickly included him. 'Did you find everything?'

'Eventually,' Moses said. He unloaded his supplies on the bed.

Cigarette in mouth, the old man picked up a tin of sardines, tore off the packaging, slipped the key over the metal tab, and deftly unrolled the lid. Then he crushed his cigarette out and reached for a fork. Just by watching him you began to get an idea of how many tins of John West sardines he must have eaten in the past (and how many tins of John West sardines he would probably eat in the future). He ate rapidly but with finesse, spearing whole fish with a single lunge of the fork and inserting them into his already revolving jaws. Drops of tomato sauce splashed on to his beard and lay there glistening like berries. When he had finished he put the two empty tins on the windowsill behind him, wiped his fingers on the sheet, and lit a cigarette. The meal had taken him slightly less than three minutes.

'Now then,' he began, and the efficiency with which he had disposed of his sardines carried over into his voice, 'you asked me a question. You asked me what was wrong with the village.' He suppressed a smile. 'I could answer that question with one simple word. Can either of you guess what that word might be?'

Both Moses and Mary shook their heads.

'Fear.' The old man pronounced the word with immense relish. 'Fear.' He paused to pick a sliver of fish from between his teeth. He seemed, at the same time, to be savouring the taste of the word. 'But that is to begin at the end,' he went on. 'It has taken me a good forty years to arrive at that simple conclusion. And before you can arrive there, you have to know everything. Or almost everything. If you want to understand completely, that is. So what I'm going to do now, if you're agreed, is to give you a brief history of New Egypt. The history I started once, but never finished. And remember one thing: nobody – and I mean *nobody* – has ever heard this before.'

And so he began to talk.

And they perched on their hard chairs and watched the slow upward trickle of smoke from his constant stream of cigarettes.

The sun strained through the cloudy windows. The afternoon faded.

They listened to his voice.

A voice roughened by years of chainsmoking and loneliness, but an articulate voice because he had, in his time, delivered lectures in the village hall and sung in the church choir.

A voice issuing from a mass of filthy sheets and crushed cigarette packets and empty sardine tins.

*

He described the people of New Egypt. Their limited horizons. Their inbreeding. Their sterility. He dissected them without pity, without prejudice. He threw their organs around on his bloody marble slab. He showed how apathy was like castration, how it had made them impotent. All his frustrations, all those months of silence ('You're the first people I've spoken to since August'), came spilling out. His concave hands scooped at the soupy air like ladles. His beard quivered. He had come alive.

His excitement reached a peak when he turned to the subject of the police. The Pharaohs of New Egypt! He exposed their hierarchy, their hypocrisy, their own peculiar brand of fear.

'It's their job,' he explained, 'to see that the village behaves in an ordered and harmonious way. But how do you define order? If I had to define it, I would say that order is morale, system, purpose. Order is rising at dawn, regular mealtimes, mowing your lawn. Order is brisk trading and a growing population. Order can be heard, for example, in the crying of a newborn baby or the chimes of an ice-cream van. In New Egypt, though, you won't find any of those things. *There is no order.* So what do the police do? They're forced to include in their definition of the word positive actions *of any kind*. Order is defined as the opposite of apathy. Order is energy, initiative. And it's in this way that drunkenness, fraud, theft, arson, rape, even murder come to be welcomed by the police as being ultimately beneficial to the community. Something has *happened*. Somebody has *done* something. Crime is proof that the village is alive and kicking. Crime is order.'

'Crime is order?' Moses laughed. 'I like that.'

The old man lifted one stained finger. 'Except when it becomes part of an escape-attempt, of course. You see, the establishment of order here in New Egypt presupposes one simple fact: the continuing existence of the village itself. Let one person leave and in no time at all you'd have everybody leaving. Hey presto, no New Egypt. It would become a gap on the map, a ghost village, a sociological monument. A community of twenty-nine policemen with no one to protect and nothing to enforce. That's why they do everything in their power to keep us here. You remember I told you that we grow up with our own nursery rhymes? Well, I'm going to give you an example of what I mean. This is one of the most well known. If you were to walk past the village school during lessons, chances are you'd hear it floating out of one of the classrooms. Every child in the village knows the words. Your mother,' and he turned solemn eyes on Moses, 'used to sing it all the time.'

He pulled himself up in bed, cleared his throat and began to sing. The tune reminded Moses of 'In the Bleak Midwinter'. Equally mournful, equally forlorn. The song would normally be sung by the high clear voices of children. The old man's voice, ravaged and gravelly, gave it new bitterness, added poignancy.

The world is a dream,
It will always be so.
Our life is a stream
With nowhere to go.

The sky's always crying,
The willow tree weeps.
We're living, we're dying,
We're here for keeps.

The wind comes to stay,
The rain and the snow;
They're here for a day
Or a week, then they go.

But we're here for life,
From our very first breath;
Come trouble, come strife,
We're here until death.

The world is a dream
That we never had.
Our life is a stream
Of tears so sad.

We do nothing but dream,
It will always be so.
Things are just as they seem.
We have nowhere to go —

No sooner had he finished singing the last line of the song than he broke down and began to cough again. His head jerked forward repeatedly as if somebody was shoving him in the back.

'I shouldn't sing,' he gasped.

Mary left the room to fetch some water. Moses could only look on helplessly as the old man struggled for breath. The old man described the village so objectively that it was easy to forget that he *actually lived* there. When he told stories and sang songs he was describing himself. A life of soiled sheets and furniture in boxes. A life of squalor, withdrawal and gloom. *We're here for life. We're here until death.*

Mary returned with a glass of water.

'Thank you,' the old man whispered. He drank, then he collapsed against his pillows. He let his eyes close. A few drops of water trembled in his beard.

When he opened his eyes again he said, 'That was the first time I've sung anything in seven years.'

'Well, you sang beautifully.' Mary said. 'Really quite beautifully.'

'You know, people used to think that song was anonymous,' he told them, 'but I did a bit of research and I discovered that it was written by a man called Birdforth.' He paused and glanced at them significantly. 'Birdforth was chief of police from 1902 to 1916.'

Moses's eyes widened at the sinister implications.

'That's right,' the old man said. 'Brainwashing. Propaganda. All quite deliberate. And very, very insidious.'

He gulped at his water. 'You see, most people don't even realise. They can't be bothered to realise. It's easier not to. But every so often,' and his eyes flickered like dark agile fish in the deep lenses of his glasses, 'every generation, perhaps, somebody a little bit different comes along. Somebody with their own private vision. Somebody with a dream. Fanatics, you might call them. And they're the people the police have to watch out for. Because they're the people who will, at some point in their lives, throw caution to the winds, fly in the face of everything they've ever learned, and try to do the one thing that nobody has ever done before: escape.'

He gave them examples: 'Tarzan' Collingwood, Mustoe the greengrocer, Tommy Dane. Something that had been cloudy in Moses's mind now began to sharpen, resolve itself, assume a shape. Until he could restrain himself no longer.

'Old Dinwoodie,' he cried.

The old man's voice cut out in mid-sentence. 'How do you know about that?'

Moses began to tell him the story of the drive through New Egypt in

July. Mary had heard it already; she excused herself and left the room.

When Moses had finished, the old man lay back, his fingers plaited on his beard, his eyes trained on some far corner of the room. 'Well, well,' he murmured. 'If that isn't a curious twist of fate.'

'Where's old Dinwoodie now?' Moses asked.

The old man hesitated. 'He's dead.'

'Oh no.' Moses stared at the floor.

'Don't blame yourself. If you hadn't helped to stop him escaping, somebody else would have. He would never have got away. Not old Dinwoodie. He was doomed from the start. I told him so myself and he never spoke to me again after that. There's no point feeling guilty about it. You didn't even know what was happening.'

Moses nodded. He tried to believe what he was hearing. But what damage you could do, he thought. What damage you could do when life blindfolded you.

'Was he a friend of yours?' he asked.

'No, not really.' A bleak smile passed across the old man's face. 'In a place like this you don't have any friends.'

Mary returned with a tray. On the tray stood three mugs, a tin of powdered milk and a green china vase.

'I couldn't find a teapot,' she explained, 'so I improvised.'

The old man shaded his eyes with his hand. 'Is that tea?'

'It is.'

'Where on earth did you find tea? Last time I looked – March, I think it was – I couldn't find any. Not a single leaf. Where was it?'

'Under the sink.'

'Good lord. Was it? Good lord. How extraordinary.'

Mary poured the extraordinary tea. The old man cradled his mug in both hands. He sipped noisily, his moustache extending over the rim.

'Christ, this is damn good,' he said. 'Uncommonly good. I'd almost forgotten what tea tasted like. *Bloody* good.'

'Something I've noticed,' Mary said. 'All your escape stories are about men. Haven't any women ever tried to get away?'

'Women?' The old man wedged his mug into a fold in the blanket. 'There was one woman.'

He lit a cigarette and leaned back. Smoke filtered out of his nostrils. He was taking his time. He knew he had an audience.

'Her real name was Miss Neville,' he said, 'but we all called her the mad lady. She lived behind the church. Strange house. Dark-red bricks and all the window-frames painted green. She had a withered leg so she couldn't get about very much. She walked very slowly with two sticks, or sometimes she used crutches. You hardly ever saw her. She loved animals, especially birds. Storks used to land in her garden and, once, a flock of swallows hibernated in her kitchen instead of flying south for the winter. She had a special way with birds. She could talk to them and they understood her. Most people in the village thought she was some kind of witch. The children were frightened of her.

'I was frightened of her too, but I was curious. One day – I suppose I must have been nine or ten – I went to visit her. I just walked up the drive and knocked on her front door. There was no answer, so I went round to the back and peeped in through her French windows. And there was old Miss Neville sitting in a high-backed chair. She was clapping her hands. Not rhythmically, the way you might clap to music, but a sort of double clap, as if she was summoning a servant. Her hair kept falling in her eyes, I remember, and her eyes were glowing yellow in the dark room, and her mouth was hanging open. She looked very strange, transported almost. For a moment I couldn't work out what on earth she was doing. Then I saw the birds –

'There were about eight of them, all the same size, dark grey, and when Miss Neville clapped her hands they rose into the air, all at the same time, straight up into the air like helicopters. And every time she clapped her hands they performed a new trick, a new manoeuvre. They flew round and round the room in perfect formation. They hovered in mid-air. They did all kinds of symmetrical things. I couldn't believe my eyes, of course. I just stood at the window and stared. I completely forgot that I had no business to be there. And I suppose she must have seen me because the next thing I knew the door opened and she was standing in front of me.

' "What do *you* want, young man?" she said. "I came to visit you," I said. "Did you?" she said. "*Did* you indeed? Well, I suppose you'd better come in then, hadn't you?" She had this queer way of stretching her neck out and looking down at you sideways. She was wearing a huge shapeless dress. As big as a tent, it was. And dark green, with little bits of velvet stuck all over it.

'She hobbled back into the room on her crutches and I followed her. I have never been to a zoo, but her house smelt the way I imagine a zoo to smell. Sweet somehow. A curious mixture of musk and chicken-feed and manure. You know, I've never forgotten the smell of old Miss Neville's house. And the *mess*. Feathers, balls of fur, bird-lime, mouse-droppings, cat-hair, frogspawn – you name it. I'd never seen anything like it. I suppose it *was* a zoo, really.

'She gave me a tour of the place first. Animals everywhere. "Look where you're going," she told me. "I don't want you treading on any of my family." Some of the rooms had straw on the floor. Others had sawdust. She had covered the floor of one of the rooms about a foot deep in mud. It had grass and plants and flowers growing in it. It was just like being outside. Wasps buzzing around. Bees too. She had two bathrooms and both the bathrooms were like aquariums. Full of fish. On the third floor she had a snakehouse. A room that had been heated to a special temperature. Absolutely crawling with snakes. Ten she had, including a python. The whole room seemed to be alive and slithering about. And then there were the birds, of course. She let them fly all over the house. Wherever we went, they landed on her head, her hands, her shoulders, or talked to her from some perch up near the ceiling. Sometimes she waved them away, saying something like, "Not now, not now."

'Anyway, after she had showed me round, she insisted that I stayed for tea. "I expect you'd like some lemonade, wouldn't you," she said. "Little boys like lemonade." I told her that I liked lemonade very much. So she led me along a gloomy passageway and down a flight of steep stone steps. We went through a door and she switched on a dim light. We were in the cellar. I looked round and saw rows and rows of bottles. They were all lying in racks like wine, but they weren't wine, they were lemonade. She had stuck labels on all the bottles and every label had a year on it, the year that she had bought that particular bottle. Some of those bottles of lemonade were thirty years old. "I like to have lemonade in the house," she said, "just in case the vicar drops in." In her book, you see, vicars always drank lemonade. Vicars and little boys. She selected a bottle for me and held it up to the light. "1919," she said. "A rather good year, don't you think?" I thought it best to agree with her. So, for tea, I drank lemonade that was nearly twenty years old, ate a few stale wafer-biscuits, and talked to Miss Neville, who sat there with a dove perched on her head the whole time. She was bats, of course, but really very kind. Afterwards I thanked her and went home.' The old man paused and scratched his beard, the part that nestled under his left ear. 'Now remind me. Why was I talking about Miss Neville?'

Moses grinned. 'You were going to tell us about how she tried to escape.'

'Of course I was. That's right. Christ, I'm getting old. Completely forgot.' The old man tapped a cigarette on his thumbnail, stuck it in the corner of his mouth and lit it. The empty packet joined dozens of identical empty packets on the shelf above his bed. 'It must have been a year or two later. 1938, 1939, something like that. A policeman, I don't remember which one, found Miss Neville lying in a field on the outskirts of the village. It was dawn. She had broken her hip. She was wearing some sort of leather harness round the top half of her body. No sign of any sticks or crutches anywhere. After being taken to the doctor, she was interrogated by Peach. She didn't deny having tried to escape. In fact, apparently she told him that the only reason she had left it until so late in her life was because she couldn't bear to be parted from her animals. Then he asked her the obvious question, "How did you get as far as that without your crutches?" "I flew," she said. "*Flew?*" Peach said. "My birds," she said. "They carried me."

'And you know something?' The old man leaned forwards, his speech accelerating. 'I believe it. After what I saw in her sitting-room that afternoon I definitely believe it. There was a magic about that woman. Not strong enough to break the spell of the village, perhaps,' and his hand twirled in the air again, 'but what could be that strong? Can you imagine, though? Miss Neville being carried through the sky at dawn by a flock of birds. Like a parachute. A parachute of birds. What a sight that must've been! What a magnificent sight!'

Moses gazed through the window. He was trying to imagine a woman in a huge green dress flying through the sky. It was difficult. In this village he found himself approaching the limits of his imagination.

'What happened?' he asked. 'I mean, how did it happen, d'you think?'

The old man shrugged. 'Nobody really knows. She must have fallen, that much is obvious. Perhaps the birds lost their grip. Perhaps something frightened them. I don't know. In any case, she was dead in two years. Complications with the broken hip.'

'Sad story,' Mary said.

'Sad, but not so very strange. Everybody fails, you see.'

Moses smiled. 'Not everybody,' he said, 'surely.'

'Well, no,' the old man admitted. 'Not everybody, I suppose.' He shook his head as if he still found the whole thing pretty hard to believe. 'You see,' he went on, 'most people fail because they think that escape's impossible and the police are infallible. When you're faced with those two beliefs, it paralyses you. Escape is a dream, a song you sing, a story you tell, but not something you ever seriously think of doing. Not if you've any common sense. Anybody actually attempting to escape steps beyond the bounds of reality. They become unreal, even to themselves. They dress up as Tarzan, they build toy bombs, they pretend to die. No wonder they fail. In the end, all they succeed in doing is making the police museum the most interesting place in the village. The secret is to *accept* all that conditioning, be realistic about it.'

Moses looked puzzled. 'Realistic? I don't follow.'

'I gave up the idea of trying to escape myself,' the old man explained.

'I knew I couldn't do it. It was beyond me, quite literally. I decided to help somebody else escape instead. My son. You. And the whole time I was planning to get you out I was realistic about it. Because it wasn't my freedom that was at stake. Because I had nothing to lose. As for you, well, you were too young to know what was happening, too young to have been weighed down, disabled by all those stories about the outside world, too young to be able to experience that sense of becoming unreal to yourself. If I failed to get you out, you wouldn't go to pieces or turn into an alcoholic or end up in the mental home. You simply wouldn't know any better. So you made it. The plan succeeded. And that's what's sustained me all these years as I've watched others fail around me. That and the idea that I might finally have got one over on old Peach – ' The old man began to chuckle to himself. His cigarette shook in his curved brown fingers.

Moses now asked the question he had been dying to ask. 'But *how* did you do it? *How* did you get me out?'

'Oldest story in the world,' the old man told him. 'There's a river that runs past the village. You may have noticed it. It's about a mile away, across the fields. There's one particular bend in the river where the current suddenly moves from the riverbank out into midstream. I tested it with twigs and cans. I waited for the right weather conditions, a misty morning, then I left you there, floating on the river in a basket made of pitch and rushes.' He smiled. 'Moses, you see?'

Moses shook his head in wonder. Then he looked across at Mary and knew that she knew what he was thinking. That pattern of light and shade. That sound of running water. Real memories.

'So David was right all along,' he said.

'Who's David?' the old man asked.

'David was one of the boys at the orphanage. I had a fight with him because he went round telling everyone that I'd been found by a river.'

The old man laughed, and, once again, the laughter triggered a fit of coughing. It shook him harder this time. His chest rattled like a bag of dice.

Mary held the glass out to Moses. 'More water,' she said.

When he returned, she had propped the old man up on his pillows. The old man's arms lay outside the blanket, limp, stringy, palms up.

'Are you all right?' Moses asked him.

The old man nodded, but didn't trust himself to speak.

Nobody had turned the light on in the room. The air had thickened, a haze of greys and blues, partly darkness, partly smoke. Hands and faces showed up pale, almost phosphorescent. A radiator began to tick in the corner.

'Those bloody sardines,' the old man muttered when he had recovered his breath.

He lit another cigarette. His face looked gaunt and dented in the stark orange flare of the match. His perversity resembled Mary's, Moses thought.

'I think we ought to leave you now,' she was saying. 'You should rest.'

The old man nodded.

'Are you sure you're going to be all right?' Moses asked.

'I'm fine.' The old man spoke in a whisper now. 'I've talked too much, that's all. I'm not used to talking, you see.'

'And you sang.' Looking down at the old man, Moses suddenly had an idea. 'Why don't you come with us?'

'I thought you might say that.'

'Well, why not?'

The old man sighed. 'It's not quite as simple as that.'

'All you have to do is get in the car.'

The old man shook his head. 'Listen, I've told you about the people who live in this village. I've told you what they're like. Well, I live here too. I'm one of them. I'm the same as they are.'

'But you're different. You – '

The old man cut in. 'I'm the same. Look at me. Lying in bed for years on end. I'm the same.'

Moses lowered his eyes.

'Don't push him, Moses,' Mary said. 'He has his own life here. And you have yours somewhere else. That was his gift to you.'

Moses looked up at the old man. 'I wanted to help you, that's all.'

'You have helped me. By coming here. By letting me know that you're alive. You've no idea how much that means.'

Moses said nothing.

'Perhaps you'll visit me again,' the old man whispered, 'sometime.'

'Of course I will.' Moses paused. 'There's one more thing I wanted to ask you. That pink dress. The one in the suitcase. Did it belong to my mother?'

'Yes, I gave it to her, but she never wore it.' The old man smiled sadly. 'It was a dream of mine to take her dancing in that dress.' He lifted a hand, let it fall again.

'A dream of yours? Like that caravan?'

Fans opened at the corners of the old man's eyes. 'Like the caravan,' he said. 'We had a lot of dreams, Alice and I. But you were the only one that came true.'

Moses bent down and kissed his father on the forehead.

'Something you should do,' the old man said, mischief now in his dark eyes, 'is to go and see your gravestone.'

'*Gravestone?*'

'Yes, gravestone. How else do you think we explained your sudden disappearance? You died, remember? You drowned in the river.'

'I see.' Moses had taken in so much during the past few hours that he felt as if he was about to overflow.

'If you run into a policeman, it might be best to pretend that you're just passing through. And don't, for God's sake, mention your name. As I said, you're supposed to be dead. If they find out you're not, well, it could be dangerous.'

'I'll be careful,' Moses promised. 'Are you sure you're going to be all right?'

'I've lived here alone for twenty years. I'll be fine. Oh, and Moses – ' the old man held his cigarette away from his lips and a slightly embarrassed smile appeared there – 'next time *you* can talk.'

*

'Well, that wasn't so bad, was it?' Mary shifted into second. The car began to scale the hill that led to the graveyard.

'I don't know,' Moses said. 'I feel a bit dazed.'

She nodded as if that made sense to her.

'You were very quiet,' he said.

'It was your scene. I didn't have a part.'

He watched her driving. You had a part, he thought.

A silence followed. The sun, setting behind an oak, punched fierce orange holes in its black, almost metallic foliage. By the time they passed through the cemetery gate the colours in the sky were vanishing. Still, they found the grave easily enough. Moses knelt down in the grass and tried to decipher the inscription. Mary wandered off to look at the church.

It was true what he had told her. He was having trouble finding room to store everything he had heard that afternoon. The places where it should have gone were already crammed with all kinds of junk from his own life. And yet so much of what he had heard, it seemed, was his own life too. He would have to squeeze it in somehow. It was a strange idea. Like trying to put foundations in a building that had already been completed. Unsettling. He heard footsteps behind him. He turned round, expecting to see Mary. Instead he saw a policeman.

'Good evening, sir,' the policeman said.

350

Moses thought it wise to match the policeman's politeness. 'Good evening, officer.'

'A pleasant cemetery.'

'Very pleasant.'

'Even at night.'

There was just the suggestion of an interrogative in the policeman's amiable remarks, as if he didn't really understand why somebody should be visiting a cemetery at night and would quite like to know.

Moses hesitated.

Suddenly the policeman's forefinger flew up to his chin and stuck there. 'Forgive me if I'm mistaken, sir,' he said, 'but aren't you the gentleman who assisted PC Marlpit in the Dinwoodie case?' His eyes glittered against the brooding sky.

Moses was too surprised to lie. 'How did you know that?'

The policeman's forefinger edged from his chin to the side of his nose where it slid rhythmically against the fleshy curve of his nostril. 'PC Marlpit described you in great detail. He was, I believe, quite struck by your appearance. PC Marlpit is one of my oldest friends. We shoot together.'

'Shoot?'

'Pheasant,' the policeman said, 'and grouse, when they're in season. Otherwise bottles in my back yard.' The way he lowered his eyes and smiled, he might just have given away a slightly embarrassing secret.

'Interesting,' Moses said.

'Something occurs to me. If you were to accompany me to the police station, I'm sure the Chief Inspector would be delighted to meet you and thank you personally for your part in the unfortunate affair.'

'I don't know. We really ought to be getting back.'

'We?' The policeman scoured the air for evidence of a second person.

'She's looking at the church,' Moses explained.

The policeman nodded to himself. His eyes returned to Moses's face. 'It would take up very little of your time, sir. The station is just behind us. A minute's walk away. If the lady wouldn't mind, that is.'

'If the lady wouldn't mind what?' Mary said, appearing out of the darkness.

'Going to the police station,' Moses said. 'The Chief Inspector would like to thank me for what I did in July.'

'Splendid,' Mary said. 'I've never met a real Chief Inspector.'

The policeman smiled modestly as if the Chief Inspector had been an invention of his. 'That's settled then.' He rubbed his hands together. 'If you'll just follow me.'

'What are you trying to do?' Moses hissed at Mary as the policeman moved away across the graveyard. 'Get me arrested?'

'What for? Coming back to life? Not being dead?'

Mary's voice was calm, but the calmness hid currents of excitement. He knew this mood of hers.

'Besides,' she added, 'don't you want to meet this famous Peach? Aren't you curious?'

'No.'

The policeman turned round. 'I'm sorry?'

'Nothing,' Mary said.

'I'm sorry. I thought you were talking to me.'

'No,' Moses said. 'We weren't.'

The policeman dropped back to join them. 'It's my hearing, you see,' he explained. 'It's very acute. Take music, for instance. When I listen to music I always have the volume on zero. That's quite loud enough for me. But my wife,' and he chuckled nasally and shook his head, 'she can't understand it. She says what's the point of listening to music you can't hear.'

Moses and Mary exchanged a look behind his back.

They were climbing a steep flight of stone steps now. The police station, a red-brick building with tall narrow windows, seemed to be positioned high above the rest of the village. Only the church tower came close. A chill wind rose. The trees shifted and dipped, hiding the scattered lights below. For a few seconds the village no longer existed.

When they reached the front door, the policeman stood to one side, his face polite and blue in the light of the frosted-glass POLICE lamp. 'Please,' he said. 'After you.'

They walked into a spacious draughty hallway paved with green linoleum. It smelt of bleach, polish, disinfectant. The antiseptic stench of power.

'As you can see,' the policeman said, indicating several of his colleagues who were gathered at the far end, under the clock, 'this is a twenty-four-hour operation.'

I bet it is, Moses thought.

'I beg your pardon?' the policeman said.

'I didn't say anything,' Moses said.

'Forgive me,' the policeman said. Using the heel of his hand, he banged first one ear then the other, let out a brief but violent guffaw and, excusing himself, marched over to the duty desk where he exchanged a few words with a police officer whose face looked as if it had been hit several times by a hammer.

'The Chief Inspector will see you immediately,' he called out. 'Won't you come this way?'

He led them down a green corridor which, despite being lit by rows of white fluorescent tubes, gave the impression of dimness. Pipes bulged on the ceiling like veins. Moses heard a long drawn-out groan come from somewhere. It hung on the air, then silence and their footsteps took over, seemed to collaborate, pretend the groan had never been uttered.

'I don't like this place,' he whispered in Mary's ear. 'I don't like this place at all.'

They stopped in front of a door that looked like the door to a strongroom. Grey metal plates. Rivets. The words CHIEF INSPECTOR PEACH stencilled in black. The policeman knocked in a way that suggested both firmness and awe. A deep voice told them to enter.

Peach was seated behind a monumental bureau desk. His hands lay loosely clenched on its polished surface, flanked by piles of paper and trays of pens.

'This is the gentleman who assisted P C Marlpit in the Dinwoodie case,' the policeman announced. 'He just happened to be passing through, sir.'

Did I say that? Moses wondered.

'Thank you, Grape.'

Peach rose majestically and eased round his desk, but when he saw Moses standing there something curious happened. His entire body stiffened. His eyes seemed to freeze over. Ice and menace in his gaze. Moses steeled himself for some kind of impact. But then the moment passed, the chill lifted, and Peach was extending a plump hand.

'Delighted to meet you, er – '

'Shirley,' Moses said.

'Unusual name for a gentleman,' Peach observed.

'*Mr* Shirley.'

'Ah, *Mr* Shirley.'

They both laughed quickly.

'And this,' Moses said, ushering Mary forwards, not a trace of hesitation now, 'is Mrs Shirley.'

Peach took Mary's hand in both of his. 'Of course. Delighted, Mrs Shirley.'

While Peach was shaking hands with Mary, Moses stared at him. Peach was an amazingly pear-shaped man. His cheeks were wider than his forehead and his hips were wider than his shoulders. He had a bully's crewcut, and his drooping lower lip made him look as though he wouldn't believe a word you said. Moses knew he would have to watch himself. It wasn't only Peach either. There was that constable standing by the door.

He could hear what you were saying even when you weren't saying anything.

Peach waved the couple to a matching pair of seats and returned to his leather chair behind the desk. 'PC Marlpit informed me of the part you played in the apprehension of Dinwoodie, and I must say that I'm very glad to have the opportunity of thanking you in person.'

'Not at all,' Moses said. 'It was nothing.'

'If only all the members of the general public were so co-operative,' Peach crooned.

Peach was a sort of oral masseur. It was a sensual pleasure to listen to his genial rumbling voice and he knew it. He used its soothing modulations to soften you up. He lulled you into a false sense of security. And then he pounced. Framed portraits of his predecessors hung on the wall behind his head like warnings. One of those stern men would be Birdforth, Moses was thinking. The sly and lyrical Birdforth. 1902–1916. He glanced across at Mary. She seemed to be ignoring the danger. Or, if not ignoring it, flirting with it.

'I'm only sorry I missed out on all the excitement,' she was saying in a breathy version of her voice.

Peach smiled at her indulgently. 'And where were you at the time, Mrs Shirley?'

The way he posed this question – so benign, so *interested* – you would never have guessed that it had been used a million times before, and nearly always during police grillings. So casual, this Peach. So dangerous.

'Oh, I was at home,' Mary laughed, 'with the children.'

She was good at this, Moses saw. She was better than he would ever be.

'A mother's work,' Peach mused. 'More difficult even than a policeman's, wouldn't you say?' He swung a few degrees on his chair to include Moses. 'You're fortunate, Mr Shirley, to have such a charming and conscientious wife.'

Moses smiled graciously. 'Just as a matter of interest,' he said, 'how *is* PC Marlpit?'

Peach picked up a paperweight (a cluster of houses trapped in clear acrylic) and revolved it in his fingers. 'PC Marlpit's a fine officer,' he said, 'but he does tend to get a little excitable at times – '

'I noticed,' Moses said.

' – so I have to ground him occasionally, take him off active duty and give him some quieter employment here in the station. You may laugh at this, Mr Shirley, coming from the city as you do, but life in a village breeds its own peculiar tensions and stresses. Most of my officers are rested from time to time.'

'No, I understand that.' Moses smiled. 'Well, please give him my regards when you next see him.'

'You can do that yourself.' Peach rose smoothly to his feet. 'After the way you helped us, I thought the least we could do would be to give you a brief tour of our police station. In the course of the tour we should come across PC Marlpit. I believe he's on duty today.'

'How wonderful,' Mary said (overdoing it a bit, Moses thought). 'I've always wanted to see the inside of a police station.'

'Most people do their best to avoid it.' Peach tucked the corners of his mouth in so that tiny humorous dimples appeared in his cheeks.

Mary put a hand on Peach's arm. 'Very witty, Chief Inspector. I've never thought of it like that.'

Smiling, Peach ushered them out of the office.

He showed them round at a leisurely pace. He pointed out features and facilities with graceful movements of his hands. He seemed particularly proud of what he called *the residential quarters*. They comprised a large bedroom with four single beds, a common-room which boasted a colour TV and several leather armchairs, and a kitchenette complete with a breakfast bar and the biggest toaster Moses had ever seen – with its curved stainless steel top and its spindly splayed legs, it looked like a spaceship and toasted twelve slices at once.

'Hungry policemen,' Moses said.

'Yes,' Peach said. 'They like their toast and marmalade.'

He combined these bland remarks with glances of chilling power, taking place at the edge of Moses's vision, sensed rather than seen.

Moses was beginning to feel uneasy. He tried to distract Peach with questions. He pointed to a corrugated-iron building on the far side of the courtyard. 'What's that building over there?' he asked, though he knew perfectly well.

Peach peered through the window as if he wasn't quite sure which building Moses was referring to.

Moses nudged him with the words, 'That corrugated-iron building.'

'That,' Peach said eventually, 'is the police museum, Mr Highness.'

Too shocked to speak, Moses stared at the Chief Inspector's back. He knew Peach could hear the fear in his silence. His heart was banging against his chest like a fist. Peach could probably hear that too.

'Mr Shirley,' he said, and knew he had hesitated too long. 'My name is Mr Shirley.'

Peach swivelled, his eyes close-range, the colour of guns. 'I *do* apologise. I don't know what I was thinking of.'

Moses stepped past him to the window. Say something.

355

'Would it be possible to see the museum, Chief Inspector?'

'I'm afraid not. The museum's closed at present. For renovation work.' Peach's lies were even smoother than the truth.

'Pity,' Moses said. 'Some other time, perhaps.'

Peach turned away, tugging on an earlobe.

He took them through a sort of operations room next and there, on a converted ping-pong table, stood a detailed scale model of New Egypt. Moses hovered above the village, looking down. He could see everything that the old man, his father, had described: the house where the mad lady lived, the stretch of field the greengrocer had tried to cross, the rushes growing beside the river – even the elm outside his father's bedroom window. And how many more stories there must be, he thought, unknown or still untold.

'We had it specially built by the people at Hornby,' Peach breathed over his shoulder. 'What do you think?'

'All you need now,' Moses said, 'are a few little flags to show where the enemy are.' He snickered at his own joke.

Peach withdrew. 'And this,' he called out, moving towards a door that had the word ACCOUNTS stencilled across its one glass pane in black capital letters, 'is where we keep Police Constable Marlpit.'

The door rattled open in his hand. Marlpit was bent over, neck exposed as if for a guillotine, face two inches from the top of his desk. Either dozing, Moses thought, or subjecting his figures to the closest possible scrutiny.

'Marlpit,' Peach boomed, 'I have somebody to see you.'

Dozing, Moses decided, as Marlpit jerked upright, his eyes unnaturally wide, a caricature of alertness.

'Oh – yes – ' the constable stammered. Saliva welled behind his teeth. 'Most certainly. What a surprise. What a pleasant surprise. How are you, sir?'

'Very well, thank you,' Moses said.

They shook hands.

'And your young ladyfriend?' Marlpit grew brighter by the second like a bulb that's about to burn out. 'How's your young ladyfriend? Delightful girl, I thought.'

Peach stepped in diplomatically. 'This, Marlpit, is Mrs Shirley. Mr Shirley's wife.'

Marlpit blushed from the neck upwards. He removed his helmet. The colour rose past his eyebrows, beyond his hairline. 'Oh – I – very pleased to meet you, madam.' He bowed two or three times in a way that made him look, for those few seconds, peculiarly oriental.

'You'll have to forgive him,' Peach whispered as he pulled the door shut.

'He's still in a state of some confusion, the poor fellow.'

You're a sadist, Moses thought, and I don't like you. But he smiled as if to say he quite understood.

'Well, that just about wraps it up.' Peach's chest swelled as he breathed in. 'Except for the cells, of course.'

'Oh, we *have* to see the *cells*,' Mary said.

Peach led them into a short passage with grey walls and a concrete floor. 'Now, as you might imagine, there isn't a great deal of crime in New Egypt so we only have two cells.' He spread his plump hands. 'One for you, Mr Shirley, and one for your wife.'

Moses stayed well back from the doors. You never know.

Mary had already peered inside. 'Why are there tables instead of beds?' she asked.

'That's a good question. We used to give our prisoners beds. Used to, that is, until one man tore his mattress-cover into strips, fashioned a primitive rope out of them and – ' Peach jerked one clenched fist away from his neck in an unmistakable gesture. He turned to face Moses. 'The man's name,' he said, 'was Dinwoodie.'

'How awful,' Mary said.

'Most unfortunate,' Peach agreed, still staring at Moses. 'One of those things.'

Moses said nothing.

'So now the prisoners sleep on tables,' Peach said. 'It's better to be on the safe side, don't you think?'

'Quite,' Mary said.

Peach escorted his two visitors to the front door of the police station. 'Once again,' he said, 'thank you for your help.'

'Thank *you*,' Mary said, 'for the wonderful tour.'

They all shook hands again.

Then Peach suddenly took a step backwards and looked Moses up and down in an extremely cunning way. 'Have you ever seriously considered a career in the police force yourself, Mr Shirley?'

Moses was flabbergasted. 'Well, no – '

'A man of your imposing size and initiative,' Peach continued seductively, 'would be a credit to any branch of our organisation. You would make a magnificent policeman, I'm sure. What do *you* think, Mrs Shirley?'

Mary took Moses by the arm. 'I don't think it's ever crossed his mind – has it, darling?'

A sickly smile spread over Moses's face.

'Well, if you should ever consider it, feel free to get in touch with me.'

Peach was rubbing his hands together, radiating good nature. 'I don't have any great influence, of course, but I would be happy to go through the details with you. Think about it, anyway.' He raised a hand, turned on his heel, and was gone, all in one fluid, smoothly executed manoeuvre.

Still arm in arm, Moses and Mary walked back down the steps.

'Going to join the force then, are you, Mr Shirley?' Mary teased him.

But Moses didn't even smile. 'He knew,' he said.

'He knew what?'

'He knew who I was.'

'Peach?'

Moses nodded.

'How could he know that?'

'I don't know. But he did. I felt it right away. Something, anyway. And then he called me Mr Highness, sort of by mistake. He was testing me, I suppose.'

Mary pulled away from him. 'When did he call you Mr Highness?'

'Oh, he was clever. He waited till you were on the other side of the room. He chose his moment perfectly. He's a real cunning bastard.'

Mary stood among the tombstones, hands on her hips now, two lines engraved between her eyebrows. 'I don't understand this, Moses. How could he possibly know?'

'I've no idea. But he did. He definitely did.' He looked round, his right eye twitching, then he whispered, 'That's why he came out with all that stuff about joining the police. It was like he was saying, you belong here, your place is in the village.' He stepped backwards, almost tripped over his own gravestone. 'It was like a threat. But in code.'

The wind lifted. Leaves scuttled across the path.

He looked at Mary, but Mary seemed at a loss for words. Here was something that even she couldn't explain.

'Come on,' he said, 'let's get out of here.'

*

He opened the window an inch, let the slipstream take his cigarette. The air had cooled, sharpened. They were driving through remote countryside, a landscape of hollows and copses, secrets and ambiguities. Not a house for miles. The headlights soaked up endless twisting road.

Mary had insisted on taking the scenic route back, one of her oldest rules being never to do the same thing twice.

'But it's so dark,' he had pointed out.

'So what? It's the principle of the thing.' Mary had been at her most dogmatic.

'But you can't see anything when it's dark. What's the point of taking the scenic route when you can't see anything?'

She had dismissed his arguments with the words, 'Don't be so pedantic, Moses.'

And he had sighed and given up.

He had wanted to put distance between himself and New Egypt, he had wanted the comfort of other cars, larger towns, crowds, but Mary drove north then east, the loneliest road she could find. Through the rear window he watched the village sink into its dip in the land, a few weak lights extinguished by the rising ground. They had got away. And London lay ahead, beyond those trees. Soon the headlights, so ostentatious now, would dissolve in the city's orange glare. In retrospect, his fear seemed melodramatic, absurd, almost hilarious.

They had been driving for about fifteen minutes when the car suddenly swerved, bumped against the lip of a ditch and stalled.

'Fuck,' Mary said.

She banged the steering-wheel with the heel of her hand.

'What's wrong?'

'The clutch. Something's happened to the clutch.'

'Let me have a look.'

Moses flicked the interior light on, then reached down with his left hand, his head resting sideways on Mary's thigh.

'Shit,' he said. 'The cable's snapped.'

'Can you mend it?'

'No.'

They stared at each other.

'Now what?' she said.

He consulted the map. 'We're miles from anywhere.'

'You're joking.'

'No joke, I'm afraid.'

'Fuck.'

'Well, don't blame me,' he said, 'I wasn't the one who wanted to do the scenic route.'

She glared at him.

He looked down at the map again. 'And you know what? One of the nearest places is still New Egypt.' He allowed himself a soft sardonic laugh. 'There's only one place that's nearer and that's Bagwash. What I suggest we do is ditch the car and walk to Bagwash. It's about five miles.'

'What's this Bagwash? Sounds like a launderette.'

'It's a village. It's got a church, a pond, a Roman remains – an obelisk – '

'Sod the obelisk. What about a garage?'

He gave her a withering look. 'You can't tell that by looking at a map.
Come on, Mary. You ought to know that.' He knew she hated the word
ought – she thought it ought to be removed from the English language –
but he wanted to provoke her.

'Why?' she said. 'Why ought I to know that?'

'Because you've been driving longer than me. Much longer. Because
you're older.'

'You bastard.' She twisted in her seat and swiped him with her driving-
glove.

He poked her in the ear with his finger. 'Much older,' he said.

She began to beat him about the head with her handbag. It was a
deceptive handbag. It looked ladylike, but it could hold a litre of vodka,
no problem. It hurt.

In retaliation he seized her nose between finger and thumb. Her mouth
opened. He stuffed it with a tissue. 'Bless you,' he said.

Their frustration slowly distilled, first into laughter, then into sex.

Afterwards Moses said, 'The light was on the whole time.'

'I always fuck with the light on,' Mary said. 'I like to see what I'm
doing.'

'But anyone could've seen.'

'I don't care.'

'What if Peach – ' Moses didn't finish his sentence.

Mary leaned back against the door and looked at him. 'What is it now,
Moses?'

'Nothing,' he said.

*

After walking for twenty minutes they reached a junction. BAGWASH $4\frac{1}{2}$,
the signpost said.

'Four and a half miles,' Mary groaned. She sat down on the grass mound
at the foot of the signpost and began to take off her shoes.

'What are you doing?' Moses said.

'My feet hurt.'

'Oh, Christ.' He moved out into the middle of the road. He looked first
in one direction, then in the other. No cars. Not the remotest suggestion
of a car. Not even the feeling that a car might once have passed this way.
They were going to have to walk.

'Come on, Mary.' He took her by both hands and pulled her to her feet. 'It's only about an hour.'

'My legs are half the length of yours,' she said. 'Two hours.'

He studied her as closely as was possible in the extreme darkness. 'They can't be half the length,' he grinned, 'can they?'

They stood face to face and measured legs.

'All right,' Moses conceded five minutes later (during which time comparison had also been made between their mouths, and between one of Mary's breasts and one of Moses's hands), 'one and a half hours.'

They began to walk.

High hedges hemmed the road in on both sides. Sometimes the wind blew and trees became haunting instruments. Otherwise silence. When they talked, the night sounded like an empty room. When they didn't, Moses heard noises. The blood in your ears, Mary reassured him. But Moses was thinking of Peach, the stealthy Peach, he was imagining the Chief Inspector following in their tracks, rubbing his plump hands together, he was hearing the sinister whisper of skin on skin, so when Mary stopped and said, for the fifth time, 'What's that?' he walked on, snapped, 'Nothing.'

'It is,' she cried. 'Look. Headlights.'

He swung round and saw two yellow trumpets playing over the dark landscape. He stepped back into the ditch. Shielding his eyes, he could just make out the shape of a truck. One wheeze of its brakes and it had obeyed Mary's waving arms and stood, shuddering, asthmatic, on the road. He moved sideways out of the glare. A man with a square face leaned out of the cab, a shiny leather cap pushed to the back of his head.

'Our car's broken down,' Moses said. 'Any chance of a lift?'

The man told them to hop in.

Like drunkenness the relief then. Moses sat between Mary and the man in the cap and talked non-stop, raising his voice above the wail of the engine.

'We just spent the day in New Egypt. About ten miles down the road. Do you know it?'

The man shook his head. He drove with his arms draped round the wheel, his hands almost meeting at midnight.

'My dad lives there. I hadn't seen him for ages. Not since I was a baby actually. Then we met a couple of policemen. Got a tour of the station and everything. One of them even offered me a job. Then the clutch went on the way back.'

The man nodded.

'Best thing, we reckoned, was to try and get to Bagwash. Think it would've taken us all night if you hadn't come along.'

The man lifted one stubby hand off the wheel and scratched his jaw. 'You from London?'

'That's right.'

'What were you doing on that lane then?'

Moses rolled his eyes towards the roof. 'We were taking the scenic route back.'

'Not quite so scenic when you break down, is it?'

It was a joke and both Moses and Mary laughed and their laughter carried them through the village of Bagwash and dropped them at the gates of a modest country hotel.

'It's the only hotel round here,' the man told them. 'If I was you, I'd stay the night here, fix the car in the morning. There's a man in the village, name of Fowler. Phone him up. He might do it.'

They thanked him for the lift and the advice, and watched as a curve in the road snuffed his tail-lights out.

In the hotel lobby, Mary asked for a telephone. 'I want to call Alan,' she told Moses.

'What are you going to tell him?'

'I'm going to tell him that we've broken down in the middle of nowhere and that we can't get back tonight.'

'It sounds awful. It sounds like you made it up.'

Mary smiled and spread her hands. 'It happens to be true.'

While Mary went to telephone, Moses registered as Mr and Mrs Shirley. The charade he had invented for Peach seemed to have taken on a life of its own.

'That's odd,' Mary said, appearing at his elbow a moment later. 'There's no answer.'

'Maybe he's gone out or something.'

She pushed her lips forward, shook her head. 'No, he said he was staying in this evening. He had some work to do.'

'Maybe he changed his mind.'

Mary didn't look convinced.

'Look, you'll be home by tomorrow lunch-time,' Moses told her. 'And, anyway, you've been away for longer than this before without calling.'

'I know,' she said, 'but something doesn't smell right.'

*

What a day it had been. There seemed nothing for it but to get terribly drunk. After all, as Mary reminded him, it was their first night alone together.

They began with cocktails in the hotel bar, then switched to gin and tonics and carried their gin and tonics, ice ringing in their glasses like chimes, into the dining-room. Mary chose a table in the darkest corner and ordered a bottle of wine.

Moses leaned back in his chair. It felt like weeks since Mary had appeared at the top of the stairs in her black wool coat and her jewels and announced that she was going to change his life. He had been living on his nerves all day and they were beginning to fray and buckle, they were beginning to say, Go and live somewhere else for a while. Hopefully, though, there would be no more surprises. Please, he begged. No more villages. No more fathers I didn't know I had. No more Peach.

He finished his gin and tonic and, seeking distraction, looked into the room. There was a sudden fluttering of napkins over by the window, as if two white birds had spread their wings only to discover that they couldn't fly. Another couple had sat down to dinner. The man wore a blue blazer. Crest on the breast pocket. Anchors on the buttons, no doubt. The woman, younger by at least ten years, wore a garish red blouse. Ruffles spilled fussily over her bust. They talked so intimately, these two, that the candle on their table scarcely flickered. Their hands clasped across the condiments. Their eyes locked as if they found each other captivating. But something failed to convince. Each time the waitress came by they flinched, withdrew their hands, turned their faces up to hers with stupid eagerness. They were like two bad actors. Ham love.

The wine arrived and Moses turned his attention back to Mary.

'Well,' she said, pouring them both a glass, 'now that we've dealt with the past, what about drinking to the future?'

'The future,' Moses said.

They both emptied their glasses.

As Mary poured again, Moses leaned forwards. He began to spin his knife round on the tablecloth.

'Did I ever tell you about the policeman?' he said.

'What policeman?'

'It happened about four months ago. While I was out. This policeman came looking for me, apparently. He knew my name. He asked Elliot if I was living at The Bunker. Elliot wouldn't tell him. So he hit Elliot. Out of the blue. Knocked him right over. Then he disappeared.'

'Who was he?'

'That's just it. Nobody knows. And Elliot had never seen him before.' He swallowed a thoughtful mouthful of wine and went back to spinning his knife around. 'I've got a hunch, though. About who it was, I mean.'

'Who then?'

'Peach.'

'Moses,' Mary laughed, 'you heard what your father said. Nobody ever leaves that place.'

'Well, how come he knows who I am then?'

'I don't believe he does.'

'He used my *name*, Mary.'

'I didn't hear that.'

'And the way he looked at me – '

'I'm sorry, Moses. I just didn't get the impression that he knew who you were. I think you're being – '

'Of course you didn't,' Moses hissed. 'He's an *actor*. Not a second-rate actor like those two over there,' and he jerked a thumb in the direction of the two lovers, 'a *real* actor. A professional.'

Mary held her elbow in the palm of her hand. Her cigarette pointed at his face. She watched him calmly through the rapid spiralling of smoke. 'I don't know what you're trying to prove,' she said.

'I'm not trying to prove anything. I'm just saying, suppose he did leave the village. Suppose,' and he paused for a moment, 'he came after me.'

Mary shook her head. 'That's called paranoia, Moses.'

'Is it?' he said.

*

An hour later they were both laughing drunk.

'And what about,' Moses was almost weeping, 'and what about when Marlpit said, "And how is your young ladyfriend?" and Peach said, "Marlpit, *this* is Mr Shirley's *wife*."'

Uncontrollable hysterics.

Then Moses suddenly said, 'Oh, *shit*.'

'What is it?' Mary asked.

He groaned. 'I just remembered. The young ladyfriend. I was supposed to be meeting her tonight. We had some things to sort out.'

Mary's eyes mocked him for a moment. 'So call her.'

'I think I'd better.'

He clambered to his feet. The table rocked, the carpet tactfully absorbed the sound of falling cutlery. On his way to the lobby he meandered past the two lovers. They seemed drunker too. Less stilted, anyhow. Less tense. Red Blouse was ordering a trifle.

'I shouldn't really,' she was saying, 'but – ' and her lips disappeared coyly into her mouth. What a naughty girl.

Blue Blazer came to the rescue, his chair a white charger now, his fork a lance. 'Well, it isn't every day, is it?' His smiling teeth glistened beneath his RAF moustache. He could almost taste the sweet sponge and jelly of her thighs. 'In fact,' he said, 'I think I'll have one too.' The wicked bugger.

Still shaking his head, Moses found the pay-phone in the corner of the lobby. He lit a cigarette. He dialled Gloria's number with a finger that seemed too big for the holes. The number rang and rang. No reply from Gloria. He dialled Eddie's number next. He was supposed to be going too. No reply from Eddie either. Now what?

The clock above the reception desk said ten to eleven. They would probably both be at the club by now. So phone the club. But what was the name of the club? The Blue something, he remembered. Yes, that was it. The Blue what, though? Elliot would know, he thought. He dialled Elliot's number. No reply again. He slammed the receiver down. What the fuck was going on?

He put his cigarette out. Suddenly his mouth tasted of wine and ashes. He swallowed. The taste remained. There were two worlds. One here, one out there. Nobody at home out there. Nobody listening. And him standing here, marooned in this one. A shiver ran the length of his spine. This second world, the world where he had been born, the world where he had already died once, where he could die again, crept up his nostrils, crept into his lungs, like gas. He felt the greedy breath of policemen on his neck. He turned. Nobody there.

He fought loose, won a moment of clarity. Directory Enquiries, he thought. He dialled 192. A woman answered.

'Please can you help me?' he began.

The woman laughed. 'I'll try.'

'I'm looking for the number of a club in Covent Garden,' he said. 'It's called The Blue something.'

'That's a funny name.'

'I mean – '

'It's all right, love. I know what you mean. Now, let me see. The Blue something – '

He could hear her humming.

'I suppose people don't usually talk to you,' he said.

'Oh, you get the odd one or two.'

It sounded snug on the other end of the phone. It was like talking to somebody who was in bed. Somebody who had just woken up and was still drowsy and smothered in blankets. Warm as warm skin. He could've listened to her talk for ages. He could've fallen asleep in her voice.

'There's one man,' she was saying, 'he rings me up and he asks me what I'm wearing – '

'What do you tell him?'

'Sometimes I tell him the truth. You know, white blouse, black skirt, shoes that leak. Other times I make things up. Once I told him I was wearing a ballgown – '

Moses laughed. 'You don't mind him asking?'

'No, I don't mind. If it keeps him happy. We laugh a bit. You know. You get on faster if you make people laugh.'

'It's funny, but I like listening to your voice.'

'Thank you. You're not going to ask me what I'm wearing, are you?'

'Not tonight.'

A soft laugh. 'Here you go, love. How does The Blue Diamond sound?'

'That's it,' he said. 'You are clever.'

'Don't. It'll go to my head.'

She gave him the number and he scribbled it down.

'Well,' he said, 'I suppose I'd better ring off now.'

That made her laugh again.

'It's been very nice talking to you,' he said. 'It really has.'

'The Blue Diamond,' she said. 'You take care now. Those night-clubs – '

'I will. Speak to you again sometime.'

'Goodbye.' She hung up.

He suddenly regretted not having asked for her number. There were millions of operators and he would probably never get her again. But imagine asking for the number of someone who works for Directory Enquiries!

He smiled as he dialled The Blue Diamond. The first four times he got the engagement ring or whatever it's called. The fifth time he got through.

'Blue Diamond.' A male voice this time.

'I want to speak to Gloria, please,' Moses said. 'She's singing at your place tonight.'

'She isn't here yet.'

'OK, can I leave a – ' Bip bip bip. Moses felt his pockets for change. He fed another two 10ps into the slot. 'Hello? I'd like to leave a message please.'

'Go ahead.'

'My name's Moses. I've had a breakdown – '

'Is that nervous or mechanical?'

Moses smiled. 'Mechanical. Listen, my car's broken down in the middle of nowhere so I'm not going to be able to make it tonight, OK?'

'Sounds a bit lame, Moses.'

'Well, it's true. Oh, and could you send her my – ' Bip bip bip. He felt his pockets again. No more coins. He slowly replaced the receiver.

Love, he thought. Send her my love.

*

Placing his hands on the table, Moses lowered himself towards his chair, missed by six inches and sat down rather heavily on the floor. He peered at Mary through a blur of condiments. 'Mary,' he said, 'I think I'm a bit drunk.'

'You took for ever,' she laughed. 'What happened?'

'Been in different worlds. Talked to,' and he hauled himself up on to his chair, 'very nice operator.'

'Did you get through?'

'Through?'

'Your call, Moses. To your ladyfriend.'

'No, not really. Nobody there.'

'I'm going to try Alan one more time.'

While Mary was away, Moses tried to establish an upright position for himself, using, as reference points, the blue china cabbage on the mantelpiece, the distant figure of Red Blouse (a suggestive fleck of whipped cream just to one side of her lips – Blue Blazer gazing, sighing, fantasising), and a picture of a white horse cantering through peppermint surf, but every time he focused on something it multiplied, had twins, triplets, quadruplets, who began to run away as soon as they were born. He couldn't keep up. He had lost this one. The entire room suddenly took off on a victory lap.

A rush of blackness, but it was only Mary sitting down.

'Any luck?' he said.

She shook her head.

He thought he saw traces of abandonment on her face. Smooth damp places. Sand abandoned by an outgoing tide. Some kind of ebbing.

'You all right?' he asked.

She downed her brandy. 'I'm going upstairs.'

He stayed at the table for a moment, then moved off jerkily in Mary's wake, as if attached to her by a long and invisible rope that had only tightened, taken effect, when she was twenty feet away. Umbilical, she would've called it. He fetched up at her side in an upright heap. Eyes vacant with alcohol. One arm held away from his body like a wing. For balance. Staring at the carpet, he wondered why anyone in their right mind would take vomit as a design motif. If he was sick, he thought, and he was sick carefully enough, maybe he could fit his sick into one of those obscene recurring patterns and nobody would ever notice.

'You go on,' he said. 'Just got to ask something.'

He found their waitress in the lobby. She stood below him gazing upwards. She was very small. Tiny balls of light (reflections of the electric chandelier above) rolled about on the lenses of her glasses. He wanted to take her head in his two hands and tilt it until the silver balls stopped on the two black centres of her eyes. Instead he asked her for a local telephone directory. She produced one from behind the reception desk.

'And two more brandies, please,' he said.

She rolled the silver balls that were her eyes and moved off down the corridor.

He thumbed through the directory until he reached H. The same old routine, with one crucial difference: this time there had to be a Highness – Highness G, 14 Caution Lane, New Egypt. He read the names out loud to himself – 'Hardware, Haseldine, Havana, Head – ' he skipped a couple of pages – 'Hick, Higgins, Hilton – ' He must've missed it. He began again. Using his finger because the names were jumping. But no. No Highness. He straightened up, wrapped his hand round the lower half of his face. It could only mean one thing. His father didn't have a phone.

On a whim, he looked up Peach. There were three Peaches, but none of them were Chief Inspectors. None of them lived in New Egypt either. Curious. Unless Peach was ex-directory, of course. He nodded to himself. Peach was cunning on two legs. Peach would be ex-directory.

The waitress returned with the brandies. 'Did you find what you were looking for?'

He shook his head. He had wanted to ask his father an urgent question. He had wanted to know how Peach could possibly have discovered his identity. But now he had no way of reaching his father, not without returning to the village, and he wasn't sure he wanted to risk that. Now he would never know. He began to walk towards the stairs.

'Sir?' the waitress called out. 'Your brandies.'

*

Wallpaper like warfare. Salvoes of red roses exploding round his ears. Two brandies balanced in one hand, he ran up the corridor and burst into the wrong room. Red Blouse had changed into Pink Slip. Blue Blazer was no longer Blue Blazer; Blue Blazer hung over the back of a chair.

'Oh, excuse me,' Moses said, and, backpedalling, hit his head on the door.

'No, that's all right,' Pink Slip said, slipping into Beige Robe (though, for Moses, she would always be Red Blouse). 'Just leave them on the table, would you?'

Moses gaped at her. 'What?'

'Just leave them on the table,' she repeated.

'But they're mine.'

'I beg your pardon?'

'They're mine,' Moses said. '*I* bought them.'

It was Red Blouse's turn to gape. 'Aren't you a waiter?'

'No,' Moses said. Glancing down at his white shirt and his black trousers, he began to understand the misunderstanding. Red Blouse had obviously been too engrossed in Blue Blazer to notice Moses sitting in the corner of the dining-room. So it's true, he thought. Love is a bad play and all the actors are blind.

Meanwhile Red Blouse was staring at him and all the time she was staring at him her mouth was opening wider and wider until it seemed that something must emerge. And finally it did. It was a scream. A scream so powerful that it wiped out the entire world. For some indefinable length of time (two or three seconds, perhaps – or a century, who knows?), there was no world, only scream. The scream of Red Blouse. Then it ceased and there was void, such as there was at the beginning of time before the world existed. Then the world crept back, shell-shocked, wary.

Moses began to slide backwards round the edge of the door, but he delayed long enough to see Blue Blazer (White Birthday Suit) catapult from the bathroom, skin trailing steam, trip on a pair of shoes ('Are you all right, daaaaargh – ') and nosedive into the carpet (Pink Buttocks, Brown Mole).

'Sorry,' Moses said, melting into the corridor. 'Terribly sorry.'

Mary lay diagonally across the bed in the next room. 'Did you hear somebody scream?' she said, her voice sleepy with alcohol.

'Scream?' Moses closed the door softly behind him. 'No, I don't think so.'

'That's funny. I could've sworn I heard somebody scream.'

He knelt down beside her. 'Brandy,' he said.

'How nice.'

'Undress me,' he whispered.

Removal of evidence.

He reached over and switched off the light.

'No light?' she said. 'But I always – '

'It'll make a change,' he said, 'won't it?'

Sex. The perfect alibi.

*

Mary woke early the next morning. She dressed with a series of deft silent movements and left the room. In the lobby she made enquiries as to the whereabouts of a Mr Fowler, then she set off down the hill on foot. Mr Fowler, the village mechanic, proved most obliging. He told her he would tow the Volvo himself. He could have a new clutch cable fitted by midday, he assured her, twirling his spanner as a philanderer might twirl his moustache. 'Leave it to me,' he said.

When she returned to the hotel, Moses was awake. She gave him the good news.

'That's great,' he said. 'Why don't you try Alan again?'

'No, I don't think so.' She came and sat on the bed. She was ninety per cent air this morning. Her fingers skimmed across his skin like a breeze. 'Let's go and have some breakfast, shall we?'

Ten minutes later they sauntered into the dining-room. Blue Blazer and Red Blouse were sitting at the same table by the window. No trifle fantasies today. No clasping of hands, no glances moist with furtive lust, no sweet nothings not disturbing candle-flames. No nothing. Only eyes lowered as if in shame. Blue Blazer spreading brittle toast, Red Blouse fingering the pleats in her skirt. Had Moses broken the spell by bursting in on them like that? Perhaps. But what a feeble spell then.

As Moses poured himself a cup of coffee he remembered having woken in the night. He had been lying on the counterpane, a chill on the surface of his skin. Naked. Dehydrated. No idea where he was. He could hear the radio going, low volume, something about the death of a famous comedian. He remembered feeling his way out of his dreams and across the room. Running the cold tap. Gulping two glasses of water straight down. Then, moving back towards the bed, he had paused, curious suddenly about the view from the window. He had imagined a vast dark sky, vaulted as the inside of an umbrella, and stars like punctures in the fabric, leaking weak light from behind, and the night air hissing, the night air seeming to escape, and then, below, the land falling away, hills and valleys rolling away in waves, unseen dogs barking, sleeping farms, a dim ribboning of lanes, wave on wave of invisible black hills and valleys, breaking against a distant silent horizon. When he parted the curtains he jumped back. A graveyard pressed its face to the glass. Cold gnarled stones up close. A thin tree beckoning. The stealthy bulk of a church. He hadn't liked seeing this. He hadn't liked seeing it alone in the dead centre of the night. He had hurried back to bed, huddled against Mary. He had buried himself in her untroubled warmth, in her oblivion.

He watched her now as she smoked and ate toast at the same time, as she swallowed the remnants of her coffee. He knew that he could admit fear to her. Admit weakness. Smallness. Anything. And that was what it was about, wasn't it?

'I still need you, you know.'

She looked up. 'Why do you suddenly say that?'

'I was just thinking,' he said. 'I remember you saying, a few weeks ago, in that graveyard it was, I remember you saying that it wasn't you I needed but my parents, my real parents, and that I'd only be able to decide whether I needed you or not after I'd found them. Well, now I've found them, one of them, anyway, and I've thought about it, and I've decided – I still need you.'

Mary smiled and came round the table and gave him a cool lingering kiss on the mouth. Out of the corner of his eye he saw Blue Blazer and Red Blouse pretending not to notice.

After breakfast they linked arms and walked outside. They followed the road that ran alongside the graveyard wall. A fresh wind blowing, laundered clouds.

'What a lot there is to tell Alan,' Moses said.

Mary pulled the hair away from her mouth. 'I shall tell him everything,' she declared, her chin in the air. '*Everything*.'

The general, he thought. *His* general.

'I know you will,' he said. He had expected her to respond like that. He knew she couldn't tolerate restrictions of any kind. Restrictions were death to her, the stones over the wall.

Everything went so smoothly that morning, as if those few hours belonged to a different weekend altogether – Mary even allowed him to take a photograph of her (usually she shielded her face with a hand and cried, 'No pictures,' or asked him why he was threatening her) – and the sight of Mr Fowler standing in front of the hotel with the car when they returned from their walk seemed like a part of this.

He greeted them with a lopsided grin. 'Good as new,' he called out, patting the bonnet.

Mary thanked him for his trouble and wrote him a cheque.

Later they passed him on the road, his arms flexing at the elbows, the morning light hitching a lift into the village on his brilliantine black hair. They waved at him and he waved back.

*

'I want some normal life,' Moses said, as they eased into the heavy traffic on Camden High Street. 'Could you drop me here?'

His gaze had fallen on the green wooden stalls of the vegetable market, the pyramids of tomatoes and oranges, the rows of aubergines, the spiky clusters of pineapples, and their colours seemed to plane the uneven surfaces in his mind, the parts that hadn't slept enough. The sun divided a heap of newspapers into equal halves of light and shadow. A bare arm reached up and opened a third-floor window. Was that a tin whistle in the distance? He wanted to drift, mingle, breathe. It would be breaking precedent, of course – it would be the first Sunday in almost four months that he hadn't been to Muswell Hill – but hadn't they already broken precedent by spending the night together and besides, as Mary herself might have argued, what was precedent for?

She stopped the car opposite the tube station and, stretching across, hands resting on the wheel, kissed him once on the lips. It was a strange kiss – formal, barren, unlike her. A kiss with no history and no future. A kiss that said goodbye and nothing else. Her mouth had shut in his face like a door and she had withdrawn deep into the house to tend to something more pressing. He thought he understood as he got out. Now she was nearing home he had taken second place to her family. He leaned on the window. Stared at her.

'You look tired,' he said.

She nodded.

'I'll call you in the week.' He never usually said things like this to her. It was that kiss. It had unnerved him somehow. He felt the car move fractionally against his body.

'See you soon, Mary.'

He lifted his hands, stood back. She drove away. Hunched over the wheel. Like somebody driving in thick fog. He watched the car shrink, a metaphor for her withdrawal. He shrugged. Turned away. Leaving her to drive into a tragedy that he could never have foreseen because all the important things are shocks that take place on either side of your imagination.

It was Sunday afternoon.

He didn't call her until the following Wednesday.

*

'I'm home,' Mary announced.

Her voice hung on in the air, a slowly dying thing.

She stood perfectly still, her hand on the edge of the front door, and listened to the empty house. The creak of a stair under no footstep. The automatic click of the kitchen thermostat. The wind testing a window in the living-room. She recognised the sounds, but she had never heard them on a Sunday before. How peculiar.

'How peculiar,' she said out loud. And felt a rope begin to tighten round her throat.

She took a few steps forward, down the hall, and stood in the kitchen doorway. They had the presence of inhabitants, those sounds. They had grown out of all proportion in her absence. In this silence.

She walked across the room and opened a window. Cold air flowed in over the back of her hand. Raised the hairs on her forearms.

There ought to be a note, she was thinking. But there was only a pot of cold tea. A jar of marmalade. A dirty plate.

Then a sound that didn't belong. A guest sound.

No, not guest.

Intruder.

She turned round.

'Mrs Shirley?'

A policeman and a policewoman stood in the kitchen doorway. Their eyes blinked like the wings of butterflies. She stared at them and saw such nervousness.

'He's dead,' she said, 'isn't he?'

CRIME IS ORDER

Elliot had gone away for a few days. Business, Ridley said. *Business?* Moses thought. Hiding, more like. But he kept the thought to himself.

It took him until Tuesday night to pin Elliot down.

'You know that policeman who was looking for me?' Moses said, lowering himself on to the corner of Elliot's desk. 'What was he like?'

'I told you,' Elliot said. 'He was a big bloke.'

'A big bloke. That really narrows it down, doesn't it.'

Elliot heaved a sigh. 'All right, he was old. Sixty, maybe. Maybe older. Tell you one thing, though. He had a punch like a fucking train.' His hand moved gingerly across his waistcoat.

'What did his hair look like?'

'Hair? Grey, I think.'

'Long? Short? Curly?'

'It was short. Sort of a crewcut.'

Moses felt his heart stall. 'What about his eyes?'

'Oh, fuck off, Moses. How am I supposed to notice his eyes? I wasn't in love with the geezer, was I?'

Moses walked to the window. He stared out over the rooftops, his hands in his pockets. Car headlights wiped across his face. 'Ridley was there, wasn't he?'

'He turned up after the bloke ran off. I don't reckon he saw much.'

'Do us a favour, Elliot. Get him up here for a moment, would you? It's important.'

Elliot blew some air out of his mouth. 'The things I do for you, Moses. And what do you do for me, eh?'

'I get hit on the head, that's what I do for you.'

Elliot sighed. He reached for the phone and dialled an internal number. 'Is Ridley around? Yeah? Well, tell him Elliot wants to speak to him. Yeah, now.'

A few minutes later the office door opened and Ridley appeared. He looked from Elliot to Moses and back again. 'So what's the problem, chief?'

'You remember that copper who came round a couple of months ago?' Elliot said.

Ridley rolled his head back. He remembered.

Moses jumped in. 'D'you remember what he looked like?'

'Didn't see him, did I?' Ridley scratched his forearm. It sounded like somebody sawing wood. 'Heard his voice, though.'

'What was it like?'

'Deep. Fucking deep.'

'Thanks, Ridley.' Moses turned away. Sixty, crewcut, deep voice. That clinched it.

When Ridley had left, Elliot said, 'What's this all about, Moses? You know who the copper was?'

Moses was staring out of the window again. At the place where Peach must, impossibly, have stood. 'Yeah, I know who he was.'

'So who was he?'

'It won't mean anything to you.'

'What's his name?'

'Peach. Chief Inspector Peach.'

'Peach? I never heard of no fucking Peach.'

'You wouldn't have.' On his way out Moses paused by the door. 'One thing, Elliot. If you see him again, don't be too gentle, all right?'

Elliot threw his cigarette out of the window to its death. 'I don't think you need to worry about that, Moses.'

Moses walked slowly down the stairs. Peach in London. Peach asking questions. Why? Moses needed to talk to somebody. And the only person who would understand was Mary. He tried to reach her that night, but there was no reply.

*

The next day he tried again. It was three in the afternoon and he was standing in a call-box in Soho. Dead ducks rotated on a stainless steel spit ten feet away. A green neon sign – SPANKERAMA – flashed in a curtained window. Somebody had scratched the words GOD and FUCK into the red paintwork above the phone. With a coin, probably, because the O was a pyramid and the U looked like a V-sign. A copy of the *Sun* soaked up urine on the floor. BIG FREEZE CHAOS, the front page said. The freak cold snap earlier in the week had thrown the whole of Central London into chaos: rail services cut, traffic snarl-ups, hyperthermia. Moses shivered as he dialled. Somebody picked up on the other end. He pressed his waiting coin into the slot.

'Hello?' he said.

'I was wondering when you were going to call.'

'Mary?' He hardly recognised her voice. It sounded so emaciated. As if it had been sent to a concentration camp for voices. But that only delayed him a second. 'Mary, something's happened. I've found out who – '

'Wait a moment, Moses,' her voice cut in, gathering strength. 'Listen to me. Just slow down and listen to me.'

The next five seconds were like watching a punch in slow motion: soft ripping as the fist split the air, then the sudden jolt as everything speeded up, happened too fast, as the punch connected.

'Alan's dead. He died on Saturday – ' Her voice crumpled as it hit the sixth word.

Moses let his forehead fall against the cold glass of the phone-box. A different kind of shivering now. The pips went. You have to pay to go on thinking, he thought. He pressed another coin into the slot, then looked at the groove on his thumb that the coin had left behind. He was noticing things like that now. Things he usually skimmed over. The word *dead* did that. It turned you into a camera. Automatic pictures: those red ducks revolving in the window; that slush in the gutter; the words GOD and FUCK. God and fuck. That just about summed it up.

Saturday . . .

They had driven south to look for his parents. They had broken down on the way back. Mary had tried to phone Alan. She hadn't got through. And no wonder. Alan had been dead the whole time.

'Mary – '

'It's all right, Moses. I'm still not used to saying it.' A wry toughness in her voice. Almost cavalier, she sounded.

'Shit, I don't – I don't know what – '

'It's all right.'

Silence again. Their relationship hadn't been built to withstand anything like this. One moment they were sailing along, the next they were clinging to the wreckage. He pressed his forehead into the glass. Icepack-cold. Numbing. He wanted to see her, but he could only see the darkness behind his closed eyes. The colour of mourning. The colour of her clothes. Maybe he *was* seeing her.

Tap, tap.

Somebody was tapping on the glass. He opened his eyes and saw a pair of black shoes. Then a grey pinstripe suit and a furled umbrella. Finally a pinched indignant face. He turned round, faced the other way.

'Can you hear me?' Mary said.

'Yes.'

'I want you to listen to me and try to understand what I'm going to say.'

He could hear the bravery in her voice. It made his voice catch when he answered her. 'I'm listening.'

Tap, tap.

'I don't want to see you, Moses. Can you understand that?'

'I think so.'

Tap, tap, tap.

'Don't call me and don't write. I need some time.'

'OK.'

Tap, tap. TAP, TAP.

He covered the mouthpiece with his hand and pushed the door open.

'I'm in a hurry,' the man with the umbrella said. 'Could you please – '

'Wait your fucking turn, all right?' Moses forced the words out, one syllable at a time, through clenched teeth. He pulled the door shut again.

'Hello? – Moses? – '

'It's all right. I'm still here.'

'Do you understand what I've been saying?'

'Yes.'

'Do you understand why?'

'I think so. I'm trying to.'

'That makes me feel a lot better.'

'Good.'

Tap, tap.

'I'm going to hang up now, Moses.'

'OK.'

Tap, tap. TAP.

'Goodbye then.'

'Goodbye, Mary – and take care – '

But she had already hung up.

He listened to the dialling tone until it cut off. Then only void. A distant sputtering, like outer space.

Tap, tap, tap.

TAP, TAP, TAP.

He replaced the receiver and pushed the door open. He snatched the man's umbrella and, with a kind of weary strength, hurled it towards Cambridge Circus. It cartwheeled through the icy sky, spinning black on grey, and landed in the middle of Charing Cross Road. He thought he heard a discreet snap as it was crushed by the wheels of a passing cab.

'Hey,' the man cried. 'You can't just – '

'I just did,' Moses said.

And walked away. No smile on his face. Not even a backward glance.

*

South from Soho.

It had always been a favourite walk of his. It used all the senses. The sultry neon of strip-joints, arguments in Chinese, rack on rack of foreign magazines, the forest-fire crackle of pork frying, a million brands of cigarettes, cauliflowers bowling along the gutters, snatches of crisp disco-funk from curtained doorways, the steamy reek of Dim Sum whisked into the street by ventilator-fans. He usually dawdled. This time, though, he walked fast, automatically. A turbulent mixture of emotions drove him along like high-octane fuel. If he slowed he would explode. He didn't understand this impetus they gave him. He was no mechanic.

He suspected that he made an impression on the city that afternoon. His size, his haste – both excessive. As he burst into Piccadilly Circus he saw one tourist point and giggle. 'Look at that English. Crazy, no?'

Yes, crazy. He had this exaggerated sense of his own power – as if, simply by walking across London, he could alter the course of history. On Haymarket he stepped out in front of a chauffeured limousine. The limo swerved, threw its passenger's bald head against the window. Afterwards Moses thought he had placed that bald head. It belonged to a senior cabinet minister. Would the minister now make an uncharacteristically shaky speech in the House of Commons?

Moses crossed Trafalgar Square on a diagonal, ignoring the traffic lights, the screech of brakes, the horns. He didn't even stop to swear at the pigeons (something he had got into the habit of doing recently). He stormed straight into Whitehall, oblivious, vacant, irresistible. The horseguards fought to control their mounts as he passed. No doubt several of the tourist snaps taken at the time would come out blurred. Shame. He wondered if he had rattled any of the windows in 10 Downing Street. He hoped so. Oh, for a million like me, he thought. Did the Ministry of Defence report any slight earth tremors? It didn't seem beyond the bounds of possibility. Not even Elliot, friend and benefactor, could put a stop to the projectile that Moses had become. He advanced to meet Moses, hands outstretched in greeting, only to be unceremoniously brushed aside and left spinning on his heels, like someone in a cartoon.

Moses didn't slacken his pace until he reached his bathroom. Never had he needed the soothing properties of his bath more urgently. He soaked for an hour and a half, waiting for calmness to descend, hardly daring to think. He lay in the bath until the water turned cold for the third time, until all he could see was a faint orange glimmer on the surface.

Alan dead.

Excluded from Mary's sorrow, confined to his own. That and the swirl of water as he stirred an arm or a leg. How close he was to that original memory of his.

Alone. The darkness. The sound of water. Dimly he began to understand his fascination with baths.

Later he walked into the bedroom, lay down on the bed and fell asleep.

*

He woke two hours later, sticky and confused. Dreams he couldn't remember rustled in his head like tissue-paper. His mouth tasted sour. His anger had curdled, turned to defiance. He picked up the phone and weighed it in his hand. After a moment's hesitation, he called Jackson.

A fumbling on the other end, then a stammered, 'Hello?'

'Jackson?'

'Moses!' Jackson cried. 'I haven't seen you for ages. How are you?'

'Not too good at the moment. What're you doing tonight?'

'Tonight I'm busy. What about tomorrow?'

Moses hung his head, said nothing.

'Why?' Jackson went on. 'What's wrong?'

'Nothing. I just feel like seeing someone.' Moses allowed himself a wry smile. 'It's a pity I can't see that ghost you're always going on about. That'd be better than nothing.'

Jackson produced a silence so incredulous that Moses wondered what he had said.

'What ghost?' Jackson asked eventually.

'The ghost you told me about. The ghost that was sitting next to me. You know, on the sofa,' and Moses pointed at the sofa, as if it proved something.

Another silence from Jackson, equally incredulous.

'You do remember,' Moses said, 'don't you?'

'I hate to disappoint you, Moses, but there isn't any ghost.'

Moses gaped into the phone. 'What?'

'There isn't a ghost. There never was. I made it up.'

'You what?'

'I made it up. I thought you might be lonely living up there all by yourself, so I invented a ghost for you – '

'But the coat-hook – ' Moses broke in. 'The chair – '

'They were just props, that's all. It was a story, you see.'

Moses sank on to the windowsill. He didn't know what to say.

'Sorry if I messed you around, Moses.' It sounded as if Jackson meant it.

'That's all right,' Moses said. 'It's my fault. I mean, I was the one who believed it, wasn't I?'

'Of course you believed it. You needed to.'

Needed to? Moses was about to mock when he recognised a sort of wisdom in what Jackson was saying. Moses had never thought of himself as lonely before, but didn't it make sense? Certainly he felt that way now. Typical of Jackson to pick up on something like that. Jackson had sensitivity, insight. He was a fund of delicate perceptions and responses. Back in August Moses had asked Louise whether there was anything going on between her and Jackson. Louise had smiled. 'Well?' he had said. 'Is there?' 'Sort of,' she had replied. 'What do you mean, *sort of*?' Louise had shrugged. 'I slept with him once.' 'And?' 'And what?' 'And what happened?' Louise's smile had deepened, become private. 'He kissed my feet,' she said.

Moses could see Jackson now, almost as if they were in the same room. Those narrowed eyes, that enigmatic smile. A buddha, that's what Jackson was. Nervous and wiry and not gold at all, but a buddha just the same.

'You still there, Moses?'

'Yeah, I'm still here. Just thinking, that's all. You know, it's funny, but you're absolutely right. Even though I didn't think about her much, I kind of got used to the idea of her being there. I wasn't living alone. I was sharing with this woman who I never saw.'

'Well, now she's moved out,' Jackson said. 'Think of it like that.'

'Yeah.' Moses laughed softly to himself. 'You know something, Jackson? I didn't like people using her chair.'

'Sometimes, Moses,' and Moses could hear Jackson smiling, 'just sometimes, you really take the biscuit.'

'Yes,' Moses nodded. 'Yes, I suppose I do.'

After he had hung up he leaned back against the window and sighed. With every phone-call, another loss. First Mary, now the ghost. Only the past for company.

He decided to risk one last call. He dialled Vince's number.

'Yeah?'

Vince was home. Good.

'Vince? It's Moses.'

'So what.'

'I need a favour.'

'No.'

'Just shut up and listen for a moment, will you. I want to get out of it.'

'When?'

'Tonight. Now.'

'What the fuck's going on?'

'None of your business. Can you organise it or not?'

Vince said nothing for a few seconds. Weighing up possibilities, no doubt. Sometimes Moses thought there must be scales in Vince's mind. A gram of this, a spoon of that. Everything measured out in little envelopes.

'Tell you what,' Moses said. 'I'll meet you in that pub opposite you. About eight. You know the one I mean?'

''Course I fucking know. It's my territory.'

'See you in a bit.'

'Hang on. How long're you going to be there?'

'Till I fall over.'

'This sounds like fun,' Vince leered.

'I doubt it,' Moses said, and hung up.

*

Moses arrived first, as he had expected to. Vince only did two kinds of waiting. He waited for his dealer, and he waited for girlfriends who had left him to come back. His dealer always showed, the girlfriends rarely did. Mere friends didn't rate as a priority.

Moses ordered a Pils and settled in a quiet corner. He was drinking to get drunk, drinking fast and with determination, so he would be able to sleep that night. He wanted time to pass, distance to happen. Like when you doze on a train. He sat there pretending the pub was a train.

Several stations later Vince turned up. He grinned at the debris of empty bottles on the table. That was what he liked to see.

'Shit,' he said. 'Must be my round.'

Unheard-of for Vince, this, but Moses didn't even crack a smile.

Vince obviously hadn't heard about Alan's death and Moses wasn't going to break the news to him so he felt weighed down at the beginning by stuff he couldn't offload, but as they moved from drink to drink and pub to pub, ever deeper into a world where objects and people Xeroxed themselves in front of his eyes, he floated free of all that. Time concertina'd, every action danced. He talked to Vince without saying anything, which was how most of his friends talked, which was how Vince, especially, talked, which was why he had called Vince in the first place. Vince didn't ask questions. Vince wasn't interested. They went to the Gents together to take Vince's sulphate and there was sufficient intimacy in that: two pairs of shoes showing under a single cubicle door.

At midnight they were leaving a basement wine-bar somewhere in Chelsea. Moses had been delayed over a discrepancy in the bill. When he climbed the stairs he found Vince wrestling with part of the décor. Some kind of framed print.

'What the fuck're you doing, Vince?'

'What's it look like?'

'You've got no idea, have you.'

'Give us a hand then.'

'Get out the way.' He shoved Vince aside. He gave the print one swift tug and it came away from the wall. A screw scuttled down the stairs and round the corner.

He ran up the stairs and turned left on to the street. When he reached the corner he stopped to inspect the print. It was an airbrush drawing of a Coca-Cola bottle. He leaned it against an iron railing and was just turning to ask Vince why he had such fucking awful taste when somebody grabbed his arm and swung him round. There were about three policemen standing there with about another three policemen standing behind them. He almost said Hello, Hello, Hello. He didn't, but the thought made him grin.

'Oh, so we think it's funny, do we?' one of the policemen said.

Fuck off, Moses thought.

Another picked the print up off the pavement and examined it with great interest as if he was in the market for that kind of thing. He probably was.

'Is this yours?' he said.

'Certainly not,' Moses said. What an insult.

'Where did you get it from then?'

'Over there.'

'Over where?'

'That wine-bar over there.'

Where was Vince? Moses wondered. His bloody idea. He glanced over his shoulder and saw Vince being questioned by some other policemen. It was unclear exactly how many.

'That your mate, is it?'

He didn't like the way they kept jumping to conclusions so he didn't say anything this time. He had the impression – a dim impression, submerged in pints and pints of alcohol – that he had said too much already. He silently cursed that honesty of his which always floated to the surface when he was drunk.

'I think,' the policeman with the print said, 'that we'd better return this to where it belongs.'

The policeman who was holding Moses reached for his walkie-talkie and, just for a second or two, his grip on Moses's arm relaxed. Moses jerked free and made a break for the nearest side-street. Darkness flowed round his body like fur. Lights bounced on either side of him. Like swimming, this running. So effortless and smooth. Ridiculous, actually. He wanted to stop and laugh. His idea (inspired, he thought, by memories of Top Cat) was to hide in a dustbin until the policemen blundered past and then dart off in the opposite direction. But when he turned the corner he couldn't see a single dustbin. Not one. No dustbins? he thought. Where do they put all their rubbish? He was still running, but the confidence was draining out of him. Dismay filtered into his bloodstream. Escape began to seem less and less feasible. As he looked over his shoulder to see where the policemen were, his foot caught the raised lip of a paving-stone and he went sprawling. The next thing he knew, there were half a dozen policemen kneeling on his back.

'Got you, you bastard.'

'Resisting arrest, eh?'

'You're in big trouble, you are, mate.'

Their breath stank of triumph and sour milk. He tried to look round to see exactly who the breath belonged to, only to have his face rammed sideways into the pavement.

'Don't you bloody move, smartarse.'

'You're in big trouble, you are.'

He didn't move.

'All right, get on your feet.'

How could he do that? At least five of them were still kneeling on his back.

'I said get up, cunt.'

He laughed. 'You told me not to move.'

He shouldn't have laughed. A fist (or something designed for a similar purpose) crashed into his kidneys. He gasped. These were hard men, he realised. They would smile at you and then knock the teeth out the back of your head if you smiled back.

'Got a right one here.'

'He's in big trouble, he is.'

'Come on, get up.'

They eased off his back – unwillingly, it seemed to him – and gripped him by the arms. All right, he thought. I'll get up.

They marched him back towards the wine-bar, two in front, two behind, one on either side. Everything bar handcuffs. Two squad cars waited on the road, engines idling. The crackle of walkie-talkies. Blue whirling lights. A small crowd gathering. This can't be real, he thought. This can't all be for me.

They passed Vince skulking in a doorway. He made a face, powerless, apologetic, and shrugged. There weren't any six policemen kneeling on *his* back and calling him bastard, Moses noticed.

They escorted him back through the door, down the stairs (past the two ragged holes and the telltale rectangle of clean white wallpaper) and into the bar. One policeman stood guard over him while two others held a conference with a squat middle-aged man who was, presumably, the manager. The few people left in the bar stared at Moses with open curiosity.

He heard the word *prosecute*. Heav–y. He exchanged a brief glance with the manager. The manager's eyes were loaded with scorn and disgust. Oh, come *on*, Moses wanted to say. I wasn't going to *steal* that thing. Who'd want to steal anything that corny?

'He liked the place so much,' the girl behind the bar was saying, 'that he had to take a piece of it with him.'

Now that hurt. He remembered smiling at her earlier in the evening and he remembered her almost smiling back. She wouldn't even look at him now. She went on polishing glasses, her eyes screened by her hair, her lips twisted in contempt.

Some kind of decision was reached. One of the policemen pushed him through the bar, up the stairs and out on to the street. A squad car drew alongside. The policeman spoke into his walkie-talkie.

' – have successfully apprehended the criminal – '

Criminal? *Criminal?* I'm not a criminal, Moses thought.

Oh yes you are, said the policeman's face.

Moses was bundled into the back of the car. He had to sit between two policemen, his shoulders drawn together, his arms dangling between his legs. The lights of the King's Road raked through the interior as they moved away. He felt a sudden sense of elation at the novelty of it all.

'See that shop?' he cried. 'That's where I bought these boots!'

The two policemen in front exchanged a glance.

What was wrong with them? Moses wondered. They'd made their arrest, the tension was over, why couldn't they loosen up, have a bit of fun? He stared at them one by one, these four policemen who didn't know how to enjoy themselves. Where was wit? Where was laughter? Where, if nothing else, was job satisfaction? He wanted to entertain them, but all his jokes fell on stony faces.

Then a frightening thought occurred to him. So frightening that he was almost too afraid to ask.

'You're not Peach's men, are you?'

Both the policemen in the back stared straight ahead, expressionless, unblinking.

'You know. *Peach. Chief Inspector* Peach.'

Not a flicker of recognition.

'He runs a police station. Somewhere down south. Pretty small operation by your standards, I suppose.'

Still nothing.

'You really don't know him?'

'Don't know what you're talking about, mate,' the driver said.

'Well,' Moses said, 'that's a relief.'

But then he thought, they *would* say that, wouldn't they. If they *were* Peach's men. He tried another tack.

'Where are you taking me?'

They wouldn't say.

He leaned forwards and peered at the fuel gauge. Almost empty. Not enough to get to New Egypt then. Thank God for that.

'Hey,' he said, 'careful you don't run out of petrol.'

'I think you'd better shut it,' the policeman on his left said.

'Oh, *life*,' Moses exclaimed. 'I was beginning to think you were all dead. Bit worrying being driven along by four dead policemen.'

'*Christ*,' the driver muttered.

The car swung left into a narrow backstreet. Now Moses knew he hadn't been kidnapped by Peach, he began to relax, take in his surroundings. They passed a girl with blonde hair standing by the side of the road. She looked at him as if she knew him. He waved. The girl smiled. Her smile reached through the closed car window, past the taciturn policemen, and into Moses's heart, where it glowed. There is nothing to beat the smile of a girl you have never seen before, he thought.

'Peach offered me a job, you know.' There was something about the silence of these policemen that made him talk. 'He said I'd make an excellent police officer. No, *magnificent*, he said. What d'you think of that?'

Before anyone could reply they had pulled into the kerb and parked. Moses was manhandled out of the car and on to the pavement. Seen in the bleak light of the street-lamps, the policemen had hard closed faces, the kind of faces that believe in duty, violence, Margaret Thatcher, and a good chauvinistic fuck on Friday nights.

'You know, I don't like Peach very much,' he laughed, 'but I like him better than you lot.'

The grip on his upper arm tightened. He would have a bruise there in the morning – and it wouldn't be the only one either.

*

He was escorted into a grey room with bare walls and no windows. Two policemen in regulation shirtsleeves stood on either side of a solid wooden desk. One was tall and sallow; a few strands of black hair had made the lonely journey across the top of his bald head. The other, stockier, had a bull neck, sloping shoulders, and a blur of ginger hair on his forearms. They had already taken his name and address (they had taken his belt too, and they had dropped it into a transparent plastic bag which made the belt look important and rather dangerous, and meant he had to hold his trousers up by hand). Now they were telling him to take off his boots. Try it sometime when you're drunk. Hold on to your trousers with one hand and reach down for your laces with the other. Impossible. Either your trousers fall down or you do.

After two or three attempts he said, 'I can't.'

The tall policeman walked round the desk and stood over him. 'Take your bloody boots off, Moses.' The Moses was a sneer.

The stocky policeman laughed. 'Are you a bit Jewish by any chance, Moses? Are you a bit of a fucking yid?' He draped his forefinger across his nose as he spoke.

'None of your business,' Moses said. For which he was shoved in the back by the tall policeman. He keeled over, landed face down on the floor.

'Take your boots off, Moses.'

'I thought it was only blacks you beat up,' Moses said, and instantly regretted it. A highly polished shoe smashed into his ribs.

'Didn't hurt you, did I, Moses?'

'You're making things difficult, Moses Bloody Highness.' The tall policeman read these last three words off his official form as if Bloody was Moses's middle name.

'So are you,' Moses said.

'I suggest you shut your mouth and get on with it.'

Both the policemen had voices that grated like machines for grinding the organs, bones and flesh of cattle. They would make mincemeat of him if he wasn't careful. He thought of Mary's voice and almost cried. He fumbled with his boots again, managed to undo one of the laces.

'Look at that. He did it.'

'Amazing.'

'Now do it up again.'

'What is this?' Moses said. 'Kindergarten?'

'You don't deserve to be treated any other way – '

'Bastard.' The stocky policeman liked to finish off the tall policeman's sentences for him. They were a real team.

Moses tied the lace. 'Now what?'

'Now take your boots off.'

He muttered under his breath. He untied the lace again. Then he stood up. He let go of his trousers, gripped his left boot in both hands and began to hop round the floor. It just wouldn't come off. His trousers slipped down to his knees, tied his legs together. He fell over again.

'I'm bored with this game,' he said.

'You're not doing very well, are you – '

'Jewboy.'

'Not quite so fucking smart as you thought.'

'Oh piss off, will you?' he said. Anger was beginning to seep through the many layers of his drunkenness.

A shoe pinned his wrist to the floor.

'We don't like that kind of language.'

'Specially not from a stupid cunt like you.'

The tall policeman moved towards him, a sheen of sweat on his high balding forehead.

'I'm going to report you two,' Moses said.

'Did you say report?'

'Yeah. To Chief Inspector Peach.' Bravado now, bluff, anything.

'Peach,' one of the policemen scoffed.

'You piece of shit,' said the other, and landed a shoe just above Moses's left eye.

'Haha,' Moses said. Red and orange planets whirled across the darkness as he closed his eyes. One of them looked like Saturn. 'If I said Manchester, would you start dribbling?'

The shoe landed again, somewhere on the back of his thighs.

'Crime is order,' he shouted as they came at him again. 'A policeman said that.'

'I'll give you crime is order.'

'Crime is order, my foot.'

Two different shoes landed simultaneously in two different and tender places.

'All right, that's enough.'

'Peach's important,' Moses murmured. 'Peach's my friend. He'll be down on you like a ton of bricks.'

But the policemen had gone and he was alone.

Cold lino floor. Distantly aching body. One grazed hand beside his face, the redness too close to his eyes. Unwillingness to move.

Cold.

*

It was some time before the door opened again.

'Would you come this way, please?'

Moses had propped himself against a wall. He turned his head and saw a young police officer with a soft face and freckles. His voice polite, almost subservient. Classic interrogation technique, Moses thought. One moment he was bastard, the next he was sir.

'What've you got lined up for me now?' But the alcohol and the drugs had worn off and he felt drab and slow, utterly incurious. Police procedure – the exhaustion, the monotony, the waiting – had tranquillised him; he would submit to each new development quite passively.

'Fingerprints,' the new policeman said.

Wincing, Moses climbed to his feet. He followed the new policeman out of the room, down a corridor that smelt like a hospital (and no wonder, he thought, feeling his injuries), and into a room that was as cluttered as the previous room had been bare.

The policeman produced a packet of Embassy Number One. 'Like a cigarette, Moses?'

Suspicious, Moses searched into the policeman's freckled face; it contained nothing but innocence. 'Thanks,' he said. 'You smoke the same brand as my dad.'

The policeman lit the cigarette for him. While Moses smoked, the policeman prepared a flat oblong tin and several printed sheets of paper.

'Give me your hand,' the policeman said.

Moses raised an eyebrow and crushed his cigarette out.

'The fingerprints,' the policeman explained with a grin. 'It's easier if I guide your hand. Unless you've done it before, of course.'

'No,' Moses said. 'This is my first time.'

He watched as the policeman took his fingers one by one and carefully but firmly rolled them from left to right, first across the ink-pad in the oblong tin, then across a sheet of paper that had been divided into squares, one for each finger. He realised that he was collecting the kind of information that Vince specialised in. That fucker. This was all his fault.

Afterwards, when he was washing the ink off his fingers, he said over his shoulder, 'You know, I think you're OK.'

The policeman grinned.

'Seriously,' Moses said. 'I've come across quite a few policemen recently and you're one of the nicest I've come across.'

The policeman's grin broadened. 'Thank you,' he said.

'What's your name?'

'Harry.'

'Not Dirty Harry?'

'That's an old joke, Moses.'

'Sorry, Harry. People always make the same jokes about my name too.' Moses dried his hands on the towel provided. 'Hey, Harry. I was thinking of becoming a policeman. What d'you reckon?'

Harry shook his head slowly. 'I think you'd better forget the idea.'

'Why's that, Harry?'

Harry pointed at the fingerprints on the table. 'I don't think they'd look too good on your application form.'

Something sank in Moses. A slow lift in the tower-block of his body. Going down. 'Oh yeah. Shit. I suppose you're right.' Then he turned and looked appealingly at Harry. 'But I would've been tall enough, wouldn't I?'

'Oh yes.' Harry squinted up at Moses. 'You would've been tall enough, all right.'

After the fingerprints came the mug-shots. One frontal and two profiles were required. Harry sat Moses down in a metal chair, then crouched behind his camera. He told Moses which way to look and not to smile.

'So I have to look serious, do I?' Moses said.

'That's right.'

'Can't have our criminals smiling, can we?' Moses composed himself, assuming an expression of great, if slightly wounded, nobility. His chin raised, he thought momentarily of Mary again.

Harry straightened up. 'You can relax now.'

'I bet those were pretty good pictures,' Moses said. 'Could you get me a few copies?'

Harry laughed. 'I'm afraid not. It's against regulations.'

'Shame, that. Are you sure?'

'I'm sure. Now there's one last thing, then you can go. You have the right to make a written statement. You don't have to, you understand. But you can. If you want. It's entirely up to you.'

Moses considered the proposition for a few moments, then he said, 'Yes, I'd like to. I feel like writing something.'

Harry sighed. He gave Moses a biro and the appropriate form (with its heavily ruled lines, it looked like the bars on a cell if you turned it sideways), and left the room. When he returned five minutes later with two cups of coffee he peered over Moses's shoulder. He sighed again.

'What's wrong, Harry?' Moses said. 'Don't you like it?'

Harry peered over Moses's shoulder again, then he frowned and scratched his head. 'Are you sure you want to do this? You don't have to, you know.'

Moses read through what he had written so far. At some points he nodded, at others he chuckled. It made a good story. He decided to cross out the bit about the policemen's breath smelling like sour milk. That probably wouldn't go down too well in court.

'Yes,' he said, 'I want to do it. One thing, though. What do I say about being beaten up by those two policemen in the other room?'

Harry took a deep breath. 'That's a very serious allegation, Moses.'

'It's not an allegation, Harry. It's the truth. Have you seen my eyebrow?'

'I understood,' Harry said slowly, 'that you sustained that injury while resisting arrest.'

Moses subjected Harry to long and careful scrutiny. Then he drew a line, very deliberately, under what he had written. 'In that case,' he said, 'I've finished.'

'Don't worry,' Harry said as he signed the statement, 'it'll be all right.' (It wasn't all right. Two weeks later Moses appeared at Horseferry Road Magistrates' Court. The judge told him he was childish and irresponsible, and fined him £50. He almost charged him with contempt of court too. For leaning on the dock. The judge had white hair and a bright pink face. Moses had never seen anyone who looked so consistently furious.)

'You can collect your things now,' Harry said. 'There are some friends of yours waiting for you.'

Moses tossed his polystyrene cup into the waste-paper basket. 'Thanks, Harry.' He paused by the door. 'Just think. We could've been working together.'

Harry grinned and scratched his head.

'Not any more, though. Eh, Harry?'

'Goodbye, Moses.'

'See you, Harry.'

Moses walked back to the duty-room where he was handed his personal effects. Through a window of reinforced glass he could see Vince, Eddie and some new girl of Eddie's. She was wearing skin-tight red and white striped trousers. The officer on duty seemed to think that she was something to do with Moses.

'Blimey, look at that,' he drooled. 'You're a lucky bastard.'

'Arrested, beaten up, my Wednesday night ruined,' Moses murmured. 'Oh yes, I'm a lucky bastard all right.'

But the officer didn't seem to hear him. Still mesmerised by those stripes.

Moses buckled his belt with great relief. How nice to have two hands again. Amazing invention, belts. He had always taken them for granted in the past. Not any more.

He met his friends on the steps of the police station like a hero returning.

It was just after two in the morning.

They all went dancing.

*

Everybody who came into contact with Mary during the six days between Alan's death and the funeral seemed, either openly or covertly, to be congratulating her on the way she was coping. *Coping*. The word nauseated her. The way she saw it, that kind of sympathy came from the same family as condescension, a distant relation, perhaps, but still family, and if there was one thing she couldn't stomach it was being condescended to, however obscurely. She thought she knew what they were picking up on, though. They were picking up on surface stuff: her dry eyes, her efficient manner – her armour, in other words. She wore a lot of lipstick and kohl. She wore stiff fabrics too, nothing that swirled or floated, nothing vague. Her airiness had evaporated completely. She displayed instead a kind of ironic practicality that verged, at times, on callousness. 'No, the funeral's happening very quickly,' she heard herself inform a neighbour on the phone. 'Apparently not many people died in Muswell Hill last week.' Inside, though, she was still trying to get used to the idea that she had been cheated. Her. Cheated. Her *anger* at that. She wanted to whirl round and, levelling a finger, cry, 'Don't think you can pull the wool over *my* eyes.' But you can't talk to death like that. Death doesn't have to listen to anyone.

She saw only the necessary people – the priest, the funeral directors, Alan's father. She made an exception for Maurice. He came round on the Tuesday. He didn't treat her as if she was ill, or wounded, or mad. He simply looked at her across the table without pity or embarrassment, the slow bones of his hands cradling a cup of tea, the right shoulder of his grey jacket worn shiny by long familiarity with dustbins. That stare of his spread a safety-net that she could fall into. Those hands made her feel strangely comfortable. She even smiled as she said, 'I want you to take all Alan's clothes away with you.'

'You mean dump them?' he said.

She shook her head. 'No. I want you to have them.'

The dustman lowered his eyes.

She watched his hands wander on the surface of the table. She thought of plants moving on the bottom of the sea.

'I know you never really spoke to Alan,' she went on, 'but you would have liked each other. I know you would. I can't imagine anyone I would rather give his clothes to. Please take them, Maurice. Who knows,' and she surprised herself by laughing, 'some of them might even fit.'

'You do me good,' she told him as she showed him to the door. 'Come again, won't you?'

'Next Tuesday suit you?' He grinned at her. It was one of his jokes.

'Next Tuesday's fine.' She watched him shamble down the garden path, his feet flapping on the concrete as if his ankle-joints needed tightening.

Her smile lasted.

When his lorry had turned the corner, she walked back indoors, stood by the phone. Facts, she thought. Facts, not emotions. She knew roughly what had happened to Alan. She knew that he had collapsed on Ealing Broadway at about two forty-five on Saturday afternoon. She knew that he had died of a thrombosis, a hardening of the artery walls which, according to the doctor who signed the death certificate, ought to have been detected years before. ('*Ought?*' she had wanted to scream at him, this placid careful man, because he had, for those few minutes, represented the entire profession to her. 'Why *wasn't* it then? Why *didn't* you?') Now she needed to know *how* it had happened. She needed an eye-witness account. She needed to be able to see every detail.

She dialled the police in Ealing. After twenty minutes of being transferred from one extension to another, after repeating her story at least half a dozen times, she was given the number of a Mrs Hart (a name that Moses must have run his finger over a thousand times, she thought, while searching for his own). Mrs Hart, she was told, had been present at the scene of her husband's death and would be able to provide her with the information she required. That same afternoon she drove to Ealing. Mrs Hart lived in a walk-up council block not far from Ealing Broadway. The stairs smelt of urine and then, higher up, of meat-fat. Mrs Hart's flat was on the fourth floor.

When Mary knocked on the door of number 72, an old woman with silver hair answered. 'Mrs Hart?'

The old woman nodded.

'I'm Mrs Shirley.'

'They said you was comin'.' Mrs Hart ushered Mary into her lounge. 'Wos your name, love?'

Mary told her.

'Mine's Ruby. Ought to've been born on Valentine's Day, didn' I?' Her narrow eyes gleamed like an animal's – trust rather than cunning, though.

They sat down on a brown and yellow sofa. A gas fire bubbled in the corner.

'I'm sorry about your 'usband.' Ruby laid a hand on Mary's wrist. 'It's a bloody world, isn' it?'

Mary nodded. 'I wanted to ask you what happened that afternoon. What you saw. It's so hard not having been there.'

'I can imagine, love.' Ruby shifted to face Mary, her hands folded like gloves in her lap. 'Well,' and she took a deep breath, 'I was on me way to the shops. Fifteen minutes' walk from 'ere. It's the steps, see. Murder on me legs.' She rolled her eyes and Mary smiled. 'I was walkin' up the main road when this bus come along, number sixty-free I fink it was. There's nobody at the stop, but the bus stops anyway, to let somebody off. Then this gentleman goes past me, well, I mean you can tell, can't you, an' 'e's shoutin' an' wavin' an' all sorts for the bus to wait for 'im like. The driver sees 'im runnin', but you know what some of them drivers're like, right bloody bastards if you excuse me language. Wos 'e do? 'E puts 'is foot down, dun 'e. Well,' another deep breath, 'the gentleman, 'e carries on runnin' 'cos the bus is goin' pretty slow, then all of a sudden 'e keels over. Jus' keels over right there on the street. I fought 'e must of tripped or summin' so I goes over to 'elp 'im up like. 'E's lying on 'is back in 'e, wiv 'is eyes open but sort of starin' an' 'e sees me an' 'e smiles an' 'e says, "Stupid," 'e says an' I says, "Wos stupid?", finking 'e means me an' 'e says, "Fancy slippin' on a banana like that," an' I look round for a banana an' there in't no banana is there an' I look at 'im an' I'm about to tell 'im there in't no banana an' what's 'e talkin' about banana but then I look a bit closer like an' I see 'e's dead. Well, there's all these people shoutin' about get a nambulance an' I says, "Wos the point of a nambulance, 'e's dead in 'e." An' 'e was wan 'e. Frombosis, the doctor said. Nuffin' to do wiv no banana.'

Tears were falling from Mary's eyes. Alan had died alone. Among strangers. Without understanding. She had been so far away. Too far away to comfort, to explain, to reassure. That degree of distance from someone she had been so close to. It dismantled her armour. Her make-up ran, her body crumpled in Ruby's arms. That one weekend away had opened up a gap for ever. She couldn't leap over or build a bridge. She could only sit at the edge and pour her tears into it. One day, when she had cried enough, perhaps she would be able to swim across. She would be returning from that weekend for the rest of her life. Even on her deathbed she still wouldn't quite have reached home.

'You poor darlin',' Ruby murmured. 'It's a bloody world.'

As Mary drove back to Muswell Hill, a strange thought occurred to her. A middle-aged man – try, she told herself, to see him objectively, even if only for a moment – collapses on a busy street. A woman bends to help him. The flow of pedestrians is interrupted. A crowd gathers. The traffic jams as cars slow down and drivers peer through windscreens. One of the city's main arteries is blocked for maybe thirty seconds. The traffic police appear. They gesticulate with their immaculate white gloves. The cars move on. The crowd disperses. The street regains its rhythm.

But there are no traffic police in the middle-aged man's veins.

The blockage is permanent.

He dies.

Yes, she thought. Alan had articulated, on a large scale, the drama that had taken place inside his own body. He had externalised his death. She

wanted to tell him that, she wanted to see the expression on his face –
when she thought of things like that she always told him – but she could
only have told him if he was still alive, if the whole thing had never
happened, and then there wouldn't have been anything to tell. Grief's
vicious circle. He was dead, and you could go round and round, but you
couldn't go back. There was no reversing up a one-way street like death.
No sir, there was a big ticket for that.

*

The day before the funeral a wreath of white flowers and wild ferns was
delivered to the house in Muswell Hill. Alison carried it into the kitchen
and laid it on the table.

'It's from Moses.' She read the note, then looked across at Mary. 'Isn't
he coming tomorrow?'

Mary was standing in front of the mirror. She tilted her head sideways,
adjusted an earring. 'No,' she said.

'Why not?'

Mary didn't answer.

'He's entitled to, isn't he?' Alison said, not querulous exactly, but
insistent. 'I thought he was – ' and she paused – 'a member of the family.'

Mary recognised her own words. She chose not to acknowledge them.
'He doesn't know about it.'

'What?' Rebecca was lingering in the doorway. 'He doesn't know that
Daddy – '

'He doesn't know about the funeral,' Mary cut in.

'Why not?' Alison persisted.

Mary turned from the mirror. This was the point at which the truth
became too complex, too unwieldy, to manage, at the moment at least, and
lies, the lackeys that they were, presented themselves, oily and obsequious.
And so she said simply, 'I didn't tell him,' which closed the door in the
face of her daughters' questions and the lies that wanted to serve as answers.
The two girls seemed to accept this, despite the look they swapped behind
(or almost behind) their mother's back. Alison murmured something about
not being able to breathe; she moved away and opened a window. Rebecca
did something nervous with her feet. Mary forced herself to leave the room.

The tension stayed with her. At four in the morning she threw on a silk
dressing-gown and walked out on to the terrace. Such a wind. She filled
her lungs with fierce air. Clouds, great jagged sheets of steel, clashed
overhead. The moon showed briefly, dented and blackened, the bottom of
an old saucepan. They told her no stories, nothing she could use to explain

her withholding, her dishonesty, not even to herself. She stood on the terrace and listened to the crash and jangle of the night until she, too, seemed turned to metal by the cold, until the wind had blown all thoughts from her head. Towards dawn she slept.

In the morning she opened the doors of her wardrobe, and the rows and rows of black clothes that she saw there immobilised her. It's almost as if I've been preparing for this moment, she thought. It's almost as if I've spent my entire life preparing for this death, this grief, this widowhood. With every black dress bought, with every black accessory received. Preparing, preparing. She dropped on to the bed, remembered her mother on a rare visit to London saying, in that deliberately puzzled voice she could put on (as if grappling with a problem to which she could imagine no possible solution), 'I simply do not understand this *love-affair* you seem to have with black.' She couldn't think what her reply had been. Something withering, no doubt. But now the sight of all that black crushed and sickened her. When Alison walked in twenty minutes later, she still hadn't moved.

'You've got to get dressed, Mary,' Alison said. 'The car will be here soon.'

Mary didn't look round. 'I'm going to wear white.'

'You can't. It's just not the right time for something like that.'

Perhaps she responded to the panic in her daughter's voice. 'Not the right time,' she repeated. But with no irony, no venom. Without another word, she submitted to Alison's choice of dress.

*

When a funeral happens, people don't usually say, 'It's a nice day for it,' but if it had been a wedding or a picnic or a flower-show, Mary thought, that's what they would have said. Last night's wind had cleared the sky of clouds. As they drove from the church to the graveyard in their hired grey limousine, they passed old men on benches, hatless, sucking on their teeth, women in gardens pinning wet clothes to the wide thin smiles of their washing-lines, shopkeepers in their doorways, slit-eyed against this unexpected sunlight. So many people out. The world and his wife, she thought. And then, moments later: the world and his widow. Not self-pity, this. Accuracy.

The car turned in through black wrought-iron gates.

'Excuse me,' she said suddenly, 'but I'd like to walk the rest of the way, if you don't mind.'

Their chauffeur, a man whose face was as rigid as the profile on a coin, stopped the car. She stepped out. Her children followed. She looked about her, recognised the cat that was dozing on a headstone. She breathed, almost with relief, the familiar air of the cemetery. She had walked its paths so many times. With Alan, with the children, and, most recently, with Moses. If Moses had come to the funeral he might have been surprised, even disappointed, she thought. He would have expected some less formal, less conventional event, unaware of how the process is designed to carry you, like a raft, away from the wreckage of someone's death, away from that whirlpool it creates, to carry you as effortlessly as possible into calmer waters where you can begin to think again. It was a funeral like a million others before it. The usual words, the usual music, the usual moments of solemnity. For once, too, she fitted in because everyone was wearing black. It almost seemed to her as if they were imitating her. Which, in their grief, perhaps, they were.

They reached the graveside. Now the priest began to recite the traditional phrases. They have beauty, she thought, staring away into the sky. A used beauty, a worn beauty, like stone steps worn smooth and slightly concave by five, ten, twenty centuries of feet. They were phrases everybody passed through. There were no exceptions. At least they contained that truth. We're all pretty ordinary, she thought. All pretty ordinary when it comes down to it. That's what the phrases said.

Her eyes drew closer, moved over the faces of her children.

Sean stood at the head of the grave. Hands clasped, hair combed, pale. Awkward in a black jacket, and trousers that itched. He would be waiting for something dramatic to happen, something to fix the day in his memory: a partial eclipse of the sun, a riderless horse galloping between the stones, an explosion in that house beyond the cemetery wall. His eyes would be aching with the constant fruitless quest for symbols. Her gaze passed to Alison. Alison's hair glowed under a black headscarf, mere embers of the fire it usually was. She seemed to be examining the brass handles on the coffin. Then her eyes lifted, moved across the polished wood, paused on that discreet metal plaque. She would be thinking how new everything looked, how horribly new and clean. And how Alan had always hated anything that looked new. How he had loved old things, things with stories in their surfaces, things with histories. Death had turned him into someone she didn't recognise. Rebecca was standing next to Mary, so Mary couldn't see her face. She could only feel the grip of her daughter's hand, a grip that tightened as a cluster of gulls suddenly rose screeching against a screen of evergreens.

Lumps of mud thudded on to the coffin lid, dirt on the cleanness that Alison abhorred. Like somebody knocking on a door. *Knock, knock.* Who's there? *Dad*. Dad who? *No, not Dad. Dead.* Mary thought she saw Sean's leg begin to tremble. She could imagine him running, running over this grass that was bumpy with other people's dead, running to escape the trembling. She felt Rebecca's grip tighten again and watched her as she leaned forwards, peered down into that fascinating oblong hole in the ground. It was so deep it made Rebecca shiver, feel dizzy; she almost lost her balance.

Then they were walking towards the limousine and the expressionless chauffeur who was waiting to drive them back to the house where there was to be, as Rebecca had whispered disbelievingly to Alison the night before, *a party because Dad's dead.*

*

Two days later Mary stood in front of her wardrobe again. She had decided that everything black had to go. Dresses, underwear, accessories – the lot. She removed her black clothes from their hangers, their shelves, their drawers, and dropped them, one by one, on to the bed behind her. The heap grew and grew until she caught herself staring, exactly as her mother would have done, with incredulous uncomprehending eyes. Oh how it all turns round, she thought.

She counted sixty-one separate black items in all (not including shoes) and was astonished at the power they gave off, the history they contained. Some dated back over twenty years to the summer when she had first met Alan (a silk blouse she bought on Bond Street in 1959), others were as recent as her affair with Moses (a pair of elbow-length gloves with pearl buttons that he had found for her at Camden Lock). She gave them the time they deserved. She let the memories flow out of them, through her, and back again, then she packed them into plastic dustbin-liners (also black).

Her first instinct had been to take her clothes along to a charity shop, but she had quickly changed her mind. She wanted them destroyed, not passed on (it horrified her to think that she might see somebody walking down the street in a dress that Alan had given her), and she wanted to supervise the destruction herself. She wanted to see them disappear with her own eyes. She wanted to know exactly where they had gone.

As dusk fell that Sunday afternoon she hauled the bags down to the end of the garden. She built a fire out of newspaper, a drawerload of Alan's memorabilia, and the remains of the old garden fence. She sat on the upturned water-tank and fed the clothes into the flames, one item at a time, with a pair of tongs. The wools crackled like dry foliage, the synthetics shrivelled and dripped. The smell was awful, something like singed hair, and the smoke that unravelled past the knitting-needle branches of the sycamore was as black as the clothes themselves. Exorcism, she thought.

Sean, who loved fires, must have noticed the orange glow from his bedroom window. He stood in the shadows by the hedge and watched as Mary lifted a fifties' stiletto into the air and placed it carefully in the centre of the blaze. The crocodile skin flared.

'What are you doing?' he asked.

She didn't take her eyes off the fire. 'I'm burning a few of my old clothes.'

He moved closer, stood at her shoulder. 'The black ones?'

She nodded.

'Why the black ones?'

Her voice dropped a register. 'Because that phase is over.'

*

'What's got into you?'

Elliot stopped Moses on the end of his finger. It was Sunday night. Draughts in the doorway of The Bunker. The cold neon glow that Moses called morgue light.

Moses stared at the finger (he had learned a trick or two from Ridley), but the finger didn't waver.

Nor did Elliot's eyes. 'I don't see you for weeks, then you walk straight past me, nearly fucking knock me over. What's the idea?'

Moses didn't know what to tell him. He lowered his eyes. 'My mother died,' he said eventually.

'You what?'

'My mother. She died.'

Elliot stepped back, hands on hips. He looked round, looked back at Moses. 'Your *mother?*'

'You know,' Moses said, 'that woman you saw. Wearing a black dress. Getting on a bit – ' His voice tied up.

'She was really your mother? Come on.'

'She was. She really was.'

'She was really your mother? And she's died?' The news had pulled Elliot's features wide across his face.

Moses just nodded.

Elliot spread his palms in the air as if testing for rain. 'Why didn't you say nothing, Moses?'

Moses shrugged. 'I was too upset.'

Now Elliot couldn't find words.

'Look, I'm really sorry about the other day,' Moses said. 'I was in a real state. I didn't mean to – '

'No. No, no, no.' Elliot dropped his head, lifted his hands to ward off the apologies. 'Listen. I don't know what to say, you know? I mean, I know how close you were – '

Moses gave him a questioning look.

'You know, the time I saw you both on the street,' Elliot said, 'kissing and that.'

Moses considered his feet. 'Yeah, we were pretty close.'

'Look,' and Elliot placed a hand on Moses's shoulder, 'if there's anything I can do just give me a shout, all right?'

Moses nodded. 'Thanks, Elliot.'

As he unlocked his front door and began to climb the stairs he didn't feel that he had in any way lied to Elliot.

*

He went and stood by the window. Sunday again. One week since that trip to New Egypt. He could no longer go to Muswell Hill. Not today, maybe not ever. He wondered what to do with himself now that so much of his life had been destroyed.

He crossed the room to his desk and opened the top drawer. He took out a pile of photographs. A record of the days he had spent in Muswell Hill. He sat down at the desk and switched the lamp on. He stacked the photographs face-down. For a moment they reminded him of cards and he remembered Madame Zola and he thought, Maybe I can use the photos as a sort of tarot pack, not to predict the future but to explain the present. The present had been happening so fast recently that it had left him bewildered, punch drunk, breathless as the runner who comes in last. A throwback to his schooldays, that feeling of falling behind. Still looking for his games clothes when the rest of the team had already left for the pitch. If only he could have borrowed somebody else's, but nobody else's fitted. He shook his head. Driftwood from childhood.

He began to turn the photos up one by one. He arranged them in neat rows until they covered the surface of his desk. He had dozens of Alan and Alison and Sean and Rebecca. The only photos he had of Mary were photos of her back or the tip of her nose. She had always refused to let him (or anyone else, for that matter) take photographs of her. When threatened with a camera (she called it threatened), she issued statements like, *Don't be a user*, or, *Why are you trying to steal pieces of me? I will* not *be stolen.* Once, when shown a picture that someone had taken of her without her knowledge, she had thrust it back with the words, *That's not me.* She had a whole arsenal of names for people who took photographs: they were thieves, they were voyeurs, they were necrophiliacs. Aim a camera at Mary and you saw her at her most scathing, her most dogmatic.

Ten days before, she had visited him at The Bunker and he had asked her, 'Why won't you ever let me take any pictures of you?'

She had been studying his parents' album with a detached curiosity, one eyebrow permanently raised. She looked up. 'Why should I?'

'I don't know. To be remembered, maybe.'

'I don't want to be remembered. I want to be alive, real, flesh and blood, not,' and she brushed a photograph of Alice with the disdainful backs of her fingers, 'not this.'

But, with Mary, wherever there was a rule there was an exception, and it only took him a moment to locate it in his memory. Exactly one week later. That Sunday morning in Bagwash. The wind blowing. Clouds like clean washing. After breakfast they had walked out past the graveyard. And she had let him take a photograph of her.

'All right,' she had said, leaning back against the wall, 'this is your big chance. Make the most of it. There won't be another.'

'Pose,' he had laughed. 'Come on, you ought to be good at that.'

Suddenly he knew how to fill this empty Sunday evening. He reached for his camera and began to wind the film back, even though he had only used half the pictures. He snapped the back open and pulled out the canister. Then he disappeared into the makeshift darkroom that he had built in a cupboard off the bedroom.

Two hours later, in the dim red light, he watched Mary's image emerge. He bent his head close to the tray of chemicals like a craftsman working with minute and precious materials. I'll never be able to show this to her was the thought he produced.

He stared at the photograph. Prophecy? Coincidence? Nonsense? He couldn't decide. She stood just to the left of centre-frame. In that voluptuous black dress of hers – it draped around her body, dropped almost to her ankles – she looked faintly Victorian. A stone wall ran behind her, waist-high, crumbly as shortbread. Her left arm reached down at an angle to her body, her left hand resting on the top of the wall as if to balance her. On one side her dress pressed itself against her, on the other it billowed out into the air. The bodice and the skirt formed two separate black triangles. Her right hand had flown up towards her hair, a spontaneous, almost girlish gesture, charged with grace, entirely natural. It looked as though she was holding on to an invisible hat, or as though some wonderful notion had just occurred to her. He remembered watching her through the camera, waiting for the right moment (she may have hated cameras but at least she understood right moments), and thinking how, for those few seconds, she had seemed to fly in the face of the world. And he had caught that elation of hers. That spontaneous groundless elation.

He tried to remember what else they had said, if anything, but no words came. Only afterwards she had walked towards him, dress swirling, and, smiling, she had said, *Photographer*, because she still thought of photography as theft, as exploitation, as necrophilia. And had, in a way, been proved right. For here she was, in this silent picture, an unknowing tragic heroine. Ahead of her, two or three hours ahead of her, lay the discovery of her husband's death. And behind her, behind her all the time, stretched a skyline of white marble, a sinister city with tombstones for buildings, because the wall she was leaning against was the wall of the cemetery. And if he half-closed his eyes her dress became a ship of death, two black sails mounted on the slender mast of her body, and the wind blowing through the picture filled her sails, blew her towards her sombre destination. And she was laughing, looking happier than he could ever remember –

No, he would never be able to show her the picture. He stared and stared at her in her black dress (happiness dressed in sadness) and thought again of the curious exchange which had taken place that weekend. She had given him his past and lost her future. A father traded for a husband. She had always seen what she had with Moses as a kind of bouquet thrown at the feet of her marriage, as a tribute, a celebration. Now it had become a wreath laid at the base of a memorial. The marriage had kept their relationship alive. The death of the one had killed the other.

He pinned the picture to the washing-line above his head so it could dry. If nothing else, he had a memento of Mary.

What was it she called photographs?

That's right: little deaths. Every photograph a little death.

Memento *mori*.

How fitting, he thought. And smiled bitterly to himself.

*

Alan dead. Mary inaccessible.

His father also inaccessible.

And Peach at large.

For days on end Moses stayed indoors. At night dreams ran round the inside of his head like men in padded cells until he had to turn the light on, get up, walk about. Times like that, sleep was a foreign country and he didn't have a passport. He came close to calling Mary, even Gloria, but he always resisted, his hand an inch from the phone. This was his to deal with.

It was as if everything that had been lying dormant for twenty-five years had surfaced at once, reworked into new nightmare formulas. The old man, his father, lying supine on an altar, delivering, between deep inhalations from his cigarette, a lecture on some high-flown subject that Moses couldn't make head or tail of, and priests approaching from dark corners of the church with knives because the lecture was, so they said, heretical. Or Moses standing at the bottom of a deep pit and his mother, eyes and mouth blacked out, rolling down the slope towards him, rolling over and over as children do, but never reaching him. Or Mary being ambushed and raped in a baroque hotel by a gang of policemen. He woke exhausted every morning. He felt top-heavy, listless, surfeited. He stared out of the window, watched different types of weather affect the view. He let Bird in, fed him, let him out again. Once or twice he took long walks through unknown streets. (He sometimes sensed that he was being followed. *That's called paranoia, Moses.* He would turn aggressively, only to realise that it was his past catching up with him.) But mostly he just made quick forays to Dino's for milk and bread and eggs, or to the Indian off-licence for cans of Special Brew. He got drunk alone. He watched his black and white TV until the screen hissed with a blank grey fury. Then he knew it was time to try and go to sleep again.

Elliot steered clear of him, perhaps out of respect for his grief, perhaps because he had more pressing problems of his own. Whichever it was, Moses was grateful. Some kind of natural understanding existed between them. Their interiors, he felt, had been constructed along similar lines, by the same architect, you might almost have said, and when certain doors closed they didn't open again, not for anyone, not until the right time came. Visitors would be greeted by a DO NOT DISTURB sign and three or four bottles of rotten milk. Some days Ridley's whistling floated up past his window. Haunting, authentic, so he could imagine himself in Africa or Norfolk – somewhere else, at any rate. He listened and he travelled. Comforting, he found it. That illusion of distance from things. When his friends rang he used one of Eddie's old lines: 'I'm having a couple of weeks off.' It meant you'd been overdoing it. They accepted that. It was language they understood.

How he ached, though. Nothing like the way he had ached when Gloria told him about sleeping with Eddie or when those two policemen beat him up. No, he ached as if he had been emptied out, emptied of everything. A real disembowelling, this time. Nothing theatrical about it. No tourists.

The loss of Mary, the loss of those Sundays. Bargains had been struck behind his back, he found himself thinking, and wondered if Mary was thinking the same way. He had had no say. He wanted say. In future, anyway.

And always in the attic of his head this long silence. Then a scurrying, a gnawing, a scurrying. Then long silence again.

Peach.

Peach with some sinister idea in mind.

Peach who would stop at nothing.

He remembered something Mary had said to him that night in Bagwash. 'You,' she had said, levelling a finger, 'you floated out of the village and you floated back again. That's what you do, Moses. You float. You know what I call you?' She had laughed. Her silver fillings flashing in the candlelight. 'I call you the lilo man. You'd better be careful someone doesn't come along and puncture you.'

And he had said, 'Mary, that's what I'm afraid of.'

She was right. He could see the dangers of sitting tight and waiting. Only the bad things came. He had to take action. Evasive action. Now.

Ten days before Christmas he called Leicester.

'Auntie B,' he said, 'can I come and stay for a while?'

SUDDEN DEATH

As soon as Peach saw Moses standing in his office he knew that he would have to kill him. There was no agonising involved. He wasn't even conscious of arriving at a decision. The thought came to him so complete, so ineluctable, that it almost seemed premeditated. It was as if it had been there all along, waiting for the right moment to reveal itself.

It was winter now, and winter was a good time to think about killing. Peach's favourite season, winter. The merciless cold. The crisp precise air. The trees stripped of all that dressy foliage, reduced to their essentials. No vagueness, no hesitation there.

Moses had to be killed. Fact. The question was, how?

Problems of accessibility. On the one hand Peach could wait until Moses returned to the village as he was bound to do now that he had, presumably, found his father. Do the job on home ground, so to speak. Delegate even. Hazard would take care of it. On the other hand a second visit from Moses might have dangerous repercussions. Say he talked. Say the truth of his identity leaked out. There was no telling what might happen then. And what if Moses brought that rather vulgar woman with him again? What would Peach do then? Kill her too?

No. He would have to act before Moses returned. And that meant another trip to the city. He didn't relish the prospect, but he had no choice. And even then it wouldn't be easy. People knew his face now. That black fellow. Moses too. For obvious reasons he couldn't afford to be seen by either of them. This thought struck him: he wouldn't be able to get close enough to Moses to kill him in any one of the usual ways.

Problems.

If only he had reacted more efficiently when Moses appeared in his office. What an opportunity that had been. What a *gift*. But he had been caught napping. Ah, the slow brains of an old man. Alertness draining out of him like blood. There had even been a moment when he had doubted the reality of what he was seeing. Some kind of optical illusion, he had thought. A mirage, a ghost, the spirit of the pink file. Some such nonsense. But Moses hadn't vanished. No shimmer in the air, no puff of smoke. Moses had been real. And Peach had made a quick recovery.

But still.

He had let him go.

He wished he could talk to Dolphin. He needed a younger mind, a sounding-board. He wanted to share the burden. Unthinkable, though.

404

How could he tell Dolphin that he had broken the very rules that they were supposed to be enforcing? It would shake Dolphin's faith in him. It would undermine the infrastructure that he had spent so much time and energy building. He couldn't do it. He would have to work in isolation. Well, perhaps that was nothing new.

But as the days went by he made little progress.

The idea of a letter-bomb excited him briefly. It failed to stand up to close examination, however. Firstly, it could be detected by the post office and traced back to him. Secondly, it was unreliable. Moses might only lose his eyesight or a hand. And Peach wasn't interested in anything less than death. One hundred per cent guaranteed death.

November became December. His deadline (Christmas Day) was less than a month away. He found his attention wandering and couldn't call it back.

'You look tired,' Hilda gently observed.

As if he didn't know! He had looked in the mirror. The pressure showed in the marshy grey terrain of his face, the soft yellow pits under his eyes.

Another time she asked him, 'Is everything all right?'

Stupid bloody question.

'Yes,' he snapped. 'Why shouldn't it be?'

*

And then, as if he didn't have enough on his mind already, Pelting Day loomed.

Pelting Day – a village custom, supposedly dating back to the Middle Ages. Every year, at the beginning of December, the police of New Egypt held a lottery to determine which of them were to be subjected to the rigours of pelting. Only the Chief Inspector could claim exemption. Three days before Christmas the three officers who had drawn the unlucky numbers were marched down the hill to the village green. Tradition demanded that they looked impeccable: full dress uniform, combed hair, boots polished to a high gloss. A jeering crowd assembled at the foot of the hill to greet them. Children capered around in masks, chanting rhymes. Then the serious business of the day began. A fourth policeman secured his three colleagues in the stocks. And there they remained for at least an hour while they were pelted with ripe tomatoes, raw eggs, rotten fruit, anything that came to hand, provided, of course, that it was soft and unpleasant.

During his lifetime Peach had seen various people abuse the spirit of Pelting Day. Tommy Dane, for one. Teeth vengefully pinned to his bottom lip, arm springy as a whip, Tommy had pelted PC Bonefield with hard-boiled eggs, light-bulbs and lumps of coal. 'You little devil,' Peach could still hear Bonefield screaming, 'I'll get you.' 'Come on then,' Tommy had said, cool as you please. And let fly with a handful of manure. Poor Bonefield had trailed home that evening with two black eyes and a chipped incisor (for which he was reimbursed from the New Egypt Police Fund). As always, Tommy Dane had taken things a little too far. In recent years, however, things had gone to the other extreme. Pelting Day had lost its appeal, its popularity. Hardly anyone bothered to come any more. 1979 had been a fiasco. When the three chosen policemen had arrived at the bottom of the hill they found the place deserted. No jeering crowd. Nobody at all, in fact. They were placed in the stocks as usual. And then they waited. After a while two small boys appeared. One of them had an orange in his hand but, instead of hurling it at a policeman, he peeled it and ate it. 'I don't like that game,' the boy had told the inquisitive Peach. 'It's boring.' Shortly afterwards they left.

1980 could well be just as laughable. With Dinwoodie dead (he had always pelted with extraordinary vigour), Highness still confined to his bed and Mustoe an alcoholic, the village had shrunk further into itself. The members of the younger generation, from whom a little spunk might have been expected, seemed even more listless than their parents. They watched TV. They slept a lot. They behaved like old people. The eighties promised nothing but bleakness.

Now Peach disliked Pelting Day intensely – the whole idea of an organised and legitimate assault on police dignity was offensive to him – and he longed to abolish it but, at the same time, he understood its value. It allowed the villagers to let off steam in a relatively harmless way. It helped to create order in the community. And it was good PR. He couldn't afford to let the tradition die out. So, this year, he found himself in the curious and uncomfortable position of having to breathe life into something that he would much rather have seen dead.

He proposed two innovations: firstly, that one of the three policemen to be pelted would now be selected by a special committee of people from the village, and secondly, that Pelting Day would become the setting for a winter fair with the ritual of pelting as its jewel. He set up a sort of think-tank to generate ideas. It comprised PC Wilmott, Brenda Gunn, Joel Mustoe Junior and, of course, himself. The meetings went surprisingly well considering. In part this may have stemmed from Peach's pre-occupation with other matters (he wasn't his usual acid domineering self, he was too busy trying to think of ways to kill Moses). In part, too, this may simply have reflected the wisdom and judgment he had shown in selecting the members of the committee. The only moments of friction occurred during the third meeting. Not, as you might expect, between the police and the villagers, but between Mustoe and Brenda Gunn. Mustoe had challenged Brenda's suggestion that the police should finance the mulled-wine stall.

Mustoe said, 'Why should the police pay for it?'

'Why shouldn't they?' Brenda snapped. 'Pelting Day is organised by the police. It's a police tradition. It's obvious they should pay for it,' each point accompanied by a brisk emphatic slap on the table.

Peach could only hear them dimly. There was a chainsaw in his mind. A deafening howl as it bit into the black side-door of The Bunker.

'Exactly,' Mustoe was saying. '*They* organise it. They've *done* their bit. Now it's our turn.'

'Oh, don't be a ninny.'

'They organise it,' Mustoe went on, 'because we can't. Or won't. Nobody here does anything except complain, get drunk and kill themselves. Sometimes this village really makes me sick.'

'Welcome to the club,' Brenda sneered.

'And that includes you, Mrs Gunn. Why don't you kill yourself too? Might as well, really, mightn't you?'

Brenda leaned back, hands flat on the table. 'Strikes me,' she said, 'that we've got three police officers sitting at this table.'

Mustoe bridled. 'What do you mean by that?'

'I mean that you, Mr bloody Mustoe Junior, are behaving like a bloody policeman.'

'Brenda,' P C Wilmott was attempting conciliation, 'I don't think you're being very constructive.'

'*Constructive?* Who the hell're you to talk? All you've been doing all week is polishing Peach's boots with your face.' Brenda leaned over the table on her man's forearms – solid marble pillars resting on the twin plinths of her fists.

Wilmott's shiny face reddened.

Up until that point Peach had been plunged deep into a world of nightclubs and murder. He had been doodling on his notepad. Sketches of nooses, knives, garottes, guillotines, machine-guns. A rack here, a bazooka there (if only he could get hold of one of those!). Injunctions printed in hostile black block capitals: KILL, THROTTLE, GAS, ANNIHILATE. And several onomatopoeic representations of the noises people make when they're dying. AAAARRRRGGGGHHHH, for instance. MMMPPPFFFF. And GLOPGLOPGLOPGLOPGLOP (blood pumping out of a slashed throat). But, despite the carnage going on in his mind, he had been listening with one ear. When Brenda turned on Wilmott, he heaved himself into the fray.

'The police will pay for the mulled wine,' he declared. (At that moment he couldn't have cared less who paid for the bloody mulled wine. If this year was anything like last year it wouldn't cost much anyway. How much mulled wine could half a dozen New Egyptians drink?) 'Happy, Brenda?'

Brenda was breathing hard through her nostrils. Still glaring at Wilmott, she sat down.

The meeting concluded with a discussion of the feasibility of donkey-rides. Peach returned to his own rather more violent speculations.

By the end of the first week in December they had come up with a sufficient number of ideas. Peach disbanded the committee. Brenda Gunn and Mustoe Junior, working in conjunction with Sergeant Dolphin and a handful of constables, were put in charge of implementation.

'Leave it to me, sir,' Dolphin said. 'There'll be no fiasco this year, I promise you.'

'That,' Peach sighed, 'remains to be seen.'

*

'Are you ready, dear?'

The gilt mirror on the hall wall showed Hilda in the foreground tying her headscarf and Peach waiting in the shadows by the front door, where the coats hung.

'I'm ready,' he said.

She dabbed her nose, her cheeks, her chin – final nervous touches with the powder-puff – then snapped her compact shut. She was wearing the wool suit she kept for special occasions. A muted shade of burgundy. It brings my colour out, she was fond of saying.

They walked down Magnolia Close towards the village green.

'Pelting Day,' she sighed. 'It only seems like yesterday – ' Since the last one, she meant.

He murmured agreement.

When they reached the grass, he gave her his arm. He looked about him. A cool clear afternoon. A bone-china sky, the most fragile of blues. Wood-smoke in the air. The damp turf blackening the tips of Hilda's shoes. She held herself very upright as she walked, braced almost, as if she was facing into a stiff breeze, as if she expected life to jostle her. But it wasn't that, Peach knew. It was anticipation.

'Oh, look,' she cried. 'A bonfire.'

He had told her nothing of the plans for Pelting Day this year. Had he wanted to surprise her, or had he simply not bothered? He so rarely surprised her with anything these days. He could blame it on his age or the pressures of work. Other men did. But he knew that wasn't it. If he was honest he had to admit that it was pure negligence. A scaling down of gifts and attention. And Hilda's expectations falling too, settling. Like dust after a building's been razed to the ground. He turned to look at her. His vision dissected her. He saw wide eyes, a parted mouth, the struts in her neck. An almost girlish excitement. A brittle pitiful delight. He thought her reactions exaggerated, and felt guilty for thinking so. Once it would have seemed natural. Now it bordered on the grotesque. His fault, really. He did so little for her. He *felt* so little. At times he had to cajole himself into feeling anything at all. His love for her seemed to have fallen to bits like one of those joke cars. Touch the door and the door drops off. Whoops, there goes a wheel. Ha ha ha. He wanted suddenly to reassemble it. But that would take time. Time spent together. After he had killed Moses, perhaps he would retire.

A child scuttled out of the shadows, scattered his thoughts. The child wore a mask. An old man's wrinkled face, a bald head, wisps of stiff white hair. Young eyes glittering beneath. This travesty pointed a finger at him and chanted:

> *Peach, Peach,*
> *Down to the beach,*
> *Drown in the sea,*
> *Then we'll be free.*

Then ran away sniggering.

Peach stood still. His lower lip moved in and out.

'You mustn't take it so seriously, dear,' Hilda said. 'It's only Pelting Day.'

Her voice, intended as a balm, had no effect.

The bonfire threw great pleading arms into the darkening sky. The damp wood hawked and spat. Strapped to a chair on the peak of the fire sat the effigy of a policeman. One of the old APRs. They watched the straw face catch. It blazed, turned black. They moved on.

The area between the fire and the eastern edge of the green bustled with stalls and sideshows. There were coconut-shies (the coconuts wore tiny blue helmets), bran tubs, dart-throwing contests, donkey-rides, hoop-la (very difficult to ring the policemen on account of the size of their boots), trestle-tables loaded with homemade pickles and preserves, a mulled-wine tent (run by Mustoe Junior), a GUESS THE WEIGHT OF THE CHIEF

INSPECTOR AND WIN A SURPRISE GIFT competition ('Thirty-five stone,' Peach heard somebody say as he went by. Very funny), and a palm-reader (Mrs Latter from the post office, her face caked in lurid make-up).

'It's marvellous,' Hilda cried. 'You *have* done well, darling.'

He nodded. The unstable orange light of the fire made everyone look predatory, fiendish, medieval. The laughter, the smoke, the gaiety, exhausted him. He hated surrendering control like this.

They had reached the clearing in front of the pub. The stocks stood there as they had stood for centuries. Lanterns hung from poles. Garlands of coloured bulbs had been draped around the trees. The Pelting Day Illuminations.

'So who's in for it this year?' Hilda asked in a whisper.

He had no time to answer. A roar went up. Somebody had glimpsed a movement on the hill. A suggestion of blue in the darkness. A wink of a silver button.

'*They're coming! They're coming!*'

People pressed towards the stocks from all directions. The Peaches were jostled, pinned from behind by the expanding crowd. Three policemen, accompanied by Sergeant Caution, arrived in the lit arena. Wolf-whistles, cat-calls, applause. Marlpit had drawn one of the unlucky numbers. Poor Marlpit. His eyes twitched in their sockets and dribble glistened on his quivering chin. Wragge trailed behind him, skin white like the inside of potatoes. Peach was rather glad that Wragge was going to be pelted; the boy needed taking down a peg or two. When invited to choose a third policeman, the villagers had settled on Sergeant Hazard. Unanimous decision, apparently. And a popular one, too. Everybody feared and hated Sergeant Hazard. He had terrorised the village for years. Only a month ago he had carried out another of his infamous (and unauthorised) dawn raids, this time on Mr Cawthorne, the postman.

Peach remembered Hazard's report, delivered with brutal frankness and meticulous attention to detail in the privacy of Peach's office:

'I kicked Cawthorne's door down at precisely five a.m. on the morning of November 19th,' Hazard began. 'Cawthorne appeared at the top of the stairs in his dressing-gown and slippers. He seemed frightened. "Who's that?" he called out. "Come down here and find out," I replied.' Hazard chuckled, scratched the side of his great dented face. He enjoyed his work, no question of that. 'I stamped on his radiogram, just to hurry him up a bit. Cawthorne shuffled downstairs. His face was greenish-grey, the colour of guilt, if you know what I mean, sir. "What are you doing in my house?" he asked me. I hit him in the mouth. Then, on second thoughts, I felled him with a chopped right hand to the kidneys.' Hazard repeated the punch for Peach's benefit. The air gasped. 'I watched him groaning for a while. He had resoled his slippers with pieces of green carpet, I noticed. The cheap bastard. I went and stood over him. I pointed at him. "I suspect you," I shouted, "of harbouring plans to escape." "On what grounds?" the bastard said. "On what grounds?" I said. "I'll give you on what grounds." I stepped on his hand and twisted my boot. Like I was crushing out a cigarette, sir. He screamed. "That's *confidential*," I said, "isn't it, Mr Cawthorne?" "Yes," he whimpered. "That's better," I said. "Now then, I think I'll just have a quick look round, if you don't mind."' The 'quick look round' had lasted almost two hours, resulting in further damage both to the postman and to the postman's house.

After listening to this report Peach leaned forwards and threaded his fingers together on the surface of his desk. 'Yes,' he said, 'but why Cawthorne?'

Hazard seemed surprised by the question. Then he said, 'He's the postman, sir.'

'The postman? I still don't follow.'

'So was Collingwood, sir.'

'Ah, I see.' And Peach nodded slowly, smiled to himself. A little far-fetched, perhaps. A rather flimsy pretext, some might say, for such a violent attack. Still, there was no accounting for the mysterious workings of precedent, especially in a place like New Egypt. And he had been pleased to see an element of rationale creeping into Hazard's brutalities. 'Very good, sergeant. Very good.'

But now, of course, Hazard was paying for it.

Peach watched Sergeant Caution bolt the struggling Hazard into the stocks. Hazard was muttering. Curses, presumably. Obscenities. Death-threats. When all three policemen had been secured in position, Caution stepped aside and gave the signal for the pelting to begin. Pandemonium. A hail of soft missiles. The crowd broke into a raucous version of the famous 'Pelting Day Song':

> *Throw tomatoes*
> *Throw a pear*
> *At a policeman*
> *If you dare*
>
> *Throw some peaches* (laughter)
> *From a tin*
> *Watch them trickle*
> *Down his chin –*

A cabbage bounced off Hazard's forehead. His face shook with volcanic fury. His eyes, bloodshot, scanned the crowd and noted names. There would be violence, Peach realised. There would be reprisals. He knew his Hazard.

He waited long enough to see a ripe tomato burst on Wragge's cheek, he watched Wragge wriggle as a clot of seeds and juice slid down inside his tunic collar, then he turned away. He didn't want to witness another second of his men's humiliation.

Throw some apples
Throw some eggs
Hazard's had it
Stop, he begs.

Just keep throwing
More and more
That's what Pelting
Day is for –

Taking Hilda by the hand, he began to push his way through the crowd. Cheers scored the air as if to celebrate his departure. He found that he was trembling.

'You look cold, John,' Hilda said. 'Perhaps a glass of mulled wine?'

'Yes. Thank you.' He tucked his double chin into his collar.

'A pretty good turn-out, wouldn't you say, sir?'

He turned round to see Dolphin standing beside him. In Dolphin's arms, the most enormous pink bear that he had ever seen.

'Better than I expected.' Peach's eyes shuttled between Dolphin's face and the monstrous bear. He had known all along that this winter fair was a mistake. Look at the effect it was having on his men.

'I won it, sir. In the hoop-la.' Dolphin bounced the bear in the crook of his arm. 'My daughter's going to love it.'

That may well be, Peach thought, but for Christ's sake stop carrying it around like that. It's bad for credibility.

Hilda tiptoed back with two glasses of mulled wine. 'Oh, Sergeant Dolphin. If I'd known you were here I would've brought you a glass too. It's *very* good.'

Dolphin sketched a bow. 'Very kind of you, Mrs Peach. But I'm on duty.'

'And that, I suppose,' Hilda scintillated, 'is your new partner.'

Dolphin became foolish. 'My new partner? Oh yes. I see. Haha.' He grinned down at his bear.

Peach now took his deputy aside. 'Any trouble?'

'Not really, sir. Mustoe's in the pub. Pretty far gone, as usual. Telling everybody what he thinks of Pelting Day. Says it's a put-up job. The police just pretending to be human for a few hours. That kind of thing.'

Peach tutted. Though Mustoe was right, of course.

'Apart from that – ' bugger all. Dolphin finished the sentence in his head out of respect for the Chief Inspector's wife who was standing beside them. He turned his mouth down at the corners to indicate that there was nothing he couldn't handle. 'Most people seem to be here.' He looked left and right as if about to cross a road. 'Amazing turn-out. Never seen anything like it.'

'Yes. I suppose so.' Peach was only making minimal contact. He was wondering whether this new lease of life, these new high spirits, could have anything to do with Moses Highness's recent visit. Had word got out? 'You haven't heard any rumours, have you, Dolphin?'

'Rumours, sir?'

'Rumours that might – might be subversive?'

Dolphin frowned. 'I don't quite understand you.'

'Never mind.'

Another roar from the stocks. Hazard had just opened his mouth to swear at Cawthorne and promptly had it filled by a lump of bread soaked in sour milk.

'All I can say is, I'm glad it's not me,' Dolphin said.

'Quite,' Peach said. 'Well, I should be getting along.' He took one step then, confidentially, over his shoulder, whispered, 'I should leave that toy somewhere until you come off duty, Dolphin. Otherwise people might not take you seriously.'

Dolphin knew him well enough to detect the presence of a command beneath that quiet suggestion. Nodding, he moved away with Hilda. They stopped by the fire for a moment to warm their hands.

He gazed at the charred effigy crouching at the centre of the fire. Of its own accord and sparked by something he couldn't yet identify, his mind began to slip forwards, incisive, remorseless, as if unleashed. It had picked up some kind of trail or scent. Something in the atmosphere (the fairy lights? the jangling music? the clamour of voices?) had reminded him of the twenty-four hours he had spent in London. Something buried in those twenty-four hours, he now knew, could help him solve the problem of how to kill Moses.

He began to scrabble at the loose earth of his memories. The blonde girl on the train? No. That Asian boy in the middle of the night? No, not there. His meeting with Madame Zola? Not there either. Then he remembered the enigmatic landlord of that pub on Kennington Road. Terence, wasn't it? Somewhere in that conversation, perhaps.

He sifted more carefully now. Words, gestures, nuances. *Bit shady, by all accounts.* No, it had come later. During the second drink. When Terence opened up a bit. When Peach asked him, 'What else do you know about the place?'

'Well, there've been some pretty mysterious goings-on – ' The landlord liked to leave his sentences hanging. At times he had reminded Peach of people in the village.

'How do you mean?'

'Vandalism, for a start.'

'Vandalism?'

'There's been a series of break-ins.' Terence ran the tip of his tongue along his moustache to signify the delicacy of the subject. 'Too many for it to be a coincidence, if you know what I mean – '

'What kind of break-ins, Terence?'

'Oh, I don't know exactly. Let's just say there's been talk of a vendetta, though.'

Peach was still staring deep into the fire. His eyes were smouldering now. Everything had clicked.

He handed his glass to Hilda. 'I've got to go.'

'Where are you going?'

'Home.' He was already ten yards away, walking backwards. 'Something very important, dear.'

'I'll come with you.'

'No, no. It's all right. You stay here. Enjoy yourself.' The fire threw black streamers of shadow across his face. 'I'll see you when you get back.'

Then he was running away over the grass, leaving Hilda standing by the fire in her burgundy suit with a glass of mulled wine in each hand.

When he reached his study he unlocked his bureau and pulled out the pink file. His heart was hammering against the bars of his ribs. He sat down, unfastened the top button of his tunic. He shuffled through his papers until he found the plans he had drawn up a few weeks before. Plans of The Bunker.

'Yes,' he breathed. 'Just as I thought.'

The Bunker had no fire-escapes. The only way out of the fourth floor, so far as he could see, was down the stairs and through the black side-door. So if a fire started on the ground floor ...

He smiled.

There would be a fire at The Bunker. A tragic fire. He could see the headlines now:

Nightclub Blaze
Leaves One Dead

Or perhaps:

Man, 25, Dies in Mystery Inferno

(And if that black bastard got killed too, so much the better.)

There would be nothing to connect Peach with the fire. Nothing to implicate him. He would burn the pink file beforehand, though. Just to be on the safe side. It would have served its purpose, after all. There was a nice symmetry about that. The file. The nightclub. Both pink. Both burning.

A sudden blast of heat passed across his face.

Why wait?

Why not do it now? Leave tonight. Return first thing in the morning. Nobody would miss him. It was Pelting Day. Turn the chaos to his advantage. Leave now. No time to tell Hilda. Tell her tomorrow. Explain the whole thing then. He would think of something. He was Peach.

He leered. Yes, why not?

A Christmas gift for Moses.

Death.

Hands trembling with strange electricity, he hurried from the room.

*

'Pelting Day,' Mustoe sneered. 'What a bloody fiasco.'

He had been sitting in The Legs and Arms all day. He had drunk himself into a stupor at lunch-time and slept it off during the afternoon. Now he was drinking again. Pints of beer and whisky chasers. He was alone except for Lady Batley, who hadn't moved for hours, who never did, and Brenda Gunn, the bitch who ran the place. Brenda usually ignored him but on this occasion, perhaps because she had been on the Pelting Day committee herself, he seemed to have touched a nerve.

'Oh and I suppose your life isn't,' she muttered.

'Isn't what?' he grinned.

'A fiasco.'

'Oh,' and he threw up his hands, pretended to cower, 'oh, *Mrs Gunn*.'

'It's a success this year, actually.' Brenda folded her arms. 'A real success.'

'*Success*.' Mustoe snorted into his glass, then raised it ceilingwards. 'To the success of Pelting Day.' He swallowed his double whisky in a single gulp. 'My arse,' he added, and slipped sideways off his stool, very slowly, like a ship going down. Waves closed over his head.

Brenda took away his glass and wiped the bar.

'Fiasco?' Lady Batley quavered suddenly. 'What fiasco?'

Then he heard a voice calling him, calling from somewhere far above. 'Dad? *Dad?*'

He peered over his anorak collar. Managed to fit his flaccid lips around the words, 'Piss off.'

'Come on, Dad,' the voice said. 'It's time to go home.'

'There's no such thing.' As time? As home? Both, he thought, sweeping them savagely aside like empty glasses.

'Something's happened, Dad,' came the voice again. 'Something strange.'

He rolled over and sat up. Bracing a hand on his knee, he clambered to his feet. He stared down with revulsion at his eight-year-old son. Conceived during the preparations for escape in 1972. Conceived as a result of those bloody stomach exercises. A living reminder of his own failure. How he loathed the child who he had, in his own tortured bitterness, insisted on calling Job.

'What's strange?' he snarled.

The boy looked up at his father with eyes the colour of ploughed fields. 'They're saying Peach has disappeared.'

Mustoe lowered himself on to his stool. His son's words seemed to tap some hidden reserve of sobriety.

'What did you say?' he said.

*

It was three in the morning. Elliot sprawled on his grey dralon sofa. A glass of Remy balanced on the fourth button of his waistcoat. He was drinking in the liquid harmonies of Manhattan Transfer. To somebody walking into the office at that moment Elliot might have looked the picture of relaxation, but that somebody wouldn't have heard, as Elliot heard, the whirr of brain-wires, or felt, as Elliot felt, the chafing of one layer of skin against another. Elliot had said good-night to Ridley half an hour before in the foyer. He had been intending to lock up straight away and go home. But when he searched his pockets he realised that he had left his keys upstairs and when he found his keys on his desk he saw the pile of letters and when he thought about the letters he poured himself a stiff brandy, put a record on the stereo and lay down on the sofa.

Now he shook the sofa off, stood up. He walked over to the pool-table and set up the balls. He broke, put a stripe down. He played himself, and the physics of the game slowly altered his frame of mind. He could concentrate now. His cool pool-brain began to plan strategies.

When the music stopped – that five-second gap between tracks – he thought he heard something downstairs. The three-syllable creak of the double-doors. And remembered now that he had left them unlocked. He leapt across the room and killed the volume on the stereo. And stood motionless, lips ajar. Not a sound now, but the kind of silence that follows sound. This had been happening slowly for a long time. He felt a curious relief as he reached for the short pool-cue.

Half a dozen steps (executed so lightly and smoothly that they all ran together) took him to the door of the office. He pushed on the wood with spread fingers. An unmistakable smell drifted into his nostrils. Petrol.

He ran down the stairs, turned the corner into the last flight, and stopped, three steps above the foyer. A policeman stood by the double-doors. He held a pink paraffin can in his hands. There was something gluttonous about the way he was splashing petrol against the walls, as if the petrol was sauce and the walls were a meal he could hardly wait to eat.

'So,' Elliot breathed, 'it's you.'

A casual tilt of Peach's brutal head. The quills of his crewcut glinting. His grey eyes grinned from the cover of their heavy lids and his bottom lip slid unceasingly against his top one, in and out, in and out. And Elliot realised. The bloke was mad. Stark fucking mad. And would do anything.

'You're going to burn,' Peach said.

Elliot sprang across the foyer. His pool-cue hissed through the air and cracked Peach on the side of the head. Peach tottered sideways, dropped the pink can. Then he began to laugh. Before Elliot could hit him again, he brought out a box of matches, struck one, and tossed it on to the floor. Elliot jumped back. Fire grew up the wall like a fast orange plant.

'Goodbye,' Peach whispered. Blood ran a red hand down the side of his face.

Elliot backed towards the door. But he wanted one question answered.

'It's not me you're after, is it?'

Peach was still laughing.

'It's Moses you want,' Elliot said, 'isn't it?'

'Oh, yes,' Peach leered, 'he's going to burn too.'

'No, he isn't. Because he isn't here.' Now it was Elliot's turn to laugh. 'You've fucked it, fat man. You've really fucked it this time.'

Peach sucked air in through his gritted teeth. Then he shook his head from side to side and let out a guttural howl of rage. He lunged at Elliot, clubbed him on the forehead. Elliot staggered backwards through the double-doors.

Snow was falling outside. Snow, of all things. White on the white of his Mercedes. He unlocked the door and scrambled in. Through the smudged windscreen he saw Peach collapse on the pavement. Smoke poured from the door of the club. A window screeched open somewhere above.

He started the engine, crashed the gears, stamped on the accelerator. He spun the car round the corner. The lights were green on the main road. They had to be. He wasn't going to stop for anything. He wasn't going to stop for a long time. And when he did he would probably be somebody else.

*

A tightening in Peach's chest. Blackness pulsing along the edges of his vision. Something lurched inside him. Slack not being taken up. He wiped at his forehead and his fingers came away wet. Blood or sweat, he didn't know.

Tightening, tightening.

Arms over his face, he crashed through the air as if it was glass. He thought he felt snow on his face. Soft cold petals settling.

One reeling upward glance. Some sort of wedding in the sky.

Snow.

He could hear the blood rushing through his body. Or. Trees moving. Darkness advancing. Some kind of second night falling.

The pain, when it came, split his body in two as an axe splits wood.

Then he was lying on something cold. His palm flat on – was it stone? He couldn't understand why the floor of his study had suddenly turned to stone. Then he remembered, and wanted to forget again.

The moisture from the pavement soaked up into his uniform. A welcome enveloping coolness.

Thoughts would not start. Sentences buckled while under construction. Words floated out of context.

He knew, though, that something final was happening. The metallic taste of something final on his tongue.

His left arm hurt. A massive invisible weight pinned him to the cool ground. He could no more move than he could have flown. Snow nursed his wounded face.

He felt the presence of fire on his skin and in his memory. He saw a crouching figure wrapped in sheets of flame. He had to burn the evidence. Had to. Had he?

He tried to get up but felt he was standing already. Leaning against a cold wall. If he stood up he would fall over. Logic. Somebody had been playing with the world.

Buildings, trees, leaned over him.

Someone appeared. Pressed against the warped shape of everything. Corn and husk. Hands closed in prayer. Flowing upwards and inwards in sickening curves. A woman. Her head blending with the tops of – or perhaps just the sky. Was that Hilda?

'Hilda?'

He couldn't hear his voice, couldn't tell if he had spoken. Only this rushing sound as if the night, the whole night with him inside it, was travelling somewhere very fast.

Now she was speaking. He strained to hear. Her mouth opened and closed like the mouth of a fish. Stretched at the corners sometimes. Painful. Water spilled out of his ears.

Her head moved closer, liquid at the edges. Was it Hilda?

He had to talk. He could see the words, but couldn't get a grip on them. Slippery as fish and his lips like clumsy hands.

'Tell Dolphin,' he wanted to say. 'Tell him Moses is alive.'

Simple.

Had he said it then?

Had Hilda understood?

Ah, so many pieces missing from this jigsaw.

He tried again. The same words. And something else.

'And tell him – '

Everything was caving in above him. The pain, the weight of the sky, the woman's face, came crashing down through the darkness. He only had seconds.

' – to kill Moses,' he cried.

The woman held his head in her cool papery fingers.

She watched his lips turn the colour of his uniform.

She knelt there until she could no longer feel her legs, until the fire-engines blared round the corner.

The snow in her hair melted and ran down her face.

'Christos,' she whispered.

The man was dead.

*

Still clutching his giant pink teddy-bear, Dolphin swayed up the garden path. He was singing.

Oh I do like to be beside the seaside
Oh I do like to be beside the sea —

Policemen weren't supposed to sing songs about being beside the seaside (or being anywhere, for that matter – apart from New Egypt, that is), but seven pints of homebrew with Hazard and the boys had washed away his usual circumspection. They had been celebrating the end of Pelting Day. A triumph, it had been. His triumph, in many ways. The most well attended Pelting Day in living memory. And if that didn't deserve a celebration, what did? So they had celebrated. And now he was drunk. And when he was drunk he liked to sing songs about water. Sea-water, preferably. The ocean. Those expanses of water where his namesakes swam, expanses so vast that they filled his somewhat limited imagination many times over. Ocean. What a wonderful watery word.

'Ocean,' he said. 'Ohhhhsssshhhun.'

His wife, Laura, opened the door. 'Ssshhh,' she said.

'Ohhhhsssshhhh – ' he began again. Thought she was joining in, you see.

'Roger, *please*. Mrs Peach has phoned three times. Where've you been?'

'Who?'

'Mrs Peach.'

'What's *she* want?'

'She's worried. The Chief Inspector's disappeared.' She scraped a few strands of hair away from her creased white forehead.

'*Disappeared?* Where?'

'If she knew that,' Laura said, 'he wouldn't have disappeared, would he?'

Dolphin let this piece of sophistry sink without trace in the swirling waters of his drunkenness. He lifted his right wrist. 'Laura, it's two-thirty in the morning, for Christ's sake.'

'The Chief Inspector's been missing since nine o'clock, Roger, and you can leave Christ out of it,' said Laura, who was religious.

Dolphin sighed.

'Where've you been all this time anyway?' she went on. 'And what's *that thing*?'

He pushed past her and walked into the dining-room. Then he wondered why he had walked into the dining-room. Peach had disappeared. Peach had been missing for almost six hours. Peach never went missing. *Nobody* ever went missing. This was bad. Very bad.

He had stopped in front of the mirror. When he looked up he suddenly saw the new Chief Inspector of New Egypt standing there. The new Chief Inspector of New Egypt was holding a giant pink teddy-bear. He would have to get rid of it, he decided. Otherwise nobody would take him seriously. Putting the teddy-bear down, he walked back into the hall. Then he picked up the phone and dialled Peach's number.

In future fluffy animals would always remind him of death.

THE WOODEN TRIANGLE

'Thank you for driving me to the station like this.'

'Don't be silly, Moses.' Auntie B's face never lost its china stillness, its placidity, even when she chided him. 'It's been lovely to see you. You'll come and see us again, won't you?'

Now she was being silly. That hint of uncertainty (the legacy of his having discovered his real father?). He dismissed it with, 'Of course I will.'

He had spent Christmas in Leicester – he had stayed over two weeks, in fact – grateful for the warmth, the soft ticking of clocks in the hallway, the small-scale dramas (the cat moulting, a blocked drain, a wine-stain on the dining-room table). He had eaten three meals a day and slept ten hours a night. Uncle Stan and Auntie B knew nothing and in their ignorance he found relief. His unease dissolved in their everyday routines. He left London behind, as he had once left the orphanage behind, and felt a great calmness settle. He told them about the contents of the suitcase, the trip down to New Egypt, the meeting with his father. He described his father as a sort of eccentric invalid and the village as one of those dull places in the middle of nowhere that nobody ever leaves, and was surprised at how much truth his carefully censored version of the facts contained (he only hid what might have worried them; about Peach, for instance, he said nothing). They listened and nodded, made all the right noises. They asked very few questions, thinking it no business of theirs, perhaps, or simply content with the parameters he had set. They had never tried to expand their role into areas where it didn't belong, and they didn't now. Their occasional references to the subject, though oblique, told him all he needed to know about the way they were thinking. For instance: 'Well,' Auntie B had said one night (and her eyes never once wandered from the TV screen), 'you know you can always come here, Moses. You'll always have a home here.' He knew. Or as now: 'You'll come and see us again, won't you.' Of course he would.

'Thank you for everything, Auntie B.' He leaned over, kissed her on the cheek. 'See you soon.'

He walked through the damp acidic air of the station – its draughty arches and its stained dripping brick had always reminded him of urinals – and boarded the train to London. His eyelids prickled. It was nine in the morning.

He was looking forward to late nights again. He wanted to sit at his fourth-floor window and feel the music ride up from below and gaze at those golden zips of light that ran down the slim dark buildings of the city. He wanted to thrash Elliot at pool, drink Eddie into oblivion, drive Vince to hospital, tease Jackson about the weather. He longed to be back. Where things happened. Among friends. He had even invented one or two strategies for dealing with the Peach threat (he would park his car further away, fit extra locks on the doors, buy a toy periscope for the kitchen window), and if they were a bit frivolous it was only his new confidence asserting itself.

Sensing his impatience, perhaps, the train left several seconds early. The magic rhythm of its wheels on the tracks soon made misty Leicester disappear and a pale-blue sky unveiled itself. A pocket-torch sun clicked on, pointed out neat lawns, a car glazed with dew, the red slant of a rooftop. It was like somebody big looking for somebody small, he thought. Ridley looking for Gloria, for instance.

Gloria.

The night before he left for Leicester he had covered that last fatal inch to the telephone. He had dialled her number. He regretted it now. He had been drinking (well, drunk). He had hardly been aware that it was her number that he was calling. That was bad. All his bluster vanished the moment he heard her voice, leaving him exposed, shrunken, pitiful. It was the first time he had spoken to her since Talent Night. That seemed like months ago. Probably was.

'Hello?' she said.

'Hello. It's me.' This false gaiety in his voice. Game-show presenter. Just awful.

'Who's that?'

'Moses. You know. *Moses.*'

Forget it. Hang up now.

'Oh. Hello, Moses.'

Too late.

It sounded, though, as if she was using a name that she was only *pretending* to recognise, that, in reality, she couldn't put a face to, that didn't *mean* anything. She sounded like a receptionist. He felt like a stranger (with no appointment). He couldn't think of what to say next. Or why he had phoned, for that matter.

'Look, I just rang up to see if you got my message.'

'What message?'

'I left a message at The Blue Diamond last weekend. No, the weekend before. I think. Sometime, anyway. You were singing there.'

'Oh, The Blue Diamond. Yes. No, I didn't sing there in the end. I cancelled.'

'Oh, that's all right then,' he said.

Thanks for telling me.

'Did you go?'

'No. My friend's car broke down. In the country. I couldn't get back. That's why I left the message that you didn't get.'

'Oh.'

Why was this so difficult?

'Look,' he said, 'I'm going away for Christmas. To my foster-parents, I think. So I probably won't see you for a while.'

He thought he heard soft laughter on the other end. Had he said something funny?

'Well,' she said, 'have a wonderful time, won't you.'

Just like that. She wasn't interested. She wasn't remotely fucking interested. He lapsed into silence, bit his lip.

'Hello?'

'I'm still here.'

That was the trouble with telephones. No time to think. No time to not say anything. Mary was right about telephones.

'When are you going?' Gloria's impersonal voice again.

He thought. 'I don't know exactly. Tomorrow maybe. Or the next day. I don't know.'

'So what are you doing tonight?'

He gulped, sensing a trap. 'Nothing, really. Just staying in.'

'Oh.'

'Look,' he quickened, 'maybe I'll see you when I get back, OK?'

'OK,' and just a trace of tired intimacy in, 'if that's what you want.'

She was like water. You could throw stone after stone and the surface always formed again. Perfectly, unbearably smooth. There was a pressure building inside him and no valve that he knew of.

'I suppose so,' he murmured. He saw himself reflected in the uncurtained window, all the hollows in his face filled with shadow.

'Ring me when you get back,' she was saying. 'Have a wonderful time, won't you.'

She hung up.

He stared at the receiver, a useless furry buzzing in his hand, then flung it against the wall. An explosion of red plastic. One fragment ricocheted, nicked his cheek as it flew past. He touched his face and his fingertips came away bloody. He would have the scar – a miniature triangle, a crocodile tear – for the rest of his life.

Then, only yesterday, at breakfast in Leicester, he had received some mail from Italy. His name and address had been scrawled in black ink, the letters spiky, rushed. He hadn't recognised the handwriting. He had sniffed the envelope. It hadn't smelt like anyone he knew. That should have told him something. When he tore the letter open, a postcard fell out. He scanned it rapidly for a signature. Gloria X X.

Now he took the postcard from his coat pocket and examined it again. A picture of a square in Florence, probably a famous square judging by the ancient yellow buildings and the groups of multi-coloured tourists. In the top left-hand corner he noticed an empty pedestal. This couldn't have been intentional on Gloria's part; he had never mentioned his statue theory to her. Still, a touch of irony there. It seemed to undermine what she had written, make it laughable. He read it anyway. She said she was sorry about their last phone-call; she'd taken some sleeping-pills because she'd been having trouble sleeping. She told him she missed him. She thought they ought to get together in the New Year.

He wondered.

He glanced out of the window and saw a mass of dark cloud, two strands lifting away into the sky, tousled by a night of restless sleep. There was no mistaking that head of black hair on that pale-blue pillow.

The train slowed, switched tracks, drew into St Pancras.

Still staring at the sky, he knew that it wouldn't be long before those black clouds (all that now remained of Gloria) were blown away.

*

Walking down Charing Cross Road, he thought he heard somebody call his name. He turned round, saw nobody, felt stupid. He was about to walk on when he caught sight of Alison waving at him from the other side of the road.

She waited for the lights to change, then ran towards him.

'Alison.' He stooped to kiss her cool cheek. 'How are you?'

Four weeks of mourning had done nothing to diminish the glory of her red hair. He could tell from her forehead, though, that she had been through a painful time. Instead of the four seagulls he remembered, one distant albatross flying alone.

'Where've you been, Moses? I've been trying to call you,' she said, all in one breath.

He gestured with his suitcase. 'I've been away – '

'Have you got time for a cup of coffee?' Her eyes moved from one part of his face to another with some urgency.

He said he had.

They ducked into the café opposite Foyle's. Flustered by this chance meeting, Moses almost hit his head on the lintel. Such a small world. They took a table by the window, faced each other across a silence of yellow formica and red plastic ketchup containers shaped like tomatoes. A shaft of sunlight struck through the plate-glass, set fire to Alison's hair. She blinked, shifted sideways into the shadow. Her hair went out. Waiting for her to begin, Moses felt for his cigarettes. He lit one.

'It took me a while to work it out,' she said finally.

He realised from the candour in her eyes that it was no use pretending he didn't know what she was talking about. She either knew or had guessed everything. How had she found out, though? He absent-mindedly flicked his cigarette. The ash rolled across the table. Alison scooped it up in a paper napkin and tipped it into the ashtray. She glanced up, noticed him watching her.

'Sorry,' she said, with a smile that contrived to be both embarrassed and ironic. 'It's a bad habit of mine, clearing up after other people.'

'It's all right.' He was still staring at her. She had just reminded him of an evening in Muswell Hill. Mary sitting crosslegged on the carpet. One elbow resting against the arm of the sofa. A lit cigarette poised between the fingers of that hand. She had waited until everybody was looking then, quite deliberately, she had tapped the end of her cigarette so the ash landed on the sofa. Alison had left her chair and brushed the ash into the nearest ashtray with her hand. Mary had waited until Alison sat down then, smiling, she had done exactly the same thing again. Alison had sighed and left the room. Now, once more, Alison seemed to be taking the parental role – concerned, long-suffering, responsible – and Mary was the daughter who had misbehaved. With me, he thought. 'How did you find out?' he said.

Alison rubbed at the surface of the table with her fingertips as if she might see a clear beginning there somewhere. 'It was about two weeks ago. Vince turned up at my flat. I don't know how he found out where I was living.' She frowned. 'Trust him, though.'

Perhaps it was that red hair of hers, glowing like a beacon in the suburbs, Moses thought. He imagined her hair would cause her a lot of anxiety in the future and that, as the years went by, her forehead would become a sanctuary for birds of all descriptions, some settling at the corners of her mouth and eyes, others flying in formation, their wings etched deep in the pale sky of her skin.

'He was out of his head, of course,' she was saying. 'Said he hadn't slept for five days. Drunk and God knows what else. I didn't want to know, you know? He told me some story about a girl called Debra.' That innocent enquiring glance again. 'She'd left him or something – '

'Is that true?'

Alison shrugged. 'I don't know. Anyway, it's beside the point.'

Moses smiled into his cup.

'Then he started on about me. I should've known he was going to do that. I shouldn't have let him in at all.'

'He would've just broken in.'

But Alison hadn't heard him. She was hearing Vince's voice. 'He said it used to be me and him and what'd happened to the and.'

'What and?'

'That's what I said. "What and?" I kept asking him. "The and between you and me," he said.' She was staring straight ahead and smiling as if she could see through the café wall to a peaceful horizon. 'Sometimes he's got a way with words.'

Moses waited for her to come back.

'Anyway,' and her voice drew nearer again, 'I said there wasn't an and any more, I said he might as well forget it, and he got really shitty, he really worked himself up, you know, the way he does, and started calling Mary all kinds of names – '

'Mary?'

'Oh yes, he always blames Mary. I don't know why. He says she turned me against him, told me he wasn't good enough, that kind of thing. All a pile of crap, really.' Though she would never get Vince to believe that. 'He really hates her, you know.'

'I know,' Moses said. 'He's told me.'

'The names he called her. Incredible.' She shook her head. 'He said she was spoilt, pretentious, immature – ' she was ticking the words off on her fingers – 'jealous, vindictive, and then he said, "I don't know what Moses sees in her – "'

Moses looked up sharply from his cup.

'I know,' Alison said. 'It had exactly the same effect on me. Vince didn't actually know anything, you see, but it was the way he said it that made me think. He went on and on about what a bitch she was, but I wasn't listening any more. All I could think about was you and Mary, all those times you came round to our house as if you were a friend of the family when really – '

'I *was* a friend of the family, Alison. I liked you all. I still do. It wasn't just – '

'I'm not attacking you,' she cut in. 'I'm just working it out for myself, that's all.'

She stared down at her hands. Moses glanced out of the window. The sky had darkened. Lights in the shop windows now, lights in the offices.

427

'I thought about you not coming to the funeral,' Alison began again, 'about you suddenly not coming to the house any more. And the way Mary won't talk about you now, like you never existed or something. It puzzled me for ages, until Vince said what he did. Then it all just suddenly fell into place.'

Moses thought of Vince's jigsaw and smiled.

'It was obvious, really. I don't know why I didn't see it before. Too close to it, I suppose. The way she kept going round to visit you. Because she never lied about that, you know. She never pretended she was going shopping or visiting a friend – '

'She *was* visiting a friend.'

' – and I admire her for that, though I don't know what Dad – ' For the first time, her eyes lost their coolness, their clarity. Her lower lip began to tremble.

'I think he knew,' Moses said.

'And then there was that awful weekend. Sorry, but I can't seem to help talking about it. And you were so close to us – ' Three tears rolled down her cheek, one after the other, and dropped on to the yellow formica. 'We were looking for you everywhere. And *even then* I didn't realise.' She dabbed at her eyes with a tissue, sniffed twice.

'The car really did break down, you know.'

Alison nodded. 'Anyway, I haven't said anything to Mary,' she said, her grey eyes clear again (she was one of those people, he realised, who cried invisibly, whose eyes didn't swell or redden, whose make-up never ran). 'I don't think it's the right time, do you?'

He shook his head, though, quite honestly, he doubted whether it would make any difference to Mary. Alison's 'right times' would never be hers.

As they paid at the counter, he noticed an old woman sitting at the table behind the coat-rack. A plastic mac, hair in a bun, a cup of tea.

Alison heard his startled exclamation. 'What is it, Moses?'

'Nothing.' He turned away. 'I just thought I saw someone I knew.'

Outside on the pavement they hesitated, drawing out this chance meeting of theirs. Suddenly there seemed to be something final about what would otherwise have been a perfectly casual goodbye. Now he was no longer seeing Mary, now Alison was no longer seeing Vince, they had nothing in common. He couldn't imagine what would bring them together. Only chance again, perhaps. He watched her staring first at the traffic then at her shoes. As he watched, a single snowflake (predicted by Jackson?) settled on the concrete beside her foot and melted. That sprawl of black cloud he had seen from the train loomed overhead. Everyone was walking faster now. Snow.

Finally she lifted her head. 'Moses,' she said, 'was it serious?'

The albatross beat its great wings on the pale wastes of her forehead and he seemed to hear its cry, very faintly, in the darkening air above. It was the cry of someone waking to a cold and muddled world and not wanting to be awake, wanting to pull the sky over their head like a blanket, wanting to close their eyes, go back to sleep again. He thought of Mary and saw no pictures, only the vaguest of silhouettes, a shadow in the distance, the blackness of her clothes. But he could still remember times when they had laughed until they ached.

'No,' he said. 'No, I don't think so.'

*

He waited for Alison to disappear up the street, then he turned and ran back to the café. He stood in front of Madame Zola. Her black eyes slowly lifted to meet his. He had forgotten how they drew you in until you were all vision and no body.

'Ah,' she said. 'You.'

'You remember?'

'The past is clear. It's only the future that isn't clear.'

Moses smiled. Same old Madame Zola. 'I'm having trouble with them both at the moment.' He peered into her cup of tea. Three-quarters full. 'You must've been here a long time.'

She nodded. 'You remember also.'

'How could I forget? You started all this.'

She waved a hand in front of her face as if brushing cobwebs aside. 'I started nothing, but,' and she gave him a curious look, 'I have something to tell you. You aren't leaving now.'

She had this way of pitching a sentence halfway between a question and a command. 'No,' he said, 'I've got plenty of time.'

'Come, sit down,' and she motioned him to the chair opposite. Her gesture reminded him of a papal benediction. He sat down.

She leaned over the table, clutching her cup in both hands. It might have been the only solid object in the room. 'I saw a fire,' she whispered, 'and a dead man.'

'No! Where?'

'Ah yes, that's so strange.' Her eyes slid away from his. 'You know the pink building? It happened there.'

Moses stared at her. 'The pink building? You mean – '

She shook herself out of her dreaming skin and hissed, 'A dead man, I said. He died in front of my eyes.'

'Who was he?'

'I don't know his name. But he was a policeman – '

'*A policeman?*'

'I held his head so,' and, lifting her shoulders, she tucked her elbows into her rib-cage and spread her palms, the tips of her little fingers touching, 'and he died in my hands. In these same hands you see now. And for some moments I thought time, he was running away, and it was fifteen years before, and my Christos – ' Her voice cracked like a dam and the dark valleys of her eyes flooded. Moses put out a hand, but she shook her head, staunched the flow with a soiled tissue. 'I had troubles with the police,' she went on. 'So much troubles, you don't know, and all because this man, he died in my hands – '

'You said something about a fire, Madame Zola. What about the fire?'

She seemed to rouse herself. 'Yes, yes. The fire-engines, they came. Clang, clang, clang. Two fire-engines.'

'And the building? Is it burned down?'

'No, it's not destroyed. It cannot be destroyed. Not yet. There are many colours it must be before it can rest. It was never orange, I think. No. I'm certain it was never orange – '

She had lost him. He pushed his chair back. 'Madame Zola, I'm sorry, but I really have to go.'

'You know,' she sighed, 'sometimes you think you have all the time in the world,' and with her gnarled hands she fashioned a globe out of the dingy air, 'and then suddenly you have no time at all. Ah,' and, shaking her head, she lifted her cup and wet her top lip.

*

Falling softly as feathers, the snow tickled the serious faces of businessmen. Bare-headed office-girls wore white flowers in their hair; winter could seem tropical. Moses ran towards Trafalgar Square. Thoughts raced through his head; they kept cornering too fast and spinning off. He jumped a bus at the lights outside South Africa House.

'Come on,' he whispered to himself, as it ground and floundered down Whitehall. '*Come on.*'

He wiped a hole in the condensation and peered out. He saw a woman stumbling along the pavement in a fur coat. Rich, she looked, but deranged. Eyes of glass. Her hands were outstretched in front of her, palms upwards. Resting on them, as on an altar, lay a pigeon, its neck slack, its head lolling – dead, presumably. There was a dignity, a mystical dignity, about the way she bore this dead pigeon along the street, past the Houses of Parliament, through a group of tourists gathered by the railings; he imagined a silence must have fallen as the red sea of anoraks parted to let her through. On other days he might have asked questions – What was the history of the woman and the pigeon? Where was she taking it now that it was dead? Could there be some kind of special pigeon cemetery in the area? – but as the bus lurched towards Lambeth Bridge, wheels slipping on the curve, gears clashing, he realised that no questions applied.

A woman with a dead pigeon.

That wasn't a mystery.

That was an omen.

*

The black double-doors of The Bunker exploded outwards, snowflakes and waste-paper flying, and Ridley appeared, head flung back, fists bunched. His movements were so violent that they threw the air around him into a state of chaos. Moses thought he felt the shock-waves as he crossed the road.

When Ridley caught sight of Moses he glared and, for a moment, Moses was included in the bouncer's terrible rage.

'Where the fuck've you been?'

Moses swallowed. He began to explain, but Ridley cut him off with a horizontal slash of his hand. The question, it seemed, had been a rhetorical one.

'I don't fucking believe it,' were Ridley's next words. He looked up and down the street as if he expected the object of his anger to manifest itself. It would have to be a very foolish object, Moses thought, to do that.

He turned his attention to the club. A sorry sight. Smoked-glass windows shattered. Fire-blackened frames. Glimpses of a burnt-out interior. The fourth floor seemed to have escaped, though. His own side-door looked untouched.

'What happened exactly?' he asked.

Ridley swung round, jaw muscles rippling. His giant gold earring spat light. Snow melted on his face, ran down it like sweat. 'How much do you know about this?'

'I wasn't here. I heard there was a fire. And somebody died.'

'Yeah, it was a copper.'

Moses nodded. 'I heard that too.'

'You heard a lot. Did you hear what his name was?'

Moses shook his head.

'Peach. His name was Peach.' Ridley stepped back to judge the effect of his words. 'Yeah, I thought that might interest you. And you know something else? They think he started it.' He stared at Moses as if he expected some kind of explanation, but Moses could only stare back.

'Are you sure he's dead?' Moses asked finally.

Ridley liked that. His laughter struck the walls of the houses opposite. Moses thought of thrown rocks.

'He's dead all right,' the bouncer said. 'Heart attack or something. I had to go down the station. Answer questions and that. They get a bit upset when a copper snuffs it.'

Then his anger returned, tightened the skin across his face. The bones seemed to shift beneath like continental plates. An immensely slow, immensely powerful grinding.

'There's something else,' he said between his teeth. 'Looks like Frazer's done a runner.' And, whirling round, he charged back indoors.

The avalanche of footsteps on the stairs told Moses that Ridley was heading for the office. He paused inside the door and looked round. He scarcely recognised the foyer. Scorched, gutted, flooded with water. A stench of damp ashes, charred wood, singed cloth. He squelched across the carpet, began to mount the stairs.

When he walked into the office, Ridley was brandishing a sheaf of brown envelopes. 'I found these,' he said.

They were letters from creditors and banks, unpaid bills, and summonses, some dating back to the summer. One letter from somebody called Mr Andrew Private and dated December 7th threatened Elliot with 'legal action in the near future', should he fail to repay his 'substantial debt' immediately. The tone of voice was tired, indignant – a reasonable man at the end of his tether; clearly not the first letter that Mr Private had written to Mr Frazer.

'I never realised,' Moses said, though, even as he spoke, he remembered the one-sided phone-calls, the talk of old ghosts from the past, and then the string of anonymous threats – the white arrows, the nursery rhymes, the blood and the shit. Yes, it all added up. 'He's gone for good, hasn't he?'

'He owed me too, the bastard,' Ridley growled. 'Four hundred quid. If I ever get hold of him – '

He flexed his right fist, and his bones creaked in the abandoned room like the snap of dry twigs in a wood; the anaconda tattooed along the muscle of his forearm swelled grotesquely as if it had just swallowed a goat.

Elliot must've been desperate, Moses thought, to have risked incurring Ridley's anger. Either desperate, or very, very foolish. Maybe even both. Ridley would crush Elliot like so much garlic and use him to season his next meal.

'When did you last see him?' Moses asked.

Ridley scowled. 'Saturday before Christmas. Tarted up to the eyeballs he was. Looked like a fucking pimp.'

Moses had to grin.

'Fucking pimp.' Ridley scraped his hair back from his forehead. 'Wouldn't surprise me, come to think of it.'

They took one final look round the office. Elliot had taken nothing with him. He had even left his beloved pool-table behind. The balls had scattered to all four corners of that flawless baize. Moses picked up the wooden triangle and turned it absent-mindedly in his hands. While the balls sat inside the triangle they looked neat, tight, safe. Lift the triangle and they suddenly seemed to huddle there, unprotected, vulnerable. Then the white ball struck and broke them up. And so the game began. He wondered which pocket of the country Elliot had darted into. A wanted man, obviously. Businessman, patron, dandy, cheat, absconder. Whereabouts unknown. Last seen looking like a pimp. Moses secretly wished him luck. Or perhaps he made his own, like Mary.

Moses moved over to the window, leaned against the sash. The snow, denser than before, was being driven diagonally across the glass, so it felt as if the whole nightclub was hurtling sideways and upwards at breathtaking speed into the last night of the year. As he gazed down into the street, the present slackened its grip, his mind drifted, and he saw himself returning by chance at some unspecified time in the future.

It was many years later and he was travelling south across London. He was a good deal larger now than he had been in his youth – so large, in fact, that the taxi-driver had made some crack about charging him an excess baggage tariff on his body. Moses had taken no offence at this. He had smiled and settled back, almost filling the three-man seat entirely. One short-cut through the back streets of Lambeth, however, brought him lurching forwards in a commotion of flesh, all his complacency gone.

'Could you stop, please?' he cried, rapping on the glass partition. 'Could you just stop here for a moment?'

The driver pulled into the kerb and watched in his wing-mirror, engine snickering, as Moses climbed out, quite agile considering, and stood transfixed on the pavement, his size now obvious as the wind pressed his lightweight raincoat to the left-hand side of his body. He was gazing up at a building that had once been pink. It was orange now, but the paint had peeled and faded, stained by exhaust-fumes, rain, the feculence of birds. The entrances had been barred with padlocked metal grilles, and most of the ground-floor windows had been punched out; white star-shaped gaps showed in the black smoked-glass. A litter of newspaper, leaves and mangled beer-cans had fetched up in the main doorway.

And the pigeons had returned. He could hear their muffled chuckling and mumbling coming from an open window on the fourth floor. 'Bastards,' he muttered, fists tightening. Time, it seemed, hadn't diminished his loathing of pigeons.

He shook his head gently. Memories collided like soft toys in a packing-case, a few eyes missing, a few limbs coming unstitched at the joints, a few holes where the stuffing showed through, but otherwise intact and safely stored away. It must have been – what? – 1980. Around then, anyway. How quaint the 19 sounded now.

The wind lunged savagely, whipping his coat away from his legs, banging a loose sheet of corrugated-iron somewhere, whirling rubbish into a hectic spiral in the doorway. An empty beer-can clattered across the pavement towards him. It began to drizzle.

He became aware of the meter ticking away loudly behind him, ticking like a direct personal threat, as if, at any moment, it might blow his fragile memories to smithereens. Nostalgia was a luxury, it told him, and had to be paid for.

He scrambled back into the taxi, slammed the door behind him and, after one last glance at the abandoned orange building, continued on his journey.

*

The wind howled as it caught the edge of the building. The place smelt old already, stale, almost sweet, like a dying man's breath. Moses turned back into the room. His time there, he now knew, was over and that saddened him, but he said nothing; Ridley would have little use for anything so sentimental, preoccupied, as he seemed to be, by thoughts of money and revenge.

They left the office and walked back down the stairs.

'If I was you,' Ridley shouted over his shoulder, 'I'd get the fuck out of here before the pigs show up again.'

Moses murmured agreement.

'Specially with *your* record,' Ridley added.

'Oh, you know about that?'

A remote smile crossed the mountainous landscape of Ridley's face. 'I reckon you've got a couple of days,' he said when they reached the street. 'Maximum.'

It was his world, this world of violence and debts, and he spoke with careless authority. He zipped his sleeveless quilted ski-jacket, shoved his hands in the pockets, and tipped his head skywards. The snow avoided it, frightened.

Moses shuffled his numb feet.

'Hey, Ridley,' he said suddenly, 'there's something I've been meaning to ask you.'

'Yeah?'

'Where'd you learn to whistle like that?'

Deep lines appeared at the corners of the bouncer's eyes. It was like watching ice crack on a frozen lake. 'My old man,' he said.

'Really?'

'He was a brickie, a boxer, did a bit of everything. He was a magic whistler, always was. He could do about over a hundred different birds. Most of them I never even heard of. I used to copy him when I was a kid. One day he said to me he said, "It's a good thing you're learning to whistle." "What you on about?" I said. "Well, you never know," he said. "Might come in handy one day." And he looked at me, real crafty, like. Couple of days later I asked my mum what he meant and she said he beat some ex-middleweight champion in a fight once by whistling at him.'

'Seriously,' he added, when he saw the smile forming on Moses's face. 'Apparently he beat him by whistling at him, very soft, between punches. Confused him, like.'

'I don't reckon you need much help when it comes to a fight, Ridley.'

'No, well. Like my dad said. You never know, do you.'

Fifty yards away, on the other side of the road, Dino paused outside his shop to marvel at the sight of these two abnormally large men laughing. If laughter was 58p a pound like tomatoes, Dino was thinking, I could make a real killing there. And it would be nice selling laughter. A lot nicer than selling yoghurt or fish-fingers.

'Well,' Ridley said, 'I'm going to get out of here.'

Moses nodded.

'Good luck, Moses.'

'You too, Ridley.'

Ridley lowered his arm across the road and stopped a cab.

After Ridley had left, Moses felt more alone than he had felt all day. But then he saw Dino waving at him from the other side of the road, two leeks in his chubby Greek fist.

'Happy New Year, Moses,' Dino pronounced it Maoses, as always.

Moses grinned and waved back. 'Happy New Year, Dino.'

A NOTE ON THE AUTHOR

Rupert Thomson was born in Eastbourne, England on November 5th 1955. His mother died when he was eight. Soon afterwards his father sent him away to boarding-school. At sixteen he won a scholarship to Cambridge where he studied Medieval History and Political Thought. One week after graduating he went to New York. While there he was almost adopted by a 63-year-old homosexual alcoholic. He escaped to Hollywood. When he returned to New York some months later he looked for the old man, but the old man had disappeared. From New York he went to Athens where he taught English. When he arrived back in London he noticed that most of his friends from university were wearing suits. It was time to get a proper job. He worked for almost five years as a copywriter in various advertising agencies. He retired in 1982. He gave his flat to a friend and left the country. During the past four years he has worked as a caretaker, a farmhand, a barman and a bookseller. He has lived in Siena, Berlin, New York (still no sign of the old man) and Tokyo. *Dreams of Leaving* is his first novel.

A NOTE ON THE TYPE

This book was typeset using Ehrhardt, a typeface based on a design by the Hungarian Nicholas Kis (1650–1702) who worked as a punchcutter in Amsterdam from 1680 to 1689 at the height of the Dutch Republic. A set of his matrices was acquired by the Ehrhardt foundry in Leipzig, hence the name adopted when the modern face was cut.

The type has all the sturdy Dutch character of the *Goût Hollandais*, the characteristic type-style of the latter part of the seventeenth century. The relatively narrow, densely black letters also show the influence of German Black Letter type.